Romance Collection

THE ONLY WAY TO KICK OFF YOUR SUMMER HOLIDAY!

If you enjoy *playing games*,
want to find out *what Phoebe wants*,
or even go *undercover with the mob*
then look no further...

Check out these three BRAND-NEW
sexy and sassy stories!

DIANNE DRAKE

Dianne's background is in music and nursing, with college degrees in both. Her hobby and passion is antiques – she collects antique European oil lamps, vintage American kitchen utensils, and brooches from everywhere, circa 1600-1900. Besides her passion for antiques, Dianne has a passion for animals – all of hers are rescued from animal shelters. Her household is made up of one husband, Joel, one college-aged daughter, Jennifer, three cats and three dogs.

ELIZABETH BEVARLY

Elizabeth is a graduate of the University of Louisville and achieved her dream of writing full-time before she turned thirty! At heart, she is also an avid voyager who once helped navigate a friend's thirty-five-foot sailing boat across the Bermuda Triangle. She'd love to have her own sailing boat one day, a beautifully renovated older model forty-two-footer, and to enjoy the freedom and tranquillity seafaring can bring. Elizabeth likes to think she has a lot in common with the characters she creates, people who know life and love go hand in hand.

CINDI MYERS

Cindi believes in love at first sight, good chocolate, cold champagne, that people who don't like animals can't be trusted and that God obviously has a sense of humour. She also believes in writing fun, sexy romances about people she hopes readers will fall in love with. In addition to writing, Cindi enjoys reading, quilting, gardening, hiking and downhill skiing. She lives in the Rocky Mountains of Colorado with her husband (who she met on a blind date and agreed to marry six weeks later) and three spoiled dogs.

The
Summer
Romance Collection

Dianne Drake

Elizabeth Bevarly

Cindi Myers

*M&B™ and M&B™ with the Rose Device
are trademarks of the publisher.*

*First published in Great Britain 2006
by Harlequin Mills & Boon Limited, Eton House,
18-24 Paradise Road, Richmond, Surrey TW9 1SR*

THE SUMMER ROMANCE COLLECTION
© by Harlequin Books S.A. 2006

The publisher acknowledges the copyright holders of the
individual works as follows:

Playing Games © Dianne Despain 2005
Undercover with the Mob © Elizabeth Bevarly 2004
What Phoebe Wants © Cynthia Myers 2004

ISBN 0 263 85072 2

049-0606

*Printed and bound in Spain
by Litografía Rosés S.A., Barcelona*

Playing Games

by
Dianne Drake

To Janie,
the real spunk behind the heroine
in this book.

1

A Little Friday-Night Waiting & Shrink-baiting

"WELCOME TO MIDNIGHT SPECIAL, sugars. Are you ready for something special? Because if you are, you've certainly come to the right place. Doctor Val has something *extra-specially* special for you tonight."

Roxy Rose gave her sound engineer, Doyle Hopps, the nod, and the program started on cue with caller number one, a thirty-something hubby-done-her-wrong from Olympia. Make that cheating husband number fifty-six for the week. Roxy always counted them—the cheating husbands. Just in case she landed a book deal somewhere down the line she wanted to be accurate. Not that she was planning on writing a book, like that obnoxious Doctor Edward Craig seemed to do about every two minutes. But she wasn't ruling out anything because her career was on a big-time growth curve lately, and all those hanky-panky-ing husbands and two-timing boyfriends came in at a whopping fifty percent share of the calls.

Love 'em, hate 'em…she definitely counted on that loose zipper legion for some nice, fat ratings. And either way, Roxy needed them. They were one of the main reasons she was eyebrow-deep in building her new dream home…a million dollars' worth of cement, steel and glass, along with a to-die-for panorama of Puget Sound.

"Eighteen years, Doctor Val. That's how long I've been

with him. I've kept myself up physically, stayed good in bed…at least I thought I was good in bed, until he started hunting down other beds. I've held down a full-time job, raised the kids. For eighteen *long* years. Then I find out he's cheating on me. And it's not like she's some younger bimbo. She's older…my age, and married, with four kids. So what's he seeing in her? I mean, if she was twenty with a tight ass, I might be able to understand it, but she's not!"

Astrid hit the bleep button as the *a* word popped out, then gave Roxy the thumbs-up to indicate she'd caught it. They were on a seven-second delay for such slippages.

Nodding, Roxy returned the thumbs-up to her friend. Best friend, actually. Astrid Billings—long auburn hair, figure of a goddess, the one who really looked like what Val sounded like—had come with the show when Roxy had inherited it from her predecessor.

"Whoa," Roxy said, her Doctor Valentine drawl slow and Southern, even though she was Seattle-born and raised and didn't have a drawl, slow, fast or otherwise. "Just calm down, now. Okay? Take a deep breath and pour yourself a big ol' glass of wine. In fact, why don't all of you go ahead and do the same." Roxy nodded at Doyle to cue up the music, then purred into the microphone, "Be right back. Don't you go away. Valentine's counting on you." Settling back into her chair, she took off her headset and gave Doyle the *I need a drink in a bad way right now* sign— the invisible cup tilting to her mouth, then tilting and tilting and tilting for emphasis. Unfortunately, Roxy's invisible cup wasn't filled with wine. Never was on air, hardly ever was in real life.

"Anything in particular?" Doyle asked from his booth.

"Anything wet. Other than that, I'm not picky." Roxy looked at the monitor for the seconds left in this break. A one-minute break already one-quarter gone, meaning she didn't have time to get it for herself. Or she would have.

"Told you we needed a wet bar in here, Rox," he said, grinning through the glass at her. His booth was large, full of all kinds of gizmos and gadgets. Hers was tiny, big enough for a desk and not much else. "A pitcher of margaritas right now sounds pretty good to me."

"Yeah, and with margaritas, you get Roxy dancing on the desk. Tap water's okay."

"Tap water...*boring*. You need to live a little, Rox. I keep telling you there's more to life than business, and I, for one, would appreciate a good desk-dancin' from you."

"You got it. Tap or ballet?" Roxy laughed. Doyle was so close to hitting the nail on the head about her boring life that it wasn't funny. Two hours on air was all anybody heard, but she managed her own Valentine publicity, hunted down sponsors, and lately, went cruising for a syndication deal. So her two hours really translated into at least fourteen. And then she slept. Oh, and did some house designing.

"I was thinking something in veils, or less. Little cymbals on your fingers."

Astrid stuck her head into the booth and held up a can and a red plastic cup full of ice. "Hey, Rox. Before you put on your dancing shoes, or veils, is orange soda okay? They're out of root beer and the tap water's looking pretty brown."

"Orange is just dandy," Roxy said cheerfully, glancing back over at Doyle for the count. "Sorry. Guess the veils will have to wait."

"Promises, promises." Doyle held up three fingers on his pudgy right hand and made a zero sign with his left. "Thirty. And I ain't lettin' you off the hook for those cymbals."

Short, a speck on the plump side, with long, scraggly brown hair always hanging out of a Seattle Mariner cap, in the control booth he knew his stuff like nobody else in the business. Like Astrid, he'd been with Roxy from the show's get-go, grabbed off a sideline grunt job and given his domain on the boards. Roxy, Astrid and Doyle…the three of them together, thick and thin, yada, yada. And Roxy never forgot that. For all her quirks, she was loyal.

"I'll put them on my to-do list right after tweaking the master bath."

"Not the house again!" Doyle cracked, covering his face with his hands. "Please God, anything but the house."

"Like you won't be parking it out there when I get my entertainment room set up. Big projection TV, a sound system that'll make you eat your heart out…"

"And you in veils…"

"We don't talk veils until we talk about my house plans, and I got into some new ones today, in case you're interested." Which Roxy knew he wasn't, but he sure liked teasing her about them."And I'm thinking they could be the ones. Some pretty neat stuff."

"Twenty. And I doubt it, Rox. Not with the way you're killing every single architect in the greater Seattle area who comes within a mile of you and your house plans. Fifteen."

Well, maybe she'd fired a few. Two, three? Definitely not more than five. But they couldn't get it right. She wanted minimal with a homey feel. They couldn't manage both in the same blueprint, and the homey part always got left out. So she was doing it on her own now, with the help of a CAD—computer assisted design—program and some old Bob Vila tapes. Plus in her spare time she stayed glued to Home and Garden TV, making up a wish list. Her house on her own beach would be nothing short of perfect."Just cutting through the middle men. That's all." And sure, somewhere down the line when she roughed out exactly what she wanted, she'd go architect shopping for someone to whip it into proper form, find the general contractor, and all the rest of it. *After* she was finished with her own preliminaries.

"Cutting up the middle men's more like it." Doyle gave

her the ten sign—ten chubby fingers wiggling at her."And just when I thought you were working out your control issues. Eight, seven, six…"

"It's not a control issue, Doyle." Well, maybe. But she *was* working on it. "It's just that I'm the only one who knows everything all the time." Grinning, Roxy winked at Astrid, who'd returned to the producer booth, then acknowledged Doyle's cue. "Valentine McCarthy back with you now, feeling so nice and mellow with a wonderful glass of…" She looked at her orange soda. "Chardonnay. Do you have your glass of wine, sugar?" she asked her caller.

"Bourbon," the caller replied flatly.

Doyle tapped on the window between their booths and she glanced over. Plastered to the glass was a cardboard sign reading Control Freak with a dozen exclamation points after it.

She stuck out her tongue at Doyle, then without missing a beat went right back to her caller. "Well, whatever works best for you. Make it a double, if you have to, and while you're doing that let me tell you what I think about your bed-hopping hubby. First, I think his cheating on you is only a fling. Usually is. Just sex. Men don't leave their wives for older women with kids, unless there's a whole lot of money involved. So, does she have money?"

"Not that I know of. She's a waitress, I think."

"Good, that means it's just sex. He's simply out for some exercise. And since he's real busy exercising his male muscle in all the wrong places, you've got a decision to make. Unless you want to go through life getting taken advantage of by a bed-buzzing jerk, you can either kick him out or keep him. Either way, you've got to learn how to respect yourself so you'll believe you don't deserve what he's doing to you.

"So like I said, you can dump the bum. Hold your head

high, walk out that door, take everything you can get your little hands on, and don't look back. He's not worth it. And believe me when I tell you that, because this is an area where Valentine knows what she's talking about." Except when Roxy walked out that marriage door, the only thing in her little hands was the iron resolve to do better without him than she'd done with him. It was all she wanted, all she took. He got the three-legged card table, the brick and board bookshelves—no books, couldn't afford them—and the lumpy mattress on the lumpy floor. A good deal for Roxy all the way around.

She drew in a deep breath, preparing herself to take the other approach—something she always did since most callers didn't want advice, but rather validation for something they wanted to do or had already done. "Or here's another plan that just might work for you. If you love him—and I think you do or you wouldn't be calling trying to figure out how to fix this thing—and you want to keep him around, I think you should teach him a lesson. Revenge is so sweet. Good for the feminine ego, and if you do it the right way he won't go wandering off again." She glanced over at Astrid and smiled. "So which is it?"

"Keep him, give him another chance."

A keeper. Not necessarily *her* personal choice. "And would you like to get even with him? Teach him a lesson that really counts? One he'll remember before he drops his drawers anyplace but home?" In the next booth, Astrid was already *visibly* fretting about the imminent advice. Roxy feigned an innocent shrug. It was Friday night, after all. *Somebody* needed some Friday-night fun. "Because if you do, I've got just the right plan. One he won't be forgetting for a long, long time. I promise you."

"Yesh…"

Just great. One caller half-soused. She couldn't blame her because that's sure what *she'd* do if she had to go pub-

lic with her life. *Her life…* If she took that public, her listeners would be getting all liquored up from boredom.
"So are you ready to start teaching, 'cause this is guaranteed to be a mighty fun lesson."

"Yesh…because I don't want to be pushed around by
him anymore. And if I confront him, tell him what I know,
he'll just say he's sorry, beg me to forgive him, then we'll
be fine until he starts sneaking out again."

On that count, the caller was right. And Roxy was getting herself worked up for some good, on-air two-timer
throttling. "You're right. There sure will be a next time. If
he gets away with it this time, he'll figure he can go out
and do it all over again. Once he's had seconds, he'll want
thirds and fourths and it'll never stop."

"So tell me what to do, Doctor Val. I want to get even
with the jerk, and I definitely want to teach him a lesson."

Roxy took a drink of her orange soda, then laughed into
the microphone. It was a throaty, deep, practiced laugh. A
pseudo laugh, one that fit her pseudonym—Doctor Valentine McCarthy. Valentine was her real middle name, Mc-
Carthy her married name, although she'd dropped it right
after the divorce and hung out her license to practice as
Doctor Roxanna Rose, Ph.D. But she liked hiding behind
her pseudonym, liked hiding behind her husky pseudo
voice, too. And it fit the raven-haired, brown-eyed radio
shrink who came out at midnight, talked sex for two hours,
then went away to be just plain Roxy again. Make that
Roxy with the bright, sunny laugh—cropped-cut, blond-
haired, blue-eyed girl next door that she was. Not a thing
like her pseudo self, *thank heavens.*

All things considered though, it worked out pretty well.
For both of them.

"Well, my advice is simple. Do unto hubby as hubby
would do, and apparently has done, unto you. Have yourself a little fling, too. Then let him know about it. Does his

honey have a hunky hubby? Maybe *he'd* like to get in on some good extracurricular activity, since his little woman is already getting it on her own. Or does your hubby have a lonely hubba-hubba back at his office, down at the lodge, maybe his best friend? If he does, I say go for a young one if you have a choice—they're so eager and willing to please when it comes to a more experienced woman.

"And that's what you are. More experienced, not older. Also, finding yourself a younger man will definitely let your hubby know that you're not over the hill or otherwise checked at the door, that there's still some mighty good grazing left, even if he isn't the grazer. Oh, and leave the clues, so he'll find them. Be obvious. He deserves it."

"And if I do all of this, Doctor Val, do you think he'll leave me?"

"Honestly, he could. I've gotta be truthful about that. But if he leaves because you're doing unto him, then he wasn't going to stay around, anyway. And if he does leave, you've got options, 'cause you can do a whole lot better. But if he doesn't, I'll bet he'll think twice before he wanders off again, knowing you might be wandering off right behind him. Bottom line, dish the dirt, but have a little fun while you're dishing it. Two more can play at hubby's game besides hubby and his mistress. And call me back, will you? Let me know if it was good for you."

Roxy cued Doyle to bring up the program music. "That answer got me all hot and bothered, thinking about all the exciting possibilities that are waiting for us out there if we care enough to go out and hunt them down. So let me go cool off for a minute, then I'll be right back." She went to break. Two minutes this time.

"Her husband?" Astrid screamed over the microphone into the booth. "You told her to go out and have an affair with her husband's mistress's husband? Come on, Rox. What's wrong with you? That's crazy, even for you!"

"*You* come on, Astrid. When you were dating that guy, Buford, last year, and found out he was sleeping with three other women besides you, didn't you want some revenge? I mean, who was it that stalked him at night and poured syrup and feathers all over his car?"

"Burton, and yes, I wanted revenge. I'll admit it. But that was different. And my revenge could be fixed at a car wash."

"Yeah, you left him the ten-dollar bill under the windshield wiper, you wimp. But what I'm saying here is that the emotion's the same. We get wronged, we want to fight back, whether it's with the guy's girlfriend's hubby or a bottle of syrup. Same thing. And I just gave her an interesting way to fight back. Which she's *not* going to do, Astrid. Human nature. She wants to fix her marriage, not make it worse. But I'm betting she'll let him know, one way or another, that she knows what he's doing. And if her marriage can be worked out, that's the start of it."

"And what if she takes your advice?"

Roxy wrinkled her nose. "Then she might just have some fun. And guess what, I'll bet no one's turning me off at the break right now and going over to that all-night sports talk show. When they're talking home run, they mean home run, but when Valentine talks home run, her callers know exactly what she means."

"I love it when you two fight." Doyle chuckled. "I think people would pay big bucks to see you do it in person…in syrup and feathers."

"Somebody gag him," Roxy yelled, glancing up at the computer screen, checking for the name of the illustrious Doctor Edward Craig. Not there yet. Kind of a surprise because the spicier calls always brought him out.

"Gag *you*, next time you pull something like that," Astrid muttered. "And next time you want something to drink, get it yourself."

"She's baiting him," Doyle quipped. "That doctor dude. That's just her way of asking him to come out and play."

"And he's ringing the bell right now," Astrid announced over her microphone. Part of her job was to screen the calls—letting in the good, keeping out the bad. And her order was to always move the self-important Doctor Edward Craig right to the top of the call-in queue. Not because Roxy particularly liked him, because she didn't. But the ratings! He brought 'em, she loved 'em. A match made in broadcaster's heaven.

"So maybe I bait him a little...."

"A little?" Doyle sputtered. "Honey, you throw out the chum and he eats it up like a hungry shark. And you enjoy it, even if you won't admit it."

"Oh, yeah. I enjoy it all right. Just like brussels sprouts. My mom fixes me brussels sprouts when I go home and I eat them because I have to, but they give me gas." Roxy thought about Doyle's notion that she liked the great Eddie Craig's calls, then dismissed it as ludicrous. He was a sprout, that's all. Necessary, not gratifying. And he did cause a fair amount of gastric upset from time to time, even though somehow she always managed to walk away satisfied. In a professional sense, of course.

"Come on, Eddie, let's see what you've got cooking for me tonight," she said, checking his name on the monitor. Yep, he was there, first name on the top of the list, and ready to go. "Whatever it is, it's going to be way better than brussels sprouts."

"Good evening, Valentine. You're in rare form tonight."

At the sound of his voice, Roxy wrinkled her nose at Astrid. The man did come on so darn strident sometimes. Like sending her copies of the fifteen billion books he'd written—the ones still in the carton in the trunk of her car. *Unopened.* "Good evening, Doctor Craig. And let me just correct one thing you said before we go any further. I'm *always* in rare form. Not just tonight." Something about his voice, that little Boston/British accent thing he had going on, made her voice go even sexier than her normal Valentine sexy. If dark chocolate could talk, it would sound like Edward Craig.

Roxy glanced down at the dark-chocolate truffle on her desk. Every night, right about this time, she got the craving.

"Rare form, maybe. But rare doesn't necessarily mean good. Not when you do such a disservice to your listeners with your advice."

"My advice, Doctor Craig?"

"Keep it nice," Astrid warned over the headphones. "We've got a couple of potential new sponsors listening in."

Roxy slapped a sweet smile on her face just for Astrid's benefit. "My advice, Doctor Craig, is what my listeners want. Or they wouldn't call me, would they." She felt a chill, awaiting his voice. Strange effect, but it happened a lot. She chalked it up to the adrenalin rush of a battle. "So what would *you* have me do?"

"I'd have you give the previous caller sound advice instead—"

"Yeah, yeah, *Eddie*," Roxy interrupted. "We know your broken record. Get counseling, get counseling. But what good's counseling going to do a cheating husband? It's not a problem in his head. It's in his pants. Actually, let me re-phrase that. There wouldn't be a problem if it *was* in his pants. You know a counselor's going to charge her a couple hundred bucks an hour, and you know as well as I do that cheating hubbys don't go to counseling. So she goes there by herself, plunks down all that money, and for what?"

"To fix her marriage."

"Might be better spent if she could *fix* her hubby. But that's not going to happen, so what I'm suggesting is an inexpensive alternative—revenge sex, *Doctor*."

"And you really believe a knee-jerk reaction like revenge sex, *Doctor*, is sound advice for working through an indiscretion? By the way, do you really think revenge sex is a good label to put on what you're advocating? That oversimplifies a serious problem."

"Knee-jerk?" Instinctively, she looked down. The left knee of her jeans had a hole in it. The right was frayed. Not exactly the Valentine image she put out there. "And whatever do you mean by *sound* advice? Personally, I think my advice *sounded* awfully good. Oh, and if you don't like to call it revenge sex, I'll be glad to go with make-good sex, getting-even sex, do-unto-cheatin'-hubby sex. Take your pick." This was getting particularly good between them tonight. Somehow she'd known it might when she'd given that little piece of revenge-sex advice to the caller.

"And you don't think the wife plays a part in the husband's actions?"

Oh, Eddie. You really opened yourself up with that one. Roxy glanced over at Astrid and winked. "A wife may play a part in the marital problems, but you and I both know it's not always marital problems that send a man into another woman's bed. So unless the wife actually drives her husband to his mistress's door, and says, 'There you go, dear. Go have a good time, and I'll be back in an hour to get you,' she's not playing a part in his cheating. It's a solo gig, Doc. He opened that door by himself, and he walked through it, and claiming she pushed him through it is a cop-out. Bottom line is, when he's cheating it's all about sex. Motivations don't matter. So if that's what it's about for him, why can't it be about that for her? I certainly think the first time he drops his pants for someone else he's inviting his wife to do the same, if that's what she wants to do."

Edward let out an impatient breath meant to be heard on air. "Having an affair because she's been hurt—what will that accomplish, *Doctor*, except to cause more hurt?"

"Sex, *Doctor*. Not an affair. And the only hurt it could

possibly cause—since she's a consenting adult—will be her husband's, who deserves to be hurt for what he's done to her. Like they say, an eye for an eye...or in this case...a romp for a romp."

"Which will drag her down to her husband's level. That, Valentine, solves nothing."

Which was true, at least in Roxy's thinking. But Roxy's thinking wasn't Valentine's, and sometimes that little tug-of-war got rough. But, all for the ratings... "Quite the contrary, Doctor. It will serve as a catharsis. Surely, as a shrink, you realize the value of a good catharsis every now and then, don't you?"

"As a *shrink,* Doctor McCarthy, surely you realize that catharsis is not an act of revenge, but an act of release—"

"And a good orgasm's not a release, Eddie? If that's what you think, then I'd say you don't get around too much, do you?"

"An emotional release," Edward said defensively, then nervously cleared his throat. "I'm talking about an emotional release, if you can forget about the sex for a minute."

"Forget about the sex?" Roxy replied in her deepest, huskiest, sexiest voice. "Doesn't sound like you've been having too much fun." Roxy smiled, impressing a mental mark in her imaginary column. "Like I said before, you must not get around, because an orgasm can be as much of an emotional release as a physical one, and there are studies to back me up on that one, *Doctor.*" She added a second mark. "Think about it...Edward. Think about the last time you enjoyed that release...with another person, I mean." She scrunched her nose at Astrid, at the thought of the pompous Doctor Craig indulging in that scenario. "Wasn't it a wonderfully satisfying emotional surrender, as well as the obvious physical enjoyment?"

"It might have been, but this isn't about me, *Doctor,*" he said, his voice so dark-chocolate it gave her goose bumps.

She glanced at her truffle. Never, ever until *after* Edward, but she wanted it so bad right now. "Isn't it, *Doctor?*" she purred, claiming her third mark. "It's about your ideas of right and wrong, which, like it or not, are affected by your life, your loves, your sexual experiences, and vice versa. My caller was hurt, she needed to vent, and yes, she needs to feel like she has some control in the matter. As a relationship counselor you know this, or you should. What I suggested, Eddie—a little revenge sex—gives her back some of that control. To me, that's a pretty simple solution. You know what they say about two playing that game, and maybe when her husband finds out she's been playing— and you know he'd never suspect she would, men never do—he might just rethink his playing if he wants that marriage to work out. If he doesn't and he leaves, she's better off without him."

"Adultery, Doctor McCarthy, is never the solution. Not to any problem. It's only a means to compound it."

It was time to end this now. He was drifting off into levelheaded land, where it was hard to combat his real logic with Val sense. Meaning she had to cut him off before Edward succeeded in besting Valentine. That was not what her listeners wanted.

Roxy drew in a steadying breath, and looked to Astrid for her end-the-segment signal, but instead got the stretch sign, meaning she was going to have to roll this all the way to the next commercial break. "Adultery isn't an issue for the husband, since he started it, Doctor, so don't make it an issue for the wife, too." She twisted toward Astrid, and gave her the slash-throat signal, but Astrid shook her head.' Roxy shook *her* head emphatically, but Astrid countered with a nod to which Roxy mouthed the words, "You're fired." Astrid responded with a gesture Roxy knew was coming and turned away from before she saw it.

"I wouldn't have to make it an issue for the wife, Doctor McCarthy, if you hadn't given her license to go out and do what feels good simply as a way of getting back at her husband. But you did, and now…"

"And now nothing," she countered. "It's sex, Doctor Craig. Sex for the sake of getting even. Nooky for nooky, and that's all it is, so don't blow it out of proportion, okay?" A little over the top, she thought. Roxy had personal reactions. Val didn't. Not ever. So, it was time to take a deep breath, refocus and bring Val back to the front of the line before Roxy went reactionary again and torpedoed the ratings.

"You know, Edward…" She whispered his name this time. Drew it out, turned it into husky need and silk sheets and promises. "It's Friday…a little after midnight now. You should be in bed with someone…in bed and making mad, passionate love. You should be sweaty, and gasping for air, and on the verge of an orgasm so explosive you can literally feel the earth move. And afterwards, you should be sipping champagne in a bubble bath with her…I'm assuming it's a her…and kissing her toes, feeling that familiar stirring down under the bubbles…the stirring that won't let you make it all the way back to the bed this time. But you're not. You're on the phone debating sexual advice with a radio psychologist instead of indulging in some of those mighty fine pleasures yourself…pleasures I would certainly be indulging in if I weren't working." Yeah, right. Pleasures she hadn't had since—she couldn't remember when. "So I'm wondering, Doctor Edward Craig, why aren't you?"

She shut her eyes, envisioning a wildly sexy Doctor Craig on her beach—she always envisioned him as wildly sexy—then jerked her eyes back open and glanced at Astrid, imploring her to end this thing. Which Astrid did with a slash gesture across her throat, laughing at the same time. Just in the nick of time, because that last image on the beach took deep root, wouldn't go away even when her eyes were open.

"It's not always about sex, Valentine," Edward continued. "Sometimes it's about making love. And that, my dear, is always the best sex, physically and emotionally. But we'll save those fine distinctions for another night, if that's okay with you." With that, he clicked off.

The image of him on her beach still floating around in her head, Roxy grudgingly gave him a mark for that last remark. He deserved one every now and then. After all, Edward Craig translated into good rating points.

And good fantasies, when she let him. Very good fantasies.

"Be right back, sugars," she said to her listeners. Then she grabbed the truffle, popped it into her mouth, and sank back into her chair to savor the taste.

2

Still Later, and Not a Creature Was Stirring, Except…

DRIP…DRIP…DRIP. Roxy shifted her stare from the computer screen, where she was designing the Rose Palace—her future home on the Sound—to the leaky kitchen faucet. An upright, with a nice, graceful, swan-curved neck and one handle. Drip! "Damn," she muttered. She'd called that maintenance guy about it twice now. Begged him to come de-drip the durn thing. She'd been pretty blunt about how much it was annoying her, too, and how she really needed him over there as soon as possible. Which was yesterday, when it wasn't even so much of an annoying drip as an occasional one.

So what if her call did have the dual purpose of drip-busting *and* getting an up-close and personal look at the man? Preferably from behind. Admittedly, she'd watched him a time or two. Or more. From the peephole in her door, from the elevator, in the lobby. He was the kind worth stopping and staring at. Gorgeous bod. Tight. She was betting six-pack abs under his T-shirt. A real appealing package in her 3D life—dull, dreary, dismal—even if all she got to do was look. Looking was good, though. Safe. Uninvolved. Easy.

Too bad she hadn't taken that road the first time. But the appeal of a starving artist had seemed romantic at age twenty. Wore off fast, thank heavens. Funny how her work-

ing three jobs so that he could stare out the loft window
and think about painting had a way of doing that.

So now she only looked. And Mr. Handyman was a
looker well worth the effort. She was thanking her leaky
swan-necked for choosing to slaver at that propitious moment, even if, so far, the plumbing Galahad had not come
running to her watery rescue. All things considered, she
thought she'd been pretty patient about waiting for him to
haul his lethally fabulous butt through her front door to
obliterate that damned dribble. But now it was getting ridiculous. The drip was running amuck and Roxy was actually more interested in a solution than the butt! Such a
sad state of affairs. And pathetic.

Pathetic but true, Roxy. Admit it. Here it was, 3:30 a.m.,
and the damnable drippity-drip was so loud she just knew
her snoopy neighbor on the other side of the wall would
start banging out a Beethoven symphony. From day one
in her apartment—was it only a month now?—he, she or
whatever had pounded whenever Roxy sneezed, blinked,
or when the light in her fridge came on. She did try hard
to stay mouse quiet. Didn't wear shoes, listened to music
only through headphones, didn't swing from the chande-
lier. The wee hours had always been good to her, and getting home at two-thirty every morning all wide-eyed and
raring to do anything other than sleep furnished her with
oodles of time to design her new house.

Until she moved in here. And Mr. Gorgeous Handyman
cruising the hall in his drop-dead tool belt didn't offset the
inconvenience of having her nights interrupted by the
Pounder.

Her house…. Roxy smiled, just thinking about it. It
would be good. Better than that, it would be all hers with
her own personal brand on every single aspect of it. She
liked that, the total control, at least at this stage of the planning. The house that Roxy built, or would build, as soon

as he got over here and took care of that demon drip from the very bowels of hydrous hell. It was driving her insane right now, not to mention ruining her creativity! And just when she was all set to choose between marble or granite on the...no, wait. That couldn't be right. Marble or granite dining room chairs? Where'd the bathroom vanity go?

That demented demon drip stole it!

Roxy's gaze shifted back over to the culpable faucet, the one devising its next move against her, and she scrunched her face into an I-dare-you-to-drip-one-more-time glare. Fat lot of good that did, because at that very moment the fiendish faucet morphed itself into a living, breathing entity, one blatantly defying her to do something about it. *Okay bitch, you asked for it. Take this...* Drip! One single, solitary drip! A laugh! That's what it was. The faucet Lucifer was laughing at her. Ddd...ri...ppp! This time an exclamation point after the laugh! "That does it," she snapped. Roxy stormed across the kitchen floor and smacked the faucet with her open palm. "Ouch," she squealed, pulling her hand back and shaking it. Didn't phase the drip at all. In fact, the dribbles started coming in punctuated pairs. *Drip, drip! Ha, ha, ha! Drip, drip! Ha, ha, ha! Double-drip dare ya!*

Of course, Pounder on the other side of the wall started right up.

"Now I lay me down to sleep, I pray the Lord for earplugs, please," Roxy muttered, pulling open her junk drawer to see if anything in it was up to the task of silencing the one-handled dribble monster. A wrench, a sledgehammer, a stick of dynamite! As she expected, though, there wasn't a single, solitary usable thing in there—only a red plastic flashlight with dead batteries, naturally, some emergency candles with no matches, of course, and a fistful of wooden skewer sticks, not that she'd ever skewered a thing in her life. Well, maybe Pounder once or twice...in her dreams. But nothing labeled drip-fixer.

Frustrated that a pipe wrench hadn't magically materialized when she needed it, Roxy started to slam the drawer shut, but caught herself in the nick of time, gently pushing it back into its place lest the wall-banging dervish on the other side started all over. Then she glared at the dreaded wall, "I hate this place, I hate this place." Close her eyes, click her heels three times and maybe she'd land in the Rose Palace.

But mercifully, this apartment was only a temp—a refuge from the rodents and roaches and fleas, oh my! in her former apartment. And it was a quick hop to work as well—a stopgap until the Rose Palace was built, which she hoped wouldn't be more than a year down the road. Provided *he*, the fixer of drips, ever got his pipe wrench over here.

Drip…ka-drip…ka-drip…drrrripppp…

"Okay, that's it!" Roxy didn't care what time it was. She'd already been reasonable with the guy, it didn't work, so now it was time for him to come play on her turf during *her* hours. And she had his number. Right at the top of an important phone numbers list stuck to her fridge, just below her fave food deliveries—pizza first, then Chinese. So, *he* was about to make a little home delivery himself, substituting tool belt for pepperoni, and a pipe wrench for egg roll. It was time for Mr. Dazzling Derriere to get over there and prove just what he was good for, other than filling out his jeans in some really unbelievable ways.

"Six-three-three," Roxy repeated the phone number from the list as she dialed. "You'd better be home…with *all* your tools ready to go." She drummed her fingers impatiently on the countertop as the first four rings went by unanswered. By the sixth ring, she was tapping her right foot. "Two more rings, then I'm going to…"

"Hello." The voice was a little jagged, a little thick, a whole lot gruff. And sexier than anything she'd ever heard at 3:38 in the morning. Or any other time of the morning, for that matter. This guy could be worth two truffles, she thought. *But I'll trade you two truffles for one fixed drip.* That's how desperate she was!

"Is this building maintenance? You *are* the handyman, aren't you?" She didn't even know his name. Hadn't bothered asking. No need, since enjoying the marvelous view had been more than enough for her—until now.

"Call back in the morning."

Certainly not a very friendly response for someone who dealt with the public, Roxy thought. "In the morning I'll need an ark. You don't happen to have one handy, do you? Or some bailing buckets?"

"Huh?"

"My faucet's leaking. More like gushing all over the place. By morning my apartment's going to be flooded." Well, maybe that was a slight exaggeration, but demented drips called for desperate measures. "I need someone to come over here *right now* to fix it, before it starts leaking through the floor into the apartment below." Well, maybe another teensy, weensy exaggeration. But if that's what it would take to get him over there…

"Do you know what time it is, lady?" He was making no attempt to hide his irritation. "Because if this isn't an emergency…" Bordering on downright hostile. But still so sexy she was thinking junk food. Always the infallible substitute.

"Well…" Roxy shrugged, then looked at the bug-eyed, tail-ticking cat clock on the wall. "Yep, I know exactly what time it is. I know what time it was when I called before— both times. And I called at respectable times then—you know, during the day, when you had that message on your voice mail saying to leave a message, that you'd call right back. But that didn't work, did it? Since you never called back, and you never came over. So this time I thought if I called in the middle of the night when you'd probably be sleeping, I could wake you up and talk to you directly." Roxy shut her eyes, trying to conjure up his sleeping image. Dark and brooding, hair tousled, sheet coming up only to his waist. Strong arms, naked chest… He wasn't wearing a stitch of clothing under the sheet because men like that always slept in the nude. Or they should, anyway. Damn waste of a lot of good maleness if they didn't. God, she needed a Twinkie. "And since you're up right now, why don't you come on over here and do something about the drip? Okay?" With or without clothes.

"I'll put you on the list for first thing in the morning," he grumbled.

A turndown? He was actually refusing after she pleaded her case so eloquently? Well, that wasn't good enough. If she had to suffer the drip, so did he. Roxy gritted her teeth for the next round. "Which is when? Nine o'clock? Ten o'clock? It can't wait that long. It's already oozing through the floorboards. You'll be getting a call from my downstairs neighbor any minute."

"Then go stick your finger in the dike, lady. That'll hold it until morning."

Roxy's foot began its impatient tapping again. At this rate there really would be a flood before he got over there. "So, will a bribe work on you?" she blurted into the phone. Drip, drip. "Anything I have, short of sexual favors." Of course, if he came over there the way she'd pictured him in bed… "Just please, come and take care of it right now. Okay? Or bring me a pipe wrench so I can do it myself."

"You ever used a pipe wrench, lady?"

"Well, no. But how hard could it be? You clamp it on the pipe then twist."

"All that leaks isn't in the pipe."

"Hey, I've got plenty of Bob Vila tapes and I know how to use them." The only response to what she thought was a reasonable request was an audible, and very vexed, sigh. So she continued. "And if you let me use your tool I'll promise not to ever call you at three-thirty in the morning again."

"Three-forty," he grunted. "And no way in hell are you touching my *tool*."

Touching his tool… Boy, oh boy, the ideas that came with that. The ideas and the images. *You wish I'd touch your tool, Mr. Handyman!* "Three-forty," she agreed. "So if your tool is off-limits, that means you're coming over and doing it yourself. Right?" It was beginning to sound promising, from a purely plumbing perspective, of course.

"Who the hell are you, and where the hell do you live?"

So he wasn't very friendly. Brooding and temperamental types were good, too. Especially when they packed a pipe wrench. And right now, the wrench was all she really wanted. "Roxy Rose. Apartment five-B."

"Five minutes." Then he hung up.

Five minutes—just enough time for him to get dressed. Damn! Another fantasy shot to pieces.

On her way from the kitchen into the dining nook she used as her office, Roxy passed by a large hall mirror and stopped, then hopped up on a plastic step to appraise her face. Whoever had hung that mirror must have been hanging it for Amazon women, because in her full five-foot-two glory she could just barely see her face. In fact, the mirror chopped her off at the nose, giving her a clear shot only of her eyes and forehead. So she'd bought the step. Easy solution. Just the way she liked things—easy.

Roxy smiled at the reflection and pushed her tangle of uncombed hair back from her face. "It's a natural look, trendy-chic," she always claimed, when friends asked why it was sticking out in odd directions, different odd directions. Truth was, she didn't like the bother of fixing it, and she'd owned that disarrayed look long before it *had* become trendy-chic. "Oh well," she sighed. "It's not like this is a date." Besides, no one had ever accused her of being a trendsetter—not in Roxy-mode. Roxy was no-fuss, no-muss, no makeup, with no particular concern over it. Trendy was Val's gig, one she used for special appearances, photo shoots and the like. Geez, those mugs of her on the city buses. All over Seattle. Here a Valentine, there a Valentine, everywhere a Valentine. And all those billboards. Yikes! There were certain stretches of road she assiduously avoided because she loathed and detested being looked down upon by the pseudo-her camouflaged up to fit the public perception.

Hopping off the step, Roxy wondered if now would be a good time to get Mr. Beautiful Buns to lower the mirror, since he was already going to be there with his tools. Doesn't hurt to ask, she decided, kicking her step back to the wall. Probably wouldn't hurt to throw on a tighter T-shirt, either.

"WHO'S THERE?"

"It's three forty-five, lady. Who do you think it is?"

"Can you show me some identification please—slip it under the door?"

"Lady, the only ID I have on me is my pipe wrench. So open up or I'm going back to bed."

Smiling, she knew what ID she wanted to see. Yeah, like she'd really ask him to turn around so she could take a look. *Only in your dreams, Rox.* "Well, hold out that pipe wrench where I can see it," she said, opening the door an inch. And there it was, his tool thrust right out there at her, and right behind it bare chest. Bare chest every bit as good as his backside. The she-gods were loving her tonight because this was pure, glorious male potency at its best. "Okay, I'm going to trust that that's a pipe wrench." Not that she had even looked at the wrench.

"It's a pipe wrench, lady, so do you want me coming in

and using it, because I'm two seconds away from going back across the hall to bed. Which is where I should have stayed in the first place."

Mercy, mercy, please come in and use it. "Across the hall, as in you're my neighbor?" Through the crack in the door, Roxy's eyes wandered from his chest, down the low-riding jeans to his bare feet then back up to his chest. Hairless—somewhat surprising, since men with black hair usually had a fine mat on their chest. But his chest was boldly bare, showing off his flat, rippled stomach. *Oh, my heavens, a six-pack!* "I guess I've just been too busy to meet—"

"Your leak, lady?" he interrupted, his lack of interest in neighborly chitchat made abundantly clear by his testy intonation.

Roxy's eyes went back up to his face. Except for the furious scowl it wasn't bad—not bad at all. Probably the first time she'd looked past his…endowments, and she sure liked what she was seeing. Whiskey-brown eyes, dark eyebrows, and that nighttime shadow of stubble. *Now, that would be something real nice to wake up to.* She remembered waking up to Bruce. He looked more like the bad end of a mop in the mornings. "Please come in…um…neighbor." She unlatched the chain, opened the door and pointed to the kitchen. "It's through the living room…"

"I know where the kitchen is," he snapped, his testiness booting up another notch.

"I guess you would…did you mention your name, by the way?"

"Ned," he grunted in passing. "Ned Proctor."

"Well, Ned Proctor. Welcome to my apartment." Stepping back as he whooshed by, Roxy caught a trace of his scent. *He smells great, too. Could this get any better?* He was like a fresh splash of something bold and virile, unlike her one and only date in the past three months. What was his name? Michael? Or was it Rupert? Whichever…he'd shown up smelling like an array of discount cologne samples, and she'd sneezed her way around the first block with him before jumping out of his car and hoofing it all the way home—in the fresh air. It took a whole month for her aching sinuses to completely recover from that redolent attack.

"It's been driving me insane," she said, watching from the doorway while he tried to manipulate the faucet's single handle to stop the drip. "And that won't work. I've tried." For Ned, it was scarcely dripping now. Barely one drop every five seconds, and a puny little drip at that. An ugly plumbing conspiracy meant to make her look silly.

"You couldn't have lived with *that drip* until morning, *Mizzz* Rose?" Glancing down at the floor, he shook his head, letting out the impatient sigh she was already coming to know quite well. "It's not exactly pouring over, getting ready to flood the apartment below, is it?"

"I'm on…a project. All the dripping was breaking my concentration."

Frowning, Ned glanced across at Roxy's makeshift, make-a-house desk area next to the pantry. "It needs a washer, and I don't have a washer." He tucked his tool in the waistband of his jeans and headed for the door. "Tomorrow."

"Tomorrow? Come on, Ned. I've been calling you for days."

"One day, two times," he grunted. "And you were on the list."

"Well, I don't want to go back on the list."

"First thing in the morning."

"I sleep all morning."

"Then I guess you'll know what it's like to be awaken during a sound sleep, won't you?"

Not to be thwarted on this, the night of her bathroom design, Roxy scooted in next to Ned and yanked at the faucet handle impatiently, hoping to… Well, she wasn't sure

what she hoped to do other than what he wasn't doing—
which was fixing it. But the only thing that happened was
a drip that doubled in both frequency and resonance. "So,
now what?"

"I'd tell you to live with it, but that's not going to get
me back to bed any quicker, is it?"

"My contract said maintenance emergencies twenty-
four seven. All I need is a lousy washer."

"All you needed *was* a lousy washer, lady. Heck if I
know what it needs now, and I'm not going to find out
until morning. What time did you say you get up?"

"Ten."

"Then I'll be here at eight." He grinned at her. "G'night."

"But what about the leak?"

"Wrap a towel around it, for Pete's sake." He pulled the
pipe wrench out of his waistband and handed it to her.
"I've changed my mind...be my guest."

The wrench slipped from his hand and landed with a hollow thunk on the old wood-and-linoleum countertop. "Well,
now you've done it," Roxy warned, her face poker-straight.

"Done what?" he asked.

"Ten...nine...eight...seven..." Pounder next door
started up on the five count, and the beat went on for
nearly half a minute. "That," she said, smiling. "That's
what I was warning you about. And this." She opened a
drawer then shut it, not particularly loud, either. With that
came the encore, a sequence half again as long as the first
chorus, accented, at the end of the performance, by one last
clap that knocked an old, black trivet right off Roxy's wall
and into the sink. "So like I was saying, Ned," Roxy continued, without missing a beat, "it's driving me nuts—the
dripping—and I have a lot of work to do tonight, and if
you can please stop it for me, I'd be grateful."

"How often does *that* happen?" he asked, nodding at
the wall.

Roxy shrugged. "Not more than three, four times a night." Grinning, "Someone over there's a Listening Tom. Too bad for them it's only my kitchen and not my bedroom." Yeah, right. Sounds from the Roxy Rose boudoir were guaranteed to put anybody to sleep, including Roxy Rose herself.

Ned cleared his throat, turning back around to face the sink. "And what do you do every night to annoy her? Georgette Selby's her name, by the way. She's eighty-two. Sweet. Bakes chocolate chip cookies. Used to be a schoolteacher."

"Normally, it's just breathing." Roxy grabbed up the pipe wrench, but he yanked it away from her. "Once in a while I eat Twinkies, and I have this little TMJ thing in my jaw…it sort of pops occasionally."

Stepping back over to the sink, wrench in hand, Ned bumped into Roxy. "I'm going to bend down now, Miss Rose. Take a look under the sink. If you don't mind moving back…"

Did she mind stepping back to get a better look at him bending down? About as much as she minded chocolate and orgasms and lots of money. "Just trying to see what you're doing so I can do it myself next time. So tell me what you're doing," she said, struggling to reign herself back in.

"Turning off the water at the valve. That'll stop the drip and when I get back over here at seven-thirty…"

"Eight."

"*Seven*, I'll get everything fixed up the right way."

"Think it's gonna work for tonight? No more drip?" The valve handle was tight and she watched him put extra muscle into his next twist—translating into something so sexy on his backside that it almost made Roxy squirm right out of her skin. Damn those baby-making hormones, anyway. They sure were in overdrive tonight. *Success now, the rest later*, she reminded herself. "Need another…" a slight tuchus wiggle caused her to gulp "…another tool?" she sputtered. *Okay, Rox. Success now, blah, blah, blah. Remember?*

"There!" he declared, rather than answering her question. "That should hold it, temporarily." Ned's head had barely cleared the open space under the sink when the valve groaned a plumbing obscenity, then let the full force of a geyser rip, shooting water everywhere—the walls, the ceiling, Roxy, Ned. Springing to his feet, Ned yanked the faucet handle, only to have it break off in his hand. No simple fixes now. It was a full-out water cataclysm in need of some instantaneous plumbing surgery, and Ned's only surgical instrument or know-how, it seemed, was a pipe wrench that clunked to the floor when he leapt back from the deluge.

Scrambling to avoid the fat force of the spray, lest she be caught up in a full-frontal wet T-shirt look, Roxy darted into the bathroom, grabbed up an armful of towels, and dashed back into the kitchen only to find Ned standing there in the middle of Niagara Falls clutching a cell phone, staring down at his pipe wrench. "Don't just stand there," she cried. "Stop it. Turn something. Or plug something up."

Ned shrugged. "The plumber will be here in a few minutes."

Shaking her head, Roxy stared at the kitchen wall, awaiting the inevitable. And sure enough, before she could even blink, Georgette "Pounder" Selby commenced doing her thing, this time, it seemed, with two fists, and perhaps, a foot.

3

Monday Night and All Is Dry

"WELL, HE'S NOT BAD to look at, but with a pipe wrench he's lethal, and not in a good way." Three nights since the great flood and Roxy's apartment still wasn't back to normal. To his credit, Ned had sent in a water damage restoration crew, and nothing was permanently ruined. Just soggy.

"And he didn't come back after he did all that?" Astrid handed Roxy the broadcast notes for the night. Nothing out of the ordinary—a new sponsor, a proposal from station management to add another hour of programming at the top end of her show, which didn't make a whole lot of sense since her show was called *Midnight Special* and not *Eleven o'clock Special.* "They might as well make me drivetime," she snorted. Drive-time, either morning or afternoon, was a coveted slot. But a deadly one for Roxy's show since her late-night topics weren't even close to drive-time subject matter.

"They know you won't do it," Astrid said, "but they keep hoping."

"They're lucky they get two hours of me a night. And they know that!" Of course, she was lucky to get those two hours, and *she* knew *that.* Hiring someone who'd jumped right from clinical counselor to talk-show host in the blink of an eye, and without any radio experience, had been a big risk for her station owners. And now, backing her in a syndication deal, and letting her continue to broadcast from their facilities was a heck of a nice thing to do. Of course, she would own that show, with a piece of it going to Astrid and generous compensation to her station owners, so it was a win-win thing all the way around. She hoped. Gosh, did she hope.

"So you said he wasn't wearing a shirt when he came over?" Astrid waved at Doyle who was settling into his chair in the engineering booth, ready to scarf down a pizza.

"Nothing but jeans, and I swear…" she raised her hand into the air as if swearing a solemn oath "…I was good. I mean this guy is…like…the best thing you've ever had in your dreams—or fantasies—right there in my apartment in the middle of the night. And all I can do is stand there practically drooling. Not that he would have noticed." Roxy waved at Doyle, too, then sat down in her chair. Still thirty minutes until air. She spread out her latest house plans on the desk. Coming along pretty well, except that aviary where the kitchen should go. "Then I didn't even see him in the hall all weekend. Not once. I mean, he's right across from me, so I kept watching, but I don't think he even opened his door all weekend. Worse than that, he sent this big, burly plumber over—the kind whose pants didn't quite make it up to his belt line by a good four inches. Believe me, that's not the bare butt I wanted to be seeing in my kitchen. But it's fixed, so I may never see him again. The handyman, not the plumber, who I *never* want to see again."

"So unfix something," Astrid suggested. "Then call him back over."

Roxy laughed. "You've been hanging around me too long. I already did that this morning. The bedroom window doesn't seem to open anymore. Imagine that."

"Bedroom?" Astrid raised her eyebrows. "Nothing subtle about that, is there?"

"Mind if I interrupt you two with some work matters and do sound levels now?" Doyle asked, still chewing his last bite.

"Check away," Roxy answered, then laughed. "Which is what I'll be saying to Mr. Pipe Wrench in a few hours, I hope."

"In the middle of the night again?" Astrid asked.

"Best time. Just ask Doctor Val. I think for once the two of us would agree on something." Roxy folded her latest house plans and crammed them in her canvas briefcase. "I think I may have to go buy another home design program. This one seems to have some kinks in it."

"Could you squeeze in a couple of promos before we go on?" Astrid asked. Then turning to the engineering booth window, she asked Doyle, "Think we could get them in? I know I shouldn't be springing this on you at the last minute, but management wants a couple of spots to stick on in evening drive-time. They think it'll tap a new audience."

"Always drive-time," Roxy sighed. "But if it brings 'em in, what the heck."

"Just give me five, and I'll be good to go," Doyle called back.

One pizza slice left, he was obviously debating whether to cram it down or leave it for later. Knowing Doyle, he'd go for the cram and order a whole 'nother pizza for later. "Extra cheese," Roxy said. "Thin crust. I'll buy."

He winked at her before he bit into the last slice. "You bet you will, *sugar.*"

"Here's the copy. Go over it a couple of times before you do it." Astrid plunked some papers down in front of Roxy.

"I prefer to *do* it spontaneously," Roxy called after her.

"Just as long as you get the name in…"

"I know. Five times."

"Seven, if you can. Plus the time it comes on."

"Like anybody listening in drive-time will still be up to hear me." These were the people who did Monday through Friday, nine to five. According to market research they were heading to bed after the eleven o'clock news, so there was no chance she was reaching the right audience with drive-time promos. But free advertising was free advertising. "So Doyle, are you ready?"

"For you, babe, I'm always ready. Let me cue up then I'll give you the count."

He was on the five count when Roxy picked up her copy and looked at it for the first time.

"One," from Doyle.

"Good evening, sugars. This is Doctor Val reminding you to tune in tonight as we talk about love, sex, and all the other little things that rock your world…and mine." Including a building maintenance man who was a solid ten on the rock scale. "I promise to have an extra-specially good show for you tonight, but you won't know how good until you turn me on." Ad-lib time because the rest of it was drivel. "And I do so want you to turn me on." Much better. Much more Val. "So stop by and check me out on *Midnight Special* at…well, midnight. The best hour of every night for *everything*. I'll be waiting for you, sugars."

Doyle gave her the cut sign, and Roxy wadded the copy and lobbed it into the trash. "I know, I only got the name in once, but they'll get the drift."

"*And I do so want you to turn me on*," Doyle mimicked. "Doctor Val, raising erections all over the interstate. I can just see all the accident reports. So is the next promo better than this one?"

"Aren't you the critic?" Astrid snapped at Doyle.

"Hey, I call 'em as I hear 'em." Doyle gave the cue sign for the next promo just as Roxy slid the copy sideways until it flittered down into the trash can. One more ad-lib coming up, but this one all the way.

"Hello out there in rush-hour traffic. This is Doctor Val with two pieces of advice for you. One is listen to my program, *Midnight Special*. You'll be amazed what you'll hear in grown-up time when we can talk about the good things, the sexy things you'll never hear on your way home from work. And the other piece of advice is drive naked, sugars. Makes the whole experience much more fun, especially if everybody else commuting right along with you is driving naked, too. So try it, then call me tonight at midnight and let me know if it was good for you, 'cause, if I'm the one commuting next to you, I'll be watching, and it'll sure be good for me. *Midnight Special* every night at…midnight."

Roxy turned to Astrid. "Got the name in more."

"And you've got two minutes to do the right one," Astrid yelled from her glass booth. "Doyle, erase that last mess and get ready for the correct promo."

"Yeah, Doyle," Roxy said, grudgingly grabbing the copy from the trash. "Cue me up to do the really good one. The one that will put everybody to sleep."

Smiling, he gave her the sign, and Roxy read, "This is Doctor Val reminding you to listen to *Midnight Special* every weeknight at midnight. On *Midnight Special* we're full of all kinds of surprises…" She couldn't help herself. "And on *Midnight Special* we like to talk real dirty. Lots of sex on *Midnight Special*. So if you like sex, if that's what makes you hot at midnight, you'd better tune in and listen to just how hot it can get on *Midnight Special*. 'Cause sugars, Valentine gets hot every night on *Midnight Special*. That's *Midnight Special* every weeknight at midnight." She made a slashing gesture at Doyle and grinned at Astrid. "Seven times, count them. So is that better?"

"After work, the real thing. And Doyle's locking the doors so you can't get away," Astrid grumbled, sitting down in her chair.

"You didn't really expect me to stick to plain old boring, did you?" Roxy countered.

"Boring pays the—"

"I know," Roxy said. "It pays the bills, but it doesn't attract the listeners. And without listeners, there's no program, and without a program we're all slapping burgers on a grill somewhere down on the waterfront." Astrid with her business degree, Doyle with one in engineering and Roxy's in psychology—the trio couldn't flip a burger together. But the burger-flipping imagery was good, she thought. "So I do what I have to do to keep us in this job." She laughed. "And deep down you know I'm right, even though you won't admit it. So just edit it, okay? Whatever you thinks works."

"Five minutes," Doyle said.

Roxy glanced up at the clock, wondering momentarily if Doctor Craig would be calling tonight. For sure he would if her ad-libbed, driving naked promo made it out on the air. Too bad Doyle had erased it.

Then briefly, Roxy imagined Ned Proctor driving naked.

ALMOST MIDNIGHT. He was tempted to turn on the radio and listen to the reigning queen of babble, since his plan to wander across the hall and ask Roxy Rose how her plumbing was doing went down the dumper when she went out a couple of hours ago. Going back across the hall… He'd been wanting to do that for several days now, but he needed some distance between himself and that whole humiliating faucet incident. What was he thinking, anyway, strapping on a tool belt and playing handyman? "Good disguise, Ned," he muttered, plodding to the fridge for a beer. Three now, on an empty stomach, and he was getting a little buzz. But he didn't care, since all he was going to do was settle in. "Bet she really bought that handyman bit hook, line and bailing bucket," he added sarcastically.

He'd been watching *Mizzz* Rose for the past month, since she'd moved in. Quick glances in the hall mostly.

Cute as hell. Sexy, actually. She was like an approaching electrical storm, all full of spark and sizzle. And sure, she was a little off center from normal, in the sense of the women he usually dated, anyway. They were all pretty much run-of-the-mill—good-looking, a lot taller, a whole lot more sophisticated. But *Mizzz* Rose fascinated him. Had since the day Oswald, the building super, had rented her the apartment across the hall from him and she burst into it like a tornado sweeping through a wide-open Oklahoma plain.

Sure, he'd wanted an introduction to her. Just not the one he'd gotten. There was no turning back from an embarrassment like that one, and no conceivable way to undo it, except maybe switch apartments. Which was as easily said as done, since he owned the building. Unfortunately, it was full right now, with a pretty long waiting list. Nothing open except the boiler room in the basement. So he was staying put for the time being, abject humiliation notwithstanding.

"So do I avoid her, Hep?" he asked his Siamese cat. She was named after Katharine Hepburn—elegance galore with a set of big claws. "Or just pretend it didn't happen?"

Hep's answer was a guttural *I don't give a damn* growl, as she strutted through the kitchen, back arched, tail up, in search of a fluffed pillow for her nighttime nap.

"You're right. Just ignore it." Plodding back into his study with his beer and a bag of chips, Ned looked at the jumble of words on the computer screen, decided to call it a day, hit save then backed it up. No reason killing himself over this one. It wasn't like he hadn't cranked out a dozen books just like it before. Pop psychology had a way of bringing out all kinds of issues in people who'd never before had an issue until they read one of his books. To date, twelve bestsellers—the reason he could afford this building. A good investment, his financial guy had told him. Not that he wanted to be a landlord, because he didn't. But he had to do something with the money he was making. And real estate was as good as anything else. Gave him a place to live, too—an upside that didn't matter much, since he'd managed to get along for thirty-five years·without getting himself too entangled in the usual trappings.

"Well, what will she be doing tonight?" he asked Hep, as he settled into his trusty ten-year-old recliner to listen to Doctor Val McCarthy. Pretty much everything that came out of her mouth was wrong. Bad psychology, bad advice, bad reasoning. But what the hell. She killed a couple of hours, and he sure liked her voice. It was a nice one to hear last thing before he nodded off.

"Welcome to *Midnight Special*, sugars. Are you ready for something special? Because if you are, you've certainly come to the right place. Doctor Val has something extra-specially special for you tonight."

"That's what she thinks," Ned snorted, stretching out in his chair and turning off the floor stand reading light.

"So tell me, what's on your mind," Val continued.

"Don't worry. I *always* do." Callers number one, two and three all rang with cheating spouses, boyfriends or both. And Val pretty much rang true with her advice, which was becoming predictable, Ned thought. Same ol' same ol'. Of course, how many ways could you spin it? You either dump them or you keep them. He chuckled. Or sleep with their significant other's significant other. That certainly wasn't a theory he'd seen in any of the books he'd read. Or written!

"Just be true to yourself," Valentine said, wrapping up a conversation he'd apparently spaced out on. But she was right. Too bad he'd missed it. "There are more big hunks out there for you if you want to go looking. Make sure you're looking in the right place, though. Someplace without a wedding ring, because if you get yourself hooked into that again, like you did last time, you'll end up like you are now, wondering why he's wandering. Now Doctor Val's gonna go treat herself to something sweet for two minutes. So sugars, I'll be right back, better than ever."

"Two minutes, Hep? So she can go look under a rock for more advice?" Chuckling, Ned grabbed his cell phone and punched in the number for *Midnight Special*. "I have a question for Doctor Val," he said, when a live voice came on. His *Ned* voice, only a little higher, because he didn't want anybody he knew hearing him call that hack. It was a little slurred, too, he noticed, thanks to that beer buzz he had going and a rasp of exhaustion. "But it doesn't involve a cheating spouse. Do you think she'll answer my question, anyway?"

"And the nature of your problem is?" the voice on the other end asked. They always qualified the callers. Some made it through, a lot didn't. He kept his fingers crossed.

"Met a woman I'd like to impress, but the first thing I ever did was pretty damned inept. Performance anxiety, I'd guess you could call it, and now I'm embarrassed to see her again. I just want to know some ways I could start it over between us. Or if I *can* start it over." Sure, he'd twist it until it sounded like this was about bad bed performance. *But never, ever let 'em know how he'd failed with a pipe wrench.* Man, oh man, talk about bored silly, doing something like this. But since Roxy wasn't home, he wouldn't get the do-over he'd been plotting all weekend in case he ran into her again. Shutting his eyes, Ned cringed.

"You'll be caller number one in the next segment," the screener told him.

"That's fast." Actually, this wasn't the call he'd intended to make. It just sort of slipped out. But what the hell! Go for it, anyway.

"Well, normally we hold that slot for someone else, a program regular, but apparently that's not happening tonight, so you're in luck. Just make sure you turn off your radio, okay? And no swearing or graphic words, because we'll have to cut you off."

Two minutes later, he got the cue. "Hello, sugar. And what can Doctor Val help you with tonight? I understand you sort of embarrassed yourself the first time you were with her and you're looking for a way to redeem yourself? Is that it?"

Ned cleared his throat, not so much because he was nervous, but because he was preparing to raise the pitch a tad more, just in case Roxy was listening. Bad with a pipe wrench *and* getting advice from a radio shrink. Two strikes for sure. "I've wanted to meet her for a while," he began. "And I finally did. But something happened, and yeah, I guess you could say I embarrassed myself."

"How? We're all on your side, so tell us the juicy."

"Let's just say it was something that comes naturally to most men, and I thought I could do it, but I found myself lacking in the skill. And she was definitely in need of that skill, but I had to call in someone else to help her out when I couldn't, well, take care of the job." Ned smiled. *Should be interesting.*

"You say you called in someone else to finish up for you?"

"That's what happened, but that's not why I called you. I just wanted your opinion on whether or not I should try it again with her. If you think she'll have me back. And how you might suggest that I go about it after humiliating myself like I did the first time."

"Well, I'm not a medical doctor, but I do know that it happens to all men at one time or another. No need to be embarrassed. And I've got to admit that Doctor Val is somewhat amazed at the lengths you'd go to for that woman of yours. Calling in someone else to finish—don't think I've ever heard that one before. But if it was between three consenting adults, I guess that's okay. I'm curious though. Since you were the one at the starting gate, wouldn't you rather be the one at the finish, too? And since you were her first choice, I'm assuming she'd like *you* to go the distance with her. So does she? Does she want you there with her at trophy time?"

"That's the problem…I really don't know. After what I did…"

"Give it another shot. I mean, this gal is really lucky to have someone so considerate, someone who cares about her pleasure and fulfillment more than he does his own. And I'm betting she'll be glad to have you back. Just make sure you take a little blue pill with you next time. Okay, sugar? Go on and knock on her door and tell her you want to give it another try."

"WHAT WAS THAT?" Roxy asked Astrid on the next break. "I mean, he's sending in the second string. Think the high and mighty Doctor Craig was listening? 'Cause I'd sure like to hear what he has to say on the subject. Especially since it's not *me* being off the wall for a change."

"He's in the queue. Just called in," Astrid said. "And he was listening. In fact, he's raring to go."

Roxy smiled. "Should be interesting."

"Twenty," Doyle called. "And if you give me the last caller's name, I'd be glad to stand in for him sometime when he needs that second string."

"I'll bet you would." Roxy laughed. "You and every other guy listening tonight, *except* Doctor Craig, who wouldn't even volunteer to stand in for himself."

"Five, four, three…" Doyle gave her the cue to go.

"Well, Doctor Craig. Welcome back. You're a little late, and I was beginning to think you were cheating on us, plying some other late-night talk show with your refutable advice."

"Not a chance, *Doctor*. Not after what I just heard. Your callers need someone to set them straight—"

He sounds a little tired, she thought. Probably exhausted himself coming up with a response. "Straight? You mean after I bend them, *Doctor?*" She glanced at her dark-chocolate truffle. Someday she was going to make that man buy her a whole box of them!

"After you bend their ears with *your* refutable advice."

"Come on, Doctor. Don't hold back. Tell me what you really think."

"I think, *Valentine,* that you wouldn't be so excited with the prospect of a pinch-hitter if you were the one committed to the regular hitter. You know, committed as in love."

Roxy leaned back in her chair and smiled at Astrid. "Sounds like you want to get into my personal life, Edward. Is that what you're trying to do? Catch a little glimpse of Valentine at home…in the bedroom?"

"Believe me, over the months I've caught that glimpse, and I threw it back."

Wow! Pretty peckish, even for him. Roxy scrunched her nose at Astrid, like she was smelling something bad. "You're forgetting, my caller was the one who'd already come up with a solution to his problem. At least his problem in the sack. And while that might not work for you, it seems to be working for him."

"If it's working so well, then why did he call you?"

"Maybe because he wants some advice on how to set things right between them, sexually."

"So you told him to go take a pill and all his sexual problems will be over."

"He wants sex, Doctor Craig. That's all he asked about. Sex. Not love everlasting or some other storybook fairy tale. He likes the gal, and he wants to know if he should try it with her again."

"I know we come from completely different disciplines, but tell me, Valentine—would you let your man line you up with someone else if he couldn't perform?"

Her man...*if only.* "You're assuming I'd get myself involved with a man who couldn't satisfy me, which is an incorrect assumption." Actually none of them had satisfied her, and she didn't mean in the physical sense. But that was none of his business. "In terms of an early relationship—mine, yours, my caller's—you simply don't know what will satisfy you. You have an idea what you'd like, what you've liked in the past, but when you're clean-slating it with someone new, it's always a great big question mark. My caller got to that great big question mark and unfortunately he turned it into a great big *huge* question mark, so I told him it's worth taking another chance on. Simple as that. Nothing ventured, nothing gained."

Roxy winked at Astrid, then continued. "Unless you're burying your head in the sand, Edward, there are signals, hunches, tinglings telling you this is someone you want to pursue. And tinglings are the best indicators. The kind that start at your toes and don't stop. Haven't you ever met a woman and started tingling right away?"

She'd certainly started tingling the instant she saw Ned Proctor standing outside her door. Maybe even before that, when he was so grumpy on the phone. Or even before that, passing in the hall, or watching him through her peephole. Whatever the case, there had been tinglings. Strong ones. Still were when she thought about him.

"But your caller wasn't talking about tinglings," he countered.

"Wasn't he? Something made him want to go back and try again, and it sure wasn't good sex since he had to bring in the second string. And since you, Edward, are always the champion of hanging around, trying to work things out, which is what I told him to do, I don't know how you could argue the point. Even though what my caller's doing isn't the way you'd do it..." Or the way *she'd* do it. "He deserves a do-over." And she was betting Doctor Edward

Craig had never, ever had a tingling or he'd know it was worth doing over.

"The way *you'd* do it, Valentine?"

Roxy leaned a little closer to the microphone. "The way I'd do it, Doctor Craig, is open to a whole lot of possibilities, many of which, I'm sure, you've never considered." Possibilities she wouldn't mind exploring with her not-so-handy handyman.

"Actually, the only one I consider is love, Valentine. That's the only thing that comes with all those possibilities you talk about."

Love? Well, that wasn't one of *her* possibilities, no way, no how. But score one for him, anyway. When he was right he was right. Even though she'd never admit it. "You almost sound like a romantic, Doctor. But of course, I know better. You write books that espouse all that academic thinking, and your readers walk away, what? Happy? Enlightened? Glad their pockets are lighter by the cost of a book? Sorry, Doc. You're still not ringing…*or tingling* my bell. And I'm sticking by what I said earlier. My caller needs to go back and try again. And take the pill with him, if that's what it takes."

"And I'm sticking by what I've said time and time again. You've skirted around the only truly important issue. But then, you always do, don't you, Valentine?"

Doyle gave Roxy the slash-throat signal, then a five count into a commercial break. Good timing. The hard and fast rule for Edward Craig's calls was that she *always* got the last word.

"What I skirt, Doctor, is being close-minded about issues my callers consider to be serious problems. That's all we have time for tonight. Thanks for calling, again." Then she was off. Truffle time!

"Whoa," Astrid said, stepping into Roxy's booth. "You two almost agreeing there?"

"Not agreeing," Roxy argued.

"But getting pretty darn close. I mean, you guys were just a couple chapters off from being on the same page. Good thing you still managed to find a way to argue about it, because the last thing our listeners need is Valentine and Edward in bed together."

"Yeah, like that's going to happen. The guy's a snore. The only thing in bed with him is a pillow."

"But it was close, Rox. You know it."

"So I agreed with him tonight…on some points. Big deal. And he was right…on some points. That caller needed a lot more than a little blue pill to fix his problems, but that's all Valentine can do—hand out the snappy fixer-upper, which is not necessarily the best one."

"Is this really about that caller?" Astrid asked. "Because you're sounding more like Roxy than Val right now."

Yeah, because she was Roxy right now. Roxy tingling over Ned. "Just tired." And full of expectations and anticipations and not sure what to do with them. "Not my usual self, I guess."

"Want me to stick in a rerun for the last half of the show so you can get out of here and go find your usual self?"

"Nope. I'm okay. Just pour me a root beer and I'll do better next segment." Roxy saw Doyle's ten-second signal and asked Astrid, "What's up next?"

"In a nutshell, big-time mamma's boy, age forty-two. She's seventy-five. He's unmarried, two of them live together. He wants a life, she won't let him have it, and *don't you dare* tell him to take his balls back from her like you did last time one of them called, okay?"

She crossed her heart, grinning. "Promise." And just when she thought she might have some fun. "Welcome to *Midnight Special*, sugar. I understand you have a little problem with your mother? So before we get started, let me just say one thing." She really hated mamma's boys. They were all whiners. Didn't listen. Made excuses. Got defensive. Horrible on the ratings. Her listeners turned them off, went to get a snack, have sex, grab a beer, or all of the above. "Mamma needs a man, junior. Even at her age, she's still got it in her. So you go out and find her one, ya hear? Find her one who will give her some good, hot mamma sex and I'll guarantee she won't be bothering you about whatever she bothers you about, and you'll be able to go out and get some good, hot junior sex for yourself."

She smiled at Astrid, giving her the thumbs-up. Val was back, all the way.

4

No 3:00 a.m. Cat-Nappin' for Roxy

NIGHTS LIKE TONIGHT WERE made for the dumper, and Roxy didn't dwell on the show once it was over and she was home. Done, finito, put to bed and that was it. Edward got all the points, damn him, she got none.

"Get Eddie off the brain," she muttered, padding over to the peephole for the tenth time since she'd been home. "Time to think about you-know-who." Except you-know-who wasn't out there. Worse than that, he wasn't in her apartment. So, to call him, or not to call? She wanted to. Wanted to really bad. That's all she'd thought about all night. Probably one of the reasons why she'd hadn't ripped apart the good Doctor Craig like she should have. But now that she was on the verge of calling Ned, she was actually nervous about going through with it. Nervous, indecisive, weak-willed, just plain chicken. Which was just totally bizarre because normally if she wanted it she went after it. And she wanted it, but her feet were lead. So were her fingers. Couldn't dial the phone. Couldn't go across the hall. Couldn't even open the durn door so she could hang out in the entryway hoping he'd see her. *Hi Ned. I've just been hanging out here in the doorway for thirteen hours hoping you'd notice me sooner or later.* Go figure! No control issues here because she had no control.

"Well, no Twinkies for you tonight," she said. It was the

only decision she'd been able to make since she got home. That, and just giving it up for the night and going to bed. "Good place for us chickens, huh?" she said, plopping down in bed, and looking up at the window she'd superglued shut earlier. "Stupid. Really stu—"

"Rrrooww!"

"What the…" Roxy jumped straight up, looked around, saw the cat. It was in the corner of her bedroom, shredding the seat cushion in her rocking chair with its claws. "Who are you?" she asked, not sure whether to get up and toss the cat out, risking the same fate as her cushion, or simply let it continue wreaking its havoc undisturbed. "Kitty, tell me. What am I supposed to do here? What's the protocol?"

The cat merely glared at her for a moment, then turned tail and lay down, apparently intent on spending the night where it was.

"You have a home, cat?" she asked. "Someone I should call?" Like it would answer her. "I'll bet someone's really missing you right now." Missing it, like missing a toothache. "So why don't you run along home." Cats were supposed to be sweet and cuddly. This one had goblin eyes that glowed pure, luminescent evil in the dark. "Home, you know, the place where people feed you. Where people actually like you."

No clues on where that was, but suddenly, inspiration hit, and she wanted to kiss the kitty for it…almost. "And I know just how to find out where that is," she said, picking up her bedside phone. *Ah, the lead fingers suddenly work.* Punching the numbers she'd memorized the first time she'd dialed them, she was prepared for a ten-ring wait, but amazingly, Ned picked up on the second.

"Yeah, what do you want?" he said, his voice a little gruffer than she remembered his 3:00 a.m. voice to be last time.

"It's about a cat."

"Pet deposit's five hundred bucks," he snapped. "Write a check, leave it under the office door in the morning."

"I don't have a cat, but somebody does, somebody who's missing one. So do you know who's missing one? And what should I do about the one who broke into my apartment?"

"I suppose you want me to come over there at…"

"Three-oh-three," Roxy supplied, smiling. Providence was also smiling a little, it seemed. Serendipity in the form of one cranky cat.

"Three-oh-three…and figure out where the cat belongs. Is that correct, *Mizzz* Rose?"

So *he* remembered *her* voice. Promising…very promising. "You have a list of pet owners in the building, don't you? This one's such a sweet little kitty, and I'm sure somebody's heartbroken over losing him." Sweet as straight lemon juice with a vinegar chaser. With claws! "And while you're here, I have this window that sticks. Maybe you could bring your tools."

And come without your shirt. She glanced at the irritated feline, its claws extended a good two feet and envisioned the cat scratches the beast could rake all over Ned's chest. "Better wear your shirt," she said grudgingly. Damn that cat, anyway.

TWO HOURS' SLEEP. It bit through some of the exhaustion, but barely took care of the beer buzz. *Well, Ned, it's what you wanted.*

Problem was, he couldn't figure out why he wanted it. It wasn't like he had time for anything else. He didn't. It wasn't like he was in desperate need. He wasn't.

But simply knowing Roxy was right across the hall made him…tingle. *Thank you, Valentine, for that description. For once you were right.*

"SO WHERE'S THE CAT?" Ned growled at her from the hall-way. A softer growl than last time, though, and she liked him in soft.

He was wearing the T-shirt, smart man. Too bad, but he did have on some nice, tight jeans as the consolation prize. For the first time since, well, since she'd closed the door on Ned last Friday night after the faucet fiasco, Roxy was feeling like Roxy again. All weekend she'd drifted between edgy and wistful and downright sloppy sentimental, one emotion chasing right after the other until she'd finally opted to sleep it off. Of course, sleeping came with dream-ing, tossing, turning and a stiff neck. Which made her grumpy, which was just a hop, skip and a jump away from edgy, wistful, and downright sloppy sentimental. Round and round and round she goes... Amazing how one cranky handyman could do that to her.

"It's in my bedroom." Never in her life had an invitation been so easy! Too bad it was only about a cat. "And I sup-pose you know where it is, don't you? The bedroom, not the cat. Who's in the corner of the bedroom by the way, sitting in a rocking chair, ripping up my fake-silk cushion." Of course, having him follow her down the hall into the bed-room did have a certain appeal to it. Being carried by him down the hall and into the bedroom had an even better ap-peal, but she wasn't sure she could manage that one...yet! *But Ned, Doctor Valentine McCarthy prescribed one big, hand-some man to sweep me off my feet and carry me straight to bed.*

"So how did this alleged cat get in?" He scowled down at her, but it was only a facial rumple, with nothing in his eyes to indicate he was put out, angry or otherwise provoked.

"I don't have an *alleged* clue. I was just getting ready for bed and there he was, sitting in the chair, glaring at me. Kind of reminds me of the way you glare at me, come to think of it."

"She," Ned corrected.

"Huh?" What was that? A twinkle in his eyes? Was he actually twinkling at her, or was it the lighting?

"Nothing. Just lead me to the cat."

Well, the *getting him into the bedroom* part of the fantasy was coming true, for starters. The rest would have to take care of itself once they were there. Yeah, right. *Like I'm really Valentine.* "My window's stuck. Thought maybe you could pry it open while you're there." Suddenly, she really wanted to be Valentine. Sexy, sophisticated, no doubts in the world about what would happen next. Val would spirit him right into bed, forget the cat, and in the morning they wouldn't even have morning hair…talk about a fantasy. Although he would look absolutely magnificent in morning hair, morning stubble, morning anything. Geez…where was Doyle's "Control Freak" sign when she needed it, because right now she sure needed some control.

Especially now that Ned was giving her a twinkle. "It's at the end of the hall, the bedroom on the right, the first cat you come to." Following him into the bedroom she kicked herself every step of the way.

ALMOST, Ned thought, standing in the bedroom doorway, tool belt slung over his shoulder. He'd sure been thinking about what would happen once he crossed the threshold, but she had that Bambi in the headlights look, one he hadn't seen since he'd given Sally Ann Stojowski her first kiss, complete with tongue…they'd been thirteen at the time. But because he had ideas of something far better than a first kiss, complete with tongue, with Roxy, he decided it best to turn off that headlight. Only for now, he hoped.

"So, do you know that *alleged* cat?" Roxy asked, pointing to it sitting regally blasé amid the remnants of pillow in the corner of the bedroom.

Ned snapped off his momentary regrets and took a quick look at Hep's handiwork, cringing at the damage,

since, after all, he'd been the one to slip her into Roxy's
apartment. Well, maybe *slip* wasn't the best choice of
words here. Earlier, just after he'd turned off that lunatic
Doctor Val, and right before he'd dozed off, he'd decided
to take a look at Roxy's kitchen faucet. Purely a professional house call, of course. And Hep just happened to be
in his arms at the time of the *alleged* inspection. So what if
he'd inadvertently left her behind, intending to go back
later and get her? *Mizzz Rose, I don't suppose you've seen my
cat wandering around in your bedroom, have you? I may have
lost her earlier, when I was in there for professional purposes
only.* Good thing she'd called him over because that was
infinitely better than him on his hands and knees in the hallway, begging to be let in. "I know the cat," he said stiffly.

"And would you know how it got in?"

"Apparently she got in when the door was open at some
point." Good evasion. Not a lie, exactly. More like the truth,
in a circuitous kind of way. He stepped into the room and
tossed his tool belt casually in the chair, sending the cat
scampering.

"Well, gee. You'd think I'd notice something like that,
wouldn't you? A cat getting in? Guess I should be more attentive when my door is open…or closed and locked. You
never know who or what's wandering in or out, do you?"

"She's harmless." Except with soft, fluffy pillows, floor-
length drapes, bathroom throw rugs, bath towels, cash-
mere, angora, wool, wooden door frames…

"So tell that to my dearly departed pillow." Roxy
crossed the room and pointed to the window over the bed.
"It's stuck. Guess I've never tried opening it since I moved
in. Think one of your tools might do the trick?"

Man, oh man, she was cute. Standing there in her short-
short jean cutoffs and T-shirt, she certainly wasn't his typical type, *or what he thought was his typical type*, but this past
month, every time he'd seen her in the hall, in the foyer,

from his peephole…well, suffice it to say there'd been a few typical *man* reactions. Hep was the proof of that, using his poor, innocent cat to *allegedly* worm his way into Roxy's apartment. That was some pretty hefty alleging and scheming…scheming worthy of Doctor Val. The kind she'd actually approve of, probably even make suggestions for improving upon. *Skip the cat, and curl up naked on the pillow yourself.* Actually, that thought had crossed his mind a time or two.

"I mean, I'd really like to let in some fresh air tonight, if I could get the window open."

He heard the words but his mind was still on curling up naked somewhere…anywhere in her bedroom. Nice thought. But not tonight. "Fresh air?"

"Remember…stuck window? Big tool to open it?"

"Let me see if I can jiggle it open first." *So climb on in her bed and do it…the window, not her.* Since the window was centered in the middle of Roxy's cushy king-size mattress, Ned crawled over it, then grabbed hold of the handle and gave the window a good, hard yank. One that should have opened it up straightaway, but didn't so much as budge it. One more try, one more great big nothing. Shades of the broken faucet. His second attempt at being handy was already bombing. "Must be painted shut," he said, clearing his throat uncomfortably. "Could you hand me that screwdriver from my belt?" The belt he sure wished he had on. He glanced at the chair where he'd dropped it. *Dumb, Ned. Really dumb.*

Without missing a beat, Roxy grabbed a screwdriver and bounded right into bed with him. And before he could tell her she had a Phillips head, and he needed a flat, she was wiggling in so close it didn't matter which screwdriver he had because he didn't have enough room to do anything with it, anyway. In bed with Roxy…that would have been a very nice place to be, except…well, he couldn't think of an *except*. It was a very nice place to be, period. "I need a flathead, the big one," he mumbled, sounding like a tongue-tied ten-year-old.

"The big one?" she asked.

"Uh-huh," was all he could manage. *So where's the snappy comeback when I need one?* Talk about being a Bambi in the headlights.

"Guess I need to study up on your tools, since you seem to be over here in the middle of the night using them a lot, lately. And thanks for getting that faucet fixed, by the way. No more drips." Roxy crawled back out of the bed and stood alongside it. "And my project is coming along much better because of it."

He'd taken a look at her *project*. Just briefly, since it was printed out and lying on the counter right next to her sink, and he *was*, after all, checking out the sink. For an architect, she was pretty bad. Horrible. Bizarre. What architect in their right mind would ever put a cupola *inside* the house? "So did you get that house plan done yet?"

"You saw it?"

More like was struck blind by it. "I noticed it the other night." He took the large flathead and wedged it between the window sash and the sill. "Kind of an odd place to put a cupola, but if that's what they like…"

"They who?"

"Your clients. I mean, I assumed you're an architect."

"You're observant, Ned. And my *client* decided to scrap the cupola altogether. Kind of cramped her style. Of course, I guess there's an advantage to having all the essentials in one convenient area, don't you think?"

"I've never considered a cupola an essential on an ultramodern." He laughed. "I'm a little more traditional than that." Finally, a nice conversation—one, he hoped, that would deflect her attention from his ineptitude.

"Four predictable walls, a normal roof, cement slab,"

she said. "And don't forget the white picket fence. That's the trademark of the traditionalist, isn't it?"

"Something like that." Screwdriver in place, Ned tapped it with the palm of his hand, hoping to break loose the paint that was holding the window down. But nothing chipped away, nothing even budged. So he hit it again, harder. Same results. "Really stuck," he muttered. *Cue up even more disgrace, the man still can't get the freakin' window open.* Could he do anything else wrong here? he wondered. And to think only minutes ago he'd had all kinds of expectations.

"I like the nontraditional, myself. Like that house you saw on my computer. Lots of open spaces, angles. It's going to be steel and cement. Lots of glass."

"Like an office building." He tapped again, this time with a lot more force, and the only thing that happened was the paint on the wooden window frame chipped away when the screwdriver slipped. Glancing over his shoulder to see if she was watching, which she was, he made one more addendum to his ever-increasing level of abject humiliation. By now she was probably wondering what kind of clod he'd be in bed. Actually, he was beginning to wonder that himself.

"Like a home. People always put tags on things that are outside their norm. And I try to throw away the tags. So who's to say what has to look like what? Whether a cupola belongs on an ultramodern, inside or out?"

"Your client, I suppose." He repositioned the screwdriver. "And that's all that matters, really. If that's what your client wants, then that's what your client gets. Me, however…I like traditional, and that includes the picket fence, and even the cupola…outside." Then he hit the window with such force the screwdriver slipped off the wood frame, clobbering the glass above and shattering it into hundreds of tiny, jagged shards that splayed out all over the top half of Roxy's bed. "Dammit," Ned muttered, jumping back from the flying glass.

Roxy jumped back, too, clean away from the bed. "Let me go get my vacuum cleaner. And stay right where you are. You're barefooted, and you'll cut your feet to ribbons if you get off."

Shutting his eyes, Ned expelled a hard, angry, humiliated breath. Oh, sure, he'd wanted an invitation into her bed. He'd thought about it for days. Somehow, though, a vacuum cleaner had never entered the picture.

GOOD NIGHT FOR Georgette "Pounder" next door, as it turned out. She never let up during the vacuuming, then went into overtime when Ned nailed a piece of plywood over Roxy's former window. Somewhere around 3:35 Georgette stopped, luring Roxy into a false sense of security, because somewhere around 3:37 Pounder actually came pounding on Roxy's front door. She was cute, in a granny sort of way—shorter than Roxy by a couple of inches, probably not even ninety pounds soaking wet, and with sweet, little ol' granny-gray, curly hair. "You either can the damn noise, lady," Pounder growled in a voice that certainly wasn't granny-sweet. Kind of reminded Roxy of the beasty voice in *The Exorcist*. "Or I'm havin' you thrown out on your ass. Got it?" Pounder stormed back over to her apartment muttering expletives that would make any sailor blush, leaving Roxy wondering if the chocolate chip cookies *sweet* little Georgette baked were safe for Ned to eat.

"Want some coffee?" she asked Ned, careful not to raise her voice lest Pounder came back to make good on her threat.

"Sure, if it's no trouble. I'll be done here in just a couple of minutes. And I've got some of Georgette's cookies across the hall—"

"Twinkies," Roxy interrupted. On her way to the kitchen, she took a quick detour by the dictionary. Cupola...a small structure on top of a roof or building. No way she'd designed a cupola...or had she? Taking a quick look at her house plans as she poured the coffee, Roxy saw it—a cupola in her kitchen. Cupola...cupboard? So maybe a cupola could have been a unique touch. "How do you take it?"

"Black." He dropped down onto a kitchen chair. "Find the cupola?"

"I didn't lose the cupola." Handing him his coffee, Roxy grabbed the box of Twinkies from her cupboard, not to be confused with her cupola, and tossed it onto the table. The living room would have been cozier, but the casualness of a kitchen was nice too, especially going on four in the morning without an intimate moment between them in sight. "Are you always up so late?"

"Nope. And, technically, I'm not even up right now." Ned unwrapped his first Twinkie. "And I'm not eating Twinkies with you at this ungodly hour, either."

She shoved another Twinkie at him. "So tell me about the cat drop. On purpose, I'm assuming, unless you can prove otherwise."

"If I say yes, are you going to read a whole bunch of hidden meanings into it?"

"Maybe." Roxy laughed. "If you think I should. So should I?"

"I'm not sure yet. Can I get back to you on it?"

"You know where I am, how late I'm up and apparently how to get in." Promising. He wasn't exactly leaping over the table at her, but he wasn't ruling it out, either. "But skip the cat, okay? A nice, subtle pipe wrench says it all, and it doesn't tear up my pillow. And about that window, you're not going to get in trouble for it, are you? With the building management or owner? Because if you are, I could just say I'm the one who..." Glued it shut. About as subtle as a cat. "Broke it."

"No trouble that I can't handle. So tell me, Roxy Rose,

what kind of trouble you get yourself into in the middle of the night."

Sounded promising. Shoot, it sounded downright leading. "I got grounded a few times. My parents...they didn't like me wandering around all night. I thought it was because I made too much noise, then when I was older I realized they thought I was listening at their bedroom door."

"You seem like the type who would." He grinned. "Am I right?"

Roxy grinned back. "Parents *never* have sex, Ned. Everybody knows that. So why would I want to listen at their bedroom door?"

"Curiosity." His fingers wrapped around the second Twinkie, then he shoved it at her.

"Curiosity...well, let's see. It didn't kill the cat, did it. I believe you deposited her in my bedroom." She shoved the Twinkie back.

"So do you listen at bedroom doors, Miz Rose?" Ned arched his eyebrows suggestively. "And what do you hear?"

"Only if I'm on the right side of the door, Mr. Proctor. And believe me, the only thing I've heard lately is a ferocious, growling cat. Meaning, I'm not involved, if that's what you were asking." She sure hoped he was.

He unwrapped the Twinkie, broke it in equal halves and slid Roxy's half across the table. "I was, and I'm not either...involved. And the only ferocious growling I've heard lately comes from that radio whack, Valentine McCarthy. And take it from me, a growling cat is much safer."

Roxy's heart skipped a beat. This was not where she wanted the conversation to take them. "I've heard she's supposed to be really good. Really popular. Cute. Smart. Nice voice. Great wardrobe. Good shoes. Nice hair. Very successful." So she couldn't help applauding herself. What of it?

"Then you don't listen to her too much, do you?"

Ned popping his half of the Twinkie into his mouth just

about popped her eyes right out of their sockets. Talk about sexy! The way he chewed, his jaw moving so slowly, so seductively…his eyes never leaving hers, it made her forget who, what, when and where for a second. No words, nothing except the zing of pure sexual awareness between them until he finally swallowed, then he glanced away to pick up his coffee cup, effectively breaking the Twinkie love spell he'd cast on her. "Huh?" she asked, still basking in a bit of the afterglow.

"Do you listen to her? Valentine McCarthy?"

"Uh-huh." Still basking in the heat of that moment, she needed a fan but that would be an admission she didn't want to make. "Sometimes," Roxy admitted, going for her half of the Twinkie. Nothing like drowning a few pent-up frustrations in that wonderful creamy filling. "She's pretty good entertainment. And popular." Afterglow fading now, she was about to launch into a dissertation on market shares and where her program ranked, but that might send up a red flag, and right now the only flag she wanted to send to Ned was white—surrender.

Ned laughed sharply. "Well, you're right about that one. She's popular. Her face is plastered everywhere—billboards, the sides of city buses. So I guess if that's the way she wants to waste her Ph.D."

"Waste?"

"Hack advice."

"Entertainment."

"Bad entertainment."

"So bad *you* listen to it." This was certainly disappointing. Splitting a creamy filling with a guy who hated her other half wasn't the best getting-to-know-you she'd ever had. So maybe it was a good thing they weren't meeting each other halfway across the table to explore the many uses for that creamy filling. "So would I be wrong in assuming you're not a big Val fan?" Yeah, yeah, yeah. Like she didn't already know the answer. But under that Val-hating exterior… Well, she really liked the rest of it. Hope springing almost eternal here, even if it was about to get slapped back in her face.

"Nope. I'm not a big fan. Just a curious listener when I can't sleep. She's a little too off the wall for me. She does have a certain appeal for the masses, though, I'll give her that."

Doable! Not nearly as harsh as it could have been. It kept him in the ballpark, anyway. And she was sure glad she hadn't spilled the Valentine beans yet. On the bright side, her resolve was safe with him. Career first—and Ned? She was tucking him in the TBD category—to be determined. "Because you're a traditionalist, right?" Time to put Val away for the night.

"Something like that. So tell me about this *untraditional* house you're designing."

Ned crossed one leg over the other, settling back in his chair. "You've designed others?"

"Especially lately. Seems like it's the only thing I design."

"But do you like what you do?"

"I love what I do." That wasn't a lie. "Took me a while to find my niche, and I'm really happy there." Sure, she had been a clinical psychologist for a while, and it had been a good gig. Lots of patients to see, lots of problems to counsel through. Nothing that gave her a thrill. But the first time she'd uttered "Welcome to *Midnight Special*, sugars," she'd discovered a great gig. That thrill she'd always lacked. Then, when she'd had to make the permanent choice between good and great, good got left in the dust. "For a while I thought I wanted to be firefighter, a nurse and an ice skater, in that order, then for a little while all at the same time. Then there was the Egyptologist phase, but I don't particularly like excavating and getting gritty."

"I'll admit to firefighter, Egyptologist and cowboy."

"So you could have been a firefighter on an Egyptian ranch."

"I've never mastered camel-riding."

"How did you end up…" Oops. Tactical error asking a *bad* handyman why he wanted to be a handyman. "Actually, it's none of my business. We don't need to talk about it."

Ned laughed. "You mean you're not dying to ask the handyman why he's such a klutz?"

Wow, what a nice laugh. Deep and rich and full of earthy undertones…so much so Roxy felt goose bumps start crawling up her arms. "Maybe I am. But that would be kind of rude, wouldn't it?"

"Like listening at bedroom doors?"

"Okay, so I'm asking. Why *are* you a handyman, Ned? Especially when you're not very handy. And I don't mean that in a bad way," she added quickly.

"Like hell you don't." He grinned. "And don't go turning all red."

The blush *was* creeping up. Being blond there was no way to hide it. And hers was sooo bright red. "I, um…"

Ned ripped off the lid of the Twinkie box and handed to her to use as a fan. "I'm not a handyman, by the way."

"But you have a tool belt." She fanned frantically for about ten seconds, until the heat started to subside.

"Borrowed."

"Can you get arrested for impersonating a handyman?"

"In my case, probably yes. But I own the building, since you didn't ask. And a few other properties. Oswald, the guy who runs it, also does the maintenance, but he had his appendix taken out a few weeks ago and he's still on medical leave. So I decided to do it for him."

She remembered Oswald from the day she moved in. Nice man. Scrawny, nervous type. Definitely not any tool belt potential in him. Not like with Ned. "Then I'll bet you're costing yourself a small fortune hiring someone to fix the messes you fix."

"Well, let me just say Oswald's getting a raise, now that I have a better appreciation for his talents."

He glanced over at the bug-eyed cat clock that read ten till five. "I know you're better at the wee hours than I am, but I really do have to get going. Even *bad* handymen need to catch a few zzzzs every once in awhile." Ned pushed his coffee mug aside. "Sure hope it was decaf," he said, standing.

Roxy smiled sheepishly. "Next time, I promise." And in spite of his lack of affinity for Val, she sure hoped there would be a next time. Men this easy to eat Twinkies with didn't come along very often. "But you can't go until you fess up on the cat."

"Boy, are you going to be embarrassed when you hear how logical my explanation is." He laughed. "I bet you're thinking there's some ulterior motive in it, aren't you?"

"Isn't there?"

"Hey, I was just doing my job, making sure the plumber fixed the leak. Instead of getting under the cabinet myself, I stuck my cat in there, figuring if she came out dry the leak was fixed."

"Well, gee. What an innovative use for a cat. So tell me, how did you manage to leave her here?"

His face was dead-straight while his eyes were laughing. "I thought that should have been pretty obvious to you. Couldn't tear her away from your pillow." With that, he retrieved Hep and went home.

5

What Seagulls Do on Tuesdays

"IT'S SO ISOLATED OUT HERE, and it doesn't get any better each time we come out," Astrid said, faking a shiver. "You need something civilized popping up somewhere—a Curves, a Starbucks, two Starbucks, for God's sake. I mean, privacy's nice, I'm all for it and everything, but I also like a little something around me besides…nothing." She gestured to the open expanse all the way around them. No houses in sight, no highways, not even a byway, whatever the heck a byway was. Just plain nothing. "I think I'd be scared to death living out here all by myself like you think you're going to do. Which I'm betting you won't."

"Like I *know* I'm going to do." Sitting on her own beach towel, Roxy dug her toes into the sand, wiggling them around in the warmth, then shaded her eyes with her hand and looked out over the water…a few drops of it her very own. It was a beautiful afternoon, crisp and blue. Perfect weather in an ever-changing climate, and she loved that. Loved this land. Loved the house that would someday stand on this land. Loved all the things that scared Astrid. No, she wasn't afraid of being alone out here. In fact, she looked forward to it, even welcomed it. "You're a hopeless urbanite. A hopeless chicken urbanite, and I don't expect you to understand why I'm doing this."

"Oh, I understand all right." Astrid slapped some sunscreen on her bare arms. For a September afternoon, it was warm, sunny. Not quite summer any more, not quite fall, either. An ideal day for doing what they were doing… basking. "You lost your mind, that's why you're doing this. The real estate agent was a hunk. He brought you all the way out here, seduced you, put some crazy notion in your head that sex in the sand is the best, so you bought the place. Right? He did some mighty fancy selling and you took whatever he had to offer, including this lump of godforsaken clod."

Roxy laughed. "Close. She was older, three grandkids, bonsai hobbyist, reads romance novels, talked about retiring soon."

Astrid capped the sunscreen and pulled on a wide-brimmed straw hat. "Sympathy factor? Trying to add a little something to her retirement kitty?"

"As it turned out, I added a lot. But I liked the land. Loved it. And so far I don't have a clue if sex in the sand is the best, but I'm sure hoping to find out." Maybe with Ned? Now that was something to look forward. A house *and* Ned out here. Talk about perfect.

"And you thought about it for what, two minutes, before you signed on the dotted line?"

"Five." Love at first sight. Six months later now, and still no regrets. "Would have been quicker but I couldn't find a pen."

"Like I said before, you lost your mind." Astrid lay back in the cabana chair and tipped the hat to cover her face. Sun and freckles were a disastrous combination.

"Hey, I've got to agree with Astrid on this one," Doyle slipped in. "You've never lived anyplace but in the city since I've known you, and somehow you just don't strike me as a beachy kind of gal, Rox. You're way too city for all this seclusion. You'll turn into a damned hermit."

"More like hermit crab," Astrid muttered from under her hat.

"So I used to be way too city," Roxy corrected. "What of it? This is what I've always wanted and didn't think I'd ever have. And no one was more surprised than me when I was actually able to buy this place. Now that it's mine I'm getting beachier by the day, and the city in me is beginning to convert. So if that means hermit to you…hey, I'll do hermit."

She tried to get out here every few days. Didn't always make it, and sometimes she made the hour-each-way drive only to claim five or ten minutes. Nevertheless, she always devoted some part of every day to getting herself out there on a permanent basis—whether it was being there in person so she could simply sit and dream, or staying holed up in her apartment and working on the house plans. Today it was being there with her friends—naysayers and cynics that they were—and she was wishing she'd asked Ned to come along, too. Or instead of. But she'd already asked them, and exposing him to any part of her Val side yet was way too risky, especially since Roxy genuinely liked Ned's company. And maybe she even had a few expectations of the tinglings she felt when she was with him.

"So I was thinking about putting the house on the knoll over there." Roxy pointed to a raised grassy patch at the edge of the sand. "House on the hill so I can look down on my domain." She laughed, nodding at the boulder where Doyle was perched. "Think I'll put my turret right where you are. I hear they're great for domain-surveying."

"A turret on that warehouse you're building? Excuse me, that was last week. It's an office building this week, isn't it?" Doyle asked. "For cripes sake, Rox. You're sitting on the edge of a bedroom community. Their houses are so freakin' traditional, it looks like a Norman Rockwell. And you really think they're gonna let you go ultra-whatever the hell it is you're doing?" He shook his head skeptically. "They don't even allow poppy seeds on their rolls, Rox, and you really think they're gonna allow you on their outskirts?"

"When he's right, he's right," Astrid chimed in. "That house is going to be one great big boil on somebody's butt."

"Well, like it or not, I'm taking that boil to the zoning board pretty soon," Roxy defended. And yes, it was going to be one great big struggle. The town board was already nipping at her heels, sending its pit bull, *actually more like its schnauzer,* William Parker, out every few days to issue vague warnings against what she was going to build. Yeah, right. Warnings based on rumors started by an architect she'd canned—an architect who lived in Shorecroft. Since she'd pink-slipped him, speculative tongues had been wagging nonstop, and so the village schnauzer, who also happened to be the village manager, was sicced on her. "And the ace up my sleeve is my property line—one toe beyond the Shorecroft village limits. They may have a say, but they can't stick me with community building covenants." Thank heavens!

Doyle snorted. "Sure hope you aren't holding your breath on that one, Rox. Politicians are politicians, and once they get a look at what's on your table they're going to pick it up and chuck it into the Sound, then come up with a law to cover their collective butts later."

"And that's what friends are for," Roxy snapped. "Support."

"And honesty," he snapped back. "The town who-has have a reputation that's a whole lot more irritating than a prickly heat rash, Rox. And I'll guarantee once you take those house plans to them for approval, the only thing you're going to walk away with is a great big prickle."

"Like you know."

"Like I know. I'm a small-town boy, came this close to being a who-ha, myself." He held up his hand, measured an inch with his thumb and index finger. "And if anybody knows who-ha, it's me."

"Well look, quasi-who-ha. It's not like I'm building some kind of Ripley's Believe It or Not out here. I just want a plain structure, nothing fancy, nothing even outlandish."

"Meaning you're getting rid of the estuary in the den?" Astrid laughed.

"It was an aviary in the kitchen, not an estuary in the den. And out here it's all aviary," Roxy said, looking up at the seagulls flying overhead. They knew her now. Expected her to bring cookies like she did every time she came.

"With an aviary you get bird crap," Doyle grumbled. "And I guarantee you'll be hating it out here once you've got all those birds trained, because all they'll do is eat your cookies then fly over your house—your mostly glass house in case you need reminding, Rox—and drop a big old load of appreciation down on it. Sure hope you've got a great big squeegee handy, because you'll be needing it."

"Or maybe I have a good friend with a great big squeegee who won't mind coming out here and helping me," Roxy retorted. She was thinking Ned, and not necessarily in a big squeegee sense, either.

"I'm betting after a month out here with the birds you'll be running right back to urbanity as fast as you can, kissing the sidewalk every step of the way." Doyle spread a blanket on the sand, then plopped down on it, making sure the eats were well within his reach. Lately they'd turned this weekly pilgrimage of theirs into a picnic of sorts, and he was already groping for the fried chicken before he had completely settled in.

"You can have your urbanity," Roxy commented, pulling the lid off the red-and-white bucket for him. Picnic the easy way. Grab it from the drive-through. So totally her lifestyle these days, she didn't even have to think twice. Which was one of the reasons she wanted to get out here so badly—she *wanted* to think twice. Living in the big city simply didn't nourish that. Not for her, anyway. "I'll take this any day." She glanced sideways at Doyle, who had a chicken leg in each hand, and was eating from left hand to right. Well, most of it, anyway.

"I'm getting tired of all this city Rox, country Rox non-sense. I vote we talk about your handyman," Astrid said, holding out her plate to Roxy for a breast.

"Not *my* handyman. And there's nothing to say. He likes Twinkies." She found the breast for Astrid, then dug out six more legs for Doyle and plunked them on a paper plate. "We talked all night, drank coffee, he broke my bed-room window, then he went home."

"Uh-huh," Astrid muttered. "So should I ask *how* the bedroom window got broken?"

"If I told you, you wouldn't believe it, so I'm not tell-ing." Roxy grinned. God willing, next time maybe there would be something to tell.

"So what you *are* telling me is that you had him right where you wanted him—in the bedroom. Was he naked?"

Doyle cleared his throat, but they ignored him.

"No, don't tell me," Astrid continued. "I want to imag-ine it my way. Big, blond, brute of a handyman with a low-riding tool belt. Boxers under that tool belt, no shirt. Six-pack, and I ain't talking beer. *And you let him go, Rox?* Are you nuts?"

"Dark, jeans and you got it on the six-pack."

"My fantasy, not yours," Astrid snorted.

Doyle cleared his throat again. "Remember me? The one who *doesn't* do girl talk?"

"Yeah, like you don't listen to every word we say," As-trid quipped. "And love it!"

"I deserve a raise, "Doyle moaned, going for a container of baked beans. "I mean, I've heard you two talking about PMS so much I get sympathetic pains twice a month."

"Not PMS. Indigestion from the way you eat," Roxy threw in.

"Okay, okay," Doyle interrupted. "You're ganging up on me, two against one. I demand that raise now."

Roxy pointed to the empty bucket of chicken, laughing. "If I give you more money, I've got to quit buying you food. Take your pick."

"Not fair," he groaned, reaching for the coleslaw.

Roxy liked being here with her friends. Liked her camaraderie with Doyle and Astrid. But maybe next time she'd bring Ned out here. Just the two of them, alone on the beach…

"Earth to Roxy," Astrid said. "You were drifting off, and I'm betting it has something to do with the handyman."

"The handyman, and the fact that he hates Doctor Val."

Doyle let out with a low whistle. "Well, doesn't that make for a dandy relationship. So I'm assuming he doesn't know what you do with your nights?"

"Nope, he doesn't know, and I'm not going to tell him. He saw my house plans and assumes I'm a bad architect, and that's where I'm going to leave it. I mean, it's not like I'm going to marry the guy or even get involved with him on a serious level. So what's the point of saying anything? Right?"

That comment drew speculative looks from both Astrid and Doyle. "So let me get this straight," Doyle said between bites. "The dude saw your house plans—the one with the bathroom in the middle of the coat closet? And this rocket scientist handyman thinks you're a gainfully-employed architect, albeit a bad one?"

"Dining room," Roxy corrected. "Bathroom in the dining room."

"My point is, the dude's gotta know you're not an architect, Rox. Not even a bad one. Which can hang okay if all he's wanting out of you is…"

"It's not hanging okay, or any other way," Roxy snapped. "We're casual. That's it. And he's not wanting anything out of me. Nada!"

"Like you're not wanting anything out of him?" Astrid popped in.

"Like I'm not wanting anything out of him except for him to fix a few things in my apartment." Ooh, such a lie. They already knew he was fixless. No wonder she never lied—she was a complete bomb at it.

"Yeah, right. And I'm ready to give up pizza for the rest of my life." Doyle eyed the chocolate chip cookies Astrid had fixed and started scooching his hand over in the direction of the plastic container. "So are *you* one of those things that needs fixing, Rox? One of the things that needs some handyman attention?"

Roxy slapped his hand and pulled the container back, not sure she would even give Doyle a cookie after that crack. "Okay, so I'll tell him what I really do. *If* we get together again, and *if* there's a reason I need to. We've only been to bed together once so far…"

"Stop right there," Astrid sputtered. "You've only been to bed once? Am I missing something here?"

"The window he broke is over the bed."

"Which brings us back to my original question, how the heck did he break the window?"

"With his screwdriver. It slipped." Roxy grinned, releasing Doyle's cookies. Talking about Ned, thinking about Ned, she couldn't do anything *but* smile. "And before you say anything else, just let me tell you he's going to have to bring out the ball-peen hammer before we take this thing to the next level." Immediately her mind went to removing the big ball-peen hammer from his tool belt, removing the tool belt from around his waist, unzipping his jeans…

"Sounds to me like someone's taking her own advice too seriously," Doyle heckled, breaking into her fantasy just when it was getting to the good part. He grabbed his cookies, then headed back to the coleslaw. "Maybe *you* should make a call tonight and see what Doctor Val has to say about it."

Roxy already knew what Doctor Val would say. *Go for it, sugar.* And for once, she half agreed with her. The other half, the Roxy half, was the problem.

"Speaking of advice, have you got any for that?" Astrid said, pointing at the beachy area just beyond where they were picnicking. It was loaded with seagulls, maybe two hundred of them, all lining up, watching them, licking their lips—if birds had lips. "They're not getting ready to go Alfred Hitchcock on us, are they?"

Roxy pitched a grocery bag full of generic cookies at Doyle. "Go toss these out there," she said, finally settling in to eat her own lunch now that Doyle was full.

"Bird crap," he muttered.

Eyeing the chicken breast she was about to eat, then getting a case of the guilts over eating one of their very distant relatives while the gulls were watching, she dropped it back in the bucket and opted instead for coleslaw, biscuits and chocolate chip cookies. "Bird crap out there unless you don't feed them, then it'll be bird crap up here."

"I'm telling ya, I really deserve that raise," Doyle grumbled, grabbing the bag and stalking out closer to the water, where the birds were congregating.

"Dump them on the ground and run," she yelled at him just as he realized that he needed to run. And he tried. Oh, how he tried. But he just wasn't fast enough.

"I'll bet we don't have a squeegee with us, do we?" she asked, setting aside her own chocolate chip cookie for Doyle, since she was, after all, the one who'd sent him off to be gull slathered that way. Not that he'd ever go near a cookie again.

But then, a cookie was to Doyle as a pizza was to… Doyle. And he *was* Doyle, after all.

TEN-FIFTEEN, and Ned was knocking at her door. Taking a look out her peephole, Roxy's heart beat a little harder. She was already fifteen minutes late getting out of there— meaning Astrid would kill her for sure—and here he was, looking *sooo* like something worth being late over, even calling in sick for. Big what-to-do quandary, when there shouldn't even be one. She'd never skipped work before, never even been tempted. But still... *Sorry Astrid, but I've come down with a bad case of the Neds. Don't think I can even drag myself out of bed tonight. Think I might have to call the Proctor to come make a house call.*

Good idea, *except* she was bringing on another big sponsor tonight, a national dot com with some pretty hefty advertising bucks to spend on little ol' *Midnight Special*, hefty bucks that would translate into even heftier ones once she made it into syndication. Which meant she couldn't afford to have Astrid stick on a Best of Doctor Valentine rerun just so she could stay home and discover the best of Ned Proctor. Not when she needed to welcome the dot com on board personally. *Take it from Valentine, you haven't experienced one of the finer joys of life until you've had your com dotted by the best dot com in the business.*

Anyway, passing off her responsibilities wasn't the way she ran her business, and as much as the tartlet parts of her were telling her to choose the handyman, *please choose the handyman*, the business parts, which were in far bigger supply, were pushing her on out the door. Into his arms? *Wishful thinking Rox, but not hardly.* Because as she brushed into the hallway, he backed away from her.

"I've got a late appointment tonight." Sure, maybe he hadn't asked, but he was skimming her shredded-knee jeans and "Born to be King" T-shirt. Was that his eyebrow raising in speculation? A twitch of disbelief on his lips? Okay, so her attire wasn't very businesslike, but she didn't owe him an explanation. It wasn't like they had anything going on that required commentary. But that eyebrow was getting to her, trying to coerce a confession right out of her. "I'm, um, working on site. Casual. Everybody's casual." So she broke under the pressure and explained. What of it?

"You're going on site this late?" he asked, flat-voiced. "Is that unusual?"

Well, at least the eyebrow went back into place. "Nope. It happens a lot. Besides like I told you, late night's my thing. Works out with my, um, clients." Switch listeners with clients, and it wasn't too far from the truth. "And right now I'm late." Durn it. "Gotta run." Double durn it.

"Before you go, you didn't happen to mis-squirt superglue on the windowsill, did you? The glazier did a measurement earlier. He said it looked like a superglue sabotage."

Busted! And, oh, no! His eyebrow was up again. "Can't recall ever mis-squirting anything." Which wasn't a lie since she'd done it on purpose.

The other eyebrow was raised now, forming a very doubting arch. Time to go on the defensive with some good offense. Arching her eyebrows right back at him, Roxy looked him straight in his mistrustful eyes. "Sounds more like something an inept handyman might do to get himself back into my apartment, wouldn't you say? Especially since he can't exploit his poor pussycat again." Good strategy, turning the tables on him like that. Doctor Val had taught her well. "And as much as I'd like to hang around and wait for your answer, *or your excuse*, I'm afraid I've got to get on out of here. I have a really mean boss who expects me to be punctual." Finally, the whole truth. She did have to get going, though. But he was so darned adorable tonight, his hair mussed, bare feet again, a tiny rip in the neck of his T-shirt. And those jeans… Wow!

"*Except*," he said, not yielding an eyebrow, "the superglue was applied before the alleged cat incident."

"Alleged superglue, and it could have been a simulta-

neous cat drop, superglue gluing. I'm betting your finger-
prints can be found on both the glue and the cat." Geez,
she had to stop this right now, or she wouldn't be going
anywhere tonight except wherever Ned wanted to take
her. And, boy, was her temperature rising. In another ten
seconds she was either going to have to strip, or hit a
cold, cold shower. At the risk of Astrid's wrath, it was definitely time to get the heck out of there. "Look, I'll be
home around two-thirty, if you want to come over and defend yourself."

"I'll bring the Twinkies."

She nodded. "The old Twinkie defense." More like
Twinkie seduction. She hoped.

"Don't forget your hard hat."

"My what?"

"Hard hat. You know, job site requirement." He turned
and padded back to his apartment.

"Geez," Roxy gasped, leaning against the wall to
steady her wobbly legs. And her wobbly heart. A little
chat in the hall and she needed a cigarette, even though
she didn't smoke.

Moments later, when the elevator doors opened onto
the first floor hall, Roxy was confronted by Georgette—Georgette with an umbrella bigger than its owner hanging on
her arm. Sharp, shrew eyes, twisted little weasel smile,
smoke rolling out the top of her head.

"You're messing with the wrong woman, missy," Georgette hissed, stepping squarely into the elevator doorway,
barring its closure as well as Roxy's escape.

She was about to be bested here. Since the woman
banged on walls, she'd probably welcome a head to bang
every now and then. "If you'll excuse me…"

"Oh, no, missy. I'll not be excusing what you do. And
you think you're getting away with it, trying to keep it a
secret, but I know. I know everything. And if I have to, I'll
be telling it all to Mr. Proctor."

She wanted to snatch that umbrella right off Georgette's arm and break it, but instead Roxy tucked her hands in the pockets of her jeans and tried stepping around her. Georgette matched her move for move, though. Wouldn't let her out. "If you'll excuse me, I have an appointment...." She waltzed to the left, so did Georgette. "And I'm late." Back to the right, followed by Georgette. "So if you'd kindly—" She stopped in midsentence, her eyes still fixed on the umbrella. Georgette was raising it slowly off her arm, in an implied threat. Her tiny little hand squeezed it as she shoved it closer and closer to Roxy's face. A mere twelve inches from Roxy's nose, she stopped and simply let the umbrella hang there, like a snake suspended from a gnarly tree branch, contemplating its next strike.

Roxy stepped to the side, trying to squeeze herself between the umbrella witch and the door. No way Astrid was buying this story. Held captive by an eighty-two-year-old with a lethal umbrella.

"Not so fast, missy!" Georgette growled, hitting the *hold* button as the alarm started shrieking the warning of an impending elevator Armageddon. "I've already complained to him about the hours you keep. Coming in so late like you do every night *always* wakes me up, then I can't go back to sleep. And Mr. Proctor assures me he's going to do something about it very soon."

A sly grin crossed Roxy's face. "Then I suppose I'll have to take my punishment from Mr. Proctor, won't I?" Maybe a spanking?

"You just keep it quiet over on your side, you hear, or you'll get a lot more than some knocking on your wall. And that's a promise." She shook her umbrella at Roxy one last time, then finally stepped aside to let her pass. "I'll tell Mr. Proctor what I know about you—your secret—and see what he has to say about *that*," Georgette hissed. "Moral turpitude, missy. Moral turpitude." She gave her umbrella a parting shake.

Moral turpitude? That one caught Roxy's attention, and she stopped and spun around to Georgette, who was getting ready to punch the fifth floor button. "And just what do you mean by that?" she asked, out-hissing Georgette's last hiss. "By my *secret?* Moral turpitude?"

The only answer was the ding of the elevator doors sliding shut.

"WELL, I JUST WISH she'd move out," Roxy said, sliding into her chair. It was burgundy leather, big, comfy, with a footrest that slid out from underneath like a recliner, but it was still a desk chair. Just one that pampered her. Her only overindulgence. The rest was standard-issue old and worn, and once she got her house done she intended to redo the studio. No, it wasn't hers in the sense that she owned it. But it was hers in the sense that she made the station a whole bunch of money. Which meant she could, and would, do what she wanted—give Astrid and Doyle better working digs. They deserved it and it was the least she could do for her team since they were as much a part of the show as she was.

"So take your own advice from last night." Doyle laughed. "You know. Fix her up with a stud and let her pound on him for awhile." He was propped haphazardly on the edge of Roxy's desk, eating a sloppy, six-meat submarine sandwich.

"So, are you volunteering, Doyle? Can I pencil you in for the two-thirty assignation?"

"The only thing Doyle's going to be penciled in for is getting those promos ready to air," Astrid said. Stepping into the booth, she gestured Doyle back into his own cubbyhole. "We've got thirty minutes to get ten of them done, and for heaven's sake, Rox, no screwing up this time.

Okay? Management wants to go with them starting tomorrow afternoon, rush hour, and we don't have time to mess around. And while we're on the subject of promos, I've scheduled you to do *Seattle SunUp* next week. Five-minute segment to promote your show."

"That would be TV," Doyle commented dryly. "Real early TV. 6:00 a.m. Bet they'll want you there even earlier than *real* early, Rox. So maybe I should stay with you the night before and make like a rooster in the morning, 'cause I'm betting you'll oversleep."

"You know what? I may already have an interesting way of keeping myself up all night without you." Add some Twinkies to her grocery list, stock up on coffee, buy some kibbles for the cat. "I won't oversleep, but with any luck I'll be late."

"Oh gosh," Astrid sighed. "All roads lead to the handyman. Again! You're getting soft, Rox. What happened to that iron resolve you're always bragging about?"

"Still there. Just taking a break."

"Handyman break," Astrid quipped.

"Actually make that a handyman *who* breaks," Doyle tossed in. Cramming the last of his sandwich into his mouth, he slid off Roxy's desk and headed into his own booth.

"Low, Doyle," Roxy called. "Real low."

"Hey, if the broken faucet fits…"

"Okay guys, back on track here. Promos. Remember?" Astrid slid the copy in front of Roxy. "Short, sweet, simple. Be a good girl, Rox, and I'll buy you a bag of cookies for those gulls."

"Ten bags." Roxy laughed. "Plain, no icing."

Sighing, Astrid headed back into her booth. "Ten bags, but I'm not gonna be the one to feed them to the gulls."

"Deal. Hey, Doyle…whatcha doing in the morning?"

"*Not* going out to your property for starters."

Smiling, Roxy imagined her and Ned and a couple hundred gulls on the beach. "He has a cat. I wonder if he likes birds?"

"Back to the handyman?" Astrid asked.

"Actually, I never got away from him."

"Well, you've got to now. Doyle, you ready?"

Doyle nodded. "But I'm not betting on Rox, right now."

"Rox is ready," Roxy sighed wistfully. For way more than drive-time promos.

NO WILD CATS TONIGHT. She'd checked twice already. No kitty, no Ned. So she had plenty of time for house plans, except she wasn't in the mood for house plans. She was in the mood for Twinkies, and not Twinkies for one.

"Well, Rox. If you don't ask, you'll never get." Roxy glanced at the printout of her plans spread out all over her kitchen table.... Nope, her mind just wasn't on architecture, except in the manly physique sense. "So I guess I'll go ask."

After she tucked away the plans, Roxy darted out her door and across the hall. "I was wondering if I could borrow a Twinkie," she said even before his door was fully open. "Since your light was on…"

"My light?"

He didn't step outside. Instead, he leaned casually against the door frame. Bare-chested, barefoot, those low-riding jeans. Like he'd known exactly how she wanted to find him. "Saw it from the street, before I came in."

"My windows are in the back of the building. On the alley. Opposite side of the building from the garage entrance."

Knees, don't fail me now. They were getting ready to wobble right out from underneath her. "Wrong turn, missed the street."

"It's a one-way alley, off a one-way street. Can't get to the garage from that direction, so you must have been…"

Looking to see if you were still up. "Looking for stray alley cats," she purred.

"Find any?"

"Not yet. But maybe you should come over and have a look for yourself."

Ned glanced down at his bare chest. "Think I'd better put on a shirt, first. Had a complaint from your next-door neighbor."

"About my secret?" Sure, she was curious. Also nervous.

"Big secret. Moral turpitude."

So far he wasn't stressing over it. That was good.

"The terrible things you do."

Glint in the eyes. She was already feeling relieved.

"Half-naked men coming and going all hours of the night. She wants me to do something about it."

Big relief! "And what would you suggest?"

"How about I nail a board over her peephole." Smiling, he took a step backwards. "Give me ten minutes, okay?"

Five would have been better.

6

Tuesday Night Temptations, Tussles & Twinkie Seductions

NED DELETED the page he'd been hopelessly stalled on all
evening, then retrieved it in case anything on it might be
salvageable. He took one final look at four hours of wasted
effort and shut down his computer for the night. Man, oh,
man, what Roxy was doing to him. Between her and her
Twinkies, and his day job with a tool belt, he was seriously
in danger of blowing his deadline. Couldn't be helped.
Roxy was infinitely more interesting than yet another pop
psychology book on relationships. It was getting old; he'd
already made enough money for this lifetime, so the lure
of another big payoff sure didn't do it for him. He needed
something to get the old creative juices flowing again.
Something new, like Roxy. And it wasn't just his creative
juices she was getting flowing. "Maybe the relationship
dude's actually getting a relationship," he said to Hep, on
his way out the door.

Twinkies in hand, Ned wandered across the hall, shirt
on this time, knocked on Roxy's door, and several minutes
later was settled in across from her. No, not in bed like he'd
hoped for, thought about, dreamed about all evening. Not
even in the living room on a nice cozy couch.

"So, did you listen to that Doctor Val again tonight?"
Roxy asked casually, pulling the Twinkie box across the
kitchen table to her.

"Some. It's good background noise." Twinkies and root beer. Kind of odd, but nice. Something he'd expect from Roxy, though. "Keeps me awake."

"And you wanted to stay awake, why?"

"Business. I had something to take care of." *Which you totally distracted me from doing.* But he wasn't going to tell her what it was. Not yet. All things would be revealed in due time, and for now he wanted to keep it simple, keep his lives separate.

"So are you a closet fan? The one who always listens, but will never admit it?"

He chuckled. "Anything but. I mean...that advice tonight, where the woman wanted more than just sex from her relationship..."

"Yeah. Where it's always straight to bed and she wants to find out if there's anything more to it than that? I mean geez, imagine that." She laughed. "She wants a little civil conversation with the guy she's sleeping with. Who would have ever figured that a woman would actually want to talk with a man, and have a man talk with her?"

"And Valentine told her to wear him out with sex before they talk about it." Ned paused, shaking his head incredulously. "They should have talked at the beginning, found out if there was enough between them to get them to that next level before they stripped and went at it."

"Point is, they didn't, and now they're stuck," Roxy countered. "And getting unstuck's going to be pretty hard to do. So she wears the guy out with sex. What's the big deal? It's not like I'm telling...um, Val's telling her to hold out on him. Just wear him out then go for the conversation. I mean, that Edward stick-up-his-butt Craig who called in said the caller's guy needs to zip and converse before he unzips again. Like that's gonna happen! Once the zipper's down, that's it. Over. Bye-bye. Talking goes right out the window. He actually said she should ask the guy where he wants to go with the relationship, which is really dumb, because he's getting what he wants already, and he's happy with where he's going. I'm not saying that talking's not good, because it is. But if you do the deed before you do the chat, chances are you'll never get back to the chat. So you might as well get everything you can from the deed." She took a deep breath, then added, "That's what Val was saying, anyway."

So Roxy's not an Edward Craig fan. Figures. Thank you very much Valentine McCarthy for that one! "And you agree with her?"

"Personally, I think a couple should get to know each other before jumping right to that next level. But that's the kind of advice you'd expect from Eddie Craig...."

"Edward," he corrected.

"From Edward Craig, not Valentine. But that's not what Val fans want to hear."

Well, so much for *his* plans. A little Twinkie, a little root beer, then maybe some jumping to *any* level. Too bad Roxy didn't have a little bit of Val in her. "Could I have another root beer?"

Roxy split the next bottle with him, although he noticed she took more than half. He liked that. Showed how independent she was, how she didn't exist solely for a man's approval. Actually, he'd figured that out the first time he'd talked to her. She was happy with herself, comfortable with who she was—no changes necessary, not to suit anyone. Yep, he liked that. Liked it a lot.

"So what's your perfect relationship, Ned? One you've had, or one you haven't had and wish you could?"

"Other than with my cat?" He took a second Twinkie, unwrapped it, split it equally with her.

"You like your relationships on equal footing, don't you?" she asked.

"You could tell that from the Twinkie?"

"Equal halves both times we've shared. Doesn't take a shrink to figure it out. If you'd given me the bigger half that means you were trying to get on my good side. Small half means you're trying to dominate me."

"Suppose I'd given you the whole thing?"

"I'm guessing it would have something to do with getting me into bed. If I wasn't full already, we might try it and find out. But I've had my Twinkie limit for the night, so we'll never know."

"I think a gal with a bigger appetite than yours would top my list for the perfect relationship."

"Appetite for what?"

"Nope. I told you mine, now you have to you tell me yours."

"One thing. You told me one lousy thing and it wasn't even a good thing."

"Then maybe I'll tell you something good after you tell me what your perfect relationship would be like." He took a swig of his root beer and settled back in the kitchen chair. "My list is pretty good, by the way." And becoming more and more defined the better he got to know Roxy.

"It had better be good, Proctor, because I don't spill my guts for just anyone. But you owe me a real one, first. Not some pitiful, lame, off-the-top-of-your-head…"

"My perfect relationship would be with someone I respect. Now you."

"Someone I can laugh with."

"Someone who shares the same core values."

"Someone who shares the same core Twinkies," she said, cramming her whole half in her mouth.

So what's that all about? he wondered. Off to a good start, then she pulled up lame.

SOMEONE HE RESPECTS? Someone with his core values? He was beginning to sound an awful lot like Eddie Craig. "So you don't think opposites can attract? Haven't you ever wanted to go to bed with someone who *doesn't* share your core values? I mean, don't you find that a little bit exciting, a variation on the same old theme? You can always go back to the same old theme, you know."

"I thought we were talking relationship?"

"And sex isn't a real relationship?" Roxy asked, heading to the sink for a glass of water to chase the last of her Twinkie. All the sugar was giving her a headache. Or maybe it was from thinking about what was going to happen once Ned met Val. Either way, her head was slamming.

"Sure, it's a relationship. Just not my perfect relationship."

"So what's perfect?" she asked. "Besides equal Twinkies?"

"Maybe unequal root beer."

"Maybe I'm not good at measuring."

"Roxy, if ever there was anybody who was good at measuring *everything*, it's you." He laughed out loud. "You're the most calculating, controlling person I've ever met."

Well, gee, like she hadn't heard that before. At a meeting just last week, the CEO of one syndication outfit she was considering told her he liked that sharky little attribute in her because it would go a long way in stomping out her competition once she got to the national airwaves. A couple of the architects she canned had some choice words on the subject too, which was why she canned them. Then Astrid and Doyle, they *always* accused her of being a control freak. *Et tu, Ned?* "Meaning you hate it." So much for that almost-relationship going any further. Her head throbbed even harder.

"Actually, just the opposite. I think it's kind of cute. Some people might be threatened, but I'm not. I mean, you look like you're always playing the angles. Something's always churning inside. Even right now. It's you and me and a bottle of root beer, but there's a whole lot more going on, isn't there?"

Besides the headache? "Maybe." Damn, he was insightful. And definitely as good as her at playing those angles. "But weren't you playing an angle tonight, when you didn't come over after I got home? You wanted me knocking on your door for a change, didn't you? *You* were controlling *me?*"

"Maybe." He grinned. "But my perfect relationship wouldn't have waited half an hour. Ten minutes tops, then she'd have been banging on my door. So since you waited thirty, was that you controlling me?"

Gosh, a while ago all she'd wanted to do was go to bed with the guy. But this little back-and-forth was almost as good as sex. *Almost*.

"Look, as much as I'd like to stay and finish this, I've got an early morning." He glanced at his watch. "It starts in about four hours with some dirty furnace vents. And God knows, with my track record, I've got to be clear-headed for it."

"So that means even if I break something right now you can't stay?" Durn it. This was just getting to the good part, and miraculously, her head was thumping less.

"Sorry, no tools."

"Meaning you'll come back tomorrow night…with tools?" She licked her lips. "*All your tools?*"

"I suppose you have another late-night *architecture* appointment?"

"Whatever pays the bills, and before you succumb to Georgette Selby's deep-seated suspicions, which I'm sure she'll be telling you shortly, if she hasn't already…no, I'm not a hooker. I may keep hooker hours, occasionally dress like a hooker, but cross my heart, my clothes never come off in the execution of my work." Roxy laughed. "And I'm not an exotic dancer, either. No sense of rhythm."

"Now I'm disappointed. I've always preferred a girl with good rhythm. Part of my perfect relationship list.

Number eight, I think. Just after good sense of direction, as in one-way alleys."

"Okay, so I was spying. A *little*. I didn't want to wake you up if you were sleeping, so I looked." Actually, circled three times, looking, hoping, praying… "So save me the extra miles tomorrow night, okay? Just be here. Bring popcorn. I'm in the mood for something salty."

"You're assuming I like salty?"

"Don't you, Ned?"

"I suppose I do get a little taste for it every now and again." Ned stood, stretched and headed to the door. Once there, he turned back to face her. "Last few days I've really had a craving for it."

Roxy followed him to the door, stopping short of pressing herself into him, then did a slow once-over, head to toe. It wasn't like she hadn't already memorized the route, because she had. But a little refresher course gave her something to tide her over until tomorrow. "Then salty it is, *sugar*."

"Sugar?"

"Huh?" Geez!

"Oh, nothing. Just hearing things."

ROXY CLOSED HER DOOR quickly.
She'd almost caught it before it slipped out, but it had passed through her lips right into the annals of their history—well, she hoped there would be a *their history*—before she could swallow it. Sugar…just a spoon full of sugar and she sounded dangerously close to Valentine. A mistake Roxy never, ever wanted to make with Ned. At least not until they were in the oohs and aahs of passion and it didn't make a durn bit of difference what she was babbling. *Oh, yes, yes, Ned. Oh, yes! I'm Valentine!* She thought about it for a minute, shook her head. Bad, real bad. With the feelings she was beginning to have about the

guy, she was going to have to work on a good way to break it to him, and pretty darn soon.

"SO LISTEN TO IT, then tell me what you think," Astrid said, plopping down on Roxy's sofa Wednesday afternoon. "First promo's going to be the tame one you did, and we'll stay tame for several days before we start letting the better ones run. Although for Val, they're pretty tame, too. We don't want to shock the listeners right at the beginning. They'll turn off the radio, or turn it down when you come on, which *isn't* what we want them to do. And besides, Valentine is an acquired taste according to the latest industry surveys. Like Limburger cheese." She wrinkled her nose. "And I've heard from Spartus Syndication, by the way. They're upping the offer since Taber's is in now. Going ten percent over, but I think we can get that to at least fifteen."

"Twenty. Then go back to Taber and get ten over that." Ping pong. And she always won.

"So it's down to those two?"

"Unless someone else can ante up. I'm open, but we're kind of reaching the top now, and I'm not sure any of the smaller players can afford us, not since Spartus *and* Taber threw their hats in the ring. But I'm certainly willing to listen to any reasonable offer, because believe me, I'm not set on this deal yet."

"You know you're going to have to do some writing, don't you? A column, maybe a book. They all do it once they're in syndication."

"Yeah, yeah. Maybe I'll hire Eddie Craig to ghostwrite me something."

"Have you ever read any of those books he's sent you? They might give you some ideas."

"They're still in the box, in my trunk, all taped up. I thought I'd use them as fire starters in the fireplace in my new house."

"At least think about it, Rox. Think about writing something, anything. Okay?"

Astrid was right, of course. She had to play all the angles to get her name out there once the syndication deal went through. *Angles*...that word again. Suddenly, the hard-boiled business Roxy melted into a puddle of sentimental Roxy. She'd seen Ned in the hall a couple times today, he heading one way, she another. And even though there was no time for anything more than a few casual words, that promise of tonight was electric between them. "So how long do I have until the great Valentine invades drive-time?" she asked Astrid.

"Probably about fifteen minutes."

"Fifteen." She nodded, grabbing a handful of house plans off the end table. "Just enough time to eliminate a couple of these." Roxy found the one she wanted to work with, and threw the others away. She pulled out the pencil that had been tucked behind her left ear, crossed one leg over the other, and studied the sheet of paper with her master bedroom plan on it. Not a bad plan. Might have been nicer if it was a master suite for two instead of one. She scribbled some larger dimensions on the corner of the plan.

"Getting better?" Astrid asked casually.

"Yeah, better. A big old box of a house for one."

"Handyman melancholia again?"

"Don't know. It could be, maybe. But there's this one really big thing between us, and believe me, the better I get to know him, the more I realize that Valentine could be a huge problem. So I'm still thinking casual."

"But you're not sounding casual. He's the one I saw on the way in, isn't he? Dark hair, nice tool belt?"

"*Really nice* tool belt."

"Hey, you gotta tell him, Rox. I know you always want to control the situation, over-control it if you can get away with it." She grinned. "But if you're not honest with him, pretty soon you're going to control yourself right out of anything you might have with him. And from what I saw, you really don't want to be doing that."

Roxy threw herself back into the sofa cushions and pulled her feet up. "So what did you think?"

"About our meeting with Aphrodite Chocolates this morning?" Astrid teased. "I think they'll be a great sponsor for the show. You can do a lot of things with chocolate in our kind of format."

"I mean about Ned. What did you think about him?"

"Well, it wasn't like we sat down and did a Q and A. But I did catch a glimpse from the backside. Figured it was him because of the tool belt. And I must say what a spectacular backside it was." She shook her hand like she'd touched something hot.

"It is spectacular, isn't it?" Roxy agreed, matter-of-factly.

"Magnificent."

"Fabulous."

"Extraordinary."

"A butt among butts." Roxy sighed wistfully.

"So?"

"So, what?"

"You know what."

"Nothing to tell." Not that Astrid would believe she'd spent the whole night talking to him. Some things were meant to be kept private though, even from best girlfriends.

"And you really expect me to believe that, Rox?"

Instead of answering, Roxy lobbed a pillow at her. "Turn on the radio. it's time for my promos."

"Captain Casey, KIJI's rush-hour guy in the sky. It's 5:05 and traffic's still backed up on Aurora near 130th Street. Fender-bender involving five cars, looks like no serious injuries, although an ambulance is still en route, about five minutes out. Police have all the cars but one pulled over into the center lane, and one lane's passable each way now.

Passable, and very, very slow—jammed up coming and
going for blocks. Lots of broken glass too, so be careful if
you decide to go on through. Looks like either 1st or 3rd
Avenues are pretty clear, beginning to take a little of the
overflow, but so far not too bad. So you might want to detour on over there and take a look. Your best bets are to exit
at 115th or 145th Streets to avoid all the congestion."

"I hate rush hour," Roxy muttered, staring up at the ceiling. "Too many people thinking they have to go someplace."

"You mean like home?" Astrid was already investigat-
ing the Aphrodites, going for all the chewy centers. *Her box.*
Roxy's was tucked away someplace safe.

"Okay, so they have a reason to be there, but I'm running out of reasons to listen to all this drive-time blather."
After the traffic report, sports was up. Something about
football…big game coming up. "But aren't they all big
games? And what makes this big game any different from
the last big game or the next one? Sheesh! Just get to the
promos, already. Spare me the quarterback hiking something between his legs to the guy behind him." Actually,
that part didn't sound bad—substitute Ned for the quarterback, make her the one behind him. Or vice versa.

Astrid glanced at her watch. "About three more minutes.
They told me it would be on at the hard break at bottom of
the hour, hard break at the next top, and the hard break at
the next bottom. Lead-in to the news spot, not the lead-out."

"One," Roxy said, holding up one finger. "That's all I'm
listening to."

"All three," countered Astrid. "And there's always the
Aphrodites to keep us going in-between."

"Who's the boss here?" Roxy grumbled.

Astrid held up a strawberry-cream filled. "Well, someone's in a big snit, isn't she? Sounds to me like someone
needs some handyman sex to calm her down. But since
you're not getting it, try an Aphrodite."

"He's really stirring something up in me," Roxy said, taking the chocolate. Admitting it out loud for the first time was not so bad. The roof hadn't fallen in or anything. She glanced up just to make sure.

"Like I haven't noticed. Is it the *L* word?"

"Whoa! We're casual here. Career first, remember? Are there any caramel centers left?"

"I'll give you a caramel if you tell me if he makes you tingle all over, and we're not talking in an orgasmic sense. Just the kind of tingling that happens when you look at him, maybe even think about him."

Not fair! One admission per customer. Astrid was way over her quota. "Maybe in my toes," she conceded, snatching the caramel right out of Astrid's fingers. "Maybe my shoes don't fit right. Too tight." Well, not quite a full admission.

"You've always said that when you meet the guy who makes you tingle…"

"*I know what I've always said.* If he makes me tingle all over, I'll know he's the right one." She popped the caramel in her mouth.

"Does he, Rox?"

Chewing, Roxy shrugged.

"Come on. Be honest, okay? Does he make you tingle?"

She shrugged again, still chewing.

"Coward!"

Finally she swallowed. "I don't have a clue what a real tingle feels like. I mean, do you know how long it's been since I even dated anyone, let alone…" Reaching for cream-filled this time, she sighed wistfully. "I'm practically a virgin again. And he's so gorgeous, Astrid. You saw him. Wouldn't you like to jump into bed with him?"

"Sure. *Hello, my name is Astrid. I'm Roxy's friend, and while she's figuring out what she wants to do with you, I get to sleep with you.*" She laughed. "I think you should let it happen, then figure it out later. You're overthinking it, which means you're sure no good to me the way you are."

"The way I am?"

"Yeah, the way you are…horny!"

Roxy grabbed the box of chocolates away from her. "You're demoted."

"Hello out there in rush-hour traffic…" Hearing the promo starting, Roxy took in a deep breath. Sure she'd protested the promos. But now that they were starting, maybe they weren't such a bad idea after all. "This is Doctor Valentine McCarthy with two pieces of advice for you. One is listen to my program. You'll be amazed what you'll hear in grown-up time when we can talk about the good things, the sexy things you'll never hear on your way home from work."

"Damn it, Rox!" Astrid squealed, pounding the sofa cushion. "I told him to get rid of that one."

"And the other piece of advice is drive naked. Makes the whole experience much more fun, especially if everybody else commuting right along with you is driving naked, too. So try it, then call me at midnight and let me know if it was good for you, 'cause if I'm the one commuting next to you, I'll be watching, and it'll sure be good for me. *Midnight Special* every night at…midnight."

"Pretty good," Roxy said, looking down at Astrid, who'd slid all the way to the floor and was curled into a semifetal heap. "And you were right about that driving naked part. It could cause…" She laughed. "A whole lot of rush-hour people to start listening to my program."

"You did that?" Astrid moaned. "On purpose?"

"Actually, no. I didn't do it. I guess that was Doyle. But I think it worked out really well. Bet they'll stay tuned for my next promo."

"We are *so* screwed." Astrid rolled over and sat up. "Management wanted it tame."

"Won't matter if it ups the ratings." No, it wasn't the way Roxy wanted to make her first splash in drive-time, but there was no doubt now that a few of the listeners would stay up past the eleven o'clock news tonight. "And I'm betting it will."

"Well, I'm betting it's *upping* something right now, a lot of somethings all over the place, and I don't have a clue if that will translate into ratings points or not." Moaning again, Astrid returned to the semifetal position.

THAT NIGHT Roxy signed on with her traditional greeting, then went immediately into a break instead of a call because of a phone logjam—every line was blinking. Astrid needed a couple of minutes to get it all organized, so Roxy used the time to prepare herself for the chaotic two hours ahead. Busy night, and her truffle was close at hand for her Eddie encounter. "They're really lighting up all over the place," Astrid exclaimed, as Roxy took a drink of water, a couple of deep breaths, and a quick perusal of the first caller's problem. Not a problem, according to the two-sentence blurb Astrid wrote up for each caller. A thank you. *Interesting.*

"We're backed up on e-mails, too," Astrid said. "Mailbox has shut down, we've had so many."

"So we'll get one of the station interns to sort through them, weed out the ones that need answering, and send an automated response to the rest." Roxy settled back in her chair and gave Doyle a friendly nod. "Ready whenever you are. Oh, and we'll discuss that little mix-up later."

He tossed his hands into the air in mock surrender. "Oops. I'm bad. Thought I'd taped over it. Guess I was wrong. But look how it turned out. You just became the talk of Seattle."

"It ran all three times during rush hour," Astrid snapped. "You were supposed to send them three *different* spots."

Doyle shrugged. "Mistakes happen. And besides, I already heard management wants Rox to retape tomorrow's promos with something a little spicier. So looks like my little mistake worked out pretty well, doesn't it?"

"Pretty well, maybe, but for starters I'm cutting off your pizza supply."

He smiled. "Harsh, Rox. Real harsh. But I don't need pizza gratification after what I saw naked on I-90. She was really *hot*, but I couldn't see much. Guess I'll have to get me a four-wheel drive so I'm sitting higher. Or maybe you could tell them, Rox, to sit up straighter, or on a couple of pillows." He laughed. "Or tell all the really hot chicks to go out and buy convertibles. Thirty seconds…"

"No one was naked," Roxy retorted. "People have better sense than to do something stupid like that."

"Twenty…then you didn't listen to the news, did you? Cops stopped people all over the place. Seattle was a veritable sea of *au naturel* this afternoon. Fifteen…"

"Yeah, well, cops stop people all the time. So what's the big deal?"

"Ten… Naked? I saw them line up some big, ugly, naked bowser down the street from my apartment, then wonder how the hell they were going to frisk him. Really nasty stuff. Guess you underestimated the power of *your* spoken word."

Roxy didn't respond. She merely shook her head and prayed for the segment to start quickly.

"Five, four, three…"

"Doctor Val back with you. And I understand the fine police officers all over the greater Seattle area were kept pretty busy today during rush hour. Getting naked, were you?" She chuckled her deliciously wicked Valentine chuckle. "Guess I'd better get right to the calls, since they're coming in faster than we can handle them tonight. Oh, and before we begin, I'd like to say hello to all my new sugars out there. Doctor Val was hoping for a few more friends to spend her nights with. "She glanced up at the board. Sure enough, one naked rush hour motorist coming up. Fifty-three—*good for her*—divorced, and Astrid had underlined the word *elated*.

"So tell me all about it," Roxy prompted. "What made it so spectacular that you had to call me?"

"It wasn't so much the deed as it was going through with it. You know, doing something to get me out of my rut. I still wear a one-piece on the beach, dress in my closet even though there's nobody else here. But when I heard what you said, I said *what the heck*. And the cop who pulled me over…he was mighty surprised. Said a woman my age should know better. But you know what, Val? Why *should* a woman my age know better? What's that got to do with anything? You get to a certain place in your life and you're supposed to do what—automatically switch your dial over to slow down?

"Well, I've been slowing down for a while now, two years divorced and that's all I've been doing. Then after I listened to your advice, something just clicked in me. There's no reason to slow down, no reason to stay in any rut. So I took off my clothes, and even though I've got to pay a pretty hefty fine for public indecency, I'm glad I did. So thanks, Doctor Val, for kicking me in my settled butt and getting me back out where I belong. Life is too short for the slow lane, isn't it?"

For once, Roxy was speechless. Life certainly *was* too short for the slow lane, and it took a naked, fifty-three-year-old divorcee to drive it home to her. "Good for you," she murmured. "Good for you."

TWO HOURS AND twenty-two calls later, Roxy hung up her headphones and stuffed her truffle in the drawer. *Strange*, she thought, signaling Doyle into her booth for a little chat.

If ever there was a topic to draw out Edward Craig, driving naked was it. But she hadn't heard a peep from him tonight. Where was the good doctor and what was he up to?

7

Flooring It On Wednesday Night—Finally!

ROXY REACHED INTO THE BOWL for a handful of popcorn. Perfect. They were sitting shoulder to shoulder on her couch, not quite touching, but close enough that she could feel his body heat, smell his aftershave. Clean and masculine. Not sweet and perfumery. Maybe that was his natural scent. She wanted to find out, but decided any more encroachment into his space would land her on his lap. And tonight Ned wasn't giving out any kind of signal that that was where he wanted her. In fact, if not for some quiet jazz music in the background, there would have been no sound at all in her apartment.

"You didn't happen to go out and drive naked today?" she finally ventured, hoping to break the ice. "I heard a lot of people did." Nice and light. Maybe it would get him out of his bad mood so she could broach the Val subject.

"She should be arrested," he muttered. *"Valentine McCarthy.* That was irresponsible of her, as a counselor, as a broadcaster."

Nope, no Val broaching tonight. Not when Ned was practically snarling. "I sure didn't think that so many people would actually take her advice…no, not advice. That wasn't advice. Just some kidding around, I think."

"The hell it wasn't advice," he exploded. "She's in the business of giving advice, and when she gives them nothing but yap, like drive naked, that's what people think she's doing. Giving advice."

"Yap?" As good as it was, Roxy pushed away the popcorn. "Did you say yap?" Damn, her hackles were rising. She didn't want them to, but…

"Yap. Trash. Reckless slabber."

And rising and rising…"Slabber?"

"Slabber. Drivel. Complete, total bull. She should have her license yanked."

Okay, it was getting personal now. Her hackles were all the way up. "Her *yap* is popular. So popular it's going to be syndicated. And if you can't accept her for what she is, turn her off."

"I would except her *yap* caused twenty-nine wrecks in rush hour today. Would have been twenty-eight if a couple of kids in the car behind me hadn't taken her yap to heart and stripped naked. While they were doing it, the driver in the car behind them was watching, of course, and somehow, at the intersection, I was the only one who remembered to come to a stop, which means I got slammed from behind, first by the car full of naked hot doggers, then by the hot doggers again when they got slammed from the rear by the gawkers. So if I want to call Doctor Valentine McCarthy's advice *yap*, I'll call it *yap*."

He was right. That promo should have never made it to air once, let alone three times, and she'd straightened it out with Doyle. Even if his little stunt had boosted ratings already, she didn't want to boost them that way. "Was it damaged much…your car? Totaled? Oh, my gosh. You didn't get hurt, did you?"

"Not hurt, except a stiff neck. And my car was dinged, but that's not the point."

Roxy could feel the point coming, and it had a really sharp end on it. "I'm sorry," she said in advance. "Really sorry, Ned." Time to get off the subject altogether, and she knew just how to do it. Reaching over to him, Roxy laid her hand on the back of his neck, then began a gentle massage. Nothing big, just a little light finger stroking on some very stiff tendons.

"That's good," he murmured. "A little higher…" He twisted around until his back was to her. "Perfect," he said, sighing. "But she has a responsibility…"

"If you want to lie down on the floor, maybe I could…" Before all her words were out, he was already on the floor, face down. Not bad for starters. Now all she had to do was keep Doctor Val out of the room from here on out, and maybe, just maybe…

"Okay if I straddle you?" she asked. Wow, had she really said that?

"If it works best for you, straddle away."

Of course it would work best for her, and if it didn't, she'd make it. Cautiously, Roxy climbed over him, keeping her knees at his hip level. Nice view from the top, she thought. Nice place to ride. Nice place to ride *naked*. Now all she needed was some nice, aromatic massage oil… No, not that kind of massage. He had whiplash, thanks to her. She owed him therapeutic.

But there were all kinds of therapeutic.

"It's mostly in my shoulders and neck," he said. "And the burn on my jaw from the air bag deploying."

"Shhh," she said, applying her fingers to his shoulders. "You want Roxy to work out the kinks, you've got to work with her." Damn, too much Val. Why was she trying to slip out here? Was it some subconscious effort to sabotage this relationship? She'd have to consult the shrink in her later, but right now… "Tell Roxy…er, me, what feels good."

"It all feels good," he murmured. Then for the next ten minutes he merely groaned as she let her fingers do the talking.

"OH, THAT FEELS GOOD." Better than good, and Ned didn't want his sour mood to get in the way of it. The day had started out bad. Computer fritzing-out, Hep hacking up a hairball for an hour, getting hit—*this* sure made it all disappear, even if he'd hadn't been able to get through to that damned Valentine tonight to give her a good, solid piece of his mind. Roxy's hands washed it all away—the pain, the stress, the need to pummel one reckless radio shrink.

"You're getting tighter, Ned," Roxy said, probing deeper into his shoulder muscles. "I can feel it. Am I hurting you?"

"Uh-uh," he murmured, enjoying the sensation too much to interrupt it with words. Thinking about Valentine was causing the stress that was tightening him up, though. And frankly, he was surprised Roxy appeared to be so taken in by her. Of course, Valentine knew what it took to reel in the fans. She was the queen of it. So in the interest of keeping his relationship with Roxy on the steadily improving course, maybe he'd just better keep quiet—for now. See how things were going to work out before he spilled his guts. After all, if she knew that her hands were giving so much pleasure to Doctor McCarthy's number one opponent, Doctor Edward Craig, those wonderful fingers of hers might start doing something to him other than working out the soreness. And with Roxy, he did want to take one of Valentine's rare pieces of good advice and explore all the possibilities…of which, Roxy Rose had so many that fascinated him. Thank God for that misadventure with a broken faucet.

"WOULD YOU MIND taking a look at the air bag burn on my face?" Ned asked, twisting over.

Roxy moved forward slightly, just until she was straddling his chest. Then she saw it. A tidy, reddish abrasion about the size of a couple of quarters tucked a little under the edge of his chin. It was hidden in his stubble, and wow, how she loved him in stubble. That was the only way she ever saw him, maybe the only way she ever wanted to see him. "Well, Doctor Roxy diagnoses a special little potion to fix it right up." She traced the burn with the tips of her fingers, a light touch that caused him to shiver.

"Then potion away," he growled.

Leaning down to his face, Roxy brushed the red area with a light kiss. "Does your boo-boo feel better now?" she asked, her cheek pressed to his.

"Not yet."

So she kissed him again, this time a little longer, then traced the abrasion with her tongue. So much restraint…both of them. She could already feel his erection pushing at her, and her erect nipples doing the same against him. Thank heavens she hadn't worn a bra tonight, just in case. "Better yet?"

"I think I may need a complete physical, Doctor. And I may have need of a few of your *other* therapies." Reaching up, he slipped his hands under her shirt and cupped her breasts. "Nice therapy," he murmured. "Think I'm feeling better already."

The first sensation of his hands on her was everything she expected, and more. "And I definitely have need of your therapies too," she gasped. Just that one little caress made her tingle. Tingle everywhere—in her toes, in her ears, between her legs. She was practically exploding with tingle. "So, *this* doctor likes to do her examinations on the floor, if that's okay with the patient." Or the bed, or the shower, or the kitchen table. Didn't matter, as long as the patient was Ned.

"*This* patient would love to be examined anywhere the good doctor wants to examine him. Anywhere…" He grinned up at her. "And everywhere."

That's all he had to say. Within two seconds Roxy's T-shirt was off and she was working on removing his.

"Also, the doctor likes to stay on top," she said, her voice so hoarse from pure, passionate excitement she almost sounded like Valentine. Durn that Valentine, always sneaking in like that.

Ned blinked at her for a moment, then laughed. "And will the patient get a sucker if he's a good boy and does what the doctor tells him to?"

"No good boys here, Ned. Only *bad* boys." His eyes were full of such fire—the whiskey hues in them glowing with embers she didn't recognize, that almost frightened her. She couldn't turn away—they pulled her in, made her want to stay longer than she'd ever stayed anywhere.

It seemed this was going to turn into more than what she'd intended—great sex on a hardwood floor. Something fast, satisfying, reckless. Roxy found herself caught up in dreamy thoughts of the next time and the time after that. But that wasn't the way she ordered her life. So she forced herself back into the moment before her little fantasy spoiled the mood. Moment to moment… "And if you're very bad, I just might have something extra-specially…" Oops. Val trying to get out again. "Extra bad for you, too. If you like bad."

"I love bad," he murmured. "Can't wait for it."

"I'll just bet you can't," she chuckled, inching down the length of him until she was straddling his legs. "Now, let me do one little thing here…." She retrieved her T-shirt from the floor and dangled it over his face, tickling his nose and lips with it. "No bra under it," she teased.

"You think I didn't notice?"

"I didn't see you staring."

"I didn't want you to." He took a deep breath. "It smells just like you."

"You already know how I smell?"

"The first time I passed you in the hall." His lips curled into a licentious smile. "You linger."

She pulled the cotton knit across his eyes. "In a good way, I hope."

"The very best way. The way a man can't forget. So are you going to tie me up with it?" Ned asked, his voice edgy with anticipation.

Yanking the shirt away from his eyes, Roxy leaned forward and brushed a flirty little kiss across his lips. "Nope. But I am going to blindfold you." She raised up slightly and caressed his face with the shirt one more time before dropping it over his eyes. In doing so, her breasts passed across his lips, and she took care to make sure her nipples visited his mouth long enough to allow him a little nibble. But just a little. Then she pulled away before he had a chance to do anything more than sigh with pleasure, and reached around his head to tie the knot.

"So I don't get to see *anything?*" he asked.

"In your mind, Ned. You'll see it all in your mind. That's the real turn-on. Of course, I've got to admit I'm sure enjoying looking at you. Have been, since, well, the first time I saw you in the hall. I've enjoyed all kinds of glimpses of you walking away this past month."

"And I've enjoyed you looking." He chuckled—low, throaty, sexy. A chuckle that raised her need to a level she'd never before felt—a chuckle that told her she wanted to race to the finish before she shattered into a million shameless pieces, and yet hold back to enjoy the journey.

"You looked good, so I stared." She leaned forward and whispered in his ear, "I stared a lot."

"So what are you staring at now?"

She whispered into his other ear, "Bad boy, Ned. Very bad boy. That's what your imagination is for. What do you think I'm staring at?" Then she kissed him, on the ear, on the jaw, on the lips. A hard kiss, so potent she could have parted happy if that was all there was to be between them. But that was just the start, as the kiss cheated Roxy of breath, of sense, of everything but the want of him. And she was so dizzy from it all....

"So when did blindfolding me come to you?" he asked, as she pulled back away from him to stop the spinning in her head.

Advice to caller number three, a week ago last Tuesday. "Just now." A part of her wanted to strip him completely naked and indulge herself in the full view of him, the total feel, the entire taste. His jeans were already riding dangerously low, exposing the glorious white band of briefs above the waist, plus a whole lot more—thank heavens he wasn't a boxers man, she hated boxers—but she wasn't ready for that yet. What she'd thought would be speedy and unconnected wasn't anymore, and for that she'd be forever grateful.

Bending over Ned, close to his face, Roxy whispered, "You don't mind being blindfolded, do you? If you do, I can think of other fun places to tie my T-shirt." With that, she twisted sideways and slid her hand along the band of his jeans, first from hip to hip, then just barely inside the fabric, skimming her fingers lightly over his belly until she elicited a gasp from him. Then she withdrew them and picked up his T-shirt.

"Take a good *hard* look, Roxy," he growled. "Does *anything* about me look like I'm minding anything you've done so far?"

She didn't look. She would have liked to, but what was good for Ned was good for Roxy. Meaning his T-shirt, her blindfold. "No advantages," she said to Ned, tying the knot securely behind her head.

"So now we begin?" he asked.

"I think we began about a month ago, didn't we?" she purred, reaching down to feel his chest. Whoa, that sure was the gorgeous chest she remembered. Bare, and so smooth. She ran her fingers lightly from nipple to nipple.

Nipples—so understated on a man, yet with so much promise. She rubbed them with her thumbs, trying to remember the exact color. Brown? No, umber…a raw, earthy color that suited his dark cast.

"That tickles," he choked, shrugging his arms up across his chest protectively.

"Good," she replied, pushing his arms back down. "It's supposed to." Then she moved to flick her tongue over first the left, then the right—what she'd wanted to do the first time she'd seen him shirtless. "Does that?"

"When it's my turn you'll get to see for yourself."

"Feel for myself," she corrected, giving him a light nip with her teeth before she pushed away. Then as a prelude, she slipped her hand down his chest and farther into his jeans than she'd gone before, brushing her fingers lightly over his erection. "And it's feeling pretty good."

"I thought you preferred bad," he said raggedly.

"Good is bad, and bad is good. And what I'm feeling right now is…" Roxy twisted to place a kiss just above his belt line as she withdrew her hand "…is huge."

His response to that was a throaty moan, followed by a shudder so intense she was surprised by it. Surprised, and aroused even more than she already was, learning that something so simple as a touch held such power.

Pushing herself back up toward his chest, Roxy continued her journey, her fingers tracing all the way to his shoulders. That's where she stopped again to explore—the muscles in his upper arms…strong, gentle. His lower arms…sinewy. His hands, fingers…all so soft…so soft she could almost feel them on her, stroking her the way she stroked him.

In good time, she thought, shivering as the goose bumps rose on her arms. "Your hands are soft," and she wanted them all over her, "like a man who's never done a day's worth of hard work."

"Like fixing a faucet?" he growled.

"I rest my case."

"Would you mind resting your case just a little lower?"

Moving back down the length of him to his stomach, she sketched the contours of its musculature with her fingertips, then followed with her tongue. The fingertips elicited a gasp of excitement from him, the tongue a hearty moan. She liked both.

Something so sexy about feeling and hearing, but not seeing. But she wouldn't see, wouldn't allow herself that pleasure…not until she knew him in every intimate detail.

"Is the floor getting too hard yet?" she whispered, unstraddling him for a moment. Time for the jeans to go, and in a way she hated for them to come off because they'd been the source of several good fantasies. But as good as he was in them, she knew he'd be even better out of them. Judging from all she'd been feeling below his waist as she straddled him, *extra-specially* good.

"Everything's getting too hard, and the floor's the least of it."

"Well, can't fix the floor but maybe I can do something for *everything* else." And off came the jeans. Her hands pulling, his pushing until they were a heap scattered who-knows-where, since neither of them could see. At least she couldn't, and she sure hoped he was staying true to his blindfold.

Of course, the visual image of him watching her when she couldn't watch him was almost as exciting as watching him. Almost…

Before Ned's briefs met the same fate as his jeans, Roxy straddled him once more, exploring his legs the same way she'd explored his chest…slowly, one sense at a time—feel, taste—until he was moaning so vigorously she feared Georgette Selby's banging might start up any minute, even though they were nowhere near the kitchen wall. "Can I be on the bottom now?" she asked.

"I thought you'd never ask." Pushing himself up, he pulled Roxy into his arms and pulled her under him almost at the same time, until he was the one doing the straddling. Then he explored her belly, her breasts with his fingertips, and traced the same path with his tongue as she'd done to him. Only his journey was much more urgent than hers, and by the time he was removing her jeans, she was responding with the same frantic urgency, arching her hips to him, writhing, throbbing, moaning.

"Ned," she gasped, reaching out blindly and frantically to pull him to her. "Please..." She needed him in her, now. The pure, aching want of him was taking over, and in the seconds it took him to find his pants and search his wallet for a condom—blindfolded—she thought she would explode. Then the unwrapping...would he ever get it unwrapped? "Let me do that," she cried, sitting up, and reaching out for the foil packet.

"My pleasure. But make sure you do that with the blindfold still on."

It was, but now she wanted it off. "You've got to be kidding."

"You weren't when you started this. I'm not as I finish it."

By the time she'd taken it out of the packet, her fingers were trembling. Then by the time she'd ripped off his briefs—*literally* ripped—her hands were shaking. "I... um...haven't..." She'd never done it before, blindfolded or not, and as she found him, and discovered the obstacle of getting that little tiny thing slipped over his great big...and in a blindfold no less, she suddenly decided on a little detour before the grand finale.

"Roxy," he moaned, the muscles on his thighs stiffening as her lips met his erection. "I can't..."

She laughed, deep and throaty. "I'll just bet you can." Moments later, just as he was about to explode, she slipped on the condom, and slipped herself over him, immodestly positioning herself to reap all the intense pleasure he could give to her. Then she began the rhythm she needed, he needed, rocking slowly at first, uttering wispy little moans that were intimate and hushed. Hers, his…theirs. Nice, unhurried…but not for very long. Because within seconds, Ned matched the rhythm, pushing up at her as she drove herself down on him. Harder, faster, their urgency unchecked. And as their moans grew louder, their thrusting more vigorous, Roxy went on ahead, exploding into an orgasm that shook the walls, the ceiling, the windows on the next floor up. "Ned," she screamed. "Yes! Yes!" And as she exploded, so did he, with the same intensity. "Ned," she screamed again as the last shudder cascaded through her.

"Roxy," he whispered in response.

Eventually, after the blindfolds were finally tossed aside, and just before the ceiling plaster started to crumble from the shaking, Roxy collapsed on top of Ned, panting and sweating, contented and quenched, and, for once in her life, without a single, solitary word to utter.

Well, without a word until Georgette Selby started banging on the wall. "What do you know." Roxy laughed. "I never knew I was a screamer. Guess you and Georgette are the first ones to find out."

No, HE HADN'T SPENT the night with her. It sure would have been nice if he had, but unfortunately, nice came with all sorts of complications Roxy simply didn't want to mess around with right now. So after they'd managed to find some very *imaginative* ways to work out the crimps and charley horses that came after all that spirited commotion on the hardwood floor—*Note to self, buy a nice, cushy rug*—they'd parted amicably. In fact, much better than an unadorned amicably. Their friendly parting at the front door, the clumsy handshake, the anti-climatic peck on the cheek had turned into a zealous bye-bye demanding another five minutes, afterwards making Roxy an unwavering believer in his fine command of the quickie.

Then after *it* was over and he was really gone, she was so weak in the knees she'd slid down the door to the floor and stayed there ten minutes to collect her wits. Even then she'd nearly had to crawl to bed.

And yes, in spite of all that bliss, and the greatest orgasms she'd ever had, Roxy was glad she was alone for the rest of the night. Waking up with Ned next to her would have been so nice, but the thought of actually sleeping in his arms and sharing the intimacies of the morning after, petrified her. Two doors and a hallway separating them was for the best. *Her best*, anyway, since career first and Ned…well, she wasn't so sure about that anymore.

Guarded and casual was okay, Roxy reasoned, as she looked out over her little piece of heaven on earth—the only thing in her crazy life that made complete and perfect sense to her. This morning she was alone there, still sort of afterglowing—not a full-fledged afterglow like immediately after the sex, but just a tinge of warm and fuzzy around the edges, hanging on more like a revered memory than an actual feeling. All she wanted to go with that were a few of the gull cookies she'd brought and a Starbucks, along with the glorious Puget Sound stretching out eternally before her. A perfect moment, and she was glad for the respite. Alone. To think.

"Okay, I give up. You win," she called to the squawking gulls, lining up fifty yards away waiting for their cookies. Grabbing a grocery bag containing the ten bags of cookies Astrid had so generously donated to the seagulls, actually the payoff for doing the promo spots correctly, Roxy wandered out to the sandy area that stretched between the grasses and the water, scattered them all over the ground, then ran as fast as she could for cover before the birds decided she looked like creamy white filling and swooped in on her for dessert.

"You keep doing that and you'll end up with thousands of them flocking out here, then you'll never get rid of them." William Parker, Shorecroft's manager, stepped over the knoll, stopping shoulder to shoulder with her. "They can be a real messy nuisance. Villagers hate them when they swarm in masses, like this. And they don't normally go away once they've been attracted by something. *Like your cookies.*"

"I like them," Roxy said. "Don't mind feeding them either, even if it's by the thousands. And I'm guessing they were here long before we were, so I think we owe them a little something for messing up their habitat. A cookie's not that high a price to pay, is it?" She crammed the empty cookie wrappers into a paper bag, then dropped it on the ground along with her shoes and the remains of her Starbucks. "So what brings you out here this morning, Mr. Parker?" Like she didn't already know. "Another stipulation on my building plans, even though I don't really have any building plans yet?"

"I'm going to cut straight to the chase here," he said, his voice cool. "And I think you need to take this seriously."

"Oh, I take it seriously, Mr. Parker. I've taken every one of your straighten-up-and-build-right letters seriously. I've taken your phone calls seriously. I've taken every bit of harassment over nonexistent house plans seriously, because I've made a huge investment in this land, and I'm not talking about the money. So it's very serious to me, Mr. Parker." She braced herself for the sharp edge, almost felt it sticking between her shoulder blades already.

"We're going to annex your property. I thought I should be the one to tell you. It's been in the works for a while, then for one reason or another never came to a vote. But at an emergency meeting last night we decided that, in the best interest of Shorecroft, we need to proceed with annexation for a lot of reasons. One being taxes. Building out here means you, and a few others who've bought property in the area, will be taking advantage of our village services, but not paying a rightful amount of the burden."

Roxy looked over at him staring into the dirt. He was a nervous man. Soft and Jello-y, balding, fortyish. No devil horns that she could see, no forked tongue either. Never looked anybody straight in the eye, not because he was shifty, but because he always looked at the ground. "You can call it a tax issue if you want, and I don't have a problem paying taxes. But that's not really it, is it, Mr. Parker?" She wasn't surprised about this. She'd known from the day she'd written the check for the property this would probably happen. This, or some other form of protest. The real estate agent had warned her that changing the status quo in places like Shorecroft wasn't an easy thing to do.

"I'm not going to lie to you, Miss Rose. It's true, there have been some concerns expressed about your plans not fitting in with the community. Frank Thomas brought it to our attention, after you fired him, that you intend to go far beyond anything we have around here. But that's not entirely it." Frank Thomas, the Shorecroft architect who'd insisted on a quaint seaside cottage. At the point she'd canned him, he was getting awfully close to a thatched roof.

"I can fight you, you know. I bought the property with stated intentions to build on it long before you lowered the annexation boom on me." Brave words, and they sounded good. But she wasn't especially convinced by them. Government bodies got away with hokey things all the time.

"Oh, you can fight us, Miss Rose. We're aware of your options, but we're also aware of ours."

"And if I build the perfect little seaside cottage? Something more in keeping with the village's image." Not that she necessarily would. But she needed some options, and compromise wasn't out of the question. Her land was certainly worth compromise. "Would that make a difference?"

He turned his head away, looking out across the water, not at her, not at the dirt. "It only just came to my attention who you are, Miss Rose. Or should I say, Doctor Valentine McCarthy. And your notoriety is…well, to be blunt, bothersome to me. We're just a quiet little community of people who want to get away from what you talk about on your radio show." Clearing his throat, he turned back, looking directly at her, maybe for the first time in all the weeks she'd known him. "Out here we don't want to drive naked, or fix up our mothers with handsome studs for the purpose of hot mamma sex." He cleared his throat again. "You use the word p-p-penis in your advice quite liberally. People in Shorecroft don't say it in polite company, and they certainly don't want to hear it. Or have their children hear it. They blush at such things, Miss Rose. And I know that may be a throwback by your standards, but we don't want your kind of influence so close by."

"Because I use the word *penis* without blushing?" Roxy laughed bitterly. 'I'm beginning to take this personally, Mr. Parker."

"I have nothing against you personally, Miss Rose. But like I told you, there were concerns voiced over your house to begin with, then when this latest information surfaced…" He shrugged nervously, looked back down at the dirt. "All I can say is, as village manager, it's my duty to address those concerns and take care of the village the best way I know how."

"Which is by annexing my property and not allowing me to build what I want to build, and hoping I'll give up and sell? I think I should be the one with concerns, Mr. Parker. Sounds like a pretty shaky way to run village business to me. But I'm not going to hold your *duty* to Shorecroft against you, like you're holding my job against me." She gave way to a disenchanted smile. "All I ever wanted was a place to watch the comings and goings of the days, a place to listen to the gulls, watch the waves, a place that would be all the things a home should be…the home that everyone in Shorecroft wants."

"I'm sorry, Miss Rose."

"So am I, Mr. Parker. I expected better from you. So who squealed on me? Can you tell me that much?" She was curious, not that it mattered now.

"E-mail. No source." That was all he said before he left.

Roxy didn't watch him walk away. Instead, she dropped back down into the grassy spot on her knoll, wondering *why now?* Why, after all this time, after all her dreams had finally started to come true, had they only now dug deep enough to find Valentine?

8

"No, I still don't know what to do about it." Sipping root beer with Astrid in the break room an hour before the show was supposed to start, Roxy was still numb from William Parker's decree earlier that afternoon, and not quite worked up to the emotional level she'd need to see this house fight through. "I went out there, fed the gulls...it started out so good, then it ended up like..."

"Bird crap," Doyle supplied, strolling in, carrying a pizza.

"Do you ever *not* listen?" Roxy snapped.

"Do you ever not turn off your mic?" he retorted, plopping the box down on Roxy's desk. "Extra cheese, double pepperoni, thin crust. Your favorite."

"Sorry. Bad day."

"So I've heard." He tossed out three paper plates and a handful of napkins.

Roxy shot him a wry look. "Yeah, apparently. And that drive naked stunt sure didn't help me any."

"Maybe not on the home front, but the front office is thrilled. They've got new advertisers lining up, advertisers that want to wrap around your promos. How awesome is that? People paying good money to put their commercials on the air next to your commercial. Price went up this afternoon, in case you hadn't heard. And there's already a waiting list. It's all about business, Rox. Your credo." Pulling up a chair, Doyle scooted in between Roxy and Astrid, then opened the box. "So have some pizza, and in case you didn't notice, I haven't even touched it yet, so you can't yell at me about that."

"I didn't yell at you about driving naked," Roxy snapped.

"Depends on what you call yelling. And like I told you before, I know I shouldn't have done it, but it seemed like such a good opportunity to give everyone a taste of the real Val. It worked out great, but I'm sorry. So are we good yet or do I need to buy you another pizza?"

Roxy relented with a forced smile. "It is working out pretty well for the program, isn't it? And yes, you do owe me another pizza. They're giving me grief on building on my property because they found out who I am and they sure didn't like my driving naked spots. And on top of that, my handyman got rear-ended by a car full of naked drivers. Nothing serious, just a fender-bender, but he was sure doing a lot of trash talking about Valentine." Of course, the fender-bender had worked out rather well. Something she wasn't about to mention to Doyle.

"Yeah, I heard you telling some of that to Astrid. The part about your property."

"They're trying to pull out the big guns to keep her from building," Astrid answered. "Hoping she'll give up and go away because they don't like Valentine."

"Like I've been telling you all along. You're city, Rox." Doyle shook his head before he bit into his first piece of pizza—actually, two pieces still joined at the crust. He swallowed almost without chewing.

"That's what you think. Just watch me." She wasn't sure what there was to watch since she didn't have a plan. Not yet. But she would. Roxy Valentine Rose didn't back down in either of her personas.

"Well, don't say I didn't warn you. They probably do secret rituals at night, incantations to cast out the evil radio-woman demons." Doyle wrestled with a string of cheese still attached to the pizza.

"Actually, they're casting out the evil radio-woman demon by annexation, not incantation, not that it matters. However they go for it, it's still going to be one great big pain in the…" Anguish causing a visible crinkle between Roxy's eyes, she grabbed for a piece of pizza while the grabbing was good, since Doyle had already staked his dibs in the way of one fleshy thumb ground squarely into the middle of pieces number three and four. "I still can't believe it," she muttered. "I own that property. They don't have the right to…" She shrugged. "I just don't know."

"So what happens next, Rox?" Astrid asked, snatching her piece.

"Maybe I can throw myself on their mercy at the next town meeting. I mean, it's not like I've done anything wrong. I bought that property in good faith, and maybe once they see that I'm not what they think I am…"

"A slut," Doyle said helpfully.

"Gee, thanks," Roxy snapped, scowling at him. "Always trust Doyle to reduce it to the bottom line."

He fingered the brim of his baseball cap in a salute.

"So maybe once they see that I'm not a…slut, they won't mind having me for a neighbor. And if they won't mind having me for a neighbor, maybe they won't mind the kind of house I want to build. But right now that's jumping way ahead of myself. So I suppose I should go to their next meeting, grovel, beg, plead, sing a chorus of 'Why Can't We Be Friends?' and tell them all I want is to get along since I intend on spending a lot of my life out there."

"Big waste of time," Doyle said, his claiming thumb heading for yet another piece. "If the seagulls don't get ya, the villagers will. They'll rise up from their graves at night…."

"And stick their thumbs in your pizza," Astrid muttered, reaching for her second piece before Doyle's thumb descended upon it.

"Got your point," Roxy said, going after *her* second piece, even though she wasn't hungry enough to finish off her first. Holding it up in the air, she said, "Peace offering for the Shorecroft annex zombies...I come in peace, bringing pizza." Fat lot of good that would do, though. The handwriting was already in the sand, the ink long since pooped upon by the gulls. "Tuesday night, Astrid. Their next town board meeting and I'm going to be there. So let's do reruns then, okay? I have a feeling I won't be in the mood to do a live show after I've been brutalized." She chuckled. "I'm afraid I'd tell the listeners to strip naked and go run through the streets of Shorecroft."

"The annex zombies versus Doctor Valentine's naked motorists. Sort of makes you wish we did television instead of radio, doesn't it?" Doyle finished his pizza then headed into his booth. "Better ratings seeing them naked than just talking about it."

"So, anything new with the handyman other than his little fender-bender?" Astrid asked, once Doyle was out of the booth. "Did he *fix* anything for you last night?"

Roxy glanced at the microphone, turned it off, then leaned over and whispered to Astrid, "Oh, he fixed, all right. In fact, he put a new spin on the word *fix*. And that's another problem."

"Oh, my God! You tingled, didn't you?" Astrid squealed so loud Doyle tapped on the glass, giving them a big, over-exaggerated shrug, meaning he didn't know what was going on, and he wanted to. Both women shooed him off with a swatting motion. "You're falling for him," Astrid continued, making sure her back was to Doyle so he wouldn't read her lips—which they both suspected that he could do. This was a strictly-between-girlfriends talk, not meant for him. "You two finally slept together and it was great. Better than great, and you're falling in love with him, but now that someone's finally rocked your world you don't know what to do about it. Right?"

"Will you keep it down!" Roxy snapped. "And yes, we did, and yes, it was, and that's as far as it goes, except I'm scared to death because it *was* nice, Astrid. Really nice. Nicer than anything I could have ever imagined *with anyone*, and I'm not just talking about the sex here. I'm talking about the two of us together. Before the sex, after the sex. Talking, laughing, whatever. It's all so good I'm totally afraid of it."

"And *sooo good* scares you, why? Because he's only a handyman and you're a famous soon-to-be millionaire radio shrink?"

"Way off. He owns the building. Several others, too, I think. But that wouldn't matter, and you know that."

"So you're afraid he won't fit into your plans? Career first, the rest later. *Sorry, Mr. Handyman, you're okay for bed but don't you get yourself involved in my life.* Come on, that's so lame, Rox. We crossed over the twentieth *and* twenty-first century marks. Women have been master jugglers for a long time now. Having it all is what it's about."

"Yeah, well lately, my juggling isn't very good," Roxy moaned. "Everything I'm tossing up is coming right back down and hitting me on the head. Like my Rose Palace…the one that's gonna have to be converted into a Rose Pup Tent if I want to live on my property any time soon."

"Hey, don't knock it until you've tried it. I've heard about some pretty neat things two people can do in a pup tent."

Roxy laughed. "I'm getting too old for hard surfaces." She rubbed her stiff lower back, remembering everything she and Ned had done on the floor. Definitely worth the pain. "Of course, working out the kinks comes with its own set of interesting possibilities."

"Not even going to ask about it," Astrid said, scooting out the door. "We'll talk later, after we're off. Unless you've got other kinks to explore."

"Later," Roxy promised, turning around and putting on her headphones. Then she wrinkled her nose at Doyle. "And in case you're reading my lips, you're not invited."

He arched his eyebrows innocently, giving her the one-minute-until-air signal. Then Astrid gave her the high sign. *It's him!* she mouthed.

After her normal sign on, Roxy went straight to the call. "Well, Edward. I thought maybe you'd forsaken us. We didn't hear from you last night." She opened her drawer and pulled out her truffle.

"And you missed me?"

"Well, of course I did, because I knew you'd have so many interesting things to say. You know, driving naked." He seemed awfully mellow. He should have snapped right to the argument, but she wasn't sure she could even drag him into it. "You didn't try it, did you? Let me guess, you tried it and you liked it."

"Did you try it, Val? Did you take off your clothes and drive around like you told everybody else to do?"

"I never get out in rush-hour traffic."

"It was irresponsible, but you know that."

"I'd prefer to think of it as liberating. Haven't you ever wanted to liberate yourself, Edward? Chuck the conventional standards and just go right out there to the end of the limb to see what it feels like?"

"Out on a limb? I've seen your face on billboards, Val. Dark glasses, long bangs, scarf around your neck, wide-brimmed hat, lots of makeup. Not much of you showing. Certainly nothing close to naked. A long, *long* way back from the end of the limb. Makes me wonder why, since *you're* so liberated. So here's the offer. When you decide you want to drive naked, give me a call. I'll pick you up and we'll do it together. And the moral of this lesson, Valentine, is if you're going to preach it, practice it. I'm betting a lot of your listeners would love to see you do what you tell them to do." Then he hung up, leaving Roxy speechless, and totally out of the mood for her truffle. Score a big one for Eddie.

IT WAS A LITTLE AFTER FOUR when Roxy finally slipped her key in the lock and crept into her apartment, trying not to invoke the wrath of the wall-banging she-devil sitting on the other side. They'd gone for coffee—her and Astrid. It was one of those tacky little all-night diners; the kind where greasy fare and awesome pie was served twenty-four seven, and one letter on the flashing neon sign was always burned out. Tonight it was an *iner,* and they'd both had a heavenly slice of cherry pie, à la mode of course, to go with the coffee. And they'd talked and speculated and what-iffed on the state of Roxy's dizzy emotions until Roxy had a dizzy headache. Then they'd said their good-nights with nothing firm figured out, except that if Roxy kept eating truffles after Eddie and Twinkies with Ned she was going to get fat—funny how they both had that sugary effect on her—and that Roxy more than liked Ned and she was getting a great big case of the guilts over hiding Val. That's why Val was always trying to sneak up on her. But Roxy already knew that going in.

Still, it was good to talk to a girlfriend…something she and Astrid didn't get to do too much these days. Work always managed to butt in. Like it would manage to butt in if she did anything more than let Ned slip in and out of her bed.

Pushing the door open, Roxy had only taken one step inside when the familiar voice greeted her from behind. "Another late-night client?" Ned asked from his door across the hall. His voice was friendly, not suspicious or accusatory. Not even proprietary, and maybe she would have liked a little proprietary…someone to watch over Roxy. *That* sure was a thought she'd never had before.

"Out with a girlfriend. Best friend." She didn't bother

turning around. "We don't get to see much of each other any more." Not a lie. She was the queen of letting assumptions ride, cloaking them in half truths, but she didn't lie.

"Georgette Selby called about an hour ago. She thought you might be sprawled out dead somewhere in your apartment since you weren't making your usual racket. She said she was concerned."

"And you? Were you concerned? Or are you checking in an official capacity, as owner of the building?" She wanted concerned. But she didn't want it.

"Well, I was a little concerned, I'll admit. But you're a big girl. You know what you're doing."

Yeah right. More like girl without a clue lately. "But you stayed up, anyway?" Promising.

"Maybe. Unless that offends your liberated sensibilities. If it does, I was catching up on some paperwork."

Liberated? Uh-oh. He'd been listening to Val, again. Thin line time, here, and she had to make sure Val didn't sneak over it. "Believe me, my sensibilities are pretty tough. Though after the day I've had, I'm not sure I have any left."

Still standing behind her, Ned raised his hands to her neck and began a gentle massage. "Anything I can do to make it better?"

"Believe me, you're already making it a whole lot better." She hadn't realized how much tension she was carrying in her body until now, and what he was doing was pure heaven. Maybe even better than sex. *Maybe.*

"Want to talk about it?"

"Nothing to talk about, except everywhere I turned something went wrong. Absolutely nothing went according to plan." He was sans shirt again, just the way she liked him. Barefooted, too. And Roxy could see the two of them on her beach, him without the shirt and shoes, his face shadowed by late-night stubble, his hair mussed. Just like he was now—the irresistible image she wanted to invite in and make love to until daylight.

"And you plan everything?"

"Everything?"

"Everything."

"Did you plan this?"

She waited for the kiss, expected it on her neck, her shoulders, anywhere. Even shut her eyes to enjoy it. But nothing…no kiss. And he even stopped the massage. "Ned?" she said, opening her eyes to make sure he hadn't gone home. He hadn't. He was in front of her now, sitting in the middle of a rug that hadn't been there when she'd left home.

"So did you?" he prompted, patting the rug, inviting her to come sit with him.

"Well, I'll admit, you got me." First Edward got her, now Ned. So big deal. Maybe a little bit of her control was slipping. For Ned, it was worth it.

"Actually, what I'd like to do is get you on the rug."

Nice rug, she thought, dropping down onto it next to him. Plush, soft, its nap deep and snugly. And it was ecru, with a gentle wave pattern throughout, woven like ocean waves…the waves she could see from her shoreline. Like he'd known. "My thoughts exactly," she said, dropping to her knees and opening her arms to him.

ROXY WAS SLEEPING SOUNDLY when Ned kissed her lightly on the forehead and went back across the hall. Not quite seven in the morning. He had about two hours in which to grab a nap, strap on his tool belt and go see about Mr. Starsiak's running toilet. Come tomorrow—Saturday— Oswald would be back to take over the building management and handyman duties, thank the divine being of building husbandry, and *he'd* be back to normal life—writing by day, doing an occasional book signing when he could fit it in, and sleeping normal hours. Well, maybe not *that* anymore since Roxy sure didn't like keeping normal hours, and he intended on keeping Roxy in his schedule— if she wanted to be kept. Good thing he'd given up his practice. It was a tough decision, but private practice and media psychology just didn't mix. And truth be told, he really liked the media psychology better. Thanks to his call-ins to Doctor Val, he actually had a couple of deals possibly in the works for himself. His own call-in radio show, maybe. Or even a TV show à la Doctor Phil. *Eat your heart out, Valentine!* Plus his books, of course. They were his bread and butter.

"So it's getting damned complicated," he said to Hep. "And I'm counting on you for some support here." Dropping down into bed without bothering to take off his jeans, Ned punched a dent in the pillow for his head then switched off the bedside lamp. "I've never known anyone like her," he murmured, as Hep kneaded a spot alongside him. "And I don't have time to get involved with her, which is a problem, because I'm going to get involved with her, anyway." He laughed, glancing at the clock. It was time to get up. "*Am* involved with her and her damn odd hours." Looking to get even more involved. Maybe even spend the whole night sometime. "And it's a damned nice rug," he said, lazily stroking Hep as both man and cat drifted off.

GOOD THING SHE DIDN'T NEED much sleep because Roxy was up three hours after her eyes closed. Still on the rug, alone, she ran her hand over the dent he'd made, and basked there for about a minute before she remembered her appointment. Two prospective sponsors before noon, sponsors she hoped to carry over into syndication. Then she was going to knock out some of the nitty-gritty with one of the syndicators. Pin them to some figures. Get them to commit to some offers—how many stations initially, if there were going to be any censorship issues. Things she had to know before she sealed the deal.

Her leisurely shower lasted about five minutes, then she dashed into her bedroom to slip into Valentine. Whoops! Big mistake. No way to explain Val if he caught her. "Geez, I've got to tell him," she said, stuffing her wig into a bag, along with her Val makeup and a very tight, slinky Val kind of dress—one that showed the cleavage she'd have to hoist up and over. Hey, it's what they expected. The package sold the show. But she sure hated the damn stilettoes.

"Look, I'll have to make a quick change somewhere else," she told Astrid, as she plodded to her door, cell phone to her ear, Valentine in the bag she was carrying.

"You haven't told him yet?" Astrid screeched in her ear.

Out in the hall now, she was fumbling through her jeans pocket for her key. "No, I haven't told him yet."

"Told who what?" Ned asked, taking the bag full of Val from her hands.

She clicked off the phone without even saying goodbye. "Told someone I, um, have an arrangement with about my credentials." Good. She spun around and looked at him. His face was pretty noncommittal. *Guess he's buying it.*

"You don't think he has a right to know?"

Talk about being in a tight spot. Right about now somewhere between that rock and that hard place looked pretty darn good. "It's complicated. He knows my, um, work. Likes it really well." Judging from the way he moaned last night, really, really well. "And pretty much he's been judging me by those merits."

"So what's the problem?"

"My, um, school." Good, good. "He hates it. Some of the core ideals between our, um, school philosophies differ, I suppose you could say. And if he knew I was, um, from that particular school, I think he'd end our arrangement based purely on that fact. You know, forget about my work and hold my school against me, even though I'm nothing like my school, and my school is…was solely for educational purposes."

"But he's seen what you do, and likes it?"

"Uh-huh." She was beginning to sweat. Face turning red. Hyperventilation coming right up. "Haven't had a complaint so far."

"And you get along well with him?"

Boy, do we! "Yes."

"Then don't tell him. Why risk a good thing when you don't have to? If he's happy with what you're doing for him, and you're happy with him, I'd say leave well enough alone. People really overcomplicate their lives sometimes, don't you think?"

Yep, he'd hit that nail on the head. And without a hammer. "But don't you think that's being dishonest, not telling him?"

"You're not lying to him, are you?"

"No, I wouldn't do that."

"Not hurting him in any way?"

She shook her head.

"Then like I said, don't overcomplicate it. Just give him what he wants, what he expects from you, and if your school ever should come up, maybe by that time he'll be so happy with what you're doing it won't matter."

Well, they were sure the words she wanted to hear. But they didn't make her feel any better. "I, um, I've got to run," she said, snatching Val from his hands. "And about tonight…I've got to work. *All night.* Sorry." She really needed some solitary thinking time.

Ned bent down and gave her a quick kiss. "Don't understand the hours, but I certainly understand the drive. I'll miss you, though."

Not as much as she'd miss him.

"BEFORE YOU SAY ANYTHING, I know. I've got to tell him."
Climbing into the car next to Astrid, Roxy tossed the Val
accoutrements into the backseat. "And I came really close
just now. Wanted to, should have, couldn't. I'm weak, I'm
a chicken."

"A chicken who's falling in love."

"It's not like that between us."

"The lips say casual, the eyes say head over heels. I'm
believing the eyes."

"You need glasses," Roxy quipped.

"Apparently, so do you. Now, the salesman's name is
Curtis Keltner. He's a little glib, and he's going to go for
the moon *and* the stars, so we've got to be firm. Keep up
the attitude that we're doing him a favor by letting him
buy time on our program."

"I know you haven't met him, but do you think he
might love me? I mean, I know I have some issues, but that
doesn't make me totally a bitch, does it? Someone like him
could love me."

"He's gay."

"Ned?"

"Curtis Keltner. The man I was trying to talk to you
about. Remember? He wants to buy time from us for his
bistro. Our first appointment this morning. Don't go soft
on me now, Roxy. He's going to wine us and dine us and
try to screw us for more minutes and less money, and with
the mood you're in right now, it's going to be pretty easy."

"But he did say I shouldn't tell him. Not if things were
going great the way they were. And they *are* going great."

"I'm not feeling good about this, Rox. You're scaring me."

"I haven't been feeling too good about it either, and it
scares *me*. But I'm afraid if I do tell him, that'll be the end
of it. And I don't want it to end."

"You're about to blow a big deal for us here."

Roxy snapped her head toward Astrid. "I've got to tell

him. I've decided. Right time, right place, and I've got to go through with it. And if you think I'm going to blow a deal with Keltner over this, ain't gonna happen, girlfriend. Roxy Rose on the personal side might be a mess right now, but when it comes to business, I'm going to have my way with Keltner, glib, gay, or otherwise."

9

A Really Beachin' Saturday Afternoon

NO NED AFTER Friday night's show. She'd asked him to stay away and he had, but she would have made room on the rug if he'd come over, anyway. She wants him, she wants him not, she wants him... Twice with Ned could still be considered a little bit of spontaneous whoopee, but three times would make it an item. While she was all for the whoopee, the item was way out there on the limb for her. The limb Edward Craig said she wouldn't go out on. *Wonder what he'd say if he could see me climbing my way out there, inch by shaky inch?* And it was definitely shaky.

Sleep was a good thing though. At least that's how she'd consoled herself as she dropped down onto the rug—*their rug*—alone and spent the night. Then by Saturday, late morning, she actually felt up to her little weekend jaunt to the beach. Brand-new day, and things weren't quite so bleak as they'd been two days ago, when Mr. Parker started leading his full frontal annexation attack. That was her property out there, durn his prudish hide. And nobody but nobody was going to railroad her into selling, submitting or otherwise compromising her dream just because she could say *penis* without blushing. Not Roxy Rose.

"Going on a trip?" Ned asked, stepping into the hall just as Roxy came out with her second armload of getaway essentials—cooler, flashlight, Twinkies...

"To the shore," she said, trying not to sound too hoity-toity. Or in her case, to an empty patch of land swooping with a bunch of seagulls. Struggling with her gear, she managed to pull shut her door. "Just carrying a few things down to my car." The rest was already there—cabana chairs, radio, change of clothes, toothpaste in case she turned it into an overnighter, which she was hoping to do, *depending on who took the hint.* She intended on taking a full weekend off—no radio promos, sponsor appointments or syndication talk, no house plans, no nothing except enjoying it. Even if her shore didn't come with shelter yet. But hey, the weather forecast was good, the air was clean, so who needed a roof? "Trying to get away."

"Looks like you're getting away for a week. Saw you taking the first load down a few minutes ago. Except for the rug, that pretty much wipes out your apartment, doesn't it?"

"I might spend the night."

"Roughing it?"

"Depends on the definition." She turned, heading to the elevator, giving Georgette Selby's door a wave as she whooshed by, even though Georgette wasn't visible. But it had become her paranoid habit, waving at the peephole. "And I love the rug, by the way. Couldn't be any better if I'd picked it out myself."

"And you're not threatened because that could be my way of trying to control you?"

She turned back around to face him. "Is it?"

"Maybe, or maybe it's just a gift."

"So maybe this is the place where we explore the ulterior motives of certain gifts."

"Like wanting to keep my bare butt off the cold floor?" He grinned. "Or wanting to keep your bare butt off the cold floor if you ever get into that position? You know, your bottom on the bottom."

"So it is a control thing?"

"You tell me."

"Most people want a little piece of control, Ned, and if you're like everybody else, you'll be stepping over that line momentarily. Prefaced by a rug, maybe."

"And what if I don't want control, Roxy? Maybe I don't buy into that kind of manipulative relationship. What if a rug is a rug is a rug, and if I'm happy to let you hang on to all the control you want?"

Then he'd be a keeper—*the* keeper. Except she didn't want a keeper. "What if I'm not wrong?" she countered, marching onto the elevator. "I'm not sure I want to risk letting in yet one more person."

"Meaning me?"

Roxy shrugged, punching the door shut button. "I'm just having a bad morning, which is why I'm running away for a little while. Leave my stuff there and I'll be back up to get it in a minute. "The door was beginning to shut. Should she? Shouldn't she? What was the matter with her? Since when had Roxy Rose gone so indecisive? "Ned," she said, stepping between the doors before they shut. "In my apartment. On the kitchen table. There's a map." Then she stepped back and let the door close. A few minutes later, when she returned for the rest of her things, they were lying on the floor just outside the elevator. And Ned was nowhere in sight.

Probably for the best.

But a kiss goodbye would have been nice.

Or an elevator quickie! *Guess we'll see, won't we?*

IT WAS A BEAUTIFUL, WARM AFTERNOON when Roxy pulled her Toyota almost all the way back to her knoll, the one she was now affectionately calling Rose Hill. First thing she did when she got out was plant her flag on Rose Hill. Well, not exactly a flag so much as a red bandana on a broomstick. But it was symbolic. She'd captured her hill, and she owned it. And no matter what anybody did, that wasn't going to change.

It took her a few minutes to haul everything out of the car—everything *except* the box of Edward Craig books. She was saving those for kindling in case she needed to make a bonfire to keep herself warm. With any luck, there'd be a much better way to keep herself toasty coming her way really soon. She sure hoped so, anyway.

A couple of trips back and forth and Roxy was finally plodding back to the Rose Hill for her last time, carrying the second cabana chair, when she noticed a bright yellow monster rolling its way over her property, coming straight at her. A Hummer! It was like one she'd seen in the parking garage. Since she and Ned didn't date in the traditional sense though—dinner, movie, anything that involved transportation—she didn't know if the Hummer was his. Looked promising, anyway.

Chair still in hand, Roxy scurried back to her little camping spot, planted the second chair next to hers, and was stretched out, sunglasses on, book in hand, when the Hummer rolled to a stop right next to her Toyota. She thought about standing up for a better look, but decided the composed approach was better, just in case it was…well, someone she really wanted to spend the day *and night* with. Totally not cool to go running over there, squawking around like a seagull after a cookie.

So Roxy remained seated and tried for unaffected, going for that day-at-the-beach kind of look by slipping on a pink, wide-brimmed straw hat. Then she listened to the padded footfalls in the grass get closer and closer, discovering with every single goose bump rising on her skin that her reaction could only mean one person. And that wasn't good, reacting to him that way. Not good at all. Even though having him there was all good.

"We could have just come together, you know," he said.

"But I didn't know if you'd be the kind who could rough it. You know, spend the whole night."

"That's what you want?"

"Believe me Ned, I don't have a clue what I want. I always thought I did. Sometimes I still think I do, but things get complicated. Which is why I come out here, to uncomplicate them."

"You own the place?"

"Every blade of grass and grain of sand." She pushed up her hat and looked up at him. "Care to share some of it with me?" She pointed to the empty cabana chair next to her, then watched Ned drop down into his lounger, kick off his shoes and begin unbuttoning his shirt.

White shirt, blue jeans, sandals... She couldn't take her eyes off him. Every button opened, even inch of flesh revealed, added more goose bumps to her already growing collection. So what if she did have this little fantasy about the two of them on the beach? And what if she had facilitated it a little? Or maybe it was her evil twin Valentine who facilitated it. And what if this is the way she'd dreamed it would start—something totally impulsive, where she snapped her fingers and he appeared out of thin air? Or in this case, rolled in, in a yellow Hummer. Same thing. Hopefully same outcome.

"You've got lots of facets, Roxy," he said, settling in.

"And you don't know the half of them." But when she got up the courage he would. Just not today. She didn't want it to end out here, if that's what happened. She didn't want those memories lingering over her land like heavy Washington humidity.

He pulled his shirt open all the way but didn't take it off. "Why didn't you just ask me? So maybe you didn't want to come out here in only one vehicle. I can understand that. You lose your control that way, and you won't put yourself in the position. But why leave the map instead of just asking me, *Hey Ned, want to cozy up on the beach with me for the weekend?*"

"I guess so it could be your decision. So I wouldn't be putting you on the spot."

"Or so I wouldn't be rejecting you on the spot? Is that it? You weren't sure you could control the situation?"

"I know how I am, Ned. Believe me, I know. But sometimes I like to take it all off. Just be simple. No agendas, no control. Only the moment." She was laying herself bare here, something she'd never done with anybody before. "I'm thirty, all alone. And I live that life just fine. I'm happy with it, in fact. Arranged it to be just what I want. Then one day you just slid in there from nowhere and for the first time I was beginning to see that no matter how I ordered my life, there will always be things that change it. Things out of my control. And I didn't ask you because, well, you were right—I didn't want to be rejected. Sure goes to the heart of my control issues, doesn't it? Where's a good shrink when you need one?"

"There's nothing wrong with wanting control. Everybody does, some more than others." He chuckled. "And you more than most. But that's okay, and I think somewhere along the way you've convinced yourself that it's not, that you've got to justify who you are. But you don't have to do that, Roxy. Your friends are your friends because of, *and* in spite of it. I'm here with you right now because I want to be, not because you maneuvered me into doing it. And I really think you should reframe the way you look at it. Think of it as determination, not control."

Roxy laughed. "You sound like a shrink."

Ned opened up the cooler sitting on the ground between them, pulled out a root beer and handed it to her, then pulled out another one for himself. "I sound like a man who's looking forward to spending the day, and maybe the night, with a great-looking chick. And I've gotta tell you, I like your choice in beaches. Couldn't have picked better myself. And I brought the rug, by the way."

"*The* rug?" Roxy finally gave in to a grin. "No promises, Ned."

"I'm not asking for promises, Miz Rose. Just a piece of chicken. You did bring chicken, didn't you?"

"What's a good picnic without chicken?" And a nice, cozy rug for two.

An hour later, after the chicken was eaten, Roxy kicked off her shoes and headed for the water. In September, there was still enough warmth left for wading, and while her property ended at the shoreline, she still considered the first few inches Rose water, and wanted to do a little toe-wiggling in it.

"Are you coming?" she asked. They'd talked about inconsequential things so far—weather, sports, how happy he was to have Oswald back on the job. And he'd never once asked her how she afforded this piece of property, which, quite honestly, surprised her. He owned real estate, so he knew the value. But so far he didn't seem the least curious. So, maybe she was wrong about him after all. Maybe he wasn't lining up to control her. Which was good…and bad. Good because she really liked him. Bad because she really liked him.

"Just wading?" he asked, catching up to her. "Nothing a little more outgoing from Roxy Rose?"

Ned was already barefoot and Roxy expected him to roll up the bottoms of his jeans, but instead he unzipped, took them off and stood there in his briefs. "Too cold for these to go, I'm afraid. Shrinkage…very embarrassing to a man. We haven't known each other long enough for you to see that kind of humiliation."

"You don't expect *me* to take off my clothes, do you?" It was still daylight, the light just barely beginning to fade.

And she'd never, ever been naked out here. Never, ever been naked outside anywhere.

"On your own property, I'd expect you have that right."

"That's what you think," she snorted. "I don't even have the right to build my house…." Oops, too much. He didn't need all the nitty-gritty details. "I'm betting that right now someone from Shorecroft is watching through binoculars."

He laughed. "Then I'm the lucky one since I get to watch up close."

"It's cold," she argued.

"Not that cold. And once you get in you'll adjust."

"I didn't bring a towel to dry off with."

"Yes you did. I saw it."

"We just ate. Don't we have to wait an hour before we go in the water?"

"Old wives' tale. And as far as I can tell, there are no old wives around here to catch us. You're not an old wife, are you?"

She shook her head, on the verge of defeat. "Once. But I got cured of that real fast."

"So then what's stopping you?"

"Propriety, for starters."

"And I thought you listened to Valentine McCarthy. Right about now I think she'd be telling you to go for it. I mean, skinny-dipping is far safer than driving naked."

Roxy laughed. He was using *her* against *her*, and *she* was winning. Only Roxy wasn't sure which she. "Except for the shrinkage. And I'm not taking off my panties."

She didn't either. Not for the ten minutes they romped like children in the water. It was a little too brisk for a good swim, not brisk enough to make them run for blankets once they dipped in their toes. So they played, splashed, pushed, shoved and after ten minutes when her nipples were so puckered and cold they were practically blue, she headed back to find her blanket, and Ned followed, showing his own signs of a good, hard chill.

"I only brought one blanket," she said, dropping down onto the rug, then crawling under the blanket to strip off her wet panties. And that was the truth. But there was no way she was telling him she had a change of clothing. That would take all the fun out of the naked-under-the-blanket fantasies she'd been having since the moment they waded into her few inches of Puget Sound.

"And…"

"And it's gonna cost ya."

"What?" he asked, pulling the waistband of his briefs away from his skin.

"For starters, my toes are cold."

"That I can take care of."

"And my knees are cold."

"That, too."

"And something else is *really* cold." She opened the blanket to him, and he practically dove in, then wrapped it around them like a cocoon. Thank heavens they had the rug.

"No shrinkage now," she murmured, giving his wet briefs a toss.

"Imagine that. So do you want me to start with your toes?"

HIS WORDS WERE BARELY OUT when they were answered with a hard, swift kiss from her. It came with such a demand he was totally surprised by it. Roxy had been exuberant and passionate before, but now there was another dimension, one he couldn't quite define. But it set his toes to tingling unlike anything he'd ever had tingle before, and he met her kiss with the same intensity she was giving him, holding nothing back, not any last scrap of him.

"I'm all wet," she finally whispered, her voice so throaty, so familiar, he felt its heat tear right through him.

"In a good way, I hope," he growled into her ear.

"In a very good way if you'd warm me up by getting on top of me." Side by side, they were wrapped so tightly in the blanket that he could feel her heart beating against his chest, feel the rush of air into her lungs as she breathed in, feel the tickle of exhalation against his neck as she let it back out.

"The lady wants me on top?" He chuckled. "Are you sure about that? Because I don't mind…."

"The lady definitely wants you on top. If you want to be on top," she added, almost shyly.

"Oh, I want," he replied, rolling off his side. "Anything to please the lady."

She nibbled his ear. "But I have other places I want you, too." Then she ran her tongue down the side of his neck and stopped at his jaw. "Good places, if you're interested."

"Want to feel how interested I am?" he asked, still sliding until he was on top of her.

She wiggled against him. "Oh, I can feel it, all right."

"You ain't felt the half of it," he growled, nestling himself all the way in between her legs.

"There's more? Bad, bad boy hiding it from me. I guess I'll have to punish you." Instead of wiggling, she ground her hips hard into his, so hard he groaned out loud. "Take that," she laughed, grinding again. "And that."

"Do you know what you're doing to me?" he gasped. Other than driving him so close to the brink he'd lost the capacity to put together cohesive thoughts.

"Making you throb, I hope?"

"Hmmm…" was all he could manage. And barely that.

"No hands," she said. "Not this time. And I want it fast. You're ready, I'm ready. I don't want to wait 'cause I've got something extra-specially fun to show you."

"Extra-specially?"

"Especially," she said. "*Es*-specially fun."

That was all it took to push his need to a raging edge,

where he wanted so much more—all the texture of her, all the taste. Underneath him Roxy was already finding her position, once again grinding her pelvis into his, only this time not to tease him but to pull him over the edge with her. She was moving so wildly against his erection now, he knew she would have her way, and very soon. And did he ever want to give Roxy her way.

"The condom?" he asked raggedly.

"I have a brand-new trick," she said. "Learned it the other night listening to *Midnight Special*. No hands."

"No hands? Then what's left?"

"Want me to tell you or want me to show you?" Roxy formed her lips into a circle and kissed him on the throat, eliciting a groan so guttural he didn't even know he had it in him.

"Oh, my…" he gasped. "You're not going to…"

"You're going to owe Valentine a big apology when I'm through with you, Mr. Proctor." Then she cheated just a little. She tore open the foil packet with her fingers. "A real big apology." And placed the condom in her mouth.

It was like nothing he'd ever felt before…. "You're killing me," he moaned as the tiny little sensations before orgasm shot through him. "Roxy…" he begged, "I can't… I…oh, thank you, Valentine!"

In the end, before his climax, Roxy found her place underneath him again, and he dove hard into her, just in the nick of time for both of them. "Ned!" she screamed, grabbing hold of his back, digging in her fingers. "Oh my…yes! Yes!" He was used to her screams by now. And if anything, they drove him closer, faster, so that his climax started shortly after hers, and they ended together. And as the last gasps came, and she went limp under him, and he went limp on top of her, Ned rolled off to the side, took Roxy into his arms, and pulled the blanket up over them, ready to snuggle. Maybe this time ready to stay there for a long time…even for the night.

The words he wanted to say, but wasn't sure she wanted to hear, were so close to the edge. Because yes, he did love her. Loved her like crazy, and that was crazy because everything he prescribed for others didn't allow for something like this to happen. Not to him, anyway. Everything he counseled was about weighing and measuring a relationship. Everything he felt for Roxy was about experiencing it. And dear God, he was experiencing it in ways he'd never come close to writing about, or lecturing about, or even believing could happen. "Roxy, I…" Before his words slipped out, a raucous cacophony of screeches and screams and shrieks split right through the mood, and he pulled her even closer to protect her as he looked out from under the blanket to see what was going on. "Don't look now, but we're not alone."

"Cookies." Roxy laughed, poking her head out from under the blanket. "Over there, in the bag. And Ned, once you dump them, run like hell."

"AM I ALLOWED to ask about him?" Ned asked, stoking the fire in the hibachi. It was past sunset now, the gulls were long gone, the air was cooling down, and dinner would be hot dogs, chips, maybe some s'mores.

"Who?" she asked, trying to sound casual, even though she knew exactly who he was talking about. It wasn't like that part of her life was a well-kept secret or anything. More like the memory less traveled. And she really hadn't intended on letting him into it. Not yet, anyway. She'd been the one to open that door, though, so maybe it was time to start cluing him in on the finer details of one Roxy Rose. Roxy first, then eventually Valentine, because that need was getting more and more urgent. He needed to know, deserved to know, *after* she let him know Roxy.

"The man who never succeeded in making you an old wife. Your ex…I'm assuming he's an ex."

"Oh, he's an ex, all right. A long, long time ago." She pitched him the package of hot dogs and rifled through the picnic basket for the buns. "It was a fling," she said from its depths. "We were young. He wanted…pretty much nothing. I wanted everything." Shutting the basket, she tossed the bag of buns on the rug. "It didn't work out. We were too different, different ambitions, different perceptions of life in general." She smiled wistfully. "Bruce was a nice man, and I was a lot worse for him than he was for me."

"And you didn't try anything to save your marriage? You know, counseling?"

She drew in a sharp breath. *Shades of Edward Craig.* "We didn't have the money for counseling, which was okay because we didn't have enough invested in the marriage to waste the money, anyway, and there really wasn't any sense in trying to put pieces back together because there were never any pieces to begin with. So we walked away, the textbook amicable parting, end of story. Didn't look back, never saw each other again. No Eddie Craig happily-ever-after."

"Edward," he corrected, his voice surprisingly abrupt. "Counseling's been known to work, you know. If you're open-minded enough to allow it."

"If you want to save the marriage, which we didn't. And I was open-minded enough for the both of us when I married him, but believe me, the door shut fast on that one. Staying together would only have prolonged the fiasco. It wasn't like we walked away hating each other though, because we didn't. We simply walked away untouched. He was a man with a strong vision of what he wanted out of life, but it wasn't my vision, and we knew, almost from the start, it couldn't work between us. But for some crazy reason, and I don't even remember what it was, we said *what the heck, let's give it a try, anyway.* But nothing clicked. Not even the sex. And I know Eddie… er, Edward Craig extols the virtues of making love over merely having sex, but we never even came close to the place where we were making love." Never came close to the place where she had feelings for him like she was having for Ned.

"Virgin, I'm guessing?"

She laughed. "More ways than one. But yes, that was when I was a chaste, young thing who wanted to wear white."

"And did you?"

"Nope. Jeans. We ran down to Vegas." And she still wanted to wear white. But she'd never admit it out loud, not even to Astrid.

"So you married the guy, pretty much wrote it off as a bust right away, but you stayed with him for a while, gave it a try, anyway?"

Roxy nodded. "Sounds pretty crazy when you put it that way, doesn't it? But yes, we gave it a try, limited edition. I mean, who goes into a marriage thinking divorce. As dumb as we were, we didn't. Of course, no one could really accuse us of thinking about anything when we got married. But since we had the piece of paper, we decided to hang out together and see what came of it. Which was nothing." Not even sex after their first couple of times. "My life changes, expands, contracts. I'm not a linear person, Ned, in case you haven't guessed. I don't walk this straight and narrow line, where I come to all the right stops at the right times—graduate from college, get married, have children. My life fans out all over the place, and maybe that's the only true vision I've ever had for myself— to keep fanning. And he was linear. I was looking for something he couldn't be."

"Are you still looking?"

"There are so many *somethings* to find, and I think life would get really boring if you set your sight on one, went after it, got it, then stopped. Like I said, I'm not linear. I don't want to miss anything. So I don't necessarily include, or exclude anything. Mostly I just wait and see, and occasionally try it out to see if it works." Roxy paused, looking up at the sky. Almost dark now. And still so many possibilities. "Now it's my turn to ask a question."

"Shoot."

"Did you ever take the plunge?"

"Nope."

She waited, but that's as far as he went. "That's it? I spill my guts all over the place and all I get from you is a simple *nope?*"

"Yep."

"So I get another question." Reaching into the cooler, she pulled out the condiments—mustard, ketchup, *no* onion. "And if all I get is a one-word answer, it doesn't count, either."

"Do you always get to make the rules, Roxy?" Ned interrupted as he opened the dogs. "How many do you want?"

She held up three fingers, then changed it to four. "Most of the time." She laughed. "Since I spend most of my life playing in my own arena, it only seems fair."

"Why your arena? Why not somebody else's?"

"Remember, I tried that? Dismal failure, and I'm not sure anybody in their right mind would want me in their arena. Not on a permanent basis, anyway. I have a tendency to bust balls."

"You haven't busted mine. Haven't even tried."

"That's because you're different. You're not…bustable. And I don't know how to explain that except…" She shrugged. "I don't know." Not so much didn't know as wouldn't admit.

"So let's say somebody who's not in his right mind comes along, invites you into his arena. Would you take a stab at it again…permanent relationship, marriage, whatever you want to call it?"

"Are you a closet shrink, Ned? Because this is beginning to sound an awful lot like some kind of analysis, when all I want is a hot dog."

He held up four fingers and waved them at her. "Analysis, which you don't believe in." He tossed the dogs on the grill, then sat down on the ground next to the hibachi. "Do you?"

"For some people...a lot of people, it works. For me?" She shrugged. There was nothing left to say except that for her, it wasn't necessary. She didn't need it, didn't want it, and her life had worked out without it. "For me, I prefer mustard on my hot dog. How about you?"

"Is that my question? Because if it is, I'm afraid my answer's only one word...ketchup."

"Figures," she muttered.

10

Things That Go Bump in Her Night

"ROXY!"

Oh no! She knew that voice, and it certainly wasn't Ned's. He was wandering around out there someplace in the dark, heeding the call of nature or something, and the last thing she expected her fire to attract in his absence was Doyle Hopps.

"Rox, are you out there?"

Maybe she could douse the fire before he saw it... Quickly, Roxy scooped up a handful of dirt and threw it on the flame, and it died down to an ember immediately.

"Come on Rox, I know you're over there!"

Damn, it didn't work.

"Rox...you-hoo!"

Not Astrid, too! Good grief, she couldn't escape them even on her day off. Hadn't they seen his Hummer parked with her Toyota and figured out that Hummer and Toyota added up to hanky-panky? "Go away," she yelled. "This is private property. Trespassers will be tossed to the seagulls."

She was stretched out in her cabana chair, trying to finish her last s'more before Doyle saw it, and thank goodness she was fully clothed when they rounded the knoll. "Didn't you bring a flashlight?" Astrid snapped, tripping her way over to the area she and Ned had set up for spending the night. Rug, blanket, a couple of pillows, some citronella candles to keep away the pests. Well, most of the pests.

"It's so dark out here, Rox. Don't you have a lantern or something?"

"It's supposed to be dark out here," Roxy grumbled. "That's the way I like it at night. Dark, quiet...*alone!*"

"We thought you might like some company," Doyle said, plopping down on the rug. "You brought a carpet?" He had a pizza box and a two-liter bottle of root beer. "Cool."

"I brought a *rug*, and get off my rug! I don't want anything spilled on it." More than that she didn't want anybody on it but her and Ned. Sentimental about a rug, maybe. Silly, probably. But it was her rug, and once upon a rug... "Get up," she snapped, impatiently. "Right now. Get up...get up!"

"Okay, okay," Doyle said, sliding off the rug onto the ground. "But you're being real bitchy about a piece of shag, Rox. Not too cool."

"It's not shag, and even if it was, it's *my* shag and I can do anything with it"—or on it—"I like, including kicking you off it." So his butt had made contact with it for what? Two seconds. That didn't count for anything more than a trial sitting which meant her rug was still, technically, unsullied by any and all unacceptable rug discommoders. And everyone but she and Ned *were* unacceptable rug discommoders, which she intended on keeping that way.

"Being out here alone's already making you nuts, Rox. You're not gonna make it through the night all by yourself. And once they start rising from their graves, it's gonna get real ugly." Automatically, Doyle handed a piece of extra pepperoni, extra cheese over to Roxy, but she declined it. She'd eaten three dogs with mustard, skipped the fourth to save room for the s'mores, along with slaw and chips, and she was already in her baggy jeans and barely zipping them at that.

"It's your favorite," Doyle coaxed, leaning over, waving it under her nose.

"Already ate."

"Are we interrupting something?" Astrid asked cautiously. "Because when you told me you were coming out here, and I asked if you were coming alone, you said yes. And when I asked if you were sure…"

"I know, I said yes, which is what I meant at the time. But I was wrong. I mean, didn't you see that yellow Hummer out there by my Toyota?"

Astrid slapped Doyle on the shoulder. "I told you we shouldn't come in the back way, like we were sneaking in or something." She turned to Roxy. "He got lost, and we ended up on the other side, over near the road to town. So he decided we should just park there and walk on in instead of backtracking out to the main road and risk ending up in the Sound or in somebody's back yard." She grabbed the pizza box away from Doyle. "I told you I should drive, but no. You said you knew the way. Now look what you've done! And I told you this was a bad idea didn't I? That we shouldn't come out here without calling first."

He grabbed the box back. "So there's enough pizza for four. What's the big deal? It's not like we walked up on them while they were still boinking."

"Boinking?" Roxy sputtered.

"Didn't I heard Doctor Val use that term the other night?" he snorted, laughing.

"You know what, Doyle…Astrid… It's a long way back and it's getting late. There's a nice little inn in town. Why don't you two go spend the night there *on me*. Okay? I appreciate your coming out here checking on me, but I promise, I don't need to be checked on." And the last thing she needed was getting her Valentine cohorts near her Roxy lover. Bad mix. Things would slip out, which was all right, but she wanted to be the one letting them slip. And at the right time, which still wasn't now.

"Okay?" she repeated. "Order room service, anything you like." She grabbed her purse, pulled out her credit card and tossed it to Doyle. "Anything. Filet mignon, two of them if you want."

"Meaning she doesn't want us here," Astrid said, kicking Doyle's foot. "So let's get out of here before she fires us."

"Want me to leave the pizza?" Doyle asked, clutching it to his chest.

"No!"

IMMEDIATELY AFTER THEY had gone, Ned returned to the fire. "You're their boss?" he asked.

"You were listening?"

"Didn't want to interrupt. Didn't want to put you in a position of having to explain anything to them…or me, if that's what you want."

"Yes, they work for me."

"Then you own your own company? Guess I missed that somewhere."

"You missed it because I never told you." Suddenly her mood for the evening, and the night, was over. She was owing him explanations now. He was expecting details. And that's where it became complicated…complicated because she was falling in love with a man who didn't have a clue who she was, and would probably dump her when he found out.

"NO, WE DIDN'T DO ANYTHING ELSE. We left right after you did," Roxy groused to Astrid. "I came home and spent the rest of the weekend doing nothing but house plans and sleeping, and I don't know what he did because he didn't call, didn't come over. Nothing. And why should he after the way I acted? Kicking him off my beach the way I kicked Doyle off my rug. I mean, it was crazy. All of a sudden the two parts of my life are together in the wrong place, and I can't handle it. So I faked a stomachache from the hot dogs and told him I had to go home."

Then she hadn't gone out, hadn't invited anybody in except the pizza delivery boy, the Chinese food delivery boy and the pizza delivery boy again. Drowning her problems in junk food hadn't been the fix she needed, though, because she'd missed him. And it wasn't just about the sex. She'd missed *him*. And she'd wanted to call him, thought about calling him, picked up the phone and put it down a hundred times, but she wouldn't do it because missing him scared her to death. Having those kinds of strong, getting-stronger-every-day feelings scared her even *more* to death. "And I know what you're going to say before you say it. I'm running away. I'll admit it. Running like a marathoner. But I can't help it. This is all so new to me, and every bit of resolve I put up so it won't happen just keeps failing me. Yeah, I want him. No, I don't. Yes, I do. And that's *so* not like me, Astrid. I'm not in control here."

"So who says you have to be in control all the time? Sometimes a nice, uncontrolled detour is just what we need to spice up our lives. And I think, right now, that's exactly what you need. Spice!"

Astrid handed Roxy the blush. A nice rosy color to go with the bluish eyeliner. Good camera appeal, even though her eyes would hide behind dark glasses for the whole five-minute shoot. Even so, the makeup enhanced her attitude. Without it she was just plain Roxy, with it she was anything but plain Valentine. Makeup to Valentine was like spinach to Popeye. "So maybe it's not about total control. I did give in to some things."

Astrid chuckled. "Dare I ask?"

"No, you *daren't*. But even on an uncontrolled detour, there's got to be some control, doesn't there? I mean, this guy drags a rug out to the beach, for heaven's sake, and I just throw myself down on it and wait for him to come take me. Which is so totally about losing control. *All* control, Astrid. And when I'm with him I don't even care. It's almost like I'm waiting for him to come take it away."

"But if you love him…"

"Who said anything about love?" Roxy snapped.

"Like I was saying, *if you love him*, control shouldn't be an issue. And like it or not, Rox, your giving it up willingly pretty much tells me how you love the guy. For a relationship counselor you're not too sharp about your own relationship, but let me give you a little piece of advice. Figure it out before he gets tired of you waffling all over the place and walks away. If he does that, girlfriend, I'm gonna kill you because beautiful butts like that don't come along every day. Neither do people who make you all gushy, and you're not too bad in a little gush. Kinda makes you seem like the rest of us peons."

Laughing, Roxy gave her Val wig a good shake then stuck it on her head. "I'm *not* gushy. Just…cautious." She considered the wild, sexy look of her uncombed wig, then decided to go with her usual, sleek and sophisticated. That's what people knew, what they expected from Val. The same—like pretty much everything else in her life.

"I love you, Rox, but you're not easy. Not for me, not for Doyle, and I imagine not for your handyman. You've got to have it your way all the time or you take your toys and go home, like Saturday night. We interrupted you for, like, three minutes tops, and you pack up your rug and hike fanny all the way home." She shook her head. "And I'm betting you didn't even think about what your handyman wanted, did you? You were angry, at us for showing up, at him for asking personal questions you weren't ready to answer, so you left. Right?"

"Someone needs to slap me," Roxy said, slipping the wires to some flamboyant two-inch chandeliers earrings through her ears.

"Believe me, another time or two with you and he probably will. For heaven's sake, Rox. Get a clue. The man loves you, or he wouldn't keep coming back for more. So all I can say is, if you don't admit it to yourself first, that *you* love him, then get yourself out on some rooftop and shout it, you're going to get everything you've always wanted, *except* him. And sweetie, a rug for one can get awfully lonely."

"It was, all weekend," she admitted sadly. That's where she'd spent most of her time. Even slept there. On a bright note, if it could be called a bright note, the house plans were done now. All the toilets were in the bathrooms, the appliances in the kitchen, the bannisters on the stairs, it was exactly what she wanted. Steel, cement and glass—no fuss, no muss. Not like her feelings, though. All fuss, all muss. She sighed the melancholy sigh of a woman who would have rather spent the weekend doing something other than a do-it-yourself CAD program. "Do you think maybe Doctor Craig might have some advice for me? Because Valentine's advice sure isn't working out, is it?"

"I'm so sorry, Rox. I really didn't mean to walk in on anything out there," Astrid said, handing Roxy her glasses. "But Doyle's in the big-brother mode with you and he really didn't think you should be staying out there alone, especially with all the trouble you're having with the locals. And since it was Saturday night and God knows I never have a date, I thought it sounded like a good idea...at the time. But I did want to call first. Cross my heart."

"Doesn't matter. Like I said, I panicked. If I were going about this the right way I wouldn't have. But I'm not, and I got myself in such a knot over how to fix the mess I'd have managed to wreck the weekend, anyway." Roxy took one final appraisal in the mirror, added another four inches to her height with some killer spikes and Valentine was good to go. "So tell me, what do I need to do out there?"

Ten minutes until air, then she'd be the sunrise sensation on *Seattle SunUp*. Another of the mandatory promos that went along with her career.

"Just promote the hell out of the show. Interviewer's name is Brianna Dean, by the way. She said the time is yours to do with as you see fit. That she'll lead you in with a couple of general questions, then it's up to Val to do what Val does best. Except no sex, Rox. Not this audience, and I'm warning you…"

"Yeah, yeah, no sex. Did you give this Brianna the regular prelim sheet of Valentine questions, or is she just winging it?" Winging it was always dangerous. Some of these interviewers went way out there in an attempt to grab a few ratings points. She chuckled. Yeah, like she hadn't done that herself.

"Sent her the sheet last week, along with your bio. She should be all set."

"And it's live, right? You did tell me that, didn't you?"

"Absolutely live, which is why you've got to behave yourself. Where's your other bra, Rox? You're too flat."

Roxy glanced down. "Way too early for cleavage. They'll just have to accept me flat." One more quick glance in the mirror showed nothing out of place. Wig okay, makeup caked on like she'd fallen in a mud puddle, extra-large shades to make up for the lack of a hat. And she did so love hiding under that hat! Yep, she was ready. "Okay, well, any time Brianna's ready to go."

Roxy tugged her Valentine-standard barely-below-the-buns skirt into place and headed down the hall to the studio. As she wiggled into her seat across from Brianna on the set, crossing her legs so that everything showing on TV was appropriate for the 6:00 a.m. crowd to see, she smiled over at the interviewer who was gulping coffee by the bucket and not making eye contact. Not a morning person, Roxy decided. "Thanks so much for inviting me," Roxy said, adjusting her Valentine voice.

Brianna blinked, then forced a tight smile. "Welcome. And I'll just ask some simple questions, if that's okay with you. You've done television before, haven't you?"

"It's the same as radio, sugar, only they get to have a look at me." Finally, Valentine had arrived.

Brianna nodded curtly, then stared at her program notes until she was prompted to go. "I'd like to welcome a special guest to *SunUp* this morning…one who's been keeping some of you up very late at night, listening to her number-one-rated radio program, *Midnight Special.* Valentine McCarthy. Or should I say, Doctor Valentine McCarthy? You are a doctor, aren't you? Because from some of the advice I've heard, well, let's just say it doesn't sound much like what someone who's earned a doctorate would give."

The camera switched to Roxy. "Ph.D. in psychology does make me a doctor," she responded, forcing a smile. Someone should have told her Brianna was a twit. "And thanks for inviting me to your little segment of *Seattle SunUp,* Bri."

"Brianna," she corrected. "And it's my pleasure. So tell me, Valentine…"

"Just call me Val, Bri. Everybody does."

"Brianna," she corrected again. "So tell me, Val, why radio junk psychology is more rewarding for you than being in a private practice, since you're obviously qualified to be in private practice, although I couldn't find any record of it."

That's because my practice was in my real name, you twit. "Well, Bri, I'm not really sure how to answer you. I suppose I could debate you on the merits of what's considered junk radio or even junk television, for that matter. Or talk to you about *Midnight Special's* tremendous ratings thanks to its extra-specially supportive listeners. Or even ask you why you're doing a tiny little five-minute segment on the early-morning news for people to watch while gargling.

But instead, let me just say that I do what I love to do. And *Midnight Special* is what I love to do, have loved doing since the first time I went on air. And I don't have to make excuses, Bri." Roxy tilted her shades down just enough to glare over the tops of them at Bri. "Or defend my choice." Her message delivered quite clearly, the shades went back up. "*Midnight Special* has a wonderful audience and I look forward to chatting with them each and every night."

"Well, Val, you do have quite the reputation for what you do *each and every night*," Brianna continued, undaunted. "Good and bad, according to some critics. Speaking of which, we have one of those critics with us this morning. A name you might recognize...Doctor Edward Craig, in person."

Doctor Edward... His name took a second to sink in, then Roxy's heart jumped all the way up into her throat and almost choked her. "Craig?" she sputtered. He was here? No way! She searched frantically for Astrid, who was standing off to the side of the set looking dumbstruck. "M-my Doctor Craig?" Roxy stammered, her Valentine voice coming out like a goose with a sore throat.

"That's right, Val. *Your* Doctor Craig. We listen to the two of you go at each other every night, and I thought it might be nice for your listeners to see you debate face-to-face for a change."

"How interesting, Bri," she managed. "Only thing is, *my* listeners are still sound asleep. But I'm sure the couple of people who are tuning in right now might find it interesting." *Okay, Rox. You can do this.* It was inevitable. There had to be a meeting. But she wanted one where she had the...control. Yikes, Ned was right about her. Astrid was right. The whole freakin' universe was right. *Doesn't matter. You can still do this.* So since they were all right about her, where was the control when she needed it? Needed it, like right now! *You have to do this.* Val could for sure, but what about Roxy? And right now Roxy was front and center, wishing she was home under her rug.

Brianna tossed her a wry look, then turned to the camera. "I'm pleased to welcome Doctor Edward Craig this morning. He's author of twelve riveting *relationship* bestsellers, including his latest book, *Looking Beyond the Bedroom*. Doctor Craig…"

"Riveting?" Roxy muttered, almost under her breath. "Guess you haven't read them, have you?" Not that she had either. But nothing about Craig could be riveting.

"Hello, Brianna. Hello, Valentine…at last we meet." The voice was behind her, getting closer and closer. "Face to face."

He stepped around the little grouping of chairs, extending his hand first to Roxy. She saw the hand, looked up, saw the chest…then the throat…the face. No, uh-uh. Couldn't be. Dreaming…this was a dream. Or she was hallucinating?

"Edward," she said, taking his hand, trying to make sure hers was rock-steady. "So nice to meet you in person, after all this time." Same hand. She knew that hand. Boy, did she know that hand. *Please let the coma come and take me now!*

"So please sit down, Doctor Craig." Brianna pointed to the chair across from Roxy. "And tell us what you think about Doctor Val as a relationship counselor."

"Not a relationship counselor, Bri," Roxy snapped, her eyes still on Ned. Did he recognize her? No signs of it if he did. "A radio talk-show host. There's a big difference. And yes, Edward, please tell us what you think about me. I'm sure the two people out there listening to this show probably haven't heard it all before." He was smiling, but it wasn't a smile she knew. It was too reserved, not sexy at all like she was used to. No humor in it, no spark, no real challenge, not like she got from Ned. So maybe it was his professional smile, and he didn't look nearly so good in it. He didn't look nearly so good in his gray wool suit as he did his jeans, either…without his shirt. Hard to imagine that gorgeous chest under that stuffed shirt and noose of a silk neck tie. Although she had to admit, now that she was getting used to it, he did look pretty good all starched up.

But this was Ned, for heaven's sake. Ned and Edward…Craig and Proctor. Ned Proctor, Edward Craig… Ned a nickname for Edward. So Edward Craig…Proctor. Doctor Edward Craig Proctor. Suddenly, Roxy laughed out loud. No wonder he'd changed his name. Doctor Proctor!

"Excuse me?" Ned quipped, raising his eyebrows stiffly. "I don't see where that's funny."

"What?" she asked, realizing she hadn't been listening to him.

"About the problems associated with establishing the sexual relationship before the emotional one. People are always eager to jump into bed right away, but not so eager to talk. Sex is easy, talk's not. And the talking needs to come first. If that's good, the rest will take care of itself later on. But you, Valentine, send out the clear-cut message every night that as long as it's good in the bedroom, the rest will work out. It's putting the cart before the horse, which is irresponsible, don't you think? Especially since every other marriage ends in divorce?"

"And you don't believe both parts of the relationship can be worked out simultaneously, Edward? Haven't you ever met someone you've been so hot for you can't sustain all that chitchat past, say, the second date? Maybe not even a full-fledged date. Maybe it's a casual encounter, and you know, say when you brush past each other in the hallway, that this is going to work out and the order it falls into doesn't matter. Then you sleep together, have sex, maybe even make love, and as that element of your relationship continues to develop over time you discover that other aspects are growing right along with it, too? That putting the cart before the horse, as you call it, really did work out?" Hard to imagine those smug words coming out of Ned, but there had been a few times when he did sound dangerously close to Edward.

"So what you're saying, Val, is that you actually believe in love at first sight? True love, the kind that won't end up as a bad divorce statistic. Just one look's all it takes and you know it's forever?"

"It happens," she admitted, not that she wanted to. Not too long ago she would have debated him on the subject, laughed at him, told him love at first sight was a load of romantic drivel. That it was really only sex at first sight. But *he'd* been the one to show her just how wrong she was about it. And yes, all it took was just one look. Which was causing her some great big problems. Bigger than she'd known just five minutes ago, when he was *only* Ned. "For some people. For the lucky ones. But it's rare, Ne…Edward. And most of the time that first look produces a hormonal drive—one that can lead to bigger, better things…things you call a real relationship. And I'm all for that. Happily-ever-after is nice." Waxing too romantic here. Val falling under the Edward charm. Bad for ratings. *Roxy* falling under the Edward charm. Bad for the heart. "So is some good, hot sex. Skip the emotions, go with the urge. Urges can be really fun, Eddie." She wrinkled her nose at him. "You ought to act on one sometime instead of always pontificating."

He smiled at her. Almost a Ned smile—the one he always used when they got into a little Valentine-Edward skirmish. "I think you're a gifted broadcaster, Val. And a good entertainer. But a deluded counselor, if you believe that starting in the bedroom makes for a solid relationship. It never does. And I'm not saying that the sexual relationship isn't important. I'm just cautioning you that if that's where it goes after a couple of dates, and there isn't a solid basis for anything else already established, the relationship may already be in trouble. Maybe even doomed to failure."

Like theirs? she wondered. Is that what he really believed? Twice together for Twinkies and nonessential handyman duties, then hot and sweaty on the hardwood floor, meant they were doomed? So maybe she'd been reading a whole lot more into it than he had. Especially if he really believed what he was saying, and from the square set of his jaw right now, he did. Meaning what *she* thought was real between them was just sex? The rug was just about sex?

Another wall for Roxy Rose. A very hard wall, judging from the size of the lump in her throat. "My radio program is offering people something they're missing in their lives, Edward. Someone to listen to them, a shoulder to cry on, someone ready with a little friendly advice. As far as my being a deluded counselor, I suppose I'd have to hear your definition of *real* counseling before I could respond to that. Because in my book, it's all relative, relative to what a person needs or wants from his or her experience. I know what my callers need and want, and I give it to them for two hours a night, Monday through Friday. No pretenses, no hypocrisy. Simple as that, Eddie. So, see ya around, sugar." Standing, Roxy unclipped her microphone and strutted off the set.

11

Close Encounters of the Catastrophic Kind

"DAMN," ROXY MUTTERED, banging her head against the dressing room wall. "Damn, damn, damn," she repeated with each bang. "Of all the rotten luck, can you believe it? Can you actually believe it?'

"I'll swear Rox, I didn't know about this," Astrid cried, once she got to Roxy. "They didn't tell me they were going to do this, or I would have..."

Roxy stopped banging and lifted her hand to rub the sore spot on her forehead. "Don't you recognize him, Astrid?" she hissed, her knees suddenly so weak she had to grab on to Astrid to stay upright. "*Him!* Edward Craig. Take a good look at him. Don't you recognize him?"

Astrid glanced up at the overhead television monitor mounted to the wall. "No," she said tentatively. "I mean he does look familiar, and he's a whole lot cuter than I thought he'd be. Actually, he's drop-dead, but I don't know him. Am I supposed to?"

"Of course he's a lot cuter. Drop-dead. Especially his backside," Roxy hissed. "*His backside, Astrid!* You know, the best-looking butt you've ever seen."

"That would be your handyman," Astrid replied.

Astrid and Roxy both looked up at the television monitor in time to catch Edward AKA Ned holding up his book, promoting the heck out of it. Brianna, the dit, was swooning all over him. She was practically unbuttoning on camera. A reaction to Ned Roxy knew oh, so well. Roxy rooted for him to hit her with the durn book—probably the only thing it was good for. "Exactly. That would be my handyman. *He* is my handyman, Astrid!"

It took a second for it to sink in, then Astrid squealed, "No way! That's him? The guy you're sleeping with? The one you're falling in—"

"Don't say it, Astrid. I'm warning you—"

"Well, I never did get a good look at his face. And judging from what I'm seeing on TV, Brianna's not exactly concentrating on his face, either." She scooted closer to the TV monitor, took another look. "No way! Valentine and Edward doing the horizontal, in the literal sense? How ironic is that?"

"Yes, way! Valerie and Edward. Talk about sleeping with the enemy."

"Whoa. Not just sleeping, but…and I'm not saying the words, but I'm thinking them and you know what they are." She laughed. "Sorry, can't help myself. Gotta say them just once. Valentine McCarthy in love with Edward Craig. Wow! Bet I can get us some ratings points out of that." She took another look at Ned. "You've done some crazy things, Rox, but this sure wasn't one I would have seen coming."

"It's not funny," Roxy snapped.

"Sure it is. And romantic. And…"

"Shut up! Just shut up."

Astrid shook her head, the laughter still bubbling in her eyes and shaking her shoulders. "So do you think he recognized you?"

"Don't think so. Bright lights, all my makeup. That stupid wig. And he didn't react to me. Of course, I didn't react to him, either, so who knows?" She glanced at the monitor again, then dropped her head back to the wall for another couple of bangs. "So what am I going to do now?" she moaned. "After I kill Brianna."

"You could march right out there on camera, take off the wig, throw yourself in his arms and confess how much you love him. And if you want to go for the big time, ask him to marry you."

"You're fired!"

Undaunted, Astrid continued, "Or Plan B, get the heck outta here before he nabs you. After that…darned if I know." Astrid started tossing all of Roxy's makeup, clothes and other paraphernalia into a tote bag for a hasty get-away. "Maybe you could read one of his books and see if he has an answer for a problem like this. You know, she love-hates him, he love-hates her." She singsonged it to the melody of the familiar Barney tune. "They're a love-hate family."

Roxy didn't wait around to take off the Valentine exterior and put Roxy back on. Instead, she grabbed her tote bag and street clothes and ran out the door. Half an hour later, still stunned, she dropped the carton of Doctor Edward Craig's books, the ones she'd been carrying around in the back of her car forever, onto her living room floor, locked every one of the four locks on her front door so *he* couldn't get in, and threw herself down onto the rug…*his* *rug*…to think.

"How could something like this have happened?" she asked, picking up his first book, turning it over to see his photo. Sure enough, there he was, Mister One and the Same. Make that Doctor One and the Same. Handsome and sexy and all Ned grinning for the camera. "He's living right here under my nose all the time, and I don't even know who he is. I'm falling in love with him, sleeping with him, having these fantasies about spending my life with him, and he turns out to be none other than…" She threw the book across the room and it hit the wall with a

thud. Ten seconds later someone knocked on the door, and
Roxy sat straight up. Georgette Selby come to cuss her out,
she hoped. Better her than Ned, because right now, she
didn't have a clue what to do about him…or with him. Or
without him.

"Rox?"

No, not Ned's voice, thank heavens.

"I heard your door slam. Can I come in?"

Doyle?

"I know you're in there."

Roxy zipped over to the door, opened it, grabbed hold
of his arm and practically dragged him inside, then shut
the door and locked it again. "What are you doing here and
what do you want?" she hissed, almost out of breath. She
ran back over to the rug and plopped down in relief. "You
saw the show this morning, didn't you? And that's why
you're here. Because I walked off."

Doyle picked up Ned's book, took a look, dropped it
back on the floor, then wandered over to the sofa, careful
not to tread upon the rug, and sat down. "Actually, I just
came over to say hello to my new neighbor." He was
dressed in baggy gray sweatpants and a black T-shirt with
the words *Kiss My*…and the image of a donkey beneath
them. So typically Doyle.

"What do you mean, new neighbor?"

"I'm moving in, right next door." He pointed in the direction of Georgette Selby's apartment. "Your neighbor
got herself into a real nice seniors' complex closer to some
of the services she needs, and I was next on the waiting list
for the building."

"Waiting list? When you recommended this place, you
didn't tell me there was a waiting list. So how did I get in
right away?" In, like, two days.

He gave her a sheepish grin. "I let you have my slot. I
was next up, this one came open and I knew you needed

a place right away, so I slipped Oswald a little cash to let you in ahead of me."

"You did that for me?" She tried smiling, even though she wasn't in the mood. Maybe would never be in the mood to smile again. But Doyle deserved the best she could manage. "Really?"

He nodded, almost shyly. "No big deal."

"Yes it is, Doyle, and I don't know what to say, except thanks." Roxy grabbed another of Ned's books out of the carton, glanced at the photo on the back cover, then lobbed it at the wall. "I wish you would have said something, though." Seemed like within the last hour, her life had started crowding in all around her in a gigantic way. Too much too close. Her two lives were colliding. "I think I owe you a pizza," she said. For Doyle, saying it with pizza always worked, and she did, after all, owe him a thank-you. If things somehow worked out with Ned, maybe a whole year's supply. Yeah, right. Like things *could* work out now.

"So you don't mind me living right next door?"

"No, you're fine. And I'm not going to be here much longer, anyway." *Maybe Georgette Selby can find me an apartment somewhere closer to the services I need.* Like stupidity-repair services. She grabbed a third book from the carton, and didn't even bother looking at the photo before she chucked it at the wall.

"Astrid called," he said cautiously.

"And?"

"And she told me what happened. That they sprang Edward Craig on you this morning."

"And?"

"And that you handled yourself pretty good, all things considered."

"All things considered," she mumbled. Doyle didn't know the half of it, and she intended to keep it that way. "I walked off the set, if that's what you want to call pretty good." Book four in the Craig series came out of the carton, and went flying into the heap with the rest of them. "So did Astrid say anything else?" Like the syndication was off, her advertisers were dropping like flies, the radio station had fired her?

"That's all, except you're pretty upset over it, and to leave you alone for a while."

"Astrid was right. I am, and I do want to be alone for a while, if you don't mind. So, I'll see you at work later, okay? And tonight, after the show, we'll have that pizza. Extra meat, *your* favorite this time."

Doyle shrugged. "Well, you know where I am. If you need anything before then, just pound on the wall. I'll be moving in all day."

SHE WAS AT THE PEEPHOLE when *he* came home. Her hundredth time at the peephole in the last couple of hours. And sure enough, there was no evil twin scenario like she'd been praying for. *He* was decked in the same gray suit, his hair combed in the same manner. And *he* didn't even look over at her apartment when he went inside his own. The door was shut—not even slammed in an angry, incensed, hostile or otherwise churlish manner—and that was it. He never came out, at least not that she heard, anyway, and she did spend most of the day with her aural faculties fine-tuned to the comings and going in the hallway. Unfortunately, they were all Doyle's, moving in some pretty clunky furniture every time she looked out.

"I'm still numb," she said to Astrid, hours later, as she was getting ready to go on air—*her air*, and she was sure going to have to fake it tonight because she didn't feel like talking to one person let alone thousands of them. "I mean, I know I've been hiding Val from him, so I really can't say anything about his hiding Edward from me. I'm not even angry about that because after everything we've talked

about—he hates Val, I hate Eddie—I totally understand it.
He's basically the same chicken that I am. But what are the
odds? Seattle's like a billion people, and *he* lives right
across the hall from me. Not only that, *he* owns my building and I'm sleeping with him.

"I want some Chardonnay for real tonight," Roxy said.
"Skip the root beer."

"Fruit punch. You don't need to go on the air all liquored up."

"Spiked? Just a little. I deserve a good buzz, at least."

Astrid laughed. "You're sounding like someone who
might agree with what Doctor Edward Craig's been saying about relationships, that the good ones are about a
whole lot more than sex."

"I *wanted* to keep it simple," Roxy moaned. "That's what
I kept telling myself. No matter how I was feeling about
him, I didn't want complications. And now I've got them
all over the place." She glanced over at Doyle who was just
entering his booth, then waved. "Am still feeling about
him," she corrected. "Not *was*. And that's another thing.
How can I feel one way about him professionally, and another personally? Is that weird, or what?"

Astrid scooted away the microphone and Roxy's mug
of fruit punch, then sat down on the corner of the desk. "If
he comes knocking on your door tonight, will you sleep
with him?"

"You mean ignore my professional feelings? Because
no matter how it turns out, one thing I won't do is put my
professional judgment aside. I need him on this program."

"I mean exactly that. All professional feelings aside. He
comes knocking, you let him in. Will that happen?"

Roxy laughed bitterly. "Truthfully, I don't know. So
much of me wants to. But now, with the way things have
changed, so much of me doesn't. And I'm afraid that it's
just sex for him, Astrid. Which is the way Val would like

it, but I'm not Val, and I was hoping…" She shrugged. "I was, and I guess I still am hoping it's more. And I don't know what I'll do if it's not." She glanced over at Doyle, who was giving her the two-minute warning, then automatically put on her headphones. "I spent all morning listening at my door. Every time I heard a noise…I mean, I wanted him to come in, but I didn't. And I was scared that he would, and now I'm scared that he won't. Silly, isn't it?"

Astrid threw her arms around Roxy. "It's never silly, being in love." Astrid and Roxy both looked over at Doyle, who was waving one finger at them and grinning.

Nodding, Roxy pulled her mic over and braced herself for the onslaught. And tonight it was an onslaught to which she wasn't looking forward. "Welcome to *Midnight Special*, sugars. Are you ready for something special? Because if you are, you've certainly come to the right place. Doctor Val has something *extra-specially* special for you tonight."

Roxy glanced up at the board for her first caller, then slashed her throat at Doyle, then at Astrid. No way was she going to take Edward Craig's call right out of the starting gate. Not tonight, anyway! But Astrid shook her head, and Doyle was giving her the speed-it-up sign. "So it looks like we have Doctor Craig to start us off this evening," she said, not even bothering to take out a chocolate truffle. "And how are you tonight, Edward?" Her voice was noticeably stiff. No usual Val flirting.

"Much better, now that we've finally met face-to-face, Valentine."

"Unfortunate little incident," Roxy said. "Having them slip you into my interview without even warning me. Not very good broadcast ethics, but I trust you made the most of the opportunity once I left. Promoted your next book, I assume?"

"I'm surprised you didn't listen," he replied, his voice totally calm and, as usual, in command. And not at all like

Ned's, she noticed. Oh, there were some similarities, now that she knew. The same deep richness, that smooth-as-silk flow, but it was different, like Roxy's voice was different from Val's. "After you left we talked about you, Valentine."

"Only good things, I'm sure." Not!

"Actually, yes. We discussed your role as a radio call-in psychologist, and how you fulfill it."

"My role?"

"As in entertainment. You *are* quite entertaining, Valentine. Frustrating, sometimes dangerous, but always entertaining."

Roxy drew in a deep breath. This could go either way. Might be fun. Might break her heart even more than it already was. "Entertaining, Edward? Well, why don't you tell me how I entertain you? In your fantasies, perhaps? Or in your dreams?" The edge in her voice was finally disappearing, being replaced by a little of the Valentine flirt. Not much! Just a little, *with caution.*

"Is that how you want to entertain me, Valentine? Is that *your* fantasy…*your* dream? To entertain me in mine?"

Damn, if it didn't sound like he was trying to seduce her right there on the radio. Nah. Wishful thinking. This was his brand of on-air foreplay. Whatever he had lined up for the main event would pack a mighty punch, one that intrigued her just a little. "My dream, Edward, or my fantasy, if you will, is not about entertaining someone in *their* dreams or fantasies. That's lonely, depressing. When I choose to entertain someone, it's on a secluded beach somewhere, just the two of us under the stars, all naked and sweaty. So hot the sex turns the sand into glass and the glass shatters into a million shards." The way it had done with them.

"Are you making love, Valentine, or merely having sex?"

"It's whatever you want to call it, Edward. I don't want to argue the details with you, since we don't ever agree."

"But it's·a very important detail, Valentine. Anybody can have hot, sweaty sex in the sand. But not everybody can make love there. In fact, very few can. And there's a difference, one you've deprived yourself of if you haven't experienced it personally."

"Choices, Doctor. We all have them to make, and we all choose differently. If you've ever had sex for the sake of sex, you'd know what I was talking about. It can be good, so good it actually deludes you into thinking it might be love. But then when you step back and analyze it, or have the truth revealed to you, you see it for what it is. Sex for sex. But that doesn't change the fact that it rocked your world for a few minutes. And maybe in those few minutes you were actually a little in love." Or completely and forever.

"But I have, Valentine. And what I know, without a doubt, is that making love is so much better than sex for sex. There's nothing to compare. One is about hormones, the other is about genuine emotions. If you've ever made love, because you were in love, you'd know what I was talking about."

"But I have," Roxy said, not intending that to go out over the air. "And believe it or not, I truly admire the people who are in love. But I'm a pragmatist about those who aren't. And I don't believe they should deny themselves one of the finer *entertainments* in life just because they haven't found a soul mate to share their genuine emotions with. And that entertainment, Edward, doesn't have to be in a fantasy or a dream. It can be on a hardwood floor and be just as good as…" As what? Making love with somebody you love? Even Valentine wasn't buying into that one this evening. Nothing was better than being with the person you love, no matter what you were doing. "…As good as you can imagine it to be." Well, maybe that didn't prove her point exactly, but it did carry her over into the first commercial break, and that's all she wanted. After that, the real callers would call in and she'd be off the hook for a couple of hours. At least until she got home.

Then, dear lord, what was she going to do about Ned?

2:46 A.M.

A phone call in the night and it wasn't Ned. Not that she wanted it to be because she still didn't know what to say to him. Not yet. She'd been too numb to figure it out. "No Astrid, I haven't even seen him tonight. Haven't heard him, haven't heard from him, haven't even caught a whiff of his after-shave." Musk, masculine. She loved it. Loved smelling it when they were making love, loved smelling it when he simply breezed by her in the hallway, even before they'd first made eye contact. "This isn't exactly how I expected things to work out between us. I mean, I don't know what I was expecting, but this sure wasn't it." *Liar. You wanted a white picket fence. You've got it penciled into your house plans.* "And now, even though I know who he is, I'm not sure I want to end it. Of course I'm not going to have much of a choice in the matter since I did actually sleep with the man on our second date which, according to him, dooms us for anything more. *His words.* We're doomed. And they weren't even real dates," she moaned. "Not like dinner, dancing, movie, monster truck rally."

"So just go over there and tell him it's the real deal for you," Astrid said. "Heart and soul forever, happily-ever-after, morning breath and bed hair don't even matter, that kind of love."

"I've never spent the night with him."

"Rox…you've got to be kidding? You *are* kidding, aren't you? Sex then adios? I'm not surprised the man predicts doom and gloom for you two. That's one of those issues we talked about. Letting the guy launch some Fourth of July fireworks for you, then sending him away. *Thanks for the great orgasm, buddy. See you next time I'm in the mood.* Big-time control issue, Rox. You don't know what to do without it. No wonder he's still on the casual wavelength. You haven't given him enough to make him switch his dial."

"I've never spent the night with *any* man," Roxy confessed, surprised to hear herself doing it. "Never."

"I seem to recall a marriage…."

"A marriage where we had separate bedrooms. We did the deed on our honeymoon, a couple of times, then he immediately checked himself into another room for the duration. It was a snore, Astrid. A big zero, and I sure didn't want to wake up to that the next morning. I always had these dreams about waking up with the man I loved. I've just never been able to…"

"Really? Never?"

"Never. And I wanted to. *With Ned.* Almost did that night at the beach…which didn't work out. It's like sex can be casual if you want to be, but spending the night in his arms can't be. Not ever. And I want to spend the night in his arms. But something stops me from doing it. Maybe the fear of waking up in the morning and finding him gone."

"So what you're telling me is that he's been giving you the kind of casual relationship you've always said you want, probably even said that to him in so many words…or actions. When all the time, deep down, you're really are a hopeless romantic?"

"Well, the hopeless part, anyway. And in all fairness *to me*, I didn't know what I wanted until I met him."

"Deluding yourself, girlfriend?"

"I'd rather think of it as naivete. I mean, how is anyone supposed to know for sure until they see it or almost have it? I always thought I wanted to be a psychologist but I didn't know I wanted to be a radio host until I got the chance." The more she talked, the worse Roxy felt. She wanted him to come over, didn't want him coming over. Did, didn't. Did… Wasn't sure. Geez!

"Bottom line time, Rox. Do you love him enough to do all the fixing yourself? Get down on your knees and crawl across the hall if you have to?"

"Maybe he won't open the door."

"Raising my finger to cut off the connection."

"Do I have to crawl?"

"Finger getting closer."

"Can't I just wait until I see him come out in the hall?"

"Finger resting gently on the button."

"Okay."

"Okay, what?"

"Maybe I do."

"Finger beginning to apply pressure."

"Knock it off, Astrid. I love him, okay. Are you happy? Love him! As in totally in love, want to have his babies and a white picket fence kind of love. And sure, I'll crawl if I have to. Is that good enough for you?"

"For now."

"That's all I get?"

"Well, I hate pink and yellow. Green's a good color with my hair. Blue's iffy, depending on the shade. And there's nothing wrong with a bridesmaid wearing a nice off-white. Or black, if it's evening. But not lavender and for heaven's sake no ruffles or bows. I won't be there if you want ruffles and bows."

"Yeah, like I'm getting married," Roxy snorted, crawling on her hands and knees over to the pile of Edward Craig books. Picking one out of the heap, she studied the photo on the back. Not the Ned she knew, but nice. There was some twinkle in his eyes. But his hair was combed and he had on a shirt, damn him! Grabbing a pen from her pocket, she did a little facial rearranging, then chucked the book at the wall. It hit with a dull thud. The same dull thud as her heart.

"Have you ever wondered if maybe you battle Edward

so vigorously because there's something sexual in *that*? I'm sure not the shrink here, but you two do have a certain chemistry, and I'm betting he knows it, or he wouldn't keep coming back for more. As Edward."

"You're fired," Roxy replied, despondently.

"You mean I'm right. You always light up when Edward's on the line. You get that little spark thing going in your eyes, gear up for battle, and as soon as he's off air, you bask in the afterglow of a truffle."

Carrying another of his books with her, Roxy crawled back over to her rug and sprawled out flat in the middle of it. "You are sooo wrong, I'm not even going to argue with you." Absently, she glanced over at the door, wondering if he knew she was home. She'd rattled her keys when she came in, dropped them, messed with the lock, dropped her briefcase twice, done a quick round of Riverdancing—all that and still no Ned. "Look, I can't think about this any more tonight and I'm tired of throwing his books at the wall. So I'm going to bed. Okay?"

"Sure you don't want to come have a jammie party with me? Unless you're planning on one with him…a jammie party *without* your jammies."

"Good night, Astrid," she said emphatically, clicking off and tossing her cell phone aside. She looked at the jacket cover photo one more time. Each one had been different, and all were good. Nice eyes, nice smile. Damn it again! *This just wasn't fair.* The *she* who promoted sex was in love, and the *he* who promoted love only wanted sex. His book hit the wall, landing in the heap with all the rest. "Like that'll fix things."

Pulling herself up off the rug, Roxy plodded over to the hall mirror. Automatically, she pulled the step out and jumped up on it, then took a good look at…her chin! He'd lowered it. "Damn him," she muttered, stepping back down then kicking the step across the hall. "He just comes and goes…fixes a mirror, buys a rug, makes me love him then, *I think you're a gifted broadcaster, Val. But a deluded counselor, if you believe that starting in the bedroom makes for a solid relationship.*" They hadn't, but it was pretty damned close. And she'd swear on every Twinkie she'd ever eaten, she really had thought it was a solid relationship.

"You hypocrite," she snapped in the direction of his apartment.

I'm just cautioning you that after a couple of dates, if that's where it goes, the relationship may already be in trouble. Or maybe already doomed to failure. And that's exactly where it had gone with them. "Only crazy me…I wasn't seeing doom there at all. But apparently you had, Ned. So I guess a couple of times on the floor is all you wanted out of this thing. So pronounce it doomed." She stomped on the floor. "Be thou doomed!"

Roxy plopped back down on the rug—his *second-time* gift to her—ran her fingers over the soft nap, shut her eyes and thought about that second time. Actually, it was the third time, wasn't it? Which meant, with their little beach frolic, they were already way over their quota. But it was a nice rug, anyway, one she'd apparently read too much into. "So Ned, do you give all your girlfriends a rug on your second date?"

Really pathetic, being so sentimental about a seven-by-nine piece of floor covering. So maybe she'd get rid of it tomorrow. Give it to Doyle as an apartment-warming gift. *It's almost like new, Doyle. Owned by a little old lady who only used it for sex twice on her way to the grocery store.* Even if she did give it the heave-ho, there was still the likelihood she'd spend the rest of her life getting mopey over any old rug on any old floor. God forbid she should go see her mom's brand-new house with wall-to-wall Berber. How would she ever explain all the sobbing?

Instinctively, Roxy glanced at the ticking cat in the

kitchen. Two fifty-four, ho-hum. No use thinking about it any longer. What was done was done. It was over.

And Ned…well, no eulogy for him. Not for the mighty Edward…the mighty hypocritical Edward, who wanted sex, not a relationship, and didn't walk the talk he talked. Yeah, wouldn't that just make a wonderful footnote for his next book. Or one of those rave reviews on the front cover. *The most exceptional book I've ever read!* Or, *I couldn't put it down once I started it.* Right, Edward. *The most deceiving pile of yap since the printing press was invented.*

Purely for spite, she went back over to his book pile, and heaved one at the wall just as someone knocked on her door. "Ned?" Roxy gasped, scrambling to her feet.

Even though she'd been thinking about this moment all day, planning it, unplanning it, chopping him up with an imaginary hatchet, now that he was here she didn't know what to do. Sure, she wanted to let him in and give him a huge chunk of her mind. But she also wanted to let him in and give him a huge chunk of her heart, too. *Them's the facts Roxy, like 'em or not!* Most of all, she wanted to see if he wanted that chunk of her heart. Or not.

"Extra meat, just the way I like it," Doyle said, shoving the pizza box into Roxy's hands. "Double-extra cheese, too. But I left off the onions. Hope that's okay."

"Huh?"

"You said you wanted us to have pizza tonight. You know, on account of my letting you have this apartment. It took me a while to find a pizza place open this late over in this neighborhood. But I did and here it is. Oh, and Rox, it's on your tab. They know you, and since you invited me… Anyway, I bought root beer, too. Actually, it's next door in my fridge. Be right back."

Flabbergasted, Roxy stood in her doorway holding the pizza box while Doyle dashed back to his apartment. Well, at least with Doyle she didn't have to face the obvious.

He'd eat himself into oblivion in about five minutes, and she'd be so exhausted watching him shove it in that when he left her place she'd sleep like a baby, if only to escape the visual reminder. Sleep, hopefully not counting pizzas.

Waiting for Doyle to return, crossing her fingers he wouldn't, but not having the heart to turn him away since it was, after all, her invitation, Roxy didn't notice Ned's door creeping open until it was too late, and he was standing face-to-face with her in the hall. Ned, not Edward. Jeans, no shirt, barefoot. So gorgeous. Grrr!

"Looks like a big one," he said, grinning.

She glanced down. "Super-size," she muttered, for lack of anything brilliant to say. "Extra meat. Double-extra cheese."

"You must be hungry."

"Got company. Old friend stopped by." Maybe telling him that was good, maybe it was bad. She didn't know. Whatever it was, though, it precluded Ned from the rest of her night, gave her more time to think things through. The look of being turned down for something that hadn't quite yet materialized into an invitation was as obvious on his face as was the bare chest she so wanted to dribble pizza sauce over. Then lick it up.

"Well, I've got work to do. Hope you and your friend enjoy it." Without missing a beat, he stepped back inside his apartment, and by the time Doyle reappeared with a two-liter root beer, she was once again standing alone in her doorway, without a trace of anyone else having just been there. Without a trace, except his after-shave. And her goose bumps.

12

Uproars and Assorted Dirty Words

"SO WHO DO YOU THINK the friend is?" Ned asked Hep, resisting the urge to look out his peephole and see. Hep merely ignored him, choosing instead to make a bed in the gray suit Ned hadn't hung up since he'd come home from his early-morning television catastrophe.

They hadn't told him he'd be going face-to-face with Valentine McCarthy. No, they'd given him an invitation to come do the short segment and promote his new book. Then Jerry freakin' Springer almost broke out. That's what Bri would have liked, anyway. But Valentine had been pretty cool about it. Much cooler than he might have expected from her.

Ned smiled. Valentine...Val...Roxy...whatever she wanted to call herself, she hadn't missed a beat with Brianna, and he actually admired her for it. Sure, he was shocked that they were the same person, although it made sense, in a peculiar sort of way. Roxy's late-night hours, some of her opinions. And they both had this over-the-top attitude. But sleeping with her? "Problem is, Hep, I don't want to walk away from Roxy, which would be the smart thing to do right now. Smart for my career, anyway. Get over her, don't look back." But not smart for his heart, and he knew he *would* look back. "So, she knows who I am now, but she's wondering if I know who she is," he said, dropping down onto the bed next to the cat who looked mildly miffed to be sharing it with anybody. "Like I wouldn't recognize the person I'm in love with, even when she's disguised as Valentine." He'd seen Valentine McCarthy's pictures plastered on billboards and buses for months, but those were flat images, and this morning, discovering Roxy in that getup…well, she was anything but a flat image. And she smelled like Roxy—that sweet, fragrant scent he could pull up from memory, even now, when she wasn't around. Knew it the moment he'd stepped out onto the set. Knew her, too, even in that disguise.

Ned chuckled. Of course, Ricky had never recognized Lucy in any of her disguises, had he? Lucy as a foreign princess, Lucy as a cabaret dancer, Lucy as a man with a fake mustache, and poor, dumb Ricky never caught on, never once recognized the woman he loved, the woman who cooked his breakfast, bore his children, made him famous. "So maybe the wise thing to do is pull a Ricky Ricardo and see how far it goes." In other words, leave it up to Roxy, let her have the control.

The more he was with her, the more he wanted what Roxy wanted. He never knew from moment to moment what that was going to be, but hey, it sure spiced up his life when he found out. So since he wanted that spice around for the rest of his life, he knew the next move had to be hers. For one thing, it would prove, beyond a shadow of a doubt, what this relationship was about. Sure, he thought he knew, especially when he was dealing with just Roxy. But now that Valentine was included in it, he had to admit there was some doubt. Not much. But some. And basically, he still trusted her to make the right decision in spite of the fact that she *was* Valentine, who, apparently, wasn't quite as wrong as he'd thought. Which he would admit to Roxy after she confessed to him.

"Lucy always pulled it off in the last few minutes," he

told Hep. Of course, sometimes Ricky just had to go in for the kiss, even when she was still mustachioed. Then he'd end up with the fake mustache on his upper lip, which didn't matter because it always came with a happily-ever-after for them. "So I guess I'll be standing in the wings with that kiss just in case she doesn't get that mustache off in time." But he did hope she'd be the one to remove it.

Pushing himself off the bed, Ned padded to the front door and looked out the peephole again, even though he'd promised himself he wouldn't. Not a creature was stirring out there, so he pulled a chair closer to the door then plopped down in it. "To think, not to spy," he told Hep, who swaggered out to see what he was doing, then swaggered back to bed when it didn't interest her.

So what if he was curious? He had a right. That was his rug over there across the hall. Well, his gift to her. And he sure as heck hadn't planned on anybody else using it…not the way they'd used it. "Just looking out for the moral integrity of the rug in question," he muttered. "Right?" After all, *she* was Val, which was an X-factor he never expected in this relationship. The Val who slept with them for sex but never loved them. But damn it, she still seemed like Roxy to him. And he didn't want Roxy over there with anybody else, on or off the rug. So sue him, he was jealous. Jealous enough he was pounding on her front door before he realized what he was doing.

"Ned?" Roxy said, smiling up at him.

The Roxy smile. *Not* the Val smile.

"Do you need something?"

"You're damned right I need something," he snapped, pushing in past her. First thing he saw was a pile of books on the floor. His books, jackets off, heaped, piled, splayed open. One of his pictures had devil horns inked in. Then he saw the rug, thankfully vacant. No clothes dropped haphazardly around it, no unidentified naked body scrambling for cover.

"What?" she asked, still standing at the door.

He took a quick survey of the rest of the apartment, and unless the unidentified *he* was in the bedroom, or hiding in the hall closet, she was alone. And the *identified* he was making one great big ass of himself. "My hammer. Can't find it with my other tools."

"Haven't seen it. Sorry."

"I lowered your mirror earlier. Thought maybe…"

"Saw the mirror, thanks. Didn't see the hammer, sorry."

"Okay…well…" The awkward moment was swelling like a water balloon hooked to the faucet. And he knew he'd better get out of there before it either exploded or she threw it at him. "I'll be getting on back, then. If you do happen to see it here somewhere…" A quick glance at the rug—no strange indentations. Thank God! So maybe it had been just a pizza date with an old friend after all. *Stupid Ned. This is Roxy, not Val.*

"Thanks again for lowering the mirror. And if I see your hammer, I'll bring it over. So, is there anything else?"

Do *you* want anything else? he wanted desperately to ask. But she was keeping her distance. Which meant he needed to keep his, too. Didn't take a shrink to figure out *this* body language. Arms folded, jaw set, body armor all shined up. "No, nothing. So, um, good night, Roxy," he said, hoping it was not also goodbye.

"Good night, Ned," was all she said before she shut her door. And standing in the hall, he heard the click of all four of her locks.

ROXY SAT BETWEEN Doyle and Astrid, who were there with her for support. The people were trickling into the Shorecroft town meeting at a crawl, driving her nuts. She repressed the urge to run into the outer hall and physically drag them to their seats, one by one, so she could get this…this…inquisition, witch trial, bogus act of occupational narrow-mindedness over with. They didn't appreciate her chosen means of livelihood, therefore, they were going to burn her house plans at the stake. "Well, they may not look like trolls under the bridge, but they're sure not going to let me cross over it without paying a mighty high toll," she whispered to Astrid. "Assuming they'll even take a toll. Maybe they won't let me over, no matter what."

Three people sat at the conference table facing her—William Parker clenching his gavel and obviously shunning eye contact with her; Frank Thomas, one of the many architects she'd fired who was making direct, gloating, eye contact with her, reveling in his power, and an older woman who was crocheting and clearly didn't care about anything going on around her. To think, her fate rested in the hands of these people! "So is the smile working on them?" she asked Astrid, without so much as moving her lips. She'd been sitting there fifteen minutes already, smiling nonstop, forcing her lips to stay curved upward so long they were beginning to go numb.

Astrid glanced over at her, then shook her head. "Nope. You didn't think it would, did you?"

"Think anything will work?"

"Sex? You take Parker, I'll take the guy who looks like he's gonna meet you in the parking lot with a tire iron, and Doyle can have grandma. Two of us should be good enough to get you the majority vote."

Roxy slapped Astrid on the arm then glanced over her shoulder to make sure nobody had overheard her. "You trying to get me thrown in jail?"

"So when are they gonna start this thing, 'cause I'm hungry?" Doyle asked, none too quietly, causing the three board members at the table to finally glance up, in unison, scowl, then return to what they were doing before. In unison.

"When they're ready," Astrid hissed.

Roxy looked over at the three of them sitting there in the

front row—Doyle, Astrid, her—their hands folded neatly
in their laps, knees properly together, backs straight—and
she had to bite her lower lip to fight back a giggle. Her attire du jour was a prim little blue knee-length skirt and a
white button-up blouse. Astrid was in the exact same
getup, and poor Doyle pretty much the same thing, substituting slacks for a skirt. They looked like a parochial-
school kids' choir. "More like when they're ready to hang
me, you mean," Roxy whispered through her smile.

She glanced at William Parker, who'd started sneaking
peeks at her from behind a manila file folder. "Not good,"
she muttered, looking over at the crocheter—a tiny, bespec-
tacled, gray-haired seventy-something who was wrestling
with an afghan that was already large enough to cover a
football field. Like William Parker, she snatched a quick
look at Roxy above the top of her wire rims, then went back
to her granny squares.

"Ugly color," Astrid commented. "Her blues clash. She
needs to stay in the true shade and get away from the
greens altogether."

"She needs to pick up that damned hammer and start this
meeting," Doyle snapped, tugging at his clip-on blue tie.

That remark was greeted by a collective throat-clearing
from the board, and several of the Shorecrofters sitting
around Roxy and crew.

"Before midnight," Doyle continued. "And you know
what happens at midnight." He widened his eyes, pulled
in his chin, stiffened his shoulder and arms, raising his
arms slowly out in front of him like a zombie.

"Stop that," Astrid said, punching him in the arm.

Both actions—Doyle's zombie and Astrid's slap—were
acknowledged by an officious throat-clearing from the
board, and pretty much from all the Shorecrofters in the
room, too.

Roxy slunk down in her seat, resisting the urge to cross

one leg over the other since William Parker might construe it as some sort of sexual advance. *Honestly, I saw her you-know-what.* "So when do we begin," she finally asked, her nerves frayed to a single, moth-eaten thread.

William Parker glanced at the crowd still creeping in behind Roxy, apparently satisfied enough of the fifty seats were filled to begin. "Now, Miss Rose." Flat voice, no intonation whatsoever. He banged his gavel. First bang didn't take since the ladies' recipe klatch in the second row behind Roxy was still going over the ingredients for the best lobster bisque ever. "Heavy cream or will half-and-half work?" were the last words that sailed out over the proceedings as William Parker banged one more time. He covered the microphone sitting on the table in front of him with his hand, then leaned forward. "Cream for flavor, half-and-half for health. Try half of each for a nice compromise."

Several people in the audience murmured agreement, a few disapproval, as William Parker shifted the microphone closer to his mouth. "As you know, we have a proposal before us tonight for the annexation of certain properties adjoining the village into the village proper. We tabled the vote at our last meeting in order to choose the village Christmas decorations—red poinsettias this year—and the meeting before that to discuss switching vendors for our swimming pool chemicals. But Miss Rose, owner of one of the properties in question, is proceeding with house plans, and in all fairness to her we need to address this issue before she goes any farther, since what we do, most likely, will have bearing on what she does out there. And just let me start off by offering my opinion. The properties before us for annexation already make use of our village services, so they might as well be on the tax rolls and pay for them."

The audience muttered a unified agreement, and Roxy already felt the hand of defeat knocking her down. Nothing she hadn't felt before she got here. But this was pretty much the death blow.

"Your comments, Miss Rose?" he continued. "For the record, are you opposed to annexation?"

The little old gray-hair glanced up from her afghan for the answer.

"My objection is not to annexation, per se," Roxy began, deciding to stay seated since this was a moot appearance, anyway. No point getting up and making a spectacle of herself. "If you want my tax money, you can have it. And actually, if I do use your village services, then I should pay for them. But what you can't have is my right to build whatever I want on my property. It's zoned for a residential structure, and I intend on building a residence, Mr. Parker."

"You may *intend* a residence, Miss Rose, but the village has strict building covenants, and after we take a vote, they'll extend to your property. And while you may think that has a certain unfairness to it, since, for all intents and purposes, you purchased that property prior to annexation, the intent to annex has been there for quite some time. And we *intend* on holding you to the same building restrictions everybody in Shorecroft is bound to follow. It's a matter of the research, Miss Rose. Our intent was on file, and if you, or your realtor, failed to find it, I am sorry. That's valuable property.…"

"Told you the dotted line was too fast," Astrid muttered under her breath. "And I'm betting your real estate agent wasn't anywhere near retirement like she told you. It was a scheme to get your money PDQ because she knew what these bastards would do to you and she didn't want you finding out."

William Parker cleared his throat as Roxy punched Astrid in the ribs with her elbow. "As I was saying," he continued, "that's valuable property and I'm sure you will have no trouble disposing of it."

"You'd like that, wouldn't you? Me selling out. Is that what this is all about? You don't want me here, and you'll do whatever it takes to get rid of me, including annexing my property, sticking me with those asinine building covenants, then never okaying anything I submit to Frank Thomas, who hates me, anyway because I fired his sorry as...him. All because you don't like my sex talk."

A round of mutterings and tsk-tsks resounded throughout the tiny chamber, and the recipe klatch got up and marched out *en masse*, even before the lobster bisque was completely done.

William Parker watched the exodus and when the last lobster-cooker was gone, turned his attention back to Roxy. "I'm sorry, Miss Rose, but like I told you in earlier discussions, it's not personal. I'm doing what I think is best for the village, and annexing your property is what I think is best. As far as approving your plans," he glanced over at Frank Thomas, "it's a committee decision."

Roxy shook her head. Pure exasperation! Sure, this was exactly what she expected, but the optimist in her had been still holding out some hope when she came in here this evening. False hope, evidently. "It's all about sex, isn't it, Mr. Parker? Sex! It makes me a pretty good living and you don't like that." She stood up, walked across the wooden floor to face him directly at his table. "You've made it pretty clear before that you have an aversion to what I do, at least in the public forum, and you're using your sexual preferences now to run me out of town. Which isn't fair, Mr. Parker. It's only a job. When it's over, I go home just like everybody else, and I really want to go home to a house on my property. A house designed the way I like it. And I'll be damned if I'll let your distaste for my job cheat me out of it. Although I must say, I was quite surprised when you were the one who came to me, because I certainly never had any intention of mixing that part of my life with this. You were the one who wanted it, though. That day out on my beach…"

Collective gasps from the audience. And one, rather boisterous "Wow!"

"So what's the big deal, anyway? What's the big deal with suggesting that someone hook up his meddling mother for sex…"

"Hot mamma sex, if I'm not mistaken," William Parker inserted.

The gray-hair at the table dropped her crochet hook, and her scowl was replaced by a smidgen of interest.

"Okay, you're right. I suggest hot mamma sex, then suddenly you don't want me living here in Shorecroft, so you covenant me, hoping I'll give up. Right?"

Chairs started moving. Some people were switching seats to get closer. Others scooted away.

"Miss Rose," William Parker sputtered. "That's not quite—"

"Right?" Roxy interrupted. "Kick me out because I can say the word *penis* in public and not even blush when I do? It's not like we all haven't said the word before. I just happen to say it in public more often than most people do, but that's what I'm paid for. What people expect to hear from me. What you've heard from me before, Mr. Parker, and I'm betting on a whole lot of different occasions."

The gray-hair dropped her afghan.

"And saying it doesn't make me a bad person. If you care to look at my house plans, you won't see one single penis in them anywhere." She hoped.

Doyle raised his fist in a power salute, but Astrid struck it down.

"Sex is what I do for a living, Mr. Parker, not who I am. And I have thousands…hundreds of thousands of people who can't wait for me to go to work every night. It's how I make a pretty darned good living, a living that enabled me to buy that property in the first place, and, hopefully, will enable me to build that house on it in the near future, if you can get past the preconceived notion that what I do is bad. Because it's not. More and more people spend the night with me each and every night, and they know what to expect from me, and I never let them down. And that's what will put some pretty significant tax dollars in your coffers. My saying penis, Mr. Parker, can pay for those freakin' red poinsettias."

"Like out there in Nevada?" the gray-hair asked.

Roxy blinked. "I'm sorry?"

"You know, those ranches out in Nevada."

Roxy drew a blank, and looked back to Astrid for clarification.

"Prostitutes," Doyle supplied, grinning. "Ladies of the evening."

"Oh, no!" Astrid sputtered, catching on while Roxy was still pondering the connection. "They don't have a clue what you're talking about, Rox. None of them, I don't think, except Mr. Parker. You're talking about the show and they think that you're a…"

Flabbergasted, Roxy spun back to William Parker. "You didn't tell them about me? After that day on the beach, I assumed you'd go back and tell them. And you didn't?" she asked, as he tried to slide under the table. "You *really* didn't tell them who I am, what I do?" she screeched, suddenly so weak in the knees she had to stagger back to her chair and sit down.

"No," he squeaked. "I wanted to respect your privacy."

"And everything I've been saying this evening, they really think I'm a…?"

"Now they do, I suppose," he squeaked again.

"Yep, Rox. They think you're a hooker," Doyle piped up, turning to watch the rest of the audience run from the room. "So, now that this thing's over, and I'm assuming they won't even let you build a sand castle here, wanna go grab a pizza?"

NED BARELY MADE IT BACK to his Hummer before Roxy stormed out of the town building. He hadn't gone inside the meeting room. She'd have seen him and her sense of independence might have been offended. And after all, this was still her situation to fix between them. If she wanted anything between them. But he'd heard everything from the hall. Every last word, every last gasp. And he had to hand it to her, she had guts. Guts in a bit of disarray right now, but guts nonetheless. Sticking his key in the ignition, Ned chuckled as his Hummer started. Ricky sure didn't know what he was missing, not loving Roxy.

FACE DOWN ON THE RUG, Roxy hadn't moved in two hours, except to breathe. And even that was an effort. If she were a drinking kind of woman she'd be drunk. But she wasn't and there was no other escape open to her, and man, oh man did she need an escape right now. "Beam me up, somebody. Please."

What a mess! "My life. Yeah, right!" she mumbled into the nap. On top of the world one minute, then climbing into that deep, dark hole she'd dug for herself the next.

She wanted to call him. Didn't want to call him. Too scared to call him. The real Roxy would have marched straight across the hall, squared her shoulders and said *Hey, Ned, you know that Valentine McCarthy you hate? I'm her, but that's okay because you're that Edward Craig I hate. So let's just skip it and get back to the real deal—Roxy and Ned— okay?*

But she was chicken. The rug was holding her down. She was coming down with a case of laryngitis. Choose one excuse. Or all three. Didn't matter, since she couldn't

do it. Not right now, anyway. Not until she was ready to
face the consequences, because it could go either way.

So for now she was safe not knowing. Safe, sorry and
sad. And stupid for thinking that she almost had it all.
That she could ever have it all. Didn't happen. No one got
it. Poor Roxy Rose. She had expectations, silly her. A career she loved, a piece of property she loved, and yes, the
most unpardonable of all expectations—a man she loved.
Way too much for any one girl to expect. Silly girl.

"Yeah, yeah," she muttered. "Way too much." But the
consolation prize, if she could console herself with it, was
that she would walk away with her career unscathed. The
home she wanted was probably a goner now. Same with
her relationship with Ned. But she had her job, and it was
getting bigger and better every day. *Here lies Roxanna Valentine Rose. She had her work.*

"Wow," she muttered, finally turning over on her back,
stretching to get a look at the ticking cat. Almost midnight.
"Wonder what words of wisdom Valentine has for us tonight."

In three years, this was the first night she'd taken off.
No vacation, no substitute, lest he or she do what she had
done three years ago when she was the substitute—snatch
the show away from the regular host. Sure, his ratings
were way down, and hers were way up. But still, it could
happen, so she always had a show or two in the can. Old
ones cut and pasted to sound like new ones, ready to go
just in case she wasn't. But until now, there'd never been
a reason to use them. Come midnight, every weeknight,
she was always at her desk, ready to utter her sugars into
the microphone. Until tonight. Listeners might not like it,
might not like the fact that the phone lines were closed
down, but they'd get over it tomorrow night, when she
was back.

Raising up just enough to grab the remote off the end

table next to the sofa, Roxy turned on her radio, then turned back over on her stomach, wondering why Ned hadn't come over. "Maybe because you rejected him, Roxy. Control freakin' bitch that you are. Doesn't take Valentine to figure it out." A control freakin' bitch without the backbone to lift the phone or crawl across the hall to him.

"Welcome to *Midnight Special,* sugars. Are you ready for something special? Because if you are, you've certainly come to the right place. Doctor Val has something *extra-specially* special for you tonight."

"I sure hope so, Val," Roxy moaned, "because I've done some extra-specially big screwing up this time."

"Doctor Val, I have this problem," the first caller began. "There's this guy I like a lot. Even love."

Me, too, Roxy thought. *Me, too.*

"That's a good start. So tell Doctor Val why you're having a problem with this guy you love."

"For starters, I haven't told him everything about me. At first it didn't matter, because I didn't know where the relationship was headed to. But now, I think we really have something, and I'm afraid if I start telling him things he should have known a long time ago that he'll leave me. I'm just so scared, Doctor Val."

"Look, I know you are. And believe me, Doctor Val is all for keeping a few little secrets in a relationship. Spilling everything can cause quite a mess, especially if you don't know where that relationship's going at the beginning."

"Which is exactly what I did," Roxy said to the rug. "Which was stupid, Val. Tell the lady how stupid it was."

"Well, sugar, there comes a point when the relationship looks like it's going to turn into more than a one or two-night stand, where you've got to fess up if you want to keep him around."

Truer words never spoken, at least by Valentine.

"And Valentine's sensing that you do. Isn't that right, sugar?"

"Maybe I do," the caller responded.

"Maybe I do, too," Roxy responded also. "And I never meant for it to go this far. But it sort of sneaked up on me. And what I thought was going to be casual wasn't. Then suddenly the secrets became important."

"And I didn't know how to tell him, so I just kept avoiding it," the caller added.

"You and me both," Roxy agreed.

"You can do one of two things here, but keep in mind, that at this stage of the game, there's no guarantee. It can go either way. You can walk away, lesson learned and vow not to do that again. Or you can tell him. Then depending on the kind of man he is, he'll either forgive you or leave."

"He's a nice man, Doctor Val. Kind, generous, and he trusts me."

"And he trusts me, too," Roxy added.

"Sounds to me like you need to do better by that man of yours," Val said. "And I think you already knew that when you called in. But you were hoping there was another way around it, is that correct?"

"Maybe," the called answered. "Something I could do without possibly losing him."

"More like probably losing him," Roxy said. "If he fell in love with the person you've been putting forward to him, then suddenly discovers you're not that person at all, there's no guarantee that the feelings he had for her will be the ones he has for you."

"Well, sugar, you could seduce that man of yours like you've never done before. Give him the thrill of his life, let him have everything his little heart desires in the bedroom, then break the news in dribs and drabs between orgasms. That might give you a headstart on keeping him, if he realizes in the middle of your confession what he'll be losing if he leaves."

Roxy flopped over and sat up. "Tell me I didn't say that," she moaned. "Please tell me."

"You go make him so weak he can't walk out that door. Make his head spin, make his eyes cross in his head, and pull out every sexual favor you know, if that's what it takes."

"No!" Roxy yelled. "Bad advice. She's giving you...*I'm giving you* bad advice. You need to sit down with the man and talk to him. Be honest. Be sincere. He might still leave, but if he does, you'll know you gave it your best shot. And sex isn't your best shot here."

"Thanks, Doctor Val. You're right, I do need to tell him. And what you're suggesting—I'm betting in the future, when I keep other secrets from him, he won't mind the confession so much."

Roxy picked up her remote and threw it at the stereo. "So if I take my advice, I'll just go across the hall, sleep with Ned, and that will make it all better." No wonder her life was so screwed up. *She'd been listening to herself.*

And no wonder Edward Craig had been nipping at Valentine's heels. They deserved some nipping.

"OKAY, HEP. I get that she's Valentine. That's cool. But what the hell does she think I am?" Ned grunted as he paced the perimeter of his living room. "*Who* the hell does she think I am? She gets me out to the beach, and like an idiot I thought it was more than what she thought it was, because once she got what she wanted, that was it. She went home. Sex on the beach, Hep. That's what it was. And I thought..." Nope. He wasn't even going to think those words. He'd been kidding himself with them long enough. So maybe she was Valentine after all, and Roxy was the character, instead of the other way around. "You know, it makes sense. I just couldn't see it. And even after I found out she was Val, I just kept on kidding myself, kept on thinking she'd finally tell me. Kept telling myself that it

was more than sex for her. That we were falling in love, because I sure as hell…" Talk about feeling stupid. "I thought
I could read people better than that, Hep."

He'd plodded to the door a thousand times in the past
hour, watching for her to come home, wondering if they
could make this better between them. But then he'd turned
on the radio and there she was, telling her caller to set the
lies straight with sex. That's all he heard, all he could listen to. It's what he expected from Val, *not* what he expected from Roxy. So maybe they couldn't be separated.

But he loved her, damn it! In spite of it all, he loved her.
And now, he just didn't know what came next.

13

Waking Up Wednesday Morning with the Ned Flu

"I'M CALLING IN SICK for the rest of the week, Astrid. Stick on some reruns for me, will you?"

"We've had a million complaints already because last night was a rerun. Your regulars recognized the cut-and-paste version, and I guarantee if they don't get somebody live on the other end of the wire next time they call, they won't be calling back. Or listening. Since we're so close to setting that syndication deal in motion, we need a warm body in your chair giving out advice."

So she was wrong, it did matter. For business, that was good; for Roxy, she just couldn't handle it right now. "Then get one," she said dismally. Sure, she could stay, go through the motions. Her heart wouldn't be in it, though, and her listeners would hear that. *Okay sugars, not to worry. Doctor Val took her own advice and it sucked.* "Your choice. I know I said I'd never use a sub, but I really do need to get out of here for a few days. So I'm trusting you to find someone adequate, *not good,* because I want a job to come back to."

"I'm guessing this is about getting away from your handyman?"

Roxy nodded. "I really wanted to fix it last night, but I was…"

"Scared," Astrid supplied. "Scared he wouldn't want it fixed?"

Roxy nodded. "You were so right. I haven't been thinking about what he wants. It's always been about me. And after that night after I kicked him off my beach, I kicked him out again when he wanted to have pizza with me. I sent him away because I couldn't face him. Didn't know how to, and it was easier for me to get rid of him. *For me,* Astrid. It was easier for me. I haven't seen him since, and it's got nothing to do with Val. It's me. *All me.* He got tired of my control issues, even though he said he wouldn't. And I can't blame him, because I'm pretty damned tired of them myself. So I just need to go away for a while and have a heart to heart with myself, figure out how, and if, I can make this right between us. Figure out how to do it in a way that's best for both of us, not just me. And I'm not very good at that." She had to figure out how to start over with Ned. Or how to live with a broken heart if he wouldn't.

"I'm so sorry about all this, Rox. Are you sure you're going to be okay?"

"I'm Roxy Rose. Of course I'm going to be okay." But there was none of the usual Roxy Rose conviction in her voice. "So let me tape a lead-in, and get out of here."

NOT EXACTLY WHAT SHE HAD PLANNED when she was packing to run away from home, but she was tired, and a nice little B-and-B just outside Tacoma suited her fine. She was already feeling a little better mentally, not being just two peepholes away from him.

Mrs. Willoughby's B-and-B was a quaint little place. Traditional, cozy charm in a nice wooded area. Even had a white picket fence, and Roxy was amazed at how much she liked it. It reminded her of Ned.

The fresh muffins and banana bread promised for breakfast made her think of Twinkies, which made her think about…well, the obvious. A bookshelf full of classics downstairs reminded her that he was a writer. No radio or television in her room. Yep, made her think of him too. And the faucet in the bathroom had a slight drip.

There was so much Ned everywhere.

Roxy slept from the moment she arrived, a little after noon, until well after eleven that night, when she finally wandered downstairs hoping somebody might be up who could point her to food. Real food, not Twinkies. Or truffles…

"Go make yourself a sandwich," Mrs. Willoughby said, pointing Roxy to the kitchen. "Then come on back out here and join me. You're my only guest tonight, and it's nice to have someone to keep me company. I'm alone now."

Alone now, like *she* was. Roxy put together a ham sandwich and headed back into the living room where Mrs. Willoughby, sixtyish and plump, snuggled into her couch, listening to her radio. *"Midnight Special,"* she told Roxy. "Ever hear it?"

"Used to," she said, wishing now she hadn't come down. Since she was eating Mrs. Willoughby's food though, she felt obligated to keep the woman company. And that included listening to the show, which she didn't want to do. Didn't want to listen to it, didn't want to think about it.

"Well, make yourself at home, dear. That chair over there's the best seat in the house." She nodded at a flower-covered, overstuffed wingback. "Sit down, get yourself comfortable." Then she giggled, sounding almost like a little girl. "You're not embarrassed about the things they talk about on this show, are you, dear? It can get pretty hot sometimes. Especially when that Edward calls her and they go at it. Talk about chemistry."

"Chemistry? More like bloodthirsty hostility, don't you mean?"

"That's not hostility, dear. I've been listening to the two of them go at it ever since he started calling, and those two, well, I'm betting in the same room they'd blow the roof off the building, and not from bloodthirsty hostility." She picked up a cup of hot tea and nodded toward the chair again. "More like sexual chemistry, dear. The kind that'll knock your socks off. Now, sit down, enjoy that sandwich. I have a chocolate cake in the kitchen if you'd like some later."

Blowing the roof off the building? Knock your socks off sexual chemistry? Is that what her listeners were hearing? "You really think they're hot?"

"Well, dear, I saw them on *SunUp* the other day. And the way that man watched her when she got up and walked away…sure miss having a man looking at me that way."

Sighing, Roxy dropped into the chair. "I think I'll turn in after I finish the sandwich, if you don't mind," she said. Only she wasn't hungry anymore.

"Welcome to *Midnight Special*, sugars. Are you ready for something special? Because if you are, you've certainly come to the right place. Doctor Val has something *extra-specially* special for you tonight. And tonight it's coming to you in the form of one extra-specially special guest host, while Valentine takes a few days off to go practice a little bit of what she's been preaching. So be gentle. I'm leaving you in good hands."

"She really gives me a good laugh sometimes," Mrs. Willoughby commented. "I hope whoever's taking over for her is as good as she is."

Frankly, Roxy didn't care. Astrid wouldn't torpedo the show, and beyond that all Roxy wanted to do was go back to bed and *not* worry about her show…her life…tomorrow—or the day after that.

"Welcome to *Midnight Special*," the dark-chocolate voice whispered across the airwaves.

Roxy dropped her ham sandwich on the floor. "I can't believe it," she sputtered, every one of her senses cracking to attention.

"This is Doctor Edward Craig, filling in for Doctor Mc-Carthy for the rest of the week."

"I'll fire her," Roxy snapped. "For real this time."

"Excuse me, dear?" Mrs. Willoughby said. "I didn't quite catch that."

"And while Valentine is off doing whatever it is Valentine does, I promise she's left you in very good hands," he continued.

"Doesn't he have just the nicest voice?" Mrs. Willoughby asked. "Dreamy. And he's a hunk. The kind you want in bed next to you. I'll tell you, if I were thirty years younger…heck, even if I *weren't* thirty years younger." She chuckled. "That's a topic I haven't heard Valentine talk about yet. Unless you count the one on hot mamma sex, but it didn't ever get around to women my age and men his age."

"She shouldn't have done it," Roxy growled. *"Astrid, how could you do this to me? You're my best friend. You, more than anybody else, know how I feel about him."* Roxy hissed out an agitated breath. "The minute I leave town, who does she go out and get?"

"So this Astrid went out and got herself a younger man, dear? Is that what you're saying? You seem pretty angry about it. Maybe a nice jigger of scotch will calm you down."

"Getting herself a younger man…it should be that simple," Roxy grumbled, scooping her sandwich up off the floor. "And I *am* angry! Furious!"

"If I were you, dear, I'd call Doctor Craig right up and ask his opinion, but he's pretty traditional, so it might not be anything you'd like to hear. But he's honest." Mrs. Willoughby set her teacup down on the end table, kicked off her shoes, pulled her feet up on the sofa and settled in for the show.

"Ha! You think he's honest? Just ask him about sex on the rug, on the door, on the rug on the beach. Ask him how honest that is," Roxy snapped, pulling her cell phone out of her pocket. She punched in the studio phone number, then drummed her fingers impatiently on the table next to her chair while she waited for Doyle to pick up. "Was that honest, hauling my rug out to the beach just so he could... Hello, Doyle?"

"Rox?" Doyle said.

"Why him?" Roxy screeched. "Of all the people she could have gotten, why him?"

"She thought it would be fun, I guess. And she was right. The lines are really lighting up tonight."

"Well, stick me in the queue for next caller up, then put her on the phone for me."

"You're not going to fire her, are you?" Doyle asked.

"That would be too good for her."

"Now I get it," Mrs. Willoughby chimed in. "Your friend Astrid hooked herself up with *your* younger man? That's why you're so angry. And I would be, too, dear. Since you're so young yourself, though, mind if I ask if he's legal?"

"He's legal, but what I'm thinking about doing isn't." Roxy waited another two minutes before Astrid came on, passing the time listening to Edward's advice to caller number one.

"So I catch him with the baby-sitter, Doctor Craig. And while they're not, like, doing it yet, she's on his lap. And he tells me she's got something in her eye and he's trying to help her get it out. So should I believe him, Doctor?"

"No way in hell you should believe him!" Roxy shouted.

Mrs. Willoughby looked at across her, giving her the thumbs-up sign.

"Sorry," Roxy muttered. "Sometimes I get carried away."

"Does he have a history of being unfaithful?" Edward asked.

"It's cheating, Eddie," Roxy snapped. "Cheating. Unfaithful is what happens when Old Faithful doesn't go off. Cheating is what happens when a hubby does! So call it as it is. Don't soft-pedal it."

"Not that I know of," the caller continued. "But this could be the first time."

"How old is the baby-sitter?" Edward questioned.

"Like that makes a difference?" Roxy shrieked. "For heaven's sake, Eddie, the man's doing the freakin' baby-sitter. Doesn't matter if he's done it before, and unless she's a kid, doesn't matter how old she is."

"Twenty," the caller said. "College student."

Roxy jumped up from the chair and started pacing the room. "Tell her to kick the bum out right now, then ask questions later, cause if daddy's got the sitter on his lap checking out her eye this time, next time it won't be her eye he's checking out."

"Marriage counseling," Edward said. "Immediately. Your marriage has some serious problems that need to be worked through before the situation gets any worse."

"New door locks," Roxy muttered. "Cheaper than counseling."

"I think you might have been a good fill-in for Valentine yourself," Mrs. Willoughby said, pushing herself off the couch and heading over to a concealed wet bar in the bookcase. "Care for a shot of scotch now?"

"I'd rather have a shot at Edward Craig," she replied.

"Rox?" Astrid finally answered the phone.

"I'm listening to it," Roxy said, lowering her voice to almost Valentine proportions. "And I'm not liking what I'm hearing."

"I thought he'd be a natural, since your listeners already know him. Some continuity, you know. And they sure as heck won't want a steady diet of him, which was one of your concerns, wasn't it? Losing your job to your sub. Won't happen with him."

"I don't care! Just kick that continuity out the door and put it on a rerun."

The phone started crackling. "Can't hear you, Rox. You're breaking up."

"Don't you dare…"

"Can't hear you, Rox."

"Astrid, you're fired. So help me, it's for real this time."

"Rox, are you still there…can't…hear…"

"Welcome to *Midnight Special*. This is Doctor Edward Craig, and what can I do for you tonight?"

His words in her ear shocked her, even though she'd told Doyle to put her next in the queue, and she pulled the phone away like it was sizzling hot, then stared for a moment.

"Hello?" he said, both from her phone and the radio across the room.

To prevent feedback, Roxy slipped into the dining room while Mrs. Willoughby slipped back onto the couch with a jigger of scotch.

"Hello," Roxy said quietly. Not her Roxy voice, not her Valentine voice, either.

"So tell me what's bothering you tonight."

"Sex, Doctor Craig. Good sex, the best sex I've ever had."

"Was it good for him?" he asked.

"Better than good. And a woman knows these things. I think it was the best sex he's ever had, too." She shut her eyes, thinking about the quivers, the moans—his, hers…. Yep, as good for him as it was for her.

"So what's the problem, other than the fact that I haven't heard anything about a real relationship mentioned so far."

"Oh, it's a real relationship, and I don't think either one of us would argue that." She chuckled devilishly into the phone. "Not the way he does *it* for me…you know, like four, five times in a row. His mouth, Doc. What he can do with his mouth on my…"

"Your what?" Edward sputtered.

"Anything, everything. And his tongue. It drives me wild, like nothing I've ever felt in my whole life. It's like fire on my skin. I'm mean, I'm getting all hot right now just thinking about it." And she was. Shivering, sweating, going weak in the knees. "I want him, Doctor, in ways I've never wanted a man before. And I've had him in ways I've never had a man before. Ways I never want to have any other man, ever again. It's like our sex is on a higher plane. All we have to do is get naked—his body touching mine, mine touching his, his hands all over me, mine all over him—and we surpass what we did together the last time. And the last time was always so good."

"Meaning it gets better every time?" Edward gulped. It was audible on air.

"Better doesn't even describe it, Doc. I mean right now, just thinking about the way he moans when I…well, there are so many things I can do that make him moan. And the way he shudders when I…well, that too. You know what makes a man shudder, don't you? It's like that and more for me, too, when he does it for me."

"It?"

"You know, Doctor. *It.* Starting with my toes and working all the way up to my… The big *it.* And it's so big for both of us it practically blows the roof off the building. That kind of sex, Doc. Do you know what I'm talking about?" Roxy smiled, cutting herself a piece of Mrs. Willoughby's chocolate cake. "Sex so great there aren't even adequate words to describe it?"

Very audible sigh. "I get the picture," he snapped. "So what's the problem?"

"You're sounding a little bothered by what I'm describing, Doctor. Obviously, you've never found yourself in this kind of situation, have you? Or you'd know what the problem is."

He didn't answer.

"Have you, Doctor?" Roxy persisted. "Because what I want to know is what makes the sex so good between us? Is it merely great sex between two people who know how to do it really well with each other—you know, the mechanical aspects. Or do you think there could be more to it? You know, maybe we have deeper feelings for each other…feelings that are driving the sex between us to that higher level? Like, if we didn't have those deeper feelings maybe the sex wouldn't be so good. *Are we actually making love, Doctor?* Could we be two people in love making love?"

Edward cleared his throat, and his voice came back a little shaky. "Have you talked about it?" he asked, clearing his throat once more. "Have you ever told him how you feel? Asked him how he feels? Explored, together, the possibility that you're in love?"

Smiling, Roxy crinkled a cellophane wrapper next to the phone. "Can't hear you, Doctor. You're breaking up."

"Honesty is the best…"

"Can't hear…" Crinkle, crinkle.

"Talk to him…."

Roxy clicked off the phone, picked up two paper plates with huge pieces of cake on them and carried them back into the living room, where Mrs. Willoughby was sprawled flat on the couch, fanning herself with one hand, hugging an empty jigger with the other. "I need cake, dear. Now!"

"Too bad we were cut off," Edward continued, "or I would have told her…"

"Yeah, yeah," Roxy muttered. "Get counseling."

His voice was resolute. "I would have told her that yes, it sounds to me like they're in love. Totally, truly, in love."

Roxy dropped her cake on the floor. "Well, I'll be damned."

"NICE PIECE OF PROPERTY," Ned said, opening a bag of cookies for the gulls. "Too bad she won't be building out here."

Doyle turned around, startled. "I didn't hear you coming."

"I didn't intend for you to." He walked out past the knoll, scattered the plain vanilla wafers, then turned back to Doyle. "Looking for Roxy out here?"

"Thought she might be here. I'm kind of worried. She's been doing some pretty crazy stuff…crazy even for Roxy." He narrowed his eyes. *"Like falling for you.* Oswald told me who you were a couple of weeks ago. I took him some beer for his recovery one night and he let it slip about you. Of course, by then, she'd already moved in across from you. I let her do that, you know. Take my place on the waiting list. She needed something real bad. Her place was a pit. But if I'd known she'd end up living across the hall from Edward Craig, I sure as hell wouldn't have let it happen. But I kept thinking it would be okay. Rox is real busy, especially lately, looking for syndicators. And she's got this business first, everything else later motto. So I figured she'd stick to it. But hell, was I way off on that one.

"I started hearing her say things about the handyman, and it wasn't Oswald. So I asked, and he told me it was you standing in for him. *You* were the one with the tool belt she was drooling over. *She was falling for Doctor Edward Craig.* Believe me, man, I was sure kicking myself for screwing things up the way I did. I mean, she's not Val. Val's tough. She can give as good as she gets. But Roxy's, well, I guess you could call her vulnerable. She always believes things will work out. She's, you know, optimistic, and naive in a lot of ways.

"Then when I heard she was falling for you, I figured once you knew who she was, with the way you always go after her on the air, you'd dump her. That Edward dude…*you*…sometimes you're a real bastard, you know. Especially since it's just radio entertainment." Doyle paused, shook his head. "And after you dumped Rox, she'd be hurt because she really was falling for you. So since it was my fault she met you in the first place, I wanted to be there to help her through it."

Radio entertainment. Damn! *Radio entertainment just like him.* Score one for the pizza guy. "So you made that arrangement for Georgette Selby?"

Doyle nodded. "She was annoying Rox, anyway, so I just found her an apartment in a seniors' place. Actually the one you own. Oswald helped me get her in. And it's real nice for her. Believe me, man, she was thrilled to get in there. Then after she was gone, I got her apartment."

"You went to a lot of trouble for Roxy, Doyle. Are you in love with her?"

"It's not like you think, man," Doyle exclaimed. "I'm trying to look out for Roxy. That's all. Like a brother. But she doesn't always listen."

"Are you in love with Roxy, Doyle?"

"Sure, I love her," Doyle admitted. "But not the way you do, dude."

"You love her so much you let the Shorecroft manager know she's Valentine, hoping that would kill her plans for building out there?"

"Okay, so I sent an e-mail and ratted her out. But it was for her own good, since she wouldn't listen to me, I swear. You gotta know that, man. I was just trying to save her from herself. I've lived in a small town like that half of my life. I know how they are when it comes to people like Rox. She was investing everything she had without taking a good look at what she'd be getting, and I just couldn't stand by and let her do that. Sure, I warned her. Over and over. But she wouldn't listen to me, didn't believe what I was saying about people like the ones who live in Shorecroft. They didn't like her house, and they wouldn't like her if they ever found out who she was. With the syndication deal getting so close, a lot more of Roxy was about to go public. In fact, if you Google her, it's already out there on the Web—Roxy is Val, Val is Roxy. So I took care of the Shorecroft problem before it went too far. Before she ended up putting more into it than she already had and ended up getting hurt."

Ned squinted up at the sun. It would have been a nice day for a picnic here with Roxy. And he missed her, which was why he'd come out here, to be close to her spirit…and her seagulls. To think—which he'd been doing for hours, sitting on top of her knoll.

Well, thanks to Doyle's moment of insightfulness, now there wasn't as much to think about as he'd thought there would be. He loved Roxy. That was it. Nothing else mattered. Sure, she was complicated as hell, but whoever said life was meant to be simple. And sure, they didn't agree on a lot of things. But the flip side was sparks and sizzle and excitement.

So he'd come prepared to do a lot of soul-searching, but all he needed was one thought of Roxy and the rest was clear. *She wasn't Val.* Just like he wasn't Edward. Roxy was who she was—a little bit of both, which made her the woman he loved. And he prayed she loved the little bit of both in him.

"I don't want her hurt, either, Doyle." Ned studied Doyle for a minute. The man protected Roxy like a pit bull, loved her, defended her. The things *he* should have been doing, instead of analyzing it like Edward would do. Meaning, Edward's advice pretty much sucked. He laughed. Valentine, *and Roxy,* could have told him that!

"I'm not some kind of perv or stalker," Doyle said. "If that's what you're thinking this is all about. And I sure as hell didn't mean for it to turn into this kind of mess for her. All I really ever wanted to do was be there, you know, as her friend. So are you going to tell her it was me? That I did her in on the property deal? Because when she finds out, you know she'll kill me, man."

"Nope. You're her friend. And she's *your* friend, Doyle. She cares about you. You're the one who's got to tell her." He had his own telling to do.

Doyle jammed his hands into the pockets of his baggy jeans and looked at the seagulls squawking over the cookies. "Like I told you, man. She's in love with you. I've seen you two in the hall back at the apartment, saw the way she looked at you, you looked at her. And I've heard the things she whispers to Astrid about the handyman when they forget I'm listening. And the damnedest part of this is, while Roxy's in love with you, Valentine's just as in love with Edward, although she'd rip out her tongue, and mine, before she'd cop to that one." He laughed. "After you two get through fighting on air, the listeners need to go light up a cigarette, the talk between you is so sexy, Doc. Not like in porno, but..."

"Chemistry," Ned said.

Doyle nodded. "We've gotten thousands of calls and e-mails about it, just haven't let Rox see them 'cause they'd have made her mad as hell, thinking she was hating you, when all the time she wasn't. And she *is* a shrink. She'd have figured it out what it was, then that would have wrecked things for the show. Wrecked them for Roxy too, but she's always said the show comes first. Of course, I believed she meant it. Guess I was wrong on a lot of things, and now I've got a lot to patch up with her if she'll let me."

"She'll let you," Ned reassured him. But would she let him?

"You *do* know that was her calling in last night, don't you? She's circling around like those stupid gulls out there, trying to figure out if there's going to be a cookie for her when she lands. So are you going to give her a cookie, man?"

"I sure as hell intend to try, but I've got a few things to patch up myself."

"Wanna go grab a pizza first?"

14

Another Night, Another Piece of Cake

"BETTER HURRY, DEAR, it's almost time." Mrs. Willoughby was settling in with her jigger of scotch while Roxy was settling in with a piece of carrot cake tonight. "You're going to call him again, aren't you? That was so exciting, knowing you were right there in my kitchen talking on the radio. I'll swear, you almost sounded like that Doctor Val."

"I may sound like Valentine, but I'm sure not like her," she replied, her glum mood not going away in spite of the yummy cake, and this was her third piece already this evening. Tonight she'd know one way or another. She had to, it was time. "Valentine would never find herself in this mess."

"I heard what you said on the radio last night, dear. So, why don't you just tell him you love him? Firecracker sex with the man you love...you'd be nuts if you didn't. Mr. Willoughby was a freight train in the sack, dear, and I was crazy about the man. Until he left me for a younger woman. I can tell you from personal experience, you just can't beat it when it's all good. But you're not going to find out if you just keep sitting here eating cake."

"And Mr. Willoughby never came back?" Roxy asked, suddenly too full to take another bite.

"Oh, he came back, dear. But I was having a hell of a good time with the plumber by then, so I kicked him right back out."

"I had a good thing going with the plumber once," Roxy said wistfully. "Loved that pipe wrench." Loved that plumber.

"Well, I prefer the chain grip pliers myself, dear. But those telescoping inspection mirrors can sure be fun, too." She winked at Roxy, then chugged down her scotch.

"And he's gone now, your plumber?"

"Yes, dear. For a couple more days. Plumbing convention in Vegas. He's checking out some new tools."

"WELCOME BACK to *Midnight Special.* Again, I'd like to thank Doctor McCarthy for allowing me to sit in for her, last night, tonight and tomorrow. And I'd also like to thank each and every one of you for calling in. Now, we have only a few minutes left, so let's make the most of them, shall we?"

So far he'd covered two cheating husbands, one wife who wished her hubby would cheat so she could have a little time off, a sex goddess who couldn't find Mr. Studly, and a Mr. Studly who couldn't find his sex goddess. Too bad this wasn't a dating service. And oh, yes. The one about hot grandpa sex. Seemed that granny had revved it up in the bedroom since she'd been listening to Doctor Val and gramps just called in to say thanks.

Ned glanced at the computer screen. One call left. Relationship down the tubes. Coming in on a mobile. Was it her? "And what's on your mind tonight?" God, he hoped it was.

"Lies, Doctor."

Ned sucked in a sharp breath. "What about lies?"

"They come between people." It was Roxy's voice all the way. "And once the lie starts, it's so hard to take it back, or change it, or set it straight. Something like that can ruin a relationship."

"So tell me about your lie."

"It didn't start out to be a lie. More like a little deception. Which shouldn't have been a big deal. I liked him, he liked me. I thought it would be casual, but it never was. Not for me, anyway. But I kept kidding myself that I'd get over it, move on, so it didn't matter what I was doing."

"And did you get over it?"

"No. And I never will."

"So what was this big lie you told him?"

"Not him. Me. I lied to myself, over and over, that I didn't love him. That all the differences between us meant I couldn't love him, or that he wouldn't love me. But I do love him, Doctor. With all my heart. Like I said, we had all these differences that scared me, all these similarities that scared me, too. So I kept on lying to myself instead of facing them. Telling myself that I couldn't have it all, that nobody can have it all. Easier that way, in case he wasn't feeling what I was feeling. Self-protection. Shielding myself from rejection."

"A little self-doubt?"

"A lot of self-doubt. I've failed before."

"We've all failed."

"I know. But I've set myself up with things I won't fail at, things I can keep under my control. Then I met him and realized what meant the most to me wasn't under my control at all. And I could fail again. So I pushed him away so that wouldn't happen."

"You mentioned you had differences and similarities that scare you. Did you ever think that these differences and similarities might scare him as much as they do you? Especially since he loves you in the same way you talk about loving him. Heart and soul and forever."

"He does?"

"He *absolutely* does."

"Me too. But I was afraid that all he wanted was casual. That's what I thought he was saying. You know, that we went so fast it couldn't be the real thing. Guess maybe I should have taken your advice and talked to him."

"*He* should have taken my advice and talked to you, because if that's what he was saying, he was wrong, and I know he's sorry for making you think that. But I think he was lying to himself, too. Thinking that because the feelings were so strong from the beginning, that it couldn't possibly be the real thing. Maybe looking for ways to make sure it wasn't in case you didn't want him the way he wanted you."

"So maybe we were both scared? Maybe because it was love at first sight?"

"He sounds like the kind of man who didn't believe in it. I think he was probably trying to dispel the romantic notion and look for something more practical. But he was wrong on that one, and you should tell him that."

"You mean tell him that there are some things you simply know without thinking about them or trying to argue yourself out of them or reasoning away the glorious rush that comes with spontaneity. No, Doctor. He's the one who should tell me."

"Sounds to me like you already know."

"What I know is that every story has two sides to it, including mine, and I'm so sorry I didn't tell him both sides to begin with. At first I didn't think it mattered, but when I realized that it did I was…"

"Chicken," he said.

"Yep. And the better it got between us the more I was afraid…"

"That it would end when you finally did let him see the other side?"

"It was killing me, and I'm so sorry."

"It was killing him, too, keeping the other half of his story to himself, and he's sorry too."

"Sounds to me like there were two great big sorry chickens in that pot, Edward."

"Two chickens who should have been talking to each other. But even though you didn't tell him, he knew both sides. A man knows the woman he loves no matter how she's dressed. And he loved you in spite of that other side, and because of it." She'd taken off the mustache herself. Finally! "So caller, he loves you, you love him. Anything else you want to talk about?"

"Well, Edward, I think he needs...deserves more. I think he deserves to know that the differences are a big slice of the relationship, something that adds to attraction. And I also think that if he's a very good boy, those differences can result in the best makeup sex he's ever had. Sex that will pop his eyes right out of their sockets and curl his toes, Doctor. Sex that will make those differences between us an extra-specially exciting part of our relationship." She was slipping back into Valentine's voice now.

"So as usual, Valentine, it's all about sex? You hear this heartfelt discussion about two people who have fallen deeply and forever in love and you take it right back to the bedroom and make it all about sex?"

"Absolutely not. It's all about making love to the person you loved at first sight and who you're going to love for the rest of your life. And I'm talking some red hot granny lovemaking way down the line, Eddie."

Roxy clicked off her phone and stepped into the booth, then took the mic from Ned. "And this is Doctor Val signing off, hoping your midnight tonight is the most extra-specially special one ever, sugars." She opened her drawer, took out two truffles and handed him one.

"You know what I was thinking?" Ned said, pulling her into his arms.

"About a rug?"

"And some Twinkies."

THREE MONTHS LATER…

"I don't want the picket fence anymore," Ned protested, perusing the house plans. "Doesn't work out there on the beach. And it's going to get in the way when I have to go out and feed your gulls." Their gulls now. "I thought you wanted a nice, unobstructed view of the Sound."

"From the bedroom."

He glanced at the prints and shook his head. "Going to be hard to do since you got rid of the windows. And as far as I know, most Victorians came with windows."

So she'd given up the cement, steel and glass. No biggie. Traditional was wonderful when it came with Ned. And once Ned's new CAD program had popped out a reasonable Victorian facsimile, the Shorecroft mob relented. A little. The house was approved, but she was forever banned from Shorecroft public functions.

"Two minutes," Doyle called, immediately pulling off the headphones so he wouldn't overhear any of the newlywed conversation. Not that everybody at the station hadn't been hearing it for the past few days. He'd fessed-up his deeds to Roxy, and to show him there were no hard feelings, she subscribed him to the pizza-of-the-month club as a thank-you for caring, even if in a Doyle-ish clumsy way. Plus she assured him, there was no way she was going syndicated without him.

She'd been honeymooning while Astrid was working out the syndication details, actually. Big details translating into lots of money. Sure, it was hard stepping back and letting Astrid take control of the deal. But she'd been caught up with a VP at Taber Syndicators lately, his butt not quite as good as Ned's, even though Astrid would never admit it, and it seemed the natural thing to do. Besides, there'd been this awesome Rose-Proctor, make that Proctor-Rose, honeymoon in the works…pup tenting out on a beach… and there was no amount of control anybody could have offered Roxy that could have compared with what was going on out on Rose Hill, in Rose Water, Rose Beach…

And there was an upside waiting for her after the honeymoon. With the pizza, Doyle got the pizza delivery girl, which looked exceptionally promising, according to Doctor Val and her new on-air partner, Doctor Edward. Collaboration—probably the only thing they'd agreed on professionally, so far. Amazing how the syndication deal exploded when that announcement hit the airwaves. Eddie and Val together… Sure, Ned was still writing by day. With lots of vigor now that he and Roxy were on the same schedule. Roxy was even thinking about picking up a pen and doing a little of that herself. Something called *An Opposite's Guide to Making Sex Even Better*. Nothing like the book Ned was writing, of course.

"So stick in a window someplace," Roxy said, looking over the program notes. Same ol', same ol', with one exception. And having *him* sitting right here in the booth with her every night, she was beginning to anticipate the fun things she might do to him during the breaks. Or during the broadcast, on the rug they'd bought for the booth. Just thinking about it made her tingle! Sliding one truffle over to him, and placing one next to her microphone, she continued, "And while you're at it, we might need some stairs to get us from the first floor to the second." Leaning into him, she whispered, "Unless you'd prefer to use a pole. And there are some extra-specially fun things I can do for you on a pole, sugar."

"I heard that," Astrid said from her booth.

"Think maybe I'll put that pole in the bedroom," Ned growled, leaning to give Roxy a quick kiss as Doyle gave them the countdown.

"Five, four, three, two…"

As the one count came down on them, Roxy took hold of Ned's hand and gave it a squeeze. "Welcome to *Midnight*

Special, sugars. Are you ready for something special? Because if you are, you've certainly come to the right place. Doctors Valentine and Edward *both* have something *extra-specially* special for you tonight."

* * * *

Make an appointment to read Dianne Drake's thrilling new Mills & Boon Medical Romance® novel. Emergency in Alaska *is available in July 2006 from all good booksellers.*

When Doctor Michael Morse comes to Alaska to find his mother, he doesn't expect to find Doctor Aleksandra Sokolov, the one woman with whom he shares a secret past...

Undercover with the Mob

by
Elizabeth Bevarly

For Wanda, Birgit and Brenda,
with thanks for welcoming me into the
M&B family

1

NATALIE DORSET WAS enjoying her usual Saturday morning breakfast with her landlady when her life suddenly took a turn for the surreal.

Oh, the day had started off normally enough. She had been awakened at her usual weekend hour of 8:30 a.m. by her cat, Mojo, who, as usual, wanted his breakfast—and then her spot in the still-warm bed. And then she had brewed her usual pot of tea—her Fortnum & Mason blend, since it was the weekend—and had opened her usual kitchen window to allow in the cool autumn morning. And then she had fastened her shoulder-length brown hair into its usual ponytail, had forgone, for now, her usual contact lenses to instead perch her usual glasses on her usual nose and, still wearing her blue flannel jammies decorated with moons and stars, she had, as usual, carried the pot of tea down to the first floor kitchen, which Mrs. Klosterman and her tenants generally used as a general meeting/sitting area. It was also where Natalie and Mrs. Klosterman had their usual breakfast together every Saturday morning, as usual.

And now it was also where Mrs. Klosterman was going off the deep end, psychologically speaking. Which was sort of usual, Natalie had to admit, but not quite as usual as the full-gainer she was performing with Olympic precision today. You could just never really tell with Mrs. Klosterman.

"I'm telling you, Natalie," her elderly landlady said, having barely touched her first cup of tea, "he's a Mob informant the government has put here for safekeeping. You mark my words. We could both wake up in our beds tomorrow morning to find our throats slit."

Mrs. Klosterman was referring to her new tenant, having just this past week let out the second floor of her massive, three-story brick Victorian in Old Louisville. Now, only days after signing the lease, she was clearly having second thoughts—though probably not for the reasons she should be having them, should she, in fact, even be having second thoughts in the first place. Or something like that. Mrs. Klosterman did have a habit of, oh, embellishing reality? Yes, that was a polite way of saying she was sometimes delusional.

Natalie had lived in Mrs. Klosterman's house—occupying the third and uppermost floor, where her landlady claimed the first for herself—for more than five years now, ever since she'd earned her Masters of Education and begun teaching at a nearby high school. Other tenants who had rented out the second floor had come and gone in those years, but Natalie couldn't bring herself to move, even though she could afford a larger space now, maybe even a small home of her own. She just liked living in the old, rambling house. It had a lot of character. In addition to Mrs. Klosterman, she meant.

And she liked her landlady, too, who didn't seem to have any family outside her tenants—much like Natalie herself. Because of the tiny population of the building, the house had always claimed a homey feel, since Mrs. Klosterman had, during its renovation into apartments, left much of the first floor open to the public—or, at the very least, to her tenants. At Christmastime, she and Natalie and whoever else was in residence even put up a tree in the front window and exchanged gifts. For someone like Natalie, who'd never had much family of her own, living here with Mrs. Klosterman was the next best thing. In fact, considering the type of family Natalie had come from, living here with Mrs. Klosterman was actually better.

Of course, considering this potential throat-slitting thing with regard to their new neighbor, they might all be sleeping with the fishes before the next Christmas could even come about. And their gifts from the new guy might very well be horses' heads in their beds. Which, call her stodgy, would just ruin the holiday for Natalie.

Putting aside for now the idea that she and her landlady might wake up with their throats slit, since, according to her—admittedly limited—knowledge of medicine, a person most likely *wouldn't* wake up had her throat indeed been slit, and the relative unlikelihood of that happening anyway, she asked her landlady, "Why do you think he's a Mob informant?"

Really, she knew she shouldn't be surprised by Mrs. Klosterman's suspicions. Ever since Natalie had met her, her landlady had had a habit of making her life a lot more colorful than it actually was. (See above comments about the sometimes-delusional thing.) But seeing as how the woman had survived all by herself for the last twenty of her eighty-four years, ever since her husband Edgar's death, Natalie supposed Mrs. Klosterman had every right to, oh, embellish her reality in whatever way she saw fit. She just wished the other woman would lighten up on the true crime books and confession magazines she so loved. Obviously, they were beginning to take their toll. Or maybe it was just extended age doing that. Or else Mrs. Klosterman was back to smoking her herb tea instead of brewing it. Natalie had warned her about that.

"I can just tell," the older woman said now. She tugged

restlessly at the collar of her oversized muumuu, splashed with fuchsia and lime green flowers, then ran her perfectly manicured fingers—manicured with hot pink nail polish—through her curly, dyed-jet-black hair. Whenever she left the house, Mrs. Klosterman also painted on jet-black eyebrows to match, and mascaraed her lashes into scary jet-black daddy longlegs. But right now, only soft white fuzz hinted at her ownership of either feature. "I can tell by the way he looks, and by the way he acts, and by the way he talks," she added knowledgeably. "Even his name is suspicious."

Natalie nodded indulgently. "What, does he wear loud polyester suits and ugly wide neckties and sunglasses even when it's dark out? Does he reek of pesto and Aqua Velva? Is his name Vinnie 'The Eraser' Mancuso, and is he saying he's here to rub some people out?"

Mrs. Klosterman rolled her eyes at Natalie. "Of course not. He wouldn't be that obvious. He wears normal clothes, and he smells very nice. But he does talk like a mobster."

"Does he use the word 'whacked' a lot?" Natalie asked mildly.

"Actually, he did use the word 'whacked' once when he came to sign the lease," her landlady said haughtily.

"Did he use it in reference to a person?" Natalie asked. "Preferably a person with a name like 'Big Tony' or 'Light-Loafered Lenny' or 'Joey the Kangaroo'?"

Mrs. Klosterman deflated some. "No. He used it in reference to the cockroaches in his last apartment building. I assured him we did *not* have that problem here, so there would be no whacking necessary." Before Natalie had a chance to ask another question, her landlady hurried on, "But even not taking into consideration all those other things—"

Which were certainly incriminating enough, Natalie thought wryly.

"—his name," her landlady continued, "is…" She paused, looking first to the left, then to the right before finishing. And when she finally did conclude her sentence, she scrunched her body low across the table, and dropped her voice to a conspiratorial whisper. "His name," she said quietly, "is…John."

Now Natalie was the one to roll her eyes. "Oh, yeah. John. That's a Mob name all right. All your most notorious gangsters are named John. Let's see, there was John Capone, John Luciano, John Lansky, John Schultz, Baby John Nelson, Pretty John Floyd, Johnny and Clyde…"

"John Dillinger, John Gotti," Mrs. Klosterman threw in.

Yeah, okay, Natalie thought. But they were the exceptions.

"And it's not just the John part," Mrs. Klosterman said. "His full name is John *Miller.*"

Oh, well, in that *case,* Natalie thought. Sheesh.

"But he tells everyone to call him 'Jack,'" her landlady concluded. "So you can see why I'm so suspicious."

Yep, Natalie thought. No doubt about it. Mrs. Klosterman definitely had been smoking her herb tea again. Natalie would have to find the stash and replace it with normal old oolong, just like last time.

"John Miller," Natalie echoed blandly. "Mmm. I can see where that name would just raise all kinds of red flags at the Justice Department."

Mrs. Klosterman nodded. "Exactly. I mean, what kind of name is John Miller? It's a common one. The kind nobody could trace, because there would be so many of them running around."

"And the reason your new tenant couldn't just be another one of those many running around?" Natalie asked, genuinely anxious to hear her landlady's reasoning for her assumption. Mostly because it was sure to be entertaining.

"He doesn't *look* like a John Miller," she said. "Or even a Jack Miller," she hastily added.

"What does he look like?" Natalie asked.

Mrs. Klosterman thought for a moment. "He looks like a Vinnie 'The Eraser' Mancuso."

Natalie sighed, unable to stop the smile that curled her lips. "I see," she said as she lifted her teacup to her mouth for another sip.

"And even though Mr. Miller was the one who signed the lease," Mrs. Klosterman added, "it was another man who originally looked at the apartment and said he wanted to rent it for someone."

Which, okay, was kind of odd, Natalie conceded, but certainly nothing to go running around crying, "Mob informant!" about. "And what did that man look like?" she asked, telling herself she shouldn't encourage her landlady this way, but still curious about her new neighbor.

Mrs. Klosterman thought for a moment. "Now *he* looked like a John Miller. Very plain and ordinary." Then her eyes suddenly went wide. "No, he looked like a federal agent!" she fairly cried. "I just now remembered. He was wearing a trench coat!"

Natalie bit her lower lip and wondered if it would do any good to remind Mrs. Klosterman that it was October, and that it wasn't at all uncommon to find the weather cool and damp this time of year, and that roughly half the city of Louisville currently was walking around in a trench coat, or reasonable facsimile thereof. Nah, Natalie immediately told herself. It would only provoke her.

"I bet he was the government guy who relocated Mr. Miller," Mrs. Klosterman continued, lowering her voice again, presumably because she feared the feds were about to bust through the kitchen door, since in speaking so loudly, she was about to out their star witness against the

Mob, who would then also bust through the kitchen door, tommy guns blazing.

"Mrs. Klosterman," Natalie began instead, "I really don't think it's very likely that your new tenant is—"

"Connected," her landlady finished for her, her mind clearly pondering things that Natalie's mind was trying to avoid. "That's the word I've been looking for. He's connected. And now he's singing like a canary. And all his wiseguy friends are looking to have him capped."

Natalie stared at her landlady through narrowed eyes. Forget about the tea smoking. What on earth had Mrs. Klosterman been reading?

"You just wait," the other woman said. "You'll see. He's in the Witness Protection Program. I just have a gut feeling."

Natalie was about to ask her landlady another question—one that would totally change the subject, like "Hey, how 'bout them Cardinals?"—when, without warning, the very subject she had been hoping to change came striding into the kitchen in the form of Mr. Miller himself. And when he did, Natalie was so startled, both by his arrival and his appearance—holy moly, he really did look like a Vinnie "The Eraser" Mancuso—that she nearly dropped her still-full cup of tea into her lap. Fortunately, she recovered it when it had done little more than splash a meager wave of—very hot—tea onto her hand. Unfortunately, *that* made her drop it for good. But she scarcely noticed the crash as the cup shattered and splattered its contents across the black-and-white checked tile floor. Because she was too busy gaping at her new neighbor.

He was just so… *Wow.* That was the only word she could think of to describe him. Where she and her landlady were still relaxing in their nightclothes—hey, it was Saturday, after all—John "The Jack" Miller looked as if he were ready to take on the world. Most likely with a submachine gun.

Even sitting down as she was, Natalie could tell he topped six feet, and he probably weighed close to two hundred pounds, all of it solid muscle. He was dressed completely in black, from the long-sleeved black T-shirt that stretched taut across his broad chest and shoulders and was pushed to the elbows over extremely attractive and very saliently muscled forearms, to the black trousers hugging trim hips and long legs, to the eel-skin belt holding up those trousers, to the pointy-toed shoes of obviously Italian design. His hair was also black, longer than was fashionable, thick and silky and shoved straight back from his face.

And what a face. As Natalie vaguely registered the sensation of hot liquid seeping into her fuzzy yellow slippers, she gaped at the face gazing down at her, the face that seemed to have frozen in place, because Jack Miller appeared to be as transfixed by her as she was by him. His features looked as if they had been chiseled by the gods—Roman gods, at that. Because his face was all planes and angles, from the slashes of sharp cheekbones to the full, sensual mouth to the blunt, sturdy line of his jaw. And his eyes…

Oh, my.

His eyes were as black as his clothing and hair, fringed by dark lashes almost as long as Mrs. Klosterman's were in their daddy-longlegs phase. But it wasn't the lashes that were scary on him, Natalie thought as her heart kicked up a robust, irregular rhythm. It was the eyes. As inky as the witching hour and as turbulent as a tempest, Mr. Miller— *yeah, right*—had the kind of eyes she figured a hit man would probably have: imperturbable, unflappable. Having taught high school in the inner city for five years, she liked to think she could read people pretty well. And usually, she could. But with Mr. Miller—*yeah, right*—she could tell absolutely nothing about what he might be feeling or thinking.

Until he cried, "Jeez, lady, you tryin' to burn me alive here or what?"

And then she realized that it wasn't that Mr. Miller had been transfixed by *her*. What he'd been transfixed by was the fact that hot tea had splashed on him. Which was pretty much in keeping with Natalie's impact on the opposite sex. Long story short, she always seemed to have the same effect on men. Eventually, they always started looking at her as if she'd just spilled something on them. With Mr. Miller she was just speeding things up a bit, that was all. Not that she wanted any *things* to even happen with him, mind you, let alone speed them up. But it was good to know where she stood right off the bat.

And where she stood with Jack Miller, she could tell right away, was that she was stuck on him. In much the same way that melting slush stuck to the side of his car, or a glob of gum stuck to the bottom of a shoe. At least, she could see, that was the way he was feeling about her at the moment.

"I am so sorry," she said by way of a greeting, lurching to her feet and grabbing for a dish towel to wipe him off. "I hope I didn't hurt you."

Hastily, she began brushing at her new neighbor's clothing, then realized, too late, that because of their dark color, she had no idea where her tea might have landed on him, or if it had even landed on him at all. So, deciding not to take any chances, she worked furiously to wipe off all of him, starting at his mouthwateringly broad shoulders and working gradually downward, over his tantalizingly expansive chest, and then his temptingly solid biceps, and then his deliciously hard forearms. And then, just to be on the safe side, she moved inward again, over his delectably flat torso and once more over his tantalizingly expansive chest—you never could be too careful when it came to spilling hot beverages, after all—back up over the mouth-wateringly broad shoulders, and then down over his delectably flat torso again, and lower still, toward his very savory—

"What the hell are you doing?"

The roughly—and loudly—uttered demand was punctuated by Jack Miller grabbing both of Natalie's wrists with unerring fingers and jerking her arms away from his body. In doing so, he also jerked them away from her own body, spreading them wide, giving himself, however inadvertently, an eyeful of her... Well, of her oversized flannel jammies with the moons and stars on them that were in no way revealing or attractive.

Damn her luck anyway.

"I'm sorry, Mr. Miller," she apologized again. "I hope I didn't—"

"How did you know my name?" he demanded in a bristly voice.

She arched her eyebrows up in surprise at his vehemence. *Paranoid much?* she wanted to ask. Instead, she replied, "Um, Mrs. Klosterman told me your name?" But then she realized that in replying, she had indeed asked him something, because she had voiced her declaration not in the declarative tense, but in the inquisitive tense. In fact, so rattled was she at this point by Mr. Miller that she found herself suddenly unable to speak in anything *but* the inquisitive tense. "Mrs. Klosterman was just telling me about you?" she said...asked...whatever. "She said you moved in this week? Downstairs from me? And I just wanted to introduce myself to you, too? I'm Natalie? Natalie Dorset? I live on the third floor? And I should warn you? I have a cat? Named Mojo? He likes to roll a golf ball around on the hardwood floors sometimes? So if it bothers you? Let me know? And I'll make him stop?"

And speaking of stopping, Natalie wished she could stop herself before she began to sound as if she were becoming hysterical. And then she realized it was probably too late for that. Because now Mr. Miller was looking at her as if the overhead light in the kitchen had just sputtered and gone dim.

Although, on second thought, maybe it wasn't the overhead light in the kitchen that had sputtered and gone dim, Natalie couldn't help thinking further.

Oh, boy…

"Mr. Miller," Mrs. Klosterman said politely amid all the hubbub, as if her kitchen *hadn't* just been turned into a badly conceptualized sitcom where a newly relocated former mobster moves in with a befuddled schoolteacher and then zany antics ensue, "this is my other tenant, Ms. Natalie Dorset. As she told you, she lives on the third floor. But Mojo is perfectly well-mannered, I assure you, and would never bother anyone. Natalie," she added in the same courteous voice, as if she were Emily Post herself, "this is Mr. John Miller, your new neighbor."

"Jack," he automatically corrected, his voice softer now, more solicitous. "Call me Jack. Everybody does." He sounded as if he were vaguely distracted when he said it, yet at the same time, he looked as if he were surprised to have heard himself respond.

For one long moment, still gripping her wrists—though with an infinitely gentler grasp now, Natalie couldn't help noticing—he fixed his gaze on her face, studying her with much interest. She couldn't imagine why he'd bother. Even at her best, she was an average-looking woman. Dressed in her pajamas, with her hair pulled back and her glasses on, she must look… Well, she must look silly, she couldn't help thinking. After all, the moons and stars on her pajamas were belting out the chorus of "Moon River," even if it was only on flannel.

But Mr. Miller didn't even seem to notice her pajamas, because he kept his gaze trained unflinchingly on her face. For what felt like a full minute, he only studied her in silence, his dark eyes unreadable, his handsome face inscrutable. And then, as quickly and completely as his watchfulness had begun, it suddenly ended, and he released her wrists and dropped his attention to his shirt, brushing halfheartedly at what Natalie could tell now were nonexistent stains of tea.

"'Yo," he finally said by way of a greeting, still not looking at her. But then he did glance over at Mrs. Klosterman, seeming as if he just now remembered she was present, too. "How youse doin'?" he further inquired, looking up briefly to include them both in the question before glancing nervously back down at his shirt again.

Okay, so he wasn't a native Southerner, Natalie deduced keenly. Even though she had grown up in Louisville, she'd traveled extensively around the country, and she had picked up bits and pieces of dialects in her travels. Therefore, she had little difficulty translating what he had said in what she was pretty sure was a Brooklyn accent into its Southern version, which would have been "Hey, how y'all doin'?"

"Hi," she replied lamely. But for the life of her, she couldn't think of a single other thing to say. Except maybe "You have the dreamiest eyes I've ever seen in my life, even if they are what I would expect a Mob informant in the Witness Protection Program to have," and she didn't think it would be a good idea to say that, even if she could punctuate it with a period instead of a question mark. After all, the two of them had just met.

"'Yo, Mrs. Klosterman," Jack Miller said, turning his body physically toward the landlady now, thereby indicating quite clearly that he was through with Natalie, but thanks so much for playing. "I couldn't find a key to the back door up in my apartment, and I think it would probably be a good idea for me to have one, you know?"

Mrs. Klosterman exchanged a meaningful look with Natalie, and she knew her landlady was thinking the same thing she was—that Mr. Miller was already scoping out potential escape routes, should the Mob, in fact, come busting through the door with tommy guns blazing.

No, no, no, no, no, she immediately told herself. She would not buy into Mrs. Klosterman's ridiculous suspicions and play "What's My Crime?" Mr. Miller wanted the key to his back door for the simple reason that his back door, as Natalie's did, opened onto the fire escape, and— let's face it—old buildings were known to go up in flames occasionally, so of course he'd want access to that door.

"I forgot," Mrs. Klosterman told him now. "I had a new lock put on that door after the last tenant moved out because the other one was getting so old. I have the new key in my office. I'll get it for you."

And without so much as a by-your-leave—whatever the hell that meant—her landlady left the kitchen, thereby leaving Natalie alone with her new mobster. *Neighbor,* she quickly corrected herself. Her new neighbor. Boy, could that have been embarrassing, if she got those two confused.

The silence that descended on the room after Mrs. Klosterman's departure was thick enough to hack with a meat cleaver. Although, all things considered, maybe that wasn't the best analogy to use. In an effort to alleviate some of the tension, Natalie braved a slight smile and asked, "You're not from around here originally, are you?"

He, too, braved a slight smile—really slight, much

slighter than her slight smile had been—in return. "You figured that out all by yourself, huh?"

"It's the accent," she confessed.

"Yeah, it always gives me away," he told her. "The minute I open my mouth, everybody knows I'm French."

She smiled again, the gesture feeling more genuine now. "So what part of France do you hail from?"

His smile seemed more genuine now, too. "The northern part."

Of course.

She was about to ask if it was Nouvelle York or Nouveau Jersey when he deftly turned the tables on her. "You from around here?"

She nodded, telling herself he was *not* making a conscious effort to divert attention from himself, but was just being polite. Somehow, though, she didn't quite believe herself. "Born and bred," she told him.

"Yeah, you have that look about you," he said.

"What look?" she asked.

He grinned again, this time seeming honestly delighted by something, and the change that came over him when he did that nearly took her breath away. Before, he had been broodingly handsome. But when he smiled like that he was… She bit back an involuntary sigh as, somewhere in the dark recesses of her brain, an accordion kicked up the opening bars from *La Vie en Rose*.

"Wholesome," he told her then. "You look wholesome."

Oh, and wasn't *that* the word every woman wanted to have a handsome man applying to her? Natalie thought. The accordion in her brain suddenly went crashingly silent. "Wholesome," she repeated blandly.

His smile grew broader. "Yeah. Wholesome."

Swell.

Oh, well, she thought. It wasn't like she should be consorting with her new mobster—ah, neighbor—anyway. He really wasn't her type at all. She preferred men who didn't use the word "whacked," even in relation to cockroaches. Men who didn't dress in black from head to toe. Men who weren't likely to be packing heat.

Oh, stop it, she commanded herself. *You're being silly.*

"Sorry about the tea," she said for a third time.

He shrugged off her concern. "No problem. I like tea."

Really.

"And don't worry about your cat," he added. "I like cats, too."

Imagine.

Mrs. Klosterman returned then, jingling a set of keys merrily in her fingers. "Here's the new key to your back door," she said as she handed one key to him. "And here's an extra set of *both* keys, because you might want to give a set to someone in case of an emergency."

Natalie narrowed her eyes at her landlady, who seemed to be sending a not-so-subtle signal to her new tenant, because when she mentioned the part about giving the extra set of keys to someone in case of an emergency, she tilted her head directly toward Natalie.

Jack Miller, thankfully, didn't seem to notice. Or, if he did, he wrote it off as just another one of his landlady's little quirks. He better sharpen his mental pencil, Natalie thought. Because he was going to have a long list of those by the end of his first month of residence.

"Thanks, Mrs. K," he said.

Mrs. K?

Mrs. Klosterman tittered prettily at the nickname, and Natalie gaped at her. Not just because she had never in her life, until that moment, actually heard someone titter, but barely five minutes ago, the woman tittering had been worrying about waking up in the morning with her throat slit, and now she was batting her eyelashes at the very man who she'd been sure would be wielding the knife. Honestly, Natalie thought. Sometimes she was embarrassed by members of her own gender. Women could be so easily influenced by a handsome face and a tantalizingly expansive chest, and temptingly solid biceps, and deliciously hard forearms, and a delectably flat torso, and a very savory—

"Now if you ladies will excuse me," Jack Miller said, interrupting what could have been a very nice preoccupation, "I got some things to arrange upstairs."

Yeah, like trunks full of body parts, she thought.

No, no, no, no, no. She was not going to submit to Mrs. Klosterman's ridiculous suggestions. Especially since Mrs. Klosterman herself was apparently falling under the spell of her new mobster. *Neighbor,* Natalie quickly corrected herself again. Falling under the spell of her new neighbor.

With one final smile that included them both, Jack Miller said, "Have a nice day," and then turned to take his leave. Almost as an afterthought, he spun around once more and looked at Natalie. "Natalie, right?" he asked, having evidently not been paying attention when Mrs. Klosterman had introduced the two of them. And, oh, didn't *that* just boost a woman's ego into the stratosphere?

Mutely, she nodded.

But instead of replying, Jack Miller only smiled some more—and somehow, Natalie got the impression it was in approval, of all things—then turned a final time and exited the kitchen.

For a long, long time, neither Natalie nor her landlady said a word, as though each was trying to figure out if the last five minutes had even happened. Then Natalie recalled the broken tea cup and spilled tea, and she hastily cleaned up the mess. And then she and Mrs. Klosterman both returned to their seats at the kitchen table, where Natalie poured herself a new cup. In silent accord, the two women lifted their cups of tea, as if, in fact, the last five minutes *hadn't* happened.

Finally, though, Natalie leaned across the table, scrunching her body low, just as Mrs. Klosterman had only moments earlier, before Jack Miller had entered the room, when they had been discussing him so freely. And, naturally, she went back to discussing him again.

But of all the troubling thoughts that were tumbling through her brain in that moment, the only thing she could think to remark was, "You said he wore normal clothes."

"He does wear normal clothes," Mrs. Klosterman replied. "He just wears them in black, that's all."

At least he hadn't reeked of pesto and Aqua Velva, Natalie thought. Though she did sort of detect the lingering scent of garlic. Then again, that could have just been left over from whatever Mrs. Klosterman had cooked for last night's dinner.

Or it could have just been the fact that she was reacting like an idiot to her landlady's earlier suspicions.

"You heard him talk," Mrs. Klosterman whispered back. "Now you know. He's a mobster."

"Or he grew up in Brooklyn," Natalie shot back. "Or some other part of New York. Or New Jersey. Or Philadelphia. Or any of those other places where people have an accent like that."

"He's *not* a John Miller, though," Mrs. Klosterman insisted.

And Natalie had to admit she couldn't argue with that. Just who her new neighbor was, though...

Well. That was a mystery.

JACK MILLER MADE it all the way back to his apartment before he let himself think about the cute little brunette in his landlady's kitchen. It had never occurred to him that there would be someone else living in the building who might pose a problem. Bad enough he was going to have to keep an eye on the old lady, but this new one…

Oh, jeez, he had behaved like such a jerk. But what the hell was he supposed to do? The way Natalie Dorset had been looking at him, he'd been able to tell she found him…interesting. And the last thing he needed was for her to find him interesting. Never mind that he found her kind of interesting, too. Hey, what could he say? He'd never met a woman who wore singing pajamas. That was definitely interesting. Hell, he'd never met a woman who wore pajamas, period. The women he normally associated with slept in a smile. A smile he himself had put on their faces. And he tried not to feel too smug about that. Really. He did. Honest.

Then he thought about what it would be like to maybe put a smile on Natalie Dorset's face. And that surprised him, since she wasn't exactly the type of woman he normally wanted to make smile, especially after just meeting her. What surprised him even more was that the thought of putting a smile on her face didn't make him feel smug at all. No, what Jack felt when he thought about that was the same thing he'd felt in junior high school at St. Athanasius when he'd wondered if Angela DeFlorio would laugh at him if he asked her to go to the eighth grade mixer—all nerves and knots and nausea.

Ah, hell. He hated feeling that way again. He wasn't a thirteen-year-old, ninety-pound weakling anymore. Nobody, but *nobody*, from the old neighborhood messed with Jack these days. They didn't dare.

Damn. This was not good, having a cute brunette living upstairs. This wasn't part of the plan at all.

So he was just going to have to remember the plan, he reminded himself. Think about the plan. Focus on the plan. Be the plan. He'd come here to do a job, and he would do it. Coolly, calmly, collectedly, the way he always did the job.

There was, after all, a whacking in the works. And Jack was right in the thick of it. He had come to this town to make sure everything went down exactly the way it was supposed to go down. No way could he afford to be sidetracked by an interesting, big-eyed, singing-pajama-wearing, tea-spilling Natalie Dorset. So he was just going to have to do what he always did when he was trying to keep a low profile—which, of course, was ninety-nine percent of the time.

He'd just have to make sure he stayed out of her way.

2

"WELL, HELLO AGAIN." The words came out sounding far more casual than Natalie felt. After all, the *last* person she had expected to run into at the Speed Art Museum was her new downstairs neighbor, Jack "The Alleged" Miller. But there he was, in all his...darkness...standing right behind her when she turned away from the Raphael to enjoy the Titian.

But she enjoyed seeing Jack even more. And not just because of the way his black jeans so lovingly outlined his sturdy thighs and taut tushe, either. Or because of the way his black leather motorcycle jacket hung open over a black T-shirt stretched tight across his expansive chest. Or because his overly long black hair was once again pushed back from his face in a way that made Natalie itch to run her fingers through it. Or because of the odd frisson of heat that exploded in her belly and shot out to every extremity, electrifying her, dizzying her, making her feel breathless and reckless, as if she were on the verge of an *extremely* satisfying—

Ah...never mind. She just enjoyed seeing him because...because... Well, just because, that was all. And it was an excellent reason, too, by golly.

Despite both her and Mrs. Klosterman's misgivings about the man's name, in the week that had passed since her new neighbor had moved in, Natalie had come to think of him as Jack. She had been able to do this because over the course of the week, she'd run into him a few times and whenever she'd greeted him as "Mr. Miller," he'd always insisted she call him "Jack, please. Mr. Miller is my pop's name."

At first, it hadn't felt right to call him that, and not just because, in spite of telling herself she was silly for doubting him, she really did find herself doubting it was his real name. But, too, he just didn't seem like the sort of man with whom one would share such intimacies like first names. If anything, he seemed the sort of man who would prefer to go by his last name, if any name at all. But "Miller" didn't suit him, either. Had his last name been something like Devlin or Steed or Deacon—or even Mancuso—*that* would have worked. Miller just seemed too...normal. Too common. Too bland. Not that Jack seemed appropriate either, but she had to call him something. Something other than "The Mobster Who Lives on the Second Floor" at any rate, which was how Mrs. Klosterman continued to refer to him.

Natalie, however, still wasn't convinced of Jack's, ah, connections. For lack of a better word. Even if she *had* heard faint strains of *Don Giovanni* coming up through the floor a few times—it wasn't like it was the theme from *The Godfather*. And even if the faint scent of garlic always *did* linger around his door—lots of people cooked with garlic, Natalie included, and it wasn't like he reeked of pesto and Aqua Velva. And even if she *had* seen him toting a bottle of Chianti up the stairs one day when he was bringing in his groceries—maybe he was just planning to make one of those interesting candles out of it. None of that proved anything. Except that he liked Italian food and opera music and that he maybe had a hobby that included hot wax.

He hardly ever used the word *whacked* as far as Natalie could tell. And not once had she seen him dragging suspiciously heavy black plastic garbage bags out to the Dumpster under cover of darkness. So that was a definite plus. And he'd worn a suit once or twice, too, she'd noticed. Boring, bland suits, too, and they weren't always black. And he wore them with neckties that were *tasteful*. Silk, even. And the toes of his shoes weren't quite as pointy as she'd first thought, and they might have been made someplace other than Italy, possibly even with man-made uppers. So there. Take that, Mrs. "I-know-a-mobster-when-I-see-one" Klosterman.

And now here he was, viewing a visiting art exhibit at the Speed Museum. Totally, totally non-Mob activity, that. Even if he did seem to be preoccupied by the Italian masters.

He appeared to be as surprised to see her as she was to see him, and suddenly, Natalie wished she'd worn something other than the flowing, flowered skirt in shades of fall, and the oversized amber sweater that came down over her fanny. She had thought the outfit feminine and comfortable when she purchased it. Now, though, it just felt frumpy. Jack Miller seemed like the kind of man who went for tight and sleek and bright, and, quite possibly, latex. Not that Natalie cared, mind you. But she did wish she had worn something different. The hiking boots, especially, seemed inappropriate somehow.

"Well, hello to you, too, neighbor," Jack said in a deep, rough baritone that belied the Mr. Rogers sentiment. "What's a nice girl like you doing in a place like this?"

Natalie looked first left, then right, then back at Jack. "It's an art museum," she pointed out. "It's a nice place."

He smiled at that. "So it is," he agreed. "I stand corrected."

She wasn't sure what he meant by that, so she pressed onward. "So you're an art lover, are you?"

He nodded, and fiddled with the program he'd already twisted into a misshapen lump of paper. Vaguely, she wondered what had made him do such a thing. It was as if he were anxious about something. But what was there to feel anxious about in an art museum? This was where people came to *escape* the pressures of the day.

"Yeah, I like art okay," he said.

But something in his voice suggested just the opposite. He seemed uncomfortable here somehow. Or maybe he was uncomfortable because he'd seen Natalie here. Maybe he was trying to keep a low profile—that was what people did when they were in the Witness Protection Program, right?—and now he was scared that if Natalie had fingered him, the Mob might, too.

Because, hey, it was common knowledge that mobsters hung out in art museums, she told herself wryly, wanting to smack herself upside the head for her Mrs. Klosterman-like thoughts. If Jack was uncomfortable, it was more likely because she'd made him feel uncomfortable by asking him what she just had. Maybe he was here because he wanted to learn more about art, and he was embarrassed to let her know how unschooled he was on the topic.

She opened her mouth to change the subject—she did, after all, completely sympathize with that whole being-out-of-one's element thing, since she'd felt out of her element since the day she was born—but he started to talk again before she had a chance.

"Yeah, I especially like the Italian masters," he said.

But again, he seemed uneasy when he spoke, and instead of looking at Natalie, he was looking at something over her shoulder, as if he couldn't quite meet her gaze. Oh, jeez, she really had caught him out with her question and embarrassed him, she realized. The male ego, she thought. It was such a fragile thing.

He was probably only saying the Italian masters were his favorite because he'd glanced down at his hastily rearranged program, where it read, in part, *The Italian Masters*. She told herself to just let the matter drop there. But there was something in his voice when he spoke, something kind of tense, something kind of apprehensive—something kind of suspicious, quite frankly—that gave her pause. And still he was looking over her shoulder, not meeting her eyes, as if he were wishing he was anywhere but here.

To alleviate his distress, Natalie decided to step in and take the lead, thereby preventing him from having to say anything that might get him in deeper than he could afford. "I like them, too," she said. "Especially Michelangelo, but we don't have any originals by him here, which is a real shame."

Jack lifted his shoulder and dropped it again in a gesture she supposed was meant to be a shrug. Somehow, though, it came off looking like strong-arming. "I like all of 'em," he told her.

Of course he did. Poor guy. He was still trying to make her think he was knowledgeable about the subject, clearly trying to preserve his male pride. Next he'd be telling her he didn't know much about art, but he knew what he liked, since that was the cliché everyone uttered in a situation like this.

"It's kind of funny, really," he said. "I know a lot about art, but I'm just not sure what I like."

Man. He couldn't even get the clichés right.

"Michelangelo is arguably the master of the masters," he said. "I mean, I wouldn't argue it, but some people might. Like you, he's a favorite for a lot of people."

Natalie wondered just how deeply he was going to wade into this stuff, and prepared herself to throw him a line if that became necessary by tossing out a few other names to him. Raphael, perhaps, or, Titian, since she'd just been looking at that one herself.

"Raphael, too," he continued, making her think maybe he'd read his program a little better than she'd first suspected. "Even if he did borrow nearly all of the Big M's repertory gestures and poses," he continued, rattling Natalie just the tiniest bit. "He was still a better portraitist. Me, though, I'm more of a Titian kind of guy, I think. He was just so great at that whole opposing the virtuosity of pigments to the intellectual sophistication thing, you know? And the distinction between High Renaissance—all that formalized and classic balance of elements—and Late Renaissance—the more subjective, emotional stuff, not to mention all those bright colors—wasn't as sharply divided in Venice as it was in the rest of Italy." He nodded. "Yeah, I like the Venetians, I think. And Uccello. You don't hear much about him, but you gotta admire the way he tried to jibe the Gothic and the Renaissance stuff. Plus, he had a really great beard. Piero della Francesca's okay, too, but his portraits have kind of a pedantry without compassion, knowwuddamean?"

Natalie blinked a few times, as if a too-bright flash had gone off right in her face. Wow. He really did know a lot about art. And he really didn't know what he liked. She was intrigued.

"I, um, I actually prefer the Flemish painters myself," she said lamely.

Jack swept a hand carelessly in front of himself. "Yeah, well, they were all profoundly influenced by the Italians, you know."

She did know. But not nearly as well as he did. "So," she began again, "you come here often?"

That something over her shoulder seemed to catch his eye again, because he suddenly glanced to the left and frowned. As Natalie began to turn around to see what was going on, Jack quickly shifted his body into that direction, taking a few steps forward, as if he wanted to block whatever she was attempting to see. Then he said, "This is my first visit to the museum. What else do you recommend I see?"

So Natalie stopped turning. But it wasn't his question that halted her. It was the way he extended his hand and curled his fingers around her upper arm and pulled her toward the right, as if he were trying to physically regain her attention, too. And boy, did he. Regain her attention, she meant. Physically, she meant. Because the minute his fingers curled around her arm, another shiver of electricity shimmied through her, right to her fingertips, and another wash of heat splashed through her belly with all the force of white-water rapids.

Jack seemed to feel it, too, because he stopped looking over her shoulder and fixed his gaze on her face, and his eyes went wide in astonishment. Or maybe alarm. Or panic. Natalie couldn't be sure, because she was too busy feeling all those things herself. And more. Desire. Need. Wanting. *Hunger.* Yes, she thought she could safely say now what it was like to hunger for something. Someone. Because that was how Jack Miller made her feel when he touched her the way he did.

"I, ah…" she began eloquently.

"Um, I…" he chorused at the same time.

"Gotta go," they both said as one.

And, just like that, they turned around and sped off in opposite directions.

And as she fled, all Natalie could think was that, for a mobster, he had a very gentle touch. Not to mention exceptionally good taste in art.

JACK WAS KEEPING a close eye on his objective when he ran into Natalie in the art museum a second time. Or, rather, almost ran into her a second time. Fortunately, he saw her before she saw him, so he was able to duck behind a sculpture before any damage had been done.

Damn. So much for staying out of her way.

This was just great, he thought as he pressed his body against the cool stone statue. Now there were two people he had to keep an eye on in this crowd. What was bad was that he would have much rather kept his eye on Natalie than on his objective. What was worse was that his eye wasn't the only body part he was thinking about when it came to keeping something on Natalie.

But he was obligated, even honor bound, to make the man in the trench coat who was studying the Matisse his priority. Because he was the person Jack had been assigned to take care of—so to speak. Not that there was any real *care* in what Jack was supposed to do to the man in the trench coat who was studying the Matisse. But he did have a job to do—and there was sort of an art to that job, he reflected—and until he could complete that job, he had to stay focused on it. Even if it was a job he didn't particularly relish completing. Especially now that Natalie Dorset was lurking around.

Lurking, he echoed to himself. Yeah, right. If there was anyone lurking these days, it was Jack. When had he been reduced to such a thing? he asked himself irritably. And why, suddenly, did his job seem kind of sordid and tawdry? He'd always taken pride in his work before. Before Natalie Dorset had come along looking all squeaky-clean and dewy and wholesome. Ever since meeting her, Jack had felt sinister in the extreme. Which made no sense, because what he did for a living was a highly regarded tradition in his family. His father, his father's father, his father's father's father back in the old country, all of them had been in the same line of work. Jack respected his heritage, and had always taken pride in his birthright. Since meeting Natalie, though, his heritage seemed almost tarnished somehow.

Which really made no sense at all, because he barely knew the woman. Yeah, sure, he'd run into her a few times this week, so he knew her a little. Like, he knew she left for work everyday at 7:30 a.m. on the dot, which meant she was punctual. And he knew she often ate breakfast and dinner with their landlady, Mrs. Klosterman, which made him think she was one of those women who felt obligated to take care of other people. And he knew she drove an old Volkswagen, to which she seemed totally suited, because it was kind of funky, and so was she. Not just because of the singing pajamas she'd been wearing that first morning he met her, but because of the way she dressed at other times, too. Like, for instance, oh, he didn't know...today. She was sort of a combination of Ralph Lauren and *Fishin' with Orlando*. And somehow, on Natalie, it worked.

And Jack knew she taught high school, because he'd seen her downstairs grading papers one evening and asked her about it. A high school teacher, he reflected again. She didn't seem the type. Hell, where he'd gone to high school in Brooklyn, a teacher who looked like her wouldn't have lasted through lunch. Jeez, she would have *been* lunch for some of the guys he'd run around with. But she'd claimed to actually *enjoy* teaching English to teenagers. She'd assigned James Fenimore Cooper *on purpose*.

And Jack knew she liked old movies, because he'd come in a couple of nights to find her and Mrs. Klosterman watching movies on TV, black-and-white jobs from the forties. Cary Grant, he'd heard them talking about as he'd climbed the stairs to his apartment. The suave, debonair, tuxedoed type. The leading man type. The type Jack most certainly was not. He preferred to think of himself as more of an antihero. Okay, so maybe he was more anti- than he was hero sometimes. That was beside the point. The point was...

What was the point again?

Oh, yeah. The point was he had no business hiding behind a sculpture sneaking peeks at a woman when he had a job to do. Especially a woman like Natalie Dorset, with whom he had absolutely nothing in common. Maybe if she'd been a combination of Frederick's of Hollywood and *Fishin' with Orlando, then* maybe his attraction to her would have made sense. Or if she'd taught exotic dancing classes instead of high school, and assigned bumps and grinds instead of Natty Bumppo. Or if she'd left for work around ten o'clock every night to serve drinks in some smoky bar. Or if she'd had breakfast and dinner with her bookie. Or if she'd driven a sporty little red number on the verge of being repo'd. Then, *maybe* his attraction to her wouldn't have been such a shock. Because women like Natalie Dorset normally didn't even make it onto Jack's radar.

She sure was cute, though.

Still, even if Jack did have something in common with her, he still had no business sneaking peeks at her. Or talking to her. Or being preoccupied by her. Or wondering what she looked like naked. But he'd only done that last thing once...okay, maybe twice...okay, five, or at most fifty times, and only because he'd had too much Chianti. Except for all those times when he'd done it while he was sober. But that was only because he'd accidentally come across *Body Heat* on cable that night. But then there was that time when he'd done it while watching the Weather Channel, too...

Ah, hell.

The point was he was only here to do a job, and that job did not include Natalie Dorset, clothed or unclothed, in or out of his bed. Or on the sofa. Or in the shower. Or atop the kitchen table. The kitchen counter. The kitchen pantry. The kitchen floor...

Um, what was the question again?

Oh, yeah. It wasn't a question. It was a fact. He could not allow himself to be sidetracked while doing this job. He would just have to avoid Natalie Dorset from here on out, and keep his focus on his target. Who...oh, dammit...seemed to have disappeared.

Jack scanned the crowded museum, starting with the last place he'd seen the man in the trench coat, invariably finding Natalie instead, then forcing his gaze away again, over everyone else in the room. There. He found him. Two paintings down from the one he'd just finished looking at. Jack groaned inwardly. Just how much longer could the guy look at paintings? Jack was ready to go for pizza. And a beer. And a naked high school English teacher.

He threw back his head in disgust with himself, only to have it smack against hard stone. He turned and realized he'd been leaning all this time against a reproduction of Rodin's *The Kiss*, and that he'd just bonked his head on a naked breast hard enough to make himself see stars.

Man, oh, man, he thought as he rubbed at the lump that was already beginning to form. This job was going to shorten his life for sure.

AS NATALIE WAS climbing the stairs to her apartment that evening, juggling two bags of groceries she'd picked up on the way home from the museum, she came to a halt in the second floor landing to adjust the strap on her purse. It had nothing to do with the fact that she heard someone inside Jack Miller's apartment talking. And she only hesitated a moment after completing that adjustment because she needed to rest. It wasn't because she thought she heard him use the word *whacked*. Because he might not have said *whacked*. He might have said *fact*. Or *quacked*. Or *shellacked*. And those were all totally harmless words.

Then again, maybe he'd said *hacked*, she thought as a teensy little feeling of paranoia wedged its way under her skin. Or *smacked*. Or even *hijacked*. Which weren't so harmless words.

Or maybe he'd said *cracked*, she thought wryly, since he could have been talking to someone about the mental state of his new upstairs neighbor.

She really had been spending too much time listening to Mrs. Klosterman this week. And she knew better than to take seriously someone who thought *The X-Files* was a series of documentaries by Ken Burns. Sighing to herself, Natalie finished adjusting her purse strap and shifted her grocery bags to a more manageable position, then settled her foot on the next step.

And then stopped dead in her tracks—and she really wished she'd come up with a better way to think about that than *dead in her tracks*—because she heard Jack's voice say, clear as day, "I'll kill 'im."

Telling herself she was just imagining things, Natalie turned her ear toward the door, if for no other reason than to reassure herself that she was just imagining things. But instead of being reassured, she heard Jack's voice again, louder and more emphatic this time, saying, "No, Manny, I mean it. I'm gonna kill the guy. No way will I let 'im get away with that."

And then Natalie's world went a little fuzzy, and she had to sit down. Which—hey, whattaya know—gave her a really great seat for eavesdropping on the rest of Jack's conversation. But when she realized she was hearing only his side, she concluded he must be on the telephone with someone. Still, only his side told her plenty.

There was a long pause after that second avowal of his

intent to murder someone, then, "Look, I had him in my sights all day," she heard Jack continue, "but there was always a crowd around, so an opportunity never presented itself."

There was more silence for a moment, wherein Natalie assumed the other person was speaking again, then she heard Jack's voice once more. "Yeah, I know. But it's not going to be easy. The guy's so edgy. I never know what he's gonna do next, where he's gonna go. What?" More silence, then, "Hey, I know what I'm being paid to do, and I'll do it. It just might not go down the way we planned, that's all."

Holy moly, Natalie thought. He wasn't a Mob hit man turned Mob informant. He was a Mob hit man period!

No, no, no, no, no, she immediately told herself. There was a perfectly good explanation for what she was hearing. Hey, she herself had wanted to kill more than a few people in her time, including several of her students just this past week, because a lot of them had neglected to do their assigned reading. So just because someone said, "I'll kill 'im," didn't mean that they were going to, you know, *kill 'im.* And that business about the crowd being around someone, that could have meant anything. And the part about being paid to do something? Well, now, that could be anything, too. He could have been paid to deliver phone books for all Natalie knew.

Yeah, that was it. He was the new phone book delivery guy. That explained all those nice muscles. A person had to be built to haul around those White Pages.

"Don't worry, Manny," Jack said angrily on the other side of his door, bringing Natalie's attention back to the matter at hand. "I came here to do a job, and I'm not leaving until it's done. You just better hope it doesn't get any messier than it already has."

Okay, so maybe he dropped some of the phone books

in a puddle and they got dirty, she thought. She could see that. They'd had a lot of rain lately. And those phone books got unwieldy when you tried to carry too many at one time. And those plastic bags they put them in were cheap as hell. It could have happened to anyone.

When Natalie stood up, she still felt a little muzzy-headed, though whether that was because of her initial fright or the profound lameness of her excuses for Jack's words, she couldn't have said. In any event, she was totally unprepared for the opening of his door, and even less prepared for when he came barreling out of it, shrugging on his leather motorcycle jacket. And he was obviously unprepared to find her lurking outside his door, because he kept on coming, nearly knocking her down the steps before he saw her.

Hastily, he grabbed her to steady her before she could go tumbling back down to the living room in a heap. But she overcompensated and hurled her body forward, an action that thrust her right into that muscular phone book-delivering body of his. And *that* made her drop both bags of groceries, which did spill out and go tumbling back down to the living room.

"Whoa," Jack said as he balanced her, curling his fingers over her upper arms to do so. "Where's the fire?"

Gosh, she should probably just keep that information to herself, Natalie thought as heat began seeping through her belly and spreading up into her breasts and down into her...

And that was when she remembered that, among the groceries she'd bought today, was a box of tampons. Oh, damn.

"I am so sorry to run into you," she said.

And then she could think of not one more thing to utter. Because Jack's hands on her arms just felt too yummy for words, strong and gentle at the same time. Hands like his would be equally comfortable sledgehammering solid rock or stroking a woman's naked flesh, she thought. And speaking for herself, she would have been equally happy watching him do either.

"No, I'm the one who ran into you, so I'm the one who's sorry," he told her, his fingers still curving gently over her arms.

In fact, his thumbs on the insides of her arms moved gently up and down, as if he were trying to calm her. Which was pretty ironic, seeing as how the action only incited her to commit mayhem. Preferably on his person. ASAP. That fire he'd asked about leaped higher inside her, threatening to burn out of control.

"I wasn't watching where I was going," he added. "You okay?"

She nodded, even though *okay* was pretty much the last thing she felt at the moment. "Yeah," she said a little breathlessly. "I'm okay. You just, um, startled me, that's all."

For a moment, neither of them said anything more. Natalie only continued to stand staring up at Jack, marveling at how handsome he was, and Jack gazed back down at her, thinking she knew not what. But she wished she did. She wished she could read his mind at that moment and know what his impression of her was. Because he was making an awfully big impression on her.

Finally, softly, "Let me help you pick this stuff up," he offered.

And before Natalie could decline, he was stooping to collect the nearly empty grocery bags and scooping up the few items that hadn't gone down the stairs. Like, for instance—of course—the tampons. Amazingly, though, he didn't bat an eye, didn't even hesitate as he picked them up and tossed them back into the paper sack. He only glanced up at her and smiled and said, "I got sisters," and his casualness about it went a long way toward endearing him to Natalie. It also convinced her she had misunderstood whatever he'd been talking about on the phone. Because no Mob hit man could possibly handle a box of tampons that comfortably. It was odd logic, to be sure, but it comforted her nonetheless.

She bent, too, then, to collect her things, wincing at the scattered strawberries. "Oh, damn," she said when she saw them.

By now, Jack was at the foot of the steps, gathering the items that had made their way down there, placing them into the sack he'd carried with him. "What's wrong?" he called up.

"My strawberries," she said. "I love them. And they're so hard to find this time of year. Not to mention so expensive when I do find them." She blew out an exasperated breath as she carefully gathered them up and placed them back into their plastic basket. "Maybe I can salvage a few of them," she said morosely.

Jack made his way back up the steps just as she was dropping the last of her groceries back into her own sack. "I'll help you get these upstairs," he told her.

"That's okay," she said. "I can manage."

"It's the least I can do," he insisted.

She relented then. "Thanks."

"Anytime."

As he followed her the rest of the way up, Natalie was acutely aware of him behind her. She knew he couldn't be watching her—with the way she was dressed, what was there to see?—but somehow, she felt the heat of his gaze boring into her. It only added to her already frazzled state, jacking up the fire that was already blazing away in her midsection. But that was nothing compared to the inferno that fairly exploded when they reached her front door.

Thanks to her nervousness, when Natalie went to unlock it, she dropped her keys, which then skittered off the top step and threatened to go tumbling down the way her groceries had. But Jack deftly caught them before they could go too far, then stepped up behind her on the third floor landing, which she'd never, until that moment, considered especially small.

But with Jack crowding her from behind, it was very small indeed. Small enough that he had to press his front lightly to her back when he stood behind her, so that she could smell the clean, soapy, non-Aqua Velva scent of him and feel the heat of his body mingling with the heat of her own. Especially when he leaned forward and snaked his arm around her to unlock her front door himself. But he had a little trouble managing the gesture, and had to take yet another step forward, bumping his body even more intimately against hers, working the key into the slot until it turned and the door opened. And every time he shifted his body to accommodate his efforts, he rubbed against Natalie, creating a delicious sort of friction unlike anything she'd ever experienced before.

Strangely, even after he'd managed to get the door open, he didn't move away from her. Instead, he continued to hold his body close to hers, as if he were reluctant to put any distance between the two of them. Which was just fine with Natalie, since she could stand here like this all night. It was, after all, the closest thing she'd had to a sexual encounter for some time. Now if she could just think of some acceptable excuse for why she had to suddenly remove her clothing…

"You, uh, you wanna go inside?" Jack asked as she pondered her dilemma.

And then Natalie realized the reason he hadn't moved away from her was simply because he was waiting for her to move first. And because she'd only stood there like an imbecile, he was probably thinking she was, well, an imbecile. Either that, or he was thinking she'd been enjoying the feel of his body next to hers too much to want to end it, and might possibly be grappling for some acceptable excuse for why she had to suddenly remove her clothing, and how embarrassing was that? Especially since he was right.

"Oh, yeah," she said, forcing her feet forward. "Sorry. I was just thinking about something."

Like how nice it would be to have her door opened this way every night. And how nice it would be if Jack followed her into her apartment every night. And how nice it would be if they spent the rest of the night rubbing their bodies together every night.

Oh, dear.

Hastily, she strode to her minuscule galley kitchen and set her bag of groceries on what little available counter space was there. Jack followed and did likewise, making the kitchen feel more like a closet. He was just so big. So overwhelming. So incredibly potent. She'd never met a man like him before, let alone have one rub up against her the way he had, however involuntary the action had been on his part.

The moment he settled his bag of groceries on the counter, he turned and took a few steps in the opposite direction, and Natalie told herself he was *not* trying to escape. As she quickly emptied the bags and put things in their proper places, he prowled around her small living room, and she got the feeling it was because he wasn't quite ready to leave. Or maybe that was just wishful thinking on her part. In any event, however, he made no further move to escape. Uh, leave.

"You got a nice place here," he said as he looked around.

And why did he sound as if he made the observation grudgingly? she wondered. She, too, looked around her apartment, trying to see it the way someone would for the first time. Five years of residence and a very small space added up to a lot of clutter, she realized. But he was right—it was nice clutter. Natalie wasn't the type to go for finery, but she did like beautiful things. After she'd graduated from college and found this apartment, she'd haunted the antique shops and boutiques along Third Street and Bardstown Road and Frankfort Avenue, looking for interesting pieces to furnish her very first place. Her college dorm had been stark and bland and uninteresting, so she'd deliberately purchased things of bold color and intrepid design, striving more for chimerical than practical, fun instead of functional.

Her large, overstuffed, Victorian velvet sofa, the color of good merlot, had been her one splurge. The coffee table had started life as an old steamer trunk, and the end tables were marble-topped, carved wooden lyres. An old glass cocktail shaker on one held dried flowers, a crystal bowl overflowing with potpourri took up most of the other. Her lamps were Art Deco bronzes, and ancient Oriental rugs covered much of the hardwood floor. Dozens of houseplants spilled from wide window ledges, while other, larger ones sprung up from terra-cotta pots. Brightly colored majolica—something she'd collected since she was a teenager—filled every available space leftover.

All in all, she thought whimsically, not for the first time, the place looked like the home of an aging, eccentric Hollywood actress who'd never quite made it to the B-List. It was the sort of place she'd always wanted to have, and she was comfortable here.

Nevertheless, she shrugged off Jack's compliment almost literally. "Thanks. I like it." And she did.

"Yeah, I do, too," he told her. "It's…homey," he added,

again seeming somewhat reluctant to say so. "Interesting. Different from my place."

His place, she knew, was a furnished apartment, but it was much like the rest of Mrs. Klosterman's house, filled with old, but comfortable things. Still, it lacked anything that might add a personal touch, whereas Natalie's apartment was overflowing with the personal. And that did indeed make a big difference.

She had expected him to leave after offering those few requisite niceties, but he began to wander around her living room, instead, looking at… Well, he seemed to be looking at everything, she thought. Evidently, he'd been telling the truth when he said he found the place interesting, because he shoved his hands into the back pockets of his black jeans and made his way to her overcrowded bookcase, scanning the titles he found there.

"Oh, yeah," he said as he read over them. "I can tell you're an English teacher. Hawthorne, Wharton, Emerson, Thoreau, Melville, Twain, James." He turned around to look at her. "You like American literature, huh?"

She nodded. "Especially the nineteenth century. Though I like the early twentieth century, too."

He turned back to the bookcases again. "I like the guys who came later," he told her. "Faulkner. Fitzgerald. Kerouac. Hemingway. I think *The Sun Also Rises* is the greatest book ever written."

Natalie silently chided herself for being surprised. How often had she herself been stereotyped as the conservative, prudish, easily overrun sort, simply because of the way she dressed and talked, and because of her job? How often had she been treated like a pushover? A doormat? A woman who was more likely to be abducted by a gang of leisure suit-wearing circus freaks than to find a husband after the age of thirty-five? Too many times for her to recall. So she shouldn't think Jack Miller was a brainless thug, simply because of the way *he* dressed and talked. Of course, she didn't think he was a brainless thug, she realized. She thought he was...

Well. She thought of him in ways she probably shouldn't.

"I'd have to argue with you," she told him as she folded up the paper sacks and stowed them under her kitchen sink. "I think *The Scarlet Letter* is the greatest book ever written."

He turned again to look at her. "I can see that," he said. "You don't seem the type to suffer hypocrites."

She wondered what other type she seemed—or didn't seem—to him. And she wondered why she hoped so much that whatever he thought of her, it was good. Then she surprised herself by asking him, "Have you had dinner yet?"

He seemed surprised by the question, too, because he straightened and dropped his hands to his sides, suddenly looking kind of uncomfortable. "No, I was just on my way out to grab something when I...when you...when we... Uh... I was just gonna go out and grab something."

She hoped she sounded nonchalant when she said, "You're welcome to join me for dinner here. I wasn't planning anything fancy. But if you're not doing anything else...?"

For one brief, euphoric moment, she thought he was going to accept her offer. The look that came over his face just made her think he wanted very much to say yes. But he shook his head slowly instead.

"I can't," he told her. "I have to meet a guy." And then, as if it were an afterthought, he added, "Maybe another time."

Natalie nodded, but she didn't believe him, mostly because of the afterthought thing. And she didn't take his declining of her invitation personally. Well, not *too* personally.

It was just as well, really. She didn't need to be sharing her table with a hit man anyway. There wouldn't be any room for his gun.

"Some other time," she echoed in spite of that.

And later, after Jack was gone and she and Mojo were home alone, she tried not to think about how her apartment seemed quieter and emptier than it ever had before. And she tried not to hope that Jack's *some other time* had been sincere.

3

TWO SATURDAYS AFTER Natalie first met Jack in Mrs. Klosterman's kitchen under less than ideal circumstances, she met him there a second time. Under less than ideal circumstances.

Since his arrival two weeks earlier, she had made it a practice to get dressed and put in her contact lenses before leaving her apartment, but, hey, it *was* Saturday—and she hadn't seen him around the place on the weekends—so she hadn't dressed particularly well today. Her blue jeans were a bit too raggedy for public consumption, and her oatmeal-colored sweater was a bit too stretched out to look like anything other than a cable knit pup tent. Nevertheless, she was comfortable. And, hey, it *was* Saturday.

On the upside, Jack hadn't dressed any better than she had. And he hadn't dressed in black, either—well, not entirely. In fact, his blue jeans were even more tattered than hers were, slashed clear across both knees from seam to seam, faded and frayed and smudged here and there with what she assured herself couldn't possibly be blood. And the black shirt he'd paired them with was faded, too, untucked and half-unbuttoned. On the downside, he had a better reason for being dressed that way than her lame *hey, it* is *Saturday*. Because he was lying prone beneath Mrs. Klosterman's sink, banging away on the pipes with something metallic-sounding that she really hoped wasn't a handgun.

Oh, stop it, she told herself. After all, not even mobsters fixed their kitchen sinks with handguns. They could blow their drains out.

Mrs. Klosterman, however, was nowhere in sight, which was strange, because she usually arrived for their Saturday morning breakfasts together before Natalie did. Ah, well. Maybe she was sleeping late for a change. It was a good morning for it, rainy and gray and cold. Natalie would have slept late herself, if her dear—and soon to be dearly departed, if he didn't stop waking her up so friggin' early on Saturdays—Mojo would have let her.

"Good morning," she said to Jack as she placed her teapot carefully on the table. The last thing she needed to do was spill something on him again, after that disastrous episode the first time she met him.

But her greeting must have surprised him, because the metallic banging immediately stopped, only to be replaced by the dull thump of what sounded very much like a forehead coming into contact with a drain pipe. And then that was replaced by a muffled "Ow, dammit!" And then *that* was replaced by a less-muffled word that Natalie normally only saw Magic Markered on the stall doors in the bathroom at school.

Okay, so maybe he would have preferred she spill something on him again. Because he sure hadn't used that word two weeks ago.

"I'm sorry," she apologized. "I didn't mean to startle you."

The legs that had been protruding from beneath the sink bent at the knee, punctuated by the scrape of motorcycle boots on linoleum. Then Jack's torso appeared more completely—and my, but what a delectable torso it was, too—followed by the appearance of his face. And my, but what a delectable face it was, too. Natalie wasn't sure she would ever get used to how handsome he was, his face all planes and angles and hard, masculine lines. It was as if whatever Roman god had sculpted him had used Adonis—or maybe a young Marlon Brando—as a model.

Of course, she reminded herself, she wouldn't have an opportunity to get used to how handsome he was. They ran into each other only occasionally, and he'd made clear his lack of interest in seeing any more of her. Oh, he was friendly enough, but she could tell that was all it was—friendliness. Common courtesy. She hadn't invited him to join her for dinner again after his initial rebuff, however polite it had been. But he hadn't brought up the "another time" thing, either. There was no point in trying to pursue something that wasn't going to happen.

Which was just as well, anyway, because she still wasn't entirely sure about who or what he was, or why he was even here. She still recalled his half of the phone conversation she had overheard a week ago, and even if it didn't prove he was up to something illegal, it did suggest he was up to something temporary. He'd told whomever he was talking to that he'd come here to do a job, and that he wasn't leaving until he'd done it. Which indicated he *would* be leaving eventually. So it would have been stupid for Natalie to pursue any sort of romantic entanglement with him. Had he even offered some indication that he was open to entangling with her romantically.

"No problem," he said as he sat up. But he was rubbing the center of his forehead, which sort of suggested maybe there was a bit of a problem. Like a minor concussion, for instance.

She winced inwardly. "I really am sorry," she apologized again.

"Really, it's fine," he told her. "I have a hard head."

Which had to come in handy when one made one's living by knocking heads together, she thought before she could stop herself.

"You're up early for a Saturday," he continued, dropping his hand to prop his forearm on one knee.

His shirt gaped open when he did, and Natalie saw that the chest beneath was matted with dark hair, and was as ruggedly and sharply sculpted as his facial features were. Nestled at the center, dangling from a gold chain, was a plain gold cross, and she found the accessory curious for him. And not just because he seemed like the sort of man who would normally shun jewelry, either. But also because he seemed too irreverent for such a thing.

"I'm always up by now," she said. "Mrs. Klosterman and I have our tea together on Saturday mornings. In fact, she usually gets here before I do."

"Mrs. K was here when I came down," Jack said. "She was having problems with the sink, and I told her I could fix it for her, if she had the right tools. I found them in the basement, but by the time I got back up here, she had her coat on and said she had to go out for a little while."

Now that was really strange, Natalie thought. Mrs. Klosterman never went anywhere on Saturday before noon. And sometimes she never left the house at all on the weekends.

"Did she say where she was going?" she asked.

Jack shook his head. "No. Should she have?"

Natalie shrugged, but still felt anxious. "Not necessarily. Did you notice if she'd painted on jet-black eyebrows, and mascaraed her lashes into scary jet-black daddy longlegs?"

Now Jack narrowed his eyes at Natalie, as if he were worried about *her*. "No..." he said, drawing the word out over several time zones. "I don't think she did. I didn't really notice anything especially arachnid about her appearance."

Wow, that wasn't like Mrs. Klosterman, either, to go out

without her eyebrows and daddy longlegs. "Gee, I hope everything's okay," Natalie said absently.

"She seemed fine to me," Jack said. "But that's interesting, now that I think about it, that stuff about the mascara and eyebrows. My great-aunt Gina does the same thing."

Aunt Gina, Natalie echoed to herself, nudging her concern for Mrs. Klosterman to the side. Hmm. Wasn't Gina an *Italian* name?

And what if it was? she immediately asked herself. Lots of people were Italian. And few of them fixed kitchen sinks with handguns. Inescapably, she glanced at Jack's hands, only to find the left one empty, and the right one wielding not a weapon, but a wrench.

See? she taunted herself. *Don't you feel silly now?*

Well, she did about that. But she couldn't quite shake her worry about her landlady. Why hadn't Mrs. Klosterman mentioned her need to go out this morning? Not that Natalie was kept apprised of all of her landlady's comings and goings, and you could just never really tell with Mrs. Klosterman. But the two of them did sort of have a standing agreement to have breakfast together on Saturdays, and if one of them couldn't make it, she let the other know in advance.

"What's the matter?" Jack asked. "You look worried. Like maybe you think Mrs. K is sleeping with the fishes or something."

Natalie arched her own eyebrows at that. Now, of all the things he could have said, why that? Why the reference to sleeping with the fishes? Why hadn't he said something like, *You look worried. Like maybe you think she's in trouble.* Or *Like maybe you think she's lying dead in a ditch somewhere.* Or even *Like maybe you think she's been abducted by aliens who've dropped her in the Bermuda Triangle along with Elvis and Amelia Earhart and that World War II squadron they never found.*

Anything would have made more sense than that *sleeping with the fishes* reference.

Unless, of course, he was connected.

No, Natalie told herself firmly. That wasn't it at all. He was just making a joke. A little Mob humor? she wondered. No, just a *joke*, she immediately assured herself.

"No, it's not that," she said. "I'm sure there's nothing to worry about. She and I usually have breakfast together, that's all, and it's odd that she didn't tell me she needed to go out this morning. But you know, you can just never really tell with Mrs. Klosterman."

Jack nodded. "Well then, since she's not here to have breakfast with you, how about I take her place?"

This time it was Natalie's turn to be surprised. Not just because of his offer, but because of the natural way he made it. Like he thought she wouldn't be surprised that he would want to have breakfast with her. So what could she do but pretend she wasn't surprised at all?

"Sure," she said, hoping that wasn't a squeak she heard in her voice. "Fine," she added, thinking that might be a squeak she heard in her voice. "Tea?" she asked, noting a definite squeak in her voice.

Jack grinned. "Actually, I'm more of a coffee drinker. But that's okay. Mrs. K put a pot on for me before she left."

Natalie nodded dumbly, just now noticing the aroma of coffee in the air. Probably she hadn't noticed it before because she'd been too busy noticing, you know, how handsome Jack was, and the way his shirt was only halfway buttoned, and how the chest beneath was matted with dark hair, and—

Well. Suffice it to say she probably hadn't noticed it before now because she'd had her mind on other things.

She watched as Jack heaved himself up to standing, tossed the wrench into the sink with a clatter, then crossed the kitchen to pour himself a cup of coffee. And why each of those actions, which should have been totally uninteresting, should fascinate her so much was something Natalie decided not to ponder. But the way the man moved… Mmm, mmm, *mmm*. There was a smoothness and poetry to his manner that belied the ruggedness of his appearance, as if he were utterly confident in and thoroughly comfortable with himself. Natalie couldn't imagine what that must be like. She constantly second-guessed herself and she never moved smoothly.

Probably she put too much thought into just about everything, but she didn't know any other way to be. Jack Miller, on the other hand, didn't seem the type to waste time wondering if what he was doing was the right thing. Or the smart thing. Or the graceful thing. Or the anything else thing. He just did what came naturally, obviously convinced it was the right, smart, graceful or anything else thing to do. And from where Natalie was sitting, he did his thing very, very well. There was something extremely sexy about a man who was confident in and content with himself and who didn't feel obligated to make an impression on anyone.

Not that it made any difference, mind you, since she didn't plan on spending a lot of time pondering the finer points of Jack Miller. Well, no more time than she already had. No more than, say, eighty or ninety—million—minutes a week.

"It's nice of you to fix Mrs. Klosterman's sink," she said as he pulled out the chair on the other side of the table and lowered himself into it. Boy, even the way he sat down was sexy.

He shrugged off the compliment. "She's a nice old lady. It's the least I can do for her. Plus, it's not fixed yet. I still have to put it back together again."

"Still, a lot of guys wouldn't see it that way," Natalie told him. "They'd tell her to call a plumber."

"A lot of guys are jerks, then," Jack proclaimed.

Not that Natalie for a moment disagreed with him, but she found it interesting that he'd make such an observation. Then again, he'd mentioned having sisters as he'd picked up her groceries last week. So maybe he'd seen them with jerk guys.

"So how many sisters do you have?" she asked him, telling herself it was only because she was making conversation and not because she wanted to learn more about him. She just wanted to show him the same common courtesy he'd been showing her, that was all.

To his credit, he seemed not the least bit confused by the segue, because he replied readily, "Four. All of 'em younger."

She smiled. "Wow. Four sisters. That must have been fun."

He twisted his mouth into something that might have been a smile. Maybe. Possibly. In the proper lighting. After a couple of mai tais. "Yeah, well, *fun* might be one word," he conceded with clear reluctance. "Another word would be damned annoying as hell."

"Actually, that's four words," Natalie pointed out.

"Yeah, one for each sister." And before she could comment further on that, he turned the tables, asking, "How about you? Got any brothers or sisters?"

She shook her head. "I'm an only child. My mother had a lot of trouble with my delivery and wasn't able to have any more kids after me." And not a day had gone by that she hadn't taken a few moments out of her life to remind Natalie of that.

"Now *that* sounds like fun," he said, "being an only child." And he was definitely smiling now. "No waiting for the bathroom every morning. No waiting to use the phone every night. No incessant giggling. No getting spied on every time you had friends over—"

"No one to share Christmas morning with," Natalie interjected. "No one to play with—or even fight with—on vacations. No one to commiserate with when you had asparagus for dinner. No one to back you up when your mother made you wear stupid clothes to school, because she was sure you were making it up when you said everyone else wore jeans and sneakers."

Jack's smile fell as she spoke, and only when she saw his...oh, she wouldn't say *horrified*, exactly...expression did she realize how much she had just revealed.

"Not that I'm bitter or anything," she hastened to add.

"Of course not," he agreed. But he didn't sound anywhere near convinced.

"It wasn't that bad," she assured him. "Just... I would have liked to have had at least one sibling. Preferably a sister. It would have made childhood much more—" she caught herself before she said *bearable*, and replaced it with "—fun. It would have been more fun."

"So do your folks live close by?" Jack asked. "I remember you said you grew up here."

She shook her head. "No, they're both gone. I lost my father to Alzheimer's when I was in college, and my mother not long after that. I think caring for him really took a toll on her, and she missed him a lot." And her daughter hadn't been enough for her to make her want to hang on any longer.

Though Natalie didn't say that last part out loud, she suspected Jack understood what she was thinking, because his expression softened some. "I'm sorry," he said.

"Yeah, me, too," she replied. "But thanks."

Although her parents hadn't been the most loving, attentive people in the world, neither had they been especially terrible. And they'd been all Natalie had, both of them moving here from other places. Any extended family she claimed lived in cities hundreds, even thousands, of miles away. She'd seen little of her grandparents and cousins and aunts and uncles as a child, and nothing of them as an adult. That was probably one of the reasons she'd bonded so quickly with Mrs. Klosterman. Her landlady was like the grandmother Natalie had never really had.

"Cousins?" Jack asked. "Aunts and uncles?"

"Scattered all over," she said. "None local. And you grew up where again?" she asked, wanting to divert attention from herself and hoping he wouldn't remember that he hadn't already told her that.

"Brooklyn," he said. But he didn't elaborate.

"And your family is still there?" Natalie asked, hoping he wouldn't interpret *family* to mean anything other than what it traditionally did.

"Most are," he said. "My immediate family is. Well, except for my sister Sofia."

Sofia, Natalie reflected. Also an Italian name. In a word, hmm...

Or, in four words, one for each sister, she thought further. *Stop being so silly.*

"Where's Sofia?" she asked.

"Vermont," her told her.

Ah-ha! Natalie thought. This proved he didn't have ties to the Mob, if his sister was living in Vermont. Hell, they wouldn't even let Wal-Mart into the state. No way would they welcome La Cosa Nostra.

"But I've got extended family spread out all over the country, too," he added. "Philadelphia. Boston. Chicago. Las Vegas. Palm Springs. More recently, Miami. And also Sheboygan."

In other words, she thought, all the places where the

Mob flourished. Well, except for Sheboygan. But then, what did she know? Maybe Wisconsin was a real hotbed of Mob activity. Just because the cheese wasn't mozzarella…

Stop it, silly.

He was surprisingly chatty this morning, she thought, considering how reticent he'd been that first day. Of course, they'd had two weeks to run into each other, and had talked informally on several occasions around the house and at the museum that day, so maybe he felt more comfortable around her.

Or maybe he was planning to off her once he'd completed the job he'd come here to do, so it didn't matter what he told her now.

Natalie sighed inwardly. This had to stop. It had gone beyond silly and was now getting ridiculous. It was just that once Mrs. Klosterman put the idea into her head of Jack's being possibly connected, it suddenly seemed like everything the man said or did had Mob implications. Had her landlady suggested Jack worked as a handyman, Natalie would no doubt be seeing references to spackle everywhere. It was just a good thing Mrs. Klosterman hadn't fingered him as a proctologist.

And, oh, she *really* wished she hadn't thought that.

"But most of my family is still in Brooklyn," Jack continued, bringing her attention back to the conversation. "The neighborhood where I grew up is the kind of neighborhood where people don't move far away, you know?"

Natalie did know. For all her traveling, she had never wanted to live anywhere but here. Particularly in Old Louisville, which was the neighborhood where she herself had grown up. She supposed a lot of people were like that when it came to their homeplaces.

"We've had our share of problems in the neighborhood, too, though," he added. "And in my family. I mean, just because a family is big doesn't necessarily mean everyone's always happy." He met her gaze levelly. "In fact, sometimes it's the big families you really have to look out for, you know?"

And something about the way he said that just sent chills down Natalie's spine. Although she was fairly certain he wasn't talking about his own blood relations when he made the comment, he still seemed to be talking about something with which he had an intimate acquaintance. A family other than his own, but a family he knew well.

But what kind of family was it? Natalie wondered. That was the question she wished she knew the answer to.

"YOU KNOW, Natalie, you should get out more," Mrs. Klosterman said the following Sunday evening as the two of them worked on a jigsaw puzzle in the living room. It was a new one her landlady had just purchased, five thousand pieces, a sweeping vista of the Alps that was almost all blue and purple and white, and which Natalie estimated would cover half the dining room table if they ever managed to finish it. But they'd probably have more success scaling the actual subject matter than they would completing the puzzle.

She pretended to be interested in whether one lavenderish piece might go with three other lavenderish pieces she'd pulled from the box. "What do you mean?" she asked.

Mrs. Klosterman lifted one shoulder and let it drop, but there was nothing casual in the gesture. But then, there was hardly anything about Mrs. Klosterman that was ever casual. Today was no exception, seeing as how she was dressed in a neon orange sweatshirt that boasted—sort of—how she was a *Bunco Babe*. At least it matched—kind of—the chartreuse running pants she'd paired it with. And her Day-Glo pink fuzzy slippers were exactly the right accessory to go with.

"It's just not right," Mrs. Klosterman continued, looking up at Natalie now. "A pretty girl like you, sitting home alone night after night the way you do."

Natalie could debate the pretty part, since her own attire—slouchy blue corduroys and an even slouchier white, men's-style shirt, and she hadn't even bothered with shoes herself—didn't have that much more to recommend her than Mrs. Klosterman's wardrobe did. Still, she did debate part of her landlady's remark.

"I don't sit home alone night after night," she denied. "Sometimes I sit home with you."

"Even worse," Mrs. Klosterman told her. "You don't need to be keeping an eye on an old lady."

"What old lady?" Natalie quipped. "I've seen you get carded."

Mrs. Klosterman smiled. "Only when the waiter is looking to increase his tip, dear."

"I could go out if I wanted to," Natalie said. "I just don't want to, that's all."

When her landlady said nothing in response, Natalie glanced up to find Mrs. Klosterman studying her with obvious concern. "That's what bothers me most," she said. "That you'd rather do this—" she gestured down at the puzzle "—than make whoopee."

Natalie smiled. "I've made whoopee before and I think it's highly overrated," she said.

Now Mrs. Klosterman smiled. "Not when it's with the right man, it isn't. When it's with the right man, there's *nothing* better than making whoopee. You just haven't found the right man yet, Natalie. And you won't find him," she pressed on when Natalie opened her mouth to object, "if you stay home every night. You need to get out more. Mingle. Go places. Meet people."

"I do get out," she defended herself. Why, just that afternoon, she got out for a walk. "And I do mingle." Why, every weekday, she mingled with scores of surly teenagers and dozens of crabby teachers. "And I do go places." Why, just last weekend, she'd gone to the museum. "And I do meet people." Why, just last weekend, at the museum, she'd met Jack Miller.

"But not the right people," Mrs. Klosterman objected.

And Natalie, alas, couldn't disagree with her there.

"You need to be more like Jack," her landlady told her. "He's hardly ever home."

Which hadn't exactly escaped Natalie's notice. What also hadn't escaped her notice was how much she'd noticed that. And it hadn't escaped her notice, either, how much she wondered what he was up to. And how she wondered even more who he was with when he was up. Or something like that.

In any event, she did wonder about Jack. More than she should, really. Not that she could help that, because he just offered her so much to wonder about. And she told herself his presence in the house had nothing to do with why, lately, she'd been even more reluctant than usual to get out more and mingle and go places and meet people.

"He reminds me a lot of Mr. Klosterman," Mrs. Klosterman began again, drawing Natalie's attention back to the matter at hand. Whatever that matter had been.

"Really?" she asked. And then, in an effort to make her landlady see how silly it was to keep insisting that her new tenant was a mobster, she added, "Was Mr. Klosterman connected to the Mob, too?"

Mrs. Klosterman uttered a soft tsking sound. "Of course not. But he was a successful counterfeiter before he met me."

"*What?*" Natalie gasped, certain she must have misheard. "A counterfeiter?"

"Oh, sure," her landlady said. "Didn't I tell you that?"

"You told me he was a milkman."

"Well, he was. He was a very successful milkman. But before that, he was a very successful counterfeiter. Well, okay, maybe not all that successful, since he put in a stretch at LaGrange Reformatory."

"What?"

"But that was before he met me."

Natalie's head was buzzing now, as if it had been invaded by a swarm of killer bees from South America. Or maybe they'd just come from Mrs. Klosterman, since those international visas were getting harder and harder to come by. But then her landlady smiled with what was obviously fond reminiscence, and Natalie softened. And she found herself wondering if maybe someday she herself would be able to smile like that. A girl could hope, she supposed.

"Mr. Klosterman turned his life around after he met me," her landlady continued a little dreamily. "Because that's all it takes, you know."

The buzzing kicked up in Natalie's head again after that, even louder this time. Yep. It was definitely coming from Mrs. Klosterman, and not South America.

"That's all what takes?" she asked, thinking she must have fallen asleep for a few minutes and missed part of this conversation. It wouldn't be the first time. Mrs. Klosterman did tend to have that effect on a person sometimes.

"That's all it takes to reform a man," her landlady clarified. "A good woman. Or, more specifically, the love of a good woman. My Edgar was headed straight for skid row when I met him. But once he realized how good life could be for the two of us if he took the straight and narrow path, he turned his back on his criminal ways and embraced the dairy industry."

"Wow," Natalie said. "That's…that's really touching, Mrs. Klosterman."

She nodded. "That's what Jack needs, too," she announced.

"To embrace the dairy industry?" Natalie asked, thinking she must have dozed off again.

"No," Mrs. Klosterman said. "Unfortunately, milkmen don't make nearly the money they used to, and their health benefits are terrible. What Jack needs is the love of a good woman to make him turn his life around."

And he was probably getting the love of a good woman right now, Natalie thought, since he hadn't come home last night. Not that she'd noticed, mind you. Just because she'd stayed up until four-thirty herself watching movies and never heard him come in, and just because she hadn't heard a sound from his apartment all day, that didn't mean she'd noticed anything. It just meant, you know, he hadn't been home. And that meant he'd been out. Probably getting some love from a good woman. Or, at least, an expensive woman. Which probably meant she was good. She might even be great. She might even be phenomenal, depending on how much he'd paid for her.

Not that Jack seemed like the kind of guy who had to *pay* for the love of a good woman, Natalie thought further. Or a bad woman, either. In fact, there were probably a lot of women—good and bad—who would have paid for a man like Jack. Women like, oh, Natalie didn't know…her.

"Well, who says he doesn't already have the love of a good woman?" Natalie asked, just now considering the possibility of such a thing. Really, for all she or Mrs. Klosterman knew, he could be married. Or engaged. Or at the very least, seriously involved with a good, and perhaps even phenomenal, woman.

"He's not romantically involved with anyone," Mrs. Klosterman said decisively.

"How do you know?" Natalie asked. "Did you ask him?"

"No," her landlady replied. "I can just tell."

Now this was something Natalie definitely wanted to hear. If for no other reason than it was bound to be amusing. "Okay, I'll bite. How can you tell he's not romantically involved with someone?"

"I can tell," Mrs. Klosterman said, "because of his shoes."

Natalie eyed the other woman dubiously. "His shoes?"

Her landlady nodded. "He never polishes his shoes. Men always polish their shoes when they have a special woman in their life."

"They do?"

"Of course they do."

"I never noticed."

"That's because you've never been seriously involved with a man," Mrs. Klosterman pointed out. Correctly, too, Natalie had to admit. "If you'd ever been seriously involved with a man, you would have noticed that he polished his shoes for you."

Natalie wasn't convinced, but decided not to provoke her landlady. It would only lead to trouble. Or, at the very least, a migraine. "Well, that's not very scientific," she said, "but I suppose it's as good a gauge as any. It's possible you could be right."

"Of course I'm right. Jack needs a woman. A *good* woman. If he found the right woman—the right *good* woman—she could make him forget all about his criminal ways. That's all there is to it."

"Mmm," Natalie said noncommittally.

Except for the part about Jack's criminal ways, to which Natalie would take exception—if she didn't think that, too, would just provoke her landlady—she neither agreed nor disagreed with Mrs. Klosterman. These days, the decision to tie oneself to another human being had to be entirely up to the individual, and it had to be based on the individual's personal experiences.

Certainly there were some men out there who would benefit from having a woman in their lives, just as there were some women out there who would benefit from having a man in their lives. But there were other people, men and women both, who got along just fine all by themselves. Natalie took pride in being one of them. Jack Miller, she felt certain, would consider himself a part of that group, too. But Mrs. Klosterman had been raised in a time when the ultimate goal for either gender was marriage and family. She would naturally think Jack needed the love of a good woman just as she thought Natalie needed to get out more and mingle. That was Mrs. Klosterman's prerogative. It didn't mean Natalie had to agree with or encourage her.

"Well, Jack might not agree with you," was all she said. "He's probably perfectly happy with his life just the way it is."

"That's only because he hasn't had a chance to see what it might be like in a different way," her landlady insisted.

"Mmm," Natalie said again.

Because she really didn't want to prolong this conversation any more than they already had. Not just because they'd never come to an agreement, but because she really wasn't comfortable talking about Jack behind his back. So she fished another lavenderish puzzle piece from the box and tried to fit it with one of the others, fixing all her concentration on the task. Thankfully, Mrs. Klosterman said nothing more about Jack, either, and instead focused her energy on the puzzle, too. But where Natalie's pieces refused to connect, her landlady managed to effortlessly join a good dozen pieces in the passage of a few minutes.

How did she do that? Natalie wondered. It was as if she

knew the secrets to the universe, the ways in which everything in the cosmos was interrelated. You could just never
really tell with Mrs. Klosterman.

"Since we missed breakfast yesterday," she said after
slipping another piece into the Matterhorn while Natalie
watched in amazement, "why don't we have dinner together tomorrow night?"

It had been a while since she and her landlady had
dined together, so Natalie nodded eagerly at the invitation.
Well, she also nodded eagerly because she knew she had
nothing else planned for the following evening. Really,
she was going to have to pencil in some mingling or something soon.

"That sounds good," she said. "Thanks."

"I'll fix a nice casserole," Mrs. Klosterman offered. "And
maybe a salad to go with."

"What can I bring?" Natalie asked.

Her landlady looked up at her and smiled. "Just bring
yourself, dear. That will be treat enough."

4

IT RAINED AGAIN the following evening, a heavy, torrential sort of rain that was more appropriate for spring than it was fall. Natalie barely made it home from work before the skies opened up with a gush, as if someone had thrust a knife deep into the belly of the clouds and ripped them open wide, spilling their innards like a gutted stoolie.

Oh, nice imagery, Natalie, she told herself. Good thing she'd finally convinced herself how silly she was being with all those mobster references.

She sighed to herself as she shrugged out of her raincoat and hung it on the coat tree by the front door. The downstairs of the house was unlit, made even darker by the thick clouds obscuring what little sunlight was left early in the evening this time of year. Maybe Mrs. Klosterman just wasn't home yet, Natalie thought. But no sooner had the speculation materialized in her head than Natalie detected the faint scent of something mouthwateringly yummy cooking in the oven. Probably her landlady had just gotten busy in the kitchen and didn't realize how dark it was outside, so she hadn't bothered with any lights. So Natalie crossed to the nearest lamp and clicked it on.

Or, rather, tried to click it on. Nothing happened, though. So she tried again. Click, click, click. Still nothing. So she moved to the end table on the other side of the sofa. One click, two click, red click, blue click. Nothing again.

Great. No electricity. Good thing the stove was gas, otherwise there would be no dinner, either, and Natalie, for one, was starving.

"Mrs. Klosterman?" she called as she made her way toward the kitchen. "I'm home! Looks like we'll be eating by candlelight tonight, huh?" She smiled as she playfully added, "Oh, well, that'll just make it more—" her words were halted, though, when she entered the kitchen and saw Jack Miller pulling a Pyrex baker from the oven "—romantic," she finished lamely.

"'Yo," he said by way of a greeting when he saw her.

She told herself that the polite thing to do would be to say *'yo*—or, rather, *hello*—to him, too, but the word got stuck in her throat. Probably because she was so preoccupied by how he looked standing there in the kitchen in his rumpled suit. His necktie was tugged loose and hanging kind of off-kilter, as if he hadn't been able to get the damned thing off fast enough, and had been rudely interrupted in the process. His hair was slightly damp, as if he'd gotten caught in the downpour, too, and was pushed back from his face in a way that showed off how long it was— longer than what one normally saw in a man who wore a suit to work, rumpled or otherwise. But what really caught Natalie's attention was how he had one hand encased in an oven mitt shaped like a lobster claw and an apron slung haphazardly around his waist—a red plaid apron that was decorated with retro-looking cats.

The scene should have been funny, she thought. But her stomach did a little flip-flop as she absorbed it, and her skin grew warm, and somehow, that response didn't seem funny at all.

"Where's Mrs. Klosterman?" she asked softly.

"You got me," Jack said as he settled the casserole on top of the stove.

Well, no, she didn't, Natalie couldn't help thinking. But it was a nice thought to have anyway.

"I just got home a little while ago myself," he added. "I thought I heard the back door slam right after I came in, but I looked around, even looked outside, and I didn't see Mrs. K anywhere. But there was a note on the table saying the casserole would be done in fifteen minutes and that there's a salad in the fridge, and that she'd be out all evening. So now I'm taking out the casserole, because it's been fifteen minutes."

He narrowed his eyes at that. "But how did she know to put fifteen minutes in the note?" he asked no one in particular. Certainly not Natalie, since she sure didn't know the answer. "How did she know I'd be home fifteen minutes before this was done? Especially since I'm usually later than this?"

"I generally get home fifteen minutes earlier than this," Natalie offered. "The rain held me up today, though. Maybe she thought I'd see the note when I arrived home at my usual time."

"Still, it's weird," he said. "I mean, if she'd put down that it would be ready at five o'clock or something specific like that, that would have made sense. But fifteen minutes? It was like she was here waiting for someone to walk through the door, and she jotted down the right number of minutes just before ducking out. But that doesn't make sense, either, because then why didn't she just wait for whoever came in and tell them in person?"

Natalie shrugged. "Gee, you can just never really tell with Mrs. Klosterman," she said, as if that would explain everything. And to Natalie, it did.

Jack evidently wasn't so easy to convince, though, because he said, "Yeah, but still…"

Nevertheless, his voice trailed off, as if he didn't want

to waste any more words on the matter. He just tugged off the oven mitt and hung it back on the peg where it normally lived. He seemed to have forgotten the apron, though, because he made no motion to remove it. And Natalie didn't want to embarrass him by pointing out that he still had it on. Especially since he looked so cute wearing it.

For a moment, they only stood on opposite sides of the kitchen staring at each other, neither of them seeming to know what to say. Finally, though, Jack broke the silence.

"Bad storm, huh?" he said.

"Yeah, this much rain is unusual for this time of year," she replied.

"Made it get dark really early."

"Even earlier than it normally does."

"Bad traffic."

"Really bad."

"No electricity."

"Not a watt."

"Does this happen often?"

"Occasionally."

And would they do nothing but make small talk all night? Natalie wondered. This was worse than when they'd first met and didn't know a thing about each other.

"So have you had dinner?" she asked, hoping to nudge the conversation into a more practical, if not more interesting, direction.

He shook his head. "No, I'm supposed to have dinner with Mrs. K."

Natalie narrowed her eyes at that. "So am I," she said.

He seemed surprised. "Oh."

"When did she invite you?"

"This morning, as I was leaving for work."

"She invited me last night," Natalie told him smugly, as if that were some kind of major coup.

He gestured toward the table. "But she wrote in her note that she'll be out all evening," he said. "Why would she invite both of us for dinner, and then go out?"

The answer hit Natalie before he'd even finished asking the question. Hit her like an avalanche barreling down from the Matterhorn, as a matter of fact. Mrs. Klosterman had invited them both for dinner and had then gone out because Jack needed the love of a good woman to set him on the straight and narrow path, and Natalie needed to get out more and mingle so she wouldn't have to spend night after night at home alone. This was a setup, plain and simple, an attempt by Mrs. Klosterman to get the two of them together. *Romantically* together. Not that Natalie would *ever* tell Jack that. There were limits, after all, to just how much one was obligated to tell a person about his landlady—she didn't care what the Department of Housing and Urban Development said.

"Gee, you can just never really tell with Mrs. Klosterman," she said again by way of an explanation, hoping he'd buy it this time.

Although he still didn't look particularly appeased by the analysis, he said, "I guess we might as well eat this without her then. While it's still hot."

"I'll set the table," Natalie offered.

But when she exited the kitchen through the other door, she found that the dining room table was already set. For two. With Mrs. Klosterman's best china. And her finest crystal. And her recently polished silver. With fresh flowers in a vase at the center. And a dozen tapers in crystal candlesticks strategically placed on the table and the buffet and the china cabinet waiting to be lit. And a bottle of what looked like very good champagne chilling in a silver ice bucket. And a battery operated boom box that was playing soft, lilting Johnny Mathis tunes.

Oh. Dear.

This, she thought, might be a trifle harder to excuse with a generic *Gee, you can just never really tell with Mrs. Klosterman* than her landlady's other idiosyncratic behaviors had been. Jack was too smart a guy not to figure out what was going on once he saw this. The minute he set foot in the dining room, he'd know they were being set up, too, and that their landlady was trying to hook them up romantically. And then he was going to run screaming for his life—or, at the very least, for the health and well-being of his manhood—in the opposite direction.

Natalie spun around in the hopes of intercepting him before he came in, thinking she could just throw some dishes onto the smaller kitchen table and sneak in here later to clear out the evidence…ah, clean up everything…later tonight. Unfortunately, when she spun around, she wheeled right into Jack. Which, okay, maybe wasn't so unfortunate after all, because he instinctively reached out to steady her, curling both hands around her upper arms in the same way Rick had with Ilsa during that "hill of beans" speech at the end of *Casablanca*, when you knew he would love her forever.

So that was kinda cool.

There was just one thing different, though, she thought as she looked up at him. Jack was way, *way* sexier than Humphrey Bogart. And seeing as how Natalie had always considered Bogey to be the ultimate when it came to sexy men, that was saying something. Mostly, she supposed, what it was saying was that Jack Miller was now the ultimate when it came to sexy men. But those eyes, those cheekbones, those lips, those nose…ah, that nose… She couldn't quite quell the wistful sigh that rose inside her when she looked at him.

Until she realized he wasn't looking back at her. No, he was looking at the dining room table. The dining room table that was already set for two—and only two—with all of Mrs. Klosterman's finery.

Oh. Dear.

"Uh…" Natalie began eloquently, having absolutely no idea how to explain this development without feeling completely humiliated.

"Oh, Mrs. K already set the table," Jack said when he witnessed the horrifying scene. "That was nice of her. She even put out some candles for us. She must have realized the power might go out in a storm like this. That was really good planning on her part," he added, thereby sparing Natalie from humiliation, mostly by being a complete blockhead.

And then he turned around to go back into the kitchen, thereby concluding the revelation portion of their show.

Unbelievable, Natalie thought. All that blatant, rampant romance, and as far as he was concerned, it was "good planning." Wow. Women really were from Venus, and men really were from some dark dank cave where they had yet to discover fire. Even smart guys like Jack Miller were absolutely clueless when it came to matters of the heart. Here was incontrovertible scientific proof. Or, to put it in layman's terms, here was a real doofus.

Oh, well, she thought. At least now she wouldn't have to make something up about Mrs. Klosterman's intentions. She could just sit back and enjoy the ambiance of a romantic meal, and be comfortable in the knowledge that she was the only one who appreciated it.

Once back in the kitchen, Jack clutched the edge of the counter and exhaled a huge sigh of relief that Natalie had obviously fallen for his ignorance about what that scene in the dining room was all about. Yeah, one thing about women—they could always be counted on to assume men were absolutely clueless when it came to matters of the heart. But any idiot could have taken one look at what Mrs. K had done out there and realized what the old lady was up to. She was playing matchmaker. And the match she had in mind to make was Natalie and himself.

Not that Jack would necessarily object to such a match under certain circumstances. Provided it wasn't a match, per se. The traditional kind of match, he meant, where two people got married and started a family and ended up fiddling on the roof together happily ever after. He'd rather do his fiddling with Natalie in the bedroom. Just not happily ever after, that was all. Well, okay, maybe happily. Maybe *very* happily, now that he thought about it. Just not ever after. Because that whole ever after concept was something he wasn't suited to at all.

He just wasn't the flowers and candlelight and Johnny Mathis type. He liked women, sure. He liked them a lot. Maybe too much, which was part of the problem. He couldn't see himself being tied to one for the rest of his life, even if she was cute and smart and funny and funky and reminded him of *Fishin' with Orlando*. Natalie was the kind of woman who needed and deserved a guy who would fall deeply and irrevocably in love with her and be with her forever. Not one who was only in it to have a good time for as long as a good time lasted. Which was all it would be to Jack.

Yeah, maybe, possibly he could see it lasting with her longer than it did with other women. Because she was, you know, *really* cute. But he couldn't see it lasting forever. Especially since he was only here for as long as it took him to complete a job, and then he was outta here for good.

And he certainly couldn't see the two of them sitting down to china and crystal and flowers and candlelight on

75

a regular basis. Not on *any* basis. Not unless it was perfectly clear that nothing, but *nothing*, would happen afterward. So as long as he played stupid about the whole romance thing, then maybe the two of them could get through the evening relatively unscathed. All he had to do was make his stupidity convincing. And hey, that shouldn't be so hard, right?

Of course, there was Natalie to think about, he reminded himself. She for sure had to have picked up on what Mrs. K was trying to do. Not only were women always homed in on the whole romance thing, but Natalie was an especially smart woman. And, all modesty aside, Jack knew she was interested in him romantically. And not just because of the invitation she'd extended to him last weekend to join her for dinner, though certainly that was what had put him on alert. But since then, whenever he'd seen her, he'd picked up on little clues here and there that let him know she was thinking about him in ways that weren't necessarily casual. Like the way she always said *hello* to him. And how she always *smiled* at him. What else could it be, but that she was interested in him romantically? People didn't just go around saying hello to people and smiling at people to be polite. She *had* to be interested in him romantically.

Sometimes, a man just had a sixth sense about these things.

So that made it doubly important why Jack had to make sure she didn't get any wrong ideas about this little dinner. He didn't want to lead her on. That would be cruel. No, instead, he'd just break her heart right up front, he thought wryly. Because that would just be so much kinder.

And with that little pep talk—such as it was—out of the way, he went to the refrigerator to find the salad Mrs. K had promised, pulled off the plastic wrap and rifled through the drawers to see if his landlady had one of those big ol' wooden spoon and fork sets that people used for tossing salads and taking up extra wall space over their stoves. When he didn't find them, he settled for a smaller, stainless steel version instead, then carried the salad out to the dining room.

Where Natalie was putting a match to the last of the candles and looking incredibly sexy bathed in the soft golden flickers of light.

Jack stopped dead in his tracks when he saw her, the termination of his movements so abrupt that the salad kept going, nearly tumbling from his fingers before he managed to regain his grip on it. For a moment, he simply could not move from the position where he had halted, because he was so transfixed by the vision of Natalie. In profile as she was, her face washed in pale candlelight, she was quite the vision indeed.

Her dark hair, which she normally wore pulled back, fell forward over one shoulder, the silky tresses curling over her breast against a crisp white blouse whose top two—no, three, he noted with something akin to gratitude—buttons were unbuttoned. As she shook out the match and straightened, the garment gaped open a bit, just enough for him to see a hint of pearly skin beneath, skin that seemed to glow almost golden in the soft illumination. She looked up at him then, and smiled, her features seeming softer somehow, more feminine, thanks to the buffing effects of the lighting.

He had been thinking since she entered the kitchen that evening that she looked every inch the schoolteacher, with her starched white blouse and flowered skirt and berry-colored cardigan sweater. But the sweater was gone now, and the blouse buttons were undone, and the skirt flowed down over stockinged feet. Natalie had made herself comfortable. And there was something inherently sexy in that.

What was really strange, though, was that usually, when women made themselves more comfortable around Jack, they didn't, you know, make themselves more comfortable. They actually made themselves less comfortable by putting on sexy contraptions like bustiers and garter belts that made Jack less comfortable, too. But in a good way.

Natalie, though, she took making herself more comfortable to heart. And her version of *more comfortable* was, inexplicably, far sexier than any other version of *more comfortable* that Jack had ever seen.

And it *really* made him uncomfortable. In a *really* good way.

"What can I do?" she asked when she saw him, her voice as soft and glowy as the rest of her seemed to be.

What could she do? he echoed to himself. What could she *do?* Oh, he could think of *lots* of things for Natalie to do in that moment. Like, she could unbutton the rest of those buttons on her blouse. And then she could slip that skirt down over her hips and legs and leave it right where she was standing. And then she could walk over to where he was standing, and take the salad out of his now numb hands and put it on the table. And then she could put *her* hands on him, and go to work on *his* buttons and *his* skirt…ah, shirt. And then she could sit herself down on the edge of the dining room table, and pull him in between her legs, and move his hands to her breasts, and stroke her fingers down over his bare chest and torso, and then even lower, until she could wrap her fingers around his—

"Not a thing," he said, his voice sounding a little strangled, even to his own ears. He cleared his throat roughly. "You don't have to do one single thing," he reiterated. "I'll just, um…" He remembered the salad then, and set it hastily on the table. "I'll go get the casserole, and then we can eat." And before she could respond, he fled back into the kitchen as if the hounds of hell were on his heels.

A funny thing happened, though, once he got there. He couldn't for the life of him remember what he had gone into the kitchen to do. Because he was too busy remembering what he'd wanted Natalie to do in the dining room.

Oh, man, he thought. It was going to be a long night.

NATALIE WASN'T sure whose idea it was to play Trivial Pursuit, but not long after she and Jack had finished cleaning up Mrs. Klosterman's kitchen, they were sitting at the dining room table again, with the board unfolded and game pieces assigned and all the candles gathered together to provide enough lighting for them to see what they were doing. Jack, ever the gentleman, insisted that Natalie should roll first.

"Entertainment," she said when she landed on the pink space. Oh, goody. That and arts and literature were her best categories.

Jack drew a card from the container and read, "Which movie took home the Oscar for best picture in 1972?"

Oh, that one was simple. "The Godfather," she answered easily. Until she realized what her answer had been. And then she felt a little *un*easy.

Ah, it was just a coincidence, she told herself. That stuff about noticing more Mob references because her landlady had put her in the right frame of mind. There was nothing more to it than that.

"Correct," he told her. "You get to roll again."

So Natalie did. This time she landed on a blue space— geography. Oo, ick. That was her worst subject. She braced herself for the question.

"What body of water connects Sicily to the Italian mainland?" Jack asked. Then he smiled. "I know the answer to this one," he said without turning the card over.

That made one of them, Natalie thought. "I have no idea what it is," she said.

"The Strait of Messina," he told her. He flipped the card over to double-check the answer, then punctuated his response with a satisfied chuckle that indicated, Yup, he did indeed know the answer to that one. "My turn now," he said. He rolled and landed on a yellow square. "Oh, I'm great with history," he said.

Yeah, yeah, yeah, Natalie thought as she pulled a card from the deck. Who wasn't? "What volcano erupted with devastating results in 1669?" she asked.

"Hah," Jack replied smugly. "That's easy. Mount Etna."

Natalie turned the card over. The answer was indeed Mount Etna. Dammit. "Where is Mount Etna, anyway?" she asked as she replaced the card in its proper box. "You being so good with geography and all, I mean," she added teasingly.

"It's in Sicily," Jack told her. "Hey, whattaya know. That's two Sicily questions in a row."

Yeah, and one Godfather before them, she thought. She was beginning to detect a pattern here....

"My turn again," he said, rolling the dice. "Sports and Leisure," he said as he landed on an orange square. "Excellent. I'm great with this subject, too."

Natalie ignored him and read, "What underdog NBA team won the National Championship in 1978?"

Jack smiled. "That would be the Washington Bullets."

She narrowed her eyes at him. There was definitely a pattern emerging here. And she wasn't sure she liked it.

He rolled again, landing on another orange space, but this time his right answer would win him a piece of the pie. "Wed-gie, wed-gie, wed-gie," he chanted as Natalie drew a card from the deck.

Doof-us, doof-us, doof-us, she chanted to herself. Oh, good.

It was a bartending question. Maybe he'd miss it. "What drink," she said, "contains both Galliano and Amaretto?"

"Oh, oh, I know this," he said. "It's on the tip of my tongue."

"Yeah, sure it is," Natalie said.

"It is, I tell ya. I know this."

"Mmm-hmm. Fifteen seconds."

He gaped at her. "Since when? There's no time limit on Trivial Pursuit."

"There is when one of the players is a smug little geek," she said.

"Hey!"

"Ten seconds."

He started to argue again, thought better of it, and put his efforts into trying to remember the name of the drink. "Ah, dammit. What's it called…?"

"Five…four…three…two…one." Natalie honked out the sound of a penalty buzzer and said, "Time!" Then she flipped the card over and frowned. "A Hit Man?" she said.

"That's it!" Jack exclaimed. "A Hit Man."

"There's actually a drink called a Hit Man?" she asked dubiously.

"Sure," he said. "It's a shooter."

Of course it was.

"My turn," Natalie said, snatching up the dice before he could get his mitts back on them. She rolled a six, which put her on a green space. Damn. Science and nature. She almost always missed those.

Jack pulled a card and read, "Which dark nebula is located in the constellation of Orion?"

Well, if nothing else, at least they were getting away from the mob questions, Natalie thought. Not that she had a clue what the answer to this one was. "I have no idea," she confessed.

"Me, neither." He flipped the card over. "The Horse-head Nebula."

Natalie felt like banging her head on the table but somehow managed to refrain from doing so. Instead, she said, very civilly, too, "Your turn." And then she tried not to flinch as she waited to see what he would land on next, and what his question would be.

He landed on pink. Entertainment. Surely there couldn't be any more questions about *The Godfather*, right? She drew a card and breathed a sigh of relief when she saw the innocuous question. "Down what street does Chicago's famous St. Patrick's Day parade march?"

Jack smiled. "I know this. Like I said, I have family in Chicago."

"So then what street is it, smart guy?" she asked.

"Wacker Avenue."

All Natalie could manage by way of a response was something that vaguely resembled a growl.

"Me again," he said, scooping up the dice. "History again," he said when he landed on a yellow space. "Hit me."

Oh, don't tempt me, Natalie thought. She drew a card, but found herself reluctant to look at it for some reason. And when she finally did, and saw what the question was, all she could do was shake her head in defeat. "What labor figure was last seen at the Machus Red Fox restaurant in Bloomfield Hills, Michigan in the summer of 1975?"

"Jimmy Hoffa," Jack said, grinning.

Natalie snatched up the box top to study it. "What is this, Trivial Pursuit the Sopranos Edition or what?"

"Ah, ah, ah," Jack admonished. "Don't be a sore loser."

"I'm *not* losing," Natalie pointed out. "Neither one of us has any wedgies. We're tied."

"But I've answered more right questions than you have," he said.

Only because the questions were all about his family, Natalie thought uncharitably. "Oh, and what a gentleman you are to have pointed that out," she snapped.

His smile fell. "I'm sorry. You're right. I'm not behaving in a very sportsmanlike manner."

Natalie felt properly chastened. "Don't apologize. I'm not exactly being a good sport myself."

"So what say we call it a draw?" Jack asked. "And do something else instead."

Natalie looked around at their poorly lit surroundings, and listened to the rain pinging against the dining room window. "What else is there to do on a cold, rainy night when it's dark outside and there's no electricity?"

And no sooner was the question out of her mouth than an answer popped into her head. A very graphic, very explicit answer that featured her and Jack. Specifically, her and Jack upstairs in her apartment. Even more specifically, her and Jack upstairs in the bedroom of her apartment. Most specifically of all, her and Jack upstairs in the bedroom of her apartment naked. And sweaty. And horizontal. Though maybe she was a bit less horizontal than he, being on top like that and yelling *Ride 'im, cowboy…*

"Uh…I mean…" she began, trying to cover for herself.

Thankful that the dim lighting hid her embarrassment, she looked over at Jack…only to discover that the lighting wasn't quite dim enough. Because she could see from his face that his brain had conjured the same answer to her question that her own had, maybe even right down to the *ride 'im, cowboy*, which meant he most certainly could see enough of hers to deduce the same thing.

Though, on second thought, maybe he was thinking something else, she realized as she studied him more intently. In fact, judging by his expression, his thoughts were even more graphic and explicit than her own. Which meant he must be thinking about—

Oh. Dear.

"We, uh…" she began, scrambling for something—anything—that might put different thoughts into their heads, "we should, um…we should, ah…clean up," she finally stated triumphantly. "We should clean up the kitchen so Mrs. Klosterman won't have to do it when she gets home."

If she ever gets home, Natalie thought. What time was it anyway? She glanced down at her watch to see that it was past nine o'clock. This really wasn't like her landlady at all. Then again, if Mrs. Klosterman was playing matchmaker, which she clearly was, who knew how late she'd stay out? She might not come home until tomorrow. Hell, she might not come home until April. And if she wasn't here to chaperone things, and with Natalie and Jack both thinking graphic and explicit *ride-'im- cowboy* thoughts…

"Yeah, clean up," Natalie repeated. "We should do that. Right away, in fact. Now, in fact. So Mrs. Klosterman won't have to when she gets home, in fact."

When she looked at Jack this time, he didn't look embarrassed *or* aroused. What he looked was befuddled. "Natalie," he said.

"What?"

"We already cleaned up so Mrs. Klosterman wouldn't have to."

"We did?"

He nodded. "Less than an hour ago. Don't you remember?"

Now, how was she supposed to remember that, when her head was filled with *ride-'im-cowboy* thoughts about Jack, huh? Honestly. Men.

"Oh," was all she said in response. Though then she did receive a faint recollection of standing next to Jack while he washed dishes, wiping them dry and stacking them neatly on the counter.

"But we didn't put the dishes and crystal away, did we?" she asked. Because she was pretty certain they hadn't.

"That's because we didn't know where Mrs. Kloster-man kept them," he pointed out.

Oh. Yeah. Right. Then Natalie noticed the china cabinet behind Jack, noted a few empty places where things had obviously been before, and realized that must be where their landlady stored everything. "Well, it must go in there, right?" she asked, pointing to the piece of furniture in question. "We can put everything back in there. It would save her the trouble of carting it all in here and putting it all away since I doubt she'll be able to do that very quickly."

And it would save her and Jack the trouble of ripping off all of each other's clothing and writhing on the dining room table naked, since she doubted they'd ever make it upstairs the way they were both looking at each other right now. Heck, they'd be lucky to even rip *all* their clothes off each other, she thought further. Then again, there was a lot to be said for making love half-clothed, she thought further still. Not that Natalie had a lot of first-hand experience with such a thing in her limited sexual knowledge—or *any* first-hand experience with it, for that matter. But giving it some thought now—which, inescapably, she did, and for several moments longer than she needed to, really—it seemed kind of, oh…incredibly, outrageously erotic.

"We could do that," Jack offered with an eager nod.

And for one brief, delirious—and incredibly, outra-geously erotic—moment, Natalie thought he was talking about the writhing half-clothed on the dining room table thing instead of the putting Mrs. Klosterman's china and crystal away thing. And in that one brief, delirious—and incredibly, outrageously erotic—moment, she felt a little light-headed. Not to mention a little warm. Not to mention a little incredibly, outrageously erotic.

But then sanity returned—dammit—and she realized he was only proposing that they do the putting away thing, and *not* the putting out thing, and she tried not to feel too suicidal over that.

It soon became clear, however, that the putting away thing and the putting out thing had a lot in common. Because putting Mrs. Klosterman's china and silver and crystal away in the china cabinet meant that Natalie and Jack worked in very close quarters, since the china cabinet wasn't especially large. Every time Natalie reached up to put something in the hutch, Jack seemed to be bending down to put something in the base, and their bodies kept bumping, their arms kept intertwining, and their positions shifted continuously into poses that, had they indeed been only half-clothed, would have led to some serious dining room table writhing.

So by the time they finished putting everything away, they were even more inclined to be putting out than they had been before.

"Gee, I wonder when Mrs. Klosterman will be getting home?" Natalie wondered aloud as she moved away from Jack and toward the dining room window, looking beyond it as if by doing so, she could conjure her landlady outside. "It's getting kind of late."

"I'm sure she's fine," Jack said. "She did say she'd be out all evening."

Natalie just hoped that didn't translate to *all night*. Because, gee, that would be Mrs. Klosterman for you. She was about to look away, then noticed something curious. The house next door had lights in the windows. And not the soft flickering glow of candlelight, but the bright, blazing light of electric lamps.

"Hey," she said. "The house next door has electricity. How come we don't?"

"You sure?" Jack asked.

He joined her by the window and bumped his body against hers again, and Natalie instinctively took a step in retreat, lest the bump lead to something else, something like, oh, Natalie didn't know...writhing half-clothed on the dining room table.

"That's weird," he said. "Both houses should run on the same power line."

He strode to the other side of the room and flicked the wall switch, looking up at the overhead fixture. But nothing happened. He went out into the living room, Natalie on his heels, and tried a light in there. Nada.

"Maybe there's a blown fuse," he said.

"For the whole house?" she asked.

He shrugged. "Could be the whole first floor is hooked up to one. It's an old house. Fuses blow sometimes."

Not since Natalie lived there, she thought. Mrs. Klosterman had had the whole place rewired when she'd had it renovated into apartments. Everything was totally up to code.

"Do you know where the fuse box is?" Jack asked.

She nodded. "In the basement."

"Show me."

She collected a flashlight from a shelf in the kitchen where Mrs. Klosterman always kept one handy, then led him down the rickety wooden steps—those hadn't been renovated along with the rest of the house—into the cold, damp basement, through a maze of stacked boxes and discarded furniture, to the corner where the fuse box was fixed against the wall. Jack flipped the metal door open and shined the flashlight on it, then shook his head at what he saw.

"What?" Natalie asked. "What's wrong?"

In reply, Jack began to flick switches, one after the other, until he reached the bottom of the second row, which threw the basement into light.

"They were off," he said. "Every last one of them. Flipped over to the off position. Now, how could that have happened?"

How indeed? Natalie wondered. But not for long. Because she knew exactly how it had happened. And if Jack was even half as smart as she was confident he was, he'd know, too. Even a man who was absolutely clueless when it came to matters of the heart knew how a fuse box worked. Because he was a man. And it was a fuse box. And God had made both—along with power tools and football conferences and overpriced sneakers and V-8 engines—on the same day. The only way those fuses could have been flipped over was if someone had done the flipping. Someone who thought Jack needed the love of a good woman, and who thought Natalie should put out...ah, get out... more.

In spite of that, she said, "Gosh, I can't imagine."

"Yeah, me, neither," he replied. Though she was pretty sure he was lying.

"It's an old house," she said, echoing his earlier statement. "Old houses can be eccentric that way." And not just old houses, either, she added to herself.

"Mmm," Jack said.

And Natalie couldn't have agreed more. Because you could just really never tell with Mrs. Klosterman.

5

"SO, HOW WAS dinner last night?"

Natalie narrowed her eyes at her landlady as she sorted through the mail she had collected from the front table on her way in from work the afternoon following her dimly lit, but nevertheless very enlightening, evening with Jack. The weather was gorgeous today, almost as if in apology for yesterday's nasty storm, cool and clear with just a hint of the oncoming winter. Natalie had responded by dressing for school in a sky-blue skirt and butter-yellow sweater, opting for flats instead of the hiking boots she donned in lousy weather. Her landlady had responded by wearing an electric purple muumuu spattered with images of pineapples and ukuleles and hula boys and the words *Aloha from Waikiki!*

"How was dinner last night?" Natalie echoed, telling herself that was *not* petulance she heard in her voice. She leveled a knowing look on her landlady. "You mean the dinner you so painstakingly took to prepare and then skipped out on? Is that the dinner you're referring to?"

Mrs. Klosterman smiled. "No, I'm talking about the nice, quiet, candlelit one I arranged for you and Jack."

"So then you admit it was a setup," Natalie charged.

"Of course it was a setup. Any fool could have seen that by the way I set the table."

"Mrs. Klosterman…"

"How did it go?" her landlady asked again, ignoring the exasperation Natalie hadn't even tried to hide.

"It went," she said succinctly.

"But *how* did it go?" Mrs. Klosterman insisted. "*Where* did it go?"

It almost went up in smoke, Natalie thought. Because after the way Jack had been looking at her there toward the end, and thanks to some of those smoldering brushes of their bodies as they put things away, she'd very nearly spontaneously combusted.

"It went fine," she said vaguely. "Though, strangely, we ultimately discovered that what we had thought was the storm cutting off the electricity was actually the result of someone having switched off all the fuses in the basement."

"Really?" Mrs. Klosterman asked, her tone of voice a little *too* amazed.

"Really," Natalie told her, her tone of voice decidedly less amazed.

"Well, what do you know about that?" Mrs. Klosterman said with a smile. "Must have been gremlins."

"Gremlins," Natalie repeated.

Her landlady nodded. "Romance gremlins. They're mischievous little buggers."

"Aren't they just?" Natalie concurred.

"So," Mrs. Klosterman said. "When are you and Jack going out again?"

Natalie arched her eyebrows at that. "What are you talking about? We have not gone out. Ergo there is no *again*. Ergo, there is no going out, either."

Her landlady looked stunned by the news. "But why not?"

"Just because we had dinner together in the building where we both have apartments, and only because we were both invited by a host who failed to show up," she added meaningfully, "that doesn't mean we're dating, Mrs. Klosterman."

"In my day, it would have meant you were engaged."

And in Mrs. Klosterman's day, women could get pregnant from public toilets, too. Natalie politely declined from pointing that out, though.

Instead, she said, with profound understatement, "Jack is very attractive, and he's a very nice man." She waited a telling beat before adding, "But. We're just not interested in each other romantically." For some reason, however, that last part of her statement came out sounding a lot less convincing than the first half of her statement.

"Oh, pooh," Mrs. Klosterman said.

"Watch your language," Natalie cautioned with a grin.

Her landlady ignored her. "I've seen the way you two look at each other."

Uh-oh, Natalie thought.

"You're definitely interested in each other."

"And you're definitely imagining things," Natalie said, hoping she sounded convincing.

"I don't imagine things," her landlady assured her with a sniff of disdain.

Oh, sure. Spoken like a woman who had just said her fuse box was broken into by romance gremlins.

Natalie expelled an exasperated sound. "Whatever happened to 'Mr. Miller is a mobster?'" she asked. "Ever since he moved in, you've been convinced he's connected. Now you want *me* to connect *myself* to him? What about waking up next to a horse's head? Or waking up with my throat slit?"

Mrs. Klosterman grinned wickedly. "Wouldn't you rather think about waking up next to Jack? Or waking up with your libido satisfied?"

"Mrs. Klosterman!" Natalie exclaimed, scandalized. It

was one thing for the older woman to make a reference to whoopee, and quite another to mention Natalie's libido. Honestly. Next Mrs. Klosterman would be telling her to *ride 'im, cowboy.*

"Mr. Miller isn't a mobster," her landlady said now with much conviction.

Not that Natalie disagreed—well, not *too* much—but she asked, "And what caused you to have this sudden change of heart?"

"It isn't sudden," the other woman said. "I've just gotten to know him better since he moved in, that's all. And I realize he's not the type of man to be a mobster." Before Natalie could ask for specifics, she went on, "He's very kind, for one thing. He fixed my sink. Offered to do it without my even having to ask him. And he's never once used the word 'whacked' since that first time he came to look at the apartment."

Well, that was a matter of debate, Natalie thought. She still wasn't totally positive he'd said *shellacked* during that phone call she'd overheard him making. Because as far as she could tell, he hadn't been doing any home improvement since moving in. Except for the kitchen sink, she meant. And that didn't involve wood finishing.

"And he works in advertising," Mrs. Klosterman added.

"How do you know?"

"He told me so."

"He did?" Natalie asked. That was odd. He'd never mentioned working in advertising to her. Not that she'd asked him about it. But he hadn't offered any information, either, and usually men could be counted on to say *some*thing about their jobs when they were making casual conversation. "When did he tell you he worked in advertising?"

"When I asked him what he did for a living."

Oh. Okay. So maybe Natalie should try going down that route next time.

"*And* he's a vegetarian," Mrs. Klosterman added, as if that trait, more than any of the other very convincing arguments she'd made, settled the matter once and for all.

"He is?" Natalie asked. "But what about the casserole last night? That had chicken chunks in it."

"No it didn't. That was soy."

"Soy?" Natalie asked, wrinkling her nose. She'd eaten soy chunks? In a word, *eeeeewwwww.*

"So you don't have to worry about waking up with your horse's throat slit," Mrs. Klosterman interrupted Natalie's thoughts before they could become too gross...by replacing them with thoughts that were even grosser. "Jack is a good man who deserves a good woman. And you," she said, pointing her finger at Natalie, "are a good woman who deserves a good man."

"I don't dispute you for a moment," Natalie said. "But I do dispute that Jack and I are right for each other, simply based on our respective goodness."

"How can you say you're not right for each other?"

How indeed? Natalie asked herself. "Well, he's just very—"

"Yes, he is," Mrs. Klosterman agreed enthusiastically.

"And I'm not at all—"

"Oh, don't sell yourself short."

"And the two of us together would just be—"

"I totally disagree."

"Besides, he's only here temporarily."

This was obviously news to Mrs. Klosterman. "What do you mean temporarily?"

Natalie was embarrassed to admit she'd been eavesdropping...until she remembered who she was talking to. "I overheard him on the phone a couple of weeks ago," she

said. "Not long after he moved in. He was talking to someone and said he was here to do a job, and from the way he
said it, I just got the impression he wasn't going to be staying long."

She'd also gotten the impression he was going to whack
someone, but she probably didn't need to tell that part to
Mrs. Klosterman. After all, he might just be here to shellac
someone. She still wasn't real clear on that. No need to be
an alarmist.

"He signed a six-month lease," Mrs. Klosterman said.

"Then maybe he'll be here six months," Natalie replied.
"But I bet he won't be here any longer than that. I mean,
come on, Mrs. Klosterman, that's a furnished apartment on
the second floor. No one stays in it for very long."

Her landlady seemed to give her analysis of the situation some thought, but she said nothing in response.

So Natalie repeated feebly, "Besides, he and I just aren't
suited to each other," and hoped her landlady believed that
more than she did herself. "Promise me you won't arrange
any more of these romantic dinners for us, all right?"

Mrs. Klosterman was clearly unwilling to make such a
pledge, but she said reluctantly, "All right, fine. I promise
I won't arrange any more dinners for you."

"Any more *romantic* dinners," Natalie clarified.

"Any more *romantic* dinners," Mrs. Klosterman repeated obediently.

"For me and Jack," Natalie added.

"For you and Jack," Mrs. Klosterman echoed.

But that still wasn't good enough for Natalie. She knew
Mrs. Klosterman too well. "Repeat after me," she told her
landlady, "I, Trixie Klosterman, promise I won't arrange
any more romantic dinners—or *any* dinners—ever again
for the rest of my life, for you, Natalie Dorset, and your
downstairs neighbor, Jack Miller, that include candlelight,

fine china and crystal, Johnny Mathis, pulled fuses and an absent landlady named Trixie Klosterman."

This time Mrs. Klosterman was the one to expel an exasperated sound, but she repeated the vow word for word. Natalie nodded, but still felt a little uneasy.

Because you could just never really tell with Mrs. Klosterman.

JACK DID HIS BEST to work late everyday—every freakin' day—the week following his candlelit, Johnny Mathis chaperoned, dinner with Natalie, just in case his landlady tried to pull a stunt like that again. Not that he had anything against Natalie—or Johnny Mathis, for that matter. But when she'd said she couldn't think of anything else for them to do in the dark besides play Trivial Pursuit, Jack had immediately found himself wanting to show her *lots* of things they could do in the dark, none of which had anything to do with trivial pursuits.

Well, okay, maybe the part about chasing her around the table could, technically, qualify for a pursuit, even though, judging by the look on her face right about then, she wouldn't have been running very fast to get away from him. What happened after he caught her wouldn't have been trivial, that was for damned sure.

But working late that week hadn't been all that hard to do, anyway, since the guy he had followed to Louisville kept making it hard for Jack to do his job in the first place. Never had he seen a man who wanted to be out in a crowd more than this guy. And being out in a crowd was the last thing he ought to be doing when there were people out there who were interested in seeing him get whacked. Of course, his being out in a crowd had probably been the one thing that had kept him from getting whacked so far, but that was beside the point. The point was that Jack had been having a tough time doing what he was being paid to come here and do, and as a result, his mood had become just a tad irritable.

Because he couldn't possibly be feeling irritable as a result of all those dreams he'd been having about Natalie. Even if those dreams *had* caused him to wake up in a tangled knot of sweaty sheets every night—every freakin' night—the week following his candlelit, Johnny Mathis chaperoned, dinner with her. Always, the dream started as that night had ended, with the two of them climbing the stairs to go to their respective apartments, and muttering awkward good-nights at the second floor landing. In his dream, though, instead of parting ways, Jack followed Natalie up the next flight of stairs and into her apartment. And there, amid the cheerful clutter of her eclectic furnishings, and often *atop* her furnishings, Jack made love to her in very creative, and not a little awkward—especially that one where they were both standing up pressed against the refrigerator—ways.

But he never woke up from those dreams feeling irritable, he reminded himself, so they couldn't be the cause of that. No, he always woke up after those dreams feeling exhausted and edgy and dissatisfied, that was all.

That last feeling, especially, had begun to eat at him more and more as the week progressed. Because the more dissatisfied Jack felt that week, the more he thought about Natalie. And the more he thought about Natalie, the more he wanted to make love to her. And the more he thought about making love to her, the more dissatisfied he felt.

It was such a vicious cycle. Among other things.

So by Friday evening, when he came wandering in from work at nearly ten o'clock, bleary-eyed and weary-boned, all he wanted to do was lock himself in his apartment, pop the top on a cold Sam Adams, turn on any sporting event he could find and do his best to *not* think about how badly he wanted to make love to Natalie.

Unfortunately, Mrs. Klosterman had other ideas. Because just as he settled his foot on the first step that would lead to his apartment and, hopefully, eventually, sweet oblivion, he heard her call out his name.

When he turned around, he saw her bustling out from the dining room waving a big, padded overnight mailer at him. He breathed a sigh of relief. Good. Just mail. No broken drains to fix when Natalie was due to come down for breakfast. No sneaky romantic dinners to eat that Natalie had been invited to, too. No suspiciously tampered with fuse boxes to go looking for with Natalie. Mail he could handle.

Until Mrs. K said, "Could you please take this up to Natalie?"

Take it up to Natalie? he wanted to echo, outraged. But taking that up to Natalie would mean seeing Natalie. And seeing Natalie would mean wanting Natalie. Of course, *not* seeing Natalie had meant wanting her, too, he reminded himself. So what the hell.

"Yeah, I can take it up to her."

"It arrived separate from the mail this afternoon before she got home," Mrs. K explained. "And I just now remembered it. Hearing you come in reminded me it was here. I'd really appreciate you delivering it, since you're going up anyway." She smiled a little sheepishly. "My old knees just aren't what they used to be, you know."

No, Jack hadn't known. But that was okay. His knees weren't all that great, either.

"No problem, Mrs. K," he said, taking the mailer from her. "You sure Natalie's home, though?"

"Why wouldn't she be?"

He shrugged. "Well, it *is* Friday night," he pointed out.

"A lot of people go out on Friday nights." Especially cute young brunettes who made guys have dreams on a nightly basis that left them feeling exhausted, edgy and dissatisfied. But not irritable.

"You're not out," Mrs. K said.

Jack wondered why he felt so defensive about her having pointed that out to him. "Well, I *was* out," he said. And he hoped he didn't sound snippy when he said it. Because if there was one thing he hated, it was snippiness. Especially when it was coming from him. Snippiness just wasn't manly.

"But I bet you were working, weren't you?" his landlady asked.

"Yeah. So?"

She smiled again, one of those benign, old lady smiles that made him feel as though she knew a hell of a lot more about the world than he did. "So nothing," she said mildly. "Just don't work too hard. All work and no play…" she began to recite.

Yeah, yeah, yeah. Like Jack hadn't heard that one a million times before.

"Besides," she added, "Natalie was down here just a little while ago, so I know she's home."

Jack wondered why his own arrival home had reminded Mrs. K of Natalie's mail when Natalie's physical presence in the place hadn't reminded her of that. Oh, well. You could just never really tell with Mrs. K. And he was too exhausted, and too edgy and too dissatisfied—and too irritable, dammit—to question it right now.

"I'll go call her right now and tell her you're on your way up, so she'll be looking for you."

He nodded, roused a tired smile and said good-night, then began to make his way wearily up the stairs—all three flights of them. As he went, he loosened his tie until it was a long ribbon of silk that hung completely unfettered around his neck, then unbuttoned the first three buttons of his shirt and tugged his shirttail free of his trousers. But in spite of his efforts to make himself more comfortable, more relaxed, by the time he reached Natalie's front door, he was strung tighter than an overtuned piano wire.

And the feeling only multiplied when he arrived at Natalie's front door to find it half open, obviously in anticipation of his arrival. So he knocked lightly, and when he didn't receive a response, pushed it open farther and entered...

...just as Natalie came striding out of her bedroom, shrugging a robe—a really skimpy, really short robe—over her naked—her really hot, really naked—body. But she wasn't quick enough to prevent him a glimpse of what lay beneath that robe. Because Jack saw just enough of her bare torso, including one bare breast—one perfect, pink, luscious breast—to make that overtuned piano wire snap clean in two.

"Thanks, Mrs. Klosterman," she said as she walked toward him, looking down and focused on tying her robe sash and obviously not realizing who had entered her apartment. "But I could have come down for it myself. I really appreciate you bringing it up—"

She glanced up then and saw Jack standing there gazing back at her like an idiot.

"Up," she finished.

Oh, yeah. He was that, for sure.

"What are you doing here?" she asked.

Besides copping a peek at your breast and battling a raging hard-on? he almost said. *Oh, not much.*

"Mrs. K told me she was going to call you to tell you I'm coming," he said stupidly. And, oh, man, he really wished he hadn't ended that sentence with the word—

"She did call," Natalie said.

Oh. Well. In that case, if this was the way she was dressed to wait for him, then Jack might as well just go ahead and—

"But she said *she* was going to bring up my mail," she added.

It took a moment for him to backtrack from his plans— they were, after all, really good plans—to process what Natalie had said. And once he did, he felt like an idiot. Of course Mrs. Klosterman had told Natalie she'd be bringing up the mail. And of course she would send Jack up here at a time when she knew Natalie would be getting ready for bed. Why hadn't he seen this coming from a mile away? Probably because he'd seen Natalie's bare torso and naked—had he mentioned she was naked?—breast first.

"I, ah…" he began. "I mean, I, um… That is, I, uh…"

But for the life of him, once he recalled Natalie's bare torso and naked breast, he simply could not get his brain to budge beyond the memory of Natalie's bare torso and naked breast. Especially since her tiny robe was made out of some kind of translucent material that clung to her body, so that he could see the faint outline of the dusky circles around her nipples, and the nipples themselves pushing against the pale ivory fabric. Even the lower curves of her breasts were apparent, he noted, and little droplets of water clung to the skin revealed in the deep V of the neckline. Her hair, too, was wet, he finally saw, pushed back from her face in damp strands, save a couple that were sticking to her neck. And in that moment, he wanted nothing more than to walk over to Natalie and unstick those wet strands of hair. With his teeth.

"You've got skin," he said vaguely. Then, when he realized how badly he had misspoken—well, not about her having skin, since she did have that…lots and lots of creamy, soft-looking, damp skin, in fact, skin that he'd love to spend the rest of the night learning more about...but that wasn't what he'd meant to say—he hastily corrected himself, "I mean...you've got mail."

Natalie looked at Jack, her heart pounding in her chest, and tried to think of something—anything—that might defuse the situation. If only she could figure out what the situation was... Besides him standing over there looking at her as if he intended to toss her over his shoulder and carry her back to the bedroom and prove something from a Bruce Springsteen song to her all night. And besides her standing there nearly naked, wishing he would hurry up and do it.

What was he doing here? He was supposed to be Mrs. Klosterman. She had just called thirty seconds ago—getting Natalie out of the shower—to tell her she was bringing up a package that had come separate from today's mail. But now Jack was here instead. And Natalie was barely dressed. And it was nighttime. Almost bedtime. This couldn't possibly be a good thing.

So why did it feel so good?

"Jack?" she said experimentally, not even sure what she wanted to tell him. She just felt like she needed to say something, and his name was the first thing that came to mind that was decent enough to let out of her mouth.

"What?" he asked.

"Why are you here?"

And why did that seem like such a loaded question? she wondered.

"I brought you something," he said.

But he didn't extend the padded mailer he was holding toward her. No, that slipped from his fingers and landed on the floor with a soft thud. He didn't react, though, as if he hadn't even realized he was holding it in the first place.

"What did you bring me?" she asked. But her voice was so soft, she almost didn't hear the question herself.

She wasn't sure if Jack did, either, because instead of answering her verbally, he crossed the room in a few deliberate strides and stopped before her. He said nothing, though, only gazed down into her eyes as if he expected her to not only know what was going on, but to be able to explain it to him, too. Natalie wished she could. But the only thing she could get a handle on in that moment was that Jack was looking at her in a way that made her want to touch him, and be closer to him. So she took a step forward, too, bringing her body almost flush with his, and lifted a hand toward his face. Then, after only a moment's hesitation, she brushed her fingertips lightly over his lower lip.

He didn't move when she touched him, but his eyes fluttered closed at the contact, and she felt his breath blow warm against her hand as he exhaled on a low rumble of satisfaction. So Natalie lifted her other hand, too, this time grazing her fingertips along the strong line of his jaw, over the rough, day-old growth of his beard.

He was so different from her, she marveled as she touched him. So much bigger, so much broader, so much stronger. His skin was coarse and dusky where hers was smooth and fair. His body was angled and muscular where hers was curved and delicate. The perfect opposite to her, she couldn't help thinking. Yet, somehow, the perfect complement, too.

He opened his eyes then, and his pupils expanded to nearly the edge of his dark brown irises. Natalie's heart hammered harder when she saw it, knowing it was an indication of his arousal. She saw her own face reflected there, her passion evident, and she waited to see what Jack would do next. He acted quickly, reaching up to grasp both of her hands in his and pull them gently away from his face. And then, before she even realized what he intended to do, he wove their fingers together and dipped his head to hers, covering her mouth with his own.

He brushed his lips lightly over hers once, twice, three times, four. She melted into him the moment their mouths made contact, thinking it must have always been inevitable that they would succumb to the heat that had been simmering beneath them since their first encounter. Jack guided their linked hands down to their sides as he slanted his mouth over hers, kissing her more deeply, more insistently, even though their bodies had yet to touch beyond their woven fingers. For a long time, he kissed her that way, exploring her mouth with his, tilting his head first one way, then the other. Helplessly, Natalie kissed him back, trying to follow his lead, but wanting to strike out on her own, too.

So she struggled to free her fingers from his grasp, and when he released them willingly, returned them to his face, to skim them lightly over his features and thread them into his hair. Jack took advantage of her exploration to do a little exploring of his own, lifting his hands to her bent elbows and tracing his fingers up her arm. She felt the heat of his touch through the thin fabric of her robe and shuddered in spite of the warmth. Then his hands traveled higher, cupping her shoulders briefly before moving inward, drawing slow lines along both of her shoulders until he reached her throat, skimming the pads of his thumbs up over the tender flesh there.

And then she felt his fingers on her face, tracing intimately along her cheeks and jaws and temples before skimming down again, to the back of her neck. He curved the fingers of both hands over her nape and cradled her jaw beneath his thumbs, then urged her head back more so that he could kiss her even more deeply. Natalie capitulated with a soft sigh, but when she tilted her head back to accommodate him, he seized the opportunity to dip his head to her exposed throat instead, and he dragged his open mouth slowly along her sensitive flesh.

He smelled of powerful man and potent pleasures, making her think of long, dark nights with just the two of them alone. He touched her with an unspoken promise of indescribable passion, tempted her with a silent vow to satisfy every dream and wish she'd ever entertained. And even though, deep down, she knew better than to let him, or any man, carry her away like that...

Natalie really wanted to be carried away. And she never wanted to return again.

Jack's mouth returned to hers then, even hungrier and more demanding than before, kissing her with such unerring ardor that Natalie began to grow dizzy. She wasn't sure when things had moved from exploration to explosion, only had a vague memory that they were supposed to be doing something other than this. But how could that be, when what they were doing felt so very good, so very right? When Jack dropped his hands to her waist, hooking them over her hips to pull her closer, she opened her own hands wide over his chest. She felt his irregular pulse buffeting her fingertips, making the muscles between feel almost alive. And still he kissed her, again and again and again, as if he never intended to let her go.

And then his hand was between their bodies, tugging at the sash of her robe in an effort to free it. Natalie recalled vaguely that she was completely naked beneath it, knew that if he succeeded in doing what he clearly intended to do, that there would be little to prevent them from seeing this thing through to its obvious conclusion. But she felt no shock, no anxiety, no desire to stop him. In fact, she dropped her own hand to brush away his and with one swift maneuver, had the sash sliding apart and the robe falling open.

And then his hand was inside it, spreading over the

bare flesh of her torso, skimming wildly over her bare belly and ribs. And then higher, closing over one breast, thumbing the stiff peak to even greater tension. She cried out softly at the caress, but he silenced her with another kiss and continued his gentle manipulation, until she thought she might very well go mad with the pleasure of it all.

And then his hand was moving again, down over her flat abdomen, hesitating only the briefest of moments before slipping between her legs. Natalie told herself to object, to remove his hand with her own if need be, but she couldn't quite rouse the offense she thought she should be feeling that he would take such a liberty. Because she was too busy feeling something else instead, a wide, hot ripple of pleasure that began where he had placed his hand and then moved outward, spreading to every cell she possessed, every nerve that could feel, every fiber of her body that comprehended ecstasy.

"Oh," she said softly when he moved his fingers against her. "Oh, Jack… Oh, please… Oh, yes…"

She took one step to the side, opening more fully to him, and he slid a finger inside her, making her gasp. Not just at the intrusion itself, but at how easily he made it. She was more ready for him than she had realized, her body already knowing things her mind had yet to understand.

"Natalie."

Her name was a soft benediction uttered against her mouth, a sigh of pure, unmitigated pleasure. But how could that be, she wondered, when she was the one feeling it? How could Jack sound as if he were as carried away as she by what was happening?

"I want you," he said. "Right here. Right now. Natalie, tell me you want me, too."

"I do," she whispered, amazed that she had even managed those two small words. "Oh, Jack, I want you, too. The same way. Please…make love to me."

He moved his finger inside her again, then withdrew it, dragging it through the damp folds of her flesh one final time before pulling it up over her belly, leaving a slick trail in its wake. Then he cupped her breast in his hand again and tore his lips from hers, bending until he could part his lips over her taut nipple and suck her tender flesh into his mouth. He laved her with the flat of his tongue and teased her with its tip, covering her other breast with sure fingers as he did so, palming her, squeezing her, until her knees threatened to buckle beneath her.

Natalie had moved her hand to his waist, had freed his belt from the buckle and was feverishly working at the zipper of his fly when a shrill, incessant beeping pierced the fragile shell of what little sanity she still claimed. But even that couldn't halt her from her actions, so intent was she on satisfying the roaring conflagration Jack had ignited inside her, and she scooped her hand into his trousers to wrap her fingers around him. But he evidently had a better handle on his emotions—damn him—because before she could even curve her palm completely around him, he pulled his mouth from her breast and jerked his body away from hers, turning so that his back was facing her.

It took Natalie a moment to understand what had happened, and for that moment, she only stood half-naked in her living room, staring at Jack's back and feeling profoundly unfulfilled. But little by little, comprehension chipped away at her delirium, until she saw that he was looking at a little palm-sized device in his hand and swearing with much gusto.

His pager had gone off, she realized then. A little plastic box filled with wires and microchips was the only thing that had prevented them from completing an act they were driven to complete by one of their most basic, most primitive instincts. Ah, the wonders of technology.

Hastily, she wrapped her robe around herself again and belted it, knotting it twice, for good measure. Then she ran her fingers briskly through her damp hair to tidy it as best she could, and she tried to remember what the hell they had been doing when things had gotten so out of hand. Or, rather, so into hand. And so hand into—

Don't think about it, Natalie, she instructed herself. *Because that way lay madness.* And it probably led to something she would have regretted in the morning, too.

Jack continued to stand with his back to her, though he had ceased his colorful swearing. He had also dropped both hands to his hips, but his shoulders rose and fell with his rapid, still ragged, respiration. Natalie decided to wait and take her cue from him, since it had been his pager that had intruded. Surely that's what Emily Post would have considered proper in a situation like…like this. Whatever the proper terminology for *this* was. Although Natalie supposed it wasn't *quite* a case of *coitus interruptus*, their respective coituses—coitusi?— had most definitely been interruptussed, that was for damned sure.

He hesitated another few beats before turning around, and when he did, his expression indicated he was feeling as, oh…*incensed* was as good a word as any, she supposed, especially since it was in keeping with that whole heat thing they'd had going on…as she was about what had happened. But she marveled even more at the state of his clothing, amazed that she had done that to him herself. His shirt was completely unbuttoned, spilling half off of one shoulder, and his belt and fly were both unfastened, his zipper completely down. His hair was a mess, thanks to the way she'd been dragging her fingers through it, and there was a red mark on his neck where she must have nipped him without even realizing it.

And seeing him looking like that only aroused Natalie all over again, because she realized she had been every bit as passionate as he, and she understood just how close they had come to—

Well. The proper term for that escaped her, too. It wouldn't have been making love, in spite of what she'd asked him to do, since love had nothing to do with whatever was burning up the air between them. But having sex didn't seem quite right, either, since that sounded so casual, and there was nothing casual about this—whatever it was— either. *Coitus* was too intellectual a label, *copulation* was too scientific, *fornication* was too puritanical and *intercourse* was too medical. That left only words for the act that weren't uttered in polite company, and all of those were much too coarse for anything she and Jack might do together.

Though when she recalled the way her body had nearly burst into flames when he stroked her and entered her the way he had, she supposed maybe those words were the most appropriate yet.

"I'm sorry," he told her, though she could detect nothing apologetic in his tone. "I have to go. It's kind of an emergency."

Well, she sure hoped so. She would have hated to think he was leaving in the middle of what had promised to be a very nice whatever it was burning up the air between them because his table was available at Outback Steakhouse.

"I understand," she said, even though she really didn't.

"I don't want to leave," he told her.

"I understand," she lied again.

"I want to stay, Natalie."

"I understand."

"Do you?" he asked. And there was something very crucial in his voice now when he spoke.

She nodded.

"Do you *really* understand, Natalie?" he asked further.

She nodded again, but with a bit less conviction this time.

He took a few steps forward, until his body was nearly flush with her own again, but without touching her anywhere. He wanted to touch her, though—she could see that plainly. Maybe even as much as she wanted to touch him. But he didn't. And she didn't, either. She didn't dare. Instead, Jack only fixed his gaze on hers, never once looking away, and she met his gaze levelly, never backing down.

"Because if I stayed here," he said, "you know what would happen, don't you?"

"Yes," she said. Because she knew very well what would have happened. And she would have welcomed it. For tonight, anyway.

"The two of us," he said, "we'd have ended up in your bed."

"Yes," she agreed. "We would have."

"Hot."

"Yes."

"Naked."

"Yes."

"Sweaty."

"Yes."

"Making love."

She said nothing to that, only because she still wasn't sure what label to attach to what they would have done while being hot, naked and sweaty in her bed. Nevertheless, she knew *what* they would have done. And they would have done it all night long. And it would have been phenomenal.

"Natalie?" he said when she didn't reply.

"What?"

"You know we would have ended up in your bed," he repeated.

"Yes," she agreed again. Because even if they wouldn't have started there, even if they'd detoured on several other pieces of furniture along the way—and maybe the floor and a couple of appliances, too—her bed was eventually where they would have finished.

"I'd rather be here with you," he told her flatly. "But I have to go. This…" He held up his pager. "This is the only thing that could make me leave you right now."

She hesitated only a moment before asking, "Will you…" She faltered, then tried again. "If I wait up for you…will you come back?"

He studied her in silence for a moment, his expression one of sheer desire, of stark need, of rabid hunger. "Do you want me to come back?"

"Yes," she said.

He didn't say anything for a moment, then, "How late will you wait up?" he asked.

She hesitated not at all this time when she told him, "All night. I'll wait up all night for you, Jack."

"Natalie…"

He did reach for her then, curling his fingers fiercely around her nape and pulling her toward himself. He crushed her mouth with his, kissing her deeply, fervently, wantonly. She closed her eyes as he plundered her mouth with his, then staggered backward when he released her. When she opened her eyes, he was gone, and she was by herself again. But she felt more alone in that moment than she'd ever felt in her life.

6

NATALIE AWOKE WITH a start on her sofa, only to squeeze
her eyes shut tight again because sunlight was pouring in
through a gap in her living room curtains and falling over
her face. The hand-crocheted throw that was normally
neatly folded over the back of the couch was tangled
around her legs, and the chenille pillow that usually sup-
ported her back when she was sitting was tucked under
her head. She opened her eyes more slowly this time and
glanced around to see what had startled her so, and found
Mojo sitting on the back of the sofa behind her, wearing his
I'm-hungry face. But except for Mojo, she saw as she drove
her gaze around the rest of the room, she was alone.

Jack hadn't come back. Even though she'd waited up all
night for him, just as she'd promised she would. Then
again, she recalled hazily as she pushed herself up to sitting, he hadn't ever really *said* he'd be back, had he? Not
in so many words. But his actions of the night before had
said differently. She remembered that very clearly. If ever
there had been a man who wanted something, it was Jack
last night. He'd wanted Natalie. So why hadn't he returned
for her?

She told herself it must have been because whatever had
called him away hadn't allowed him to. That whatever the
emergency had been, it had lasted all night, was probably
still going on at that very moment, and he just hadn't been

able to get away. Surely that could have been the only thing that would have prevented his return to her. Surely it wasn't because he'd had second thoughts and decided he was better off without her.

Mojo meowed at her then, plaintively, pathetically, as if he hadn't eaten for weeks. The roundness of his outline, however, belied his complaint. Natalie smiled though, and reached up to ruffle his ears. Nice to know there were still some guys you could count on, who acted in predictable ways.

She kicked off the throw and rubbed her arms against the chill morning air that filled the room. After folding up the throw and returning it to its rightful position, she padded barefoot over to the thermostat and nudged it up a few degrees, then made her way to the kitchen to feed Mojo. After donning some pajamas and a warmer robe she returned to the living room, and only then spied the overnight mailer that Jack had brought up to her the night before. During their maneuvers, one of them must have kicked it to the side, because it was stuck half under the side of the couch.

She picked it up, wondering who had been sending her something overnight in the first place. A glance at the return address had her even more puzzled. She hadn't ordered anything from the Victoria's Secret catalog, and certainly nothing that required overnight shipment.

Tearing the express envelope open, she pulled out something wrapped in pink tissue and frowned. She carried it over to the couch and gingerly unfolded the paper, only to find a barely there confection of black lace inside, along with a card. So she opened that, too, and read what it said:

Thought this might come in handy about now. Love, Mrs. K.

Her landlady, Natalie saw, had made good on her promise not to throw her and Jack together in close quarters by inviting them to dinner. But that left the field of, oh…just about everything else…wide open. Clearly Mrs. Kloster-man still intended to get the two of them together. And now she was playing dirty.

What was ironic was that, last night, Natalie and Jack had played dirty all by themselves, and the black lingerie would have been completely unnecessary. Of course, had she opened it right after he left, maybe she could have slipped it on and been wearing it upon his return. But he hadn't returned, she reminded herself ruthlessly. Whatever his emergency had been, it had kept him all night.

She was about to rise from the couch when she heard a sound that seemed to come from downstairs. So she hesi-tated and cocked an ear to see if the sound came again. It did. Footsteps. Jack was home. He hadn't come back to Natalie's as she'd thought he would—as she'd practically begged him to do—even though she had made good on her promise to wait up all night.

So he *did* have second thoughts. He'd thought better of coming back to be with her. She wondered just how bad that was, when a man had an obvious and open invitation to return to a woman's bed specifically to get hot and naked and sweaty—free of charge, no less—and didn't take her up on the offer. Pretty bad, she decided. Clearly he'd just been caught up in the passion of the moment. Once that passion had had a chance to cool, he'd decided it would be a mistake to end up in her bed. So he'd stayed away.

Natalie told herself it was better this way, that it would have been a mistake for her, too, to do something so rash with no promise of any kind of future. Not that she needed the promise of a future to be intimate with a man—well, not a forever after kind of future anyway. But she did want some kind of assurance that being intimate with a man meant the two of them were, you know, *intimate*. In ways other than the sexual. And really, what did she know about Jack? Not much. That he was from Brooklyn originally and had four younger sisters. That he was kind and helpful to old ladies in need. That he was a vegetarian. That he knew a lot about art—he just didn't know what he liked. That he was good at Trivial Pursuit. That he could touch her in ways that made her feel wild and reckless and out of control.

Okay, so maybe she knew quite a bit about him, she conceded. It still wasn't enough to found a relationship on, even one that might not be destined for a happily-ever-after. And she wasn't the type of person to scratch an itch just because it was itchy. She wanted to treat the symptom with a long-term solution. Natalie was a relationship person. Not a one-night-stand person. And Jack, she was certain, wasn't the type to go for the long haul. Maybe it wouldn't have been a one-night stand with him. But it wouldn't have been a forever-after, either. It wouldn't even have been a half-year-after, since he'd only signed on with Mrs. Klosterman for six months.

Yeah, she was definitely better off this morning with things the way they were than she would have been had the two of them succumbed to their impetuous desires the night before.

So why didn't she feel better? she wondered. And why couldn't she stop thinking about their impetuous desires the night before? And why did she want to keep envisioning a different ending for them?

IT WAS JUST past ten o'clock that night, and Natalie was doing her best to read a novel she'd been looking forward to for months, when the phone rang, making her realize she'd been studying the same two pages for nearly a half hour. For one fleeting, hopeful moment, she thought maybe it would be Jack calling, and that he'd tell her he was sorry, he'd been out for the past twenty-four hours, and that was why he hadn't come back to her place, and no, he hadn't been home all day, she must have imagined those sounds she'd heard down in his apartment—hey, hadn't Mrs. K mentioned having gremlins or something?—but now he *was* home, so could he come back up to her place and then they could take up where they'd left off, preferably by taking off all of what they'd had left on?

Okay, so maybe it took more than a moment for her to think all that, and it wasn't such a fleeting thought. She'd still been hopeful. Alas, however, it wasn't Jack calling—it was Mrs. Klosterman. But even at that, Natalie still found herself feeling hopeful, thinking that maybe her landlady would be going back on her word and inviting her to come down for a romantic, prearranged dinner, then disappearing when Natalie got there and leaving Jack in her place. But that hope, too, died when she heard what Mrs. Klosterman had to say.

"*Notorious* is on tonight," her landlady told her. "It starts at ten-thirty on Encore. No commercials. You want to come down? I got some of that Cajun popcorn you like."

Actually, it was Mrs. Klosterman who liked the Cajun popcorn. She just used her tenant as an excuse to buy twice as much of it. Still, Natalie felt grateful for the invitation. It wasn't like she was doing anything else this evening.

"Gee, I've only seen *Notorious* about fifty times," she said. "And it's probably been at least a month since the last time I saw it. Sure. I'll come down. Just let me get dressed. I'm already in my pajamas."

"Oh, don't bother," Mrs. Klosterman told her. "There's no one home but you and me. Jack said he had a late date."

Natalie's smile fell at that, and her heart sank. She told

herself his late date had to have been arranged before the two of them had turned to each other so passionately last night. But then she couldn't help wondering if maybe it had come about *because* of last night. Maybe Jack was deliberately seeking satisfaction from someone else tonight for the desire she'd aroused in him, because he didn't want to get involved with Natalie.

And if that was the case, then it could only be because he knew Natalie was a long-term woman, and he was anything but a long-term man. So, hey, she really was better off today for having not spent the night with him last night, she told herself. Because it would be even worse to be sitting here now, having made love with him, and realize he wasn't interested in anything more than a fling.

Funny, though, how that didn't make her feel better at all.

"Natalie?" she heard Mrs. Klosterman say from the other end of the line. "You still there?"

"Yeah, I'm still here," she said halfheartedly. Where else was she going to be? "I'll be right down."

"SO JACK SAID he had a late date, huh?" Natalie asked as the closing credits for *Notorious* began to scroll down the screen, hoping she sounded nonchalant. "Did he say where he was going?"

"Nope," Mrs. Klosterman said. "But he smelled very nice when he went out."

Natalie nodded. He would smell very nice for a late date. Especially since late dates often led to all-nighters. Not that she cared, mind you. It was Jack's life. He was a grown man. He could do whatever he wanted. Even spend the night with some cheap floozy tart when he could have had Natalie instead. It was no skin off her nose. Nossirree. She'd just find some other way to put that black negligee to use. It would make a great dust rag, for instance. Or maybe she could use it in a collage. Or stuff it with pot-pourri. Or make cat toys out of it for Mojo. Yeah, that's the ticket.

And speaking of that black negligee...

"I forgot to thank you for the gift you sent me," she said to her landlady.

"What gift?" Mrs. Klosterman asked. But her blue eyes were twinkling when she said it.

"The gift from Victoria's Secret," Natalie said anyway. "But I can't imagine what you were thinking to send me such a thing."

"Can't you?"

"No," Natalie replied steadfastly. And then, before she could stop herself, she added, "You should have sent it to whoever Jack went out with tonight."

Mrs. Klosterman's eyes continued to twinkle—damn them—when she said, "Oh, that would be his new friend across the street. And I don't think the nightie would have fit him."

"Him?" Natalie echoed. "Jack's out with a guy? But you told me he had a late date," Natalie objected.

"No, I told you he *said* he had a late date, not that that was what he actually did."

"Then how do you know he's out with a guy and not on a late date?"

"Because I watched him through the curtains after he left," her landlady said matter-of-factly, as if peeking through the curtains at passersby was something she did every day. Which, of course, it was. "And if he'd really had a late date, then he would have driven off in his car to meet a woman. But what he actually did was walk across the street to Millicent Gleason's place."

"Maybe Jack has a late date with Millicent Gleason,"

Natalie suggested, in spite of the fact that Mrs. Gleason was around Mrs. Klosterman's age and opted for the same sort of wardrobe and scary jet-black daddy-longlegs eyelashes, never mind the fact that she also still had Mr. Gleason underfoot.

"Hah. Millicent wishes," Mrs. Klosterman said.

"I'm sorry," Natalie said, "but you still haven't told me how you know Jack is out with a guy."

Her landlady sighed with much gusto, clearly disappointed that Natalie wasn't following along. "Millicent has a new tenant, too," she said. "One who moved in around the same time that Jack moved in here. And I've seen Jack go over there a lot since he moved in here. And I've seen him leave the building with Millicent's new guy. And Millicent says she often hears them talking in her guy's apartment—his name is Donnie something—and sometimes laughing, as if they know each other very well."

Natalie eyed her landlady suspiciously. "Gosh, you and Mrs. Gleason seem to have picked up a new hobby over the last couple of weeks," she said.

Mrs. Klosterman shrugged. "It keeps us off the streets."

"It keeps you watching the streets, you mean."

"We're members of the neighborhood block watch. It's our civic duty."

Not that it was Mrs. Klosterman's or Mrs. Gleason's sense of civic duty that galvanized them into joining the block watch, Natalie knew. No, that would have been their sense of kibitzer duty that made them do that.

"So if Jack's only visiting a friend," Natalie said, "then why would he tell you he has a late date?"

"I have no idea," Mrs. Klosterman said. And then she smiled, as if she knew perfectly well why Jack had told her that, but she wasn't going to spell it out for Natalie.

And Natalie wasn't going to ask her landlady for the

proper arrangement of the alphabet, either. She did have some pride. Somewhere.

"Gee," Mrs. Klosterman began again, "you know, for a minute there, you sounded kind of jealous when you thought Jack was out with another woman."

"I'm not jealous," Natalie denied coolly.

"Of course you're not."

"I'm just curious."

"Of course you are."

And more confused than ever, she thought. Not only had Jack turned down an obvious invitation to enjoy what most men considered exceedingly inviting, but he'd turned it down in favor of an evening out with the guys? Wow. That was *really* insulting.

"So I wonder who this Donnie is that he went out with?" Natalie said, hoping she sounded vaguely interested, thinking she probably sounded profoundly fascinated instead.

"I have no idea," Mrs. Klosterman said. "But that's where Jack went running off to last night, too, after you and he…" She wiggled her white eyebrows playfully.

"After he and I what?" Natalie challenged. "For all you know, we were upstairs playing Parcheesi."

"Oh, is *that* what they're calling hanky-panky now?" her landlady asked. "Honestly, you young people. Always coming up with new slang terms we oldsters can't possibly keep up with."

"Oh, and like 'hanky-panky' is a term that just makes so much more sense," Natalie said.

"Don't try to change the subject," Mrs. Klosterman said.

"I'm not," Natalie denied. "The fact is, there was no 'after you and he' to begin with," she added. "There couldn't be an 'after,' because there was nothing that happened before. No hanky-panky, I mean. Or playing Parcheesi, either," she hastened to say. And she hoped her landlady believed her. Because although she and Jack hadn't technically made love the night before, they had certainly hankied their pankies into an uproar. And their Parcheesis would probably never be the same again.

Mrs. Klosterman's expression softened some, and she made an exasperated sound. "Look, I've done all I know to do to get you two together," she said. She took a breath to say more, but Natalie intercepted.

"But that's just it, Mrs. Klosterman," she said. "There *is* no together for me and Jack."

"How can you say that?" her landlady asked her.

"How can you say otherwise?" Natalie countered.

Now Mrs. Klosterman made a face at her. "It's obvious you two are attracted to each other."

Well, Natalie certainly couldn't deny that, especially after the sparks the two of them had generated last night. "Just because we're attracted to each other doesn't mean—"

"And you're both very nice people," Mrs. Klosterman added. "You'd be great together."

Not that Natalie could deny that, either, but she had a feeling she and her landlady were thinking about two different things when it came to the phrase "great together." Mrs. Klosterman was thinking in terms of couplehood, where Natalie was thinking in terms of coupl*ing*. She didn't doubt for a moment that she and Jack would be great together in bed. Hey, if last night was any indication, they'd be extraordinary together in bed. Astounding. And, quite possibly, illegal in thirty-two states. But in life? Natalie wasn't so convinced they'd be able to sustain much there.

"I'm just not sure," she told her landlady, "that there's enough between him and me to—"

She never finished what she'd started to say, because the front door opened slowly, and then, quietly, Jack came tiptoeing through it, looking as if he were trying not to make a sound, so as not to wake anyone up. He was wearing his black jeans and his black leather biker jacket again, both garments that looked as if they'd seen better days. Natalie and Mrs. Klosterman watched in silence as he very carefully closed the front door, then turned the dead bolt cautiously and spun carefully around...

Only to come to a complete halt when he saw them gazing back at him. His expression was probably the same one fourteen-year-olds wore when they'd just been caught sneaking in at four in the morning after joy-riding in a neighbor's car. But Jack wasn't fourteen years old, and he wasn't accountable to anyone. Least of all Natalie and his landlady. Nevertheless, he looked every inch the guilty party.

"I just remembered someone I have to call," Mrs. Klosterman said by way of a greeting.

Then she switched off the TV and jumped up from the couch to scurry off, leaving Natalie and Jack all alone. And all Natalie could think was that she hoped Mrs. Klosterman's call was long-distance, because it was way too late to be calling anyone locally. Of course, there were other things it wasn't too late for locally....

Jack's greeting was a bit less drawn-out than Mrs. Klosterman's had been, because all he said, very quietly, was, "Natalie."

And there was just something in his voice when he said her name the way he did that stripped away every ounce of self-preservation—and, alas, self-respect—that Natalie possessed. Before she could stop herself, she heard herself say, flat out, "Why didn't you come back last night? I waited up for you like I said I would."

He was across the room in a half dozen long-legged strides, standing before her and looking very chastened indeed. "I wanted to come back," he told her. "But I was out most of the night, Natalie. It was almost dawn by the time I got home. I figured you'd be sleeping by then, and I didn't want to wake you up."

"But all day, today, you were home," she pointed out, "and you still didn't come ba—"

"I was afraid you'd changed your mind," he said before she even finished speaking. With a soft sound of resignation, he sat down on the sofa beside her, but with a good foot of space between them, Natalie noted. Somehow, it didn't seem like a good sign. It seemed like an even worse sign when, as he started speaking again, he was staring straight ahead and not at her.

"Last night," he began slowly, obviously taking care to choose his words, "we were both a little crazy. Stuff just sorta happened without warning. And in the light of day, when you had a chance to think about it, I just figured you'd feel differently than you did last night."

"I don't feel any different," she told him without hesitation. What the hey. She'd already bared her soul to him. Among other things. In for a penny, in for a pound. Whatever the hell that meant.

He turned to look at her then, his gaze fixed intently on hers. "Then you still want to—"

"Yes."

Jack studied Natalie in silence for a moment, wanting nothing more than to sweep her into his arms and carry her up the stairs to his apartment, just like some guy from a paperback romance. But he couldn't quite bring himself to do that. She may not feel differently today, but he sure did. He'd spent the whole day thinking about last night. About the way she had felt when he'd held her, about the way she had looked and smelled and sounded, about the way she'd melted into him and he'd melted into her... God, he hadn't been able to think about anything else.

And it had scared the hell out of him, the way those thoughts—the way *Natalie*—made him feel.

When his pager had sounded the night before, he'd wanted to kill the person responsible for setting it off. But after Jack had a chance to cool down—hours and hours and *hours* later—he'd been grateful to the guy for throwing the brakes on what had almost happened with him and Natalie. Because they'd been so close last night...*so* close. So close to doing something that now, in hindsight, Jack knew would have been a mistake. Not because it wouldn't have been incredible with Natalie, but because he didn't want to be the one to walk away after the two of them made love.

And he had to walk away from Natalie, eventually. Once he finished this job, he was due back in New York for another one. He couldn't stay here. His job—his life—was a thousand miles away. And it didn't include her. It couldn't include her. She wasn't suited to the way things were with him. She was too sweet, too gentle, too decent for that way of life. She belonged here, with a guy who was sweet and gentle and decent, too. And Jack wasn't any of those things.

"But you don't still want to, do you?" he heard her ask, pulling him out of his troubled thoughts. And there was no way to mistake the hurt that punctuated the question.

What was ironic was that he did still want to. He still wanted to real bad. But he couldn't. He couldn't do that to her. And he couldn't do it to himself, either.

"You're the one who's had second thoughts," she said further. "Aren't you?"

"It isn't that," he told her.

"Then what is it?"

He wished he could think of some way to explain it to her. But that was going to be tough, when he couldn't even explain it to himself. So what he settled on was a lame, "The timing's just not right, Natalie, that's all."

She nodded at that, but he could tell she wasn't buying it. She was taking it personally. And that was the last thing he wanted her to do. It wasn't her. It was him. He was about to tell her that, but she intercepted him.

"So in other words, it's not me, it's you," she said, her voice tinged with just a touch of sarcasm now.

Oh, *great*. Now what was he supposed to say? "Really, Natalie, it's—"

"Nothing personal," they said as one.

Jack tried again. "It's just that you really—"

"Deserve better," they chorused again.

So Jack made one last effort to set things right. "But I hope we can still—"

"Be friends," she said along with him.

And if Jack hadn't already felt like a big, fat jerk—and, hey, no worries, there—then that would have definitely cinched it. Obviously, she'd heard this speech before, from some schmuck who had hurt her feelings. Now she was hearing it again. From some schmuck who was hurting her feelings.

Dammit.

"Look, don't worry about it, Jack," she said, sounding tired now more than anything else. "I understand."

The hell she did.

"And I appreciate you being honest with me," she added. "Really, I do."

Even though he wasn't being so much honest as he was being stupid.

"Let's just forget last night ever happened, okay?" she concluded.

Yeah, right, he thought. Like he was going to be able to do that. "Sure," he said anyway. "No problem."

And then a silence descended over them that was more deafening than anything Jack had ever heard in his life. What was really bad, though, was that it was a sound he knew was going to haunt him for a long, long time.

IT WAS ALL NATALIE could do to avoid Jack the following week. She left for work every morning thirty minutes earlier than usual, because she'd run into him too many times on his way out when she left at her regular time. She did all her shopping and errand-running on her way home from school, so that she could be safely ensconced in her apartment before he got home. And she made sure she never wandered out of her apartment whenever she heard Jack moving around downstairs. What was truly demoralizing, though, was that she realized her life wasn't that much different while she was trying to avoid Jack than it had been before he moved in.

She really did need to get out more, she supposed. Mingle. Go places. Meet people.

Honestly, it got to the point that week where she felt like a spy skulking around the house where she'd lived for five years, always peeking around corners before entering a room, and listening in the stairwell before going up or down the steps. At this rate, she was going to end up trying to fashion one of those spy scopes from her childhood out of hand mirrors and rubber bands and paper towel rolls. She just had to let it go.

By Friday, Natalie had had enough. And, as she would soon discover, so had Mrs. Klosterman. Because her landlady, evidently tired of the way Natalie and Jack *both* had been skulking around the house, cornered Natalie in the kitchen that evening.

"What are you doing?" Mrs. Klosterman asked when she found her.

Natalie guiltily slammed shut the drawer she had been rifling through in search of rubber bands. Nervously, she tugged on the hem of her dark green sweater and brushed at some nonexistent lint on her blue jeans. "Nothing," she said.

Mrs. Klosterman eyed her suspiciously. "I'm missing some paper towels from the pantry. You wouldn't know what happened to them, would you?"

Natalie shook her head. "Nope. Not me. Nuh-uh."

The other woman settled her hands on her hips and Natalie noticed that not only was she wearing her good red coat, obviously in preparation for going out somewhere, but she was holding a padded overnight mailer in one hand. A chill went down Natalie's spine when she saw it.

"I need for you to take this up to Jack," Mrs. Klosterman said, holding the mailer out to her.

"What, did you order him a black lace nightie, too?" Natalie asked.

Mrs. Klosterman shook her head. "No, it's one of those G-string things with an elephant head on it. He can tuck his…you know…into the trunk. I got a large. I hope it's big enough."

First, Natalie's mouth dropped open, then her eyes squeezed shut. You could just never really tell with Mrs. Klosterman. "You didn't," she finally said.

"No, I didn't," her landlady told her. "But I was tempted. It's actually a very nice pipe wrench I ordered from the Sears catalog. Jack mentioned needing one that day he was working on my kitchen drain. I figured buying him one was the least I could do to return the favor."

Natalie opened her eyes again and studied her landlady. She tilted her head to the side and saw that the return address on the envelope was indeed Sears. And she was pretty sure Sears didn't sell those elephant G-strings. So, probably, the other woman was telling the truth. Probably.

Mrs. Klosterman shoved the package forward again. "Take this up to Jack," she said insistently.

"Why?" Natalie asked.

"Because he's in the shower," her landlady told her, as if that made perfect sense, because everyone knew you had to have a very nice pipe wrench whenever you took a shower. "I just heard the water switch on," she added. "So you need to take this up to him. Now."

"Oh, no," Natalie said, shaking her head vehemently. "I'm not going to fall for that one. No way."

"Fall for it?" Mrs. Klosterman said. "What are you talking about? I'm not trying to fool you. I told you flat out what I'm doing. I ordered this on purpose, had it over-nighted on purpose, so it would arrive separate from the other mail on purpose. I waited until I heard the water kick on in Jack's apartment, and then I came looking for you. Now I'm telling you to take this upstairs to him so that when you knock on his door, he'll have to get out of the shower to answer it. And he'll be all wet and half naked, just like you were that time I sent him up to your place after I heard your shower kick on. And then, when he sees you standing there, nature can take its course."

Natalie gaped at her landlady. She couldn't believe Mrs. Klosterman was admitting to all this.

"Except that this time, nature won't get beeped," her landlady added. "Because I took the batteries out of Jack's pager."

"Mrs. Klosterman!" Natalie cried. "What if there's an emergency?"

"Oh, please," the other woman said. "He's not an ER surgeon, and he's not working for peace in the Middle East. Therefore, there is no greater emergency he needs to see to than the two of you getting together. It's ridiculous the way you two have been dancing around each other for the past few weeks. Now it's time you danced together. Preferably doing the horizontal boogaloo."

"Mrs. Klosterman!"

"I'm going out," Mrs. Klosterman said. "I have my bunco club tonight, and we're meeting at Aloe Morton's place. Aloe and I go way back, so I've finagled an invitation to spend the night with her. I won't be home until lunchtime tomorrow, Natalie," she added meaningfully. "Which means you and Jack can make all the noise you want, and nobody will hear."

And with that, she thrust the padded mailer out to Natalie again, more forcefully than ever. When Natalie still declined to take it from her, Mrs. Klosterman began to bang on Natalie's upper arm with it.

"Ow," Natalie said. Yep, it definitely felt like a very nice pipe wrench in there. No soft, elephant head G-string, that was for sure.

"Take it," her landlady ordered her. "Now."

Natalie did as she was told, holding the mailer out at arm's length, as if it were a bleeding spleen.

"Now take it upstairs to Jack," Mrs. Klosterman commanded.

"Yes, ma'am," Natalie replied as she spun around to do just that.

"And, Natalie," Mrs. Klosterman called out as she made her way to the kitchen door.

Natalie turned around. "Yes?"

Mrs. Klosterman smiled. "Have a nice time, dear. I'll see you tomorrow."

7

AS SHE CLIMBED THE stairs to Jack's apartment, Natalie told herself to just set the mailer against his front door and leave it there, then ring the doorbell and run. But then she remembered that she was a grown woman. A grown woman who did not need to be fashioning spy scopes out of rubber bands and hand mirrors and paper towel tubes. Not only would she return Mrs. Klosterman's two rolls of Bounty in the morning, but she would knock on Jack's door tonight. She would get him out of the shower all naked and wet and hot and naked and wet and hot and naked and wet and hot and naked and wet and hot and—

Oops. Her mind got stuck there for a minute.

Anyway, she would knock on Jack's door tonight, and she would get him out of the shower all...you know...and she would be mature about it. She would be totally unfazed. She would be cool, calm and collected. She would hand him his mail, and he would thank her, and then she would turn around and march upstairs and forget all about seeing him all...you know. And then she would stop skulking around her own home and get on with her life.

Squaring her shoulders, Natalie made a fist and knocked. *Rap. Rap, rap. Rap, rap, rap.* And then she waited. She shook out her hair and brushed a hand down over her clothes again because she was incredibly nervous, and she waited. Then she tucked an errant strand of hair behind one ear and shifted the mailer from one hand to the other because she was incredibly nervous, and she waited. Then she listened at the front door for the water to shut off and waited.

Okay. So being an adult was going to have a wait a few more minutes.

This time Natalie rang the doorbell. *Buzz. Buzz, buzz. Buzz, buzz, buzz.* That, finally, seemed to do the trick, because she did hear the water shut off then. Then she heard heavy footsteps padding across the floor. Then she heard a mildly irritated male voice say, "Who is it?"

"It's Natalie," she said. "Mrs. Klosterman asked me to bring something up for you."

She wasn't sure, but she thought the irritated male voice sounded even more irritated when it said what it did next, which was pretty much one of those bathroom wall words that she'd been reluctant to use for whatever it was burning up the air between her and Jack. She told herself it *wasn't* an invitation—or even a command, more was the pity—and steeled herself to see him, knowing that particular word was never going to happen for them.

"Is what you have for me mail?" he asked through the door.

"Yep," Natalie told him.

"Did it come overnight, separate from the other mail?"

"I'm afraid so."

He said that word again, louder this time, and Natalie tried not to get her hopes up.

"Come on, Jack," she coaxed. "Be a man about it, for God's sake. I answered the door when you brought my mail to me."

"No, you didn't," he said, still speaking through the door. "It was already open. And only because you didn't know it was going to be me."

"A minor detail," she told him. When he offered nothing in reply—and still didn't open the door—she cajoled, "You can run, Jack, but you can't hide. We might as well get this over with, because she's not going to knock it off until we prove to her that nothing will come of her machinations."

She heard him blow out a long, perturbed sound, then heard the thump of the dead bolt and the rattle of the doorknob. And then the door opened, and Jack stood on the other side.

All naked and wet and hot and…

Wow.

Then she realized he wasn't quite naked. He was *half*-naked. A navy blue towel was slung around his waist, knotted at one hip, and hanging down to just above the knee. He was, however, wet, deliciously so, and she could almost feel the steam emanating off of him. He smelled clean and damp and masculine, and Natalie watched, fascinated, as a single droplet of water tumbled from his broad shoulder and wound slowly down his chest, spiraling leisurely through the swirls of dark hair, exiting above his flat torso and taking a new route, circling around his dusky navel, through more dark hair, before finally ending its journey in the dark fabric of the towel.

And suddenly, Natalie felt hot and wet, too, and she wanted very badly to be naked.

So she jerked her gaze back up again, making herself look at Jack's face. But that was no help at all, because he was looking at her much as he had that night in her apartment, just before he'd reached for her and pulled her to himself.

Remembering the padded mailer, she thrust it toward him and said, "You've got skin."

"We need to talk," he said.

Which was odd, because talking was the last thing Natalie wanted to do just then.

"You better come in," he added, stepping aside.

She told herself to decline the invitation, to just throw the mailer into his living room then turn and run screaming like a ninny back to her apartment. But there was something in Jack's voice, and something in his eyes, and something in his stance—and, okay, something in his towel, too, she conceded—that prevented her from doing so. More important, there was something in *her* that prevented her from doing so. Instead, she forced her feet forward, being careful not to touch him as she strode past him, and looked at everything in the room except Jack.

Unlike Natalie's apartment, this one came furnished to the renter, which was probably another reason why there was such a high turnaround for it. People who rented this apartment were short-termers, between jobs or working here temporarily, or living here until they could afford a larger place with their own stuff. Still, Mrs. Klosterman had furnished it nicely, with solid, comfortable furniture in neutral colors. Plain cotton rugs in more neutrals covered much of the hardwood floors, and built-in shelves housed an eclectic assortment of books. The kitchen was smaller than Natalie's, and a breakfast set situated near one window constituted the dining room. The bedroom, Natalie knew, because she'd visited this apartment before when other renters had claimed it, lay beyond the living room and to the left, in the turret of the old house. It was just big enough for the bed and antique armoire that filled it.

All in all, it was a small, but comfortable apartment, made more so by Mrs. Klosterman's things. Still, it would have been nice to see a few personal touches, she thought. Something that might tell her a little bit more about Jack as a man. She made one final, quick survey of the room, searching for something along those lines, anything that might give her some small peek into his character.

And that was when she saw the gun.

It was holstered, hanging over the back of a wing chair in the living room, as if that were the most natural place in the world for it to be. A revolver, she saw, even though her knowledge of firearms was limited, to say the least. It was black and heavy-looking and ugly, and its significance was even uglier. She could only think of two kinds of people who carried handguns, and neither of them worked in advertising: cops and criminals. So which one was Jack?

The former, she hoped. But she couldn't quite quell the ripple of doubt that crept into her brain about the latter. Her head snapped back around, until she could look at Jack's face. But he was too busy shutting the door to have noticed where she was looking. Shutting the door, she saw, and locking it. And then turning to face her with his big body between her and it. And suddenly, he seemed even bigger than he had before. Stronger. More powerful. More potent.

More dangerous?

And that was when Natalie decided she couldn't be an adult about this, after all. Gosh, she would have liked to, really she would, but the gun thing on top of the towel thing—not to mention the water streaming over the chest thing—had her emotions in an uproar, and she just wasn't feeling especially mature at the moment. Sorry about that, thanks for playing, but if Jack didn't mind, she'd just go screaming like a ninny back to her apartment now.

Instead of telling him that, though, Natalie heard herself say, "Is that a gun over there, or are you just happy to see me?"

Jack's eyes widened in panic at the question, and he glanced over to where the weapon lay in full view of anyone who happened to be making a casual survey of the apartment to see if there were any personal effects that might reveal something personal about the occupant, and wow, there's a gun, which says quite a lot about the occupant, now that you mention it.

"Uh, yeah, that's a gun," he said when his gaze flew back to connect with hers. "And yeah, I'm happy to see you. Really happy, Natalie," he added. "I've been thinking about you a lot this week."

Translation, she thought, *We're not going to talk about the gun.*

"But," she began, lifting her hand to point to the weapon. Not to put too fine a point on it, but it *did* seem rather like a matter they should address. "But you have a—"

"A crush on you, yeah," Jack said, interrupting her. "I guess that's pretty obvious, huh?"

Oh, no, she thought. She was *not* going to get sidetracked like that. She was *not* going to let him sweet-talk her out of addressing the matter of the—

"Crush?" she echoed plaintively. "Really? You have a crush? On...on *me?*"

He nodded and took a step forward. "You're in my head all the time lately. Ever since last weekend, when we almost…"

Oh, yeah, Natalie recalled. Last weekend, when they almost made love, and she asked him to come back, and then he stood her up. *Get your head on straight, Natalie,* she instructed herself. *Don't be swayed by a man just because he's all hot and naked and wet and wow. He's also got a gun.*

Inevitably, her gaze fell to the towel knotted loosely around his waist, and she realized that yes, indeed, he did have a gun. And it was more than half-cocked.

"I gotta go," she said hastily. "Here's your mail," she added when she remembered that, holding it out to him. Then she added, in case she forgot to tell him, "I gotta go. Now."

But Jack didn't move. He didn't step aside so that she

could open the door herself, and he didn't take the package from her, which, naturally, made her think about his package again, which, naturally, made her reluctant to leave. Until she remembered the gun. The one that was hung…uh, the one that wasn't half-cocked. The other gun. The one that wasn't part of Jack's package.

Oh, hell…

She tossed his package…ah, his tool…ah, the thing Mrs. Klosterman had asked her to bring up to him, onto a table near the front door, then took a step forward, which she hoped he would realize meant she intended to leave. But still Jack remained rooted…ah, still he stood firm…ah, still he didn't move aside.

So Natalie said, "Jack? Would you mind?" She couldn't make herself look at him, though, because she was afraid if she saw that look on his face again, the one that was so hungry and needy and fierce, all of her resolve would dissolve.

He didn't say anything for a moment, as if he were silently willing her to look up at him. Natalie, though, kept her gaze fixed on his chest—his naked and wet and hot chest—and tried not to think about anything except being on the other side of that door.

Then, finally, she heard him reply, "Would I mind what?"

She licked her lips, swallowed with some difficulty and repeated, "Would you mind…you know…stepping aside so I can leave?"

He seemed to give her question a lot more thought than it actually required, because it took him another moment or two to reply. When he did, though, he seemed to have made a decision. It just wasn't the one Natalie had anticipated.

"Yeah, I think I would mind stepping aside so you can leave," he told her. "In fact, I think I'd mind that a lot."

She did make herself look at him then, her gaze connecting with his really for the first time since she'd entered his apartment to find him standing there in little more than a towel and a few dribbles of water. A few, very sexy, dribbles of water. But she said nothing in response to his statement, only wondered what it meant, and feared she already knew.

"I don't think I want you to leave, Natalie," he told her, his voice a velvety purr.

He lifted his hand to her shoulder, dipping his fingers beneath a shaft of her hair to lift it away from her. Slowly, he began winding it around his middle and index fingers, his hand nearing her face with every circular motion. Then his fingers were brushing against her jaw, and his palm was cupping her cheek, and he was dipping his forehead to press it against hers. His skin was warm and damp from the shower, and Natalie grew more than a little warm and damp in response. Except that it wasn't just her forehead responding that way.

"In fact," he added, his voice dropping to an even lower, even silkier pitch, "I think it would be a big mistake for you to leave."

Natalie's heart began hammering hard in her chest, rushing blood through her body at a rate that made her dizzy. Or maybe it was just Jack's nearly naked body making her feel that way. Or maybe it was her own desire to touch his nearly naked body. "Wh-why do you say that?" she asked.

He lifted his other hand to her face now, curving his warm, rough fingers over her jaw on the other side, then began to stroke her cheeks gently with both thumbs. Natalie's eyes fluttered shut as wave after wave of longing purled through her. And before she even realized she was doing it, she lifted her own hands to circle them around his wrists. But she didn't try to pull his hands away. No, she only wanted to be a part of the fiery current arcing between them.

"Because I think," Jack said, "you should stay here with me tonight. All night."

"But you have a gun…" she objected again, halfheartedly this time.

"Yeah, I do," he said. "For protection, that's all. It's no big deal. And, in case you were wondering, I have, you know, protection, too." He dipped his head again and brushed a featherlight kiss across her cheek. Then he moved his mouth close to her ear and whispered softly, "So stay with me, Natalie. Spend the night with me. Let me make love to you. Don't go."

The flame that had flickered to life inside her blossomed into full fire at his quietly uttered declaration, and she remembered how good it felt to be with a man. It had been too long since she'd wanted someone the way she wanted Jack, too long since she had been wanted in such a way herself. And then she stopped kidding herself and made herself admit that she'd never wanted anyone the way she wanted Jack. Because he made her feel things she'd never felt before. She didn't know why that was true, only that it was. And she couldn't help wondering if he felt that way about her, too.

And then she decided not to question it. Any of it. He must feel something for her, otherwise he wouldn't be asking her to stay with him. And all the rest of it, her doubts, her fears, her worries, all of that, she somehow knew then, would work itself out, make itself clear. But what really made Natalie capitulate was the fact that she wanted very, *very* much to stay here with him tonight. All night. She wanted to make love to Jack, too. She just wished she knew what would happen after they woke up in the morning.

"Don't go, Natalie," he said again.

And her own voice came to her, from a place she scarcely recognized, replying, "I won't."

Because Jack's softly uttered petition made Natalie forget about everything else. Gone were her misgivings about what kind of man he was. Gone was her fear that he would only be in her life temporarily. Gone was her worry that his feelings for her might not mirror her feelings for him. But how long those things would stay gone…

Well, that was something she chose not to think about right now, either.

She honestly wasn't sure how they ended up in Jack's bedroom. She only knew that one moment the two of them were standing at the front door talking in low tones, and the next moment, she was standing beside him in his room pondering a slice of silver moonlight that fell across his unmade bed. Silence enveloped them, save the quiet murmur of their individual breathing, which mingled and became one psalm.

And then Jack kissed her, and even that soft sound faded away. His lips on hers were sweet and gentle—more loving than passionate, more persuasive than demanding. He kissed her mouth, her jaw, her cheek, her temple. Then he bent and pressed his forehead to hers again, as he had at the front door, and the gesture was all the more endearing to her for being repeated. Then he drew her into his arms and held her close, bunching her hair in one hand again, stroking her back with the other. For a long time he only held her, just kissing her and kissing her and kissing her. The heat in Natalie's belly grew hotter, building to a fire whose flames licked at her heart. She lifted her hands to his bare chest, her fingers curling into the dark hair she discovered there, and silently begged him to pull her closer still.

He smelled wonderful, she thought vaguely as she tilted her head to the side, slanting her mouth more completely over his. So clean and musky and masculine. She traced her fingers along the strong column of his throat, loving the rough feel of the skin she encountered. Dipping her hand lower, she skimmed her fingertips over his collarbone and back up again, curving her hand around his nape. Then she tugged her mouth free from his, pushed herself up on tiptoe and buried her face in the warm, fragrant skin that joined his neck to his shoulder. The skin of his throat was warm and rough and salty, and she flicked the tip of her tongue over his neck to savor him a second time. The taste of him on her mouth sent a shiver of delight shimmying through her, and she couldn't help wondering if he tasted that good all over. Instinctively, she dropped her hand to the knot in his towel, but hesitated before loosing it completely.

Jack stilled when he realized where her hand had fallen, his hands settled on her hips by now. When Natalie glanced up at his face, she saw a man highly aroused. Perhaps almost as aroused as she.

"Do it," he said, his voice gruff, almost fierce.

But still, Natalie hesitated. It had just been so long…

"Then I'll do you," he told her quietly, seeming to understand.

She closed her eyes as he moved his hands to the hem of her sweater, but she lifted her arms as he began to draw it up over her torso, her breasts, her shoulders, her head. When her hair cascaded down over her face as he divested her of the garment completely, Jack's fingers joined hers in pushing it away again, back over her shoulders. But his hands lingered, tripping lightly over her skin, until his thumbs burrowed deftly beneath the straps of her brassiere. He lifted first one, then the other, nudging the thin bands of elastic over her shoulders, then farther, dragging them over her arms.

Automatically Natalie crossed her arms over her breasts in a misplaced act of modesty, preventing her bra from falling away completely. So Jack released the straps, but curled his fingers loosely and brushed the backs of his knuckles over the tops of her breasts. Back and forth, he skimmed them, each stroke moving his hands lower, until he wove his fingers with hers and urged her hands away. Feeling a bit bolder then, Natalie reached behind herself to unhook her bra, hesitating only a moment before allowing the wisp of white lace to fall away. For a moment, Jack did nothing, only gazed first at her bare breasts, then back up at her face. Then he smiled and lifted his hands again, cupping one over each breast—thoroughly, completely.

And then he bent his head to taste her.

The sensation was quite lovely. Natalie squeezed her eyes shut tight and enjoyed the ripple of heat that wound through her when she felt his lips moving reverently over her tender flesh. Then he opened his mouth over her more fully, and he drew the dusky peak of her breast deep inside, flattening his tongue against it. She buried her fingers in his hair to urge him closer, gasping when he nipped her playfully with his teeth. Immediately he laved the place he had gently wounded, then tugged her deep into his mouth again. For long moments, he so favored her, first one breast, then the other, until he dropped his hands to the waistband of her jeans.

He pushed the button through its hole, then slowly, slowly, oh…so slowly, he drew down the zipper, pushing aside the folds of denim, dipping his hand inside the heavy fabric to explore her own folds more explicitly. Natalie gasped at the intimate touch, the simmering heat inside her exploding into a white-hot rush. Again and again he pushed his fingers against her, tilling her sensitive flesh until Natalie began bucking her hips against his hand. Her fingers circled his ample biceps, gripping his bare arms with a fierceness that reflected the storm that was raging inside her. She felt Jack penetrate her with one finger, then two, and she heard his breath coming in gasps as ragged as her own. She was about to go over the edge, but he must have sensed that, because he withdrew his hand from her panties before she lost herself completely. He didn't go far, though, only moved both of his hands to her bare back and scooped them down into her jeans again, this time to cradle her bare bottom.

As he pulled her body forward, he leaned into her, until his pelvis was pressed hard to hers. She felt him against her, swollen and solid and ready, and she gasped to realize just how far things had gone. She wanted him now, here, like this, standing, or even to couple with him like an animal on the floor. She just wasn't sure she could make it to the bed at this point. But Jack seemed to have other ideas, because he dipped his forehead to hers again, his breathing slower now, as if he were trying to concentrate.

"The towel, Natalie," he said roughly. "Take it off."

She could no more ignore the request than she could have stopped the sun from rising in the morning. Gingerly, she lifted a hand to the terry cloth bunched at his waist, skimming her fingers along the damp fabric from one hip to the other before pausing at the tuck on one side. She glanced up at his face one last time, to give him one last chance to keep this from happening, since he was the one who'd had second thoughts about it before. His dark eyes held hers, and he nodded, and with one swift, deft maneuver, Natalie freed the towel from him completely.

She gazed at all of him after performing the task, studied each part of him, marveled at the magnificence of his body. His arms were truly things of beauty, roped with sinew and corded with veins. His chest and torso were a symphony of muscle and dark hair, his legs brawny, vibrant, powerful.

He could overpower her if he wanted to, she thought, crush her with his bare hands. Or he could touch her and caress her as he would a delicate violin. The thought that he could be so rough, and the knowledge that he would be so gentle, just made her want him all the more.

Her gaze roved hungrily over him again, traveled the length of him from head to toe, lingering at his midsection to study the full, ah…potential of his, ah…masculinity.

"Oh, my," she whispered with a reverent little smile before lifting her gaze to meet his again.

Jack smiled back. "Not yet, I'm not. But I'll be yours whenever you're ready."

"I'm ready," she replied immediately, knowing it was a lie. She could never be ready for a man like him.

But she couldn't tolerate the distance between them any longer, either. She wanted to touch him, wanted to be touched by him. Wanted to feel him inside her, his body rocking against hers in the most primitive, most basic, most intimate way. The press of his body against hers now was like something she had only dreamed about before. She had forgotten what it was like to be this physically close to a man, had forgotten how being physical with a man could make her feel—safe and secure, beautiful and loved. Even if those feelings never lasted for very long.

She wasn't thinking about that, though, as they fell backward onto the bed, because Jack was hot and hard and heavy atop her, and Natalie was consumed by a need that very nearly overwhelmed her. A need for him. For Jack. No one else would do.

He rolled onto his back, pulling her with him until she lay draped over his torso, wrapping his arms around her waist—fiercely, as if he still feared she intended to leave. Then he kissed her again, grazing one hand down the expanse of her bare back to settle it securely on her bottom, looping a long leg over her calf. Natalie tangled the fingers of one hand in the coarse hair scattered across his chest, trailing the fingers of the other down over his abdomen until she found the part of him that had so intrigued her. Cradling him in her hand, she let her fingers explore him, skimming down the full length of him and back again.

Jack growled almost ferally as Natalie touched him, still not sure how or why this was happening, but helpless to make it stop. Mostly because he didn't want it to stop. He'd never in his life experienced the overpowering response to a woman that Natalie had commanded, virtually since the moment he'd laid eyes on her. He should have seen this coming from a mile away, should have realized that first day that his preoccupation with her would inevitably lead them to bed. But he hadn't seen her coming. And he didn't know where either one of them would go after this. He only knew he wanted Natalie, and Natalie wanted him, and there was no reason why the two of them shouldn't enjoy each other for as long as that wanting lasted.

She continued to stroke him, deftly, maddeningly, until he was afraid he wouldn't be able to last any longer. Then he reached down to circle her wrist with sure fingers, and guided her hand back up over his belly and chest, holding it to his mouth so that he could place a soft kiss in the center of her palm. In response to her curious gaze, he only smiled, then settled both hands firmly on her hips and drew her up to sitting, so that she was straddling his waist. Then he cupped his hands under her buttocks and, with a soft nudge, urged her forward more.

She moved her body accordingly, but still obviously wasn't sure what his intentions were. Not until Jack had prompted her up to his shoulders, where her eyes went wide in something he thought might be panic. Nevertheless, she rose up on her knees and arched her back to give him fuller access to the prize he sought. When Jack tasted her the first time, she sucked in her breath as if fearful of drowning. When he tasted her a second time, she exhaled in a rush of pleasure. When he tasted her a third time, she moaned out loud, her body arching harder against him. Finally, though, she stilled and let him enjoy her.

For a long time, Jack did just that, loving the way she responded to every caress of his tongue. She was wild. She was wanton. She was beautiful. But then she was moving away from him, scooting back down the length of his body until the solid reminder of his desire for her halted her. Reaching behind herself, she curled her fingers firmly around him, and began to guide him toward the heated heart of herself.

Before she could join herself with him, however, Jack rolled again, shifting their positions so that she lay with her head on the pillow, her dark hair tumbling about her face making her look even wilder and more wanton than before. He wanted to be close to her when he entered her, wanted every part of his body to be touching every part of hers. He didn't want to know where his body ended and hers began. He wanted them to be one.

And that should have scared the hell out of him. Funny thing, though. It made him feel good. Better than he could ever remember feeling before. There was one thing, however, he did remember. He remembered he needed to protect them both, so that they could go on feeling this way for a long, long time.

When he was properly sheathed, Natalie wrapped the fingers of both hands around him and guided him toward the heated center of her, bending her legs and pushing her pelvis upward as she welcomed him inside. Then she looped her arms around his waist and arched her back, urging him deeper, so that Jack could only close his eyes and forget about everything except the way it felt to be with Natalie. He withdrew from her only long enough to drive himself more completely into her, repeating the action again…and again…and again…until Natalie, too, captured the rhythm and joined in the dance.

And as their lovemaking grew more furious, a frenzied sort of fever nearly swamped Jack. Farther and farther he drove himself, losing a little more of himself to Natalie with each frantic thrust. And then he did lose himself, utterly and completely, free-falling in the gale of completion that stormed around him. And then he landed, back on his bed, panting for breath. His damp cheek was pressed to Natalie's, her arms were draped weakly over his back. Her hair was tangled in his hands, and her legs were entwined with his. Her chest rose and fell in rhythm with his own, and her heartbeat buffeted madly against his.

He had gotten what he wanted, he realized vaguely. The two of them felt like one.

8

NATALIE AWOKE SLOWLY the following morning, absorbing her surroundings bit by bit. Her bed was as warm and cozy as ever—even warmer and cozier somehow, really—and her pillow was stuffed comfortably beneath her head the way it always was whenever she woke up. The faint patter of rain skipped over her window and tapped on the metal fire escape outside in a way that she had always loved hearing. Mojo was snuggled against her as he was every morning, stretched from the tips of her toes to the crown of her head, his big, heavy paw cupped lovingly over her breast and—

And that wasn't Mojo snuggled against her.

Her eyes snapped open at the realization, and she saw that not only was it not Mojo snuggling against her, but she wasn't in her own bed, either. The window against which the rain was pattering was covered by plain white Venetian blinds instead of the rose-printed chintz curtains that adorned her own. The sheets were also plain and white, percale instead of the soft flannel printed with snowflakes or cartoon mooses that she preferred once the weather turned cool. As for her mistake about her cat...

She braved a glance downward and saw a sturdy, muscular arm draped over her waist, the elbow bent and braced against the mattress, the broad hand at the end nestled lovingly under the curve of her breast.

Nope, that definitely wasn't Mojo. Last time she'd checked, he didn't have opposable thumbs.

She remembered then what had happened the night before, how she had been suckered into coming to Jack's apartment the way he had been suckered into coming to hers a few nights before, and how he had answered the front door dressed—or rather, undressed—in much the same way Natalie had been dressed—or rather, undressed—the same evening. And she remembered how neither one of them had been able to resist each other in such a state the second time. If only Natalie had had a pager, too, she thought. Then again, after the way they were last night, a whole herd of stampeding pagers probably couldn't have kept them from doing what they wanted to do.

And now here it was, the dreaded morning after. And just like in the clichés, she had no idea what to say or do. Because she had no idea how she felt, she realized. Or maybe it was just that she didn't want to think about how she was feeling right now. Because if she thought about how she was feeling, then she'd probably figure out how she was feeling—she was an educated woman, after all—and she really didn't think she wanted to know that just yet. Maybe not ever. It depended on what Jack said when it came to clichés.

Jack, she thought again. Oh, Jack. She closed her eyes again and just enjoyed the feel of him behind her, his naked body spooned against hers, touching literally from head to toe. The hand on her breast was relaxed, but still managed to feel possessive, and her head was tucked beneath his chin, so that his warm exhalations stirred her hair. When she held her breath, she could feel his heartbeat thumping against her back, slow and steady, as if he hadn't a care in the world. She wondered if he was smiling in his sleep, and found herself smiling at the very idea.

Or maybe she was just smiling because she felt so good in that moment. It was cold and rainy outside, but warm and snuggly inside. It was Saturday—*Yay, there's no school today!*—and she didn't have to be anywhere until…oh, forever. Because that was how it felt just then. As if she'd never have to do anything or be anywhere again, except lying in Jack Miller's arms for the rest of her life. And the thought of that made her happier still.

Which maybe told her everything she needed to know about how she was feeling. And that left her with nothing to think about except to wonder if Jack's feelings were anything like her own. And she *really* didn't want to think about that.

She must have been thinking louder than she realized, because he began to stir then. She thought about pretending to still be asleep, thereby avoiding any conversation that might lead to thoughts about feelings, or, worse, *words* about feelings. But there was no point in pretending to still be asleep, because sooner or later, she was going to have to open her eyes. She had to eat, after all. Not that she ate with her eyes, but they did help her find the foods she enjoyed putting into her open mouth.

Boy, she was really stretching for things to think about, to avoid thinking about her feelings for Jack.

He woke even more gradually than she had, she noticed, first breathing deeply and exhaling the breath on a long, lusty sigh. Then he *slooooooowly* stretched, starting with the hand at her breast, which clasped over her more intimately. And then his arm, which, enfolded her more familiarly, pulling her body even closer to his. And then his legs, one of which wrapped itself over hers, as if he wanted to anchor her in place with her body pressed to his and never let her go. And then his…

Wow. She hadn't realized men could stretch that, too.

She felt him moving his head then, and he dipped it into the hollow of her neck to brush warm kisses along the slender column of her throat. Natalie's heart raced wildly at the contact, her skin hot and vital beneath his touch. She reached behind herself, tangling her fingers in his hair, and turned her head in a silent bid for his mouth upon hers. He responded enthusiastically, turning her body as he kissed her until she lay flat upon her back and he was braced on his elbows atop her. He continued to kiss her like that, again and again and again, his stiff shaft pressing against her belly, the friction of their writhing bodies making him thicker still. Natalie reached down between them and cupped her palm over him, finding him damp and ready for her. Without thinking, she hitched up her hips and guided him into herself, sighing in contentment as he filled her.

His mouth never left hers as he pumped himself inside her, slow at first, then faster, harder, until his hips were grinding against hers. She wrapped her arms around his back and her legs around his waist and bucked against him, her mouth clinging to his, their tongues tangled together, until they were penetrating each other as deeply as they could. It was over more quickly this time, but was no less satisfying. In some ways, Natalie enjoyed it even more than that languid second time in the darkest hours of the night.

Jack collapsed against her, his naked body slick with perspiration, rolling until he was on his back this time, and she lay sprawled atop him. She bent her arm across his chest and settled her chin on her hand, and she looked at his face, his devilish, handsome face, and wondered how on earth she had gotten so lucky.

"I could definitely get used to waking up like this," she murmured softly when she found her voice again.

He lifted a hand to her hair, brushing an errant strand

back behind her ear. With his other hand, he reached down until he found hers, then linked their fingers together. His dark eyes met hers, and somehow she got the impression that he wanted to tell her something. Something very important. Something very serious. Something she couldn't help thinking she might not want to hear him say.

And before she could stop herself, she heard herself talking instead, telling him, "I have to ask you something really important, something really serious, something I maybe don't want to know the answer to. But I'm going to ask you anyway, and you have to promise you'll be honest with me when you answer."

Jack looked at Natalie and tried to remember just when everything between them had shifted. But he couldn't. Maybe there wasn't an exact moment when that had happened, when they'd gone from being attracted to each other to needing each other. Maybe it had been there all along, dormant, waiting for the right moment to appear. Maybe it had been there before they even met, he thought further. Because somehow, this morning, he felt as if he'd known her a lot longer than the short time he'd been in residence here. Hell, in some ways, it felt like he'd known her forever.

And he wanted to keep knowing her forever, he thought. Which could potentially present a problem. Another problem, he added to himself. So he might as well just toss it onto the pile with the rest of them.

And now Natalie wanted to ask him something, a question to which she feared receiving an honest answer. But she was going to ask it anyway, because it was important, and it was serious. Jack steeled himself for the worst. What was it going to be? he wondered. What did she want to know? Was he married? Had he ever had any sexually transmitted diseases? What was the capital of Albania? As long as it wasn't that last one, he figured he was okay. Because the answers to the first two questions were a solid no. That last one, though…

When Natalie inhaled a deep breath, Jack did, too, and he held it in anticipation.

And then she said, so quickly that it almost sounded like one long word, "You're-not-a-hit-man-for-the-Mob-are-you?"

The question hit him like a ton of cement overshoes, leaving him so surprised, he felt light-headed. Then he realized it wasn't that the question had been so surprising it made him light-headed, it was that the question was so surprising he forgot to breathe, and *that* made him light-headed. So he exhaled on a long whoosh of air…and a few nervous chuckles. Gradually, though, the chuckles turned into laughter. And then the laughter became great, walloping hilarity that nearly had him doubling over into a riotous bundle of mirth—even though *mirth* was one of those words he normally, manfully, avoided.

"A hit man for the Mob?" he repeated incredulously between guffaws. "Me?"

Natalie sat up in bed, but she pulled the sheet with her, anxiously wrapping it around herself. The fact that she suddenly felt the urge to modestly cover herself, after the indecent way they'd coupled only moments before, told Jack he really shouldn't be laughing, and that this was indeed important. So he swallowed his laughter as he sat up, too. The sheet dipped low on his waist, but he didn't care. He didn't have anything to hide. Not from Natalie.

She nodded nervously in response to his reply, but she didn't back down. "Yeah. A hit man for the Mob. You."

Oh, man, she was serious, he thought as he tried to collect his wits. Where the hell had she gotten an idea like *that*? When he was finally able to compose himself—well, a little, anyway—he asked, "What makes you think I'm a hit man for the Mob?"

Natalie, in turn, looked dubious. "Well, gee, there's that small matter of the holstered gun slung over a chair in the other room."

Yeah, okay, so he could see that making her a little suspicious. But he was no more anxious to talk about that this morning than he had been last night. Telling her he'd had a crush on her the way he had had seemed like a good idea at the time, a way to take her mind off the gun so they could talk about the attraction between them instead. But he'd been hoping they would be able to say things that would *ease* the attraction, not inflame it. He'd thought the two of them would be able to behave like adults about it. Acknowledge it was there, sure, but then refrain from doing anything about it. And okay, they *had* acknowledged it was there—hoo boy, had they acknowledged it—but instead of behaving like adults about it, they'd behaved like...

He smiled. Well, they'd behaved like animals. In a word, woof. And man, did he feel better this morning for having done it.

"Jack?" Natalie said, bringing him back to the matter at hand. Namely, the gun in the other room that she still wanted an explanation for, and which he still wasn't sure he wanted to talk about.

Why had she jumped to the conclusion he was a mobster? he wondered. Why not conclude he was in law enforcement? That would have been a lot more likely.

But before he could point that out, she hurried on, "And you've been very secretive about your job and stuff since you moved in."

He was genuinely puzzled by that. "I have?"

She nodded. "Well, you for sure never told me what you do for a living."

"You never asked me what I do for a living."

"No, but Mrs. Klosterman did," she said. "And you told her you worked in advertising. But people in advertising don't wear guns. Unless, you know, they were hired by Smith and Wesson or something," she added as an afterthought.

Damn. In hindsight, Jack supposed he should have realized that the lie he'd told to his landlady was going to come back to bite him on the ass. But what was he supposed to do, tell Mrs. K the truth about what he was doing here? And scare a nice old lady like her?

"Okay, so maybe I fudged a little bit on that," he confessed. "I panicked when she asked me point-blank what I do, and I said the first thing that popped into my head. I was afraid if I told her what I was really doing here, she might've gotten scared and overreacted or something."

"Mrs. Klosterman overreacting," Natalie said flatly, evidently choosing to overlook the *scared* part of his statement, something that kind of bothered him, since denial wasn't normally a trait he liked to find in a woman. "I'm not sure it's even possible for Mrs. Klosterman to overreact," she continued. "I mean her going about her daily routine is overreacting. It would be impossible for her to over-overreact."

"Yeah, I guess you got a point there," he conceded.

"So just what *are* you doing here, Jack?" Natalie asked, sobering again. "Why did you think Mrs. Klosterman might get scared and overreact when she heard the truth about your job? Because I have to tell you that hearing you say that makes *me* feel a little scared about your job, too."

"Natalie…" he began, still not sure what he should tell her, but wanting her to know the truth.

But before he could say any more, she asked, "Does it have something to do with that time you were on the phone talking about doing a messy job? I'm pretty sure I heard you use the word 'whacked' in that conversation. And what was I supposed to think when I heard that? How do you explain it?"

Jack had to think for a minute before he could figure out what she was talking about. Then he remembered. That night when he ran into her—literally—outside his front door, and she spilled her strawberries and other feminine necessities. He'd been talking to his boss that night, and he'd been pissed off about this assignment. "Okay, I remember that night," he said, nodding slowly. "And I confess I did use the word 'whacked' in that conversation."

"Aha," she said. But instead of looking triumphant, she actually looked pretty depressed.

"But before I explain that," he said, "*I* have a question for *you*."

"Shoot."

He arched his eyebrows at the word, and she squeezed her eyes shut tight when she realized what she'd said.

Hastily, she backtracked, "Uh…I mean…what's the question?"

Jack crossed his arms over his chest and asked, "What were you doing eavesdropping on my phone conversations?"

Now Natalie looked contrite. And for some reason, Jack liked that better. Anything was better than seeing Natalie sad.

"Thin walls?" she asked in a small voice.

He smiled. "Yeah, right." Then he decided to give her the benefit of the doubt. He had been pretty pissed off that night. And he probably had been shouting. He supposed it wasn't her fault she'd come along just when he was yelling about someone getting whacked. "Okay, yes, I did have such a phone conversation that night," he said, "and yes, I do recall using the word 'whacked.'"

"Why?" she asked.

This part, he thought, was going to get a little tricky. So he uncrossed his arms and scooted closer to her, settling both hands on her shoulders. "Natalie," he said in a very serious, very important voice.

"What?" she asked in an even more serious, even more important voice. She was starting to look worried now, which was precisely the reaction he had been trying to avoid.

"I assure you," he said softly, "that I'm not a hit man for the Mob."

She relaxed visibly at his admission.

"But I guess I should tell you that I *do* work with the Mob."

Immediately, she tensed up again.

"It's not what you think," he said quickly. "I'm not a member of the Mob. I'm a federal marshal. And I work with WITSEC. That's the Witness Security Program. More familiarly known as the Witness Protection Program. And I'm here because of an assignment."

First she narrowed her eyes at him. Then she gaped at him. "Holy moly. Mrs. Klosterman was right."

Great. Mrs. K again. Just when things were starting to make sense, too. "About what?"

"That first day I met you in the kitchen, she was telling me she thought you had been relocated here because you were a Mob informer who was about to turn state's evidence. She said there was another guy who scoped out the apartment before you rented it, and she thought he was the federal agent assigned to keep an eye on you."

Oh, well, that explained why Natalie thought he was a mobster, Jack thought. Mrs. K had a way of making the most bizarre suggestions seem totally normal. Not that she'd been off-target with that particular bizarre suggestion. Well, not *too* far off target. Just...

Ah, hell. He was getting confused again. And he needed to keep his wits about him now. Because he needed to make Natalie understand some things about his job. And about him, too.

"The guy who looked at the apartment first was a federal marshal, too," Jack said. "But he's local. He found a place for me and another agent from New York, in addition to the guy we're here keeping an eye on. They're both in the building across the street, and I'm here. Us two agents have been trying to keep this third guy—who, incidentally, *is* a Mob informer—alive until he can testify at a trial in the spring. But he's a squirrely guy, Natalie. He doesn't like being cooped up, and he keeps sneaking out on us. So we've had to be on him twenty-four-seven, keeping tabs on where he goes and what he does.

"If it makes you feel any better," he continued, "the guy I'm keeping an eye on isn't a hit man. Wasn't a hit man. He was...he *is*..." Jack sighed heavily. "He's a friend of mine, Natalie."

This time she was the one to look surprised. "You have friends in the Mob."

"Not friends, plural. Friend, singular."

Oh, boy, Jack thought. This was going to take a lot more explaining than he wanted to do right now. Because right now, what he wanted to be doing was holding Natalie. Kissing Natalie. Making love to Natalie. But he couldn't do that until he did this first. Because she had to understand what his job was like, how much it was a part of himself, how important it was for him to be doing it.

"The neighborhood where I grew up, Natalie, was a pretty rough neighborhood. But I loved it, you know? There were good people there, too—there *are* good people there, too—trying to make it a better place. But a lousy element thrived anyway."

"The Mob," she guessed.

He nodded. "They wouldn't go away," he said. "And

they kept the people who wanted something better for the neighborhood from getting something better. Donnie Morrissey was my best friend from the time I was six years old. We grew up together on the same street, did everything together. He had sisters, too, and we were like the brothers each other never had. But when we were in high school, we started to drift apart. Because Donnie got involved in some stuff he shouldn't have, and I couldn't figure out a way to get him back. Fast money, that was what he wanted. And that was what the Mob provided for him. But man, he worked for it. Did things I never thought I'd see him do. Did things *he* never thought he'd see himself do."

"And that's who you're here protecting?" Natalie said.

Jack nodded, suddenly feeling very, very tired. "He finally realized one day that maybe the life he was living wasn't the greatest life to live. He came to see me. Said he'd give us some really good information about a local family in exchange for a new identity. A new life. But he said he'd only do it if I was one of the guys assigned to protect him. He didn't trust anyone else. So what could I do but promise I'd be there for him? Just like when we were kids. When they relocated him here, to keep him safe until the trial comes up in the spring, I came with him. After the trial, once he's said his piece in front of a judge, we'll send him somewhere else."

Natalie studied him in silence for a moment, then, "Where will you send him after the trial?" she asked.

Jack shook his head. "At this point, I really don't know."

She nodded, but he didn't think it was in understanding. "And when he goes, will you go, too?"

This time Jack was the one to study Natalie in silence, and he decided she was a lot more interested in his answer to that question than she was letting on. She was looking down the road, he thought. Looking toward her future. Looking toward a future that included him. And he just wasn't sure how he felt about that. Nor was he in a position right now to really think about it. Right now, his priority had to be his job. And not just because he'd made a promise to a childhood friend, but because his job had always been his first priority, and he just wasn't sure he knew how to bump anything else into that position.

So he told Natalie the only truth he knew in that moment. "When Donnie goes back to New York for the trial, I'll go with him. And after he's testified, WITSEC will put him someplace safe, someplace far away from New York where nobody will ever find him again. But I won't go to that place with him. Chances are good I won't even know where they send him. I'll probably never see the guy again after that. His life will be somewhere else, and my job will still be in New York."

Natalie gazed at him in silence for another moment, her eyes never leaving his. Then, very slowly, she nodded once more. Jack wasn't sure if she was nodding this time because she did indeed understand what he was saying, or because she'd drawn some conclusion of her own that she agreed with more. And he honestly wasn't sure which one he preferred.

"That phone conversation you overheard that night?" he began again, wanting to finish up his explanation, not wanting to leave loose ends...of any kind. "When I said the job was going to get messy? I was talking to my boss that night, and I said that stuff about things getting messy because I knew we were having to bend the rules so much for Donnie. He's claustrophobic and can't stay cooped up for very long without going nuts. And when I used the word 'whacked,' it was because I was afraid someone was going to whack him. He's had a contract out on him since they found out he was talking to us. Someone is, in fact, trying to whack him," Jack concluded. "Just, you know, not me."

Although there had been times when he'd wanted to coldcock the guy and duct-tape him to a chair, he thought uncharitably, just to make sure he stayed put. Especially that night when Donnie's disappearance had made Jack cut things short—so to speak—with Natalie.

"So then your name really is Jack Miller," she said, surprising him again.

"What, you doubted that, too?" he asked her.

She shrugged halfheartedly. "Well, you don't seem like a John."

He grinned. "That's why I go by Jack."

She didn't grin back. "Well, you don't seem like a Jack, either."

"What do I seem like?" he asked.

"I don't know," she told him. Then she grinned a little guiltily and said, "Okay, so you seem sort of like a Vinnie 'the Eraser' Mancuso."

Jack decided not to ask how she'd come up with that one. Mostly because he was sure Mrs. K must have had a hand in it. And you could just never really tell with Mrs. K.

"Well, you're half right," he said.

"Your nickname is 'the Eraser'?" she asked.

This time Jack was the one to grin. "Nah. I'm half-Italian, though. On my mother's side. The Abruzzis."

"So your Aunt Gina is your mother's sister," Natalie guessed.

"Actually, she's my great-aunt, but yeah, on my mother's side."

"And I bet your sister Sofia's name comes from that side, too."

He nodded. "My sister Isabella, too. My other sisters,

Esther and Frances, are named after women on my father's side of the family. And I'm named after my father. And yes, before you ask, there was a lot of infighting when I was a kid, because Es and Frannie thought Sofia and Bella got much more glamorous names. For a while they tried to go by Elisabetta and Francesca, but it never stuck."

Natalie smiled again, a bit softer this time. "I'd love to meet them," she said.

Oh, boy, Jack thought. He could only imagine the fireworks if he brought a girl home to meet his family. He'd never done that before. Had never really planned, too. With Natalie, though...

He couldn't think about that now. So instead, he left the remark unremarked upon and changed the subject. "So all this time, you've been thinking I was connected?" he asked instead.

She hesitated for a moment—probably mulling over the fact that he'd chosen not to say anything about her meeting his family, he couldn't help thinking—then told him, "Well, not *all* this time. Just a little bit at the beginning there, I kind of wondered. Like maybe...four times. Maybe five. No more than twenty or so, though. Fifty at the outside. And then maybe for a few minutes again after, you know...the gun incident last night. But even then, I wasn't positive. Just a little doubtful."

"Why did you assume I was a mobster when you saw the gun?" he asked. "Why didn't you just assume I worked in some kind of law enforcement? That would have made more sense."

"Yeah, but you don't seem like someone who works in law enforcement, either," she told him.

"And I do seem like a mobster?"

"Well, no..." She shook her head, as if she were trying to physically toss out the thoughts that were going through her head. "So how long have you been a federal marshal?" she asked.

"Practically since I graduated from college," he told her. "Law enforcement has been kind of a tradition in my family. My dad's a homicide detective for NYPD. My grandfather was a beat cop. My uncle Dave, my dad's brother, was the first to become a fed. He was a marshal, too, one of the first guys to work on WITSEC after it was developed in the sixties. He got me interested when I was a kid. I always thought he had the coolest job around. He told some great stories.

"But when I got older, my reasons for joining the marshals changed," he added, sobering as one episode after another from his childhood and adolescence wheeled through his head. "I wanted to do whatever I could to stick it to those bastards," he continued, his voice coming out rougher than he intended. But that was what happened when he thought about stuff like this. "The Mob wrecked my neighborhood, Natalie, with all the crap they pulled. The drugs, the prostitution, the extortion. They recruited one of my best friends when he was still just a kid, and then turned him into a man I couldn't recognize. Another friend of mine, Leo Schatzky, disappeared one day after a coupla wiseguys went to his apartment. And a couple more roughed up his dad and his brother when they went asking questions about it. They never did find out what happened to Leo.

"I hate those guys, Natalie," he added, biting back the bitterness he always felt when he thought too much about the past. "They're scum. Every last one of 'em. And I'll do whatever I have to to get rid of 'em forever, even if it means keeping one of 'em safe long enough to rat out a bunch of others. Yeah, Donnie's coming out of it now," he said, glad for that, if nothing else. "And he's trying to do the right thing. But he'll never be the guy he was before. And he's done some things he'll probably never be able to live down. I don't want to see that happen to another decent guy."

Natalie said nothing for a moment, and Jack feared he may have said too much. Then she smiled, finally, but it was a soft, sad sort of smile, and she hooked her hands loosely over his arms.

"Your work is really important to you, huh?" she asked.

"Damn straight," he told her.

"It's almost like a life calling, isn't it?"

He nodded. "Sometimes it feels like it, yeah."

She lifted a hand to his cheek, and when she cupped her palm gently over his jaw, Jack closed his eyes and turned his face to receive her touch more fully. And almost like magic, all the bitterness was suddenly gone, and a sad sort of emptiness took its place. But emptiness was good, he thought. Because he could fill emptiness with something better than bitterness. Something sweeter. Something that wasn't quite so dark. When he opened his eyes again, he saw Natalie smiling at him, and he realized even the emptiness wasn't quite as empty as he'd thought.

"I'm sorry I even thought for a minute you could be one of them," she said. "And really, if I'd thought honestly about it, the way you just described it, I never would have lumped you in with them."

"Thanks," he said softly. "But even thinking I could be some lowlife scumbag mobster, you still sorta liked me, huh?"

She winced a little at that. "Do you think I need professional help? Maybe there's a group therapy program for people like me. 'Women who like wiseguys and the shrinks who think they're nuts.'"

He smiled. "More like 'the shrinks who wear body armor while treating them.'"

"So then you do think I need professional help."

"Nah, I just think you need to remember that what you see on TV about the Mob, it's way glamorized," Jack told her. "The real Mob's not like what they show on TV at all. Well, except maybe for *The Sopranos*," he conceded. "And another thing I think is that maybe I'm going to have my work cut out for me convincing you once and for all that I'm one of the good guys."

She gave him an almost convincing pout. "You consider that work?"

Jack's smile broadened. "Maybe that wasn't the best way to put it. But I do want to show you how good I can be."

"I already know how good you can be."

"Yeah, but maybe we better go over it again, just to be sure."

She said nothing for a moment, only considered Jack in silence, as if she were giving great thought to something. He said nothing, either, though, because she seemed to need the quiet. Finally, she said, "And what happens after we go over it again?"

"What do you mean?" he asked.

"I guess I'm trying to figure out what happens after your six-month lease expires," she told him. "After you take Donnie back to New York for his trial. Am I just going to be a fond memory to you then, Jack? Because I have to be honest with you. You're going to be a lot more than that to me."

This, he remembered now, was what he had feared the conversation would come to when Natalie had said she wanted to talk about something important and serious. And now, even though Jack had kind of seen it coming, he realized he had no idea what to say. So, again, he told her the truth. At least, it was the truth as he knew it in that moment.

"I don't know what happens then," he said. "I don't

usually think that far ahead, Natalie. I can't. I'm sorry. Right now, all I can think about is doing my job, and keeping Donnie alive. But after that…"

He shrugged, hoping the gesture didn't look too cavalier. Because cavalier sure as hell wasn't how he felt at the moment.

"I just don't know," he said again.

This time Natalie studied him in silence for a long, long time. Finally, though, "Fair enough," she said.

But Jack didn't think she believed that any more than he did.

9

THE APARTMENT THEY'D found for Donnie was a lot like the one Jack was staying in himself, except that Donnie's was on the third floor of the house across the street instead of on the second, and the furnishings weren't quite as comfortable and homey-looking as they were in Mrs. K's house. And, too, unlike Jack's, Donnie's windows had bars on them, which had been another selling point as far as the marshals were concerned. Not so much because they wanted to keep Donnie in—though had Jack known about the guy's propensity for wanting to get out, he would have made that a priority, too—but because they wanted to keep everyone else out.

So far, so good.

Of course, there had been little chance anyone would find Donnie here, even though his new, phony identity wouldn't go into effect until after the trial. He was a thousand miles away from the guys who wanted him dead, and security within the WITSEC program was very, very good. Nevertheless, they'd needed to have someone here to make sure things stayed that way. Between Jack and the other federal marshal assigned to Donnie, they'd been able to keep track of him around the clock. And they'd kept him safe, which was even more important. And not just because of Donnie's value when it came to nailing other members of the family, either. But because, especially having spent the last few weeks with him and seeing the changes his former friend had gone through, Jack genuinely wanted to see the guy end up in a better place.

And that made Jack realize how he wouldn't mind seeing himself end up in a better place, too. In fact, that was exactly what he was thinking about as he watched Donnie pace back and forth in his temporary living room across the street from the house where Jack knew Natalie was sleeping. It was 3:00 a.m., after all. What else would she be doing? Well, if *he* were there with her, he knew what she'd be doing. And he knew what he'd be doing, too. Running his hands and mouth over every last inch of her naked body. But he was here watching Donnie pace, instead. Because that was his job. Watching Donnie. And Jack's job had always come first. Always. No matter what. Funny, though, how suddenly, he didn't want to think about it nearly as much as he wanted to think about something else.

Or, rather, some*one* else.

"Donnie, sit down," he said now, when he started feeling as edgy as Donnie looked. "Jeez, it's makin' me exhausted just watchin' you."

Hell, Donnie was still wearing the rumpled trousers and dress shirt he'd had on when Jack arrived that afternoon, and all Jack had seen the guy consume since his arrival was about ten gallons of coffee. He leaned back in his chair and crossed his denim-clad ankles over each other, then crossed his arms over the black, long-sleeved T-shirt stretched across his chest. But he still couldn't relax. He was still thinking about Natalie. Across the street. In bed. Alone. Sleeping. When she should have been in bed with him, not sleeping.

Donnie ignored Jack's plea, his legs scissoring wildly as he made his way from one side of the room to the other. "I can't sit down," he said. "This waiting is starting to drive me nuts, Jack. I can't sleep, I can't eat, I can't do anything."

He had lost weight since their arrival in Louisville, Jack thought, noting Donnie's even lankier than usual frame. And he hadn't been bothered by this rampant insomnia when they first got here. That was a more recent development—ever since that night he'd paged Jack at Natalie's, right when things were heating up. If this kept up, Donnie was going to waste away to nothing before it was time to take him home for the trial.

But at least he'd be alive. Jack just hoped Donnie would be in some kind of shape to testify. Because Jack didn't want this to take any longer than it already had. He had things to do. Places to go. People to see.

Yeah? Like who? a voice inside himself piped up.

Immediately, Natalie's face materialized in his brain. And he told himself he was the one who was nuts, not Donnie, for thinking anything might come of that. His life was a thousand miles away from hers. And his life had none of the niceties and refinements that hers did. Not that Natalie Dorset was some major heiress who lived in a country estate and wore white gloves and went to garden parties, he reminded himself. But she was a nice person. A decent person. And she deserved to live a nice, decent life that wasn't tainted by the kind of people Jack had to deal with on a regular basis.

"Well, you better get used to the waiting, pal," Jack told Donnie, "because you still got three months of waiting to get through."

And Jack still had the rest of his life to get through. Without Natalie.

Donnie groaned like a rabid animal at that, and his pacing became more frenzied. Jack felt like standing up and slapping the guy silly. Hell, *he* had more to feel lousy about than Donnie did. All Donnie had to worry about for the rest of his life was a crime family with eyes everywhere taking out a hit on him. Jack had to face the prospect of a life without Natalie Dorset in it.

He was *this* close to acting on his impulse to smack Donnie silly when the other man finally stopped pacing and collapsed into an overstuffed chair. "Tell me a story, Jack," he said. "Something to take my mind off my worries."

Now Jack bit back a rabid sound. That first night, when he'd come over here because Donnie couldn't sleep, he'd spent hours trying to calm the guy down. The only thing that had helped had been when Jack started talking about their shared childhood and adolescence, dredging up one memory after another from the old neighborhood until Donnie had finally calmed down enough to sleep. But over the last couple of weeks, he'd pretty much relived both of their younger lives. He was running out of things to talk about.

"Nah, you tell me a story, Donnie," he challenged. "I've told you all mine. It's your turn to entertain me."

Besides, Jack had worries he wanted taken off of his mind now. And whatever it took—even if it was listening to Donnie Morrissey drone on and on about God knew what—he'd take it.

Surprisingly, Donnie took the command seriously. "All right," he said. "Gimme a minute to think of one." He dipped his dark blond head down toward his chest, as if he were trying hard to remember something, then lifted a hand in triumph. "Okay, I got one. The story of Angela and Gabriela Denunzio."

Jack rolled his eyes heavenward. "Not that again."

"Yeah, that," Donnie said, smiling. "The story of Angela and Gabriela Denunzio, and how they turned a prince into a frog."

As much as Jack did *not* want to revisit the Denunzio twins episode, he didn't balk at the introduction of the subject. At least it had made Donnie stop pacing, and that in itself was enough to recommend it for further discussion. Besides, it really would take Jack's mind off of Natalie. Mostly because he was the prince that had gotten turned into a frog by the Denunzio twins.

"You remember them?" Donnie asked, his smile growing broader, because he already knew Jack remembered the Denunzio twins very, very well.

In spite of that, Jack replied obediently, "Yeah, I remember them."

"And do you remember," Donnie continued, "how you wanted to ask one of them to the senior prom, but couldn't decide which one to ask, because they were both so cute?"

"Yeah, I remember," Jack said.

"And do you remember how you put off asking either one of them until you could decide?"

"I said I remember, didn't I?"

"And do you remember how you finally settled on Angela?"

"Yeah."

"And how she said no, because she was going with Tommy Finster, who asked her the week before?"

"I remember."

"So then you asked Gabriela, but she said no, too, because she was going with someone else?"

"I remember."

"And who was that, that Gabriela said she was going with?" Donnie asked then, his smile broader than ever. "I can't remember."

"The hell you can't," Jack told him.

"No, really," Donnie said. "My mind's a little fuzzy. Who was it Gabriela went to the prom with?"

"You," Jack muttered.

"Who?" Donnie asked. "What did you say? I couldn't quite make out what you said."

"You," Jack said more clearly this time.

"That's right," Donnie said, laughing. "Gabriela went to the prom with me."

"Even though you knew I was going to ask her myself," Jack reminded him.

"Hey, she was second best to you," Donnie reminded him right back. "I always liked her better of the two."

And he had, Jack recalled. Donnie had been crazy about Gabriela Denunzio, ever since junior high school. But by the time senior prom rolled around, Donnie had gotten into trouble often enough that Jack had started to think maybe his friend preferred girls who weren't so nice, and that maybe Gabriela would prefer a guy like Jack over a troublemaker like Donnie. Still, he probably shouldn't have gotten so bent out of shape over it when she'd told him she was going with Donnie instead. Maybe Gabriela had still seen some potential in Donnie or something, to have said yes to his invitation.

"And then you didn't have a date to the prom, did you?" Donnie taunted Jack now.

"No," Jack said, "I didn't."

"Because all the other girls had dates with guys who didn't wait 'til the last minute to ask them."

"Yeah, yeah, yeah," Jack said.

"You're just lucky your aunt Gina was available that night," Donnie told him.

"Yeah," Jack said. "Lucky for me."

"I thought it was great how she taught all the kids to Madison and do the Charleston the way she did."

"Yeah."

"And who woulda thought an old broad like her could put away the Chianti the way she did?"

"Yeah."

"Those were the days, huh, Jack?"

"Yeah," Jack muttered. "Those were the days."

The two men were silent for a minute, both lost in thought. But Jack wasn't thinking about the past just then. Well, not the distant past, anyway. He was thinking about the night before, when he and Natalie had held each other close, and how good it had felt to be buried deep inside her, and how it had been even better to wake up curled against her that morning. He thought about the way she looked that first morning he met her, when she was wearing those goofy pajamas. And he thought about how much fun they'd had playing Trivial Pursuit. He thought about how serious she looked when she was grading papers in the evening, and how fresh she looked coming down to go to work in the mornings. And he thought about what it was going to be like to never see or feel any of those things again.

"I wanted to marry Gabriela," Donnie said out of the blue.

Well, this was news to Jack. "Why didn't you?"

Donnie lifted one shoulder and let it drop. "Other stuff got in the way," he said.

Other stuff, Jack echoed to himself. Meaning the job. Donnie's job. His work with the Mob. He'd made that his priority, instead of marrying the woman he'd been in love with since junior high school.

"Gabriela was a good girl," Donnie said further, his voice softening some, sounding sadder. "She didn't want no part of what I got into. And I don't blame her. She never could have survived in that world. It was too ugly for someone of her delicate nature. If we'd gotten married, it wouldn't have lasted very long."

Jack started when he realized that what Donnie had just said about himself and Gabriela mirrored many of the same thoughts he'd had about himself and Natalie. Except that Donnie was right—his world really was an ugly, sordid place, and Gabriela Denunzio really was a delicate woman who could never have survived there. By comparison, what Jack did for a living was decent and honorable and safe. And Natalie Dorset was a strong, fearless woman who didn't back down from anything—not even a guy she thought might be a-hit-man-for-the-Mob.

"Gabriela's still single," Jack said. "Did you know that? She never married anyone." And neither had Donnie.

Donnie nodded. "Yeah, I know. But I blew it back then, picking the life I did over her. And even with things the way they are now... It could never work with her and me. There won't be no second chance there, pal, that's for sure."

Jack didn't know if that was true or not, but it wasn't his decision to make. Gabriela Denunzio was indeed a "good girl," he knew. More important than that, though, she'd always been a smart girl. She'd made the right choice ridding herself of Donnie when they were teenagers, because Donnie had been headed down the wrong road. But now, if Donnie got himself straightened out... Who knew if it was too late for the two of them or not?

And why did Jack think about Natalie just then?

Maybe, he thought, because there wasn't a whole lot of difference between his situation and Donnie's. Oh, for sure, he wasn't on the same sorry road Donnie had chosen to take. But his job was more important to him than anything, just as Donnie's job—however illegal—had been to him once upon a time. Donnie had indeed blown it with Gabriela. He'd missed his chance, he'd just said so himself. Was Jack going to blow it with Natalie, too? Miss his chance with her? Because his job was more important to him than anything?

"Yeah," Donnie said, pulling him out of his troubling thoughts, "hindsight really is twenty-twenty, you know? When I think about Gabriela, and the way things could have been with her and me if I hadn't chosen the life I did…" He shrugged. "I just coulda been happier, you know? Maybe had a coupla kids. A real life, you know, Jack? Not…" He threw his hands out, indicating the tiny apartment he'd been cooped up in for weeks, and which he'd stay cooped up in for another three months. "Not this. Not this uncertainty, and this fear, and being alone, and wondering if I did the right thing for the rest of my life. Who needs that, you know? But I got it anyway. Whether I like it or not."

Jack opened his mouth to say something—though, honestly, he wasn't sure what to say—when his cell phone chirped, pulling his attention away from Donnie. He thumbed the talk button and said, "Miller," then listened to a man's voice buzzing from the other end of the line. He nodded, set his jaw grimly, and said goodbye. Then he thumbed off the phone and looked at Donnie.

"Good news," he said, although that, in his opinion, was debatable. "The trial date's been bumped up. Judge has an opening next week. We need to be back in New York day after tomorrow."

As JACK UNLOCKED the door to his apartment the following morning, he wondered what the hell he was supposed to tell Natalie about this new development. A glance down at his watch told him she'd already left for school, so he couldn't talk to her now anyway. Not that having six hours to plan made much of a difference. How many ways could you say, "I have to leave, and I don't know if I'm ever coming back"?

The enormity of what was happening hit him then. He had to leave Natalie tomorrow. And he really didn't know if he'd be coming back. The trial was still a week away, but it was scheduled to run at least two weeks. And for those two weeks, federal marshals—one of whom just happened to be Jack—would have to be with Donnie around the clock. At the earliest, it would be nearly a month before Jack could come back here.

A month without Natalie, he thought. That just felt... wrong.

It was so weird, because a month ago, he didn't even know who Natalie Dorset was. And until a couple of weeks ago, he hadn't considered her more than a friend. Okay, he'd considered her more than a friend, he conceded. He must have. Because he didn't spend hours and hours thinking about any of his other friends naked. Still, until a couple of weeks ago, he hadn't known Natalie intimately.

Yet now it felt weird, unnatural even, to think about being separated from her. But why would that feel weird to him? He'd spent his entire adult life alone, and he'd liked it that way just fine. Yeah, he'd always had a girlfriend whenever he wanted one, and sometimes he'd been with one woman for months. But the thought of ever being separated from any of them for any length of time had never made him feel like this—as if he were going to be missing a part of himself. Why should it be so different with Natalie?

Because it *was* different with Natalie, there was no denying that. Nevertheless, there was no way he could get around leaving her. He had a job to do. A very important job, at that. Jack had made a promise to Donnie that he would stick by him until this thing was over. And Jack always kept his promises. Always.

But what about after the trial? he asked himself. What happened then? After Donnie had testified, and the bad guys were put away, and Donnie was given some new identity and settled in some new place with some new job, where he'd be safe, provided he followed the rules and stayed out of trouble. Donnie would be back on the

straight and narrow then, his life wide open, full of possibilities. Maybe he didn't have a second chance with Gabriela Denunzio, but he had a second chance to find another
kind of happiness. Donnie could do anything he wanted,
be anything he wanted, be *with* anyone he wanted. And
where would Jack be? Back at home in Brooklyn, with everything exactly the way it had been before he left.

No. Not the way it was before he left, he realized. Because now he'd have memories of Natalie, and he hadn't
had those before. Memories of how she looked and felt and
tasted, and of how good it had been between them. Every
night, his last conscious thought would be of her. Then
he'd go to sleep and dream about her. And every morning,
he'd wake up alone, and remember what it had been like
to wake up next to her instead.

But that was the way it had to be, he told himself. Because that was his life, and it was a thousand miles away
from hers.

Unless…he thought further.

Nah, he immediately countered himself, before the
thought could even fully form in his head. He couldn't
come back here to live. He'd grown up in the big city, with
all its hustle and its bustle and its noise and its smells.
Brooklyn was in his blood, and he lived in a perpetual
New York state of mind. *Look at me, I'm a native New Yorker*
and all that. There was no way he could survive in a little
burg like this. Even if he *had* read that the opera was doing
Don Giovanni next season. And even if the Speed Museum
did have an impressive collection. And even if Vincenzo's
restaurant downtown *did* have the best damned Italian
food he'd ever tasted in his life, with a marinara sauce his
Aunt Gina would kill to be able to reproduce.

And even if Natalie Dorset did live here.

So maybe she'd consider coming back to New York with

him? he found himself wondering before he could stop the thought from forming.

Nah, he immediately told himself again. That wouldn't work, either. Because the fact was, he wasn't the kind of guy to settle down, here, there, anywhere. Whatever he might feel for Natalie—even if it was totally different from anything he'd ever felt for anyone else—was only temporary. It wouldn't last. His feelings for other women—even if those feelings had all been totally different from what he felt for Natalie—had never lasted. And once his feelings for Natalie evaporated like the rest of his feelings for women had, he'd walk. And then he'd just end up breaking her heart.

And even if it did last, he let himself muse, the kind of work he did for a living was very demanding and time-consuming. It had long hours and lots of travel, and there were times when it could be dangerous. He couldn't ask a woman like Natalie to share a life like that with him. She had deep roots in the community where she'd grown up, and she was accustomed to safe, secure surroundings and a totally predictable life. If the two of them tried to build a life together, she'd just end up resenting him for never being around. And then she'd be the one to walk out. And he'd be the one with the broken heart.

Either way, he thought, it pretty much sucked.

At this point, all he could do was hope he could figure out some way to explain all that to her so that it made sense. And he hoped, too, that she'd understand when he tried to explain it. But he did have to figure out some way to explain all that to her. He had to make it clear to her that he was only here temporarily, and that that had been the plan all along, and that he couldn't stay any longer because his job obligations were elsewhere, and always would be. And even if his job hadn't been a factor, he was used to living in

the big city, where he could get anything he wanted, anytime he wanted it. He just couldn't stay here with Natalie.
  Could he?

10

THERE WAS LESS THAN fifteen minutes left in Natalie's last period when she turned around from the chalkboard and saw Jack standing on the other side of the window in her closed classroom door. She shut her eyes for a moment, certain she must just be imagining him out there—or, probably more accurately, just thinking wishfully—but when she opened them again, he was still there, wearing his trademark leather jacket and black T-shirt. He probably had on his black jeans, too, she surmised, not to mention the ratty motorcycle boots he always paired with the outfit, but she could only see his top half through the chicken-wire enforced glass.

He lifted one hand in greeting, then pointed to the left, where the hallway outside intersected with another in a spot that formed something of a sitting area, complete with benches and a Coke machine. He was telling her he'd be waiting for her there when her class ended, she translated.

Before he could turn away, though, and without really thinking about what she was doing, Natalie motioned him inside instead. And when she did, every one of her students turned around to see who she was gesturing to. She wasn't sure why she extended the silent invitation—she just always invited visitors in to her classroom, whoever they were. She taught juniors and seniors, who were old enough to be able to halt in the middle of class and pick up again where they left off, and sometimes visitors to class offered an opportunity to expand her students' horizons in one way or another. Plus, her last class of the day was her Literary Social Criticism class for the advanced English students and was populated with remarkably intelligent, sophisticated kids who welcomed any and all new opportunities to learn.

Some of them were sophisticated in other ways, too, Natalie knew, having grown up in some of the city's rougher neighborhoods. Which was precisely why she used this class to introduce topics that might not be suitable for other students, and why the students, in turn, learned more than they might in other English classes.

Not that she wanted Jack's presence here to expand their horizons in quite the way he had expanded *hers*, mind you. Especially since there were a handful of kids whose horizons were probably already more expanded than Natalie's were in that regard, unfortunately. Stephanie Brody, for instance, was the mother of a seven-month-old baby.

Besides, Natalie was curious about why Jack would be here, now. She'd told him about the school where she worked, of course, but she'd never expected him to drop by to see her here, particularly unannounced this way. And although she was delighted he would do such a thing, for some reason, she couldn't quite quell the frisson of discontent that shuddered through her upon seeing him.

He looked surprised by her invitation to join them in class, but opened the door and stepped through it. Some of the students continued to study him—mostly the girls, Natalie couldn't help noting—while others turned back to look at her for explanation.

"Come in, Mr. Miller," she said. "Students," she added to her class, "this is my neighbor, Mr. Jack Miller, who is also a great reader." Then, to Jack again, she said, "We were just going over some of the finer points of one of your favorite novels, Mr. Miller."

Jack looked a little flummoxed by the attention being thrust upon him by a roomful of teenagers, but he replied in an even voice, "Uh, which one would that be, Miss Dorset?"

Natalie grinned at his designation. Ooo. She kind of liked the way he said *Miss Dorset*. Maybe she should make him call her that the next time they—

Her gaze skittered nervously over her students. Well. They could talk about that later.

For now, she said, "For the past two weeks, we've been reading and discussing *The Sun Also Rises*."

Jack's eyebrows shot up at that. "Are you sure that's a good idea?" he asked.

The question puzzled Natalie. "What do you mean?"

Jack tipped his head toward her students. "Well...I mean...you know...these are just kids."

Kids being a relative term here, Natalie couldn't help thinking. After all, some of them were the result of neighborhoods similar to Jack's crime-infested one in Brooklyn. She'd wager he hadn't felt like much of a *kid* at seventeen or eighteen. "And?" she asked.

Jack fidgeted a little, looking even more uncomfortable than before. "Well...I mean...*The Sun Also Rises*," he echoed, as if that should explain his objection.

"What about it?" Natalie asked, still feeling puzzled.

"Well, it has all that..."

"What?"

"*You* know."

"No, what?"

He looked first to the left, then to the right. Then he looked back at Natalie, lowering his voice as he said, "*Bullfighting*."

Natalie smiled. "It's all right, Jack. They're seniors."

"Hey, all the more reason to avoid discussion of...*you* know."

"Bullfighting?"

He nodded vigorously. "Yeah. And there's also..."

"What?" Natalie asked.

"*You* know."

"No, what?"

Jack did that left and right thing again, then looked back at Natalie and said, "Jake's *wound*."

"It's all right, Jack," she said again. "We've already addressed the matter of Jake's impotence, which also led to a lively discussion about how much of a healthy loving relationship really is dependent on sex."

His eyes went wide at that. As if he didn't want to belabor the point, however, he hurried on, "But what about all the drinking?" he asked.

"As a matter of fact, that's what we've been discussing today," Natalie told him. "How all the drinking often brings out the worst in the characters, and how no amount of drinking makes the characters feel any better about themselves or their actions. They still feel very unfulfilled and unhappy and very much a 'lost' generation. Much as is the case with excessive drinking in real life," she added meaningfully. At least, she hoped he'd realize what it meant. That by illustrating the characters' vices as being truly destructive, it might make these *kids* think twice about turning to that behavior to quell their own unhappiness.

Jack opened his mouth to object again, then nodded, obviously picking up on her meaning quite well. Yet another way they had connected, she couldn't help thinking. And that made her feel good inside. Probably better than she had a right to feel, really. In spite of how well things had been going with her and Jack, those things were still pretty much up in the air. And even though she'd continually cautioned herself not to do it, Natalie's hopes rose a little higher every day that "those things" would turn into "*some*thing" and that the something it turned into would last forever.

Although they'd spent every possible moment together since making love that first time, they'd never made any plans beyond what they would do the following day. They had spent their nights together whenever Jack hadn't had to baby-sit his friend Donnie, sometimes at Jack's place, and sometimes at Natalie's. And they'd taken as many meals together as they could, too. Jack had even cooked an Italian dinner for her one night, creamy manicotti from his aunt Gina's secret recipe that had melted in her mouth. Natalie, in turn, had introduced him to the wonders of the chocolate pecan pie that was so popular in her hometown, and had even written down the recipe for him to take home to his aunt Gina.

And that had been the only awkward moment they'd experienced—when Natalie had mentioned Jack's "going home." Because not only had the mood of that evening gone from convivial to dismal in no time flat, but Jack had thanked her and pocketed the recipe and promised to pass it along. And that was all he had said. There had been no mention made of his returning.

"Well, don't let me interrupt the discussion," he said now. "I just wanted to let you know I was here and that I'd be waiting for you outside."

A ripple of murmurs went up through the class, most of them running along the lines of *Way to go, Ms. Dorset,* but Natalie ignored them.

"No, stay," she told Jack. "Class will be over in a few minutes. We're almost finished here. Have a seat," she invited, indicating an empty desk at the back of the room. "You might offer a view of the novel we haven't discussed yet." Because, hey, Natalie knew for a fact that Jack could for sure bullfight way better than Romero, and his wound didn't bother him *at all*.

For a moment, he looked as if he would decline, then he dipped his head forward and made his way toward the desk to which she had directed him. And as he sat down, an odd ripple of desire fluttered up Natalie's spine. Because in his black motorcycle jacket, with his dark, overly long hair pushed back from his face so carelessly, he just looked every inch the rebel without a cause. Sitting at the back of her classroom the way he was, he looked like that bad boy in high school all the good girls—like Natalie—had fantasized about, the one every girl had wished she could tame. Or, better yet, the bad boy who might make every good girl turn as bad as he was himself.

"Ms. Dorset?" one of the girls in the front row said.

Natalie jerked her gaze away from Jack to look at her student. "Yes, Ms. Pulaski?"

"You were saying?" the girl asked. "About World War One?"

Natalie backtracked to where they had left off. "Right. World War One left many men of that time feeling confused about just what it meant to be a man at that time. Those who volunteered for service marched off to war feeling very manly indeed, but many came home shocked and dismayed by the appalling things they saw and did. Some were even damaged emotionally and psychologically by what they experienced, and that compromised their masculinity. What they had once deemed a rite of manhood—going off to war—was suddenly a horror instead. In that sense, Jake's wound, which he received in the war, can be interpreted as a symbol of how that war emasculated an entire generation of men..."

Her eye on the clock, Natalie finished making her point

as quickly as she could, doing so just in time to have it punctuated by the ringing of the last bell of the day. "Before you go," she called out over the din of the students closing their books and gathering up their things, "I need to assign tonight's essay."

A handful of groans went up from around the room, but Natalie felt not one whit of contrition. They all knew the drill. They had to write a one-page essay every night for homework over something they'd read in whatever book they happened to be studying at the time. It was her way of not only making them think about parts of the book they hadn't yet discussed in class before the discussion got under way, but also, she hoped, something that would put them into the habit of writing. And writing well. The fact that even the groaners flipped open their notebooks to write down the assignment heartened her.

"I want you to write tonight's essay on what you think Jake means when he tells Cohn in chapter two, and I quote, 'You can't get away from yourself by moving from one place to another.'"

Her students jotted down the directions, closed their books, then filed out of the classroom. But not with a few fond looks at Jack from most of the girls. Natalie shook her head, but smiled inwardly. Had she seen someone like Jack when she was seventeen or eighteen, she would have been more than a little overwhelmed, too.

Jack sat in the back of Natalie's classroom, watching the students file out and marveling at how mesmerized she had kept them during the last part of her class. When he'd been in high school, the last minutes of the last class of the day had meant it was time to blow off everything except what he had planned for after school. But Natalie's students had been hanging on her every word.

And he had, too. Of course, he'd never doubted she

was a good teacher, but he hadn't given it a whole lot of thought, really. Now that he'd seen her in action, though, he was ready to nominate her for teacher of the year. Not only had she taken a book that might not normally appeal to teenagers, but she'd chosen one with subject matter that might not be appropriate for teenagers under other circumstances. Yet she'd made it appropriate, not to mention interesting.

Because she obviously respected her students, he realized. And they, in turn, respected her. He'd known the minute he looked at the kids that the majority of them came from a background similar to his own—not the best neighborhood in the world, one filled with a new opportunity to screw up your life around every corner. But they were obviously like him, too, in that they tried to do the right thing. If they were smart enough—and mature enough—to study *The Sun Also Rises*, then they were remarkable kids.

Who had a remarkable woman for their teacher.

Something cold and unpleasant settled in Jack's stomach as the thought unrolled in his head. Because the reason he had come here this afternoon was to tell that remarkable woman he was leaving. Tonight. He'd spent the day packing up what few belongings he'd brought with him and collected over the past several weeks, and tying up any professional loose ends that might be left here in town. His flight was scheduled for departure in three hours—just after six o'clock. He'd been instructed to arrive at the airport with Donnie in tow ninety minutes before that. Which meant he had barely an hour to say goodbye to Natalie.

But now, suddenly, he realized he couldn't say goodbye to Natalie.

His plan had been to come down here and tell her what

was happening, then whisk her away after class, so that they could spend their final hour together making love. He'd even gone so far as to book a room at a downtown hotel for them, and he'd already packed his car with his things so that he could leave for the airport straight from the hotel, thereby squeezing every possible minute out of that last hour. He'd wanted to make sure he and Natalie were left completely alone, without distractions. He'd just wanted to hold her and kiss her, and bury himself inside her, and feel her warmth and softness surrounding him one last time.

So many plans, he thought as the last of her students passed by him and headed out the door. He'd had *every*thing planned for this afternoon. What he hadn't been able to plan was what would happen beyond this afternoon. And maybe that was why he found himself unable now to go through with any of the other ones he'd made.

"So what brings you down here?"

Jack's head snapped around at the question, and he saw Natalie still standing at the front of the room, dressed in her teacher clothes of full, printed skirt—this one in varying hues of dark green and beige—and an oversized sweater in a dark green that complemented it. Her dark hair was swept back into a loose ponytail, and antiquey-looking earrings dangled from her ears.

She was nothing like any other woman he'd ever been involved with, he thought. So why did he hate it so much that he was going to have to tell her goodbye? She was just a woman, he tried to tell himself. A wonderful woman, sure, but still. There were lots of wonderful women in the world. So why was she the one who'd gotten under his skin?

He remembered then that she'd asked him a question, and that it had provided him with the perfect opening to tell her what he'd come here to tell her. That Donnie's trial date got bumped up. That he had to leave right away. That the two of them still had time for an intimate farewell. But he couldn't make himself say any of it. Because he knew that when he did, Natalie would want to say something, too. She'd want to ask him when she'd see him again. And Jack just didn't know the answer to that.

"I just wanted to see you," he said in response to her question, congratulating himself for being honest.

She smiled. "That's sweet, Jack. Thanks."

He shook his head. "Not sweet. True. I missed you last night. And today." And, wow, he was honest when he was saying that, too.

She glanced quickly at the door when he said it, and only then did he remember where they were. Fortunately, the hallway outside was awash with students chattering and scurrying to get out of school, clearly with their minds on other things. He stood, anyway, and strode to the front of the room, so that anything else the two of them might say to each other couldn't be overheard.

"I'm sorry," he apologized when he got there, "I didn't mean to say that out loud like that. It just sort of popped out."

Which was another thing that should be setting off alarm bells, Jack told himself. He wasn't used to being with a woman who made things "just pop out" of him. Hell, he didn't even like using the words "popped out." They weren't, you know, manly.

"Don't worry about it," Natalie said, smiling again. He really did like her smile. A lot. "Hey, I was just talking about impotence with my students, after all."

"Yeah, but you weren't speaking personally," he said. "At least, you better not have been."

She chuckled. "Ah, no. Impotence has never been a problem for me."

He growled playfully. "You know what I mean," he said.

"I know what you mean," she agreed. "And it hasn't been a problem for me."

"Damned straight."

She sighed a little wistfully. "I can't leave yet," she told him. "I'm sorry, but I have to stick around for a while."

Obviously, she was assuming he'd come here because he'd wanted her to go somewhere with him—somewhere that *didn't* involve an intimate goodbye—and the realization made him feel a little sick to his stomach. He told himself to correct her assumption, that she'd just provided him with yet another perfect opening for him to tell her that he had to leave. Tonight. In less than an hour. But something held him back.

"Normally, it wouldn't be a problem for me to take off after class," she continued regretfully, "but I have a teacher's meeting this afternoon that's going to tie me up until after five. I can't miss it, I'm sorry."

"That's okay," Jack said. *Tell her*, he then instructed himself. *Tell her you have to leave. Tonight.* But he still couldn't push the words out of his head and into his mouth.

"But if you're not baby-sitting Donnie tonight, maybe we could meet somewhere for dinner," she added earnestly.

Tell her! Jack commanded himself. He opened his mouth to do just that...then heard himself say, "I have to baby-sit Donnie tonight." Which was an answer that still kept him honest, he tried to console himself. Of course, it was an answer that was also misleading...

Her disappointment was almost palpable. "But you had baby-sitting duty last night," she complained. "Can't Douglas do it tonight?"

Douglas was the other federal marshal watching Donnie, but he wouldn't be returning to New York until tomorrow. Jack was the one designated to escort Donnie back. Because he'd promised to stay with Donnie throughout this whole thing. "He can't tonight," Jack said. Honestly. And also, you know, misleadingly. "It's up to me."

She pushed her lower lip out in an exaggerated pout. "Well, that's not fair."

Oh, she didn't know the half of it. "Yeah, well, that's life," he said, trying to inject a lightness into his voice that he was nowhere close to feeling. But, hey, at least he was still being honest. Dammit.

She opened her mouth to say something, probably something that would require Jack to commit to meeting her somewhere tomorrow, or doing something with her tomorrow, or seeing her tomorrow, so he lifted a hand to her mouth and pressed his fingertips lightly to her lips.

"I just wanted to see you, Natalie," he told her softly again. "That's why I came down here. Because I missed you, and I wanted to see you, that's all."

He felt her breath against his fingertips when he said those first words and knew that she had gasped softly at them. Funny, but they'd had the same effect on him, too, and he was the one who'd uttered them. He dropped his hand back to his side and dipped his head to hers, placing his mouth where his fingers had been, brushing his lips lightly over hers once, twice, three times, four. His heart began to pound with every new stroke, but he made himself stop before things got out of hand, and pulled himself back.

"Don't worry that the meeting will hold you up," he told her. But he lifted his hand to her face again, grazing his fingers lightly over her jaw and cheek, rubbing his thumb lightly over her bottom lip, as if by doing so, he might etch her features into his memory forever. "I've got some other things I need to do, anyway," he told her. Still being honest, bastard that he was. "Don't let me hold you up."

And then, because he just couldn't help himself, he curled his fingers around her nape and he bent toward her again, taking her mouth this time in a hot, hungry, heart-felt kiss, deep and open-mouthed. And then he pulled back from her, turning away—literally if not figuratively—and headed toward the classroom door.

"Don't rush home," he called out over his shoulder. But he couldn't make himself turn around.

"Okay," he heard her reply. But there was something in her voice when she said it that made him think she was puzzled, maybe even troubled, by their exchange. Especially when, in a softer, more uncertain voice, she added, "I'll see you when I get home, okay?"

Jack couldn't respond to that. He just couldn't. He didn't want to lie to her. But he didn't want to say good-bye, either. So, with his back still turned to her, he only lifted a hand to her in farewell. But he could feel her anxious gaze on his back as he walked out the door.

And he couldn't help but wonder if that was the last touch from Natalie he'd ever feel.

NATALIE SAW THE strawberries sitting on the floor in front of her door before she saw the note lying atop them. And not just a pint of strawberries in a plastic box like one might find at Kroger. But a wooden bucketful of straw-berries that looked as if they had been freshly picked. There must have been over a gallon of them. At first she was puzzled by their presence. She hadn't seen fresh strawberries at the grocery store since—

Well. Since that day she'd run into Jack outside his apart-ment, and they'd spilled from her bag, and then she'd in-vited him to stay for dinner at her place, and he'd declined.

And suddenly, she stopped being puzzled by their pres-ence. Because she was way too busy just then, having a bad feeling about things. Jack's appearance at school earlier had been odd. And the way he'd left her had been odder still. And now, she couldn't help thinking that things were about to go from odd to worse.

She slowed her pace on the stairs until she came to a halt at the one just below the landing. From there, she could see a piece of plain white paper, folded in half, lying on top of the strawberries. The word *Natalie* was scrawled upon it, in bold, dark, masculine handwriting. Jack's handwriting, she identified immediately. Because she'd seen it before and would know it anywhere, as well as she knew Jack himself. Suddenly, though, for some reason, she found herself wondering if maybe she knew him at all.

Oh, she really did have a bad feeling about this.

Forcing herself to take that final step up that would put her on the same level with the berries, she bent and gingerly retrieved the note. But she couldn't bring herself to open it right away. Instead, she stroked her fingertips lovingly over the letters of her name, trying to pick up some sense of Jack from them. But she couldn't. It was just letters on a piece of paper, after all. Nothing of the Jack she had come to know and—

And that was when she accepted the fact that he was gone. He must be. What else could that kiss in her classroom this afternoon have been but a kiss goodbye? She'd been confused by it at the time, but now she understood. For some reason, he'd had to cut his time here short, and now he was gone. Without even telling her goodbye. Sighing heavily, she opened the note and read what it said inside.

Natalie, it began in that same heavy handwriting. No *Dear*, not even a *'Yo*, just *Natalie*. And if she hadn't sensed it already, she knew then that she wasn't going to like what the rest of the missive said. In spite of that, she continued reading.

I'm really sorry to do this in a note, but when I came to school earlier to tell you there, I realized I couldn't. Donnie's trial date got bumped up, and we have to be back in New York tomorrow. So we're booked on a flight home tonight. I don't know how long the trial will last, or how things will go between now and when it's over. But I'll call you when I get a chance and let you know what's happening. Found the strawberries at Paul's Market and remembered how much you like them. Take care. Jack.

And that, literally, was all he wrote.

Take care, she repeated dismally to herself as she folded the note closed again. Yeah, right.

How could he have done this? she wondered as she sank down onto the top step. How could he have left town without even telling her goodbye? How could he have just written an impersonal note and dropped it at her front door? After everything they'd done together? After the way they'd *been* together?

I'll call you when I get a chance…

Oh, sure he would. If he couldn't even tell her goodbye in person, how was she supposed to believe him when he said he would call? Guys could say that to a woman's face and not mean it. No way was she going to take a handwritten assurance from a man who'd ducked out on her as a promise.

She told herself not to take it personally, then chuckled morosely over her own wording. Hadn't she and Jack already had this conversation once before? she asked herself. Hadn't she sat next to him on the sofa in Mrs. Klosterman's living room that night after they'd almost made love and heard him speak those very words? That his reluctance for anything more serious to happen between them was nothing personal? That Natalie really deserved better? And that they could still be friends?

God, how stupid could she have been? she berated herself. Jack had been sending her signals since the get-go that
had warned her off him. He'd declined her first invitation
to dinner. He'd done his best to avoid her in those first couple of weeks. Even after they made love, he'd told her flat
out that he didn't know how things would be for the two
of them once he took Donnie back to New York. As early
as a week ago, when she'd written down the pie recipe for
his aunt to take home with him, he hadn't used the opening to reassure her of his return. Not once—not once—had
he offered her any indication to think things between them
were anything other than temporary.

In spite of the way she felt about him, and in spite of the
way the two of them were together, he'd made it clear to
her that his job came first and that his life was elsewhere.
And that Natalie wasn't—couldn't be—a part of that life.
She'd hoped that maybe by spending more time together,
he'd eventually come to change his mind about that, to
think that Natalie *was* a part of his life, and that maybe he
cared more for her than he first realized. But now he was
gone, and there wouldn't be any more time for them to
spend together.

She had known he would be leaving, she reminded herself. He'd never told her otherwise. For her to be angry and
sad now was unreasonable. But she was angry and sad.
And she didn't think she was being unreasonable. They'd
been good together, the two of them. Jack had liked her—
he hadn't made a secret of that, either. And she'd liked
Jack, too. Oh, hell, who was she kidding? She'd fallen in
love with Jack. Probably before the two of them had even
made love. And after being intimate with him…

Oh, hell, she thought again. That was all. Just…*oh, hell*.

I'll call you when I get a chance, she thought again, the
words bouncing around in her head, echoing again and

again in Jack's rough baritone. Right. And that chance would come, oh…never.

She pushed herself up from the step and bent to retrieve the berries, and tried not to think about Jack. No way would she ever be able to consume all of these herself before they went bad. She'd divvy them up with Mrs. Klosterman. Give her something to remember Jack by, too, however temporary that souvenir might be. Then again, a temporary souvenir for a temporary man just seemed so fitting somehow.

Maybe she was wrong, Natalie thought further as she unlocked her front door and entered her apartment. Maybe Jack really would call her when he got the chance. Maybe the trial would be over quickly, and then maybe he'd come back. Or maybe he'd invite her up to New York for a short visit. And then maybe that short visit would turn into a long visit. And then maybe that long visit would turn into—

And that was when the memory of something very important hit Natalie, square in the middle of her brain. She remembered then that, as Jack had left her classroom that afternoon, for some reason, she'd dropped her gaze to his boots. It hadn't seemed that pertinent at the time, but it did now.

Because she'd noticed as Jack walked out the door that his boots *weren't* polished.

11

JACK SAT ON A HARD wooden bench inside one of the larger courtrooms in the New York City courthouse, listening intently to Donnie Morissey's testimony and wishing he would wrap it up soon, in spite of the fact that every new word out of the guy's mouth put some new scumbag crook behind bars. For two days, Donnie had been sitting before the Honorable Judge Genevieve Dupont and a jury of his peers, spilling his guts—and the guts of more than a few members of one of the city's most notorious crime families, figuratively speaking. What Donnie was telling the court was going to put away a good number of people and leave them to rot behind bars for a good long time, which was just about the only activity Jack could think of that suited them. Donnie was doing good. In more ways than one.

So why wasn't Jack happier? he asked himself. His job was about to get a little easier, thanks to Donnie, and since his job had always been his first priority, that ought to make him euphoric. Oh, sure, there'd always be wiseguys lining up to fill the holes these bastards left behind. But Jack and his colleagues were already on top of it. And whenever bad guys got caught and sent up the river, it was always an occasion for excessive celebration.

Funny, though, Jack didn't feel much like celebrating. Even funnier, he was barely listening to Donnie at this point. Because Jack had his mind on infinitely more important matters than the public well-being. He was thinking more along the lines of personal well-being. And how his being hadn't felt too well for the past month.

A month, he reflected again. That was how long it had been since he'd seen Natalie. Although the trial had started within days of his and Donnie's return to the city, it had been dragged out twice as long as they had anticipated. The defense had thrown up one lame roadblock after another to stall the opening arguments, until finally they'd run out of excuses. And even after things had finally gotten under way, they'd still dragged their feet. Even the prosecution had taken longer than they'd intended due to some last minute developments. But at this point, Jack honestly didn't care about any of that anymore. All he cared about was that he hadn't seen Natalie for a month. And it was really starting to piss him off.

Starting to? he berated himself. Hell, he'd been feeling irritable since his feet hit the tarmac at LaGuardia. No, even before that. Since he'd left Natalie's classroom that last afternoon he'd been in town without telling her what he'd gone there to tell her. That he was returning to New York to take Donnie back for the trial. That he didn't know how long it would take or when he'd be back. That he'd call her and stay in touch and let her know how things were going. That they could talk later, when they had more time and his head was clear of all things job-related. And then, finally, goodbye.

He was such a jerk.

None of those things had happened. Not one damned one. He hadn't been able to tell her he was going that day, had ended up leaving her that letter instead. He still hated himself for that. And he hadn't called her since coming back to New York. He'd been too chicken. Try as he might to work out something acceptable in his head to say to her, he hadn't had a clue. What did you tell a woman you'd spent a week making love to, and a month caring about, when you hadn't even been able to work up the nerve to tell her goodbye? Natalie probably hated him even more than he hated himself. If he was pissed off about not seeing her, he had only himself to blame.

"'Yo, Jack," a voice whispered beside him.

He looked up to find that Donnie had just sidled in next to him on the bench, obviously finished saying his piece.

"How'd I do?" Donnie asked further.

Jack made himself smile encouragingly. Hey, he could feel encouragement for Donnie, if not for himself. "You did real good, Donnie. Thanks."

Donnie smiled, too, but Jack didn't think he'd ever seen the guy look worse than he did in that moment. The past few months had really taken a toll on him. But now it was over. Or maybe just beginning. After today, Donnie was going to be buried in WITSEC, given a new name, a new identity, a new social security number, a new life. Jack just hoped the guy realized what an amazing opportunity that was and didn't screw it up. And he didn't think Donnie would. His friend had wised up a lot over the past few years. In spite of his youthful stupidity, he seemed determined to lead a good life now. Donnie, Jack was confident, would make the best of his second chance.

The two men sat quietly through the rest of the day's proceedings, then, when the judge called a recess until the following day, waited for everyone else to file out before rising themselves. Another marshal sat on Donnie's other side, and the three of them stood together.

The other marshal, though, turned around first, and when he did, Jack heard him say, "I'm sorry, ma'am, but you'll have to leave with the others," since, for the sake of security, the room had to be cleared before they could escort Donnie out.

Jack and Donnie turned, too, Jack only vaguely interested in who the woman might be—probably a member of the press corps wanting an interview—but when he saw her, he put his hand on Donnie's shoulder. "It's all right, Douglas," he told the other marshal. "She's a friend."

That was when Donnie turned around, too, his mouth falling open when he saw Gabriela Denunzio sitting at the very back of the room. She hadn't changed much since they were teenagers, Jack reflected, still had a mane of thick black hair and pale brown eyes and lots of dangerous curves. But as much as Jack had lusted for her and her twin sister in high school, he felt not a single stirring of desire now. Well, not for either of the Denunzio twins, anyway. His desire was all twisted in a knot and panting for Natalie Dorset, who lived a thousand miles away, and who he hadn't seen or spoken to in a month, and who he still hurt from missing.

Donnie turned to look at Jack, as if asking for permission to go to her, and Jack nodded, smiling. Douglas started to mutter an objection, but Jack cut him off with a look. "It's okay," he told the other marshal again. "Really."

And he wished he could say the same thing for himself.

He waited a few minutes while Donnie and Gabriela spoke in low tones, then, when he started to grow worried about Donnie being out in the open like this, he slowly approached the couple to express his concern. As he drew nearer, though, he couldn't help overhearing part of the exchange, and he halted to give them just a few minutes more. He knew the value of a last few extra minutes, after all. He'd spent the last month replaying that last few extra minutes he'd had with Natalie in her classroom.

"It's never too late, Donnie," Gabriela was saying. "Not if you figure out what's wrong and fix it." She pushed herself up on tiptoe and kissed Donnie on the cheek, then smiled shyly. "We have a lot to talk about before you go."

Donnie glanced over his shoulder at Jack, and Jack nodded. They'd figure out a way to make it happen. Donnie smiled his gratitude, and Gabriela murmured a word of thanks to Jack. Then she threaded her arm through Donnie's and followed Douglas out of the courtroom with Jack right on their heels.

Well, whattaya know, Jack thought as he watched the two of them walk away, their heads bent together in quiet conversation. Maybe Donnie would get a second chance with Gabriela, too. Somehow, the knowledge of that made him feel better.

THE MEMORY OF Donnie and Gabriela was still with Jack when he sat down—alone—to eat his dinner of frozen spinach lasagna and beer—alone—in his Brooklyn apartment that evening. Although he'd been back for a month, he still didn't feel like he was home.

Before his sojourn down in Louisville, he'd never paid much attention to the place where he lived. He'd moved to his apartment not long after becoming a federal marshal, and over the years had furnished it with functional furniture and all the necessities a single man required—a righteous stereo system, a refrigerator big enough to hold leftovers from Sunday dinners at his mom's and a case of Sam Adams, microwave, alarm clock, Xbox and the biggest damned TV he could find. His sisters and mother all had done their best to make the place homier whenever they came by to visit—which wasn't all that frequent—but most of their contributions had threatened to turn the place into the Spiegel catalog, and many had mysteriously disappeared over the years. All in all, Jack had always considered his place to be…fine. Nothing fancy, but it suited his needs.

Since returning to New York, though, his apartment hadn't been fine. And it sure as hell hadn't seemed to suit his needs. Every day when he came home, he found himself prowling around the place, because it always seemed like something was missing. But try as he might to figure out what was wrong, nothing ever was. Nothing had changed since he left. What had been there before was there now. Somehow, though, it still felt…wrong.

And, inescapably, he'd found himself constantly comparing his own apartment to Natalie's. Hers hadn't been any bigger than his, but somehow, it had seemed so much more accommodating. Natalie's place had looked and felt like Natalie—warm, welcoming, interesting, cozy. Her place had had personality. And it had made Jack feel good inside. Just like Natalie had.

God, why hadn't he called her?

And why hadn't she called him?

He told himself he shouldn't have expected her to call him. He was the one who'd taken off without even saying goodbye, and he'd written in his note—a *note*, for God's sake—that *he'd* call *her* when he got the chance. But a part of him had thought—or maybe hoped—that she would call him first. Natalie Dorset wasn't the kind of woman to take a goodbye letter from a jerk like Jack lying down. Wasn't she the one who'd told him flat out that she'd stay up all night waiting for him to come back, if it meant they could make love? And then, when he didn't go back, wasn't she the one who'd called him on it and told him flat out that she still wanted to?

When Natalie Dorset wanted something, she made it known. So if she hadn't called Jack, then it could only be because she didn't want *him*. And maybe, when all was said and done, that was what had kept Jack from calling her. First, it had been because he was too chicken, and he just hadn't known what to say to her. But then, as the days had gone by, and she hadn't called him, either, it had been because he was afraid she just didn't want to talk to him. Didn't want to see him. Didn't want to remember him. Because if she had, she would have called him.

Unless maybe…

Something hot and frantic splashed through Jack's belly then, and the beer he'd been lifting to his mouth slammed back down onto the table with a thump. What if something had happened to her? he wondered. What if the reason Natalie hadn't called him was because she hadn't been *able* to call him?

Why hadn't he thought about that before? he demanded of himself now. What if she'd been sick? Or hit by a bus as she walked through the school parking lot? What if she was in the hospital right now, calling out his name? *Jack…Jack…Where are you, Jack…? Jaaaaaaaack…* What if she'd been standing in line at the bank when armed robbers burst in, and what if she'd been caught in the cross fire when the cops responded and been grazed by a bullet or something? What if she'd been sitting too close to the ring at a pro-wrestling match and been beaned by a flying heavyweight? What if she had amnesia? What if she'd been abducted by aliens? What if a bunch of radical activists had broken in to Mrs. Klosterman's house and were holding Natalie and Mrs. K—and hell, even Mojo—hostage in exchange for their imprisoned leader *right now*?

Hey, it could happen.

Oh, man, he had to get back to Louisville. He had to help Natalie. He just hoped it wasn't too late…

"ARE YOU OKAY?"

The question should have been easy to answer, Natalie told herself. And it would have been, had it not been for the fact that only minutes ago, she'd been buried in a deep, *deep* sleep, but had been awakened by the brutal buzzing of her doorbell, something that had made her snap up in bed so quickly that she'd startled Mojo, who had been so frightened by being jerked out of his own deep, *deep* sleep that he'd dug his claws—all twelve of them, since he had an extra one on each front paw—into the thigh he'd been nestled against—Natalie's thigh, incidentally—which had *really* jerked her out of a deep, *deep* sleep, and then she'd tripped over a stray shoe after leaping out of bed, something that had sent her barreling into the nightstand before tumbling down onto all fours, but rattling the nightstand that way had made her glasses go careening to the floor, so while she was down there, she'd had to feel around for them until she found them, and meanwhile, the doorbell just kept buzzing frantically, and all she'd been able to think was that Mrs. Klosterman was having a heart attack, and she couldn't find her glasses to drive her to the emergency room, and then she'd finally slammed her hand down on her glasses—so hard that she'd snapped off the earpiece—but she'd stuck them on her face anyway, kind of haphazardly, and then gone limping out to the living room, where the buzzing was even louder and more frantic now, to throw open the door and find—

"Jack."

Which was another thing that made it hard for her to answer what should have been an easy question.

She took off her glasses and closed her eyes to rub them hard, certain she must still be asleep and dreaming this. But when she opened them again, Jack was still there, closer now, his hands wrapped around her upper arms. And all she could think was, *Dammit, why does he always show up when I'm wearing goofy flannel pajamas?* Because tonight she had opted for the hot pink ones that had humongous

bowls of ice cream all over them. Well, what had she cared?
It wasn't like anyone else was going to see her in them,
because Jack had left her high and dry a month ago and
hadn't called once, even though he'd said he would and—

"And why didn't you call me?" she demanded before
she could stop herself.

It was then that she noticed how hard he was breathing, and that his hair was a mess, as if he'd been dragging
ferocious hands through it for the last few hours. He was
wearing his black motorcycle jacket again, but it looked
kind of rumpled, like maybe he'd been bunching it up in
his fists when he hadn't had it on. The white T-shirt beneath it had a marinara stain on it, as if he'd been wearing
it since dinner time, which would have been… Dammit,
she couldn't do math in the wee small hours of the morning. A long time ago. Her gaze skittered down over the
black jeans and motorcycle boots—still unpolished, she
noted with some regret—and fell on the weekender bag at
his feet.

Yes, he'd come back to Louisville, she thought. But he
obviously wasn't planning to stay long.

"You shouldn't open your front door without checking
to see who it is first," he told her. Vaguely, she noted that
he was neither greeting her, nor answering her question.
"For all you know," he added, "I could have been a bunch
of radical activists who were breaking in to Mrs. K's house
to hold you and Mrs. K—and hell, even Mojo—hostage in
exchange for their imprisoned leader."

Vaguely, she noted that he was also making no sense.
Natalie narrowed her eyes at him. And she was pretty sure
she spoke for herself and Mrs. Klosterman—and hell, even
Mojo—when she said, "Huh?"

Jack smiled, a tremulous, anxious little smile. "Are you
okay?" he said again.

And there was just something in his voice when he said it that made Natalie go all soft and gooey inside. "I'm fine," she told him quietly. "There hasn't been any radical activist hostage-taking activity in the house for, oh, gosh, a couple of weeks now, at least."

"And you weren't abducted by aliens, either?" he asked earnestly.

Natalie honestly had to think about that for a minute. Not because she was trying to remember if such a thing had happened—even in her sleep-interrupted state, she could safely say that she had never been aboard a UFO— but because she was trying to figure out what the hell was going on in Jack's head. Finally, though, "Um, no," she said. "Haven't seen any aliens for a while, either."

"Any odd occurrences at the bank lately? Robberies? Cross fire? Getting grazed by bullets?"

She shook her head and eyed him with much concern. "Nope."

"Buses at the school been treating you okay?"

"Yeah…"

"Been to any pro wrestling matches lately?"

"Nuh-uh."

His gaze roved hungrily over her face again. "And you called me Jack, so you remember my name—you don't have amnesia."

Okay, now this was just plain weird. "Of course I remember your name. Jack, what's going on?"

"Ah, Natalie," he said. "I don't know what's going on. I just know I needed to see you. Right away. Make sure you were okay and everything."

"You could have just picked up the phone," she said. Then, before he had a chance to respond, she added, "Oh, wait. Maybe not. You don't seem to be too good at using the phone."

She hated herself for being sarcastic, but what was she supposed to do? A month goes by without word from him, even though he'd promised to call, and then suddenly he was at her door, waking her up in the middle of the night to ask her if she'd been abducted by aliens. Call her unreasonable, but the situation just didn't make her feel like herself.

He studied her in silence for a moment, his expression sober and not a little hurt. "I didn't call you," he said, "because I didn't know what to tell you. I couldn't figure out how to explain everything, because I didn't understand everything. I just knew I had to get back to New York with Donnie and didn't have any choice about that, and I didn't have time to work through everything else. And there was so much other stuff, Natalie. So much stuff that I wanted to say, but couldn't figure out how to say it. I just… I just… I—"

"Look, Jack," she interrupted him when he started to flounder, hoping maybe she could help him out. "You don't have to explain that part. I always knew where I stood with you, really I did. Ever since that talk we had after we made love that first time, I understood that your job was a lot more to you than just a job. And I understood that you were only in Louisville temporarily, and that you couldn't possibly stay, because your job obligations were elsewhere. You made that clear. So I totally understood."

Jack looked at Natalie, saw her mouth moving and recognized the words she was saying as being English. And he appreciated that she was trying to help him out here. But he wasn't sure he liked what he was hearing from her. Which was weird, because the words and the sentiment sounded kind of familiar to him….

"Plus," she continued before he had a chance to respond, "I knew you were used to living in a big city, where you could get anything you wanted, anytime you wanted it. I couldn't possibly have been so selfish as to expect you to stay here." She met his gaze levelly as she added, "Even if I did...even if I *do*...you know...love you."

Whoa, whoa, whoa, Jack thought. Now *these* words, and *this* sentiment, were definitely new. Now she was saying something that wasn't familiar to him at all. At least, he didn't think it was familiar. Was it?

"And I couldn't have been so presumptuous as to follow you back to New York," she went on, "because, well, you didn't invite me, for one thing. But also because I knew your job was very demanding and time-consuming, and I wouldn't have wanted you to start worrying that I might resent you someday because you were never around."

Okay, now this was sounding familiar again. But he still wasn't sure he was liking it.

"Even if I was sure that would never, ever happen, because I did...I *do*...you know...love you."

Wow. There it was again. She was saying that thing that shouldn't have been familiar—and that should have been terrifying, quite frankly—but it somehow felt like it totally belonged in the equation, and was a perfectly natural part of what was going on.

"So I understood," she went on, "that you had to go back to New York—alone—and I wouldn't have thought of trying to keep you here or follow you back there. I understood all that, Jack," she said again. "Really. I did. Honest. I totally, totally understood." She hesitated just a moment, then added, "What I didn't understand was how you could just leave me without telling me goodbye."

A loud buzzing had erupted in Jack's ears as he listened to Natalie talk, mostly, he supposed, because she had just repeated so many of the thoughts he'd had himself before leaving her, but which, strangely—or maybe not so strangely—he hadn't once entertained since returning to New York. Well, except for that part about her, you know, loving him. He hadn't thought about that before leaving Louisville. Or after he'd returned to New York, either. At least, he didn't think he'd thought about it there…

Now, though, it seemed like the only thing he *should* be thinking about. Because he realized then—or maybe he'd realized it before, when he'd gone back to Brooklyn—that that was the reason why what he felt for Natalie was so different from what he'd felt for other women. He'd never been in love with those women. They'd never felt like a part of him the way Natalie did. It hadn't hurt to lose them, because he hadn't been losing them, not really. But he *had* lost Natalie. For a whole month. And it had been hell. And he didn't want it to happen again. Because he suddenly realized—or maybe it wasn't so sudden after all—that he was in love with her. It all made sense to him now. Being in love with her was what had brought him back here. And now that he was back here…

"You understood why I left, huh?" he asked her.

She nodded slowly.

"Then that puts you one up on me," he said.

Her dark eyebrows arrowed downward. "What do you mean?"

He expelled a sound of exasperation. Exasperation for himself, mainly, because he was so dense. "I mean that maybe it took me a month to figure it out, but I finally understand now, too."

"What?" she asked. "What is it you understand?"

He took a step toward her and pulled her into his arms, dipping his head forward so that he could press his forehead to hers. "Natalie, I have missed you so much over the past month that I've felt like a part of myself was missing," he told her without reservation. "What I understand now is that I won't feel good again until I can be with you. I understand now that I don't want to lose you. And I understand now that I'll do whatever I have to do to keep us together. Because as big and exciting as New York is, there is, in fact, one thing I can't get there anytime I want it."

"What's that?" she asked.

He smiled. "You. I can't get you there. Because you're here. And you wouldn't be so presumptuous as to follow me back to New York. Which is going to be a problem," he added, pulling her closer to him still.

"Why?"

"Because I, you know, love you, too."

"Oh, Jack…"

"I want us to be together, Natalie," he told her again. "I don't care where or how or what the circumstances are. I just want to be with you. Forever."

"Oh, Jack…" she said again. But this time, she punctuated the remark by looping one arm around his neck and the other around his waist.

And oh, man, did it feel good to have her there again.

He looked around then, at Natalie's apartment in Mrs. Klosterman's house, and he realized then that he did actually care where or how or what the circumstances were. Natalie wasn't the only person he'd come to care about. Because the truth was, he'd kind of been missing his former landlady, too. And he'd been missing this neighborhood— it was a lot like the one where he grew up, only without the bad element thriving. Old Louisville was like what he'd always envisioned his own home place could be like in the best of circumstances. Only it was better. Because it had Natalie.

"Oh, Jack," she said a third time, her voice trembling. "I want us to be together forever, too. But I love it here—I don't want to live in New York. And there's Mrs. Klosterman—she's like the only family I've ever had. I don't want to leave her. But I'm afraid if you move here, you won't stay. I'm afraid this life here won't be enough to satisfy you. That you'd always regret giving up the life you have now in New York."

He cupped his hands firmly under her chin and brushed a soft kiss on her mouth. "Natalie," he said firmly. "Since I went back to New York, I don't have a life. And even if my life there could be full of riches and adventure and every pleasure known to mankind, if you're not in it, then it's nothing. Knowwhuddamean?"

Natalie smiled, and then nodded. Because she did understand. Her life would be the same way without Jack. "So then you're not just back for a visit?" she asked.

"Well, I did sort of leave a few things up in the air up there. For instance, I'm supposed to be at work in—" he looked at his watch "—about four hours."

"Oh, Jack," she said, laughing.

"But I'm due for a little vacation time. Especially after this assignment with Donnie. I think if I give them my two weeks' notice tomorrow…today…whatever…I'll be good for a month off with pay. That ought to give me time to line up something down here. Something permanent. Maybe even the same thing I'm doing now."

"But the Mob isn't a problem down here," she told him.

He grinned. "Yeah, I know. Which is something else I love about the place."

"But that's your life calling," she reminded him.

He shook his head. "Not anymore. Now my life calling is you."

He pulled her closer, until he could touch his mouth to hers, and Natalie curled her fingers into his hair and kissed him back deeply, vying with him over possession. For a long time, they only stood at her front door, each trying to devour the other, until Jack pushed the door closed with his foot. Then he took a small step forward, forcing Natalie to take a small step back. That step was followed by another, less small, step. And that one was followed by another. And then another. And another.

And with each step he took, he deepened the kiss, simultaneously tasting and testing Natalie. Little by little, he danced her down her short hallway to her bedroom, which he entered without hesitation. He dropped onto the bed and tugged her down into his lap, then pulled his mouth free of hers to look at her, as if he wanted to silently reassert his intention to stay with her forever. She smiled as she wove her fingers through his hair, nodded to let him know she believed him, then leaned forward and kissed him again.

Jack curved his fingers over her nape, cupping the back of her head in his palm, and draped his other arm over her thighs. In turn, Natalie circled his shoulders with her arms and pushed herself closer, tangling her fingers in his hair as she kissed him more deeply still, with all the wanting and the longing that had been building for so long. He responded by opening his hand over her thigh, squeezing it hard before dragging his fingers up over her leg and under her pajama shirt, then settling the splayed fingers of his other hand possessively over her fanny.

When she murmured low in response to his touch, he pressed his palm more firmly over her derriere. And when she shifted on his lap, he groaned, swelling to life against her. The hand that had dipped beneath her top prowled higher, moving forward to cover her breast. And when she pulled her mouth from his to whisper his name, he pressed his mouth to the sensitive skin of her neck.

As he palmed her sensitive flesh, he pushed her top up under her arms, nuzzling the fragrant skin between her breasts before running the tip of his tongue along one plump lower curve. Natalie caught her fingers in his hair and tipped his head backward, but Jack leaned forward again and drew her nipple deep into his mouth. This time she was the one to tip her head backward, and then her body began to fall backward, halting only when he braced his arm against her back to prevent her from tumbling out of his lap and onto the floor. He held her that way while he tasted her, his mouth closing over her breasts again and again, his tongue at once insistent and indolent, generous and demanding. Finally, though, he chose one breast and held it firmly in his hand, focusing his attentions on it completely, until, unable to tolerate the threads of delight unraveling inside her, Natalie cried his name out loud.

Only then did Jack withdraw. After he pulled her pajama top over her head, she clawed at his shirt until it was off. Liberated from the garment, Jack pushed Natalie back onto the bed, settling his body between her legs, and weaving his fingers through her hair.

"I love you," he said simply. "And I will always love you. Do you believe me, Natalie?"

She nodded, knowing unequivocally that it was true. "And I love you," she said. "Forever, Jack. Forever."

He sealed their promises with a kiss, a long, hard, thorough kiss that illustrated their love for each other quite clearly. Then Natalie felt his hand working its way between their bodies, untying the drawstring of her pajama bottoms and tugging them down. He continued to kiss her as he dipped his hand inside the soft flannel, then beneath the cotton of her panties, until he located the dampened heart of her. He swallowed whatever scant protests she might have offered—not that she really wanted to offer any—with another kiss, then drove her to near madness with his eager and expert caresses.

Natalie stilled at his touch, enjoying the lazy exploration of his fingers. But soon, she began to move with him, arching her hips off the mattress, opening her legs wider to encourage him further. He kissed her neck and her shoulder, dragged his tongue along her collarbone, sucked her breast into his mouth again. And then he penetrated her with one long finger, sliding it in deep, making her gasp as a shudder of heat rocketed through her.

And then Jack was skimming her pajama bottoms and panties down over her thighs and knees and ankles, until she was lying naked beneath him. But he was still half-dressed, damn him, which she simply could not have, so instinctively, almost incoherently, she reached for the fly of his jeans and jerked the button and zipper free. Then she shoved her hands beneath the waistband at his back to grasp the hot, taut flesh of his buttocks, before peeling the worn denim down. And then she felt his hard heavy shaft nestled between her legs, and she knew she was almost home.

Bending her knees, she pushed herself forward and wrapped her fingers around the heated length of him, stroking him none too gently, and loving the way he grew harder still in her hand. This time she was the one to sheathe him before guiding him to herself, but this time he was the one who pushed himself inside. Natalie gasped at the depth of his penetration, feeling fuller and more complete than she had ever felt. Before she had a chance to grow accustomed to having him inside her, he withdrew, and before she could protest, he slammed into her again.

This time she cried out loud at the power of his possession, the sound of his name surrounding them both. Jack thrust against her again...and again...and again, increasing his rhythm with every push, rocking his hips against hers with a pulsing regularity that very nearly drove her mad. Then Natalie began to move, too, her body seeming to respond on its own, sensing what Jack needed from her, and taking what she needed from him in return...

The faster they went, the more Natalie began to un-ravel, and she yielded to her response quite willingly, let-ting it run wild. Just when she thought she would lose herself completely, Jack rolled until he was beneath her, bucking savagely up to meet her, penetrating her more deeply than she ever could have imagined.

Once more, he upped the intensity of his movements, until Natalie became lost in the waves of ecstasy breaking inside her. With one final thrust, they cried out together, then she leaned forward and kissed him—kissed him as if she needed him for life itself. But the touch of her mouth on his brought her back to herself again. And she knew she was right where she belonged—with Jack. Forever. The way he belonged with her. As he relaxed beneath her, he wrapped his arms around her and pulled her down to lie beside him.

And Natalie knew then that their happily-ever-after had begun.

Epilogue

THE SATURDAY morning the week before Natalie's wedding dawned hot and humid, as most July mornings were in Louisville, and it stayed hot and humid all day. But that was all right, because she and her husband-to-be had a lot to do around the house they'd moved into scarcely a month before, so they'd be hot all day anyway. Of course, they'd been hot pretty much daily since they moved in together—sometimes twice daily. And once three times, but it had been especially hot that day. And several times they'd been hot on the dining room table, one of those times being only half-clothed. And those instances of heat had had nothing to do with the weather outside.

Right now, however, they were getting hot not through illicit acts, but through honest labor—of which there had also been many occasions. Jack was busy painting the second level of the big Victorian house they'd purchased in Old Louisville, and after he finished that, he had to get to work on the main staircase. It still needed to be shellacked.

Natalie, in the meantime, contented herself on doing some work on the exterior of their new old home. For the most part, the house was in good shape, its foundation sturdy and much of its hardware original. But the previous owners had let the place go until it was tired-looking and outdated. Any necessary changes were merely cosmetic, but there were plenty of cosmetic changes necessary.

She had spent much of the past week stripping and then painting the screened-in back porch, and she was determined to finish giving it a second coat of crisp, white paint by day's end.

When she took a break to stretch and wipe the perspiration from her face, she glanced into the backyard of the house next door and found her new neighbor taking advantage of the sunny day to work in the garden.

"Good afternoon, Mrs. Klosterman!" she called to her former landlady, who looked up at the summons and waved back in greeting. "Your peonies look beautiful!" she added, pointing at the fat red and white blossoms that grew along the property line.

"Thank you!" Mrs. Klosterman called back. "I'll bring some when I come for dinner this evening."

Natalie smiled. She and Jack had issued a blanket invitation to their former landlady when they'd moved in, and every Saturday, Mrs. Klosterman joined them for dinner. It was the least they could do to pay her back for everything she'd done for them.

Jack came outside then, carrying two tall, sweaty glasses of iced tea. "Thought you could use a break as much as I could," he said as he extended one toward Natalie. "'Yo, Mrs. K!" he added when he saw their neighbor out in the yard. "Don't work too hard in this heat!"

Mrs. Klosterman waved a negligent hand at him. "Fear not, dear! I only work hard enough to keep myself out of trouble!"

Jack chuckled quietly. "That's a matter of debate," he said too quietly for their neighbor to hear.

Natalie swatted him playfully. "Hey, sometimes her trouble works out pretty well. Look at us."

He smiled. "Yeah. Look at us."

Okay, so maybe, to the casual observer, they didn't look

all that great at the moment, Natalie in battered cutoffs and a paint-spattered tank top, and Jack in torn jeans and a paint-spattered T-shirt. Natalie knew they looked very fine indeed to each other. Jack, she thought, was especially easy on the eye, with the sleeves of his T-shirt rolled up to reveal salient biceps and brawny forearms, the threadbare cotton stretched so tight across his chest she could see every bump and ridge of his muscular torso. She watched as he lifted his glass to his mouth for a generous taste, his throat working powerfully over the swallow before he lowered the glass again and wiped his mouth with the back of his hand.

And suddenly, the day grew even warmer than it had been before.

She still couldn't believe he was hers, still couldn't quite come to terms with how she had found love with a man like him. Then again, she reminded herself, he was everything she'd always said she wanted in a man: smart, loving, gentle, kind. He was the sort of man who would love her happily ever after. He'd made a big sacrifice, moving away from his home and his family, just to be with her. But she was his family now, and he was hers. Someday, when they were ready, he'd be a wonderful father, too. But for now, she was quite content to have him all to herself. The two of them together made a very good family indeed.

She glanced next door as the thought unfolded in her head and smiled. And Mrs. Klosterman, too, she thought. She was definitely part of their family.

"So is your Uncle Dave all set to come down?" Natalie asked Jack as he drained his glass.

"He can't wait. He made me promise to take him to Churchill Downs while he's here. The guy loves the ponies. Too bad the horses won't be running. He'll still enjoy it, though."

Natalie nibbled her lip in thought for a moment. "You know, Mrs. Klosterman likes the track, too," she said. "Maybe we could make it a foursome one day."

Jack eyed her thoughtfully for a moment, turned to look at their neighbor, then looked back at Natalie and smiled. "Uncle Dave likes the ladies, too," he said.

"Really," Natalie said.

"Yeah, really. And he's got a boatload of stories to tell about his experiences working with WITSEC. He knew a lot of the big-name mobsters."

"Yeah?"

"Oh, sure," Jack said. "Dewey 'the Knife' Delvecchio. Fat Tony Mazzoni. Murray the K—"

"Murray the K wasn't a mobster," Natalie interjected.

"Murray Kaminski? Sure he was," Jack said.

"Oh. I was thinking of a different Murray the K."

"And then there was Lefty 'the Lemon' Barker. And Joey 'the Kangaroo' Madison."

Natalie gaped at him. "There really is a mobster named Joey the Kangaroo?" she asked, recalling that she'd used that very name when jesting with Mrs. Klosterman that first day she met Jack.

"Yeah. Bail jumper," he said.

Of course.

"I bet Mrs. K would really get a kick out of some of Uncle Dave's stories," he added.

"I bet she'd really get a kick out of Uncle Dave," Natalie said.

Jack's grin broadened. "I bet she would, too. 'Cause you know, you can just never really tell with Uncle Dave."

Oh, yeah, Natalie thought. Uncle Dave and Mrs. Klosterman were going to get along *great*. Maybe even as well as she and Jack.

But that was another story.

*Get hot and steamy every month with
Mills & Boon Blaze® and look out for
Elizabeth Bevarly's*
Indecent Suggestion
coming to Blaze in November 2006.

*Friends become lovers in this
red-hot office romance!*

What Phoebe Wants

by
Cindi Myers

For Pam Hopkins
who never gave up on this one.

And special thanks to Wanda Ottewell for
giving Phoebe a chance.

1

MY GRANDMOTHER ALWAYS TOLD ME, you make your own luck. As if luck was something that could be baked like a cake or sewn like a shirt. Of course, my cakes could be used as first base down at the ballpark, and my ninth-grade home-ec class voted me "girl most likely to do bodily harm with a sewing machine." This could explain why I haven't had much luck lately, of any kind.

Which would you say is worse: being dumped by your husband who then takes up with a twenty-four-year-old cocktail waitress who has a stomach tight enough to bounce quarters off, or sitting in a cubicle that smells of cigar smoke and sweat, listening to a shiny-faced car salesman try to make you a "deal"?

Having recently endured both, I'd have to say it's something of a draw. The whole sorry business with my husband dragged on longer, but in its own way, the ordeal with the car salesman was just as tedious.

"Now, I know a woman like you is concerned about finding something dependable." The salesman nodded sagely and gave me a toothy grin. He had a bad comb-over and his deodorant had long since packed up and hitched a ride out of town. "I mean, what good is a great deal on a vehicle if it leaves you in the lurch?"

Left me in the lurch. That's what Steve did when he walked out. Just calmly packed his bags and said, "I know you don't want me here if I'm not happy." As if his leaving was all about his concern for me, and not about his own pathetic midlife crisis.

"You see what I'm saying, Ms. Frame? My only concern is that you leave here today happy."

There was that word again—happy. At this point in my life, I was beginning to think the whole pursuit of happiness shtick was highly overrated. "I just need something that will get me where I'm going and doesn't cost more than six thousand dollars." I twisted the straps of my purse in my hand.

The salesman made a face as if he'd just sucked a lemon. "Six thousand. Now, I don't know if we're gonna find much for six thousand." He leaned toward me, his yellowing teeth looming large in my vision. "Do you have a trade-in?"

I blinked. "A trade-in?"

"Another car? Do you have another car to trade in?"

"Yes. It's...uh, it's parked down the street." The maroon Ford Probe had died at the corner of Anderson and Alameda, smoke spewing from under the hood. An alarming sequence of pings and rattles issued from the engine before it gave a last gasp and simply quit altogether. I had sat there for a long moment, head on the steering wheel, too disgusted to waste tears. Then I'd gathered up my purse and keys and started walking.

Walking is a relative term in Houston in late August. It was more like swimming through the heavy, humid air. Heat radiated up from the pavement, through the soles of my sandals. Sweat pooled in the small of my back and my hair clung damply to my forehead. As I walked, I tried to think of new epithets for Steve, who had driven away from me in a brand new black Lexus, leaving me with the twelve-year-old Ford.

I'd started alphabetically, with addlepated asshole and was up to middle-aged midget-brain when I saw the sign for Easy Motors. That was it. I'd buy a new car. Or at least one that was newer than the recently departed Ford.

The salesman—the nameplate on his desk said his name was Hector—grabbed a form off the corner of the desk and began to write. "So what are you trading in?"

"It's a 1990 Ford Probe. Maroon."

"Maroon." He wrote down this information. "Mileage?"

"One hundred and seventy thousand."

His frown got a little tighter. "Car that old, that many miles, most I can give you for it is five hundred dollars."

I blinked. Wasn't he even going to ask if it ran? I bit my lip, fighting a decidedly inconvenient attack of conscience.

Hector apparently mistook my silence for reluctance. "Six hundred. Most I can do. Take it or leave it."

I swallowed hard. "Where do I sign?"

I had never bought a car before. My father had purchased the first vehicle I'd driven, an orange Gremlin formerly owned by a dog trainer. Every time it rained, the car smelled of wet poodle. Steve bought the maroon Probe for me for Christmas one year. I'd wanted a blue Mustang, but he had surprised me with the Probe and I thought it would have appeared ungrateful to protest, though I could never look at the car without thinking of dental work.

"All right, then." Hector pushed back his chair and stood. "I'll show you what I've got in your price range."

For the next hour, I followed Hector around the lot as he showed me red Volkswagens, yellow Chevies and a lime-green car of indiscernible lineage. "Now darling, this is the perfect car for you," he said, patting the hood of the lime-green model. "Very sporty."

I stared at what looked to be an escapee from the bumper-car ride at the carnival. "I could never drive anything that color."

Hector took out an oversize handkerchief and mopped his forehead. "Well, honey, I wouldn't say in your price range you can afford to be picky. Besides—" he patted the car again

"—it's proven that cars this color are in fewer wrecks. Why do you think they paint fire engines green these days?"

A flash of blue caught my attention. That's when I saw it. My dream car. "What about that one?" I pointed toward a blue Mustang at the back corner of the lot.

"That one?" Hector rubbed his chin. "Yeah, I forgot about that one." He straightened. "Sure. I could make you a deal."

We walked over to the Mustang. It had a dent in one door and tired-looking upholstery. I slid into the driver's seat and turned the key. The engine coughed, then turned over. "Honey, I'd say it's you." Hector leaned in the window and grinned.

An hour later, I drove off the lot in the Mustang. I didn't really care that it was a ninety-six model or that it had a bumper sticker that read Onward Through the Fog. The important thing was that it was blue, the color of the dream car I'd never gotten. I'd taken it as a sign. I was on my own now, calling all the shots. And, by God, I was going to have that blue Mustang—my dream—dents and all.

THERE ARE TIMES WHEN I CONSIDER not having been born with pots of money to be a gross injustice. Just inside the door of the employee lounge at the Central Care Network Clinic where I work is a banner that proclaims: Two Million in Profits and Climbing! Whenever I see this, I feel majorly annoyed. Not only had I not been born with money, I had managed to find a job that guaranteed I wouldn't be getting my share of that two mil. Next to nurses' aides and janitors, transcriptionists are at the bottom of the hospital hierarchy.

But hey, I was young and single and had a new car, so what did I have to complain about, right? *Yeah, right,* I thought, as I boarded the elevator heading up to my cubicle in the family-practice section of the clinic the next day. I pasted a fake smile on my face as I entered the elevator. My mother had always told me I should smile even when I didn't feel like smiling because it would help me to develop the "habit of happiness." I preferred to think a permanent smile gave people doubts about your sanity, and thus they left you alone.

Family Practice was on the eleventh floor of the steel-and-glass high-rise in the Texas Medical Center complex. At every floor, the elevator doors parted and more people poured in as others exited. I found myself pushed farther and farther toward the rear of the car, until my nose was practically buried in the shellacked updo of an orthopedics receptionist.

I always got nervous when the elevator was this full. What if there was too much weight for the cables? What if it stopped between floors? Would we suffocate? Just last week Mary Joe Wisnewski from pediatrics had been stuck between floors for an hour.

And here I was, packed in like a teenager at dollar-a-car night at the drive-in. Two drug pushers—also known as pharmaceutical salesmen—hemmed me in on either side. I couldn't even move my arms.

So, of course, I had an itch I needed to scratch. On my butt. I shifted from one foot to the other, trying to ignore the persistent tickle on my right cheek as the elevator ground to a halt to take on still more passengers.

The tickle developed into a pinch. The hair on the back of my neck stood at attention as I realized the reason for my posterior disturbance. Some guy had his hand up my dress! He was poking and prodding my cheek like a baker testing dough. Or maybe he was a plastic surgeon who thought I was a likely candidate for a buttocks-lift.

I shifted, trying to move away from him, but in the packed elevator, it was impossible. The invisible groper started working on my other cheek. "Stop that!" I yelped.

My fellow passengers regarded me curiously, and there was a decided leaning away from me. Fury choked me.

Where did this pervert get off feeling me up like that? I'd show him.

I shifted my weight to my left leg and swung my right foot back, connecting solidly with the joker's kneecap. If I'd had more room, I would have aimed higher. As it was, he grunted and let me go. The doors opened and I surged forward, elbowing two old women out of the way as I broke for freedom.

I stood beside a potted palm in the corridor and tried to see into the elevator, to identify the man who'd groped me. But the doors shut before I could make out anyone. Sighing, I adjusted my purse on my shoulder and headed for the stairs to hike up the three floors to Family Practice.

"Phoebe, you're late." The office manager, Joan Lee, shoved a stack of patient folders into my hands. "Dr. Patterson is in rare form this morning." Standing four foot eleven inches in a size-one Jones New York suit, Joan looked like a geisha who'd gotten lost on her way to Wall Street. Her voice was soft as silk, but her backbone was diamond-hard steel. Insurance companies quaked at the sound of her name, and even the most bullheaded surgeon addressed her respectfully as "Ms. Lee, ma'am."

"He wants those charts on his desk by noon," Joan continued. "So you'd better get busy."

"No problem." I shifted the folders to my left arm and headed for the coffee machine for a fortifying cup. "Barb and I will split them up and have them done by eleven."

"Sorry, but Barb can't help you. I had to put her on the front desk this morning."

I turned, empty cup in hand. "Why? Where's Kathleen?"

Joan shook her head and disappeared around the corner. Dr. Patterson's nurse, Michelle, joined me at the coffee machine. "Kathleen was dismissed," she whispered as she spooned creamer into her cup.

I raised my eyebrows. "Turned him down again, did she?"

Dr. Patterson had been badgering the receptionist to go out with him for weeks now —despite the fact that both of them were married, and not to each other.

Michelle shrugged. "I guess so. Or maybe he decided to move on to greener pastures and didn't want her hanging around."

"Michelle, the doctor needs you in room three." Joan hurried past us, dragging a loaded lab cart. "Phoebe, don't forget those charts have to be done by noon."

"I can do it if the system cooperates. When is the new transcription system supposed to be installed?" I called after Joan's retreating back.

"Soon. You'll have to make do until then." She disappeared around the corner, test tubes rattling in her wake.

I headed for my workroom at the back of the office suite. Windowless and cramped, it resembled the supply closet it had once been. A long counter had been installed to hold the two computers and transcription equipment, and a single filing cabinet provided a place to stash my purse. Nothing fancy, but it was quiet, out of the flow of traffic and no one cared how many empty coffee cups or Diet Coke cans I let pile up as long as I got my work done on time.

I booted up my computer and popped the first tape into the transcription machine. Dr. Patterson's Texas twang filled my headphones. "The patient is a well-developed young woman of sixteen, presenting with pain in the left patella." I rolled my eyes as I typed. Patterson was always going on about the beauty or physical developments of his female patients. If they were over twenty-one he'd note if they were married or single and if they had any children. I wondered if he was making notes to himself for future reference.

I busted butt and finished the last of the tapes at ten after twelve and was fastening a printout onto the front of a patient chart when the intercom buzzed. "Doctor Patterson would like to see you in his office," Joan announced.

I groaned. What was he going to do, chew me out for being ten minutes late? "If he didn't go on so much about how big a patient's boobs or behind were, he'd shave half an hour off my transcription time," I muttered as I gathered up the charts and headed for the doctor's lair at the other end of the office.

Dr. Ken Patterson was a tall man with the broad shoulders and thick neck of a former football player. He, in fact, had been a linebacker for the University of Texas before deciding on a career in medicine. His hairline had receded in twin widow's peaks, frosted with gray, which only added to his distinguished good looks. Patients talked about how charming he was, but I thought there was more smarm than charm in the good doctor.

"Here are the charts you wanted." I deposited the stack of file folders on the corner of his desk. It was a massive mahogany piece that was big enough for a grown man to stretch out on. Rumor had it that Patterson had made good use of that space with more than one woman. Frankly, I was glad it wasn't my job to polish the thing. I turned to leave, but Patterson caught me by the arm.

"What's your hurry?" Still clutching my arm, he reached back and pushed the door closed.

I frowned. I didn't want to end up like Kathleen, with bills to pay and no job, but neither did I want to end up as Patterson's next plaything. "I have a lot of work to do," I said, trying to pull away from him.

"Yes, I've noticed how tense you've been lately." He released me, but continued to block my path to the door. "I think maybe you've been working too hard."

"I'm fine, really." I tried to dodge past him and collided with Albert, the life-size skeletal model grinning cheerfully from his stand next to the desk.

Albert clanked and swayed like a macabre set of wind chimes. At Halloween we dressed him up and stationed him by the reception desk with a bowl of candy, but the rest of the year Albert was a mute observer of the goings-on in Patterson's office. If those bones could talk...

"The real reason I wanted to see you is I have a question about one of the notes you transcribed for me." Patterson walked around the desk, seemingly all business, but I didn't let down my guard. He pulled a folder from a stack in his out box and beckoned me toward him. "It's right here. Please take a look and tell me what you think this means."

I leaned over the desk, staying as far from Patterson's octopus arms as possible. Fortunately, I could read upside down. "Patient is recently divorced, suffering from nervous strain." I looked up at Patterson. "I'm certain that's what you said on the tape. Is there something wrong?"

"Not wrong, but I couldn't help thinking how well that phrase describes your own situation." He pressed the tips of his fingers together and looked down his nose at me, as if I'd suddenly developed a rare disease. Or a third breast. "You know, Phoebe, not only am I your employer, but I think of myself as your physician, as well. It's obvious to me that since your divorce, you, too, have been exhibiting signs of nervous strain. I believe I can help you."

I started backing toward the door. "Dr. Michaels over at County General is my doctor."

For a man of his size, Patterson was amazingly quick. He came around the desk and pulled me to him in a bear hug. It was like being caught in the elevator doors, my ribs creaking, my breath cut off. "I find you so attractive," he murmured, and began kissing my neck. Wet slobbery kisses. You'd think a man who considered himself a modern-day Don Juan would have a better technique. I struggled, caught tight in his crazed grip.

Nose buried in my neck, his ear brushed up against my lips, pink and vulnerable. I know how to take advantage of a good opportunity when I see it. I bit down hard.

He screamed like a woman, a high-pitched shriek that was probably heard two floors away. I shot out of his arms and was standing by the door by the time he straightened up. He had one hand clapped over his ear and his eyes were wet. "Why did you do that?" he asked, seeming genuinely puzzled.

"Did I mention I have this thing about being held against my will?" I turned the doorknob. "I'm going to pretend this never happened," I said. "But if you so much as lay a hand on me again I'll report you to the AMA, the TMA, the BBB and anybody else who'll listen."

"Phoebe, Phoebe, Phoebe." He started toward me again, arms outstretched, pleading. "I know you've been without a man for months now. Surely you must need the physical release—"

I was out the door before he finished the sentence. My feet pounded down the carpeted hallway in time with my furiously beating heart. "What I need is to be left the hell alone," I muttered as I rounded the corner, headed toward the front office. Joan was going to hear about the doctor's latest shenanigans.

I didn't see the man at the end of the hallway until it was too late. I had a fleeting impression of broad shoulders and dark hair before I barreled into him. Papers scattered as he was shoved back against one wall. He struggled for balance, holding on to the only support available—me.

2

"GET YOUR HANDS OFF OF ME!" I swatted at the stranger as his fingers clutched at my dress.

"You're the one who ran into me, lady." He righted himself and stared down at me. He was quite tall and, in a better mood, I probably would have thought he was handsome, with his tousled dark hair and heavy-lidded eyes. He was fairly young, midtwenties, I guessed.

"You should watch where you're going," I snapped.

"I could say the same to you."

We glared at each other, both rumpled and out of breath. Not unlike two people in the aftermath of a particularly vigorous round of sex. I swallowed. Now why had I thought of that? Except, of course, that he was a particularly handsome man, and those dark eyes of his seemed to look right through me, as if he could tell I was wearing my best Givenchy underwear.

Stop it! I ordered myself. I glanced around, hoping someone would come to my rescue. The office was eerily silent and I realized everyone else had gone to lunch. Me and handsome Hank here were alone, except, of course, for the lecherous doctor.

I smoothed my hands down my sides. The thing to do was to stay calm and collected. That was me. Ms. Cool. "If you're here to see the doctor, his office is back there." I pointed down the hallway.

"Actually, I'm looking for a Phoebe Frame." The man

glanced around us. "Maybe you could point me in the right direction and I promise to stay out of your way."

"Phoebe Frame?" I felt my face warm. "Uh, what do you want with her?"

"Not that it's your business, but I'm here to install a new transcription system. She is the transcriptionist, isn't she?"

"Yes." The word came out as a squeak. I straightened and tried to look indifferent. "I'm Phoebe. If you'll follow me, the transcription room is right this way."

I marched past him, down the hall toward my cubicle. By now it felt as if my whole face and neck were on fire. And red is not my best color. Not that I cared what handsome Hank thought of my looks, but...

I stopped at the doorway to my cubicle and whirled to face him. "You haven't told me your name."

"You didn't give me time." He offered me a card. "Jeff Fischer. My friends call me Jeff, but you can call me Mr. Fischer."

All right, maybe I deserved that. I cleared my throat. "Look, I'm sorry about, well, about just now. I was very annoyed at someone and you were in the wrong place at the wrong time."

He set his briefcase on the counter and opened it. "Yeah, well, I guess you weren't hired for your personality anyway, huh?"

"I said I was sorry."

"Forget about it."

"Oh, that is so like a man."

"What are you talking about?"

"You insult me, and then you try to blow it off as if it isn't important."

"Hey, you insulted me first."

"I did not."

"Yes, you did. You accused me of trying to grope you when I was only trying to keep my balance."

"You *were* groping me." I flushed, remembering the feel of his hand on my breast. "Though I'll admit, you probably didn't do it on purpose."

He looked up at the ceiling, addressing some invisible being. "She admits she's wrong. That must be a first."

"How can you say that? You don't even know me."

He grinned. "No, but I'd like to." He stuck out his hand. "Let's start over. I'm Jeff Fischer. Nice to meet you, Miss Frame. Or is it Mrs.?"

"It's Ms." I shook his hand, ignoring the flutter in my stomach at his touch. Maybe I was just hungry. "Nice to meet you, too, Mr. Fischer."

"I thought we were going to be friends now. Call me Jeff."

"All right, Jeff. I'll, uh, just leave you to your work."

"Sure you don't want to stick around? You could tell me what I'm doing wrong."

"No, I think I'll go to lunch." I backed toward the door. With any luck, Jeff wouldn't be here when I got back. The last thing I needed right now was a young, handsome man with a sarcastic sense of humor.

Or maybe it was the *first* thing I needed. Sometimes the two extremes aren't that far apart.

ON THURSDAYS, I ALWAYS HAVE LUNCH with my friend Darla. After the morning I'd had, I figured our lunch would be the one spot of sanity in my day. A tall blonde with an Ivana Trump updo, Darla is not only my best gal pal and chief partner-in-crime, she's also my hairdresser—the only person who knows my real hair color—and the keeper of all my secrets.

"You got new wheels!" she squealed as I pulled to the curb in front of Hair Apparent, the salon where she works. She climbed into the passenger seat. "What happened to your old ride?" She flipped down the passenger side visor and fluffed her bangs in the makeup mirror.

"The Probe died yesterday afternoon, smoke pouring out from under the hood and everything."

"So you just walked down the street and bought a new one?" Darla's perfectly plucked eyebrows rose in amazement.

I shrugged. "It was either that, or call a taxi."

I turned into the lot of Taco Loco and found a parking place. Darla followed me inside and we slid into our usual booth. "I never knew anyone who decided to buy a car and just did it," she said. "I mean, aren't you supposed to research these things? Take test-drives?"

The waitress set two glasses of iced tea and a basket of hot chips in front of us. "The usual?" she asked.

"The usual," we chorused. Chicken chalupas with guacamole. Best in the city. I turned back to Darla. "That's how Steve bought cars. How my father bought cars." In fact, it was how every man I knew bought cars. Did that make it right?

Darla raised her glass in a toast. "To Phoebe's new wheels," she said. "May they take you places you've always wanted to go."

I liked the sound of that, even if I had yet to figure out where it was I was headed. "What's new with you?" I asked.

She suddenly became very interested in the placemat in front of her, eyes avoiding mine. "Well..." She pursed her lips. "I heard some news today. Something I don't think you'll especially enjoy hearing."

I sipped my tea and tried not to look too interested. News meant gossip and it felt unseemly to appear overeager to indulge in something that, after all, was supposed to be a vice. "News about what?" I asked after a moment.

"News about Steve and Miss Just-a-waitress."

Darla's nose for news had discovered that the teenybopper

Steve had started dating three months into his midlife search for "happiness" worked at the Yellow Rose, one of those cabaret places euphemistically known as gentlemen's clubs. The girl—Tami—swore she was "just a waitress," though from what I had seen, she was certainly well qualified to wear tassels, or whatever sort of excuse for a costume was customary for dancers in those places. "I don't want to hear it," I said, and shut my mouth firmly, as if to hold back any sign of the curiosity that was already spreading over me like a rash.

"You're going to find out sooner or later." She leaned across the table, her voice soft. "And I think it's something you'd much prefer to hear from me."

My stomach quivered. I hated this—hated caring what Steve and his girlfriend were up to. My goal in life was not to care, to be serene and happy and above it all.

But I wasn't there yet. I took another swallow of tea, trying to wet my too-dry mouth. "What is it?"

Darla studied her perfect manicure. "Just-a-waitress came into the shop today."

I waited, but apparently Darla required some sort of reaction before proceeding. "Did she have an appointment, or just drop by to say hi?"

"She had an appointment. With Henry." She made a face. "Good thing it wasn't with me, or she'd have walked out bald."

I held back a snicker. Tami had gorgeous long blond hair. The idea of her without that crowning glory had a certain nasty appeal. "So what's the scoop? Did she get dreadlocks, or a pierced nose?"

Darla shook her head. "Didn't you say Steve never wanted children?"

There went my stomach again, acting as if I'd just plunged five stories in the front car of a roller coaster. "Yes. I mean, no, he never wanted children. He said they would make things too complicated."

I put a hand over my belly, not even realizing until it was too late that I'd done so. In the early days, I'd thought I'd change Steve's mind, that one day we'd have a family. Even as recently as last year, I'd been telling myself we had plenty of time. "What are you saying, Darla?"

"I'm saying Steve's life is about to get pretty complicated. Just-a-waitress is four or five months gone."

I counted back in my head. That meant it had happened after our divorce six months ago. We'd been separated six months before that. Plenty of time for me to get over the guy, right? Why should I care what he and his girlfriend were up to?

"You don't look so good." Darla leaned forward and studied my face,

"I'll be okay in a minute," I managed to squeak out.

"Okay is a relative term." She frowned. "You want to talk about it?"

I shook my head. No, I wasn't okay. And no, I didn't want to talk about it.

The waitress brought our food and I focused on adding salsa to my chalupa, glad of an excuse not to say anything. Even if I'd wanted to spill my guts to Darla, I didn't think I could have found the words to describe how I felt.

Something ugly and black had attached itself to my insides, some slimy emotional specter that was, in turns, angry and disgusted. I'd put off having children because Steve didn't want them, yet our divorce papers were scarcely cold before he knocked up some other woman. Outside, I was mute, lips welded together by pride. But inside, I was screaming.

"So, what are you going to do now?" Darla scooped guacamole onto a chip and popped it into her mouth.

Last I heard, murder was still illegal. I sighed and laid aside my empty spoon. "What can I do? I have to get on with my life."

She eyed me critically. "Starting when? It's been six months since the divorce and almost a year since Steve walked out. Have you been on a single date?"

"Just what I need—another man in my life." I shook my head. "No, thank you."

"They aren't all bad. You like Tony, don't you?"

Tony was a truck driver Darla referred to as her rustproof lover—"heart of gold and buns of steel." He was also a genuinely sweet guy. "You got the last good one," I said.

"Oh, come on. You're still young. Attractive. You could find someone nice."

I shook my head. "Who would I date? In my job all the men I meet are either old, sick or married." The image of a certain studly computer installer popped up to call me a liar. Okay, so Jeff Fischer was gorgeous and I hadn't noticed a ring on his hand. He was also young and sarcastic and I hadn't exactly wowed him with my charm. "I don't need another man in my life," I said, stabbing a fork into my chalupa for emphasis.

"Just think about it," Darla said gently.

I nodded. "I'll think about it." But thinking and doing are two entirely different animals, aren't they?

I RETURNED TO WORK AFTER LUNCH and discovered the cubbyhole had been ransacked. My computer processor sat in the hall, my transcription machine balanced atop it. My monitor occupied my chair and half a mile of cable coiled around the doorway like so many snakes prepared to wrap around my ankles.

I picked my way through this maze and stepped into the room, only to be confronted with one of the finest specimens of male *gluteus maximus* I've ever been privileged to see.

The butt in question wasn't naked, more's the pity, but the

expertly tailored slacks molded around it did a nice job of showing it to advantage.

"What are you staring at?" The rest of the man in question emerged from beneath my desk.

"Jeff! Uh, hello." I moved over and pretended to be interested in a stack of computer manuals. "Was I staring?"

He pointed a screwdriver at me. "You were staring. And smiling."

"I'm just delighted at the prospect of finally getting the new transcription system installed." I kept my eyes on the manual, pretending to be reading, but I was really trying to identify the cologne he was wearing. Something spicy, faintly exotic...

"I didn't know you read Chinese." He'd risen and was looking over my shoulder.

I glanced down at the booklet in my hand. Rows of Chinese characters danced across the page. I snapped the booklet shut. "I was studying the diagrams." I pointed to the snarl of cables streaming out from under my desk. "Don't you think you should do something about all that?"

"Your usual sunny self, I see." He kneeled and began fiddling with something under my desk. "And here I thought we were going to be friends."

I didn't want to be friends with Jeff Fischer. He was too young, too good-looking, too full of himself, too *male*. Men were not at the top of my list these days. I kicked at the tangle of cables. "How am I supposed to get any work done with everything scattered all over the place like this?"

"I'll have it all back together in no time." His head disappeared beneath the desk once more.

"With this new system, you'll be faster than ever." He reached up and patted the desktop. "Have a seat and keep me company."

I backed toward the door. "Maybe I'd better leave you alone to do your work."

"I work better when I have a pretty woman to talk to."

I resented the flutter that ran through my stomach. As if a compliment from a smart-ass like him meant anything. I told myself I was only staying because if I went back up front Joan would put me to work labeling urine samples, or filing test results or some equally odious chore.

So I took a seat on the desk, next to a canvas satchel that spilled tools across the desktop. It wasn't the most comfortable position. My feet didn't touch the ground, which left my legs swinging practically in Jeff's face. Why had I decided this was a good day to wear my chartreuse-with-white-polka-dots slip dress?

"That's better." Jeff's gaze traveled from my exposed knees to my ankles. "Very nice."

He grinned in a way that might have been lecherous on someone who didn't already look like an Eagle Scout. "How old are you?" I blurted.

He arched one eyebrow. "Old enough to know my way around."

"No really. How old?"

"I'm twenty-six." He said it as if he was announcing a winning Lotto number. "How old are you?"

"Too old for you." I inched farther away from him.

"I prefer experienced women." He went back to operating his screwdriver.

Experienced? Was that anything like a used car being "experienced"? Or did I look like a woman who'd been around the block a few times? "What makes you think I'm experienced?"

"Let's just say you don't strike me as a recent escapee from a convent."

"Someone told you I was divorced. That Michelle—"

"No, I didn't know that. I was thinking more about the hickey on your neck."

I clapped my hand to my neck so hard the skin stung. Heat washed over me and I knew my face was bright red. "I do not have a hickey!" Where would I have gotten one? I hadn't been intimate with a man since.... A sick feeling washed over me as I recalled my prelunch wrestling session with Dr. P. The bastard.

Jeff stood and dropped the screwdriver into the tool bag. "It's not that noticeable," he said. "It's just above your collar, right...there." His finger brushed across my skin, a feather touch that made every nerve ending vibrate with awareness. I took a deep breath, trying to regain my composure, but all that did was draw his spicy, exotic, masculine scent into my lungs. I stared at the V of naked chest showing in the open throat of his shirt and fought the insane urge to plant a kiss right...there.

Hormones. That had to be it. They were like ants. They'd been fine, not bothering me at all in the year since Steve had called it quits. Content to go about the business of doing whatever hormones were supposed to do in the body. And then the stud here had disturbed them. One touch from him and the hormones had come to life like an anthill stirred with a stick. And they apparently weren't going to calm down anytime soon. I wouldn't be safe around any being with a hint of testosterone. The next thing I knew, I'd be leering at old men in elevators and flirting with the teenager behind the counter at McDonald's.

"I have to go." I slid off the desk, scattering three screwdrivers and a socket set in my hurry to escape.

I fled to the ladies' room and contemplated my red face in the mirror. Wincing, I pulled back my hair and studied the purpling love bite. "That no-good Dr. Lech. I ought to—"

"Phoebe, hurry up in there." Michelle pounded on the door. "I have to go."

I grabbed my purse and groped through it, in vain hope I'd find a scarf to cover the evidence of a definite lapse in judgment. But I didn't wear scarves. I searched the supply cabinet mounted over the toilet. Nothing but half a box of tampons, two cans of hair spray, six rolls of toilet paper and a pink toothbrush. Short of wrapping toilet paper around my neck, I was stuck.

I opened the door and sidled past Michelle, my head down so that my hair fell forward to cover the side of my neck. "Are you okay?" she asked.

"I'm fine. Do we have any bandages?"

"Sure. In the lab. Over the sink. Did you cut yourself?"

"Just a paper cut," I mumbled, and hurried to the lab.

I was studying my reflection in the paper-towel dispenser, making sure I'd covered the mark, when Michelle came into the lab. "You got a paper cut on your neck?"

I straightened and tugged my collar a little higher. "I, uh, was carrying some charts and one slipped." Was I a pathetic liar, or what?

Michelle laughed. "Reminds me of high school. We used to put Band-Aids over hickeys. As if everyone didn't know what was under there." She picked up the blood-draw tray and turned to leave, but paused in the doorway. "You'd better watch those paper cuts, Phoebe. A girl can't be too careful, you know."

She giggled and left the room. I sagged against the counter. Great. Now the whole office would think I'd been up to something. If only I *had* been up to something. At least I'd have great memories to go along with the hickey.

The staccato tap of high heels on linoleum announced Joan Lee's approach. "What are you doing hiding in here?" she asked. She peered closer. "What is that on your neck?"

"Vampire. Met him in the park last night. I'm thinking maybe I ought to go home in case I suddenly develop a desire to start biting people."

Joan frowned. "There are no such things as vampires. Besides, you can't go home. Dr. Patterson wants to see you."

"Speaking of bloodsuckers..."

Joan frowned. "He's in his office. Don't keep him waiting. He has patients to see."

When Joan heard humor was contagious, she was the first in line to be immunized against it.

3

RELUCTANTLY, I MADE MY WAY to Dr. Patterson's office.

Albert grinned at me from his usual post. Someone had crowned him with a Houston Astros ball cap. "Orange is not your color," I told him. "It does nothing for your complexion."

"Good afternoon, Phoebe." Dr. Patterson looked up from a patient chart. "Did you have a pleasant lunch?" He frowned. "What's wrong with your neck?"

"You're what's wrong with it." I glared at him. "When you groped me earlier, you gave me a hickey."

He blinked, his expression bland. "Obviously, you're delusional." He consulted the papers in his hand, suddenly all business. "I'd like you to help me with some research I'm doing for my upcoming presentation at the annual Texas Medical Association conference. It's a tremendous honor to be selected and my presentation must be perfect."

Right. This was all about him. What else was new? "I'm a transcriptionist," I said, trying to match his chilly demeanor. "I don't see how I could help—"

"I'd ask the receptionist to take care of it, but until we hire a new one, that position is vacant and I can't wait to prepare this presentation." He handed me a sheet torn from a yellow legal pad. "Besides, you're not busy right now, not with the new transcription system being installed. All you have to do is conduct a Web search for the topics listed here."

I frowned at the list of medical terms on the paper. "I'm not sure what these mean."

"You're welcome to use my reference books to look up anything you need." He nodded toward an oak bookcase against the far wall. "And I'll be happy to assist you when I have the time." His smile was just short of a leer.

I folded the sheet of paper. "Would this assignment involve working late?" _With you?_

He moved toward me. "I promise you'll be rewarded."

I prepared to dodge out of the way when Joan Lee appeared in the doorway, trailed by a drug pusher in a gray suit. You hang around doctors' offices long enough, you can spot these guys and gals. Expensive suits, perfectly styled hair, imported sports cars—everything about them screams big bucks, including their perfectly straight, gleaming white teeth. Those teeth were always on display as they grinned and glad-handed their way through the office. They passed out pens and sticky notes like candy. Sometimes they even passed out candy. At Christmas, they brought elaborate gift baskets, which the doctor usually kept for himself.

I didn't intend to let this interruption derail our discussion. With any luck, the pusher would be in and out in a few minutes and I could tell Patterson exactly what he could do with his little extra "project."

I drifted to the bookcase and pretended to be interested in the _Merck Manual._

"I brought those samples you asked about, doc." The salesman's voice boomed through the office as he opened his sample case.

Patterson glanced at me, but I kept turning pages in the big green book, feigning avid interest in a description of contact dermatitis.

"Great, Jerry. Thanks a lot."

Jerry pulled out a cardboard tray of little boxes. Each bottle would contain a few pills of medication, meant to be handed out as samples to patients, who would then be convinced enough of the drug's benefits to opt for a full prescription. "Everything they say about this stuff is true," Jerry gushed. "It'll sure put pep in your pecker."

By now I had a pretty good idea of what drug Jerry was peddling. Sure enough, every box in that tray was emblazoned with the familiar blue tablet and a capital *V*.

To my secret delight, a stain of red crept up the back of Patterson's neck. He hastily shoved the samples in his desk and ushered Jerry from the room.

As soon as they were gone, I replaced the *Merck* on the shelf and rushed to the desk. I opened the drawer and took out the tray of little boxes. Sure enough, it was Viagra. As if the doc needed any more pep in his pecker.

I didn't have time to open all the little boxes and empty each bottle, so I dropped the whole tray in the trash can beside Patterson's desk and carried it out with me.

I passed Joan in the hall and she gave me a curious look.

"I thought since I wasn't busy, I'd try to clean up a little around here," I said.

At the end of the hall, I ducked into the ladies' room and emptied every bottle in the toilet. Then I stuffed Patterson's trash can in the supply closet and sauntered back into the corridor, humming to myself. My bad mood had vanished. I felt almost giddy. I didn't know what had come over me. I'd never done anything so daring in my life.

I pushed aside a momentary nudge of guilt by telling myself that Patterson deserved this small payback after the way he'd treated me. Women everywhere would be thankful if they knew what I'd just done.

I passed Jeff near the end of the hallway. "What are you looking so smug about?" he asked.

I gave him what I hoped was a mysterious smile. "My

mama always said nothing would make your day like doing a good deed for someone else and she was right."

He angled himself against the wall, blocking my way. "What good deed did you do?"

I shook my finger at him. "Oh, but it's more virtuous to do your good deeds in secret."

"Since when are you virtuous?" He reached out and stroked the bandage at my throat. "Barney. Definitely your style."

I fought against a blush. "It was all we had. They're very popular with kids. Would you like one?"

His voice was a low rumble that set up vibrations in my chest. "I can think of a few things I'd like from you, but a Band-Aid isn't one of them."

My knees suddenly felt wobbly. I fought the urge to hold on to him for support. "Dream on," I said, sounding a little out of breath.

He leaned closer, a decidedly wicked grin making him more handsome than ever. "Sometimes dreams come true, you know."

He let me by him and I tottered to my room, which was miraculously back together. A mixture of victorious exaltation and frustrated desire made me giddy. So Jeff wasn't right for me? A woman could flirt, couldn't she? I probably needed the practice. And putting one over on "Dr. Love" was enough to make anyone happy.

I sank into my chair. Yes, from now on I wasn't putting up with crap from anybody. I was declaring a one-woman revolution. I reached for the phone and punched in Darla's number.

"Darla, I want to make an appointment. I need a color job."

"Okay. Let me make sure I have some Bashful Blonde in stock."

I glanced at my reflection in the darkened computer monitor. "Forget the blond. I'm ready for a change."

"A change? What kind of a change?" She sounded alarmed.

I twirled a lock of hair around my finger. "I think I'm ready for something more exciting. More daring." My grin widened. "I'm ready to be a redhead."

AT FIVE O'CLOCK ON THE DOT, I escaped from work, leaving Jeff on his hands and knees in my office, threading computer wire along the baseboards. "Leaving already?" he asked as I walked past.

"I have an important appointment."

"Another hot date with the vampire?" He had a way of arching one eyebrow when he said something meant to tease me that made my mouth go dry.

Hormones, I reminded myself. *Just those damned hormones.* "Next time I see him, I'll drive a stake through his heart."

Jeff put a hand over his heart. "Remind me to never rub you the wrong way."

You're never going to rub me the right way, either, I thought, but did my best to keep the sentiment from my face. Jeff Fischer was sexier than any man had a right to be, but he was also six years younger than me. Not that much older than Just-a-waitress. Wouldn't Steve laugh if he thought I was having my own midlife crisis?

With that thought souring my mood, I drove to Hair Apparent. It was one of those huge places with six stylists, two manicurists, a tanning booth and a massage therapist. The year before, they'd added the words Day Spa to their name and prices had shot up twenty percent. But I stayed with the place because of Darla. It's hard enough to find a friend these days, and even harder to find a good hair stylist.

Darla greeted me with what looked like a giant, economy-size bottle of ketchup in her hand. "What do you think?" she asked, holding up the bottle so that a beam of sunlight from the front window struck it. "It's called Ravishing Ruby."

"It looks like ketchup." Maybe my decision to be a redhead had been a little hasty....

"It looks better on. Trust me." She shoved me into a chair and wrapped me in a plastic cape.

"What's with the Barney bandage on your neck?" she asked as she fastened the cape.

"You don't want to know." I grabbed a magazine off the counter beside the chair and opened it at random.

"There are two people you do not keep secrets from in this world—your hairdresser and your best friend. I happen to be both, so spill."

I didn't have to look in the mirror to know my face was redder than my hair was going to be. "I had a run-in with Dr. P. this morning. Apparently, he's got the idea that I should be his next conquest."

She frowned. "The lech. But what does that have to do with the bandage on your neck?"

"He, uh, apparently thought it would be cute to leave his mark on me," I said grimly.

"No! A hickey?" Darla's squeal silenced every other conversation in the room. Chairs swiveled in our direction and the other stylists froze, combs and scissors poised as they waited for the next revelation.

I sank down in the chair. Darla began combing out sections of hair and everyone else went back to work. "That man's got a lot of nerve. You ought to report him."

"Yeah, like that hasn't been tried before. It never does any good. He's this big respected doctor and I'm just some sex-starved receptionist." I frowned at my reflection in the salon mirror. "No, the best thing to do is to just stay out of his way until he gets tired of it and decides to pick on somebody else."

Darla's scowl let me know what she thought of that strategy, but a good friend knows when to keep her mouth shut. She shook the ketchup bottle and began squirting color onto my hair. I closed my eyes. It looked like the fake blood they used in movies. I could always tell people I'd been the victim of a tragic accident.

"What did people at work say?" she asked.

"Most of them didn't notice. The only one who gave me a hard time about it was Jeff."

"Jeff? Who's Jeff?"

I opened my eyes. "This kid who's installing my new transcription equipment."

"Just how old is this kid? And is he good-looking?"

I shifted in the chair. "Too young. Twenty-six."

"Oooh. Twenty-six is a good age in men. They're too old for fraternity parties and most of them still have all their hair. He's handsome, I'll bet. He must be, or you wouldn't have ignored the question."

I picked a piece of lint off the cape. "I wouldn't call him ugly." Tall, muscular, thick brown hair, dark brown eyes—no, that definitely wasn't my idea of ugly. "It doesn't matter what he looks like."

"He's that good, huh? So, are you gonna go out with him?"

"I'm not going out with him. He's just a kid." I swiveled the chair around so suddenly Darla missed my head altogether and a big blob of the fake-blood-looking hair color landed on my shoulder and dripped down the front of the cape.

Darla wiped at the spilled color with an old towel. "Twenty-six is not a kid. And he's only six years younger than you. Just because you married an old man when you were nineteen doesn't make *you* old. Besides, haven't you heard that younger men and older women are more compatible sexually? There was a therapist on *Oprah* last week talking about it."

Maybe six years didn't sound like much to most people, but it felt like more than six years to me. I was mature for my age. Though come to think of it, that doesn't sound like the compliment now that it did when I was nineteen. "Darla, he's installing some computer equipment in my office. There isn't anything sexual about that."

"Sure there's not." Her expression told me she didn't buy it. "He's just a hot young stud who is interested enough in you to notice a love bite from another man on your neck and comment on it. And you've just spent ten minutes protesting how impossible it would be for you to have the slightest interest in him. That's longer than you've talked about any man other than Steve the sleaze."

I glared at her in the mirror. She laughed. "All right, I'll drop the subject if you tell me one thing."

"What's that?" I was still suspicious. Darla had a way of getting confessions out of me that I didn't want to give.

"Did this Jeff guy have anything to do with your sudden decision to become a redhead?" She pointed at my reflection in the mirror. "And be honest."

"It didn't have anything to do with Jeff." I smoothed the cape across my lap. "I've thought about this for years."

"Then why didn't you do it before?"

"Steve wouldn't let me." Even as I said the words, I knew they sounded pathetic.

"What did he do, lock you in the house and threaten to take away your car keys?" She shook her head and made clucking noises under her tongue. "Sorry. I just can't stand it when men try to tell their wives what they can't do with their hair or their clothes or anything like that. It's like they think women are children who need to be kept in line."

"Steve always told me he liked my hair just the way it

was," I said wistfully. In fact, the first thing he ever said to me
was "Hey beautiful, do blondes really have more fun?"

Okay, so it wasn't a great pickup line. I was nineteen at the
time. Steve was thirty and I thought he was suave and sophisticated. I didn't care what he said to me as long as he said
something.

"Well, I'm glad you decided to do this." Darla set her minute timer and grinned at me. "It's going to look great. So why
now? What happened to make you decide to do it today?

I managed a smile in return. "You might say I owe it all to
some samples of Viagra."

"Viagra? The sex pill? Are they giving it to women now?"

"Nope. And a certain troublemaking man won't be taking
it, either." I told her about swiping the doctor's samples and
dumping them down the toilet. "It was sneaky," I concluded.
"But it sure felt good."

"Sneaky? It was brilliant. And it serves him right, the old
lecher."

"I'm sure he'll just get more samples, but it makes me feel
like I have a little power over him now. I know his big secret."

"Speaking of secrets, I have some more news about your ex
and Just-a-waitress."

I squirmed in the chair, remembering the last "news" Darla
had told me. "I'm not sure I want to know."

"You're going to know soon enough, anyhow. When she
was in here she also told Henry that she and Steve-o are getting married."

My stomach clenched and I locked my jaw, freezing my
face into what I hoped was an indifferent expression. I
shouldn't have been surprised, considering that they were
going to have a baby, but the information hit me like a punch.
"Oh, hon." Darla put her hand on my shoulder. "You didn't
really want him back, did you?"

I shook my head so hard little drops of color spattered

across the front of Darla's smock. "No. Never." I *didn't* want
him back. But Steve marrying someone else was the final evidence that a chapter in my life was over. He was moving on,
but what was I doing? I lived in the same house, held the
same job, did the same things and I was still alone.

"Come on over here to the shampoo bowl." Darla nudged
me toward the back of the shop. "If you like, I do a pretty
good rendition of 'I'm Gonna Wash That Man Right Out of
My Hair.'"

A bit of a smile broke through my gloom. "I don't think
that's necessary."

She patted my shoulder. "You'll feel better once you see the
new you. I guarantee a certain younger man is going to be hot
for you once he sees you in red."

"It's been a long time since anyone was even lukewarm," I
said. "I don't see why Jeff should be any different."

"But you want him to be, don't you?" She put her face close
to mine, staring into my eyes. "Don't lie, Phoebe Elaine
Frame."

I shrugged. "Sure, I'd be flattered if some gorgeous young
stud thought I was all that. But it's not going to happen."

"It could."

"Even if it does, I don't think it would be smart to get involved with him."

She turned on the water and tested the temperature against
her wrist. "Who said anything about smart? What you want
at this point in your life is fun. You haven't had nearly
enough of that lately. Sounds like young Jeff could be just the
ticket."

One way or round trip? I wondered as warm water cascaded
over my scalp. Or did it really matter? If I was only going
along for a pleasure cruise, did it really matter where it took
me or how long it lasted?

4

I HAD A HARD TIME KEEPING my eyes on the road on the way home that evening. I kept tilting my head to look in the rear-view mirror at the stranger who stared back at me. Oh, she had the eyes, mouth and nose I was used to seeing when I looked at my reflection, but she also had a gorgeous head of shiny, copper-colored hair. I smiled every time I saw this "other" me. Suddenly, my eyes were bluer, my skin looked creamier. And all because of a change in hair color. "Who would have thought?" I murmured, and forced my gaze back to the road. I couldn't wait to show off my new look at work tomorrow. What would Jeff say?

I smiled, imagining his reaction. I was still smiling when an ominous *clunk* sounded from beneath the hood, followed by a horrifying grinding noise. I put on my blinker and steered onto the shoulder. The grinding grew louder and I shut off the engine and stared out the front windshield. A bitter odor wafted up through the air-conditioning vents.

A string of choice curses fought to climb up my throat, but what came out of my mouth was "OhGodohGodohGod." I bailed out of the car and hurried to pop the hood. The acrid odor was stronger. Was it my imagination, or did the whole engine appear to be leaning to one side?

I backed away, eyeing the car warily. The urge to kick something was strong, but I'm superstitious about cars. I think they can sense when you're upset with them, and mechanical failure is their chief way to get back at you.

Yeah, I know people *say* cars can't think, but who says they don't have intuition? The minute you begin to hate one, they know it and will make your life miserable.

I stomped to the shoulder and looked out at the traffic flying past. Someone would stop soon and maybe they'd have a phone I could use to call a wrecker.

A pickup sped by so close its tires slung gravel at me. A chorus of catcalls and whistles sailed toward me.

Cars honked. Men whistled. One made an obscene gesture. Another man yelled that he was in love with me. Women looked the other way. Some even changed lanes so they wouldn't have to drive on my side of the road. But no one stopped.

So much for chivalry or Good Samaritans. I searched the shoulder for a good-size rock. The next idiot who made a rude suggestion was going to get it in the windshield.

I'd found what I thought was a good weapon when a black pickup slowed and pulled in behind me. "Thank God," I said, walking toward the truck. "I thought no one was going to st—"

The door opened and a pair of long legs in tan slacks emerged, followed by a pair of broad shoulders and strong arms. I swallowed and grinned weakly. "Hello, Jeff. Imagine meeting you here."

He took a long time looking at me, his gaze traveling from the tips of my pink-painted toenails to the top of my coppery hair. "I like it," he said at last. "Very sexy."

I wasn't sure if he meant my new hair color or me in general, but I didn't dare ask. "What do you know about cars?"

"A little."

I followed him around to my upraised hood. He looked at it for a moment, then leaned in and wiggled something. Then he slammed the hood. "Broken motor mount," he said.

"Is that expensive to fix?" Who was I kidding? Everything about cars is expensive to fix.

"Shouldn't be too bad. How long have you had the car?"

"I just got it yesterday."

"Then it should be under some kind of dealer warranty. I'd take it back to where you bought it." He slipped a phone from his shirt pocket. "We'll call a wrecker to tow it to the dealer."

"Won't they be closed?" It was almost seven.

"If it is, the wrecker driver can leave it in the yard and you can stop by tomorrow to arrange everything." He punched in a number. "What's the name of the dealer?"

"Easy Motors. Over on Alameda."

He made a face, then spoke to someone on the line. "Ben? This is Jeff Fischer. I've got a friend here who has a Mustang with a broken motor mount. Can you tow it for her to an Easy Motors, over on Alameda?"

He gave the driver directions, then disconnected. "He'll be here in ten minutes."

"Thanks." Now that the car was taken care of, it felt awkward standing here with him. Cars raced past, stirring up dust that blew back at us in a hot wind.

He took my arm and steered me toward his truck. "Let's wait inside."

The truck was clean and relatively new. It smelled of leather and Jeff's cologne. I sat on the edge of the seat, next to the door and found myself imagining what it would feel like to lie back in that cool leather seat, with Jeff slowly undressing me....

See what kind of trouble hormones will get you into? I crossed my arms and my legs and wondered if Jeff would think I was strange if I asked him to turn up the air conditioner. The air in that cab was definitely too warm.

"So, Red." He turned toward me, grinning. "Did I ever tell you I have a thing for redheads?"

My heart pounded. "Uh...what kind of thing?"

He slid his hand along the back of the seat, toward me. "I think they're very...exciting."

"Sorry to disappoint you, but I'm not an exciting person." But I was definitely getting excited. I squeezed my legs together and tucked my hair behind my ears. "So, did you finish installing the transcription system?"

His grin never faltered. "Don't think you're going to get rid of me that easily. I'm under contract to stick around and teach you how to use the new software."

I swallowed hard, imagining hours spent in my little cubicle with Mr. Testosterone. "I've been a transcriptionist for years. What's to learn?"

His eyes darkened and his voice lowered. "Oh, I'm betting I could teach you a lot."

He moved a little closer. I couldn't decide whether to scream or throw myself at him. Throwing myself at him was definitely winning out when a horn sounded behind us and a purple-and-black wrecker pulled alongside.

We climbed out of the truck and met the wrecker driver beside my car. He was a whip-thin man with long gray hair pulled back in a ponytail, his denim work shirt rolled up to reveal arms corded with muscle. "Hey, Jeff. How's your old man?"

"Doing great, Ben. Thanks for coming out. This is Phoebe Frame."

Ben nodded, then turned to the car. "You bought this from Easy Motors?"

I nodded. "I've only had it since yesterday, so it's still under warranty—isn't it?"

Ben made a noise that might have been laughter. "Good luck getting anything out of that bunch."

I retrieved my purse and Ben hooked the car up to

the wrecker. I started to climb in beside him, but Jeff pulled me back. "Ben can take care of it. I'll drive you home."

I didn't think that was a good idea, but before I could say anything, I heard clanking chains and tires on gravel and Ben pulled out into traffic, my Mustang hoisted behind him like the catch of the day.

"Okay. Thanks." At least driving, he'd have to keep his hands to himself. As for me, I could always sit on *my* hands.

"I'm starved. Let's get something to eat."

Eating was too much like a date. I was not going to date Jeff. "I really need to get home," I said.

"You have kids?"

The question jolted me. "Uh...no."

"Good."

Good? "Why is that good?" Was the world infested with men who didn't like children?

"It means you don't need to get home. And everybody has to eat, don't they?"

We ended up at a place called Pizza Junction, which combined Old West decor with Italian food in a sort of spaghetti Western theme. "You've eaten here before?" I asked as we made our way past bales of hay festooned with braids of garlic.

"It's very good." He slid into a booth and I sat across from him. "I recommend the Lariat Special."

I ordered a Diet Coke and agreed to split the Lariat Special with Jeff. He apparently wasn't a man who believed in small talk. As soon as the waitress brought our drinks, he looked me over and asked, "How long have you been divorced?"

I stripped the paper from a straw and wadded it into a knot, avoiding his gaze. "Six months. We were separated six months before that." Anticipating the next question, and wanting to get it over with, I added. "We were married twelve years."

"Was it your idea, or his?"

I had to hand it to Jeff; he had nerve. I imagined him tackling computer problems this way: find out everything you can so that you approach the problem armed with information. I could have told him these things were none of his business, but why bother? It wasn't as if I had any real secrets to hide. "It was his idea. He said he didn't want to be married anymore." I swished my straw around in my Diet Coke. "He has a young girlfriend now."

He took a long pull on his beer. "He's crazy."

"Because he left, or because he took up with a younger woman?"

"Both. What could a younger woman offer that you couldn't?"

He sounded so certain of right and wrong here. So naive. "You don't understand now, but one day you will. Of course, right now, younger women for you are in high school."

He leaned back against the booth. "I've always been partial to older women."

"Then go visit the nursing home."

He grinned. "Touchy, touchy. You know what I mean."

The arrival of our pizza saved me from having to find an answer to that. Jeff was telling me he was interested in me and I couldn't deny the powerful physical attraction I felt for him.

As we worked our way around the pizza, I turned the conversation to safer topics. I found out Jeff owned the company that distributed the software I was going to be using, as well as a number of other medical and dental programs. He had a small office with a few employees and spent most of his time in medical offices, selling or setting up new systems.

"Is every office as much of a soap opera as ours?" I asked.

"Pretty much." He looked thoughtful. "They're mostly

women, you know, so it's always interesting for a new man to enter in to the mix."

"I'd think you'd enjoy the attention."

His grin returned. "Oh, I do. I certainly do."

He managed to eat most of the large pizza, and there wasn't an ounce of fat on him that I could see. I'd confined myself to two pieces and hoped all that cheese wouldn't translate itself into an extra inch on my hips by Friday.

It was almost nine o'clock by the time Jeff drove me home. I sat against the passenger door, staring out at the dark streets and thought of all the times some boy had driven me home from a date in high school. I had the same feeling now, that sort of jittery, sick-to-my-stomach sensation, anticipating whether or not he would kiss me, and what I would do if he tried. You'd think, at my age, I'd be over that kind of nervousness, but apparently it had come back to haunt me, like post-adolescent acne.

I had my door open seconds after the truck turned into my drive, but Jeff was almost as quick. "I'll walk you to your door," he said.

He came around the truck and tried to take my arm, but I shied away. "What's wrong?" he asked.

"Nothing." I fumbled in my purse, looking for my keys.

"You've been jumpy all evening. What's your problem? What is it about me that you especially don't like?"

"It's not you in particular," I said, and headed up the walk. "It's just...I haven't had the best of luck with men lately."

"Not all men are jerks like your husband."

I thought of Dr. Patterson and the man who groped me in the elevator. "Just most of the ones I know."

I started to unlock the door, but he covered my hand with his own. "I'm not like them."

I sighed. "You say that, but your mind works like theirs."

"How can you say that? You don't even know me that well."

He was leaning very close, and his eyes were dark with a desire that both frightened and thrilled me. "I know you're probably going to try to kiss me right now," I whispered, any intention I'd ever had of refusing him vanished from my mind.

He took a step back and shook his head. "I don't think so. The mood you're in, you'd probably bite my lips off."

He turned away and I sagged against the door. "Good night, Phoebe," he called when he reached his truck.

When he was gone, I let myself inside. I told myself I'd talked my way out of a tight spot. After all, I really didn't want to start anything with Jeff.

But the part of me that never lied wished I'd let him kiss me.

5

THE NEXT MORNING, I was waiting at Easy Motors when they opened the doors. A teenage receptionist with allergies greeted me with a smile that soon faltered when I told her I'd bought a car there a few days before and now it needed a repair.

"You'll have to talk to Frank," she said, reaching for the phone. "He's in charge of that."

In charge of what? I wondered.

"Mr. A-dams," the receptionist whined into the phone. "We have a customer out here with a prob-lem."

A few moments later, a man in a rumpled brown suit came into the room, hand extended. His grin was too large for his face, wrapping around his cheeks toward his ears. "You're the owner of that little Mustang they towed in last night, aren't you?" he gushed. "Darling car. I can tell by looking it suits you to a tee. Come into my office and we'll fix you right up."

He wrapped his arm around my shoulders and steered me toward a glass-fronted cubicle that reeked of stale cigars and onions. Sweeping aside a stack of dog-eared repair manuals, he pushed me into a folding chair and took his own seat behind a green metal desk. "Now, how can we help you?"

I tried a smile of my own. "It's simple, really. I bought my car here two days ago and last night it broke down. A friend told me it looked like a broken motor mount. So I had it towed here to be fixed."

Friendly Frank nodded and plucked a multipart form from a stack on his desk. "We can do that. We can do that. Fix you right up." He began writing furiously on the form, pausing twice to punch numbers into an ancient adding machine at his side. The machine whirred and clacked and unreeled a stream of yellowed paper. Frank added a final figure and pushed the form toward me. "Sign at the bottom and we'll get right to work."

Numbers danced down the page in cramped script. My gaze fixed on the figure at the bottom. "Four hundred and seventy-two dollars!" I shoved the paper back toward him, gasping for breath. "I'm sorry. I must not have made myself clear. This repair should be covered under the dealer's warranty."

Frank's smile vanished. "Your car is seven years old, and there's no such thing as a warranty on a car that old."

"But I've only had it two days."

He leaned back in his chair, arms crossed over his chest. "I don't make the rules, lady. I just enforce them. Now, do you want the repair or not?"

"Not!" I stood. "I'll take the car somewhere else."

"Fine." He handed me a second form. "That'll be eighty-nine, ninety-seven."

"For what? You haven't done anything."

"Storage fees."

"This is outrageous."

"Don't blame me because you bought an older car. You should have opted for one of our premium models."

"This is not my fault," I protested.

"What do you know about cars, Mrs. Frame?"

I glared at him, but didn't answer.

He rose and patted me on the shoulder. "Do yourself a favor. Next time you go shopping for a car, bring a man along."

I jerked open the door and stormed into the lobby once more. "I want to see the manager," I told the receptionist.

Her eyes widened. "Mr. Adams *is* the manager."

I turned and saw Frank smiling at me. Not the cheery grin with which he'd greeted me, but the look of a sly fox.

I wanted to rip that smile right off his face. I wanted to scream, to throw punches, to do something to make him quit looking at me as if I were a bug and he was about to squash me.

I didn't have the strength to beat him up or the clout to make him afraid of me, so I did the only thing I knew to do. I gave him the haughtiest look I could manage. "This isn't the end of this," I announced, and stomped out the door.

I stalked down the sidewalk, my shoes slapping against the concrete, sending tremors up my legs. My stomach churned and my heart raced. I hated this feeling of helplessness. No matter what Frank said, Easy Motors had cheated me. But there was nothing I could do. They had my car. They had the six thousand dollars I had paid for the car. And unless I gave them more money, I wasn't going to have the money or the car again.

"Aaaargh!" I yelled in frustration. A man on a bicycle stared at me and swerved across the street to avoid me. I didn't care.

I took a deep breath and deliberately slowed my steps. "Don't fall apart, Phoebe," I muttered. "Think this through. There has to be *something* you can do."

I started to feel a little better. I wasn't going to let Frank Adams and Easy Motors get to me. If they were going to fight dirty, then I would fight dirty, too. I didn't have much experience, but I was a fast learner.

MY MOOD HADN'T IMPROVED MUCH by the time I arrived at work, but my co-workers' enthusiastic reaction to my new hair color made me feel a little better. Of course, there's always a spoilsport in every bunch. Joan Lee made a face when she saw me. "I don't think it suits you," she said. "Too flamboyant."

"I can be flamboyant," I protested.

"Transcriptionists are not flamboyant," Joan announced, as if this was a fact obvious to everyone but an idiot.

"Maybe red hair is just a start." I tossed my head in what I hoped was a confident, flamboyant manner. "Maybe I'm thinking of changing careers."

Joan shook her head and walked away. I could see my next job evaluation. *Hair color not suited to job description.*

I filled my coffee mug and headed toward my cubicle. Jeff met me in the hallway. He grinned. "I think there's a flamboyant Phoebe underneath your mild-mannered guise as an ordinary transcriptionist," he said.

The idea pleased me, but I wasn't about to let him know it. I was still a little miffed about the way he'd walked away from me last night. "Didn't anyone ever tell you eavesdropping will get you into trouble?"

He lifted one eyebrow in that sexy way of his. "Maybe I'm a man who likes trouble."

I bit back a smile and hurried past him, to my office. He followed. "Did you get everything settled with your car?"

I tightened my grip on the coffee mug. "Not exactly."

"Not exactly?" He intercepted me in the doorway. "What do you mean, not exactly?"

"The manager at Easy Motors says I don't have a warranty. They want almost five hundred dollars to fix the car, or ninety dollars to release it so I can take it somewhere else."

Jeff frowned. "Want me to go talk to them?"

"No!" Just what I needed, a man getting me out of this fix. "I'll take care of it myself."

He shrugged. "Just thought I'd offer."

I pushed past him and sat at my desk. I dug the phone book out of the drawer and flipped through it. "What are you looking for?" Jeff asked.

"Are you always so nosy?" I punched in a number and waited while it rang.

"*Houston Banner*. Bringing you the news first."

"Hi. I'd like to speak to your consumer affairs reporter."

"I'll transfer you to editorial."

An elevator-music version of "Livin' La Vida Loca" filled my ear. I swiveled my chair around and saw Jeff still watching me. After a moment a man's voice barked, "News desk. Sanborn."

"I'd like to speak to your consumer affairs reporter."

"No such animal."

I blinked. "Pardon me? What happened to Simon Saler, the Consumer's Friend?"

"He quit. Said he wanted to be a sports reporter." I heard a chair squeak and the rustle of papers. "He got tired of people writing in wanting to know where they could buy the last bottle of Coty perfume or complaining they saw a roach run across their table at Casa Lupe."

"My aunt gets her Coty from a specialty store in Dallas. And how would you like it if a roach shared your lunch?"

"Well, why didn't you say something while Simon was still here? Maybe he wouldn't have run off to write about the latest fight on the basketball court."

"But what am I supposed to do about the car dealer who sold me a lemon car?"

"You're on your own, dearie."

Fat lot of help he was. I slammed down the phone. "What are you going to do now?" Jeff asked.

"I'll think of something. Right now, I'd better get started on these charts or Joan will make me clean bedpans or file appeals with insurance companies."

"Go ahead and use your old software to get caught up," he said. "But then I want to start teaching you the new program."

I sat and scowled at the tower of folders beside my monitor, then glanced at the idle computer down the counter from mine. "Joan's going to have to hire someone to help me if she expects me to keep up," I said, and reached for my headphones.

Jeff sat on a stool and rolled it over next to me. "So, are you really contemplating a new career?"

I shrugged. "Maybe." Actually, before that morning, the thought had never occurred to me. Not that I wouldn't enjoy a more glamorous, better-paying job, but transcription was all I was trained for. "I think I'd better handle one life change at a time," I said.

"I didn't realize changing your hair color took that much out of you."

I frowned at him. "I meant my divorce."

"That was six months ago. Old news."

"Which goes to show you've never been divorced."

"I don't intend to be, either."

"What, you're going to remain single all your life?" I slipped the headphones over my head and popped the first tape into the machine.

"No. But when I marry, it's going to be for life."

"That's what I thought, too." I switched on the tape and Dr. Patterson's drawl filled my ears. I didn't want to listen to Jeff's naive pronouncements about the sanctity of marriage. I could have told him no one plans to bail out before "death do us part." Sometimes you just don't see it coming, like a head-on collision. Most people survive, but it doesn't mean you aren't a more careful driver for a while.

He seemed to get the message and left me alone after that. He fiddled with the other computer for a while, then wandered off to some other part of the office. I worked faster once he'd left. There's something disconcerting about listening to a description of an old Mr. Miller's problems with impotence while a sexy stud sits three feet away.

Just before lunch, I finished up a stack of letters to referring physicians and set out to deliver them to the various offices in the building. I could have sent them out with the next batch of interoffice mail, but delivering them in person was one of the few legitimate excuses I had for escaping my cubbyhole.

The last of my letters went to the OB-GYN office on the second floor. Dozens of fruitful women in designer maternity wear kept three physicians and twice as many nurses and techs busy. I could never look at the "wall of fame" beside the reception desk, with its photos of smiling moms and dads with their newborns, without feeling a pang of sadness. I kept telling myself I still had plenty of time to have kids, but there was that pesky matter of needing someone to be the father. I wasn't crazy about diving back into the whole relationship thing any time soon.

"Thanks, Phoebe," the receptionist, Beverly, said when I handed her my letters. "I think I've got some for you, too."

While Beverly went in search of the letters, I turned my back on the family photos and surveyed the waiting room. A trio of women in various stages of pregnancy sat reading copies of *American Baby* and *Modern Maternity*. The nurse came to the door and beckoned one woman and she levered herself out of the chair and waddled toward the exam room. There was something familiar about her long blond hair, her glowing skin....

I clutched the edge of the reception desk, overcome by the urge to scream or puke, I wasn't sure which. The lovely Madonna waddling away from me was none other than Just-a-waitress Tami, the future Mrs. Steven Frame.

"Here are those letters. Thanks for waiting." Beverly

shoved a stack of envelopes toward me. She frowned. "Are you okay? You look a little pale."

"I'm...fine," I lied. In any case, there was no medical cure for what ailed me.

I pretended to look through the letters, trying to collect myself. The print on the envelopes blurred in a haze of rage. A woman waddled up to the desk and handed Beverly some paperwork. "Thanks, Mrs. Alexander," Beverly said. "How are you feeling today?"

"Having a first baby when you're forty is a lot harder than I thought it would be," Mrs. Alexander said. She patted her expanding belly. "But the doctor says I'm doing fine."

I jerked my attention from the letters and stared at her. She was obviously pregnant, but she didn't look like the other glowing young things in the office. Her hair was streaked with gray, and tiny lines radiated out from her eyes. "You're really having a first baby at forty?" I blurted.

She smiled, apparently used to dealing with idiots like me. "Yes. My first husband and I never had children. I thought it was my fault. But when I remarried and my new husband wanted a baby, I thought, why not give it a try?" She laughed. "Turns out there's nothing wrong with me finding another man didn't cure."

She waddled back to her chair and I hurried out of the office. Forty. She was eight years older than me and having a first baby. I still would have gladly strangled Steve if he'd been anywhere in sight, but I felt a little better. I had a lot of good years left. Years to find the right man and start a family.

I boarded the elevator and the only other passenger, a short man with an unfortunately large nose, grinned at me. "Love your hair," he said, letting his gaze drift over me. He reminded me of a basset hound who had just spotted a juicy bone. I expected him to start drooling at any minute.

The elevator stopped at my floor and I rushed out. So much for the "finding the right man" part of the equation. Of course, there was always artificial insemination.

6

THANKS TO THE TIME I'D LOST waiting on Jeff to install my new system and the fact that I was now working alone, I ended up having to stay late at the office several nights. I used to resent those extra hours on the job, but let's face it, if I couldn't improve my social life, I could at least fatten up my bank account with overtime pay.

Besides, there's something mysterious and a little exciting about being at the office after everyone else is gone. It's quiet and you have the whole place to yourself. You can go through people's desks, looking for food and learning their secrets. For instance, I once discovered a pair of crotchless panties in Joan Strictly-Business Lee's desk. I suppose she could have found them in one of the exam rooms, but why would you keep someone else's underwear around?

When no one else was around, you could look through the sample shelves to see what new products were on hand. Not that I'd take any drugs without permission. It was a sure way to get fired and besides, all the really good stuff was kept locked up.

You could play around in the lab, looking at stuff under the microscope and feeling the fake breast to see if you could find the hidden lumps. You could take apart the model of the heart and put it back together again. Granted, none of this would be considered true quality entertainment, but it beat actually working.

Of course, I did eventually have to do some typing. That

was the only creepy thing about working late. Not the work itself so much, but the fact that I was stuck back in my hidey-hole, hooked up to the transcription machine, unable to hear or see anyone approaching. I tried not to think about how vulnerable I was here alone, but, just in case, I always kept a canister of Betadine Spray beside me. It wasn't Mace, but I figured it would at least slow a guy down.

I was well into Patterson's rollicking description of a football scrimmage that resulted in injury to the right wrist of a high school junior when I had the sensation that I was being watched. Goose bumps rose along my arms and the hair on the back of my neck prickled. Patterson's voice still droning in my ear, I grabbed the can of Betadine and swiveled to face the door....

Patterson looked down at the splotch of Betadine quickly spreading across the front of his shirt. "Did I look like I needed disinfecting?" he asked.

"Y—you startled me." I set aside the can and switched off the machine. "What are you doing here?"

"I have a presentation to work on. I'm glad you're here to help me." He began unbuttoning his shirt. I ripped off the headset and reached for the spray can again. I might have known the person who was most likely to give me trouble had a key to the office.

"Put down that can, Phoebe," he said. "I'm only going to change my shirt."

He didn't seem to be in any hurry to do it, though. He stood around for several minutes, apparently hoping I'd be overcome by lust for his naked chest. It wasn't a bad chest, but the fact that it belonged to Patterson made it completely undesirable.

"I like your new hair color," he said. "Red suits you."

"Uh...thanks." I bent over the stack of charts, pretending to search for something.

"Why don't you come into my office and we'll get to work," he said.

As if I was going to fall for that. "I really stayed late to catch up on my transcription," I said. "So I won't be able to help with your project."

"But I really need your help." He put his hand on my shoulder. "I'll see that you're amply rewarded."

I cringed. Did he think sex with him was reward enough, or was he actually willing to pay for time in the sack? I thought about the Viagra I'd flushed and wondered if he was that desperate. Either way, I'd heard enough. "I'm not interested." I shrugged out of his grasp. "Go hit on someone else."

"Phoebe, I'm hurt that you would think me so shallow." He put his hands on my shoulders again and began massaging. "I care about you as a person."

I lurched out of my chair, spray can in hand. "Touch me again and I'll aim for your eyes."

He stepped back, chin jutting out like a kid whose mom just told him he couldn't have another cookie. "I don't appreciate your attitude," he said huffily.

"Well, I don't appreciate yours. Leave me alone or I'll report you."

He glowered at me. "Do that and I'll simply say that you came on to me. Who do you think they'll believe, a redheaded divorcée in a short dress or an esteemed colleague?"

He had me there, though I wasn't about to admit it. "This isn't the 1960s," I said. "Even divorcées in short dresses can have clout, if they talk to the right people." *Like who?* I wondered, but kept that thought to myself. The only way I was going to keep my job and keep Patterson in line was to make him think I knew what I was talking about.

He looked me up and down with an expression of pure contempt, then turned away. "We'll see about that."

I slumped back into my chair, clutching the can of Betadine

to my chest. My heart was pounding so hard I could feel the vibrations through the can. I wanted to run home and take a shower. I wanted to leave this office and never come back.

But why should I do that? I sat up straighter, good old anger blotting out my revulsion. "Why should I let a bully like that push me around?" I muttered.

"Do you always talk to yourself?"

I gasped and whirled around to find Jeff standing in the doorway. "What are you doing here? Don't you have a home to go to?" I snapped.

"I came by to pick up some equipment I left and saw your light." He walked over to the counter and picked up Patterson's abandoned shirt. "Did I come at a bad time?"

"It's not exactly a good time." I slumped in my chair.

He wrinkled his nose. "What's that smell?"

"Betadine. It's a disinfectant."

He looked at the shirt again. "I saw Dr. Patterson in the hallway. He wasn't wearing a shirt."

I didn't say anything. Let him think what he liked.

"Looks like somebody thought the good doctor needed disinfecting."

"Shh." I glanced down the hall. "He'll hear you."

"No, he won't. He left. Didn't look very happy, either." He dropped the shirt into the trash can and leaned back against the counter, facing me. "I think I'm beginning to get the picture."

"You don't know anything." I turned to the computer, but I could still see him, long legs stretched out in front of him, perfectly relaxed. Why shouldn't he be relaxed? He was a man.

"That's a little harsh, don't you think?" He picked up the can of Betadine and studied it. "I'm guessing Patterson got a little fresh and you blasted him. End of story."

As if it were so simple. I glared at him. "If you think that's the end of the story, that shows how much you don't understand."

He crossed his arms over his chest. "Then why don't you help me understand?"

He looked so smug. So sexy. So *young*. How was he ever going to understand how I felt? Anger clawed at my throat, anger at Patterson and Steve and Frank Adams and the anonymous elevator groper and men in general. I stood and poked Jeff in the chest, as if I could poke a hole in that self-assuredness that seemed an inborn thing with men. "No one ever threatened to take your job away if you didn't sleep with them, did they?" I snapped.

He didn't flinch, just kept his irritatingly calm gaze locked to mine. I moved closer, leaning over him, trying to intimidate him. "No one ever turned every conversation they had with you into some kind of sexual word game, did they?" I slid my hand along his thigh and pinched, hard. "No one ever felt you up in an elevator, did they?"

Anger flashed in his eyes and he reached for me, but I darted away. He stood and came toward me and I avoided him. I slipped behind him and circled his throat with my hands, and stood on tiptoe to whisper in his ear. The spicy, exotic scent of his cologne swept over me like a drug. My voice was husky when I spoke. "You never had to be afraid when you went out at night just because you were a man, did you?"

He started to turn, but I put my hands on his shoulders and held him, then slid my hands down the hard column of his back, to that perfectly toned backside. I was breathing hard, anger edged out by fear and manic desire. I was sick of being pushed around by men; now was my time to push back. "No one ever tried to cheat you because you were a man, did they?" I squeezed him, hard, and this time he succeeded in turning to face me.

He reached for me, but I caught his wrists and held them, made strong by the wild emotions that had been building inside me for too long.

I pressed him against the edge of the counter, fitting myself between his straddled legs, pinning his arms alongside him. I could feel his erection against the crux of my thighs and felt distanced from myself, as if the real Phoebe was standing across the room, watching this wild-eyed redhead do these things. "Do you know what it feels like to want to fight back and not be able to?"

I leaned forward and put my lips on his. I don't know what I thought I was doing. Maybe I only meant to excite him and draw away, to frustrate him with the strongest power a woman ever has over most men.

Then I made the mistake of looking into his eyes. What I saw there wasn't fear or loathing, but naked lust. A raw hunger that made me tremble in the deepest part of myself.

Thoughts of revenge and retribution fled, replaced by an overwhelming need. A need to feel, to act, to be alive in a way I hadn't been alive in a long, long time.

We tore at each other's clothes, grappling in our urgency to touch, to taste, to feel each inch of exposed skin. We spoke, not in words, but in sighs and moans, in grunts and soft, throaty murmurs of passion. We traded places and he lifted me to the counter, spreading my legs wide to enter me deeply, fully. I closed my eyes and threw back my head, losing myself in the intensity of the moment. In the distance, I heard a keening cry that rose in pitch and volume. Then I realized I was the one crying, and gave myself up to the sound and the rhythm, riding it like a wave to a collision against emotion and sensation that left me both energized and weakened.

We clung together for a long time afterward, eyes closed, bodies pressed together, until the air conditioner's chill crept over our warmth. I opened my eyes at the first feelings of coldness, and ugly reality descended like a dark cloak.

I struggled away from him and reached for my clothes. I turned away from him, hopping on one foot as I tried to step into my underwear while fighting the urge to run away.

"Phoebe." He reached for me, but I wrenched away.

"I'm sorry," I said, choking on the words. "I didn't mean for that to happen."

"It's all right." He was still naked, standing in the middle of the room as if this was a perfectly normal way to carry on a conversation.

"It's not all right." I found my dress and slipped it over my head, fighting with the zipper.

He put one hand on my shoulder and with the other, drew up the zipper. He gently patted my back. "Don't be upset."

Easy for him to say. Maybe this sort of thing happened to him all the time, but it was definitely a new ball game for me. With shaking hands, I collected my purse. "I have to go."

"I'll take you home." He reached for his trousers.

"No. I'll get a cab."

I ran, taking advantage of the time it would take him to dress. Avoiding the elevator, I headed for the stairs, descending eleven flights and arriving in the lobby breathless and shaking.

I found a taxi and collapsed into the back seat and closed my eyes. Every nerve vibrated with the memory of Jeff's touch. The scents of his cologne, the lingering too-sweet odor of Betadine and the musky aroma of sex clung to me like an invisible garment. My muscles ached from unaccustomed exertion, and a stickiness between my legs reminded me that we hadn't used a condom. Oh, God, what if I ended up pregnant?

I shook my head, refusing to think about that tonight. The

taxi pulled up in front of my house and I handed the driver a
ten and didn't wait for my change. All I wanted was to hide in
my darkened house, to take a shower and try to convince myself that I hadn't just made the biggest mistake of my life.

7

IT'S AMAZING WHAT A SHOWER, pajamas and a pint of Ben & Jerry's can do for you. As I scooped out a heavenly spoonful of Bovinity Divinity, I felt my grip on sanity returning.

What you need, I told myself, *is to look at this objectively. Maybe you've made too big a deal of this. You're both adults.* I dug out another spoonful of ice cream.

It's not as if Jeff is some stranger you picked up in a bar. He's made it clear he's interested in you. So what if you took the lead with a man for a change? He didn't seem to mind.

The phone jangled, and I stared at it, heart in my throat. *Oh, God, don't let that be Jeff.* I didn't want to talk to him. I *couldn't* talk to him.

Click. *Hello, this is Phoebe. If this is a telemarketer, leave your number and what time you eat dinner and I'll call you back. If you're calling about a bill, the check is in the mail. If you're a friend, leave a message and I'll call you back.*

"Phoebe. Phoebe, pick up the phone. I know you're home. I want to know what everyone said about your hair."

I let out my breath in a rush and picked up the phone. "Hello, Darla."

"It's about time you answered. What took you so long?"

"I was screening my calls."

"Ohhhh? And why is that?"

"Umm. Didn't feel like talking."

"Come on, Phoebe. Something else is going on. I can hear it in your voice."

I tucked my feet under me and tried to find a comfortable position on the sofa. "Hear what?"

"*Who* don't you want to talk to? A man?"

I sighed. Darla was going to find out the truth sooner or later. I could never keep anything from her. She could have taught the CIA a few things about interrogation. "Jeff," I said.

"Jeff!" Her voice rose in a squeal. "What happened? When? Tell me everything."

I squirmed. "I was working late tonight and Dr. Patterson was there and hit on me again and I'd barely gotten rid of him when Jeff came by and I was really ticked off."

"So you had an argument?"

"Well, sort of."

"And now you're sorry." Darla was full of sympathy. "Don't worry. Apologize tomorrow. Take him to lunch and make nice."

"It's not quite so simple." I twisted a lock of hair around my finger. "We started out arguing and then we sort of...got physical."

I heard the sharp intake of her breath. "Oh, Phoebe, no! Jeff *hit* you?"

"No! Not...not that kind of physical."

The silence was so long I thought maybe we'd lost our connection, then Darla gasped. "Oh! You mean—sex? Right there in your office?"

I nodded. "Uh-huh."

Darla giggled. "So, how was it? Is he a stud or what?"

How was it? My skin tingled from the memory. "It was...wild. I didn't mean for it to happen, it just did. One minute we were arguing and the next we were tearing each other's clothes off."

"Ooooh, wild-animal sex. I love it."

"What am I going to do? I didn't mean for it to happen."

"It happened, so go with it. He's a single, good-looking

guy, you had great sex—why not just go with the flow and see where this takes you?''

"He's six years younger than me! We have nothing in common.''

"I'd say a strong physical attraction is a good place to start. And what's wrong with a younger man? He's a nice guy, isn't he?''

"He *is* a nice guy. But...'' I chewed my lower lip.

"But what?''

"But I don't think I'm ready to get involved with anyone else right now. Every time I turn around these days, some man is trying to take advantage of me. Did I tell you the car dealer is holding my new car hostage?''

"No, and quit trying to change the subject. Just because your ex-husband and your boss are assholes, doesn't mean all men are bad.''

"Don't forget the car dealer. And the guy who felt me up in the elevator.''

"You got felt up in the elevator? Are you wearing a new perfume or something? Something that drives men wild?''

"I wasn't wearing anything.''

"That would do it, too. But isn't it a little chilly?''

How is it someone who drives me absolutely crazy can always make me laugh? "You know what I mean. And you know what I mean about Jeff, too. I don't think jumping his bones at the office is a good way to start off.''

"He might not agree with you.''

"Exactly. How am I going to face him again and tell him I didn't mean to start anything? That I'm not interested in a relationship or an affair or whatever you want to call it.''

"A fling.''

"What?''

"You could call it a fling. You know, sowing a few wild oats. After all, you were just a kid when you married Steve.''

"Fine. Call it a fling. A one-night fling. Now it's over. But how do I make Jeff understand that?"

"If he works with computers, he must be reasonably intelligent. I'd just tell him."

"Just tell him?"

"Are you having trouble hearing tonight? Yes, just tell him—Jeff, it was great, but I don't want to be involved with anyone right now. Thanks and goodbye. Practice a few times in front of the mirror."

"And you think that'll work?"

"Well, he could always get down on his knees and pledge his undying love for you, but I think that only happens in the movies. Real life is usually more practical."

I took a deep breath. "Okay. I'll do it. Thanks."

She yawned. "No problem. Let me know how it goes. Now I have to get my beauty sleep."

I hung up the phone, collected the empty ice-cream carton and deposited it in the trash. I'd tell Jeff I wasn't interested. It was so logical, so simple. So scary. All I had to do was find the guts to pull it off.

ANY COURAGE I EVER HAD DESERTED ME the next morning, and I took the coward's way out. I called in sick to work. Maybe a day apart would cool things off between me and Jeff. Maybe next time we met, I could face him calmly and take Darla's advice to simply tell him how I felt.

Maybe I'd hit the Lotto jackpot and never have to go back to work again.

Meanwhile, I still had to find a way to get my car back. I poured a cup of coffee, grabbed the phone book and started dialing. Better Business Bureau, American Automobile Association, my insurance agent. I told everyone I could think of my sad story about my car. They all clucked their tongues and shook their heads and basically let me know that I was an

idiot who didn't have enough sense to know when I was being cheated. "Maybe you should take the bus from now on,"
my insurance agent told me. "A car is a big responsibility."

"It's not a dog," I said. "I'm not going to leave it out in the
rain to starve."

He made more meaningless sounds of sympathy and told
me maybe I should just pay the money to get the car out of
hock. "Consider it a lesson learned the hard way."

I slammed down the phone. How many lessons did a person have to learn before she could graduate, or at least move
up to the next grade?

I picked up the newspaper and flipped through it, hoping
to find notice of a class-action suit against Easy Motors or an
ad for a consumer agency that specialized in helping women
who'd been swindled.

"Why did Simon Saler have to become a sports writer?" I
whined to myself. "*He* would have helped." For the past five
years, Simon's homely but friendly face had smiled out at me
from the top of his column "Consumer's Confidant." He'd
helped people retrieve precious wedding dresses from clean-
ers who'd skipped town in the middle of the night, gotten a
new paint job for a woman who had ended up with a pea-
green house and extracted eloquent apologies from multina-
tional corporations that had screwed consumers. He was my
hero, and when I needed him, he was gone. Wasn't that just
like a man?

Where did the paper get off not hiring a replacement for Simon? Maybe I wasn't having any luck as far as my car was
concerned, but I could at least let the paper know how I felt.

I found a pad of paper and a pen and wrote an impas-
sioned plea for the return of the "Consumer's Confidant." I
told the whole sorry story of my car, and how no one had
been willing to help me. *People think they're justified because
they're "following policy" or playing by the rules,* I wrote. *But just*

*because something is legal doesn't mean it's right. I will continue to
fight until this wrong is righted.*

I looked at the words on the page. *I ought to cut them out and
tape them to the bathroom mirror,* I thought. To remind me that
I was on my own now. Nobody else was going to fight my
battles for me. Not Steve or Simon Saler or the BBB. I was a
one-woman army now.

When I'd finished the letter, I slipped it into an envelope
and dropped it in the mail. After a morning of fruitless complaining, writing that letter made me feel as if I'd done something constructive. Maybe it wouldn't do any good, but at
least I felt better for having had my say.

By this time, it was after twelve. I debated going out for
lunch, but with my luck, I'd run into Joan Lee at Taco Loco
and she'd find out the case of stomach flu I'd pleaded wasn't
as severe as I thought.

So I settled on a tuna sandwich. I was in the kitchen mixing
up the tuna when a sound from the living room made the hair
on the back of my neck stand up. I could have sworn I heard
a footstep. I froze, spoon poised over the mayonnaise jar, and
listened. *Creak…creak.*

What was someone doing in my house in the middle of the
day? I looked around for the phone, but the cradle was
empty. Then I remembered, I'd taken it into the living room
when I was thinking about calling Darla.

I heard the sound of the desk drawer sliding open. Whoever was in there wasn't even trying to be quiet. They probably thought they were alone, that I was at work and they
could take their time. Maybe I could use that to my advantage.

I laid aside my spoon and crept across the kitchen to the
knife rack and slid the biggest carving knife out of its slot.
Then, brandishing the knife like a sword, I tiptoed to the door
and eased it open.

A tall, dark figure was hunched over my desk, pawing through the papers. As I watched, he shut the drawer and dumped the pencil cup on the blotter.

"Hold it right there!" I shouted.

Pencils flew everywhere and the cup bounced off the carpet. The bandit yelped and whirled to face me. "Phoebe, what are you doing here?"

I sucked in my breath and stared, goggle-eyed. "Steve?"

8

"WHAT ARE YOU DOING HOME?" Steve sounded annoyed. "You're supposed to be at work." He tilted his head to one side and studied me. "What did you do to your hair?"

I put one hand to my slightly mussed hair, then lowered it, determined not to get sidetracked. "You first. What are you doing breaking into my house?"

"I wasn't breaking in." He dangled his key chain at eye level. "I still have a key." He tucked the keys back into his pocket and frowned. "Put down that knife. You look ridiculous."

I laid the knife aside. It felt ridiculous holding it on him. Even after a year apart, Steve's sudden appearance stirred feelings in me. Not love. Not hate. Just...recognition. I shifted my weight to my right side. Having him here made me nervous. He didn't have a right to be here, and yet, to some part of my brain, he looked at home in the living room we'd once shared. "What's wrong with knocking?"

"I didn't think you were home. Where's your car?" He looked around the room, as if he might find the Probe parked there.

"In the repair shop." Technically true, I suppose. "So you thought I wasn't home and decided to break in."

He stuffed his hands in his pockets and pursed his lips in a look of impatience. "Now, Phoebe, it's not like that." He frowned. "You looked better as a blonde."

"Who asked your opinion?" I smoothed my hair again. "I happen to like it better red."

He shook his head. "You don't have the right personality for a redhead."

"Shows you didn't know me so well after all." Hah! Take that. My smile was downright smug.

Did I mention that Steve is forty-three? He's an accountant at a big oil and gas firm downtown. Wears nice suits, has his thinning hair cut and styled—and I happen to know, colored—at a posh salon in the Galleria. In some ways he's a very handsome man, but I'd learned long ago that he had some very unhandsome attitudes. "Don't try to talk your way out of this one," I said. "You had no right to open that door and you know it." I reached for the phone. "You'd better leave now before I call the police." And after that, I'd call a locksmith. I shuddered. How many times before had he come by when I wasn't home and pawed through my things?

"Now, Phoebe, let's not fight." He crossed the room and took the phone out of my hand as easily as if he'd been taking an empty soda can from a child. "Just because we're divorced doesn't mean we can't be friends."

I suppose I could have put up a fight, screaming and making a scene. Steve hated scenes and he'd always retreat if I threatened one. But he must have come here for a reason and I wanted to find out why. "What are you doing here?" I asked.

He glanced around the living room again, whether avoiding my gaze or searching for something, I couldn't tell. "I came by to get something I left behind when I moved out."

I wrinkled my forehead, puzzled. Steve had carted away a whole moving van full of crap when he moved out. Everything from a drawerful of gym socks to every tool in the garage. Later, when I'd wanted to hang a picture in the living room, I'd had to use the heel of a shoe to hammer in the nail.

"If you're talking about the three-year collection of *Playboy* up in the attic, I threw it away a long time ago."

He winced. "Those could have been worth a lot of money."

"Is that what you were looking for? Old magazines you could sell for a few bucks?" I leaned against the back of the sofa. "Number-crunching business that bad these days?"

He stared at the floor, working his jaw as if trying to get the words out. Finally, he looked at me. "I want the ring."

"What ring?" Every nerve in my body went on red alert. I only had one ring Steve could have been interested in. He wanted his grandmother's diamond solitaire. The ring he had given me when we got engaged. It was a beautiful ring, in a 1920's art deco setting, the one piece of really good jewelry I'd ever owned.

"I want my grandmother's ring."

"My engagement ring." I'd stashed my wedding band in the safe-deposit box the week after the divorce was final and hadn't looked at it since. But I kept the diamond, and still wore it occasionally. I associated that ring with happy times, with young love and the early years, when our marriage had held so much promise.

His lips tightened in a grim line. "That ring is a Frame family heirloom."

An heirloom he hadn't cared one fig about until now, when he was going to get married again. When he was going to have a family. My stomach hurt. "Our divorce decree said all jewelry was mine to keep," I said, my voice tight, strained.

He looked pained. "Phoebe, don't be unreasonable."

"I'm unreasonable? I'm not the one who broke into this house with the intention of stealing my ex-wife's jewelry."

"That was my grandmother's ring."

"It's mine now."

Little beads of sweat sprouted on his forehead. He rocked back and forth on his heels. "I'll pay you for it."

I almost smiled at that. Steve had to be desperate to offer to spend money on me. Just-a-waitress must have heard about the ring and been pressuring him to get it for her. "I don't want your money."

The line of his jaw tightened. "I'll buy you a new ring."

He would buy me a cheap cubic zirconia in a ten-carat setting. I hadn't lived with the man twelve years without learning the way his mind operated. I shook my head. "No. I like *that* ring."

His expression shifted again, to one of desperation. "Phoebe, that ring has great sentimental value to me."

I snorted. "Since when are you sentimental?"

He looked offended. "Becoming a father does that to a man, I guess."

The words were like a match to the anger that smoldered within me. "I thought you didn't want any children," I snapped.

"I've changed my mind."

The truth was there on his face, taking my breath away. He didn't want *my* children. "Get out!" I ordered him.

"No. I'm not leaving until we talk this over like adults."

He still held the phone, but I had an extension in the bedroom. I was on my way to it when the doorbell rang. I went to answer it, grateful for the interruption. After talking with Steve, I probably looked sick enough to fool anyone at the office, and even a delivery person would be a good excuse to get rid of Steve.

The one person I wasn't prepared to find at my door stood grinning at me. "Jeff!" I gasped. "What are you doing here?"

"I brought you some chicken soup." He held up a brown paper bag.

I felt weak in the knees, whether from the reminder of the last time I'd seen him—naked and gorgeous—or the knowledge that now I had to deal with two difficult men at the same time.

"Phoebe, why don't you introduce me to your friend?" Steve had followed me to the door and was smirking at Jeff. I could see that accountant's brain of his assessing Jeff, adding up how old he must be.

"Jeff, this is my ex-husband, Steve. Steve, this is Jeff. He's installing a new transcription service at the office."

Jeff didn't look pleased at that description, but what did he expect? *Steve, this is the man I had wild passionate sex with last night.*

They shook hands, both men doing that guy thing where they try to squeeze the life out of each other's fingers. Judging by the pained look in Steve's eyes, I'd say Jeff won.

Jeff handed me the soup and touched my shoulder. "How are you feeling?"

"I've been better," I said truthfully. And things were getting dicier by the minute. I glanced at Steve. "Steve was just leaving."

Steve smirked. "Anxious for me to go, are you?" He glanced at his watch. "I guess you have to take advantage of these lunch hours, don't you?"

I felt like throwing the hot soup in his face, but that would only prove what he insinuated was true. Instead, I took his arm and urged him over the threshold.

"I intend to get that ring," he said under his breath.

"I won't let you bully me. Not this time."

He left and I shut the door and sagged against it.

"Are you all right?" Jeff asked.

I couldn't think of a good answer. There were days when I thought I might never be all right again.

He looked away, but I didn't miss the look of disgust on his face. "What did you ever see in that guy?"

I pushed away from the door. "Sometimes I ask myself that

question." I carried the soup into the kitchen and he followed. I set the bag on the counter and slumped at the table.

Without asking me, he took the soup carton from the bag and put it in the microwave. Then he hunted through the cabinets and pulled out two bowls. I watched, thinking I ought to protest, but I didn't want to. The truth was, I could use company just now.

And for some reason I felt the need to defend my marriage. To prove that I hadn't been a total idiot to choose Steve in the first place, or to stay with him for all those years. "He was different when we first married," I said.

Jeff didn't look convinced. "What did he want?"

"A ring." I rubbed my finger, where I used to wear the ring all the time. "It belonged to his grandmother, and he gave it to me as an engagement ring. He's getting married again, and I guess he wants it for his new wife."

"And you don't want to give it up."

"Why should I have to give it up?" I slammed my hand onto the table. "Dammit, he took everything else he could get his hands on. He didn't even care about the ring until now."

"Hey, I didn't say you were in the wrong." He sat down beside me, almost, but not quite touching. I was grateful for that. If he'd touched me, I might have broken down.

"I didn't mean to snap at you," I said. "It's just...so frustrating."

"Yeah." His voice had a huskiness to it that made me think he wasn't talking about the ring anymore.

The microwave dinged and he got up and filled the two bowls with soup. He brought them to the table with a waxed-paper sleeve of saltine crackers and two glasses of orange juice. I was reminded of when I was a little girl, and stayed home from school with a cold. This was the lunch my mother had always served me. It was a funny feeling having someone else take care of me, after so many years.

"You'd make a good nurse," I said, only half joking.

"I'm better at fixing computers than people."

We ate in silence, the one thing we hadn't mentioned—the events of last night—hanging like a ghost between us.

Finally, I pushed my empty bowl away. "I'm glad you came over," I said. "This gives us a chance to talk away from the office. About last night—"

"Don't." He put his hand over mine. "If you're going to say anything about how it shouldn't have happened or it was wrong, or anything like that, don't. I wanted it to happen. And I'd have made sure it did, sooner or later."

"Why did you want it to happen?" I looked into his eyes, hoping to find the answer there. What did this gorgeous guy see in me? "You hardly know me. There must be women your own age—"

He smiled. "You act like we're a whole generation apart, instead of a few years." He leaned closer. "How old was your husband?"

I knew what he was getting at, but I knew lying wouldn't do any good. After all, he'd seen Steve. "He's forty-three."

"Eleven years older than you. And that didn't matter to you when you married him."

"How did you know...?"

He grinned. "Michelle told me."

I looked down at the table. "A younger man is different." Even as I said it, I knew it was ridiculous. I slid my chair back and stood, needing to get away from him. "Look, my life is a little screwed up right now. I'm not a person you want to get involved with. What happened last night—"

He held up his hand to stop me, but I pushed on. "It was incredible. Wonderful even. But I can't let it happen again. I have to get my life in order, to figure out what I'm doing here. I don't need another man confusing me."

He stood and came to stand beside me. "At least you admit we were good together. I'll consider that a start."

I stared at him. "Didn't you hear what I just said? I don't want to start anything with you."

"Too late. It's already started." He grinned. "But I'm a patient man." He leaned over and kissed me, the briefest brush of his lips that sent heat coursing through me. "But I'll warn you," he whispered. "I don't play fair. I don't intend to make it easy for you to stay away from me."

9

I HADN'T CONSIDERED what walking into my little workroom the next day was liable to do to me. I strolled in, unsuspecting, cup of coffee in one hand, a doughnut in the other, and the first thing I saw was a stack of papers, the top one wrinkled by what I knew to be my own naked butt. I had perched right there, on the edge of the counter, while Jeff had his way with me.

I flushed at the memory, not with embarrassment, but with a fierce longing to repeat the experience.

Don't be an idiot, I told myself. *Wild, uninhibited sex with a man you hardly know is not a sensible activity for a woman trying to put her life back together.*

Not to mention, if Joan ever found out we'd been doing the dirty on the patient charts, she'd have us both out on the street faster than I could type a resignation letter. I tossed the rumpled chart to one side and dropped into my chair. *Deep breaths*, I reminded myself. *This is just a room. Your workroom. It's not some sexy boudoir.*

Except that all I could smell when I took that deep breath was Jeff's cologne. I grabbed my coffee cup and took a long drink. "God, I'm pathetic," I moaned.

"It can't be that bad."

Coffee sloshed onto my skirt as I squealed. "Jeff! I—I didn't expect to see you."

"But now that I'm here, aren't you glad?" He smiled and held his arms wide.

I looked away, my heart beating double time. I might not enjoy being caught in the middle of all these whirling emotions, but at least I was getting a great aerobic workout.

"You'd better get that out before it leaves a stain." The next thing I knew, he was kneeling in front of me, sponging at my skirt with a handkerchief. If he kept that up, I was going to melt into a puddle right here in this chair.

"Is the air-conditioning on the blink?" I said panting. "It seems awfully warm in here."

He stilled and our eyes met. "Yeah." He licked his lips—gorgeous, moist lips that begged to be kissed. "It is a little warm all of a sudden."

"What are you two doing in here?"

We jumped apart as Joan entered the room. She looked at each of us in turn, lips pursed in disapproval.

"I was just getting ready to start training Phoebe." Jeff stood against the far wall, hands in his back pockets.

I could think of a few things he could train me in...but I pushed that thought aside. "Did you need something, Joan?"

"Doctor wants to see you in his office right away." She turned and left, her heels tap-tapping down the hall.

I shoved up out of my chair. "I'd better go see what he wants."

Patterson was using a pair of surgical scissors to trim his nails when I walked into his office. He gave me a smile that was more of a smirk. "Well, Phoebe, it's nice to see you decided to grace us with your presence today."

I gave myself credit for not making some snide remark just then. But I kept my cool. "Joan said you wanted to see me."

He leaned across the desk and shoved an eight-inch high stack of charts toward me. "I'd like you to transcribe the marked sections of each of these charts for me."

I gaped at the pile of files, which bristled with pink sticky notes. It would take hours...days...to go through all of those.

"I won't be able to get to them right away. I have to train on the new software, and catch up on the work from yesterday."

"Then I guess you'll have to work overtime." He stood and handed me the stack of charts. "I need these for my presentation at the TMA conference."

The charts weighed like a stack of bricks in my arms. "This doesn't have anything to do with my turning down your advances, does it?" I asked, though I already knew the answer.

His expression hardened. "I have no idea what you're talking about. And if I hear any hint of you bringing it up again—to anyone—you will be out of a job."

My stomach clenched. I had no doubt Patterson would carry out that threat without blinking an eye. "Yes, sir," I said through clenched teeth.

I walked as fast as I could back to my office and tossed the files onto my desk, sending them skidding across the counter to collide with the monitor where Jeff now sat.

He looked up, one eyebrow raised. "Something wrong?"

"Patterson's given me all this extra work to do. I think he's trying to get back at me for turning him down the other night."

"Why don't you just report him for sexual harassment? File a complaint with the Medical Society or something?"

I slapped my hand against my forehead. "Gee, why didn't I think of that?" I gave him a withering look. "I'm not totally stupid, you know."

He swiveled to face me. "Then why don't you do it?"

"Oh, sure." I picked up the phone and spoke into the receiver in my best Miss Priss voice. "Hello, Harris County Medical Society? I'd like to report that one of your members seems to think boinking the boss is part of my job description. Yes, the doctor has a fine reputation as a physician. Me? I'm a transcriptionist. Yes, I'm divorced. My skirt? I'm not sure the length of my skirt has anything to do with this. Did I ever encourage the doctor's advances? Absolutely not! Oh, but he says I did? He said what? That in the aftermath of my divorce, I turned to him for advice and comfort? That's ridiculous! Well, no, I don't think anyone actually *saw* the doctor make advances toward me. Yes, it is my word against his. Yes, I suppose you're right."

I hung up the phone and looked at Jeff. "The Medical Society is one of the biggest old-boy networks around. Believe me, they're going to look after their own, and a complaint by one lowly transcriptionist isn't going to mean anything to them."

He frowned. "I think you're exaggerating. After all, there are women in the Medical Society, too. Surely they'd take your side."

I shook my head. "They're doctors first, then women. They had to be to get as far as they have. Not only that, a lot of them are married to doctors and they live in fear of women like me seducing their husbands." I pulled out my keyboard drawer and slid a pile of charts toward me. "If I complained, all I'd end up with is a reputation as a troublemaker and a spot in the unemployment line."

"So what are you going to do?"

I shrugged. Hadn't I just told him there was nothing I could do? It wasn't as if I liked being helpless. But in this case, I knew I was. "I'm going to avoid being alone with the good doctor and watch my back."

He slid his chair over next to mine. "I'll be keeping an eye on Patterson, too. If he lays a hand on you, I'll bust his chops."

Oh, boy. I took a deep breath. I should have seen this coming. Men are *so* predictable sometimes. I mean, they sleep with you once and suddenly they're like cavemen, beating their chests and booming "You my woman now." I looked down my nose at Jeff, doing my best impression of every stern schoolteacher I'd ever had. "There's something we need to get straight right now," I said. "What happened the other night, in here, doesn't give you any kind of claim on me. And it doesn't give me any claim on you. Understand?"

He nodded, but the knowing look in his eyes said he didn't really believe it. *Oh, God, a romantic! That was worse than a caveman. Now he probably thought because lust had got the better of our common sense, we were meant for each other.*

"Quit looking at me that way!" I snapped.

"What way?" A smile tugged at the corners of his mouth and he scooted his chair even closer.

"Like you're thinking nasty thoughts about me."

The smile came out full force and he waggled his eyebrows. "Maybe I am."

I laughed. How could I keep from it when he looked so silly—part sexy stud, part endearing boy? "All right, Prince Charming," I said when my giggles subsided. "Why don't we get to work?"

For the rest of the morning, we worked side by side as he showed me the ins and outs of the new transcription software. I'd expected working with him again would be awkward, but I actually enjoyed myself. Jeff was a good teacher, much more patient than I would have been.

Yes, I was very much aware of him—of his thigh brushing against mine when he leaned forward to show me how to adjust the volume; of his breath, warm on my neck when he prompted me to hit the command keys; and of his cologne, filling my senses with memories of those wild, passionate moments in his arms. But that heightened awareness was like the thrill of a roller-coaster ride without the danger. Desire buzzed through me like an electric current, making me feel that much sharper, more alive, ready for anything.

I had just aced my fourth tutorial when he reached out and

snagged my hand in his. "Is this the ring?" He stroked his thumb across the diamond.

"That's the one." I eased out of his grasp and held my hand up to the light. "Isn't it beautiful?"

"It's beautiful on you."

I quickly looked away from his out-and-out admiration, which had gotten me into trouble in the first place. For whatever reason, this young guy found me attractive, but that was no reason to lose my head, or to think that anything positive could come from this.

"It's time for lunch," I shoved back my chair and stood.

"Let's go somewhere together." He stood also. "I hear the Warwick has a great café downstairs."

And great bedrooms for rent upstairs, I thought. I shook my head. "I have some errands to run." I slipped my purse over my shoulder and got the hell out of there, before the bedroom-eyed boy made me change my mind.

Only one elevator was working today. I wondered who'd got caught in the other one this time. Word was one of the neurologists had been trapped last week and missed his tee time. He was threatening to sue the building owners.

The working elevator's doors parted and Darla hurried out and almost bowled me over. "Ready for lunch?"

10

DAMN. I'D FORGOTTEN TODAY was Thursday, my regular date with Darla. "I don't have time for lunch," I told her. "I have to get over to the car lot."

I started toward the open elevator, but she put a hand on my shoulder, holding me back. We watched the doors slide shut and the elevator descend without us. "You have to eat."

"I really have to get over to the car dealer." I punched the down button again.

"She wouldn't go to lunch with me, either."

Jeff came up behind us and put one hand on my shoulder. Darla's smile widened and a slightly dazed look came into her eyes. "Who are you?"

"Darla, this is Jeff. Jeff, this is my best friend, Darla." I watched, getting a good look at Jeff from Darla's point of view, as a stranger, without prejudices. Well, except that she knew he and I had had sex, and that it had been a fantastic experience, but not one I wanted to repeat.

The truth was, Jeff was a damn good-looking man. Not movie-star handsome, but real-man handsome, with a strong jaw, thick hair, just the right amount of muscle and a way of looking at a woman that made her feel like Eve and Aphrodite and Princess Diana, all rolled into one.

"Well, *I'd* certainly go to lunch with you," Darla cooed. The elevator arrived again and the doors split open. "But right now, Phoebe and I have some things to talk about." She grabbed my hand and pulled me onto the open elevator.

She waited until we'd descended three floors before she spoke. "I can see why you jumped his bones. What a hottie!" She fanned herself.

"Jeez, Darla. You make it sound like *I* seduced *him*."

"From the way you described it to me on the phone, it was a mutual seduction."

I folded my arms under my breasts. "It was nothing of the sort. It just...happened."

"Uh-huh. You know, you really need to learn to be more comfortable with your sexuality. There was a doctor on *Oprah* the other day who was talking about just this thing...."

By the time we reached the lobby, I had a list of three books and two movies I should read or view to rid myself of my latent guilt about my sexuality.

We bought hot dogs from a street cart and walked over to the fountain in front of the Warwick Hotel to eat them. It was one of those rare fall days when the weather in Houston is perfect. The muggy heat of summer has faded and the damp chill of winter hasn't yet set in. Office workers had turned out in droves to enjoy the sunshine and cool breezes. A busker was playing energetic blues by the fountain, his open guitar case littered with change from an appreciative audience.

"Your hair looks great," Darla said as we waited in line for our dogs.

"Thanks." I couldn't help but smile. "I never got this much attention when I was a blonde."

"Maybe it's not the hair. Maybe it's the new Phoebe. The improved, kick-ass version."

I laughed. "Right. I think it's the hair. I haven't done much ass kicking lately."

"I don't know about that. The old Phoebe would never have had her way with a gorgeous hunk like Jeff."

I blushed. "Don't remind me." I still couldn't believe I'd gone after him the way I had. Or that it had felt so good.

We took a seat beside the water. "So what's Jeff like?" Darla asked. "Is he a nice guy?"

I shrugged. "He's nice." I took a bite of hot dog and chewed thoughtfully. "Too charming for his own good," I added after I'd swallowed.

"I like him. You shouldn't worry about the age difference or what people think." She popped a bite of hot dog into her mouth. "Or what Steve thinks. Not that he even has to know about it. It's none of his business who you go out with."

I winced. "He already knows. I mean, not that Jeff and I are dating—which we aren't. But I think he suspects something is going on. Which it isn't."

"Steve knows about Jeff?" Her eyes widened. "How did he find out?"

"Jeff came to the house when Steve was there and they didn't exactly hit it off."

"Oooh, two stallions fighting over the mare. I'll bet *that* was interesting."

"I am not a mare. And I'd hardly call Steve a stallion." Jeff, on the other hand...

Darla waved aside my protest. "I was speaking figuratively. I just heard a guy on the radio. He's written a new book that explains all human relationships in terms of the behavior of farm animals." She leaned toward me. "Did you know that pigs have the longest orgasms of all domestic animals?"

"And what am I supposed to do with that little tidbit of information?" I shook my head in exasperation. "If Steve and Jeff behaved like animals, it was more like two grumpy bears."

"What was Steve doing at your house anyway? Did you invite him over?"

"God, no! He broke in."

"He broke in?" Darla's shriek sent three pigeons fluttering

into the air. A woman across from us looked up from her book and frowned. Darla made a face at her and turned back to me. "Steve actually broke into your house? Why?"

"He wanted his grandmother's ring." I held out my hand, showing her the jewel in question. "It was my engagement ring and the divorce settlement gave it to me, but now that he and Just-a-waitress are getting married, he wants it back."

"Tell the cheapskate to go buy a new ring." Darla wadded her hot-dog wrapper into a ball. "And Jeff came by in the middle of this? Just paying a social call?"

"I called in sick to work and he stopped by to check on me."

"That's so sweet. I told you I liked him." She patted my arm. "See, Tony isn't the only nice guy left in the world."

I frowned at the remains of my hot dog. My feelings about Jeff were too mixed-up for me to talk about right now. I didn't even want to think about them. Why did relationships have to be so complicated? "Darla, do me a favor," I said. "Just shut up. Okay?"

She grinned. "You do have it bad, don't you?"

I glared at her, but she kept right on grinning, as if she knew something about me even I didn't know yet.

THAT AFTERNOON, I HEADED OVER to Easy Motors for another try at freeing my car. I armed myself with a list of places I'd filed complaints, and a T-shirt I'd had made up that read I Bought a Lemon at Easy Motors. I'd wanted it to read Easy Motors Cheats Customers but the clerk at the T-shirt store had persuaded me that the car dealer could sue me for that, whereas stating I bought a lemon from them was closer to fact. "Are you a law student?" I asked as I paid for my finished shirt.

He grinned. "Nah. I watch a lot of Court TV."

Hector was on the lot with a customer when I walked up,

and he about dropped his teeth when he saw my shirt. The black shirt with fluorescent green lettering was hard to miss. He left his potential buyer and hustled over to me. "You can't wear that here," he growled.

I tried not to look as nervous as I felt. "It's a free country. And I'm merely stating the truth." I looked around the lot. "Where is my car, by the way?"

He looked evasive. "You'll have to ask Frank about that."

"Good, I'll do that." I marched to the office, past the gaping secretary, and into Frank's office. He was just about to bite into a meatball sub when I burst through the door, and my sudden entrance sent a meatball spurting out the side to roll across his desk.

"You!" He stood, still clutching the sandwich in one hand. "What are you doing here? And get that shirt off!"

"Do you think my being topless would distract the customers from the fact that you're cheating them?"

His face was the color of the sauce oozing out the sides of the sub. "It's bad enough you write to the papers, now you come around here harassing us, too. I'll call the police." He reached for the phone.

"The papers?" I blinked. "What are you talking about?"

"They printed your letter in today's edition." He punched in three numbers and barked into the phone. "I want a cop over here right away. I've got a customer who's making trouble."

The words sent a jolt of fear through my middle, but I told myself the police wouldn't take such a complaint seriously. Besides, I wanted to find out more about my letter in the paper.

While Frank mumbled into the phone, I leaned over and looked into his trash can. Sure enough, peeking out from beneath a fast-food wrapper was this morning's edition of the *Houston Banner*. I fished it out and stared down at the editorial page, with my letter displayed prominently in the middle. *Woman distressed over poor treatment at car dealership* read the headline.

My smile got bigger the more I read. There were my words, in print for everyone to see. Or at least everyone who read the paper. And there was my name at the bottom. Phoebe Frame. It had never looked so good. Not even on a check.

The door opened behind me and one of Houston's finest strolled in. He was the poster-boy image of a cop, the kind you see on TV shows: young, tall, muscular, of an indeterminate but decidedly ethnic background. He looked slightly annoyed at having been called out on this piddly call. "Mr. Adams? You having some sort of problem here?" He glanced at me and I gave him what I hoped was a friendly smile.

"No problem, officer," I said. "I just came to talk to Mr. Adams about my car."

The officer glanced at my shirt and grinned. "I read about you in the paper." He turned to Frank. "Why don't you just give this lady her car back?"

Frank squared his shoulders and tried to look dignified, but since he was still holding the limp meatball sandwich in one hand, the effort was wasted. "If she wants her car back, she can pay me three hundred and fifty-nine dollars and eighty-eight cents in storage fees."

"Three fifty-nine?" I squeaked. "You told me eighty-nine, ninety-seven before."

"That's eighty-nine, ninety-seven a *day*." He shook his head. "I ain't running no parking garage here."

"It seems to me you two ought to be able to come to some kind of compromise," the cop said.

"He's holding my car hostage," I said.

"I won't be bullied by a customer." Frank jabbed his finger toward me. "Now I want you to escort her off my property this minute."

"You don't have to do that." I laid the paper back down on Frank's desk. "I was just leaving." I laid my list of complaint organizations alongside the paper. "Here's a list of places with whom I've filed complaints about Easy Motors. I imagine you'll be hearing from them soon." I waggled my fingers at the two men and sauntered out of the office. If I swayed my hips just a little more than necessary, it was only because I was feeling pretty satisfied with myself. I didn't have my car back yet, but I hadn't let myself be bullied into accepting something that was blatantly wrong, either.

Outside, I raised my fist in the air triumphantly. "I have not yet begun to fight," I said.

A taxi mistook my victorious gesture and screeched to a halt in front of me. What the heck? I climbed in back and told the driver to take me to the closest newsstand. I needed about twenty copies of today's issue of the *Houston Banner*.

I TOOK TEN COPIES OF MY ARTICLE to work on Monday and, for about five minutes, everyone was impressed. Then one of the drug pushers came in with fresh Krispy Kreme doughnuts and I was old news. I took a copy of the paper and a fresh doughnut back to my work space and ate while admiring my words all over again.

Jeff wasn't around today. He had another client to take care of. And here I thought I was the only one! Though I didn't like to admit it, I missed him. Aside from the fact that I wouldn't consider dating him, I'd begun to think of him as a friend. At least I could talk to him and he listened and even seemed to respect my opinion about things. But maybe that was only because he wanted back in my pants. You never can tell with men.

About ten o'clock, I was the office celebrity all over again when a florist's delivery came for me. The arrangement of sweetheart roses and carnations was sweet and showy at the same time, and brought out a satisfying chorus of envious oohs and ahs and jealous looks from my coworkers.

"Who's it from?" Michelle asked as I unpinned the card from the pink satin ribbon around the vase.

My heart beat wildly as I slit open the envelope. Would it be too much to hope they were from Jeff? But then, everyone would give me a hard time about it and Joan might feel compelled to lecture me on the office policy on relationships with contractors—which no one knew about but her.

I took a deep breath and read the card. "From a secret admirer." A thrill ran through me and I squinted at the handwriting. Did Jeff make his *S's* like that?

"Ooh, how exciting!" Barbara peered over my shoulder. "Who do you think it is?"

I shook my head. If Jeff wanted to send me flowers, wouldn't he say so? He hadn't been shy about declaring his feelings before now.

"Maybe a patient has a crush on you," Michelle said.

"Or a friend?" Joan snatched the card from my hand and turned it over. "It's from Casa Verde florist. Why don't you call and ask them who sent them?"

"I already thought of that." I grabbed the card and stuffed it back in the envelope. Actually, I hadn't thought of it before she said anything, but I'm sure I would have.

I picked up the flowers and carried them back to my office. Then I dialed the number for the florist. "Hi, my name is Phoebe Frame and someone from your shop just delivered some flowers to me at the Central Care Network Clinic—Dr. Patterson's office.... Oh, yes, they're beautiful. I love them. But the card doesn't say who they're from and I wondered... Yes, I'll hold."

I hummed along with the Indigo Girls and admired the waxy sheen of a pink rose in the arrangement. What is it about getting flowers that makes a woman feel so special?

Would a man feel the same way if I sent him a bouquet? I shook my head. No, men appreciate something they can eat or wear.

"Hello?" The florist clerk came back on the line. "Those flowers were ordered by a man named Eddie."

I frowned. "Eddie who?"

"Doesn't say. Just Eddie. I wasn't here when he came in."

"It doesn't ring a bell, but thank you." I hung up the phone and looked again at the card that had come with the flowers. Who the heck was Eddie and why was he sending me flowers? I buried my nose in the bouquet and sniffed appreciatively. What the heck? I might as well enjoy them while I could. Whoever he was, Eddie was obviously a man with excellent tastes.

I set the flowers up on the filing cabinet and stepped back to admire them. The only thing better would be if Jeff were here to see these. *I wonder if he'd be jealous?*

11

I DECIDED AS LONG AS I had the ring out, I ought to get it cleaned and appraised. If Steve made any more offers, I could come back at him with the true value—a price I was pretty certain he was too cheap to pay.

The only jewelry store I knew that did appraisals was in the Galleria. This is the fanciest mall in Houston, home to Neiman Marcus, Nordstrom, Saks and an indoor ice rink. When you get tired of looking at all the high-dollar items for sale, you can sit at tables overlooking the rink and watch all the would-be Tara Lipinskis practicing their spins and leaps.

The old jeweler's eyes lit up when I showed him the ring. "Oh, yes, a very fine piece." He put his fingers on either side of the band. "May I?"

I let him slip it off. He fished a loupe from his pocket and fit it to his eye. "Art deco," he said. "Possibly even Tiffany. The stone has a very fine color and a nice cut." He raised his eyes and handed the ring back to me. "If you'd like to sell it, I could offer you five thousand for it."

I blinked. That much, huh? Steve would never shell out that much cash for this when he could buy Just-a-waitress a new one for half the price. "No thank you," I said. "It has a lot of sentimental value for me. But I would like to have it cleaned."

While he took the ring into the back to clean it, I wandered through the shop, admiring all the necklaces, bracelets and earrings I'd never be able to afford. Still, it was nice to dream....

A young couple walked in, holding hands. She had the blond, blue-eyed good looks and fresh-faced complexion of a high school cheerleader and the business suit he wore didn't fit him as well as his old football uniform probably had. I could read their whole story on their faces: high school sweethearts, he was out of college now and working in his first real job. They'd just gotten engaged and had come in to pick out a ring.

Sure enough, they stopped in front of the display of wedding sets. A grandmotherly clerk greeted them with a smile, then offered congratulations.

I drifted away, not wanting to intrude on this private moment. But I couldn't help glancing back toward them. The clerk pulled out a tray and the girl oohed and aahed over the selection. After a moment, she pointed to one and her young man removed it from the slot in the case and slipped it onto her finger.

The light in her eyes illuminated them both. He looked at her with a besotted expression and then they kissed, a sweet, tender touching of their lips I had to look away from.

I blinked back tears, cursing my sudden turn toward sentimentality. Steve and I had probably never looked that sappily at each other. Maybe that was the problem.

"Mrs. Frame, I have your ring now." I accepted the ring from the clerk. The stone shone with blinding brilliance. It looked like a ring worth five thousand dollars and I was tempted to keep my hand covered as I walked down the street, lest anyone try to steal it.

I glanced down the counter at the young couple once more. She was holding out her hand, admiring the simple solitaire on her ring finger. Her ring probably wasn't worth a third of mine, but I knew she'd never trade places with me for a whole roomful of diamonds.

AFTER I LEFT THE JEWELRY STORE, I decided to have a look around the mall. I hadn't been here in a long time, though once it had been my favorite hangout. As I said before, it had all the poshest stores, and that magical wonderland atmosphere that all the best malls have. As if everything you needed to make dreams come true could be found somewhere amongst the rows and rows of brightly lit stores.

When I was a little girl, my family would make a special trip to the Galleria each Christmas, to visit Santa Claus and to look at all the decorations: towering nutcracker soldiers and giant golden angels, a Christmas tree as tall as a building, covered with candy garlands and lavish ornaments and a little train that gave rides around Santa's village.

Even in the middle of summer, the Galleria still had some of that Christmas magic for me. When I was a teenager, Darla and I came here almost every Saturday. We'd check out the latest sales at The Limited and Gap, then head to the ice-skating rink. Even when it was a broiling one hundred degrees outside, the ice rink was cool, in every sense of the word.

My girlfriends and I would wear our shortest skirts to skate, and when a cute guy was around, we'd twirl and twirl, until we were dizzy. The boys would hang out along the side of the rink and watch, hoping to catch a glimpse of the girls' underwear.

I stopped and watched a teenage girl skate a lazy figure eight. She looked so young and graceful, with her long brown hair flying out behind her. The kind of girl the guys would stop and watch.

Funny, I hadn't thought about skating in years. I wondered if I could even stand up on the ice anymore. Steve hadn't liked to skate, so we'd never come here after we started dating.

I watched the girl turn and head back up the ice toward me. Why had I let Steve keep me from something I'd enjoyed so much? I tightened my grip on the railing around the rink. I wasn't going to do that anymore. I wasn't going to let anyone else decide what I would do or not do. I'd do the things I wanted and if they didn't like it, they could lump it.

MY MOTHER USED TO SAY "trouble comes in threes" but in my case it was more like multiples of three. An ordinary day for me meant at least one minor crisis, and lately I'd had more than my share of major ordeals. If there's any kind of balance in the universe, somewhere my alter ego is sailing through life completely untouched by chaos.

This thought didn't give me much comfort, however, the morning I reached up to adjust my shower and the shower-head broke off in my hand. As hot water cascaded over me, I screamed and groped blindly for the faucet. "Stop! Stop! Stop! Aaaargh!"

By the time I had the water shut off, my bathroom was flooded. I pushed my wet hair out of my eyes and stared up at the jagged end of the pipe that protruded a scant quarter inch from the wall. I looked at the equally jagged end of the showerhead in my hand. "Something tells me Super Glue isn't going to be enough to fix this."

I finished rinsing off under the tap, then dried off and went in search of the phone book. Houston has plenty of plumbers. I flipped to the last page of the listings and called Zaragosa Plumbing. My theory is that AAA Plumbing and Acme Plumbing get all the business from the people who are too lazy to look any further. I thought if I picked someone whose name began with a Z, I might have a chance of getting him to come to my house before next Christmas.

I explained my problem to the woman who answered the phone. "He can take a look at it this afternoon," she said.

"What time this afternoon?" I asked.

"He don't have a schedule like a bus. This afternoon is as close as I can get."

"Oh. It's just that I have to work." If I took another day off, Joan was liable to have a full-blown conniption.

"And you think maybe Mr. Zaragosa spends his afternoons down at the bowling alley? You ain't the only woman in Houston with plumbing problems, lady. The city's eat up with bad pipes."

I thought about telling the woman that Mr. Zaragosa wasn't the only plumber in Houston, either, but I had a feeling I wasn't going to have much better luck with someone further up in the alphabet. "All right. Tell him to come by this afternoon." I gave her the address, then went to get dressed for work.

My luck wasn't all bad that day. City buses were on time for a change and I showed up at the office with a full minute to spare. I had just about worked up the courage to tell Joan I needed the afternoon off, when Michelle told me the dragon lady had a dentist appointment after lunch. Back in my cubbyhole, I did a victory dance. Saved by tooth decay.

At twelve twenty-two I ran up the walk and fitted the key into my front-door lock. Surely the plumber had stopped for lunch and I'd have time to grab a bite before his arrival.

I could have prepared and eaten a five-course meal before the Zaragosa Plumbing truck rattled into my driveway at three forty-five. A short, thick man climbed out of the cab. His black T-shirt barely fit over the muscles of his arms, and even the denim overalls he wore strained against his broad chest. Wrenches, pieces of pipe and a large hammer poked up out of the top of the canvas tool bag he carried. "Mrs. Frame?" he asked.

"Yes. Thank you for coming."

He stuck out a meaty hand. "Vince Zaragosa. I understand you got a problem with your shower."

"Yes. It's right back here."

I showed him the busted showerhead. He turned it over in his hand and shook his head. "I'm betting these pipes are pretty old."

"The house was built in seventy-eight," I said.

He nodded. "What did I tell you?"

I watched from the doorway as he planted both feet in my bathtub and stared up at the pipe protruding from the wall. "Can you fix it?" I asked anxiously.

He looked back over his shoulder at me. "Lady, I can fix anything but a broken heart."

I figured, on that note, I'd better leave him to his work. I retreated to the kitchen and cracked open a Diet Coke. I wondered how much this was going to cost me. I'd heard plumbing was expensive.

I was still musing on this when Vince Zaragosa strolled into the kitchen. He laid a faucet handle in front of me. "This was gonna go any minute," he said. "You'd better let me replace both handles and the spigot, too."

I stared at the round, faceted handle. "Um, how much is this going to cost?"

"Less now than if you wait until you've got water spewing all over the place and I have to come out here at night or on a Saturday on an emergency call."

"How much?"

He wiped his hands on a rag and stuffed the rag into his back pocket. "The whole thing, like new, two hundred and eighty-seven dollars."

I swallowed. "Oh, wow."

"You think that's too much? It's one of the best rates in

town. Those guys over at Acme would charge you three
twenty-five and not even blink an eye."

I stood up, so I could look him in the eye. Since we were almost the same height, this was easy. "Mr. Zaragosa, are you
being straight with me?"

"Straight as a preacher," he said solemnly.

I swallowed. "Because I have to tell you, I've heard of cases
where repairmen take advantage of women because we don't
have any good way of checking out what you're telling us."

"You think I'm taking advantage of you because you're a
woman?"

"I'm not saying that's what you're doing. I'm saying it's
been known to happen."

He nodded, and started muttering in Spanish. *Oh, God, I've
done it now*, I thought. *I've offended him.* He'll tell every
plumber in Houston about this, and I'll be washing my hair
under the faucet for the rest of my life.

"Let me show you something." He pulled his wallet from
his back pocket and flipped it open. I figured he was going to
take out his license and make some speech about his integrity.
Instead, he unfolded a string of photos that cascaded almost
to the floor. "This is Seraphina, my oldest daughter." He
pointed to a smiling girl in a graduation cap and gown.

"This is Lucinda. That's her wedding picture. And that's
Estelle and the twins Maria and Sophia. The last picture there
is the baby, Pilar."

I admired the photos. "They're all very pretty. But, uh,
what does this have to do with my plumbing?"

He refolded the pictures and replaced the wallet in his
pocket. "I have six daughters, Mrs. Frame. And the woman
you talked to on the phone? That's my wife, and you probably figured out, she don't take nothing off nobody. You think
a man who has to answer to seven women is going to try to
get away with cheating one?"

I smiled, and he smiled back. "I guess not," I said. "Do you take Visa?"

An hour later, I was the proud owner of all-new shower fittings. "They give you any problems, you call me back," Mr. Zaragosa said as he packed up his tools.

"Thanks." I signed the charge slip and handed him his copy. "And thanks for not getting upset when I questioned the charges."

He waved away my apology. "I know you were just looking out for yourself." He handed me his card. "You need anything else, you let me know."

I looked down at the card and laughed. There, in black letters beneath his name, was a slogan. I Can Fix Anything But a Broken Heart. "Goodbye, Mrs. Frame," he said as he stepped out the door. "You take care, and remember, not every man is out to take advantage of you. There are still some of us good guys left."

JEFF WAS SUPPOSED TO COME BACK to the office the next week to continue training me, but he sent a message that he had to go out of town. I was sick with disappointment. I didn't want to care about him, but obviously the guy had really gotten under my skin.

But then, most of my feelings were contradictory these days. I found out for sure that I wasn't pregnant from my wild night of whoopee with Jeff. I should have been overjoyed, but instead I burst into tears as I hunted under the counter for the box of tampons. Even single motherhood sounded better than no motherhood at all, and at the rate I was going, I might never find a guy decent enough to marry, not to mention love.

I blamed Steve. Why not? He had behaved like a jerk and deserved all the blame I could heap on him. After all, he'd been the one who didn't want a family, who had swept me off my feet when I was young and vulnerable, then abandoned me when some of that youth and vulnerability faded.

A week after my visit to the mall, I received a certified letter from a lawyer, along with a proposed "resettlement" which granted Steve the right to his grandmother's ring and me four thousand dollars.

I read the letter twice to make sure I understood it. Steve must want the ring pretty badly to fork over that kind of cash. But I didn't care about the money. That ring was mine and he had no right to take it away.

I wadded the letter into a ball and launched it toward the kitchen trash. Two points!

Then I went and fished it out and smoothed out the wrinkles the best I could. Not that I intended to take him up on the offer, but you never know when a letter like that might come in handy.

I looked around my desolate living room. Friday night and here I was all alone. There was only one thing to do: time for a pity party.

Like any good shindig, the success of a pity party hinges on food and entertainment. Fortunately, I had all the ingredients close at hand: ice cream (the good stuff, none of that diet stuff will do), hot fudge, popcorn with extra butter and wine of your choice. I prefer a nice Pinot Grigio, but if you're going for the pizza and cheese-curl party food, a nice Lambrusco goes well.

For entertainment, I raided my stash of videos. The weepier, the better. *An Affair to Remember*, *Titanic*, *Casablanca*.

I put on my flannel jammies, popped the corn, dished up the ice cream, poured the wine, grabbed a box of tissues and punched the play button. Who needs real men when you've got Cary Grant, Leonardo DiCaprio and Humphrey Bogart right in your living room?

I'd just reached the scene where Humphrey Bogart tells Ingrid Bergman they'll always have Paris when the phone rang. I started to let the machine get it, but hoping it was Darla—or maybe Jeff, not that I really cared, of course—I snatched up the receiver on the third ring. "Hello?"

"Is this Phoebe Frame?" asked a masculine voice on the other end of the line.

I frowned. "Who wants to know and what are you selling?" Didn't these phone solicitors ever take a night off?

"Mike Dawson from the *Houston Banner*. I wanted to see how it's going with your fight against Easy Motors. Do you have your car back yet?"

I set aside my half-eaten dish of ice cream and hit the pause button on the video. "No. They're still holding it hostage."

"Have you talked to them since we published your letter?"

"I went by there the day the letter came out. The manager had a copy of the paper in his trash can. He wasn't too happy to see me, I tell you."

"What did he say?"

"He called the police and tried to have them haul me away." I smiled at the memory of Frank's red face. "The officer just asked him why he didn't release my car."

Mike Dawson laughed. "What would you think of going over there again tomorrow, with me and a photographer? I'd like to do a follow-up story for the paper. Our readers really love this kind of thing."

"What kind of thing?" A woman making a fool of herself?

"You know, David and Goliath. The underdog fighting the big company."

I didn't think Easy Motors was exactly a "big company" but I got his drift. "Sure, I'll go back over there," I said. "I'm not giving up until I get my car back."

"That's the spirit. I'll meet you there tomorrow morning at eleven."

I hung up the phone and stared at the bowl of melting ice

cream. I had just agreed to have my picture in the paper. I was going to let the whole city, including the many people who never read the letters in the editorial section, know that I'd been made a fool of by both my ex-husband and a sleazy used-car dealer. Oh, God, what was I thinking?

I shut off the video and slumped down on the sofa. I could not go tomorrow. The reporter could do the story without me. He could talk to Frank, take pictures of the dealership...

And I'd be sitting here without a car.

Or I could go. I could wear my Lemon T-shirt and tell my side of the story to anybody who'd listen and maybe, just maybe, I'd do some good. Maybe I'd even get my car back. At the very least, I'd show Easy Motors that I wasn't a pushover.

I drained my wineglass and carried the melted ice cream into the kitchen. Forget the movies. I had to get ready for tomorrow. I was David going into battle and I needed to marshal my forces and plan my attack.

At the very least, I needed to wash my hair and do my nails for my media debut. A woman has to have her priorities straight, after all.

12

THE NEXT MORNING, I met Mike Dawson and the photographer, Sheila Mills, across the street from Easy Motors. He laughed when he saw my shirt. "That's great. The readers will love it."

Frank didn't love it, though. When the receptionist announced my arrival, he stormed out of his office, his face the color of a ripe eggplant. "I told you not to come here harassing me again," he said.

"I brought a couple of friends I want you to meet." I turned to Mike and Sheila. "This is a reporter and a photographer from the *Houston Banner*."

The color drained from Frank's face as he stared at the camera. Sheila took advantage of his momentary shock to snap off a couple of pictures before he barricaded himself in his office. "No comment!" he shouted through the closed door.

"You'd better leave," the receptionist said. "He's not going to come out as long as you're here." She smoothed her hair and smiled, showing all her teeth. "Before you go, would you take my picture?"

We retreated outside to the street corner, where Sheila took a few shots of me holding a sign I'd made that read Give Phoebe Her Car. As people stopped for the light, I handed out copies of the letter I'd sent to the paper to anybody who'd take one. People honked their horns and waved, and pretty soon a crowd had gathered. The manager of the Dairy Freeze on the opposite corner sent me a free soda and said I was good for business. Half a dozen workers from the car wash down the street gave me a sun visor and posed holding my sign.

A Channel Two news van pulled up and a perky blond reporter interviewed me. I gave her one of my letters, and recited my tale of woe. This celebrity business was actually kind of fun. Why had I been so worried about embarrassing myself? I was doing great.

A black Lexus pulled even with the curb and I offered the driver a copy of my letter. The smoked-glass window slid down and Steve gaped at me. "Phoebe, what are you doing?"

The Channel Two reporter stuck her microphone in Steve's face. "What do you think of Ms. Frame's campaign to receive fair treatment from Easy Motors?" she asked.

"I think she's crazy." He glared at me.

"This is my ex-husband, Steve Frame," I said to the camera. "He's the man who left me without a decent car to drive, and without enough money to buy a new one."

A chorus of boos issued from my fan club, which consisted mainly of six Mexican car-wash workers and two winos who had wandered over to see what all the excitement was about. Steve shut his window and sped away, burning rubber.

From time to time, Frank looked out the front door of Easy Motors and scowled for the camera. The crowd hissed and shouted obscenities in English and Spanish. At one point, we even had people doing the wave, and chanting, "Give Phoebe her car." Any minute now, I expected someone to start up a chorus of "We shall overcome."

By twelve-thirty, I'd given away all my letters, and the car-wash workers had to get back to work. The news van packed up and left and the winos wandered away in search of a better party. Mike shook my hand. "Great story, Phoebe. I hope it gets you your car."

"Thanks, Mike. I appreciate your help."

I was crossing the street toward the bus stop when a black pickup pulled up alongside me. The window slid down and Jeff grinned at me. "Want a ride?"

I couldn't think of a good reason to say no, so I opened the door and climbed in. To tell you the truth, I was glad to see him. The office had been a dull place without him around.

His week away hadn't dimmed his charm or dulled his looks. He had a healthy tan and sun had highlighted his dark hair. Instead of slacks and button-down shirt, he wore jeans and a T-shirt, and he hadn't bothered to shave. Looking at him made me weak in the knees. It ought to be against the law for a man to look that good.

"What are you doing in this neighborhood?" I asked, trying to distract myself from my decidedly impure thoughts.

"I was out running some errands and heard about you on the radio, so I decided to drive over and see for myself."

"You missed all the excitement." I grinned. "Channel Two was here."

"Think it'll help you get your car back?"

I shrugged. "I figure it couldn't hurt." I realized we weren't headed toward my house. I turned toward him. "Where are we going?"

"It's after lunch. I thought you might be hungry."

We ended up at an icehouse on Telephone Road, one of those places with a gravel parking lot and garage-door sides that roll up to let the breezes blow in. The air smelled of hot pavement, cigarettes and smoke from the barrel barbecue cookers lined up six abreast out back. Conjunto music blared from the jukebox and two old men in cowboy boots, faded jeans and tank tops played pool for quarters under a whirring ceiling fan.

We ordered paper plates piled with smoked brisket, beans and coleslaw, and sweating long-neck bottles of beer. We ate at a wooden picnic table in the shade of a spreading live oak, sitting on top of the table with our plates beside us, our feet propped on the bench.

We didn't say much while we ate, just enjoyed the smoky nirvana of perfectly cooked brisket and peppery sauce, washed down with beer so cold it made the muscles at the back of my jaw ache. I was still flushed from the thrill of the morning, of my temporary celebrity and the feeling that, for once, I'd gotten the best of a man who had tried to take advantage of me. I didn't have my car yet, but I'd made a good start. At least I'd gotten someone to listen to me and take me seriously.

Jeff drained his beer bottle and tossed it toward an old oil drum that served as a trash can. He leaned back on his hands and looked at me for a long while, saying nothing.

"What? Do I have barbecue sauce smeared on my face?" I brushed my cheek, but felt nothing.

The corners of his mouth lifted in the beginnings of a smile. He really did have great lips. Lips I couldn't look at without thinking of kissing him. "What?" I demanded again.

"Just admiring the view," he said. "You're a very pretty woman, Phoebe Frame."

I gave him a thoughtful look. "Your middle name isn't Eddie, is it?"

"No. It's Wayne." He frowned. "Why?"

"No reason." I started to get off the table, to put a little more distance between his too sexy good looks and honey-smooth voice, but he grabbed my hand and pulled me back. "I see you still have the ring." He stroked the jewel with his thumb.

"Steve is still trying to get it. He had his lawyer send me a letter offering four thousand dollars if I'd give it up."

He whistled. "That's a pretty good chunk of change."

I jerked my hand away from him. "It's not about the money."

He looked puzzled. "The ring means that much to you?
"It's a nice ring."

He sat forward, elbows on his knees. "You could buy a nice one to replace it with the money."

I knew what he was too polite to ask. He wanted to know why I wanted a ring that my ex-husband had given me. Why did I still want that tie to Steve?

I didn't know how to answer that question. Maybe I wanted the ring because it represented the good years of my marriage, when Steve and I had been in love. For that one brief time in my life, the future had looked full of promise. It wasn't wrong to want to hold on to that, was it?

When I didn't say anything, Jeff changed the subject. "Go out with me this evening. We could go dancing."

I think I would have enjoyed dancing with Jeff, swaying arm in arm to something soft and sultry. I shook off the fantasy and straightened my shoulders. "I can't. I have to work."

"Work? It's Saturday."

"Yeah, and I have a dozen charts to transcribe for Patterson." I shrugged. "Besides, I could use the overtime to pay for all those copies of my letter I handed out today."

"I don't like the idea of you alone there with Patterson."

"I'll be all right. If I'm lucky, he won't even show up."

He slid off the table and pulled out his keys. "I tell you what, I'll come with you."

"Don't be ridiculous." I stepped back, alarmed. "I don't need a baby-sitter." I also didn't need the distraction of thinking about the last time we'd been alone in that office.

"I won't distract you. I have some work of my own I need to do."

"Jeff, I really don't think that's a good idea. Especially after last time." There. I'd said it. Or at least let him know that I hadn't forgotten.

He grinned. "We could try the lab this time. Or the doctor's office. That's a big desk he has." He waggled his eyebrows suggestively.

I burst out laughing, shaking my head. "Jeff, no! I really do have to work."

He took my elbow and steered me toward the truck. "Fine. I promise to let you get your work done if you promise to let me come with you."

"And if I don't let you?"

He slid his hand down my back, sending instant heat to every erogenous zone on my body. "I promise to do my damnedest to make you forget anything having to do with work."

I swallowed. This was a choice? "I have to work," I said weakly.

He squeezed my bottom, making me jump. "Great. We'll both work now." He unlocked his truck and opened the door for me. As I climbed into the cab, his hand brushed my bottom again. "But I promise we'll play later," he whispered, his breath tickling the back of my neck and making me wish my common sense would take a vacation. Far away. At least until I'd gotten Jeff out of my system. Like say, maybe in the next ten years?

DESPITE HIS SUGGESTIVE TEASING, Jeff was a man of his word and he left me alone in my workroom once we reached the office. I started in on my stack of charts and he disappeared into another part of the office, doing who knows what.

The longer I worked, the more annoyed I became with Patterson. Compiling all these chart notes was just busywork, the equivalent of being made to write "I will not shun the doctor's advances" five hundred times on the blackboard. I doubted he'd even use the information in his presentation.

This was the first time Patterson had been asked to speak at the conference, and you'd have thought he'd been asked to star in his own daytime talk show. The most favored patients got a blow-by-blow account of his invitation to speak, and the rest of us heard about it almost hourly. He couldn't return calls just now because he was working on his talk. He couldn't review a supply order because he had to research his talk. He couldn't interview a new transcriptionist because he was too busy preparing for his talk.

"The talk" had taken so much of his attention he'd almost—but not quite—slowed down his constant pursuit of the feminine form. At least he'd limited his advances toward me to those times when we were alone, with the occasional leer in my direction. But unless something happened to change him, he'd be back in top form after the conference.

An hour and a half into the afternoon's work, I took a much-deserved break and went looking for Jeff. I found him in the last place I'd expected him to be—Patterson's office.

In fact, he'd made himself right at home. He was sitting behind the doctor's bed-size desk, tapping away at Patterson's personal computer. "What are you doing in here?" I asked.

"Promise not to tell?" With one finger, he tapped out a string of letters and numbers and hit Enter.

"That depends." I perched on the edge of the desk. "Is it something interesting and too juicy to keep a secret?"

"Hardly." He hit another series of keys, then swiveled the doctor's high-back leather chair around to face me. "I'm snooping."

"You mean...hacking?"

"That's a crude term for it, but yes."

I grinned. "Find anything good?"

"I was hoping he might have kept a log of his conquests, or his Web browser would be full of naughty sites he'd visited, or I'd find a cache of secret love letters to some high-muckety-muck's wife." He shook his head. "But I didn't find anything but boring medical files and financial data."

"Patterson's a slime, but he's not dumb," I said.

He picked up a pencil and began turning it over and over in his hand. "He's arrogant. Arrogant people think they're too good to get caught, so they make stupid mistakes. You wouldn't believe the stuff I've found on people's computers."

"What do you do when you find out something naughty?"

He shrugged. "Nothing. It's none of my business. But for Patterson, I might make an exception."

I glanced over my shoulder, as if I half expected the good doctor himself to come bursting in. "What would you do if you found something dirty about him?" I asked.

"I'd use the information to blackmail him into leaving you alone."

His expression was all hard lines—jutting jaw, eyebrows knitted fiercely together. A true knight, risking, if not his life, then his reputation, to protect me. I was touched. And more than a little turned on.

"You'd do that for me?" I asked, the quaver in my voice betraying my emotions.

He looked away, a flush of red creeping up from his collar. "Yeah, well I didn't find anything, did I?" He leaned over and punched the power button. The screen image shrank to a pinpoint of light, then vanished.

He shoved up out of the chair and moved out from behind the desk. "Finished with your work?"

I shook my head. "Hardly." I stretched my arms over my head, arching my back. "I just needed a break."

He came up behind me and began massaging my neck. It felt so good, I almost groaned. The man had magic hands. Strong, but gentle. Every knot melted away at his expert touch. I sagged against him, eyes closed. "You could have a second career as a massage therapist."

"I don't do this for just anybody, you know." He slid his

hands over my shoulders, until they covered the tops of my breasts. My nipples stood at attention.

There are times when a conscience is more curse than convenience, and this was one of them. "Jeff..." I said in warning.

He took his hands from me and stepped back. "I know, I know. But I can't help wanting to touch you."

I looked at him, trying to see beyond the charming exterior to the man within. "Why? What does a young, good-looking guy with his own successful business see in an older, recently divorced woman who's overdrawn on all her credit cards and can't even get her car out of hock, much less her life in order?"

He grinned. "I find your modesty so charming." He shoved his hands in his pockets. "Seriously, you don't give yourself enough credit. When I look at you, I see a woman who's been dealt a bad hand but who's rising above all that. You haven't let the bad things make you bitter."

I crossed my legs primly. "I'm sure there are plenty of non-bitter women your own age out there."

"Yeah, but I have this thing for old women like you." He put his hands on the desktop, on either side of my thighs, trapping me. His chest brushed the tips of my breasts and he stared into my eyes. "I figure if I play my cards right, in a few years I can live off your social security and take advantage of all the senior-citizen specials at restaurants."

"You're making fun of me," I breathed.

"Uh-huh." He dipped his head and covered my mouth with his own, pressing his body more fully against mine.

I didn't want this to be happening, but I couldn't make it stop. I didn't know if Jeff was right for me, or what direction my life would take next, but, right now, none of that mattered up against the fact of this man touching me, calling forth sensations from my body that had been shoved aside or forgotten or maybe had never even existed before.

"Jeff," I whispered. I'd meant a protest, but it came out like an endearment.

"Phoebe." My name was soft on his lips, warm and breathy and heavy with meaning. My hands slid back, sending a stack of folders and a stethoscope sliding to the floor. He brought his hand around to my back to support me, and I threw my arms around him, silently telling all doubts and misgivings to take a hike.

"One of these days, we're going to have to try a bed," Jeff mumbled as he pushed me further back on the desk and fumbled with the snap of my jeans.

"There are eight other desks, four exam-room tables and a gurney in this office." I grinned at him as he found the catch on my bra and unhooked it. "It could be a while before we'll even need a bed."

"Should we try for them all tonight, or pace ourselves?"

"I'm betting you give out before I do." I grinned and tugged at the hem of his T-shirt.

"I don't know. A young stud like me might be too much for an old lady like you." He stripped off his shirt, and my smile was lost in a flood of desire, and not a little bit of triumph. This magnificent man wanted me. He didn't care if my breasts weren't as perky as they'd once been, or if I had more cottage cheese on my thighs than the average dairy case. He wanted to be with me. To love me.

I leaned back and struck a provocative pose. "Come here, big boy. Let's see if you can keep up."

It's no secret, forbidden pleasure is an aphrodisiac all its own. I suppose making love on the boss's desk is the equivalent of making out in your parents' car. It's naughty, there's a chance you might get caught, and that makes it that much more fun.

It isn't particularly comfortable, though, and by the third time some office gadget poked me in the rump, I was ready to cry uncle and suggest we head for a hotel. Jeff shoved the stapler out of the way and laughed. "I've got a better idea."

And that's how he ended up on the desk, giving me the ride of my life. That was so much fun, we tried the chair, which was quite a moving experience, once we discovered the rollers had no trouble traveling on carpet. I was all ready to give the gurney a go when Jeff admitted he needed a rest. "I'm vanquished," he said, wrapping his arms around me and pulling me to the carpet.

I rested my head on his chest and giggled. "What's so funny?" he asked.

"I have a confession to make."

"You mean...you're not a virgin?"

I pretended to punch him. "No, my confession is that I've never had so much fun making love."

He patted my shoulder. "Then I'd say you've got a lot of catching up to do. And as soon as I've recovered, I'll get back to making up for that deficit."

I kissed him long and hard, letting him know just how much I approved of that idea. One kiss led to another, and we were so wrapped up in the moment, we almost didn't hear footsteps approaching down the hall.

"What's that?" Jeff raised his head, listening.

"What's what?" I giggled, and tried to pull him down to my level once more.

He shoved up onto one elbow and looked toward the office door. "Someone's coming."

13

I HEARD IT THEN, TOO. Shoes thudding on the hall carpet, headed this way. "Oh, my God!"

Knocking heads and bumping elbows, we scrambled for our clothes. "We've got to get out of here!" Jeff whispered, eyes wild.

"In here." I grabbed his hand and dragged him toward the bathroom. He stopped long enough to shove the chair back into place and toss the stethoscope onto the desk. We pulled the door shut behind us just as Patterson strolled in.

Stifling a squeak of fright, I urged Jeff toward the shower stall. We stood behind the black vinyl shower curtain, clutching various articles of clothing about us. "What's he doing here?" Jeff croaked.

I shrugged, and strained my ears to listen. I heard desk drawers opening and closing, papers rattling, then a long silence.

"He must have left," Jeff whispered in my ear.

I nodded, still too afraid to move.

"Come on. I think the coast is cl—" Jeff had his hand on the curtain, about to pull it back, when the bathroom door opened and Patterson stepped in.

We froze, staring at each other in bug-eyed fear. I don't think I even breathed. Any minute now, Patterson would rip back that curtain and demand to know the meaning of this. I suppose I could have told him the plumbing wasn't working at my house and I'd decided to take a shower, but I didn't think he'd buy the part that Jeff was just trying to save water by joining me.

The curtain never moved. I heard the sound of a zipper, then the cascade of water into the toilet. Patterson whistled while he peed. I swear, does going to the bathroom make men that happy or are they just trying to distract themselves?

With this thought in mind, I made the mistake of looking at Jeff. He grinned and puffed his cheeks out, miming whistling. I clamped my teeth together, stifling laughter, and telegraphed threatening messages with my eyes. Inside me, laughter expanded like popping corn, threatening at any moment to explode.

At last, Patterson left us. We listened as his footsteps retreated, then waited through half a lifetime of silence before either of us moved. "I think he's really gone this time," Jeff whispered.

I nodded, feet still stuck to the bottom of the tub.

"Why don't I get dressed and go check? If I run into him, I can always tell him I was checking the network."

I nodded again. Jeff pulled his shirt over his head, then nodded toward my hand. "Could I have my briefs, or are you saving them for a souvenir?"

I looked down and saw that I had mashed Jeff's briefs into a golf-ball-size wad. "Sorry." I handed them over and pawed through the other clothes in my arms. "If I have your briefs, where are my panties?"

We couldn't locate them, so I ended up putting on my jeans without underwear. It felt naughty and sexy, and I prayed I wouldn't get anything caught in my zipper next time I went to the bathroom.

Jeff left and I finished dressing. Sometime between pulling on my jeans and fastening the strap of my sandals, the reality of my situation hit me. If Patterson had walked in even five minutes earlier, he would have caught me rolling around na-

ked on the floor of his office with a man who was technically
a co-worker. I'd risked my job and my reputation, and for
what? For an hour or so of bliss with a man who couldn't be
serious for more than a few minutes without cracking a joke?

I sagged against the bathroom sink, my buoyant mood vanished. I had to face facts: Jeff was a great guy. A lot of fun to
be with. But he was not ready to settle down and start raising
a family. And I was.

"All clear." He stuck his head around the corner of the
bathroom. "Oh, and I found these." He held up a pair of pink
cotton panties.

I grabbed the underwear and stuffed it into my pocket.
"Where were they?"

His grin widened. "Hanging from the top of the ficus plant
in the corner. I guess you threw them there in all the, um, excitement." He pulled me close and nuzzled my neck. "Speaking of which...want to try out the gurney?"

I shook my head and gently pushed him away. "I think I'd
better go home now."

"Good idea. We can try out your bed."

"I'm going home alone."

"Alone?" He looked surprised.

I nodded. "I've had enough excitement for one night. I
need a little time alone to try to figure things out."

He shook his head. "You think too much. Everything
doesn't have to be analyzed, you know."

"Most of the mistakes I've made in my life have come from
not thinking enough. I don't want this to be like that."

"This? You mean us?"

I nodded. "Yeah, us." I brushed back my hair and tried not
to look as upset as I felt. "You're fun to be with, Jeff. You
make me feel good. But I'm not sure if that's what I need to be
doing right now."

"You said yourself you hadn't had enough fun before."

"Not enough fun in bed." I glanced at the jumbled desktop. "Or out of it." I straightened my shoulders and tried to look stern. "Common sense goes out the window when I'm around you. I'm not sure that's a good thing."

"I can be sensible, Phoebe. Give me a chance."

A chance to do what? Screw up my heart, and maybe my future? I ducked under his arm and out the door. "Go home and rest," I called over my shoulder. "I'll see you Monday."

He didn't answer right away. I was almost to the end of the hall when he called out, "Good night, Scarlett."

I whirled around. "Scarlett?"

He shrugged. "Scarlett O'Hara. Isn't she the one who said 'I'll think about it tomorrow'?"

"I thought she said 'fiddle-dee-dee' and 'I'll never go hungry again.'"

"That, too." He straightened. "Good night, Phoebe. I'll let you run away from me this time, but one of these days I won't let you off so easily."

I fluttered my fingers at him. "Fiddle-dee-dee." Then I hurried away, heart pounding. Damn right I was running. But I was also leaving a little bit of myself behind, soaked into Jeff's skin and tucked in next to his heart.

I WOULD HAVE PREFERRED to stay home the next day and mope and eat chocolate, but I'd promised Darla I'd go to the final game of Tony's big bowling tournament and help cheer for Tony.

"So, Phoebe, are you ready to cheer our boys on to victory?" Darla, in pink capri pants and a green-and-white T-shirt that read Go Ace Trucking Tigers across the front, hurried over to me when I arrived at the bowling alley. "Here, you'll need these." She handed me a pair of green-and-white plastic pom-poms.

"Cheerleading? For bowlers?"

"Hey, if football and basketball can have cheerleaders, why not bowling?" Tony winked at Darla. "Besides, we've got the best-looking supporters in this place."

Which wasn't saying much, considering this was not exactly a bunch of highly trained athletes. From the number of pot bellies within view, I'd say this crowd's idea of weight lifting was to hoist a few schooners of beer.

I shook the pom-poms. "I always wanted to be a cheer-leader."

"Well, now's your chance." Darla raised her arms over her head. "Give me a *T!* Give me an *I!*"

"What's she doing?"

A familiar masculine voice sent a shiver down my spine. I turned and found Jeff standing behind me. "Hi," I said. "I didn't know you bowled."

"I haven't tried it in years."

"Then what are you doing here?"

"Darla invited me." He nodded toward my friend, who was finishing up her cheer by executing the splits. "Apparently this tournament is a really big deal."

"Apparently." I turned back around so he couldn't read the expression on my face. The smell of him was still on my skin and the memory of our lovemaking glowed technicolor bright in my brain. Now probably wasn't the best time to be making objective decisions about our relationship.

Jeff came around the bench and sat next to me. "Does it bother you that I'm here?"

I assumed what I hoped was a casual expression. "No. Why should it bother me?"

"You don't look too happy to see me."

"I'm just nervous," I said. "About the game. Why are you here? You don't really know Darla or Tony that well."

He grinned and laid his hand along the back of the bench,

his fingers almost, but not quite touching me. "That's easy. Darla told me you were going to be here."

"So you came here because of me? Why?" I was a little annoyed at the way my heart sped up at the thought. What happened to being an independent woman, relying on myself, not needing others' approval?

"I thought it would be good for us to see each other outside of work. Get to know each other better."

On some levels, we couldn't get to know each other any better than we already had at the office...in my workroom...on Patterson's desk...

"Why are you blushing?" He squeezed my shoulder and scooted closer. "Are you thinking naughty thoughts about me?"

I looked away, at a man warming up to bowl his first frame. "I—I'm embarrassed for that man," I said. "Someone should tell him double-knit slacks don't do anything for him."

We watched the bowlers for a while, saying nothing. Bowling is like a kind of dance, as if bulls or elephants or some other creature not made for dancing suddenly decided to try out a few steps. Every bowler has his or her own style, the way they dip down to deliver the ball, the way they kick their foot out at the end of their delivery.

After a while, though, I noticed the bowlers weren't the only ones getting physical. Jeff had moved his hand over until his fingers were resting on my shoulder. His touch was light at first, just a gentle stroking. Then he began caressing, kneading my shoulder. Tingles of sensation radiated across my back and down my spine. I squirmed on the hard plastic bench. "Will you stop that?" I snapped.

"Stop what?" He assumed a patently fake expression of innocence.

"Pawing me." I scooted away from him.

"Sorry." He looked sheepish and took his hand away. "I just like the way you feel."

What was I supposed to say to that? I got up and joined Darla on the sidelines. She was waving her pom-poms and bouncing on her toes. I ought to mention that Darla really was a cheerleader in high school, whereas I was too shy to try out. "Go, Tony!" she yelled. "Bowl a strike, baby!"

Tony turned to grin at her and she blew him a kiss.

"Why did you invite Jeff?" I asked.

She lowered her pom-poms and shrugged. "I thought if you saw him outside of work, in a social setting, you might change your mind about him."

"Why would you think that?"

"He's a nice guy, Phoebe."

"How do you know that?"

"I called the office the other day but you were out delivering memos to other offices or something. So Jeff and I ended up talking for quite a while." She put her hand on my shoulder. "You ought to give him a chance."

I hugged my arms across my chest. "I know he's a nice guy. He's just not right for me."

She put her hands on her hips. "Why do you say that? And don't say he's too young."

"But he is too young. We're at different places in our lives. He's still sowing his wild oats. I'm ready to settle down."

"What's wrong with sowing wild oats? You've been settled down for twelve years. Maybe it's time to try something else."

"I'm going to the snack bar. Do either of you ladies want anything?" Jeff came up behind us. I blushed, wondering if he'd heard any of our conversation.

Darla smiled at him. "No thanks, Jeff. I'm fine."

"What about you, Phoebe?"

"I'll come with you." I followed him to the snack bar,

where he ordered a beer for himself and a Diet Coke for me. He didn't say a word to me until we were on our way back to our seats.

"Phoebe—" he began.

Just then, two small, screaming boys raced past, almost knocking us backward. Jeff swore as half his beer sloshed onto the floor, then reached out one hand to steady me. "You okay?"

"Yeah." I laughed and looked after the running children. "I don't think they ever saw us."

He frowned. "Parents shouldn't let kids run wild like that."

I shrugged. "Oh, they're just being kids."

"They're just being brats."

I stared at him, startled by his reaction. "You don't like children?"

"Oh, I hear they're quite good fried."

"Jeff!"

He laughed. "It's just a joke, Phoebe."

He retrieved a handful of napkins from a dispenser and handed me half. "Do you ever think about having children?" I asked as I mopped soda from my arm.

He shrugged. "Not really."

"Why not?"

"I just haven't thought about it much."

He gave me a funny look and I decided I'd better back off. Have you ever gotten lost in a strange city and ended up in a bad neighborhood? You know that feeling you get in the pit of your stomach—equal parts fear and self-loathing because, after all, you got yourself into this? If you'd paid attention or read the map, you wouldn't be here.

That's the way I felt with Jeff. I had told myself early on not to get too attached to him. That we weren't right for each other. And now that he was proving my prediction true, all I could think was that it was too late. I wasn't going to get out of this without getting hurt.

"What about you?" he asked. "Why don't you have any children? Or is that question too personal?"

I looked away. "Steve didn't want them."

"But I thought... isn't his fiancée pregnant?"

Fiancée. The word sounded strange. It's hard to think of your ex-husband as having a fiancée. "Yeah."

"I'm not sure I understand," Jeff said.

"Join the club."

We didn't say anything else as we made our way back to our seats and pretended to watch the tournament. I know I wasn't really paying attention to the bowlers and I could feel Jeff's eyes on me. Maybe I never should have brought up the kid thing. But wasn't it better to know now, before I got in any deeper?

"Isn't it terrific?" Darla bounced over to us, eyes shining.

"Isn't what terrific?" I asked.

"The tournament. The Tigers only need thirty points to win. And Tony's up next."

I watched with renewed interest as Tony retrieved his bowling ball and readied himself. He brought the ball to his chest and stared down the lane at the pins like a general staring down opposing forces. A hush fell over the crowd as Tony brought the ball back in a smooth arc and began his approach. His feet were practically soundless as he took three strides forward and released the ball. It barreled down the lane, arcing toward the pins, a purple blur reflected in the waxed wood of the lane.

The pins exploded up and outward with a tremendous crash, the sound of their falling drowned out by the cheers of Tony's teammates. Darla jumped up and down and waved her pom-poms wildly.

"He only needs to bowl two more strikes and they win," she squealed.

"Is he that good?" I never thought a bowling tournament could be so exciting, but here I was, on my feet, palms sweating as Tony readied his next shot.

Darla shot me a scolding look. "Of course he's that good. He's the best player on the team."

"Sorry." But she didn't even hear me over the roar of the crowd as Tony bowled his second strike.

Darla's not one to hold a grudge, however, and, as Tony set up for his third shot, she came over and wrapped her arms around me. "I can't look," she whispered, and buried her head in my shoulder.

Tony brought the ball up to his chest, then back in a fluid movement. He reminded me of a slow-motion film as he stepped forward, then launched the ball. I leaned forward with him, urging the ball forward...forward...forward.

The ball struck the pins and they tumbled down, rolling and spinning away. The crowd gasped as one pin wobbled like a drunk trying to regain his balance. Over, then up. Over, then up. Around, around, around....

When it fell, Tony's teammates surrounded him, pounding his back and shouting. Darla squeezed me tight. "He did it! He did it! He won the tournament."

I grabbed both her hands and squeezed them. Tony came up and threw his arms around both of us. "Congratulations," I told him.

"Come on," he said. "We're all going over to Pizza Palace to celebrate. I'll buy you a drink."

"I'll buy you one, too." Darla glanced around. "Where's Jeff? We should ask him to go."

I looked over to the bench where we had been sitting, but it was empty. Jeff wasn't with the bowlers celebrating their victory, or over by the snack bar. "Maybe he's in the men's room," I said.

We finally sent Tony into the men's room to check, but he came back shaking his head. "He's not in there." We went outside then, but his car wasn't in the parking lot, either.

"Did he just leave?" Darla asked. "Without saying goodbye?" She looked at me. "Did you two argue about something?"

"No...well, not really."

"Phoebe, what did you say to him?"

"Darla, honey, let it drop." Tony put his arm around her shoulders. "Let's go have pizza and have a good time. Maybe the guy wasn't feeling well. Or maybe he had someplace else he had to be."

Or maybe all the talk about children had put him in a bad mood. It had put me in a bad mood, too, but I didn't have the choice of going home and sulking. I had to go with my friends and pretend to have a good time.

Why is it, just when I think I've got my life figured out, someone comes along and throws a big monkey wrench in it? It's enough to make a woman want to join a convent.

14

I DIDN'T SEE JEFF for the next week. I tried calling his office and got his answering service. "Uh, just tell him Phoebe called," I muttered and hung up.

Well. I didn't know whether to be pissed off that he was avoiding me or worried that I'd ticked him off somehow. Maybe he was just tired of me playing hard to get.

Not that I'd set out to play exactly, but I hadn't thrown myself into his arms, either.

Or maybe he was just tired of me. The way Steve had grown tired of me.

Ugh. Jeff was not Steve. And I wasn't doing anyone any good sitting here trying to second-guess his motives. Fine, next time I saw Jeff we'd have it out. I'd tell him I was ready to start thinking about maybe having a relationship with him, but he was going to have to be patient.

After all, Mama always said good things were worth waiting for. Surely I was a good thing for Jeff.

Wasn't I?

In any case, while I waited for Jeff to return my call, or at least show up at the office, I had plenty of things to occupy my mind, what with all the extra work Patterson was giving me and my repeated attempts to get Easy Motors to release my car. I'd taken to bombarding various government agencies with complaint letters, hoping to get some results, but so far, nothing was happening.

I'd searched the paper every day for the article Mike Dawson was supposed to write, but it hadn't shown up, either. To tell you the truth, I was getting discouraged.

Of course, work and the situation with my car didn't mean I didn't think about Jeff. I thought about him a lot. When he didn't return my call after a day and a half, I called his office again. This time I reached a secretary, who told me he was out of town. I hung up before she asked my name. I felt as though I was in high school again, calling boys and hanging up because I was too scared to talk to them.

I planned to spend that Saturday cleaning house and listing all the reasons why I should calm down and risk a little romance with Jeff. I planned to work up the perfect speech to announce my feelings to him—as soon as I could figure out what those feelings were.

But that's what happens when you make plans. You're just asking for someone to come along and blow them all to hell.

In this case, the person who came along was Darla, so I couldn't complain. Who wants to dust and clean toilets anyway?

Darla offered plenty of distraction. She burst into the house with a dozen Krispy Kreme doughnuts in one hand and a hefty shopping bag in the other. "Look!" She thrust the box of doughnuts into my chest, then shoved her hand under my nose, displaying a diamond the size of a large chocolate chip. "Isn't it gorgeous? Tony gave it to me last night when he popped the question."

It was gorgeous, in the way only a big, gaudy hunk of precious stone can be. "Congratulations!" I squealed, and hugged her. To tell you the truth, I'd had my doubts about Tony ever making an honest woman of Darla. After all, they'd been dating six years. I was thrilled he'd finally done right by my friend.

We celebrated with a fresh pot of coffee and half the doughnuts. "So, have you set a date?" I asked.

"Sometime in November. Before the holidays. But we're not really sure." She reached under the table and drew out the shopping bag. "That's another reason I came over here. I need your help."

She upended the bag and magazines slid across the table-top. *Bride's, Modern Bride, Bridal Guide, Wedding Planner, Wonderful Weddings.* "What is all this?" I asked.

"I've been waiting for years for this, but now that it's here, I don't know what to do." She picked up a magazine and flipped through it. "I have to plan a wedding. But first I have to decide what kind of wedding I want." She shoved a magazine toward me. "Look. This couple got married in a vineyard. The reception was a wine tasting." She tossed another issue toward me. "This one has a story about a couple who got married at a zoo."

She slumped forward, chin in her hands. "It's not enough to just get married. Weddings have themes these days. I need you to help me decide on a theme."

I looked at a picture of a smiling bride and groom posing next to an elephant. The elephant had a wreath of magnolia blossoms perched between its enormous ears. "I think I'd stay away from anything to do with animals." I shoved the magazine aside. "What do you want to do?"

"All kinds of things. The problem is, I've had too much time to think about this. When you're nineteen and get married, you've probably only been fantasizing about it ten years or so. You go for the white gown, the black tux, the church and the orange blossoms. Your mom cries. Your dad is nervous. The photographer takes forever."

That was my wedding in a nutshell. My mom fluttered around like a crazed moth, my dad chewed his fingernails until they bled and Steve locked his keys in his car and had to call a locksmith to get his tux out of the back seat. The preacher called me Penelope when he introduced us to the congregation and the best man made a lewd comment just as Steve was taking off my garter, so the wedding picture showed me with my eyes bugged out and my mouth open so wide you can see my tonsils.

"I've had too much time," Darla continued. "I'm thirty-three. I've had twenty-six years to think about this, at least. One minute, I want a traditional church wedding. Then I think a wedding on a cruise ship would be nice. Or what about a wedding in a foreign country, Jamaica or the Bahamas? I can't decide."

"What does Tony want?"

She snorted. "He wants what every man wants. He wants to elope. Ten minutes in the judge's office and you're done. I told him he could forget that idea. I want a real wedding. One I'll remember."

I smiled. "You really don't remember, you know. You sort of float around in a daze the whole day. The next morning, you wake up and look at the gold band on your finger and the man in bed next to you and you realize it really did happen. But you don't remember it."

Those magical blissful moments have all the staying power of the soap bubbles they blow at weddings now instead of tossing rice. It's a million other moments in marriage that stick in your head: the night he came home late and refused to tell you where he'd been. The fight you had when he insulted your mother. The way his face looked when he told you he didn't love you anymore.

"At least I'll have a video." Darla pushed the pile of magazines aside. "I can't think. I'm too excited to know what I want. Let's talk about something else." She folded her hands in front of her and looked at me expectantly. "So how's Jeff?"

"Jeff?" I cleared my throat and tried to sound less guilty. "He's fine. I guess."

I got up and poured more coffee. Maybe instead of brooding about Jeff on my own, I should talk to somebody about it. Darla had given me good advice about things before. "About Jeff…" I began.

She tore her gaze away from her ring. "He's coming to the clinic Halloween party, isn't he? Have you decided on a costume, yet?"

I dropped into a chair. "I hadn't really thought about it." Every year, the Central Care Network Clinic gave a huge Halloween party. Everyone came in costume, there was great food and drink and door prizes. It's one of the few things they did for employees that was genuinely fun—at Christmas, we would get an ornament with a picture of the clinic on it. This was supposed to make us feel appreciated?

"I'm not sure I want to go this year," I said. The prospect of trying to avoid both Jeff and Patterson while we were all in costume didn't appeal to me for some reason.

"Don't be silly! You have to go. If you don't go, you don't get your full share of employee benefits." She grinned. "Besides, it's your one chance to really wow everybody with a dynamite costume. So what do you think you'll go as?"

I shrugged. "I guess I could pull out the witch costume I wore last year." The pointed hat had gotten crushed when a pumpkin from the neurosurgeon's office had sat on it, but I could probably straighten it out.

"Don't be ridiculous. You should go as something you've always wanted to be. As a way of empowering yourself."

"A Halloween costume can be empowering?"

"Absolutely. It's a kind of visualization. I read an article about it in the dentist's office last month. Now come on, what's your fantasy?"

I thought a moment. "I guess what I want most is to be a strong, powerful woman who doesn't take shit from anybody. But how are you going to get a costume out of that?"

Darla looked thoughtful. "What about sexy?"

I squirmed. "Well, yeah, I want to be sexy, too. I want to be the kind of woman who has men worshiping at my feet. But no costume is going to do that for me."

A smile spread across her face. "Actually, I think I've got the perfect costume for you."

"What?"

"Oh, I'm not going to tell you now." Her grin was evil. "Leave everything to me. You're going to love it!"

Monday morning, I arrived at the office to find a picture of me cut from the paper and taped to the wall in the employee break room at the clinic. There I was, wearing my Lemon T-shirt, holding a sign that read Give Phoebe Her Car. The Easy Motors sign loomed behind me and I thought I could just make out Frank's face scowling at the entrance to the dealer's office.

"Phoebe, you're famous," Michelle said as she poured coffee. "You made the front page of the metro section."

I read the article taped below the picture. Mike Dawson had finally come through for me. He'd done a great job, too, portraying me as a crusading woman who was tired of being taken advantage of. He even got in a dig about Steve. "While Frame's ex drives a Lexus, she was left with a twelve-year-old car that promptly died six months after their divorce."

I grinned. Later, maybe I'd highlight that section of the article and mail a copy to Steve's office.

"Have you seen Albert's hat?" Barb came into the break room, the skeleton in her arms. "I thought I left it on the top shelf of the supply closet last year, but it's not there."

"I think I saw it in the cabinet over the refrigerator," Michelle said.

Barb leaned Albert against the counter and dragged a step stool over to the refrigerator. "Here it is." She waved the black-and-orange ball cap in triumph. "Oh, and here's the pumpkin lights for around the reception desk."

"Is it time to decorate already?" I asked. Halloween was...I glanced at the calendar. Only two weeks away. Yikes!

"Here, why don't you dress up your workroom?" Barb tossed a ball of spider webbing at me. "We've got rubber spiders, too."

"Just don't put the candy out yet," Michelle said. "Last year I gained five pounds and could hardly fit into my costume."

Barb looked down her nose at Michelle. "If that Elvira dress wasn't so tight, you wouldn't have that problem."

"Your bunch-of-grapes costume didn't hide anything any better than my Elvira outfit."

Barb blushed. "I was fine until some wise guy decided to pop my balloons."

Poor Barb. I'd thought her idea to tape purple balloons all over her body to resemble a bunch of grapes had been a good one, until the balloons had popped and she'd been left standing there in a purple leotard with a grape-leaf hat.

"What are you coming as this year, Phoebe?" Michelle asked.

"I don't know."

"Come on," Barb said. "You can tell us."

"Honest. I don't know. Darla's planning something for me. It'll be a surprise."

"Can somebody tell me where I'm supposed to put this?" Jeff stood in the doorway, an enormous pumpkin in his arms.

I stared at him. "What are you doing here?" I asked. *And why didn't you call me as soon as you got back in town?*

"Ms. Lee wants me to make some modifications to the system."

So much for thinking he'd come to see me. I turned away, hoping my disappointment didn't show on my face.

"Just put the pumpkin over here in the sink," Barb said. "We still have to carve it."

"Why don't you get Dr. Patterson to do it?" Michelle said. "He ought to be good with a scalpel."

"I asked him, but he said he's too busy writing his talk."

"You're looking very nice this morning, Phoebe."

How is it the way one particular man says your name can make your insides turn to mush? Nobody else acted as though they noticed anything, but when Jeff said my name, all I could think of was those moments in his arms on Patterson's desk. "Uh...thank you," I squeaked.

"Are you coming to the Halloween party?" he asked.

"Y—yes. Are you?"

He smiled, a slow, seductive smile that made my temperature go up five degrees. "Oh, I wouldn't miss it."

"She won't tell us what her costume is," Barb said. "It's a secret."

"I don't know what it is," I protested. "Darla's putting it together for me."

"You could come as a protester and wear your T-shirt." He pointed to my picture on the wall. "Have you heard from Easy Motors?"

"Not yet. But I'm going to keep after them."

"Good for you." Michelle stood and tossed her napkin into the trash. "Don't let them walk all over you."

"What is everyone doing in here?" Joan Lee appeared in the doorway. "We have work to do."

"I just came in to get the Halloween decorations." Barb put the hat on Albert and looped the pumpkin lights around his neck.

"Do the decorations later. We have patients to take care of." With that, she turned and stalked out of the room.

"Yes, Miss Lee." Jeff's voice was a perfect mimic of every robotic classroom reply I'd ever heard, but his face was perfectly solemn. He picked up Albert and marched him toward the door. "I'll get right on it."

I took this as my cue to head back to my cubby. So much for celebrity. It doesn't last, but then, what good thing does?

I'd just booted up my computer when Jeff came into my cave. "I need to look at a few things on the system," he said, taking a seat at the other terminal.

I swiveled my chair to face him. Jeff always looked at me when we were together, one of the things about him I found most flattering. Today, he kept his eyes averted. "We need to talk," I said.

"About what?" He typed in a string of letters and symbols, still not looking at me. Okay, I was getting annoyed. Glare at me, shout at me, make faces at me, but do not ignore me.

I leaned over and hit the off button on his monitor.

"What the h—" He looked at me then, anger sparking in his eyes. "Why did you do that?"

"Why did you run out before the end of the bowling tournament?"

He shrugged, and assumed that macho-guy, too-cool-for-anything-to-upset-me expression. Which was stupid because it told me he was upset. "It was time for me to leave."

"What's that supposed to mean?"

He shook his head and turned back to the computer to switch the monitor back on.

I reached over and switched it off again.

When he glared at me, I glared right back. "Try that again and I'll unplug it," I said.

He sat back in his chair, arms crossed over his chest, and continued to scowl at me. Not talking. As if I was going to let him get away with that.

"Look," I said. "I'm not a mind reader. If I said something that upset you, you'd better tell me."

"You've been saying things to me for weeks. I guess that day I was finally ready to hear."

And this was man-code for what? "What are you talking about?"

He uncrossed his arms and sat up straighter. "You've been telling me you didn't want to get involved with me, but I never believed it before that day at the bowling alley."

And he believed it now? Just when I'd changed my mind? Men! You couldn't depend on them. "I don't know what you're talking about. What happened at the bowling alley?"

"When we were talking about your ex. Steve. And his fiancée. I understood then that the reason you didn't want to go out with me was that you're still in love with him."

Obviously, this was some kind of nightmare. Or I'd heard wrong. Jeff couldn't possibly have accused me of still being in love with my ex. The lying jerk who'd dumped me in the name of personal freedom and had scarcely waited for the ink on the change-of-address forms to dry before he'd taken up with a younger, perkier woman.

"You think I'm carrying the torch for Steve?"

Jeff nodded.

I stood, too agitated to sit still. "That's ridiculous. I can't stand Steve's guts. I ought to send Tami flowers and thank her for taking him off my hands."

He shifted in his chair, confusion glazing his eyes. "Do you mean that?"

"Of course I mean it." I shuddered. Lately, I'd spent more than a little time asking myself what I'd ever seen in Steve Frame.

Jeff frowned. "You acted so odd when we were talking about Steve having a kid. I assumed that meant you were jealous of him and Tami."

"I'm pissed off that he spent all those years refusing to even discuss having children with me and now he's walking around like a candidate for father of the year. Makes me sick."

Jeff's next move surprised me. He reached out and grabbed both my hands. "Then why won't you go out with me? Don't say it's the age difference, because that's a bunch of bull. Don't say you're trying to get your life together, because I can help you with that."

I nodded. His hands felt nice around mine. Strong and warm. "Okay."

He blinked. "Okay what?"

"Okay, I won't say any of those things."

"Then what will you say?"

I smiled. "I'll go out with you."

"When?"

"Whenever you like."

He pulled me toward him. Giggling, I half fell, half sat in his lap. We kissed, a sweet, searing meeting of our lips that made me aware of how much I'd missed him.

"Hrrrmph!"

For a small woman, Joan Lee can clear her throat quite loudly. We flew apart and stared at the office manager, who fixed us with a freezing gaze. "Mr. Fischer, you are here to adjust the transcription program, not the transcriptionist," she said.

I scrambled to my feet and smoothed my dress, cursing the rush of blood to my face. "Phoebe, you are to conduct yourself in a more professional manner," Joan said.

"Of course." I turned to my monitor, hiding a satisfied grin. I felt giddy, and a little afraid, too. I'd just agreed to go on a real date with my handsome young stud. What kind of crazy thing would I do next?

15

"I'M HUNGRY. Let's get something to eat."

I looked up from my computer at six o'clock that evening to find Jeff standing over me. "Now?" I said.

"You promised me a date. I figure I'd better collect on that promise before you change your mind."

"Why would I change my mind?" I adopted a teasing tone.

"You're a woman. That's what women do."

I laughed and switched off my monitor. "That's right. So you'd better watch your step." Already my skin was tingling at the thought of the evening ahead. A whole evening with the magic man here. I wish I'd taken my vitamins. I had a feeling I might need them.

We drove to a Mexican food place and ordered cheese enchiladas. He smiled at me while the waitress arranged our food on the table. I fidgeted in the booth across from him. Sure, we'd eaten together before, but that had been as friends. This was...something different. I wanted the evening to turn out well, but I was wary of reading too much into it.

When the waitress was gone, he said, "I can't believe this is our first real date. It seems like I've known you for months."

I prodded my enchiladas with a fork. "Yeah, but all those times at the office weren't real dates."

"Come on, you liked it as much as I did."

I shrugged. "I never said I didn't. It's just..."

"Just what?"

I laid aside my fork and met his gaze. "I'm not sure what

kind of relationship we have going here. Are you really interested in me, or is it just a physical thing?"

"I'm really interested in you." The way he said the words, as if he was absolutely positive, sent an excited tremble through me.

"Then tell me about yourself," I said. "Not the stuff I know from the office, about your business and stuff, but about you."

He took a sip of beer. "All right. I'm the youngest of four children, the only boy." He grinned. "Maybe that's why I like women. Strong women." He scooped up a forkful of enchilada. "I'm ambitious. I like to ski. I like alternative rock and kung fu movies. I like making passionate love to a certain beautiful redhead, but then, you already know that." He pointed the fork at me. "Your turn."

"You already know about me. I'm divorced. I'm the oldest of three children. I got married when I was nineteen and thought I'd live happily ever after and it didn't work out that way. I never thought of myself as particularly strong, and, when my husband left, I fell apart."

"But you didn't stay that way."

I sighed. "No. I guess you could say I got fed up and decided to fight back. I'm still fighting."

He stopped eating and leveled a steady gaze on me. "You don't have to fight with me, Phoebe. Though I'm here as backup if you need me."

Some little icy place inside of me melted when he said those words. I didn't know whether to burst into tears or throw my arms around him and kiss him senseless. I settled for eating my dinner and acting unaffected. But my heart pounded with joy, and maybe a little fear. What was I getting into here? I really, really, really didn't want to make another mistake with a man.

A little while later, he took me home. He walked me to the

front door and started to follow me in, but I stopped him. "I think we'd better say good-night now," I said.

He looked puzzled. "Any particular reason why?"

I smiled and stood on tiptoe to kiss his cheek. "Because, I never sleep with a man on a first date."

He was still standing there when I slipped inside, but after a minute or two, I heard him walk away and start his truck. I leaned back against the door and smiled, hugging myself. Tonight had been special. For the things I'd found out about Jeff, and the things I'd found out about myself.

I thought a lot about what Jeff had said about fighting. I'd been passive for so long that standing up for myself was a tremendous rush. But had I gone overboard? How did I know when it was safe to stop the battle and get on with my life?

BY MIDWEEK, THE ENTIRE Clinic building looked like a cut-rate haunted house. Cobwebs dripped from the doorways and pumpkins grinned from every flat surface. Albert stood watch at the entrance to the Family Practice office, nattily dressed in his orange-and-black ball cap and a bow tie that played "Monster Mash" when anyone pressed the button in the middle.

The drug reps ignored Michelle's anti-candy campaign and loaded us down with candy corn, chocolate witches and those sugar-syrup-filled wax lips that taste like crap but look so wonderfully grotesque.

Jerry Armbruster, the Viagra rep, one-upped the competition by bringing in a bagful of candy fangs and what he announced was the ultimate Halloween costume. "What is it?" Michelle asked, holding up what appeared to be a large oval pillow with various straps and buckles dangling from it.

"It's a pregnancy belly." He demonstrated by strapping the contraption over his Brooks Brothers suit.

I don't think words can do justice to the image of a six-foot-tall guy with newscaster-perfect hair and polished wing tips standing there with this huge belly sticking out in front of him. "It looks like some kind of tumor," I said, giggling.

"I suppose you could think of a baby that way." He turned sideways and struck a model's pose. "It's weighted so it puts pressure on the back and kidneys, just like a real pregnancy. They were originally designed to help men develop empathy for their pregnant wives."

"You mean men actually wear these?" Barb gave the belly an experimental poke.

Jerry slipped off the fake fetus and held it up by the straps. "I think it's one of those things that sounds good on paper, but face it girls, the average man wouldn't be caught dead in one of these."

"The guys probably couldn't take it," Michelle said. "I've had three kids and, believe me, pregnancy isn't for wimps."

"The question is, what are you doing with it?" I asked.

"My company makes them," Jerry said. "They're really popular in schools these days. They use them in family-education classes to try to give teenage girls an idea of what a real pregnancy is like. It's supposed to be a great deterrent."

"I can see how it could do the trick." Michelle hefted the belly by the straps. "But what are we supposed to do with it?"

"I thought one of you could wear it to the big Halloween party. Do a pregnant ghoul or something."

"Or the pregnant bride of Frankenstein," Barb added.

"I'll leave it here and let you decide what to do with it." Jerry set it up on the counter. "Now, if I could just have a word with the doctor for a minute?"

I grabbed a handful of chocolate witches to fortify me for the afternoon and headed back to my workroom. Or my dungeon, as Jeff insisted on calling it now that it was draped in cobwebs and black crepe paper.

The intercom buzzed and Barb informed me that I had a call. I hoped it was Frank, telling me that Easy Motors had decided to return my car. Instead, it was Mike Dawson.

"So, how'd you like the story?" he asked.

"It was great. I really appreciate it."

"Has Easy Motors coughed up your car yet?"

I sighed. "No. They haven't said a word about it."

"Not to you, but I've heard plenty. They've threatened to sue me for slander."

"Oh, Mike! I'm so sorry."

He laughed. "Hey, don't worry. I know the law and I haven't done anything wrong. This is actually a good sign. It means we're making them sweat."

"Do you really think they'll break down and give me my car?"

"If we keep at them, I think they will. So what do you think about doing another story? Going back to Easy Motors and giving them some more bad publicity?"

I swallowed. Was all this doing any good, or was I just making a spectacle of myself for nothing? "I don't know, Mike...."

"Come on. Don't give up now. Aren't you tired of riding the bus?"

I took a deep breath. "Okay. If you really think it will help."

"Good girl. I'll meet you there tomorrow morning at eight. That way we'll attract the morning drive-time crowd. You'll see. This is gonna be great."

I WAS AT THE DOOR of the local Quickie Printer's by six that evening. The clerk took one look at my I Bought a Lemon From Easy Motors T-shirt and grinned. "Hey, I read about you in the paper," she said. "Did you get your car yet?"

"Not yet. But I'm working on it. I need your help."

"Sure thing. What do you need?"

Two hours later, I left with two hundred and fifty bumper stickers that read Give Phoebe Her Car. If I was going to be notorious, I figured I might as well go all out.

When Easy Motors opened at eight o'clock the next morning, the Phoebe Frame fan club was there to greet them: me, Mike and Sheila, and Darla, who had dragged Tony along to act as "bodyguard" in case Frank got too forceful with his threats. "It's the least we can do," Darla said when I protested they didn't have to do this. "Besides, I always wanted to be in the papers."

Frank was so stunned by my reappearance that he didn't react right away when I handed him one of my bumper stickers. Sheila snapped a great shot of him holding the sticker, with me grinning next to him.

News Four showed up and filmed me applying a bumper sticker to Tony's truck, and then Channel Two got into the act by interviewing me for a segment on the morning broadcast. The reporter introduced me as a "plucky young woman fighting for her rights." I didn't know which I appreciated more: being called young or a fighter.

Whether because of the time of day or my growing notoriety, an even larger crowd gathered to gawk. I waved and smiled and handed out my bumper stickers to anybody who would take one. A teenage boy put one on his skateboard, and a middle-aged businesswoman plastered one across her briefcase.

Just before nine, a hulking black-and-purple tow truck pulled to the curb and a tall, lanky man unfolded himself from the front seat. "Ben." I welcomed him like an old friend. "This is the wrecker driver who towed my car here in the first place," I told Mike.

Ben scratched his head. "I've felt kind of bad about that ever since. So I stopped by to tell you that if this bunch ever does decide to let your car go, I'll be happy to tow it over to my shop and fix it for free."

When the news went out, a cheer rose up from the crowd. Ben flushed and shuffled his feet. He didn't say "aw, shucks" but he might as well have.

At 9:15, with the crowd showing no signs of dissipating, the receptionist picked her way across the car lot. "Frank sent me out to talk to you," she said.

"Why doesn't he come out himself?" Mike asked.

The receptionist snapped her gum. "He doesn't want to be on TV or in the papers." She glanced around, then spoke to me in a more confidential tone. "To tell you the truth, I think he's a little afraid of you. No woman has ever stood up to him that way before." She giggled. "You've even got me thinking maybe I should ask for a raise."

While it was gratifying to think I had cowed Frank, that wasn't getting me my car back. "What does he want you to say to me?" I asked.

"He says he'll give you your car back now if you'll go away and promise to never come back."

I grinned. "Somebody go tell Ben to fire up the wrecker. I think this means we won."

Before the cheering had died down, Ben had the blue Mustang hooked onto the back of his wrecker and was leading a caravan down Alameda. I rode with Mike and Sheila, who wanted to film the reunion between me and my wheels. While I balked at kissing the dusty hood, I was happy to sit behind the wheel and wave out the window, grinning from ear to ear.

Ben towed the Mustang to his shop and fixed the motor mount and checked out the rest of the car for me. "She's not in that bad a shape," was his final assessment. "You ought to think about getting the radiator flushed before too long."

"I promise I'll bring it in soon," I said. "And this time, I'll pay you for the work."

He shrugged. "I'd say the publicity's worth more than the cost of that motor mount." A grin cracked his gaunt face. "Besides, it was worth it, seeing Frank Adams get his."

I was feeling so good, I decided to take the rest of the morning off. Joan didn't like it, but she stopped short of threatening to fire me. Right now, Jeff and I were the only ones who knew how to work the new transcription system. If she let me go, no one else would ever figure it out.

Darla didn't have to go in to work until later that afternoon, so she followed me back to my house and we celebrated over a lunch of take-out pizza and bargain-bin Lambrusco. "Here's to Phoebe Frame, freedom fighter." Darla raised her glass in a toast.

We clinked glasses and I took a long drink of wine. "I just liberated my car, not an enslaved country."

"You stood up for women everywhere. You showed Sleazy Motors they can't take advantage of someone just because she's female."

"Hmm. I don't feel particularly militant. Just relieved it's all over with. Besides—" I picked a slice of pepperoni off the pizza and popped it into my mouth "—I never could have done it without Mike Dawson and all the publicity he gave me."

"You don't give yourself enough credit."

"You sound like Jeff."

"Oh?" She perked up and leaned toward me. "And what does the boy wonder have to say on the subject?"

I squirmed. "Just what you said, that I don't give myself enough credit. That I have more going for me than I want to admit."

She sat back, a satisfied smirk on her face. "I'd say the man is not only handsome, he's smart. So, are you still playing hard to get?"

"Uh, not exactly." I picked at the cheese on my slice of pizza, stretching it out like a rubber band, then letting it go.

"What do you mean by that?"

"I mean, we've agreed to date."

"Each other?"

"Of course each other." I took a bite and chewed, grateful for a reprieve from talking.

"And?"

I raised my eyebrows at Darla and kept chewing.

"And how's it going?" she prodded.

"It's going all right." I was still confused by my feelings for Jeff. On one hand, I was wildly attracted to him physically, and I enjoyed his company as a friend. On the other hand, I still didn't believe I could ever have anything permanent with him.

I'd rationalized the whole thing by telling myself it was probably better to have at least one "expendable" relationship between one marriage and the next. To make sure I wasn't on the rebound and everything. Isn't that what everybody said? "I'm going to try to have fun with Jeff and not worry about what happens next," I said.

Darla froze, a piece of crust halfway to her mouth. "You, not worry?" She leaned forward and felt my forehead. "Are you okay?"

"I'm fine. More than fine. I'm just great." Not exactly happy with my life, but not unhappy, either. Some days that's the best you can hope for.

The doorbell rang and I jumped. "Expecting someone?" Darla asked.

I shook my head and went to answer it. The only people who ever came to see me, besides Darla, who never rang the bell, were school kids selling something and earnest young men in white shirts and narrow ties who wanted to talk to me about the afterlife. I always told them I had enough troubles handling this life without worrying about the next one.

My visitor today wasn't a school child or an evangelist, though there were times when I thought of him as a particular kind of devil. "Steve, what do you want?"

He pushed past me into the house. "I want the ring. It was my grandmother's and it rightfully belongs to me."

"Do you want me to call the police?" Darla appeared in the doorway to the kitchen, portable phone in hand.

"You can't have a man arrested for being in his own house," Steve said with a sneer.

"It's not your house anymore," Darla snapped.

"Steve, you'd better leave." I tried to sound reasonable, though what I felt bordered on panic. The man said he wanted out of my life—why did he keep showing up like this?

He held out his hand. "The ring."

I put my hands behind my back. "No. The ring belongs to me."

Did I mention that Steve is a master at the condescending look? He wore that look now, an expression that said he was the adult here, trying to deal with a difficult child. "You have the ring now only because I gave it to you. As a symbol of our intention to get married. We're not married anymore, so the ring is meaningless as a symbol."

It sounds so logical, doesn't it? As cold and calculated as the language in our divorce decree itself. "You gave me this ring. You can't just take it back, the way you took back your wedding vows."

He clenched his fists at his sides and anger roughened his voice. "The trouble with you, Phoebe, is that you're so good at playing the victim. This whole fiasco with your car is a perfect example. You didn't bother to tell that reporter that I was the one who bought your other car for you, that I'd given it to you as a gift. And you didn't tell him that when it came time to settle the terms of our divorce, you never said one word about wanting a new car."

I stared at him, assaulted by this twisted logic. "I was in shock. I was too stunned to think about the car."

He shook his head. "There you go again, playing the victim. And the worst part is, you don't even realize you're doing it. Even after the divorce, if you'd bothered to ask my advice on buying a car, I would have told you to have it thoroughly checked out by a mechanic first."

"Why should she bother asking your advice about anything?" Darla took a step toward him. She still had the phone in her hand and I figured any minute now, she'd brain him with it.

I tried to move to intercept her, but my legs felt too wobbly to move. "You'd better go," I said weakly.

"Not until I have the ring."

I twisted the ring on my finger. All of a sudden, it didn't seem to fit so well. Why did I want this particular diamond? I'd thought it was because it represented something important in my life, but now Steve's words had taken even that away. I slipped the ring off my finger. "Phoebe, no!" Darla cried.

I folded my fingers around the diamond and looked at Steve. "I want the money."

His eyes fairly glowed with triumph. "Send the papers to my lawyer and I'll see that it's taken care of."

"No. I want it now." I leaned over and plucked a pen from a shelf by the door. "Write me a check."

"It'll probably be hot," Darla said.

I shook my head. Steve always carried a five-thousand dollar balance in his checking account. That way, he didn't have to pay any check fees.

He hesitated, then pulled his checkbook from his pocket and wrote out a check for four thousand dollars. He handed it to me and I dropped the ring in his hand. "Maybe when you give it to Tami, you'd better tell her it's just a loan, in case things don't work out between you two."

He glared at me, then shoved past me and out the door. The sound of it slamming echoed in the awful stillness he left behind.

Darla came over and slipped her arm around me. "Why did you do it?" she whispered. "Why did you let him win?"

I looked at the empty finger where the ring had been. "He was right. The ring didn't mean anything anymore. I thought it did, but I was wrong."

She patted my shoulder. "Buy yourself something nice with the money. You deserve it."

I nodded. Sure. I could pay off my Visa bill. Buy myself some new shoes.

I rubbed the slight indentation on my finger where the ring had been. I felt strange without it, stranger still without this last tie to Steve. A chapter of my life was officially over. Time to begin another one. With Jeff? Or someone else.

Too bad crystal balls don't work. I'd have given a good chunk of those four thousand presidents to see what the future had planned for me. Call me a coward if you like, but I prefer to call it smart. If you know what's coming, you'll know when to duck.

16

"YOU KNOW A MAN IS SERIOUS when he sends chocolate." Michelle made this announcement a few days later as she delivered a giant heart-shaped box of candy to my workroom. "A bicycle courier just dropped this off for you."

I stared at the gaudy arrangement of satin bows and plastic roses adorning the top of the box. "Who sends a heart when it's almost Halloween?" I asked. "Where would someone find something like this time of year?"

"Maybe he's been saving it since Valentine's Day." Michelle deposited the box on my desk. "So is it another present from your secret admirer?"

I slipped a card from beneath the ribbon and opened it. "Sweets for my sweetie," I read. No signature.

"He's not exactly original," Michelle said. "Still, I'd be impressed if a guy sent me anything."

I opened the box and studied the assortment of chocolates within. "Do they look stale to you?"

Michelle leaned over and plucked a caramel from its slot. "Mmmmfff...chewy." She swallowed. "Maybe a little stale. But not bad."

"Michelle, Doctor needs you in room two." Joan tip-tapped her way toward us. She frowned at the box of chocolates. "All that candy is very bad for you," she said. "It sets a bad example for the patients."

"I don't think any of the patients will see it back here." I offered her the box. "Would you like a piece? The caramels are especially nice." With any luck, she'd lose a filling and be out of commission for at least a day.

"Put that away and get to work," she ordered, and retreated down the hall, Michelle in her wake.

I replaced the lid on the candy and tried to get back to work. But listening to Patterson relate the amusing story of how a three-year-old swallowed a quarter from the tip tray at a restaurant didn't hold any fascination for me.

I was restless. Edgy. As if I'd suddenly gained ten pounds and none of my clothes would fit right. My life didn't fit right. For twelve years, I'd known exactly what to expect from each day. I'd had the same house, the same job, the same marriage. Now, nothing was the same. I didn't know where I was going or where I wanted to go.

I looked around my workroom. No wonder Jeff called it my dungeon. That's exactly what it felt like. I took off my headphones and tossed them onto the counter. I had to get out of here. At least for a few minutes.

I grabbed up the box of candy and headed up front. "Where are you going?" Joan asked as I passed her.

"You're right. This candy has no place in the office. So I'm going to get rid of it."

I made it onto the elevator just as the doors shut. I had the car to myself, and took advantage of this to study my reflection in the polished steel door. "Phoebe, you need a vacation," I said to the tired-looking woman who stared back at me. "Someplace without ex-husbands, lecherous bosses or sadistic car dealers."

The elevator stopped on the second floor and a pregnant woman got on. I scarcely looked at her, I was so absorbed in my own problems. Besides, it's an unwritten rule that people in elevators don't look at each other or say anything. We all stand in our own little square of silence, facing forward and keeping our mouths shut. And, except in the case of my mysterious groper, our hands to ourselves.

Apparently, this chick didn't know the rules. After a minute, she leaned toward me. "Aren't you Phoebe Frame?"

I turned and stared into an all-too-familiar face. "You!" Just-a-waitress. Tami. The future second Mrs. Steve Frame. We'd never been face-to-face like this before. Of course, I'd thought about meeting her many times. In my fantasies, I either tore out her hair or spat in her face.

But real life isn't like fantasy. I couldn't even think of any cutting remarks. I just stared at her, goggle-eyed. The elevator stopped on the ground floor and the doors started to open, but she leaned over and hit the close button. "We need to talk," she said.

She hit the button for the seventeenth floor and, after a moment, we started back up. "I don't have anything to say to you," I said, and faced forward again.

She took a step back, and put her hands protectively on her belly. "I know you probably hate me, but you shouldn't."

"I shouldn't swear or eat so many sweets, but I haven't been inclined to give them up. Why should I give up hating you?" In fact, I was pretty ticked off that she'd expect me to stand here and listen to her. I leaned over to hit the four. I'd get off and take another elevator back down. But just as my finger touched the button, the car lurched and made a screeching noise.

Everything went silent and still. Tami looked up at the lighted display which showed the number of each floor. Both the three and the four were lit. "Why are we stopped?" she asked.

"I don't know." I started hitting buttons, but nothing happened. "They've been having trouble with the elevators," I mumbled.

"Then we'd better call."

I opened the little door in the control panel and picked up the emergency phone. "Hello, this is Building Services. If you'd like to report a maintenance problem, press one. If you need to order supplies, press two. If you have a question for janitorial services, press three...." I listened with ever-growing irritation, until the recording reached seven. 'If you'd like to leave a message, please record your name and number at the tone.'

"If I had a number, I wouldn't be calling you," I snapped. "We're stuck in the elevator, dammit." I slammed down the receiver and glared at it. Of all the times to get stuck in the elevator. If it had to happen, why couldn't it have been with Jeff? At least he would have made it...interesting.

Tami sank to the floor like a deflated balloon. I scowled at her. "I hope you don't expect me to help you up again."

"I can't stand very long," she whined. "My ankles swell."

I leaned against the opposite wall of the car and pretended not to look at her. But how could I not look at her? If you'd been in a race and lost by inches at the last second, wouldn't you look at the runner who beat you out? Wouldn't you want to know what that runner had that you didn't?

Who was I kidding? I knew what Tami had that I didn't: long blond hair, big boobs and ten fewer years in the birth-date slot on her driver's license. She also had Steve, but as far as that went, she was welcome to him.

"Go ahead and laugh if it makes you feel better," she said.

"Laugh?" I frowned. "Why would I laugh?"

She struggled to sit up straighter. "I know what you're thinking. I used to be thin and pretty, with a glamorous job, and now I'm just fat and pregnant and unemployed. While you stand over there, in your fancy clothes, with your fancy job and...and a box of chocolates. I'll bet you think you have it made." She sounded as if she was going to cry any minute now.

I tried not to let my surprise show on my face. It was true she was looking a little doughy these days, but she had a good excuse. I would have translated "unemployed" to "lady of leisure" but maybe it didn't look that way from her end.

I glanced down at the off-brand suit I'd bought on clearance two years ago. Not what I'd call fancy. And I certainly wouldn't call stuck in a closet all day typing up notes for Patterson a glam position. I did, however, have a box of chocolates. I removed the lid and offered the candy to Tami. "Would you like a piece?"

She looked at me as if she suspected I'd laced them all with poison, but apparently the lure of even stale chocolate was too much for her. She chose a piece and popped it into her mouth.

I watched her chew with cowlike thoroughness and felt a completely unexpected emotion sneak up and poke me in the stomach. Looking at this doughy, fat, stringy-haired person slumped on the floor of the elevator, masticating a stale chocolate, I felt a kind of pity. Not only was she pathetic, she had to put up with Steve. "What did you want to talk to me about?"

"This." She held up one hand.

Any sympathy that had been building for her dried up when my gaze came to rest on her left hand and I saw the ring glinting there. "I could almost forgive you for taking Steve off my hands," I said. "But I'll never forgive you for stealing my ring."

She regarded the jewel. "There's no reason for you to feel that way. It's Steve's grandmother's ring. It ought to stay in the family." She resumed her pouting expression. "Besides, Steven told me you have a new boyfriend who can buy you all the rings you want. A young, good-looking boyfriend."

I blinked. "Steve told you that?"

"He didn't want to, but I made him." She squirmed. "I think it ticked him off that you'd end up with somebody with more hair than he has. He's very sensitive about his hair, you know."

"He's sensitive about a lot of things."

She rolled her eyes. "Tell me about it. I cooked his egg too hard the other morning and he had a hissy."

I nodded. So she was already finding out about the bad side of her glamorous older man. "What did you do?"

She shrugged. "I told him if that's how he felt, he could make his own breakfast."

Now why didn't I ever think of that? I held out the box of chocolates. "Here. Have another piece."

"Thanks."

We were silent for a minute, eating chocolate. "Does Steve still leave his dirty clothes in the middle of the bathroom floor?" I asked after a minute.

"No, I broke him of that one. I told him anything on the floor went in the trash. He didn't believe me until I threw out a brand-new golf shirt."

I winced. "What did he do?"

She shrugged. "Oh, he threw a temper tantrum, but I just put on my headphones and turned up the stereo. I told him if he was going to act like a toddler, I'd treat him like one."

A snort of laughter escaped me. "You should give lessons."

She glanced up at me. "No offense, but you spoiled him. A lot of women do that. But he's coming around. Yesterday he did a load of laundry for the first time. I figure it's a start."

I could see it all so clearly now. I had spoiled Steve—waiting on him, picking up after him. I'd been...like another mother to him. No wonder our love life had suffered.

This revelation hit me hard. I felt like sinking to the floor, too, but managed to stay upright. While I was still trying to absorb this new picture of my marriage, the phone rang.

"Hello?"

"You ladies all right in there?" a man asked.

I glanced at Tami. "We're okay, but one of us is very pregnant. If you don't want her having the baby right here, you'd better get us out pronto."

"We're working as fast as we can. Don't worry."

I hung up the phone and turned to Tami. "They're working on it."

She nodded. "I've noticed people—men especially—are afraid of pregnant women. They're terrified we're going to go into labor and start bleeding on them or something. The other night, we went out to dinner and the service was a little slow. Steve told the waiter I might go into labor any minute and ten minutes later, we had a five-course meal on the table."

I nodded. "So what did you want to say to me about the ring?"

"Just that you did the right thing, giving it up. I appreciate it, and so does Steve, even if he'd never say it."

I wasn't so sure about Steve, but I was ready to let it go. Even though I hated to lose a fight, losing in this case was almost like winning. I'd cut my last ties with my old marriage and my old life. I was starting over. And being four thousand dollars richer for it didn't hurt, either.

The elevator lurched, then we started moving down. "I think it's fixed," I cried.

Tami started to hoist herself up the wall. "Here, let me." I offered my hand. She took it and I helped her stand.

She checked her watch. "That wasn't so bad."

I glanced at her, my old animosity lost somewhere between the third and fourth floors. "No, it wasn't so bad," I said. I pulled the box of candy from under my arm and held it out to her. "Why don't you take this? I really couldn't eat it all."

"Are you sure?"

I nodded. "I'm sure."

She took the heart-shaped box. "I'm already fat, so I guess it doesn't matter if I get a little fatter." She straightened and met my gaze. "I'm glad we had a chance to talk."

"Me, too."

I watched her waddle across the lobby and out the door and thought about all the funny twists and turns life can take. Maybe if I'd told Steve to fry his own eggs, he and I would still be together. Or maybe we'd have beat each other to death with spatulas.

Or maybe, everything had worked out exactly as it was supposed to. Some people believe in that kind of fate. Me, I'm not sure what I believed in, except that maybe my life wasn't so bad after all. Maybe I just had to stretch a little bit, and make it fit.

DARLA WAS MY BEST FRIEND, so that pretty much meant I couldn't kill her. But that didn't mean I wasn't tempted to strangle her when I found out what she'd planned as my costume for the Halloween party. "What am I supposed to be?" I asked, fishing a pair of tiny leather shorts out of the grocery sack she handed me.

"Just put it on. All of it." She pushed me toward the bedroom. "I can't wait to see."

When I unpacked the rest of the stuff in the bedroom, I discovered fishnet stockings, a pair of thigh-high, spike-heeled boots, a leather vest, a studded dog collar and a whip. "Darla, I can't wear this!" I shrieked.

"Yes, you can. Put it on."

Okay, so I'll admit I couldn't wait to see how I'd look in that getup. All that leather...I mean, it's a sexual fantasy waiting to happen.

I put on everything in the bag. The dog collar took a little getting used to, and I felt ten feet tall in those boots. When I finally got up the nerve to look at myself in the mirror, my mouth dropped open. I have to admit, I looked pretty hot. Those tall boots and little shorts made my legs look a mile long, and the vest was just tight enough to make my little bit of cleavage look like a lot.

The door opened and Darla leaned in. "What do you think?"

I swallowed. "I think if I wear this to the party, I'm liable to give Patterson a heart attack, not to mention the wrong idea."

"If he gets out of line, you can always use the whip." She picked up the leather quirt and flicked it at me. "Besides, who cares about Patterson? What do you think Jeff will think?"

The thought of Jeff's potential reaction sent a flush of red from my cleavage up. Darla laughed. "That good, huh?" She handed me the whip. "Then you've got to wear it."

I turned away from the mirror. "Darla, what in the world made you decide I should dress up as a dominatrix?"

"You said you wanted to be a strong woman who wouldn't take shit from anybody and a sexy woman who would have men crawling at her feet." She gestured toward me with both hands. "Tah-dah! Power, command and sex appeal. I'd say it's you."

"I have to work with these people." I tossed the whip onto the bed again. "Joan will have a fit when she sees me."

"Joan probably has a second job running her own dungeon. Come on, this could work to your advantage."

I crossed my arms over my chest. "And just how do you figure that?"

"You said yourself everyone at the office takes you for granted. Well, this will shake them up. They'll realize they don't know everything there is to know about you. They might even be a little afraid of you. And you know what they say—a little bit of fear can translate into a whole lot of power."

"Who says that?" I slipped a finger under the dog collar and scratched.

"Some professors who wrote a book about sexual power. I saw them on *Oprah*." She tilted her head and studied me. "Remember, lots of eyeliner and mascara and red, red lipstick."

"Can I at least wear a mask? At least then maybe everybody won't recognize me."

"You're no fun." Darla laughed. "But yeah, I brought a mask, just in case you chickened out. But it only covers your eyes." She waggled her eyebrows suggestively. "I made sure to leave your mouth free in case you want to reward some lucky slave with a kiss."

The thought sent a tingle through me. I couldn't be sure if it was nervousness or desire. Part of me was terrified of looking like a fool. The other part couldn't pass up a chance to play the woman in charge for a change. Lord knows, it wasn't a role I ever got to see in real life. I took a deep breath. "Okay. I'll do it. But if I end up without a job, believe me, you—"

"I know, I know. I owe you."

17

WITH MY HAIR TEASED OUT and sprayed with glitter, and a black mask covering my nose and eyes, I held out a slim hope that no one at the party would recognize me. I figured I had the element of surprise on my side. I mean, how many people would expect meek transcriptionist Phoebe Frame to transform herself into Mistress Phoenix?

By the time I got there, the party was already in full swing. A DJ in the main lobby played music that was piped to all the medical suites. Every floor had a buffet with a different theme: Mexican food, Chinese food, barbecue. There were two cash bars plus free rum punch. The top floor had been turned into a haunted house—a mad doctor's operating room with enough real medical equipment to give anybody the creeps.

All my seemingly normal co-workers had transformed themselves into everything from a thirteenth-century knight to a six-foot-tall cockroach that was more horrifying than any run-of-the-mill ghoul. I recognized my friend Beverly from obstetrics, dressed as Dorothy, with a tin man who had to be her husband, Bill. Michelle was a ghoulish nurse, complete with bloodstained uniform and a green fright wig.

Lots of people stared at me as I minced across our office suite in those impossibly tall high heels, and one or two of the men leered, but no one showed any signs of recognition. A thrill rippled through me as I passed people who saw me every day and their faces remained blank. They had no idea that the powerful, sexy woman before them was mild-mannered Phoebe Frame, forgotten transcriptionist. Let me tell you, it was a rush. I understood how superheroes could get addicted to the saving mankind shtick.

I headed for the punch bowl, and a healthy dose of liquid courage. While I ladled rum punch into a paper cup, I searched the crowd for Jeff. He'd refused to tell me what kind of costume he'd chosen. Would he be a vampire? A mummy?

Before I could find Jeff, however, Dr. Patterson found me. Only he didn't realize it was me. He was wearing a Dracula getup, complete with white tie and tails. Owing to his broad shoulders and not inconsiderable bulk, he more closely resembled a penguin on steroids than Vlad the Impaler. "Hellooo," he drawled, and flashed his fangs. "I'm Ken Patterson. Dr. Patterson. I don't believe we've met, Miss...?"

I affected a German accent in case Patterson recognized my regular voice. "Mistress. Mistress Phoenix."

Instead of putting him off, as I'd hoped, my frost-queen act only piqued Patterson's interest. "It's such a pleasure to meet you, Mistress. Uh...may I call you Mistress?"

Oh, what the hell? I thought. When was I going to be in this kind of position again? I gave him an aloof smile. "Only those who please me may call me Mistress."

He sidled a little closer and lowered his voice. "Then what may I do to please you?"

Give me a twenty percent raise? Move to Siberia? I took a step away from him. "I'm hungry," I said petulantly. "Fetch me some shrimp from the buffet."

He didn't even hesitate. "What kind of shrimp do you prefer? We have boiled and fried."

Amazing! "Boiled. And be sure to peel them."

Coattails flapping behind him, he headed for the buffet table in the next room. I took off in the opposite direction. By the time Patterson returned with those shrimp, I planned to be in a distant part of the building.

I was trying to squeeze my way through the crowd to the elevator when somebody grabbed my arm. I whirled and looked down at a pudgy guy wearing red-footed pajamas and horns, who was carrying a pitchfork. His forehead came about level with my chin and his nose stuck out from beneath his black mask like the prow of a ship. "I've been looking for you," the little devil said, grinning up at me.

I shook loose of his hand. "You must have me confused with someone else."

"Oh, no. You're the only woman I want." His grin morphed into a full-blown leer and settled on my cleavage. "I love your costume."

He reached for me again, but I managed to dodge out of his way. "Do not touch Mistress Phoenix," I said in my thickest accent, scowling at him.

He actually giggled! "I love it when you get forceful." He sidled closer. "Maybe later you could spank me?"

I felt nauseated just thinking about it. I took a step back. "Um, I have to go now. I'll be late for the...late for the next door-prize drawing."

I took off, moving as fast as I could through the crowd. It's amazing what having a whip in your hand will do for you. I was almost to the door when I heard someone calling, "Mistress! Oh, Mistress Phoenix!"

I tried to ignore him, but the crowd had me pinned and the next thing I knew, Patterson was at my side, holding a plateful of naked shrimp. "I didn't know if you wanted tartar or red sauce, so I got both," he said.

I stared down at the little pink shrimps. Sure enough, there wasn't a peel on any of them. The thought of eating anything Patterson's hands had been all over turned my stomach further. "Um, I've changed my mind." I leaned over and set the plate on a nearby planter. "I'm not hungry anymore."

The old boy wasn't fazed. He grabbed my hand and pulled me toward the center of the room. "Let's dance."

I jerked my hand away. "Mistress does not dance."

"Then I'll teach you." I watched in horror as he held his hands up over his head and swayed.

"No!" I said, alarmed. "I—I'm thirsty. I want a drink."

"There's punch over here—"

"Not punch. I want a real drink."

He stopped moving. "All right. The bar's downstairs. We'll go get you a drink. Then maybe we can find someplace quiet, where we can get to know each other better."

His fangs glittered as he grinned at me. I shuddered. "No. You get the drink for me."

"But we can go together—"

I glowered at him. "You said you wanted to please me." I stamped my foot. "I want a drink."

His shoulders dropped half an inch, then he rallied. "All right. What sort of drink would you like?"

I searched my brain for the most complicated thing I could think of. "I want a...a martini. Shaken, not stirred. Two olives. In a chilled glass."

He nodded and made an elegant bow. "I shall return."

Fine, but I wouldn't be here waiting for him. As soon as the crowd swallowed him up, I took off toward the stairs. Eleven floors in these heels was going to be a bitch, but it would be worth it to get away from Patterson.

Unfortunately, the doctor wasn't the only one intent on monopolizing my time. The little devil had climbed up onto a desk and was scanning the crowd like a sailor searching for shore. I crouched down, hunting for cover.

A long table had been set up on the side of the room, draped in a white cloth and topped with jack-o'-lanterns and bowls of candy. I duckwalked toward it, then dove under the cloth. I could creep along under here almost to the door, then make a dash for it.

Do you know how difficult it is to creep in spike-heeled boots and tight leather shorts? I dropped to my hands and knees and crawled, fish net digging into my knees. When I saw Darla again...

"Eeeek!" I squealed as a hand grasped my ankle, and whirled to find myself staring into an amused pair of brown eyes.

"Lose something?" Jeff asked.

I crawled out from under the table and stood with my nose buried in a broad, bronzed, naked chest. Well, not altogether naked. Jeff wore a leather vest, leather cuffs and a dog collar that was wider and more heavily studded than my own. And he seemed to be carrying a shield. A whiff of spicy, seductive cologne stirred my senses. I looked up, gaping. "When did you get here?"

He grinned. "I thought I recognized you." His gaze slid appreciatively over my costume. "I have to hand it to you, Phoebe, you're not exactly predictable."

"Shh." I put a finger to my lips and glanced around to see if anyone had heard. But everyone was intent on the door-prize drawing being announced over the loudspeaker. "Call me Mistress Phoenix. I don't want anyone to know who I am."

"All right. Mistress." The word hissed off his tongue like cold water on a skillet, and sent a shiver down my spine.

I stepped back to get a better look at his costume and immediately felt weak at the knees. In addition to the leather vest, cuffs and collar, he wore a short pleated skirt that showed off his fantastic legs and a pair of Roman sandals. "You're a gladiator," I said.

"You get an A." He took my elbow and steered me around

a clot of people. "So whose idea was the dominatrix getup? Yours or Darla's?"

"Darla's. She said I needed to free my inhibitions and act out my fantasies."

"Mmm." His hand skimmed down my back and came to rest on the seat of my leather shorts. "I think I like your fantasies."

I tried to put a little distance between us, but it was tough to do in that crowd. "You are not allowed to touch Mistress Phoenix without permission," I said in my fake German accent.

"And what do I have to do to get permission?" He took his hand off my bottom, but closed the distance between us until a good deep breath would have pressed my breasts into his chest.

I knew I couldn't blame my light-headedness on one cup of watered-down rum punch. I swallowed hard. "I don't think touching is a good idea right now." I glanced at the people milling around us and caught sight of Patterson scanning the crowd. He must have cut in line to get back up here so quickly. He had a martini glass in one hand, and a look of pathetic eagerness on his face. "Quick, I have to hide from Patterson." I grabbed Jeff's arm.

"I know just the place." He pulled me out the door and toward the stairs. We climbed up one flight and emerged in a black-lit hallway.

"Where are we?" I asked.

"Back entry into the Haunted House. Come on."

He pushed open a doorway and I jumped as I came face-to-face with a headless body. "Good evening," said the head, which was sitting on a table beside the body. "Welcome to the Hospital of Horrors."

"Lookin' good, Pete." Jeff gave a thumbs-up to the body.

"Thanks," said a voice from within the body's suit coat. "What are you doing sneaking in the back door?"

"I'm giving Mistress Phoenix here the VIP tour."

We walked on, squeezing past crowds that lined the narrow hallways. In one room, a bug-eyed "surgeon" was sawing off the limbs of a "patient," realistic blood everywhere. Various displays of supposedly real body parts were set out to delight the ghoulish and turn the stomachs of the squeamish. Oversize needles, wicked-looking surgical instruments and miles of bandages and fake blood added extra-authenticity to this house of horrors.

"If people go through this, they'll never want to come to the doctor again," I said as we entered the start of the tour, the waiting room, where a cobweb-covered man with a long gray beard snoozed in the corner. A sign identified him as the true horror of the doctor's office—the forgotten patient.

"Nah, people love this stuff," Jeff said, pushing open a door that led into the corridor. "Money from the entry fees goes to the Cancer Society. It's one of their biggest fund-raisers of the year."

"And how do you know so much about it?" I asked.

"I helped set up the computer-animated special effects."

"You know how to do that stuff?" I was impressed.

He gave me a wicked grin. "I have a lot of special talents you don't know about." He leaned forward, as if to kiss me, when a familiar voice sounded in the room we'd just left. "Has anyone here seen a tall dominatrix?"

"It's Patterson!" I wailed.

"Come on. In here." Jeff took my hand and pulled me down the hall, into a darkened exam room, and shut the door behind us.

The noise of the party receded into the background and, in the darkness, our breathing sounded loud and a bit labored.

Jeff slid his hand down my spine and my heart pounded wildly. "I said, no touching."

"How about kissing?" His lips brushed the back of my neck, warming every nerve ending. He pulled me close, his erection pressed into my back. "It's been a long week," he whispered into my ear. "I've missed you."

My only answer was a low groan. I turned in his arms and kissed him full on the mouth. What can I say? It was probably the only chance I'll ever have to put my hand up some guy's skirt.

Though we were both plenty turned on, we didn't feel the need to rush. We were past the first deprived-and-depraved stage and into the getting-to-know-you phase of lovemaking. So we indulged in long, slow, wet kisses and the kind of extended petting you do when you know you're going to end up having intense, mind-blowing sex. We peeled back layers of clothing, but didn't undress all the way, using the costumes to help set the scene.

The exam table wasn't a bed, but it was flat and cushioned, so it wasn't a bad substitute. And the stirrups did provide a useful place for me to rest my feet, after all.

I may have gotten a little carried away. I can't say for certain I didn't moan a little loudly. Or maybe I even screamed. But honestly, who could have heard me over the din of that party?

I would have been content to lie there all night in Jeff's arms, but the setting itself wasn't exactly conducive to relaxation. "We'd better go before someone comes in and finds us," Jeff said. He sat up and reached for his vest.

Reluctantly, I dressed also. At the last minute, I remembered to put my mask back on. "Maybe it would be better if we didn't leave together," I said.

He nodded. "All right. I'll meet you in the parking lot in fifteen minutes."

I nodded. He left first and, five minutes later, I followed. All I had to do was make it through the crowd and down to the lobby without being recognized, and I'd be home free.

By this time of night, only the serious party-goers remained. The buffets looked as if a horde of locusts had descended on them, the carved pumpkins had burned down to blackened husks and the punch contained significantly more rum than fruit juice. The DJ was fielding requests for "I Put a Spell on You" and "Werewolves of London" and those couples who hadn't sneaked off to various nooks and crannies weren't so much dancing as engaged in rhythmic groping.

I was almost to the elevator when a leering Dracula materialized at my side. "Mistress. I was so afraid you'd left without me."

I ground my teeth together and resumed my Marlena Dietrich impression. "Doctor, where is my martini?" I demanded.

He blinked. "When I couldn't find you, I threw it away."

"You could not find me? You did not look hard enough."

He actually flinched. Oh, my. This was too much fun. "Do you think I am going to make things easy for you?" I snapped. "As mistress, my job is to make things very difficult. You must prove you are man enough for me."

"Yes, Mistress. Certainly. I'll bring you another drink." He turned to go, and collided with a short, big-nosed devil.

I groaned. Why did I attract such freaks?

"Ph-Phoebe!" the little devil slurred drunkenly. "Your costume is f-f-fabulous!" He leaned toward me, a besotted smile across his face. "You're the most beautiful woman in the room."

"Phoebe?" Dr. Patterson's face paled beneath his Dracula greasepaint. His eyebrows came together, then sprang apart. "Phoebe Frame?"

"Who are you?" I demanded of the drunken devil.

"Eddie." He smiled dreamily. "Eddie Parker."

"Do I know you?" It was hard to tell when you're talking to a man who probably doesn't ordinarily run around in red pajamas.

"I work upstairs, in accounting. I see you in the elevator a lot." He leaned closer and the alcohol on his breath made my eyes water. "Did you like the flowers I sent? And the candy?"

The hair on the back of my neck rose up. My secret admirer. "You're the groper!" I said, and moved toward him.

He jumped back, and trod on Patterson's toe. The doctor had recovered from the shock of finding me out, and glowered at me. "You did this on purpose," he said. "You set out to make a fool of me."

"I didn't set out to do anything but come to a costume party," I said. "Anything else that happened, you did all by yourself."

"This won't be the last you hear of this."

"Don't threaten me." I tried to sound brave, and hoped he wouldn't notice the shaking in my voice.

"That's exactly what I'm doing." His voice was a menacing growl. I leaned away from him, shaking in my boots. "You'll be sorry you ever crossed me." He gave me a cutting look, then swept his cape around himself and stalked away, looking more like Dracula than he had all evening.

I stared after him, telling myself I wasn't going to make things any better by throwing up in public, though fear had whipped my insides into pudding. Would Patterson really do something to harm me? Something physical? Or would he think of something worse?

"Mistress, now that we're alone we can talk."

I turned to Eddie, who was still grinning at me. "Get lost!" I snapped, and raised my whip.

He tripped over his tail in his hurry to get away, and ended up carrying it in one hand and the pitchfork in the other. I made it to the parking lot uninterrupted, and found Jeff leaning on my car. "I thought I was going to have to go back in after you."

"I ran into Patterson again."

"Oh?" Jeff took my keys and unlocked my door. "Did he give you any trouble?"

"He knows who I am now. And he wasn't happy about it."

"How did he find out?"

"There's this little guy who gropes me in the elevators sometimes. Apparently, he has some kind of crush on me and he recognized me and said my name when Patterson was within earshot."

"He gropes you in elevators?" Jeff clenched his fists, as if he was ready to pound the man in question.

"Some guys get off on that, you know?" I waved the topic aside. "Anyway, Patterson is really ticked now. I think he might fire me."

"Can he do that? Fire you for coming to a costume party?"

"He'll say it's something else. That I wasn't getting my work done. Or that I have a bad attitude. Which is true." I slumped in the seat. "What am I going to do? I need this job."

"You may need a job, but it doesn't necessarily have to be this one."

"Easy for you to say. You own your own company."

"You could come work for me."

I looked up at him, trying to judge whether or not he was serious. "Right. Doing what? I don't know anything about computers."

"You know about the transcription program. You could train people in the offices where I install it."

"No, thanks. It's bad enough that we've worked together here. The last thing I'd want is for you to be my boss."

"You'd be in for all kinds of extra benefits." He caressed my shoulder.

"I could sue you for sexual harassment."

"Promise?"

He reached for me, but I pushed him away. "I think I've had enough excitement for one night. I just want to go home and think about this."

"You mean brood."

"Don't knock it. It's one of the few things I'm good at."

He leaned over and kissed me on the cheek, a sweet, comforting gesture. "You're good at a lot more than that, Phoebe. Don't you forget it."

He opened the car door and slid out. "I'll call you."

I nodded and started the engine. "Good night, Jeff. And thanks."

"Thanks for what?"

"Mainly for not being a jerk-off, like every other man I know."

He stepped back from the car. "I think I'll take that as a compliment."

I laughed and drove away. When I looked back, he was still standing there in the parking lot, a tall man in a short skirt who, little by little, was turning my life upside down.

18

I DIDN'T SLEEP VERY WELL that night, between imagining all the ways Patterson would find to make my life hell and wondering what I was going to do about Jeff. I mean, I liked the guy a lot. And the sex was great. But there ought to be something more going for a relationship than great sex, don't you think?

Me, I can scarcely think at all before my first cup of coffee. I was waiting for it to brew when someone knocked on the back door. I didn't have to guess who it was. Darla always comes to the back door, and I knew she'd be anxious to hear how her costume creation had gone over.

"Morning, Darla," I said when I opened the door. It was much too early yet to tell if it was good or not.

"Guess what?"

I blinked at her. She was wearing cat's-eye sunglasses, a pink polka-dot sundress and a bubble-flip hairdo right out of the pages of *Seventeen* magazine—circa nineteen sixty-seven. "You've been impregnated by an alien," I said.

She lowered the sunglasses and stared at me over them. "No. Have you?"

A gladiator, maybe, but not an alien. I shuffled back to the coffeemaker and stared at the black gold slowly dripping into the carafe. "What have you done to your hair?"

She patted the solid curve of the flip. "It's leftover from my costume. But it's part of what I rushed over here to tell you about."

I poured a cup of coffee for me, then filled a second mug for

Darla. "Tell. Just don't expect much response until the coffee kicks in."

She accepted the coffee and followed me to the table. "Tony and I have decided on a theme for our wedding. We got the idea from our costumes last night."

I looked at her hair again. "You went as Barbie and Ken?"

She laughed, a sound that was entirely too cheerful to be made before noon. "No, silly! We went as Elvis and Priscilla. We're going to have an Elvis wedding! Isn't that fantastic?"

Fantastic was not the word I'd have chosen. Different, maybe. Innovative. Well, how about downright weird? "An Elvis wedding." I furrowed my forehead trying to imagine Tony as Elvis. "Young, sexy Elvis, or old, fat Elvis?"

"Young and sexy, of course."

"But...Tony doesn't have any hair. I'm pretty sure Elvis had hair."

She waved aside this minor discrepancy. "Tony's going to be a bald Elvis. He can do the sideburns, you know. And you should see him in his black shirt and gold chains."

"What exactly is involved in an Elvis wedding?"

"That's what I need your help with. We have to decide on all the details. The dress is easy. I'm going to wear a white lace minidress and go-go boots. Tony's going to grow his sideburns and wear black. But you have to help with the rest."

The last thing I felt like doing was planning a wedding. But maybe this is what I needed to get my mind off my own problems. And really, how hard could this be? "You could rent a pink Cadillac for the ride to the reception," I said.

"That's a great idea. See, I knew I could count on you. Do you have any paper? We should write this stuff down."

Somewhat revived by the coffee, I went in search of a notebook. I found one in the living-room desk and was on my way back to the kitchen when the doorbell rang. I hesitated. It probably wasn't anyone I wanted to talk to, but still...

I stood on tiptoe and peered through the peephole. A big brown eye stared back at me. My lips instantly produced a smile, though I'd have sworn I didn't have one left in me.

I opened the door and grinned like an idiot at the man standing there. "Jeff, you're out and about early."

He was wearing jeans and a polo shirt, but in my mind's eye, he was still in his gladiator's costume. Parts of me woke up just thinking about it.

"I stopped by to see if you were okay."

The words made me feel all sappy and squishy inside.

"Aww, isn't that sweet?"

I might have been thinking something along those lines, but it was Darla who actually spoke. She strolled into the living room, beaming at us both. "Why wouldn't Phoebe be okay?"

Her smile slipped away as she glanced from me to Jeff and back again. "Did something happen at the party last night?" she asked. "Or afterward?"

Jeff stepped into the room and shut the door behind him. "Hello, Darla. Do you have any more of that coffee?"

We all trooped into the kitchen and emptied the coffeepot, then started another one brewing. Darla fussed with sugar and creamer, then sat at the table and fidgeted until she looked like Barbie with a bad case of PMS. "Are you going to tell me what happened last night, or not?" she demanded at last.

Jeff glanced at me. I nodded. What the hell?

"Dr. Patterson really went for that dominatrix getup you fixed up for Phoebe," he said.

She rested her chin on her hand and studied him. "And what did you think of it?"

The smile that spread over his lips was positively lethal. I had to bite my lip to hold back a moan. "I liked it," he said, in a voice that suggested my costume ranked just behind breathing on his top-ten list of favorite things.

Darla stuck her tongue out at me. "What did I tell you?"

"The problem is, Patterson liked the costume entirely too much," I said. "He didn't realize it was me in it."

"If he didn't know it was you, what's the problem?"

I squirmed. "You might say I got a little too into the role."

"What—did you hit him with your whip or something?"

"Not that into it! No, I just ordered him around. Talked down to him. He ate it up."

"Sounds like fun to me. Giving the bastard a little of his own medicine."

"Trouble is, Patterson found out it was Phoebe, after all," Jeff said. "Now he's flamed."

"Ooooh." Darla's lips formed a perfect O. "What did he do?"

"Nothing, yet," I said. "But I have a feeling Monday is not going to be a good day at the office."

Darla leaned over and patted my hand. "Don't worry. I'm sure you can find another job."

"Yeah, I know. But it's such a hassle. I mean, when is it going to end? My life has been one big hassle ever since—" I stopped and glanced at Jeff.

"Ever since your divorce? Hey, I'm a big boy. You don't have to protect my tender feelings." He sipped coffee, looking thoughtful. "I think life is mostly hassles. It makes the good times stand out that much more."

Maybe that's why the time I spent with Jeff had come to mean so much to me, though I wasn't ready to admit that yet.

"I should come back some other time." Darla slid out of her chair and started toward the door.

"Don't go." I felt like a louse. Here she'd come to me with

wonderful news and I'd been about as enthusiastic as a slug. "I want to help you with the wedding."

"Wedding?" Jeff, who was standing now, also, looked at Darla. "Who's getting married?"

"I am," she said.

"Congratulations."

She grinned. "Thanks. Just before you came in, I was telling Phoebe that Tony and I have decided on an Elvis wedding."

"An Elvis wedding?" Somehow, he managed to keep a straight face.

"Yes. With Elvis music and decorations and stuff. Phoebe said we should get a pink Cadillac to take us to the reception."

"Are you going to serve fried-peanut-butter-and-banana sandwiches?"

"Hey, great idea! And RC Cola and MoonPies."

"You'll have lots of music to choose from. 'Love Me Tender,' 'Teddy Bear,' 'Only You'..."

"I have to write this stuff down." She grabbed up the pad of paper I'd brought in from the living room and scribbled madly. "This is all great. Wait till I tell Tony." She ripped off the sheet of paper and stuffed it into her purse. "I really do have to go now. I have a ten-thirty perm at the shop." She gave me a quick hug, then rushed out the door. "Blue Suede Shoes" blasted from her car as she roared away.

"You don't think she'll have the bridesmaids dress like the inmates in 'Jailhouse Rock,' do you?" Jeff asked.

"I don't think she'll go quite that far." I leaned back against the kitchen counter and studied him. "What now?"

"What do you mean, what now?"

"I'm not sure how to take you, Jeff. I mean, what do we really have going on here besides a series of quickies at the office?"

"I'd like to think that we're friends."

I folded my arms across my chest. "Friends?"

"Very good friends." He leaned against the counter beside me.

"Is that all?"

"I suppose that's up to you. You're the one who's always protesting we won't work as a couple."

"I guess I can't figure out if you're leading me on, or if it's the other way around," I said.

"Are you asking me if my intentions are serious?"

The old-fashioned language made me blush. Or maybe it was just knowing that I was putting him on the spot that embarrassed me. "I guess that's what I'm asking."

He looked down at the toes of his shoes and didn't say anything for a long moment. The coffeepot gurgled, a dog down the street started barking and I wished fiercely I could take back the question. It's true that sometimes ignorance is bliss.

At last, he raised his head and his eyes met mine. "I guess my answer is that my intentions are as serious as you want them to be."

What kind of answer is that? Apparently, the only answer I was going to get, since he didn't elaborate. Instead, he took my hand in his and rubbed the knuckle of the third finger. "Why aren't you wearing the ring?"

I'd never thought of myself as having particularly dainty hands, but they looked small and delicate against his broad palm. "I sold it to Steve for four thousand dollars."

"I thought you said it meant more to you than money."

I took my hand away and busied myself rinsing coffee cups. "I guess I lied."

"What did he say to get you to let him have it?"

"Oh, no." I shook my head. "I'm not going to tell you all my secrets."

"I'd settle for even one." He moved away, toward the door to the living room. "Just because I've got a Y chromosome, doesn't mean I'm the enemy. If you're going to be angry with men, be angry with the ones who deserve it."

Before I could answer, he left the room. I was still drying my hands when I heard the front door slam, and the sound of his truck starting.

I stood there with the dish towel in my hand and thought about giving in to a good cry. But I was sick of crying. Sick of whining and moaning about what I didn't have. I knew a better way to fight these blues.

I went into the bathroom and put on some makeup and combed my hair, then picked up my purse and headed out the door. You've heard the saying, haven't you: when the going gets tough, the tough go shopping. Well I had four thousand dollars to spend.

MONDAY MORNING I walked into work wearing a Narciso Rodriguez suit and Manolo Blahnik sandals. If I was about to be unemployed, I was determined to go out in style. Besides, there's nothing like a new outfit to give a woman a boost of much-needed confidence.

On the elevator ride up, I felt someone staring at me. With a feeling of dread, I turned and scowled at Eddie. He grinned. "You're really looking hot this morning, Phoebe." He sidled up to me and lowered his voice. "Would you have my love child?"

"Eddie, I know where a lot of sharp scalpels are kept," I said. "Don't make me use one."

He blanched and sidestepped to the other end of the car. When we reached my floor, I took a deep breath and held my head up as I strode into the office. "Oooh, don't you look snazzy," Michelle said as I passed her.

The office looked as though the building itself was suffering from a bad hangover. Crepe paper drooped from the ceiling and burnt-out jack-o'-lanterns squatted in various stages of decay. Albert leaned drunkenly on his stand, his bow tie half-off, his hat missing altogether. Joan stood in the middle of the office, hands on her hips, frowning at the general chaos. "Take away these pumpkins at once," she ordered, though it was unclear to whom she was speaking. "And get rid of that crepe paper."

I retreated to my office and began undecorating. I rolled cobwebs into balls and wondered if I'd even be around to string Christmas lights.

I tried to get some work done, but aside from a few notes from hospital rounds, there wasn't much to keep me occupied. I debated confronting Patterson myself, and putting an end to this torturous waiting.

At ten o'clock, Joan paged me and told me the doctor wanted to see me. I walked down the hall to his office like a fifth grader on her way to the principal's office. When I opened the door, he looked up from his desk. "Ah, Phoebe. Or do you prefer Mistress Phoenix?"

"The dominatrix getup was just a costume." I forced myself to move closer to the desk. I didn't want him to know how nervous I was. "It was just a gag."

"Too bad." He returned his attention to the patient chart in front of him. I doubted he was really reading it. He was playing a game, making me wait.

"You wanted to see me?" I prompted.

He glanced up at me, then closed the chart and stood. "Yes, I did, Phoebe. I think it's time you and I laid our cards on the table."

I frowned. I didn't like the sound of that. As far as I knew, he held all the cards.

He moved around to the front of the desk and stood with his hands behind his back. "I know the truth, Phoebe, though you've done your best to play hard to get. But Saturday night showed me your true colors."

Things weren't getting any clearer. "I told you the dominatrix outfit was just a costume," I said. "I was just playing around."

He smiled, a thin, superior smile. "You can pretend all you like, but I know the truth."

I crossed my arms over my chest and shifted my weight to one side. "And what is the truth?"

"I know you're hot for me, Phoebe. I've known it from the first day you turned me down. It's high time we quit playing around. I'm ready to accept you as my mistress. Believe me, it's a move you won't regret."

I gaped at him. If he'd just announced he was giving me a raise, I couldn't have been more stunned. My first thought was to tell him to take a flying leap, but some instinct for self-preservation, not to mention job preservation, made me choose my words more carefully. "I'm not interested," I said, and clamped my lips shut.

He tut-tutted and shook his head. "I'm disappointed in you, Phoebe. I had really hoped you would show more intelligence."

"Selling myself to the highest bidder doesn't strike me as all that smart," I said.

He looked sorrowful. "Then I'm afraid you leave me no choice but to let you go."

"You're firing me?"

"It would be impossible for us to work together any longer, considering the circumstances."

"You can't fire me. I'll sue."

He walked back around the desk and picked up the folder he'd been perusing when I came in. "This is your personnel file," he said. He pulled out a sheet of paper and scanned it, lips pursed. "Let's see. It says here that you've taken off three days in the last six months without providing either advance notice or sufficient medical excuse. You've also been late six days and left early another seven days. Yet, at the same time, you've logged almost forty hours in overtime."

"I had to work overtime to keep up with the extra work you gave me," I protested.

He leaned toward me, hands knuckled on the desk. "It has also come to my attention that you are having an affair with one of our contractors, in direct violation of company policy."

I blanched. "There isn't a company policy like that."

"If you had attended the last staff meeting, you would know that there is." He closed the folder. "In light of all this, would you like to consider my offer again?"

Only my ladylike upbringing and a lifelong indoctrination against spreading germs kept me from spitting in his face. I squared my shoulders and spoke with all the dignity I could muster. "You don't have to fire me. I'm resigning. I'll find a better job. One that makes use of my real talent." Whatever the hell that turned out to be.

19

I'D LIKE TO BE ABLE TO SAY that I made a dramatic exit from the office, but the truth was, Michelle was busy trying to draw blood from an uncooperative three-year-old, Joan was helping to hold the child down and Barb was trying to calm the hysterical mother. So I gathered my things and left without anyone even noticing I was going.

As I rode the elevator down to the lobby, I wondered how long it would be before anyone realized I'd left. Even then, would they miss me? Within a few days, some other transcriptionist would be installed in my workroom, and, pretty soon, everyone would forget all about me. Even Eddie would find another crush before too long. Maybe even someone who would return his affections.

There's nothing like being fired to put you in that kind of morbid mood. It didn't help matters any when I reached my car and found a flyer stuffed under the windshield wiper. I pulled it out, expecting one of those cheesy video-store come-ons, but instead, I read: Are you looking for a new career? Houston Technical Institute can train you for an exciting new career in medical technology, medical transcription, nursing, X-ray technology and many other rewarding positions in the medical field. Call 555-8888 to learn more.

"No thanks." I crumpled the paper into a ball and tossed it into the back seat. I'd had one "exciting" career in the medical profession and hadn't found it to be particularly rewarding. I didn't want another job that had anything to do with doctors or hospitals. But since I'd managed to screw myself out of unemployment benefits by quitting before Patterson could fire me, I had to find some kind of job, quick.

On the way home, I stopped at the grocery store and bought a box of double-fudge brownie mix and a paper. While the brownies baked, I could check the want ads for my next "exciting" new career. I would have liked to take a few days to mope, but my bank-account balance told me I didn't have that luxury.

I hung my new suit in the closet and consoled myself with the fact that I had at least one killer outfit to wear to interviews, then pulled on old sweats and mixed up the brownies. One of the nice things about being single is that if you feel like overdosing on chocolate for supper, there's no one around to tell you, you can't.

The *Houston Banner* had one of the biggest want-ads sections in the country, and you'd think those pages would be filled with great, high-paying jobs for a woman with clerical skills. Not.

Unless you call assistant manager at a fast-food joint or night clerk at the local video store the hot new careers of the future. Along with day-care workers and dump-truck drivers, these seemed to be the biggest job markets out there.

Team player needed for fast-paced business with growth opportunities. If you're up to any challenge, call us. Translation: want to be overworked and underpaid and work with a bunch of misfits just like you?

Dot-com start-up seeks creative, high-energy individuals to get in on the ground floor of this exciting opportunity. Work eighty hours a week for worthless stock options.

Exciting position in restaurant franchising. Supervise your own team and reap the rewards. Manage a burger place and have fun coercing a dozen hormonal teenagers into showing up for work on a regular basis. All the fried food you can eat.

I pulled the brownies out of the oven and poured a glass of milk. Say what you want, but warm brownies and cold milk are better than any tranquilizer. I returned to my search of the paper. Hmm, an amusement park was looking for an alligator wrestler. Did fending off Patterson's advances qualify as experience?

Disgusted, I flipped the paper over and was surprised to see my own face staring back at me. Woman Wins Fight with Car Lot read the caption. I scanned the brief story that told of my fight with Easy Motors and their agreement to release my car. "Phoebe Frame's story shows what one person standing up for her rights can accomplish."

I smiled. I had done something good, hadn't I? Too bad I couldn't turn that into some kind of gainful employment. I grabbed the scissors and cut out the photo and article. Maybe I'd make copies and include it with my résumé. Some businesses might get a kick out of having a local celebrity on staff.

I could dream, couldn't I?

I was working my way through my third brownie when the phone rang. "I was calling to see how you're doing," Jeff said.

I set aside the brownie and licked my fingers. "You know, this is becoming a habit with you."

"Does it bother you?"

I smiled. "I think I like it."

"When I stopped by the office this afternoon, Barb told me Patterson had fired you."

"I wasn't fired. I quit."

"Only because he didn't give you any choice."

I leaned back against the counter. "Oh, he gave me a choice. I could have chosen to become his mistress."

"The bastard!"

What did it mean that Jeff's anger on my behalf pleased me

so much? "He has this delusion that I'm secretly in love with him."

"Give me five minutes alone with him and I'll give him delusions."

I chuckled. "I love it when you play the tough guy."

"You seem to be taking this pretty well."

"Yeah, I guess I am, at that." To tell the truth, I felt as if I'd just taken off a too-tight girdle. "I guess that job wasn't a good fit for me anymore," I said. "It was time I left. This is going to force me to do something else with my life instead of spending it stuck in a closet in the back of a building."

"So what are you going to do?"

"I guess tomorrow I'll start sending out résumés. Maybe do some temp work until I find something permanent."

"No, I mean, what are you going to do about Patterson?"

I frowned. "I don't even want to think about that man. Besides, what can I do?"

"I heard talk around the office. Apparently, you aren't the first woman he's done this to."

I sneaked another bite of brownie. "No, there must be half a dozen of us."

"Then somebody ought to stop him."

"And you think I should be that somebody?"

"Why not? You don't strike me as a coward."

Where did he get these vaulted opinions of me? "Maybe not. But I'm not into fighting losing battles, either."

"There must be something you can do. Maybe if all of you got together—"

"Jeff, it's awfully sweet of you to be so indignant on my behalf, but, really, it's best if I just forget this and get on with my life. Patterson is holding all the cards. I don't have any proof of what he's done. And, besides, he doesn't care what us lowly peons think. He only cares about what his colleagues think. That's why this speech is so important to him. The men and women he's speaking before are the ones who count to him."

"Yeah, men like that make me sick."

I pictured Patterson standing up on the podium at the annual Texas Medical Association conference, preening in the spotlight. Those other doctors would listen to him and think what a great physician he was, and never know that he was also a lousy human being.

Sometimes brilliant ideas come from the strangest places. Like in an idle daydream while chewing a brownie. "Jeff, I just had an idea about how I might make Patterson pay for all the harm he's done."

"Now you're talking. What's the plan?"

I shook my head. "I have to see if I can pull it together first."

"Let me help."

"No. I mean, that's really sweet, but I need to handle this myself."

"You don't trust me."

"It's not that." A thrill of anticipation ran through me. "I guess you could say it's a matter of pride."

"I don't understand you. First, you don't like my suggestion to do something, now you can't wait to go after the guy."

"Maybe you inspired me." I dug the phone book out of the drawer and began flipping through it. "I have to go now, Jeff. I have some calls to make."

"Goodbye, Phoebe. Have I told you lately that you're one of the most intriguing women I've ever met?"

"Is intriguing the same thing as confusing?"

"In your case, it just might be."

I laughed. "Bye, Jeff."

"Goodnight, Phoebe. And good luck."

I hung up the phone and dug out a pad of paper. I had lots

to do if I was going to pull this off. And I'd need more than a little luck to make it happen.

I TOOK ADVANTAGE of my first full day as an unemployed person by sleeping late. After more brownies for breakfast, I polished up my résumé and headed to the copy place.

"Hey, how's it going?" The clerk greeted me like her long-lost cousin.

"Uh, hi." I faked a big smile, but she must have clued in to my confusion.

"I helped you print those bumper stickers, remember?" She pointed to a bulletin board beside the cash register. There, above one of my Give Phoebe Her Car bumper stickers was the article from the paper. "You're my most famous customer," she said. "What can I do for you today?"

"I need to make copies of my résumé."

"Thinking of using your notoriety as a springboard to a new career?"

I blinked. "Uh, yeah."

"Springboard. It's one of those 'business' words they teach us to use in this brochure." She pulled a folder out from under the counter and handed it to me.

"Twenty-three ways to energize your résumé." I glanced down the list of suggestions. Buzzwords like *springboard*, *actualize* and *optimize* jumped out at me. "Um, maybe I should read this before I send anything out."

"Let's see what you got here." The clerk held out her hand and I reluctantly handed over my masterpiece.

She read through it silently, nodding her head and making encouraging noises in her throat. "Skilled at juggling multiple tasks. What does that mean?"

"I can eat lunch and type at the same time."

"That's good. How about great organizational abilities?"

I flushed. "I was the fastest alphabetizer in secretarial school."

She grinned and returned the résumé to me. "Phoebe, you don't need that brochure. You could have written it."

She made twenty copies for me, and even supplied nice mailing envelopes. "Remember, presentation is very important," she said solemnly. "Do you need anything else? Thank-you cards? Business cards? Stationery?"

"Do you do transparencies? You know, for overhead projectors?"

"Sure. We can do photos, graphs, charts...."

I leaned forward and lowered my voice. "I'm planning a little, um, thank-you gift for my former boss," I said. "And I need your help. But it has to be top secret."

The clerk's expression reminded me of a spaniel I once had. You might be on your way to the vet to have him neutered, but tell him he would get to ride in the car and his ears perked up and he'd knock you over on his way to the garage. "I can do it."

"Good. Here's what I have in mind...."

MY NEXT STOP WAS THE OFFICE. Joan Lee met me at the front desk. "You aren't supposed to be here," she said. "Former employees aren't allowed access to the office."

"I just need to pick up a few things I left behind." I tried to move past her, but she put out her arm to block me. For a little woman, she was surprisingly strong.

"Come on, Joan, it's not like I'm going to sabotage the EKG machine or something."

"If you want anything, you can tell one of us and we'll get it for you."

I leaned against the counter. "Fine. I just need the number for Jerry Armbruster."

"The pharmaceutical rep?" Barb flipped through her Rolodex.

Joan frowned. "Why do you need his number?"

None of your business, Joan. I pasted on a fake smile. "I heard his company was looking to hire people."

"You think you could be a drug pusher?" Barb handed me a business card.

"Why not? I've watched plenty of them at work." I patted my hair. "Might have to upgrade my wardrobe and hairstyle. Get a better car."

Apparently convinced I wasn't going to sneak in and make off with a gross of tongue depressors, Joan went back to her office. When she was gone, Barb leaned toward me. "How are you doing?" she asked.

I shrugged. "Okay. Doing the whole job-hunting thing. Listen, I need a few more numbers from you."

"Sure." She reached for her card file.

"Do you have current phone numbers for Kathleen and Gail?"

Her eyes grew wide. "Joan might have them. I don't."

I made a face. "I doubt if Dragon Lady will let me have them without an interrogation."

Barb bit her lip. "Well...I'm not supposed to do this, but they're both still patients here."

"Then the numbers would be in their patient records."

She nodded and tapped her keyboard. After a few minutes, she scratched two numbers on a sticky note and slid it across the counter to me.

"Thanks." I tucked the note in my purse. "Have they hired a new transcriptionist yet?"

"No. They've decided to use a service. They even have Jeff taking out the equipment." She grinned. "Want me to let him know you're here?"

"No, that's okay."

"Barbara, don't you have work to do?" Joan stood in the doorway of her office, scowling at us.

"I'd better go," I said. "Thanks."

I was waiting for the elevator when Jeff emerged from the clinic. "Why didn't you tell me you were here?" he asked.

"I didn't want to disturb you." I glanced back toward the office. "No sense getting you on Joan's bad side, too."

"Does Joan have a good side?" He touched my arm. "How's it going?"

"Good. I got twenty copies of my résumé printed up this morning and I have a few leads for jobs."

"What about your, um, project?"

"That's going good, too."

"Still won't tell me what's going on?"

I smiled. "That depends. Can you still hack into Patterson's computer?"

"Maybe." He put his arm around me and walked me farther down the hall. "You're not thinking of doing anything illegal, are you? Like corrupting files?"

"I just want to know if you can go in and add some files. Nothing obscene or untrue," I hastened to add.

"I could probably do that, if I agreed it wasn't illegal. I'd have to come back after hours."

"Can you do it this week? Before Patterson's talk on Saturday?"

"How about Friday night?"

"That would be perfect."

He glanced back toward the office. Joan was watching us, lips pursed in displeasure. "Why don't I pick you up Friday about seven and we'll see what we can do?"

"Great. And thanks."

He grinned. "That's all I get? Thanks?"

I winked at him. "Let's see what kind of job you do, then we'll discuss payment."

I sashayed back to the elevator, with an exaggerated sway of my hips. I could hear Jeff's laughter all the way down the hall. I felt like laughing myself. So many bad things had happened; my new ability to laugh at them was probably the biggest victory of all.

20

HAVING MAXED OUT my credit card at the Quickie Printer's, I set about job hunting in earnest. Wearing my new designer duds and armed with my guaranteed-to-impress portfolio complete with newspaper clippings, I staged a frontal assault on an assortment of law offices, real-estate firms and computer consortiums. My plan was to land some sort of clerical position with enough pay and benefits to keep me in Diet Coke and coffee. I'd consider almost any field, as long as it didn't have anything to do with medicine.

I started the day with high hopes. After all, I looked great, I felt great and I did great work. What employer wouldn't be happy to have me?

Apparently, the Rose Law Firm was less than impressed. "We're looking for someone with legal experience," Anson Rose told me as he frowned at my résumé.

I scooted forward on the upholstered chair across from his desk. "I have legal experience."

"I don't see reference to that here."

"Well...I'm divorced, and that involves all kinds of complicated legal paperwork. And I once helped a friend file for bankruptcy."

He closed the portfolio and handed it back to me. "That's not quite what we had in mind. But thank you for stopping by."

The real-estate firm told me they were looking for someone with "less notoriety."

"Don't think of it as notoriety," I said. "Think of it as celebrity. Don't you think having a famous person on staff would draw customers?"

Apparently not.

By three o'clock, the oppressive Houston humidity had wilted my hair and melted my makeup. I had a quarter-size blister from my five-hundred-dollar shoes, a chip in my manicure and a run in my ten-dollar pantyhose. And I still had no job.

I sat in the car with the air conditioner running, trying to plot my next move. I could sign on with a temp agency and be the flavor of the week at a series of jobs where no one would remember my name and I'd never be able to find the ladies' room. I could buy another paper and try the want ads again.

I scowled at my own face, smiling out from the copy of the paper on the seat beside me. A lot of good it had done to bring that along. No one had been impressed by my brief brush with fame.

Who would have thought when I sat down to write a letter to the editor, it would have ended up this way? I remembered the rush I'd had that first day seeing my name in print. It was a feeling I could get used to.

I sat up straighter. If I'd been in a cartoon, a lightbulb would have glowed over my head. Well, why not see my name in print more often? Like—every day?

I put the car in gear and headed down Bellaire Boulevard, toward the offices of the *Houston Banner*.

The glass-and-steel skyscraper overlooking the muddy waters of Brays Bayou might have been an oil-company office or an accounting firm. It didn't look like my idea of a newspaper office. Newspaper offices ought to have men in shirtsleeves barking into old-style, chunky telephone receivers and crusty editors chomping on the ends of cigars. Women in padded suit jackets would hunt and peck at old upright typewriters and reporters would race down the aisle, shouting "Stop the presses."

Okay, so maybe I watch too many old movies. All I saw when I stepped onto the newsroom floor was a row of cubicles filled with glowing computer screens. A woman wearing jeans and a sweatshirt walked past, talking on a cell phone, and a guy with a ponytail was intent on a game of computer solitaire.

A receptionist looked up from her computer. "May I help you?"

"I'm here to see the editor," I said.

She did that thing they must teach in receptionist school—you know, that expression where they raise their eyebrows at you and stare down their noses at the same time. "Do you have an appointment?"

"I'm here about the consumer columnist's job."

"I'm not aware of any interviews scheduled for that position."

I pretended I was Katharine Hepburn in *Woman of the Year* and gave her what I hoped was a supremely confident look. "Then maybe he forgot to tell you." My smile was purposely insincere. "Would you just tell him that Phoebe Frame is here."

While she muttered into the phone, I wandered farther into the room. The guy playing solitaire glanced up at me. "Are you winning?" I asked.

He shook his head. "I never do."

"The secret is to cheat."

"How do you—"

"Miss Frame? I'm Gus Sanborn, managing editor."

Still playing Katharine Hepburn, I held out my hand. "I spoke to you on the phone a few weeks ago, Mr. Sanborn. You mentioned that your consumer reporter, Simon Saler, had taken another position as a sports writer."

He shook my hand and frowned. "That's right. Man still doesn't know the difference between a backdoor slider and a Baltimore chop."

"I'd like to apply for the position," I said.

"Do you know the difference between a backdoor slider and a Baltimore chop?"

I blinked. "Um, is a Baltimore chop anything like a pork chop?" I struggled to get back into Katharine Hepburn mode. "Actually, I want to apply to be your new consumer reporter."

He looked me up and down, not in a sexual way, but more as if he was measuring me for a straitjacket. "Just what makes you think you can do the job?"

I opened my portfolio and extracted the article about me. "When you told me you didn't have a consumer reporter to help me, I went after Easy Motors by myself. And I won."

His eyes widened and he looked at me again. "You're the chick with the bumper stickers?"

I smiled. "That's me. So you see, I have a proven consumer victory under my belt. And something of a reputation with your readers."

He motioned me past the row of cubicles to a glassed-in office. "Have a seat. You want some coffee?"

I sat on the edge of a plain wooden chair. "No, thank you."

"It's terrible stuff anyway." He poured a cup and settled behind the desk. "Do you have any journalism experience, Ms. Frame?"

I shook my head. "But I can type ninety-five words a minute."

He winced. "It might not seem like it sometimes, but writing generally involves more than just typing."

I flushed. "Oh, I know that. I just meant that I'm familiar with computers and different programs and things. As for the writing part, well, you printed my letter to the editor, about my problem with my car.''

He nodded thoughtfully. ''Our readers liked that letter. The whole underdog story.''

''And that illustrates how I have a creative approach to problem solving. And I'm not afraid to stick my neck out to help someone.''

He laughed. ''I'll say that.'' He tapped the portfolio. ''What about the job you have now?''

I made myself sit still and not squirm in my chair. I'd prepared for this question. ''I quit because I wanted to pursue a job that allowed for more interaction with the public.''

He leaned back in his chair and studied me a long moment. ''Maybe we could give you a try. Let you write a few columns, see how it goes over.''

''Yes!'' I jumped up and leaned across the desk. ''I'll do a great job. You won't regret hiring me.''

He rose also, holding up his hands as if he was afraid any moment now I'd launch myself at him. ''Now, I'm not promising anything. This is just a trial.''

I nodded. ''I understand. But you'll see. I'll do great.''

''All right. Well, ask Lisa to show you the way to the personnel office. You can start Monday.''

I practically danced out of his office. The man playing solitaire looked up as I passed. ''I never look that happy when I come out of Sanborn's office,'' he said.

''It's this magical effect I have on men.''

At the stunned look on his face, I laughed and floated away. I did feel magical. No more losing for me. This time, Phoebe Frame was a winner. And I'd fight anybody who tried to take that away from me.

JEFF PICKED ME UP AT THE HOUSE Friday evening, since we'd agreed we shouldn't take a chance on someone seeing my car parked at the clinic after hours. I met him at the door dressed in black jeans, a black sleeveless sweater and black boots. "You look like a cat burglar," he said.

I brushed my hands along my thighs. "I didn't want to be conspicuous. After all, I'm not supposed to be at the office."

"But we don't have to break in. I have a key, remember?"

He took my arm and walked me to his truck. "I'm not complaining, though. You look cute." He opened the passenger door, then pinched my butt as I climbed into the seat.

See, I told myself. He's not serious. This is just a game to him.

I hadn't been to the office in five days and already it seemed like a strange place to me. The rooms were eerily quiet, lit only by the greenish glow of battery chargers and emergency lighting. Someone had put out the Thanksgiving decorations: sheafs of wheat and cornstalks, cutouts of turkeys and pilgrims. Albert grinned at us from beneath a Pilgrim's hat and wide white collar.

Jeff locked the front door behind us and we headed for Patterson's office. He switched on the desk lamp and ran his hand across the edge of the giant wooden desk. "I remember the last time we were here together," he said.

I swallowed, heart thudding like a bass drum. I remembered, too. "Um, we have work to do," I reminded him.

He smiled, and switched on the computer. "Okay, what do you want me to do?"

"Find the visuals for Patterson's talk tomorrow and insert these." I pulled the transparencies out of an envelope I was carrying.

Jeff held them up to the light and let out a low whistle. "The audience ought to get a kick out of this."

"I always heard it was important to incorporate humor into a speech."

He laid the transparencies on the table. "Patterson won't think it's funny. And we'll need to scan them."

"I already had that done." I handed him a disk.

He took the disk and tapped it against his hand. "We could both get in big trouble for this."

"Maybe, but do you really think Patterson's going to want this in court?" I straightened. "Besides, he deserves to get his after all the women he's degraded and used."

He slipped the disk into the drive. "That's one thing I like about you, Phoebe. You don't let people step on you."

"I used to. I guess I got tired of it."

While Jeff worked, I wandered around the office. I swiped a mini Snickers bar from Barb's stash in her desk and looked for more underwear in Joan's office, but didn't find anything interesting.

My workroom had already been converted back to a storage closet. I looked at the stacks of file boxes and shuddered. Was I ever glad to be out of this place. What had kept me hidden back here so long?

Jeff came up behind me and slipped his arms around my waist. "I'm all done. Want to try out that gurney?"

"I've got a better idea."

He nuzzled my neck. "I'm listening."

"Why don't you come home with me?"

He raised his head and his eyes met mine. "To your house? To a real bed and everything?"

I nodded. "I think it's time we take this relationship to the next level, don't you?"

He didn't say another word, just took my hand and pulled me toward the door. My heart hammered in my chest as I followed him to the elevator. I hadn't had a man in my bed since Steve left. I was glad Jeff was going to be the first, but also terribly nervous. Not just about all the normal things—will he think I look fat, will he hate my decor, will he snore? I was scared shitless about what this move meant.

Wanting to bring Jeff home didn't mean I was in love with him or anything, did it?

We got to my house and I stood in the living room, not knowing what to do next. "Uh, would you like a drink?" I asked.

He shook his head. "No, I want to see the bedroom."

"The bedroom?" My voice actually came out as a squeak.

"That's right." He took my hand and pulled me toward the hall. "It's this way, isn't it?"

Luck was definitely with me, since not only was the bed made, but just the day before I'd picked up a week's worth of shoes and shoved them in the closet. I lingered in the doorway while Jeff turned on the lamp on the bedside table. He looked around, saying nothing. Finally, I couldn't stand it anymore. "Do you like it?"

His smile made me weak at the knees. "It's got a bed. It's got you. What's not to like?"

He crossed the room again and started kissing me, his hand reaching up under my sweater. I felt the rush of cool air across my back as the fabric lifted, and the heat of his hand against my ribs. "You're shaking," he said, his mouth against my mouth.

"I'm a little nervous."

"Why?" He looked into my eyes with real concern.

"I'm scared of being hurt." Again. I didn't add the last part, but it was there. I felt faint. This honesty thing was scary.

"I'm not going to hurt you, Phoebe." He stroked the side of my cheek. "I care too much about you to ever hurt you."

There went another cold place inside me, melting away.

I care about you, too, Jeff. So much. I couldn't say it yet, but I thought it. Loudly. I hope he got the message.

I took his hand and led him over to the bed. The way he looked in my eyes, I think he did get the message.

21

THE ANNUAL TEXAS MEDICAL Association Conference was the largest gathering of physicians in the Southwest. What with the various auxiliaries, vendors and doctors' spouses in attendance, over a thousand people filled the halls of the Albert Thomas Convention Center in downtown Houston.

So it was easy enough for me to slip in along with Jeff. He was an official vendor and had made up a fake badge designating me as his assistant. All I had to do was avoid being seen by anyone who might recognize me until it was time for Patterson's speech.

Patterson's talk was listed on the program as The Family Physician and Antibiotics: Are We Using Our Best Weapons Effectively? Jeff and I got to the auditorium early and placed neatly lettered Reserved placards on five chairs directly in front of the speaker's podium. The computer-operated slide projector was already set up, so Jeff had a chance to check out the equipment. "It should work perfectly," he said when he joined me by a side door to the auditorium.

I shifted from one foot to the other. "I think I'm going to be sick."

He patted my arm. "It's going to be fine."

How could he be so sure? I excused myself to go to the ladies' room. If my stomach did decide to give in to this queasiness, I'd just as soon it didn't happen in public.

The ladies' room was around the corner from the auditorium where Patterson was scheduled to give his presentation.

I'd almost reached it when a familiar voice distracted me. "Yes, I'm quite honored to be asked to speak," Patterson boomed.

I turned and saw the good doctor addressing a crowd of admirers. He looked especially dignified today, with a wine-red silk handkerchief in his breast pocket and a matching silk tie. He looked like the kind of doctor you'd trust to put your interests first. The kind of doctor you'd see on a TV show, lingering at the bedside of a dying patient.

Which just goes to show that, for some people, image really is everything.

"Dr. Patterson, what advice would you give our readers concerning antibiotics?" A reporter, notebook in hand, had her pen poised to record Patterson's answer.

I couldn't really see the woman, but Patterson's smile told me she was young and probably good-looking. "Well, my dear, I would say it's important to be informed as to your options, and also to find a physician you can trust. I'd be happy to discuss the subject with you further after my talk. Perhaps over cocktails?"

I ducked into the bathroom and into a stall. Instead of fighting nausea, I was battling panic. Who was I kidding to think I could fight a man like Patterson? Not only did he have all his colleagues snowed, now he had the press eating out of his hand. What I was doing wasn't going to make any difference to him, and it would probably amount to social suicide for me.

I looked up at the ad board mounted on the inside of the stall door, as if hoping to find inspiration in notices about diet pills and local radio stations. An almost naked woman smiled out at me from an ad for a prominent plastic surgeon. "Be yourself, only better," the ad proclaimed.

Below it was a stark black-and-white notice. Are you a battered woman? it asked. Call for help, and then a phone number.

I stared at those harsh words, then my eyes flickered back to the model in the plastic-surgery ad. That pretty much summed up everything, didn't it? All those subtle messages women get every day that we aren't quite good enough the way we are. And how often do we take that stuff in without a protest?

Here was my chance to make my own protest. How could I let this opportunity get away from me? I might get lucky and make a difference to somebody. Maybe even to myself.

By the time I got back to Jeff, the auditorium was filling up. Several people approached the reserved chairs and looked at them curiously, but no one said anything or made any objections. It's amazing what people will stand for if you make it look official enough.

Patterson arrived with a group of doctors who wore beribboned speakers' badges and the room grew quiet. The president of the TMA introduced Patterson with a lot of flowery praise about his expertise as a physician, etc. And that was all true. Patterson was a good doctor. He just let his personality and the way he treated his employees taint his medical skills.

Patterson stood and acknowledged the applause, then shuffled through his notes. While he was doing that, I opened the side door and let in my partners in crime: four women, all obviously quite pregnant. They wore sunglasses and big coats and made a great show of waddling to the reserved seats in the front row, where I joined them. Jeff waited by the door, ready to help us make a quick getaway.

A murmur rolled through the audience, and I thought I heard a few chuckles. Patterson stared down at us and blanched. He looked over his shoulder, perhaps for someone to remove us, but no one came to his rescue.

After a tense moment, he cleared his throat and began his

talk. "A study by Doern, et al, of one thousand, six hundred and one clinical isolates of *Streptococcus pneumoniae* showed the overall rate of strains showing resistance to penicillin at 29.5 percent, while 17.4 percent..."

I tell you, it was all I could do to keep my eyes open, but the audience was attentive enough. Though I sensed that more than a few of them were watching our little group in the front row.

"I have some slides to illustrate my points," Patterson said, and nodded for the projector to be switched on.

With an audible whir, the first slide appeared on the screen. It was a petri dish full of some sort of ugly growth. Gross, if you asked me, but the way the audience reacted, you'd have thought a photo of Linda Evangelista had flashed on the screen.

By this time, Patterson had relaxed. He knew he had everyone's attention. I imagine he was already congratulating himself on making such a good showing.

"And here we have an illustration of *Streptococcus pneumoniae* after inoculation with ciprofloxacin."

The projector clicked and a gasp rose from the audience like a cloud of steam. A woman's picture, a black bar concealing her eyes, popped up. The woman was extremely pregnant, and the typed legend under her photo read: I was seduced by Dr. Ken Patterson.

Patterson reddened, and clicked a button to fast-forward. Another woman's face appeared. Also pregnant, her caption read: I lost my job when Dr. Ken Patterson dumped me.

Frantic, Patterson clicked again. Another woman appeared. And then another. All pregnant, all confessing to affairs with Dr. Ken Patterson that had ended badly.

The room was so loud now, no one could hear Patterson's protests over the laughter and shouted questions. I nodded to my companions and we all stood and walked down the center aisle and out of the room.

Or rather, I walked. The other women did the exaggerated duck walk of the extremely pregnant, their bellies stuck out in front of them. They'd slipped out of the coats and now everyone could see the T-shirts they wore that read, I'm a Product of Managed Care.

Someone started booing, and others joined in. Two female physicians stood and were soon joined by others, men and women. Patterson put his hands to his head, as if to ward off blows. Head bowed, he scurried off the stage. The slides continued to flash overhead. Woman after woman. I was seduced by Dr. Ken Patterson.

Outside, the women and I ducked into the ladies' room while Jeff kept watch. We emerged minutes later, having shed the T-shirts and the pregnancy bellies I'd borrowed from Jerry Armbruster. Then we made a dash for a side entrance and Jeff's waiting truck.

"I don't know when I've had more fun." Kathleen, my predecessor as an object of Patterson's affections, hugged me. "Thanks for letting me in on this."

The other women agreed, and we exchanged hugs all around and promises to keep in touch. Finally, Jeff and I were alone. He shook his head. "What do you think they're doing to him right now?"

"I don't know, but I'm going to find out." I headed back toward the building.

Jeff grabbed my arm. "What, are you crazy? People will recognize you. You could be mobbed."

"I didn't do all this work, take all this risk, not to see how things turned out." I shook him off. "Call me vindictive, but I want to see Patterson roast."

It wasn't hard to locate the doctor. All I had to do was follow the sound of shouting. He was cornered in a room just off the auditorium, the press hurling questions at him. "Doctor, who were those women?" "Doctor, is it true you had all those affairs?" "Doctor, do you feel you've violated the public's trust in you as a professional?"

Patterson stammered denials, but the questions continued. The suit that had looked so dapper only moments before now seemed to hang on his frame, and his tan, handsome face looked pale and old.

"Anderson! Barclay! You know me. Tell these people that I'm a good man. These accusations have no basis in fact." He beseeched his colleagues for help. The other doctors looked embarrassed. One shook his head in a pitying gesture, then they turned their backs and left him to the wolves.

Some of the reporters turned to watch the other doctors leave, and that's when someone spotted me. "Isn't that one of them? The woman who was sitting with the pregnant women?"

The press corps surged toward me with such suddenness I was afraid I'd be crushed. I turned toward the door to get the hell out of there, but Patterson's voice stopped me. "She did this to get back at me for refusing her advances!" he shouted. "She had a crush on me and I refused her. She became obsessed with me, until I had no choice but to let her go. This is all about revenge. There's no truth in it."

"Is it true?" a reporter asked. "Did you work for Dr. Patterson?"

I tried to read the expressions on the reporters' faces, to see if they believed Patterson's accusations. One or two looked skeptical, but most were more guarded, waiting for my answer. "I did work for Ken Patterson," I said. "And he did recently ask me to leave his employment."

A murmur rose up among the press corps, and I had to raise my voice to continue. "He asked me to leave because I had repeatedly turned down his advances. That's his pattern.

He has an affair with an employee, or tries to, and if she refuses him or he grows tired of her, he fires her or persuades her to quit. You can check his employment records and see the truth."

"Lies!" Patterson shouted, but the reporters ignored him.

"Weren't you in the paper recently about your car?" one asked. "Francis something or other?"

"It's Phoebe. Phoebe Frame." I leaned forward to speak into his microphone. "I'm the new consumer reporter for the *Houston Banner*."

"Ms. Frame! Ms. Frame!" They clamored for my attention. I smiled, some of my nervousness replaced by elation. They were really listening to me. I had made a difference.

"Phoebe, you've already taken on a crooked used-car dealer," a woman said. "Is this exposure of Dr. Patterson an example of the kind of in-your-face reporting we can expect from you in the future?"

I blinked. No one had ever called me "in-your-face" before. I cleared my throat and leaned forward to address them again. Sometimes words come to you, you know? Like a gift. The moment arrives and, for once, you know just what to say. I looked out at those reporters and gave them my best smile. "I think it's safe to say that the only thing you can plan on expecting from me in the future is the unexpected."

22

DARLA AND TONY DECIDED to have their wedding at the All Faiths Wedding Chapel on Westheimer, mainly because it was close to the Knights of Columbus Hall where they'd booked their reception. The KCs won out over the Sons of Hermann when they agreed to give the happy couple a discount if they let the Knights use their Elvis-themed decorations for their next Friday night dance.

So, on a sunny afternoon in November, I found myself helping my hairdresser and best friend arrange her hair for her wedding, while strains of "Loving You" drifted from the adjacent chapel. "Do you think the sequins on the veil are too much?" Darla tugged at the sequin-studded netting that cascaded from a daisy crown pinned to her hair.

"Too much" is a relative term at an Elvis wedding. What with the minister in a white jumpsuit, decorations which included flashing Christmas lights, guitars and stuffed hound dogs, and an Elvis impersonator crooning "Don't Be Cruel" to the wedding guests, a sequined veil hardly seemed worth noting. "You look fine." I straightened the veil over her shoulders. "Beautiful."

She frowned into the mirror. "I don't know. Do you think it makes me look like I have measles?"

"No. Besides, it will be lifted for the pictures."

"That's right." She looked relieved. "I keep forgetting all these details."

"I warned you. Wedding days give you amnesia."

"Darla? Are you ready yet?" Darla's mother, wearing an aqua-and-silver formal, her white hair piled into a beehive, stuck her head into the room. "Tony's starting to look nervous."

"We're ready, Mama. Go ahead and take your seat." Darla turned to me. "Can you believe I'm doing this?"

"It's going to be wonderful." I hugged her, taking care not to crush her hair. "Come on. Let's go."

Darla's father, who had grown his sideburns long for the occasion, was waiting in the hall. I followed him and Darla to the foyer and checked my dress one last time in the mirror while we waited for our cue to go in. After looking at half a dozen chiffon numbers in eye-achingly bright sherbet colors, we'd settled on this pink-sequined minidress with white go-go boots. Retro, but not too ridiculous.

The first notes of the "Hawaiian Wedding Song" sounded. "That's your cue!" Darla hissed.

I settled my single white magnolia on my stomach and began my stutter-step up the aisle. Talk about a weird feeling. The last time I'd done this, I'd been a bride myself. My stomach had the same jittery feeling I'd had back then. Mainly, I was afraid I'd lose a heel or trip, and go sprawling down the aisle, magnolia petals flying. I took a deep breath and focused on the blinking white lights over the altar. Tony had wanted to string the lights in the shape of a guitar, but the chapel had drawn the line at that.

At last, I reached the end of the aisle, and took my place across from Tony. His head shone in the bright lights, and his dark sideburns made him look more like a pirate than Elvis, but he was appropriately misty eyed as the music switched to the "Wedding March" and Darla and her father started down the aisle. At one point, he even wiped his eyes on the sleeve of his leather jacket.

The minister stepped forward, the rhinestones on his white

jumpsuit winking in the light. "Dearly beloved, we are gathered here..."

Amazingly enough, considering the circumstances, the wedding vows were straightforward, with not one reference to "baby." Tony's hand shook as he slipped the wedding band on Darla's finger, and my own eyes got moist when he lifted the veil and kissed her. I hastily blotted the tears with my fingers, hoping I wouldn't end up looking like a raccoon.

"Ladies and gentlemen, may I present Mr. and Mrs. Tony Bosco."

As the Elvis impersonator crooned "Love Me Tender," the happy couple hurried down the aisle and into their waiting pink Cadillac for the ride to the reception.

I followed the Caddie to the hall and had scarcely stepped out of my Mustang when a round, pasty-faced man in a red beret accosted me. "Are you Phoebe? Phoebe Frame?"

I eyed him warily. In addition to the beret, he had a thin moustache, so thin it looked as if he'd drawn it in with an eyebrow pencil. "Who are you?"

"Henry." Only he said it "On-ree" with a stuffy French accent. "The caterer."

"Caterer" seemed a lofty term for the man Darla had found to make ten dozen peanut-butter-and-banana sandwiches, crusts removed, cut in fourths, as well as a gallon of fried pickles and a cake in the shape of a guitar. "What's the problem, Henry?" I pronounced it the good old Texas way.

"The plumbing, it is backed up."

"You mean the sink's stopped up?"

He shook his head. "No, I mean the facilities don't work."

"The facilities?" I frowned. "What facilities?"

"The toilet's stopped up!" His face was as red as the beret now and the fake French accent had succumbed to a strong Texas twang.

A group of well-dressed wedding guests stopped on their

way across the parking lot to stare. "Gee whiz, Henry, what's the big deal?" I said. "Grab a plunger."

I started toward the hall and he fell into step beside me. "It's going to take more than a plunger to fix this," he said. "And I've got two kegs of beer set up. This could turn into a major crisis."

Which just goes to show that there's no such thing as a perfect wedding. It's sort of like that old expression "nature abhors a vacuum." Seems to me nature doesn't care much for man-made perfection, either. Give her a bunch of people trying to put together a perfect anything—from a picnic in the park to a multithousand-dollar wedding—and nature will throw in a thunderstorm, hurricane or infestation of fire ants just to show who's boss.

Or in this case, plumbing problems. The men's room was not a pretty sight. And when I checked out the ladies' room on the other side of the wall that divided the two facilities I found out it wasn't in much better shape. "What are you going to do?" Henry asked.

What kind of a consumer advocate was I, not to mention what kind of friend, if I let a mess like this ruin my friend's wedding?

"What are you going to do?" Henry asked again.

I started digging through my purse, looking for a business card I'd stuck there weeks ago. "I'm going to call a plumber," I said.

"You won't get a plumber to come out here on a Saturday afternoon," Henry said.

I pulled out a rectangle of pasteboard and stared at the slogan written there. "This one will." Vince Zaragosa said he couldn't mend broken hearts, but he could certainly prevent one if he got out here right away.

I pulled out my phone and dialed. "Hello, Mrs. Zaragosa, is Mr. Zaragosa there? I have a big favor to ask...."

THIRTY MINUTES LATER, Vince Zaragosa was up to his elbows in plumbing hell, and I was serving up plates of hors d'oeuvres and slices of the guitar-shaped cake, along with red soda water, champagne and beer. I'd promised Vince all the cake and peanut-butter sandwiches he could eat, and free beer, if he'd come over here, but all I really had to do was mention that he'd be saving a wedding reception and he'd promised to be right over. The big romantic.

The reception music was all Elvis, all the time. Tony and Darla danced to "Can't Help Falling in Love," then segued into "Jailhouse Rock." Then Jeff danced with Darla. I watched the two of them sway to "Any Way You Want Me." Darla hadn't stopped smiling all afternoon and when she looked up at Jeff and laughed, a longing so painful it brought tears to my eyes made me drop my cake server and back away from the buffet table. I wanted to be the one in Jeff's arms, dancing at our own wedding.

Thoughts like that are nothing short of dangerous, so I decided I'd better take a break and try to pull myself together. Obviously, all this hearts-and-flowers stuff was messing with my head.

I handed my cake server over to one of Darla's cousins and retreated to a back room the KCs had dubbed the "ladies' parlor," where I'd stashed my purse. I dug out my makeup kit and touched up my mascara, but while I was standing there staring at my reflection in the mirror, I burst into tears.

"I know it's sort of tradition to cry at weddings, but you're supposed to do it in the church, not afterward at the reception."

I jumped as Vince Zaragosa emerged from the little bathroom that opened into the parlor. I sniffed and tried to wipe away tears with my fingers. "I guess I just get emotional at these things."

He handed me a snowy-white handkerchief. "Anything I can do to help?"

I sniffed and wiped away fresh tears. "Not unless you've changed your policy on broken hearts."

He settled himself on the edge of the chair, somehow looking right at home in his overalls and tool belt amongst the Louis XIV chairs and sofas. "So who broke your heart? I could fix his toilets so they never work right."

I smiled through the tears and shook my head. "It's not exactly broken. Maybe just...bruised." I took a deep breath. "I made a mistake once before and now I'm scared I'll make another one. So scared I won't let the one guy who seems to really care about me get too close."

He rested his elbows on his knees and clasped his hands together. "If this were one of them TV shows my wife gets all mushy over, this is the place where I'd offer you some kind of wise advice."

I waited for more, but when it didn't come, I said, "But you're not?"

He shrugged. "Not everything is a matter of following code and plugging up leaks. Sometimes there aren't any right answers. Or wrong ones. Sometimes you have to operate on instinct."

I frowned. "I don't know if my instincts are any good anymore."

He leaned over and patted my knee. "Yes, you do. You just have to get out of the way and pay attention. Sometimes you have to stop thinking with your head and leap with your heart."

A knock on the door startled us. Jeff stuck his head in the room and smiled at me. "There you are. Somebody told me they thought they'd seen you duck in here."

I managed a weak smile and stood. "Jeff, this is Mr. Zaragosa, the man who's saved this reception by agreeing to come out here on a Saturday to get the bathrooms working again. Mr. Zaragosa, this is Jeff Fischer."

The two of them shook hands, then Jeff turned to me. "I came to see if you'd dance with me."

The scared rabbit part of me wanted to say no, but another voice, deeper down inside, said to let this happen, however things played out. I took his hand and nodded. "I'd like that."

We left Mr. Zaragosa in the parlor. When I looked back over my shoulder at him, he smiled and nodded, as if he, at least, thought I was doing the right thing.

"You make a lovely go-go girl," Jeff said as we walked back toward the reception hall.

"I drew the line at bubble hair," I said. "But the boots are kind of a kick, aren't they?"

"You're a kick, Phoebe Frame." He led me onto the dance floor, where we slow-danced to "A Fool Such As I." I told myself it was part of the whole wedding magic, or maybe just the effects of two glasses of champagne, but I never wanted to move out of his arms.

Eventually, we did leave the dance floor and made our way back to the buffet tables. Jeff was pouring more champagne when a toddler in a frilly dress bumped up against his leg. He smiled down at her. "What's up, munchkin?"

"Daddy?" She stuck her finger in her mouth and looked around, eyes searching.

Jeff kneeled down. "Did you lose your daddy?"

She nodded and her little chin quivered.

"Awww, don't cry." He gathered her up in his arms and stood. "I'm sure we can find him."

I watched, astonished. Jeff looked so...so comfortable with that baby in his arms. So strong, and masculine and...sexy. What happened to the man in the bowling alley who hadn't wanted anything to do with children?

We didn't go far before a worried-looking man came rushing up to us. "Daddy!" the little girl crowed, and held her arms out to him.

"Amanda, what did I tell you about wandering off?" The man took her from Jeff, and pulled her close. "Thanks," he said to us, then headed back toward his table across the room.

Jeff had a pleased expression on his face. "What a cutie, huh?"

"I thought you didn't like children," I said.

He looked at me, one eyebrow raised. "Whatever gave you that idea?"

"In the bowling alley that day—you complained about those children running around."

"I don't like misbehaving children, but, as individuals, I don't have anything against them." He smiled. "I even like some of them."

We joined the other guests on the steps and helped send the newlyweds off to a honeymoon in Las Vegas with a shower of soap bubbles. "Who would have thought anything so tacky could actually be so beautiful?" I sniffed and replaced my bubble wand in the tulle-wrapped bottle.

Jeff handed me a handkerchief. "I'm sure it's a wedding no one here will ever forget."

He slipped his arm around me and together we walked back into the reception hall. "Why don't we go somewhere this evening and celebrate the happy couple?"

I glanced up at him. "You mean, another date?"

He grinned. "I could get used to it. How about you?"

I hesitated, then nodded. "I think maybe I could."

"So where do you want to go?"

I thought a moment, then smiled at the wonderful idea that popped into my head. "Do you ice-skate?"

It turned out Jeff didn't know how to ice-skate. But he didn't tell me that until we were actually out on the ice. The first time he let go of the rail, his feet slid out from under him and, arms windmilling, he crashed to the ice.

"Are you all right?" I tugged on his arm, trying to help him up.

"I think my pride's hurt more than anything." He climbed up me until he was standing again, though he still clung to my arm. "Although my backside smarts pretty good."

"Why didn't you tell me you don't know how to skate?"

"I could tell you really wanted to go." He grinned. "Besides, I thought it might be fun if you taught me."

Note to any men out there who might be inclined to pay attention: there is something incredibly sexy about a strong man who is just a little bit vulnerable.

In any case, I got all warm and gushy inside when Jeff asked me to teach him to ice-skate, and immediately became determined to turn him into the next Elvis Stojko.

Unfortunately, there was one minor flaw in this plan: Jeff didn't have any talent. I might as well have tried to teach a bull to roller-skate. He tried, I'll give him that. But every time I let go of him, his ankles wobbled, his knees buckled and his arms flailed. I figured it was only a matter of time before he broke something.

Finally, he sagged against the railing. "This isn't any fun for you," he said. "Why don't you skate by yourself for a while? I'll watch."

"Are you sure?" I backed away from him. "You won't pout?"

He laughed. "Why would I pout?"

"Steve always pouted when we went anywhere and I left him alone. He said he felt like an idiot standing there by himself."

"That's because Steve is an idiot. Now go on. Show me your stuff."

Slowly at first, then gaining speed, I skated around the

rink. "Dancing Queen" began playing over the loudspeaker, and I was immediately transported back in time to those long Saturdays when Darla and I would spend hours at this rink. My hair streamed out behind me and the blades of my skates cut into the ice in time to the music. My thighs burned with the effort and my ankles began to ache, but I didn't want to stop. Soaring around the ice was the next best thing to flying. Why had I ever given that up?

I rounded the corner and saw Jeff across the rink. He'd gotten off the ice and was standing at the rail, leaning over it, watching me, a smile on his face that made me feel weightless and full of energy. When I was almost in front of him, I tried a spin, a graceful pirouette that had once been my specialty. I twirled, faster and faster, the world a colorful blur at the edge of my vision. Then I began to slow, and everything gradually came back into focus: the other skaters gliding past, the neon of the store signs and Jeff's smiling face.

"That was really good," he said, coming to meet me as I stepped off the ice.

"Thanks." I was puffing, breathless from the exertion.

"That twirl thing you did—it looked like something you'd see in the Olympics."

I laughed. "Olympic skaters learn that kind of thing when they're still in elementary school."

"Well, it looked pretty impressive to me."

"When I was in high school, my friends and I would wear short skirts and we'd twirl like that so the boys could see our underwear."

"And they say men are the sexual aggressors." He gestured toward the ice. "Do you want to skate some more?"

I shook my head. "I think I want to get some coffee."

We bought lattes at a Starbucks that overlooked the ice rink. I sank down into my chair with a sigh. "Tired?" Jeff asked.

I nodded. "I'd forgotten how much work goes into getting ready for a wedding."

"Speaking of work, I stopped by the medical clinic this morning, on my way to the chapel."

"Oh?" Last I'd heard, Patterson had taken a sabbatical from practice, but I didn't know anything else.

"They've got a new doctor there," Jeff said. "I stopped by because she wants to put the transcription system back in."

"She?"

He nodded. "The staff is happy and I think the clinic managers hope a woman will be better, PR-wise."

I laughed. "So I guess they're looking for a transcriptionist."

"Are you interested in your old job back?"

I shook my head. "No, thanks. I like my new job."

He leaned forward. "I haven't had a chance to tell you, but what you did with Patterson took guts. I'm proud of you."

Are there many sweeter words in the English language? From the time we're toddlers being potty trained, we're always listening for those words from someone: our parents, our spouses, our friends. "I love you" gets tossed around so casually sometimes, but to be told you've made someone proud, now that's really special.

I touched my cup to his. "You know what the best thing is?" I asked. "I'm proud of myself."

"Looks like things have turned out pretty well for you."

I nodded. "I wouldn't have said it six months ago, but I think now this divorce has been the best thing that ever happened to me. It forced me to really look at my life and to try new things."

He reached across the table and took my hand in his. "Do I fit in there somewhere?"

I turned to watch the skaters on the ice. A little girl scooted by, holding tightly to her father's hand. One of these days, she'd be brave enough to let go of that hand and soar across the ice, so free.

I was feeling brave today. I turned to look at Jeff again. "What would you say if I told you I've fallen in love with you?"

Everything went still for a moment. Neither one of us blinked and the sounds of the ice rink and the mall faded away. I watched Jeff, scared to move, scared to breathe even.

Then the most wonderful smile spread over his face. Across his lips and up to his eyes. A smile that came from somewhere in his soul. "I'd say you'd made me a very happy man." He leaned forward and kissed me—a sweet, gentle touching of our lips. "I love you, Phoebe Frame," he said. "Don't you ever forget it."

I smiled at him, and at the reflection of my own happiness in his eyes. "I won't forget."

We kissed again, a long, slow kiss that said all the things I hadn't found words for yet. I held on to the advice Mr. Zaragosa had given me, and vowed to try leaping with my heart, even if sometimes it felt like skydiving without a parachute.

* * * *

Make a date with Mills & Boon Blaze® and read
Good, Bad...Better
*from Cindi Myers – available in August 2006
from all good booksellers.*

*When this good girl becomes a wild woman,
sparks really begin to fly!*

3 SEXY LOVE STORIES IN 1!

It's going to be a passionate hot summer...

A WOLF RIVER SUMMER by Barbara McCauley

Heads turn when scandalous, sexy Clay Bodine comes to town and heads straight for sensible, virginal Paige Andrews. And what Clay asks Paige to do is secretly very tempting...

HAWK'S WAY: THE VIRGIN GROOM by Joan Johnston

Mac MacReady is every man's envy and every woman's fantasy until his life turns upside down. Now he must either agree to Jewel Whitelaw's shocking proposal – or take cold showers for the rest of the summer.

THE LONG HOT SUMMER by Wendy Rosnau

Bad boy Johnny Bernard comes home to the steamy Louisiana bayou to be amazed at the desire that flashes through him when he meets prim and proper blonde Nicole Chapman.

On sale 16th June 2006

MILLS & BOON®
Live the emotion

Blaze™

SHOCKINGLY SENSUAL *by Lori Wilde*

Callie Ryder likes to shock. She even does it for a living – giving
sex advice to callers on her late-night radio show. When Callie's
on-air sex tips result in a book tour, even threats against her aren't
going to slow her down. Instead, she gets a bodyguard…

WHO'S ON TOP? *by Karen Kendall*

The Man-Handlers, Bk 1

In this battle between the sexes, they're both determined to win.
Jane O'Toole is supposed to be assessing Dominic Sayer's work-
related issues, but the sexual offers he delivers make it hard to
stay focused…

AS HOT AS IT GETS *by Jamie Sobrato*

They have an old score to settle. With that goal in mind, Claire
Elliot tracks down Mason Walker at his tropical adults-only
resort. She's determined to get him into her bed and out of her
mind once and for all. But who knew that Mason would turn out
to be so sexy and so hot?

A GLIMPSE OF FIRE *by Debbi Rawlins*

Desperate to find the mystery woman he got a glimpse of,
Eric Harmon's chasing down the sexiest female he's ever seen.
Meanwhile, Dallas Shea's having the time of her life being
chased by the hot advertising exec. He's *so* gorgeous, *so* raw, *so*
insistent…she may just allow herself to be caught.

On sale 7th July 2006

*Available at WHSmith, Tesco, ASDA, Borders, Eason,
Sainsbury's and most bookshops*

www.millsandboon.co.uk

0606/171V2

MILLS & BOON®

Live the emotion

Modern

romance™

Extra

Two longer and more passionate stories every month

STRICTLY LEGAL
by Kate Hardy

Barrister Leo Ballantyne is not the usual kind of guy
Rose falls for – strait-laced, serious and sexy… Leo's
dilemma is that Rose is of the wild variety – a vintage
clothes dealer with an allegedly dodgy past – and she
would surely play havoc with his ambitions to further
his legal career… But can he resist her…?

GETTING HOT IN HAWAII
by Kerri LeRoy

It's Jackson Banta! As successful and gorgeous as
they come – a far cry from the geek Paige knew in
high school… It's Paige Pipkin! The woman who
turned him down all those years ago. But Jackson
reckons that payback time has come – he will flirt
with her and show her what she has been missing…

On sale 7th July 2006

***Through days of hard work
and troubles shared, three women
will discover that what was lost
can be found again...***

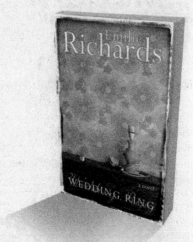

Tessa MacCrae has reluctantly agreed to spend
the summer helping her mother and grandmother clean
out the family home. They've never been close, but
Tessa hopes that time away will help her avoid facing the
tragedy of her daughter's death and the toll it's
exacting on her marriage.

At first, the summer is filled with all-too-familiar
emotional storms. But with the passing weeks each of
their lives begins to change. And for the first time,
Tessa can look past the years of resentment.

**'This much-loved family saga of insecurity and
tragic loss is compulsive.'**
—*The Bookseller*

19th May 2006

MIRA

"I was fifteen when my mother finally told me the truth about my father. She didn't mean to. She meant to keep it a secret forever. If she'd succeeded it might have saved us all."

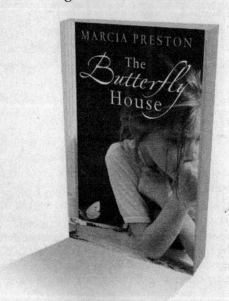

When a hauntingly familiar stranger knocks on Roberta Dutreau's door, she is compelled to begin a journey of self-discovery leading back to her childhood. But is she ready to know the truth about what happened to her, her best friend Cynthia and their mothers that tragic night ten years ago?

16th June 2006